WARRIORS

SKYCLAN & THE STRANGER

CREATED BY
ERIN HUNTER

WRITTEN BY
DAN JOLLEY

ART BY
JAMES L. BARRY

HAMBURG // LONDON // LOS ANGELES // TOKYO

HARPER
An Imprint of HarperCollinsPublishers

Warriors: SkyClan and the Stranger
Created by Erin Hunter
Written by Dan Jolley
Art and Colorization by James L. Barry

Lettering - John Hunt
Original Cover Design - Louis Csontos
Editor - Lillian Diaz-Przybyl
Managing Editor - Vy Nguyen
Print-Production Manager - Lucas Rivera
Art Director - Al-Insan Lashleye
Director of Sales and Manufacuring - Allyson DeSimone
President and C.O.O. - John Parker
C.E.O. and Chief Creative Officer - Stuart Levy

A  Manga

TOKYOPOP and TOKYOPOP
are trademarks or registered trademarks
of TOKYOPOP Inc.

TOKYOPOP Inc.
5900 Wilshire Blvd. Suite 2000
Los Angeles, CA 90036

E-mail: info@TOKYOPOP.com
Come visit us online at www.TOKYOPOP.com

Library of Congress catalog card number: 2018964872
ISBN 978-0-06-285737-8

24 EP 10 9
❖
First Edition

CONTENTS

The Rescue...1

Beyond the Code...............................85

After the Flood................................171

WARRIORS
THE RESCUE

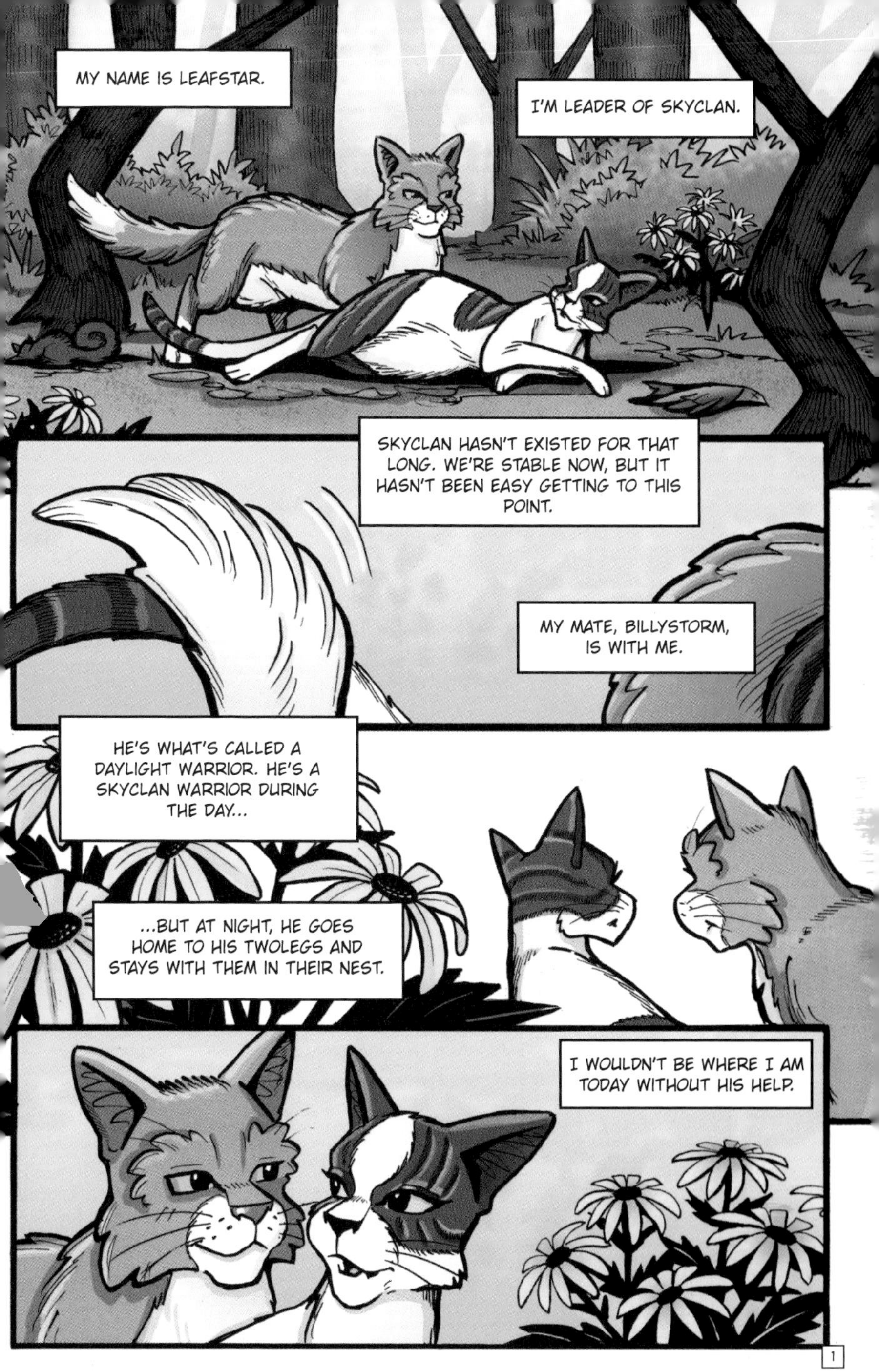

MY NAME IS LEAFSTAR.
I'M LEADER OF SKYCLAN.
SKYCLAN HASN'T EXISTED FOR THAT LONG. WE'RE STABLE NOW, BUT IT HASN'T BEEN EASY GETTING TO THIS POINT.
MY MATE, BILLYSTORM, IS WITH ME.
HE'S WHAT'S CALLED A DAYLIGHT WARRIOR. HE'S A SKYCLAN WARRIOR DURING THE DAY...
...BUT AT NIGHT, HE GOES HOME TO HIS TWOLEGS AND STAYS WITH THEM IN THEIR NEST.
I WOULDN'T BE WHERE I AM TODAY WITHOUT HIS HELP.

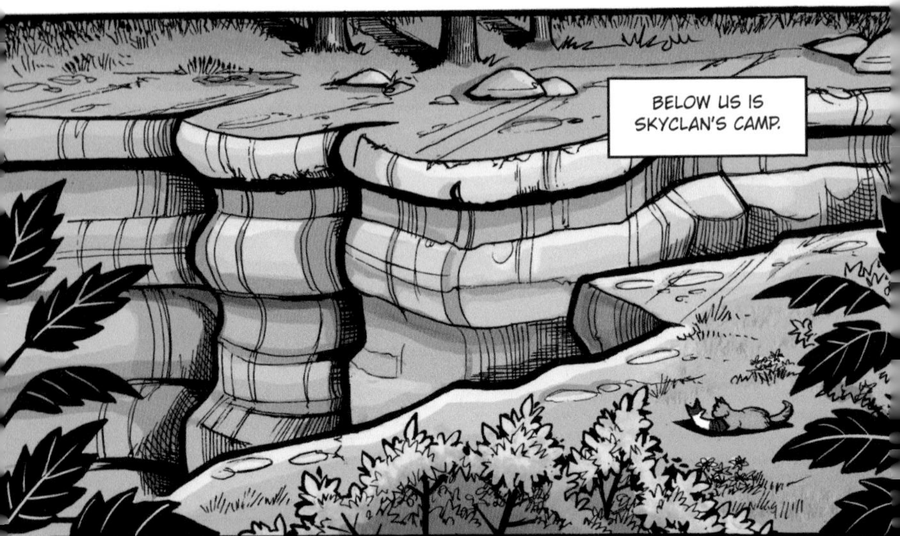
BELOW US IS
SKYCLAN'S CAMP.

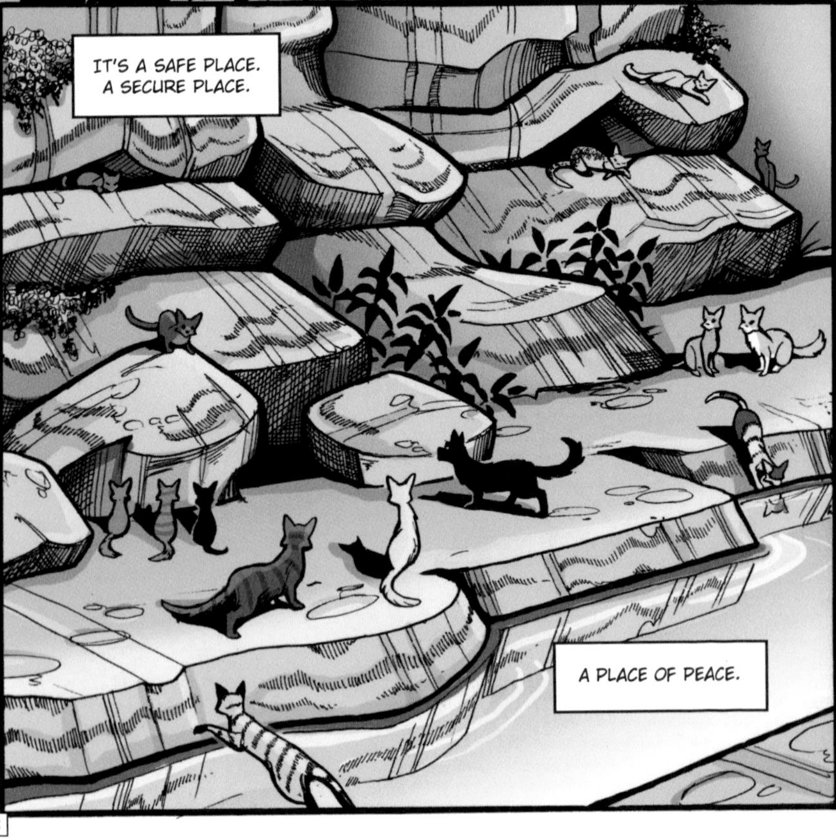
IT'S A SAFE PLACE.
A SECURE PLACE.
A PLACE OF PEACE.

NOW--ARE YOU PAYING ATTENTION?

YES, RABBITLEAP!

OKAY, YOU GATHER YOUR LEGS UNDER YOU AND SPRING STRAIGHT UP.

RIDICULOUS. BOUNCING ABOUT ALL OVER THE PLACE.

WE'RE CATS, NOT RABBITS.

YOU'LL BE AMAZED AT HOW HIGH YOU CAN GO IF YOU PRACTICE.

THE ELDER CAT, LICHENFUR, SELDOM HAS PLEASANT WORDS FOR ANY CAT, BUT SHE MEANS NO HARM.

WHAT DOES HE PLAN TO DO, LAND ON PREY AND SQUASH IT TO DEATH?

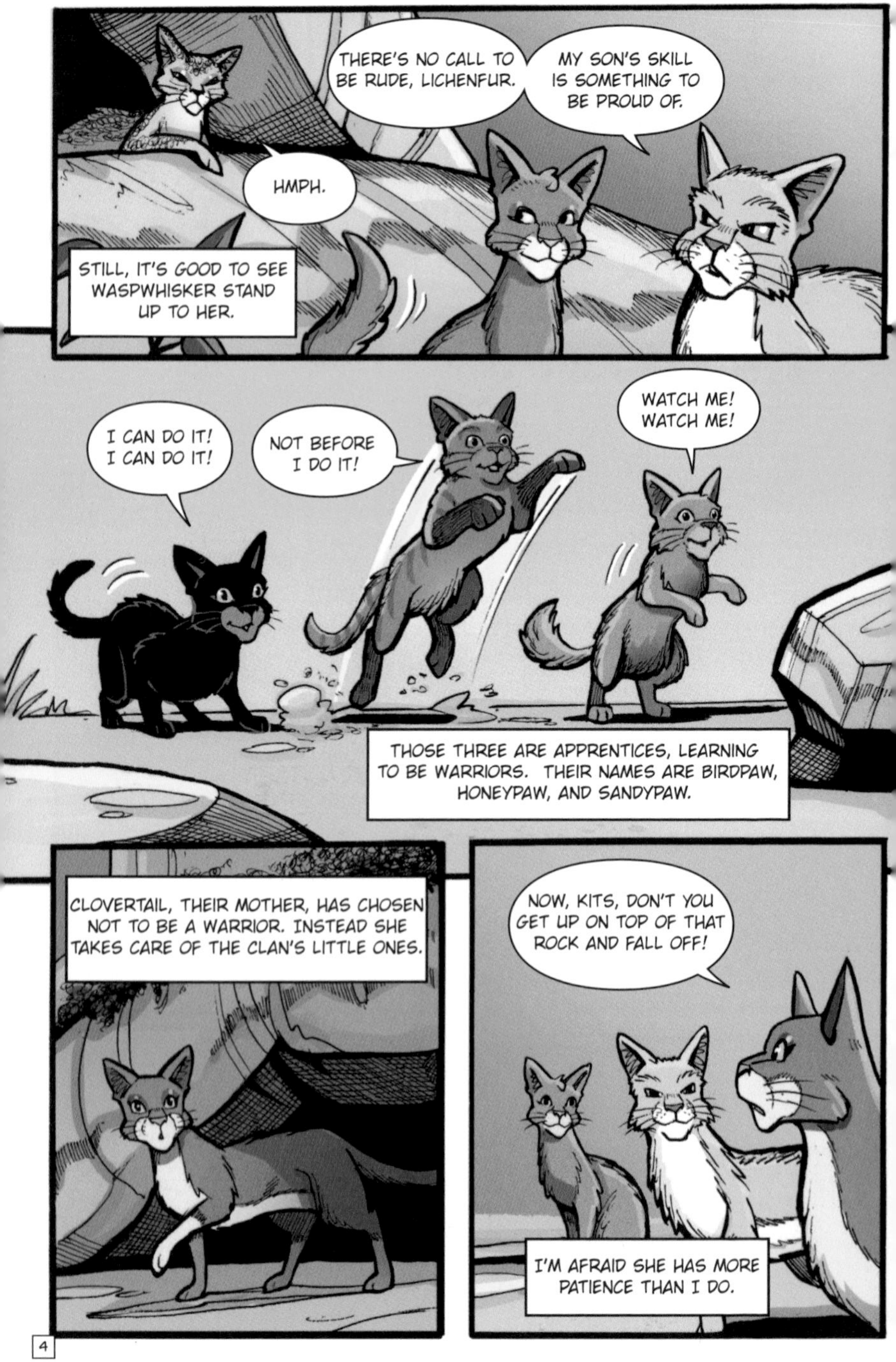
THERE'S NO CALL TO BE RUDE, LICHENFUR.
MY SON'S SKILL IS SOMETHING TO BE PROUD OF.
HMPH.
STILL, IT'S GOOD TO SEE WASPWHISKER STAND UP TO HER.
I CAN DO IT! I CAN DO IT!
NOT BEFORE I DO IT!
WATCH ME! WATCH ME!
THOSE THREE ARE APPRENTICES, LEARNING TO BE WARRIORS. THEIR NAMES ARE BIRDPAW, HONEYPAW, AND SANDYPAW.
CLOVERTAIL, THEIR MOTHER, HAS CHOSEN NOT TO BE A WARRIOR. INSTEAD SHE TAKES CARE OF THE CLAN'S LITTLE ONES.
NOW, KITS, DON'T YOU GET UP ON TOP OF THAT ROCK AND FALL OFF!
I'M AFRAID SHE HAS MORE PATIENCE THAN I DO.

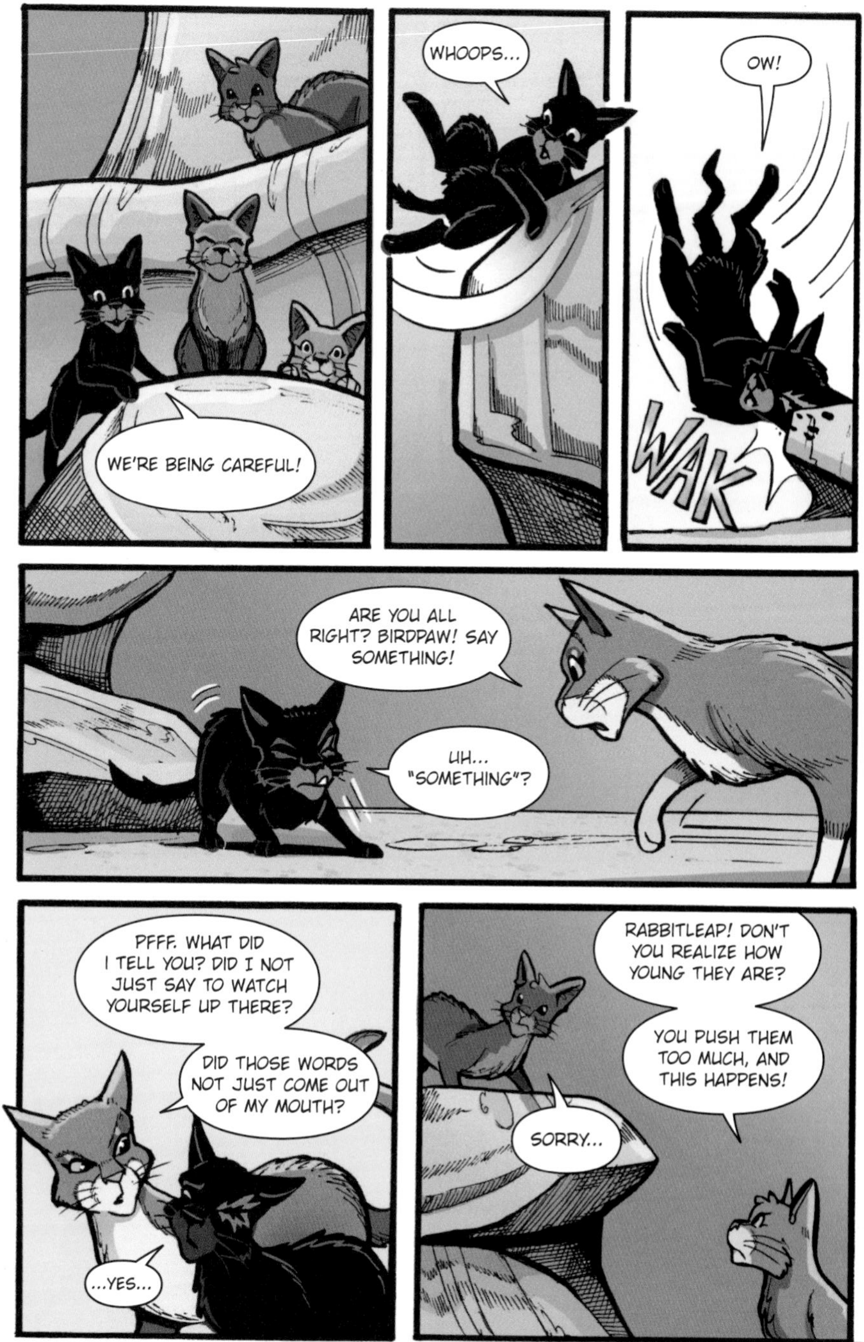
WE'RE BEING CAREFUL!
WHOOPS...
OW!
WAK
ARE YOU ALL RIGHT? BIRDPAW! SAY SOMETHING!
UH... "SOMETHING"?
PFFF. WHAT DID I TELL YOU? DID I NOT JUST SAY TO WATCH YOURSELF UP THERE?
DID THOSE WORDS NOT JUST COME OUT OF MY MOUTH?
...YES...
RABBITLEAP! DON'T YOU REALIZE HOW YOUNG THEY ARE?
YOU PUSH THEM TOO MUCH, AND THIS HAPPENS!
SORRY...

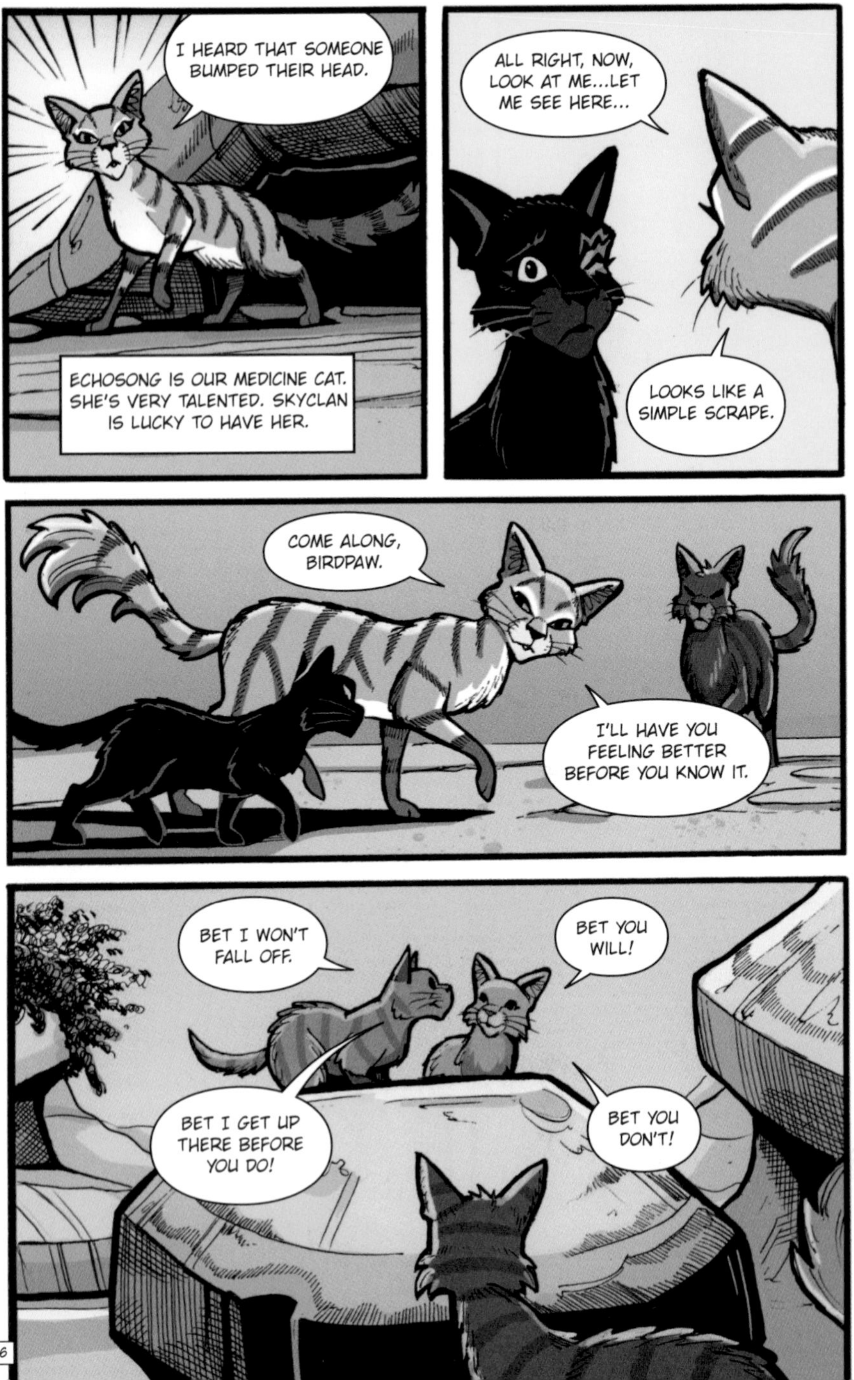
I HEARD THAT SOMEONE BUMPED THEIR HEAD.
ECHOSONG IS OUR MEDICINE CAT. SHE'S VERY TALENTED. SKYCLAN IS LUCKY TO HAVE HER.
ALL RIGHT, NOW, LOOK AT ME...LET ME SEE HERE...
LOOKS LIKE A SIMPLE SCRAPE.
COME ALONG, BIRDPAW.
I'LL HAVE YOU FEELING BETTER BEFORE YOU KNOW IT.
BET I WON'T FALL OFF.
BET YOU WILL!
BET I GET UP THERE BEFORE YOU DO!
BET YOU DON'T!

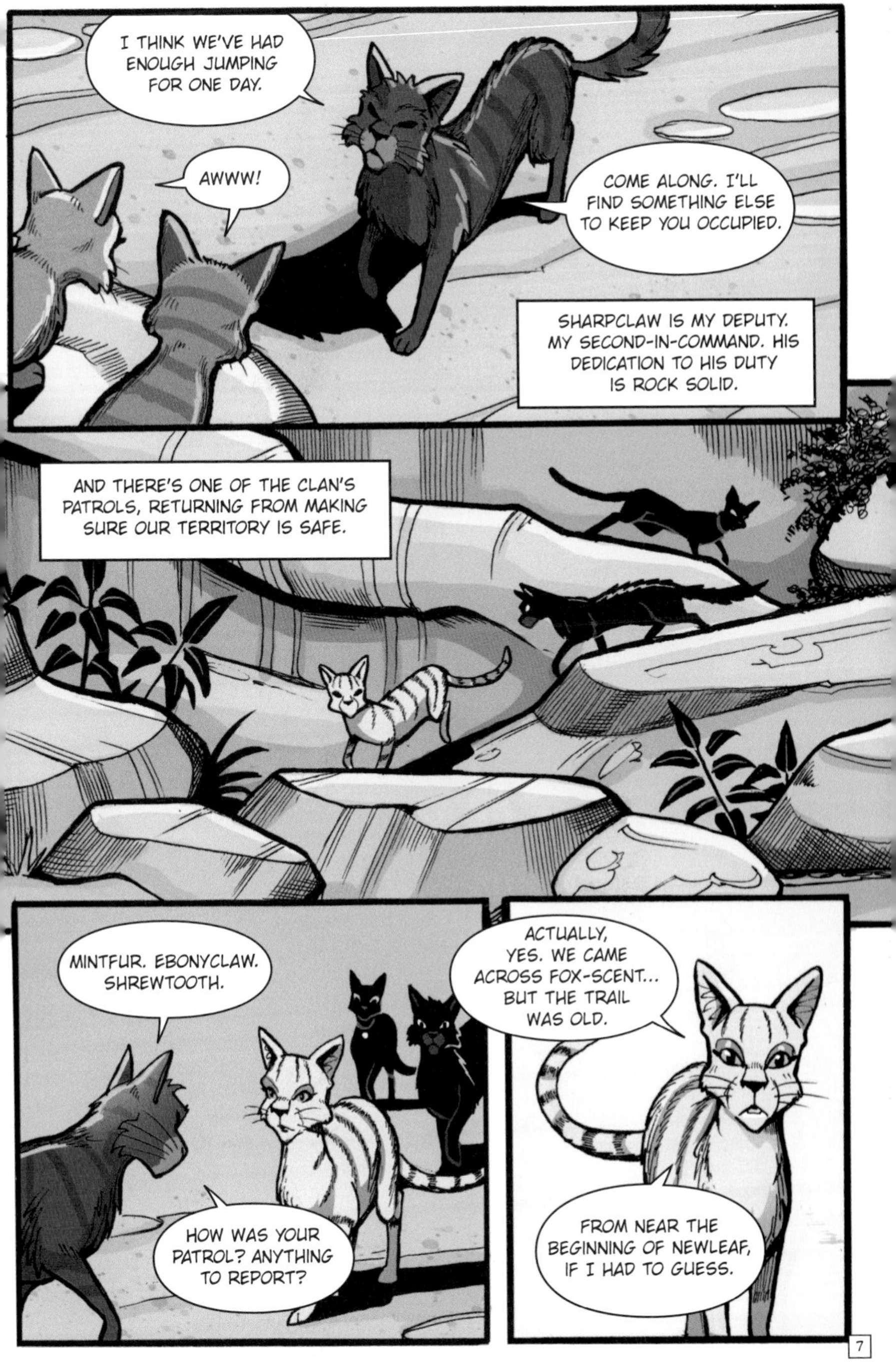
I THINK WE'VE HAD ENOUGH JUMPING FOR ONE DAY.
AWWW!
COME ALONG. I'LL FIND SOMETHING ELSE TO KEEP YOU OCCUPIED.
SHARPCLAW IS MY DEPUTY. MY SECOND-IN-COMMAND. HIS DEDICATION TO HIS DUTY IS ROCK SOLID.
AND THERE'S ONE OF THE CLAN'S PATROLS, RETURNING FROM MAKING SURE OUR TERRITORY IS SAFE.
MINTFUR. EBONYCLAW. SHREWTOOTH.
HOW WAS YOUR PATROL? ANYTHING TO REPORT?
ACTUALLY, YES. WE CAME ACROSS FOX-SCENT... BUT THE TRAIL WAS OLD.
FROM NEAR THE BEGINNING OF NEWLEAF, IF I HAD TO GUESS.

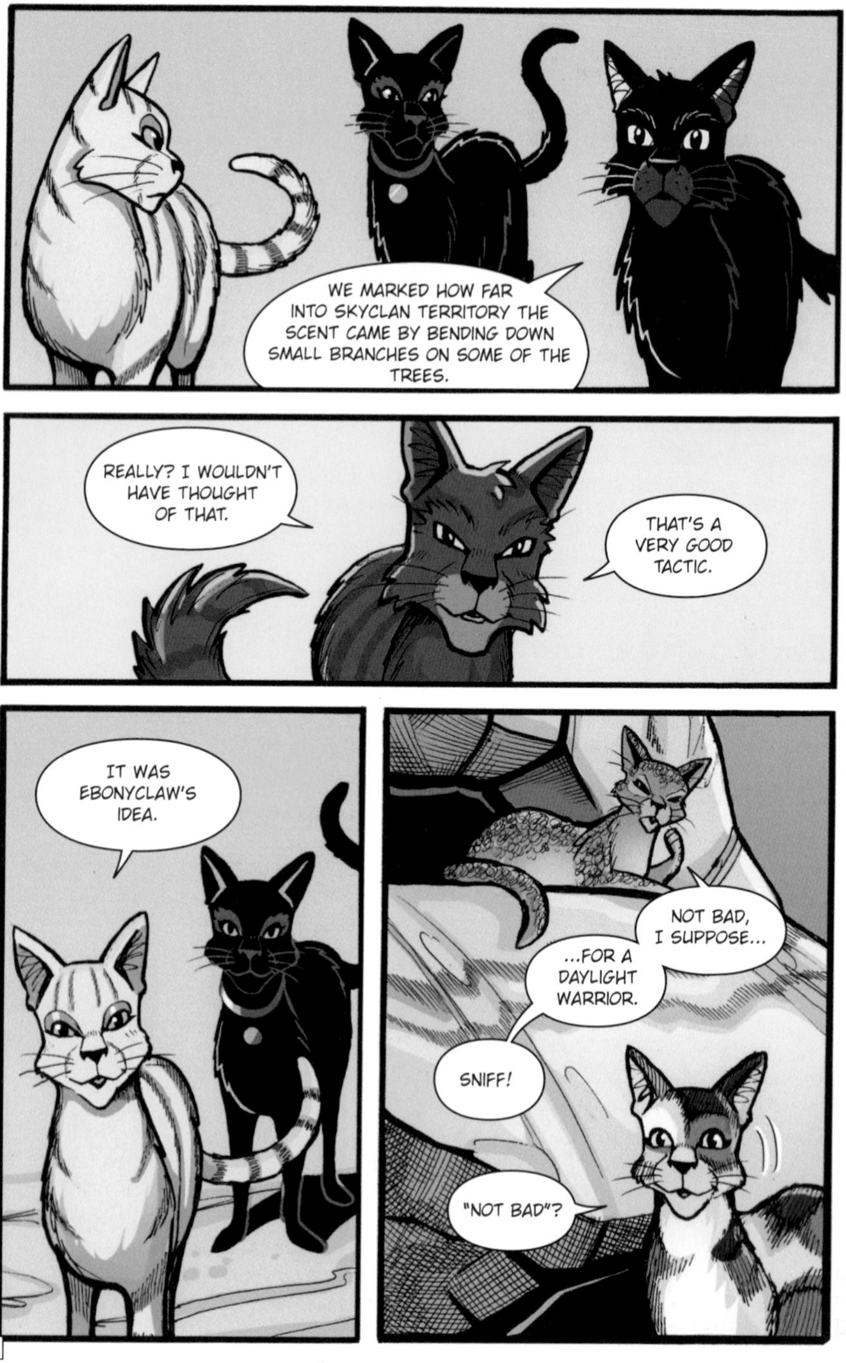
WE MARKED HOW FAR INTO SKYCLAN TERRITORY THE SCENT CAME BY BENDING DOWN SMALL BRANCHES ON SOME OF THE TREES.
REALLY? I WOULDN'T HAVE THOUGHT OF THAT.
THAT'S A VERY GOOD TACTIC.
IT WAS EBONYCLAW'S IDEA.
NOT BAD, I SUPPOSE...
...FOR A DAYLIGHT WARRIOR.
SNIFF!
"NOT BAD"?

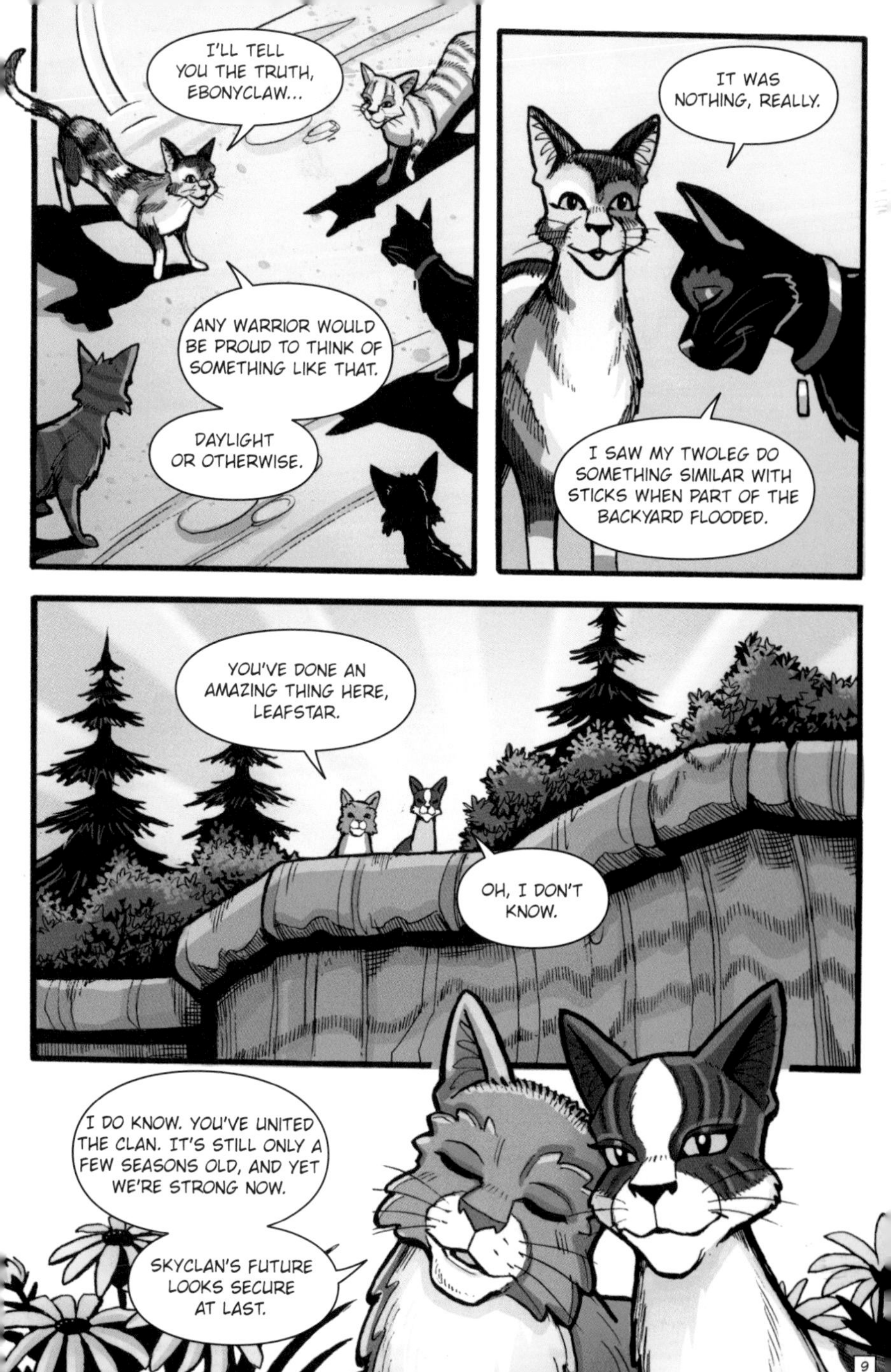
I'LL TELL YOU THE TRUTH, EBONYCLAW...
ANY WARRIOR WOULD BE PROUD TO THINK OF SOMETHING LIKE THAT.
DAYLIGHT OR OTHERWISE.
IT WAS NOTHING, REALLY.
I SAW MY TWOLEG DO SOMETHING SIMILAR WITH STICKS WHEN PART OF THE BACKYARD FLOODED.
YOU'VE DONE AN AMAZING THING HERE, LEAFSTAR.
OH, I DON'T KNOW.
I DO KNOW. YOU'VE UNITED THE CLAN. IT'S STILL ONLY A FEW SEASONS OLD, AND YET WE'RE STRONG NOW.
SKYCLAN'S FUTURE LOOKS SECURE AT LAST.

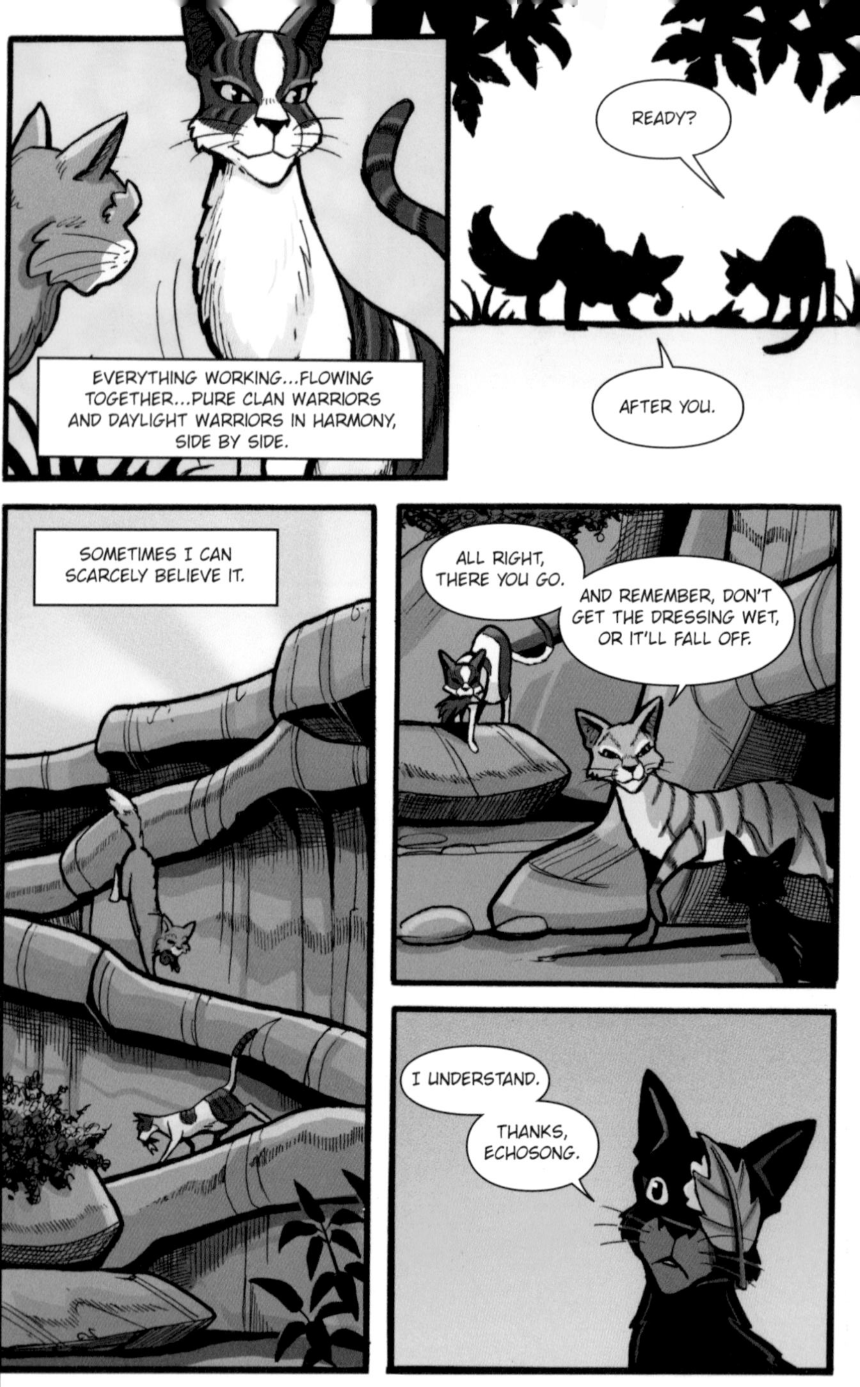
EVERYTHING WORKING...FLOWING TOGETHER...PURE CLAN WARRIORS AND DAYLIGHT WARRIORS IN HARMONY, SIDE BY SIDE.
READY?
AFTER YOU.
SOMETIMES I CAN SCARCELY BELIEVE IT.
ALL RIGHT, THERE YOU GO.
AND REMEMBER, DON'T GET THE DRESSING WET, OR IT'LL FALL OFF.
I UNDERSTAND.
THANKS, ECHOSONG.

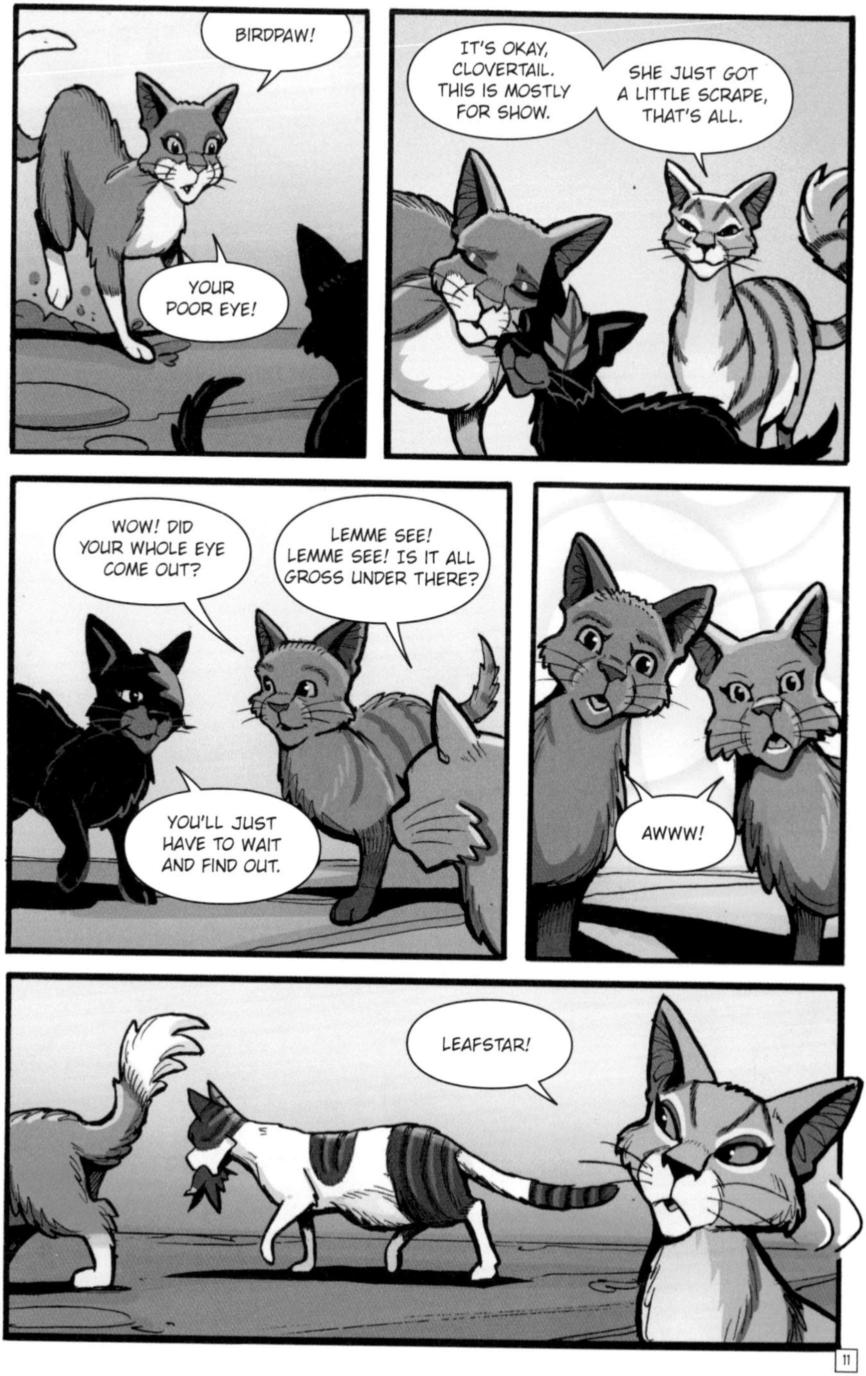

BIRDPAW!
YOUR POOR EYE!
IT'S OKAY, CLOVERTAIL. THIS IS MOSTLY FOR SHOW.
SHE JUST GOT A LITTLE SCRAPE, THAT'S ALL.
WOW! DID YOUR WHOLE EYE COME OUT?
LEMME SEE! LEMME SEE! IS IT ALL GROSS UNDER THERE?
YOU'LL JUST HAVE TO WAIT AND FIND OUT.
AWWW!
LEAFSTAR!

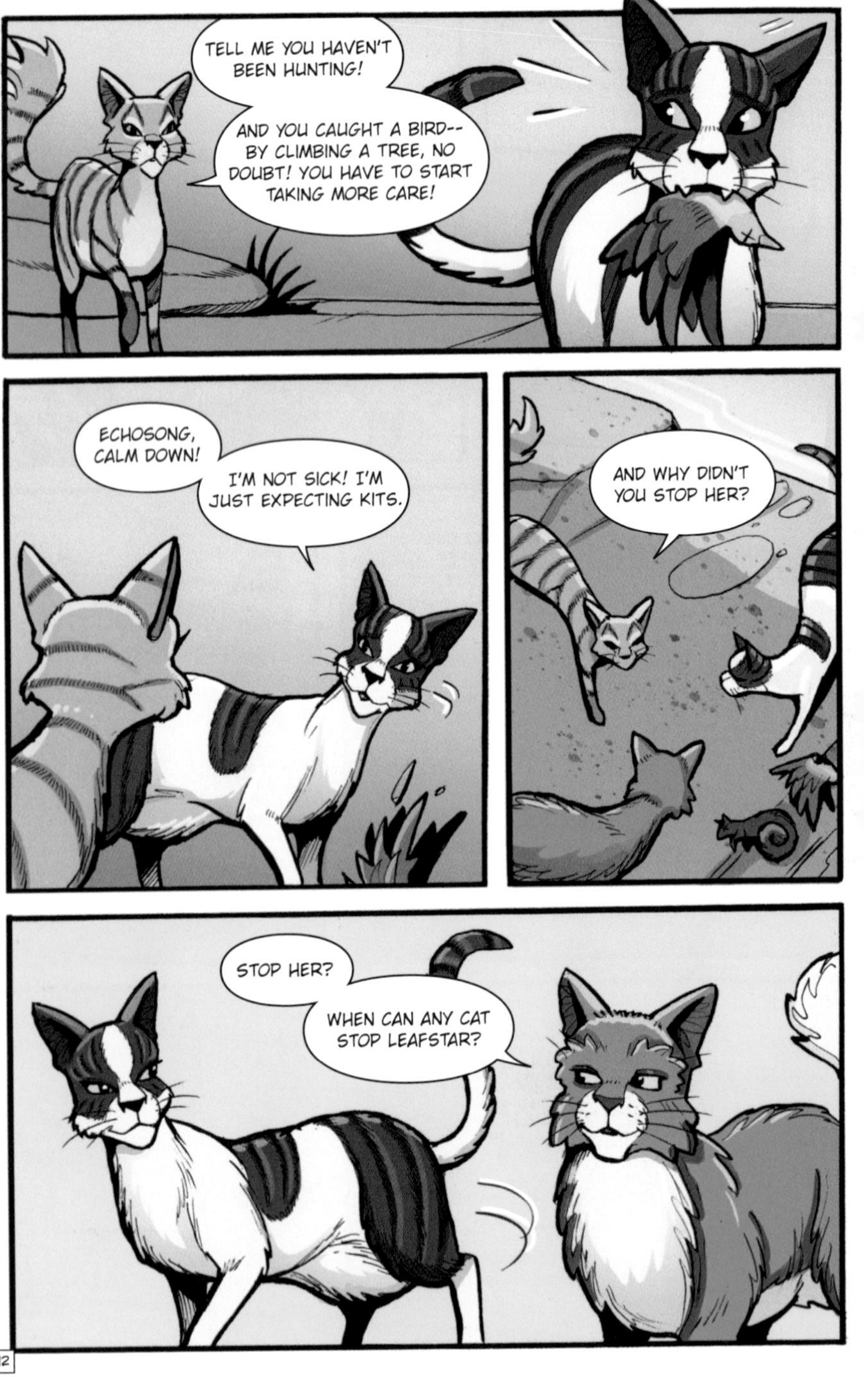
TELL ME YOU HAVEN'T BEEN HUNTING!
AND YOU CAUGHT A BIRD-- BY CLIMBING A TREE, NO DOUBT! YOU HAVE TO START TAKING MORE CARE!
ECHOSONG, CALM DOWN!
I'M NOT SICK! I'M JUST EXPECTING KITS.
AND WHY DIDN'T YOU STOP HER?
STOP HER?
WHEN CAN ANY CAT STOP LEAFSTAR?

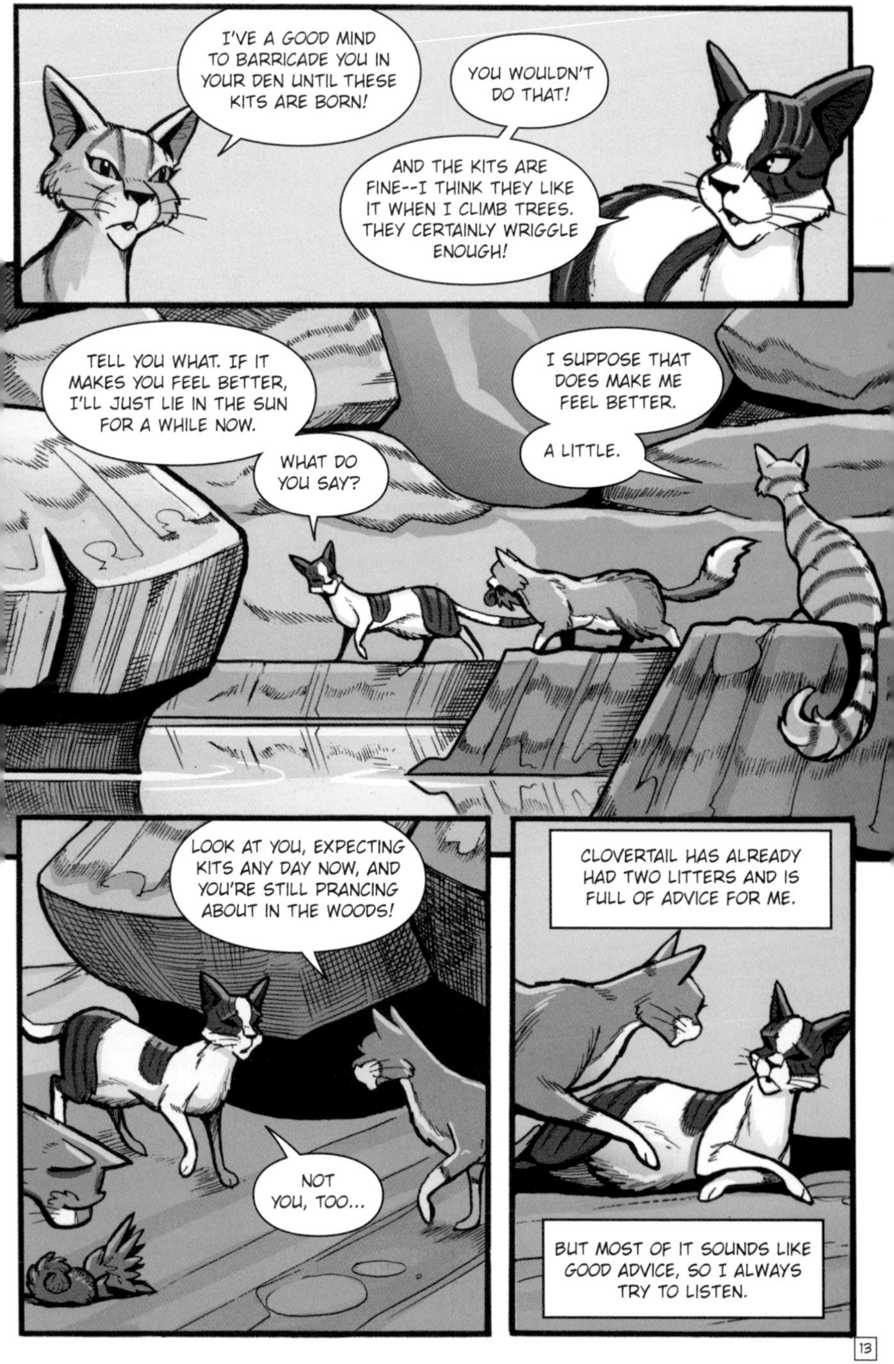
I'VE A GOOD MIND TO BARRICADE YOU IN YOUR DEN UNTIL THESE KITS ARE BORN!
YOU WOULDN'T DO THAT!
AND THE KITS ARE FINE--I THINK THEY LIKE IT WHEN I CLIMB TREES. THEY CERTAINLY WRIGGLE ENOUGH!
TELL YOU WHAT. IF IT MAKES YOU FEEL BETTER, I'LL JUST LIE IN THE SUN FOR A WHILE NOW.
WHAT DO YOU SAY?
I SUPPOSE THAT DOES MAKE ME FEEL BETTER.
A LITTLE.
LOOK AT YOU, EXPECTING KITS ANY DAY NOW, AND YOU'RE STILL PRANCING ABOUT IN THE WOODS!
NOT YOU, TOO...
CLOVERTAIL HAS ALREADY HAD TWO LITTERS AND IS FULL OF ADVICE FOR ME.
BUT MOST OF IT SOUNDS LIKE GOOD ADVICE, SO I ALWAYS TRY TO LISTEN.

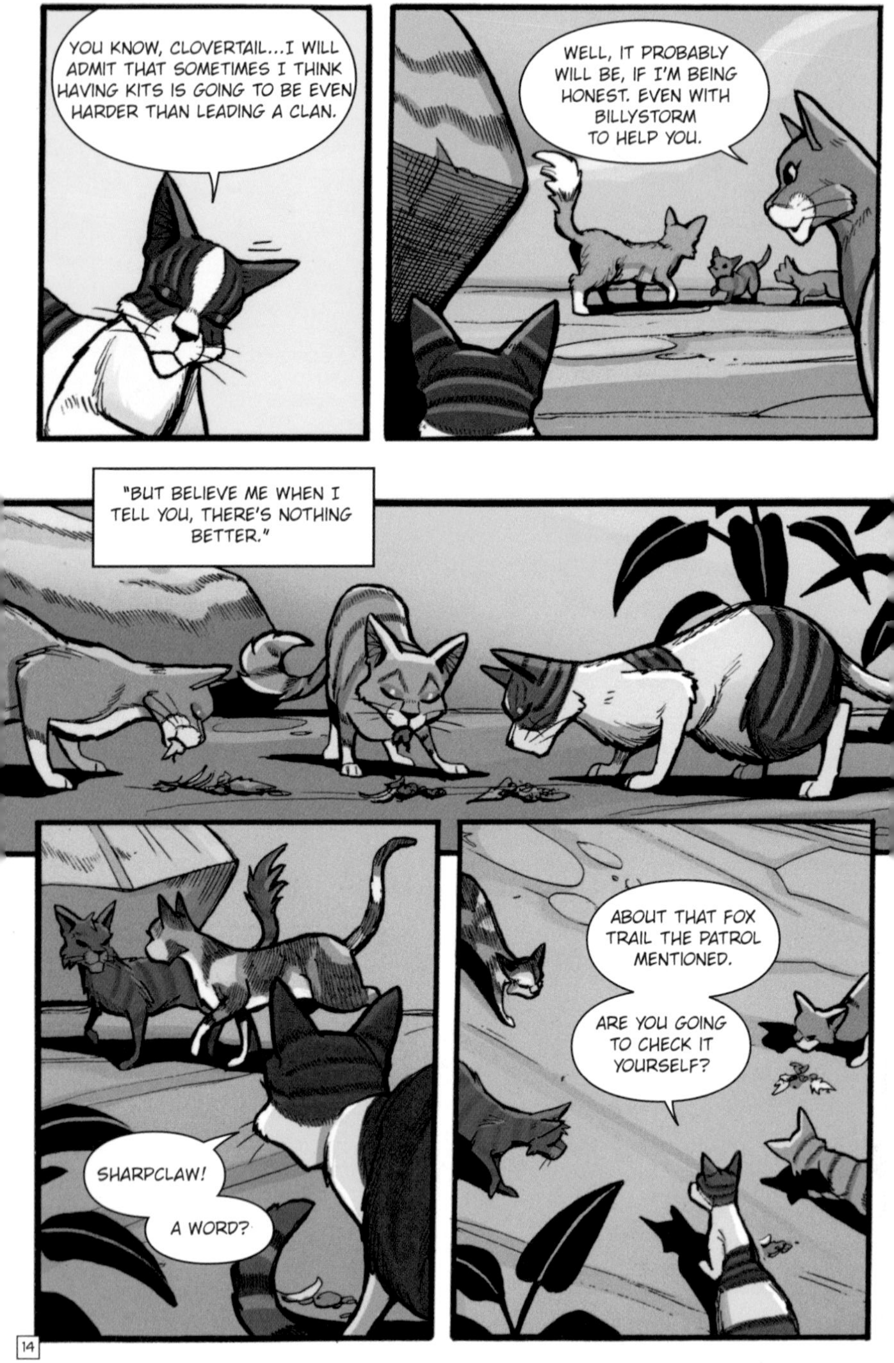
YOU KNOW, CLOVERTAIL...I WILL ADMIT THAT SOMETIMES I THINK HAVING KITS IS GOING TO BE EVEN HARDER THAN LEADING A CLAN.
WELL, IT PROBABLY WILL BE, IF I'M BEING HONEST. EVEN WITH BILLYSTORM TO HELP YOU.
"BUT BELIEVE ME WHEN I TELL YOU, THERE'S NOTHING BETTER."
SHARPCLAW!
A WORD?
ABOUT THAT FOX TRAIL THE PATROL MENTIONED.
ARE YOU GOING TO CHECK IT YOURSELF?

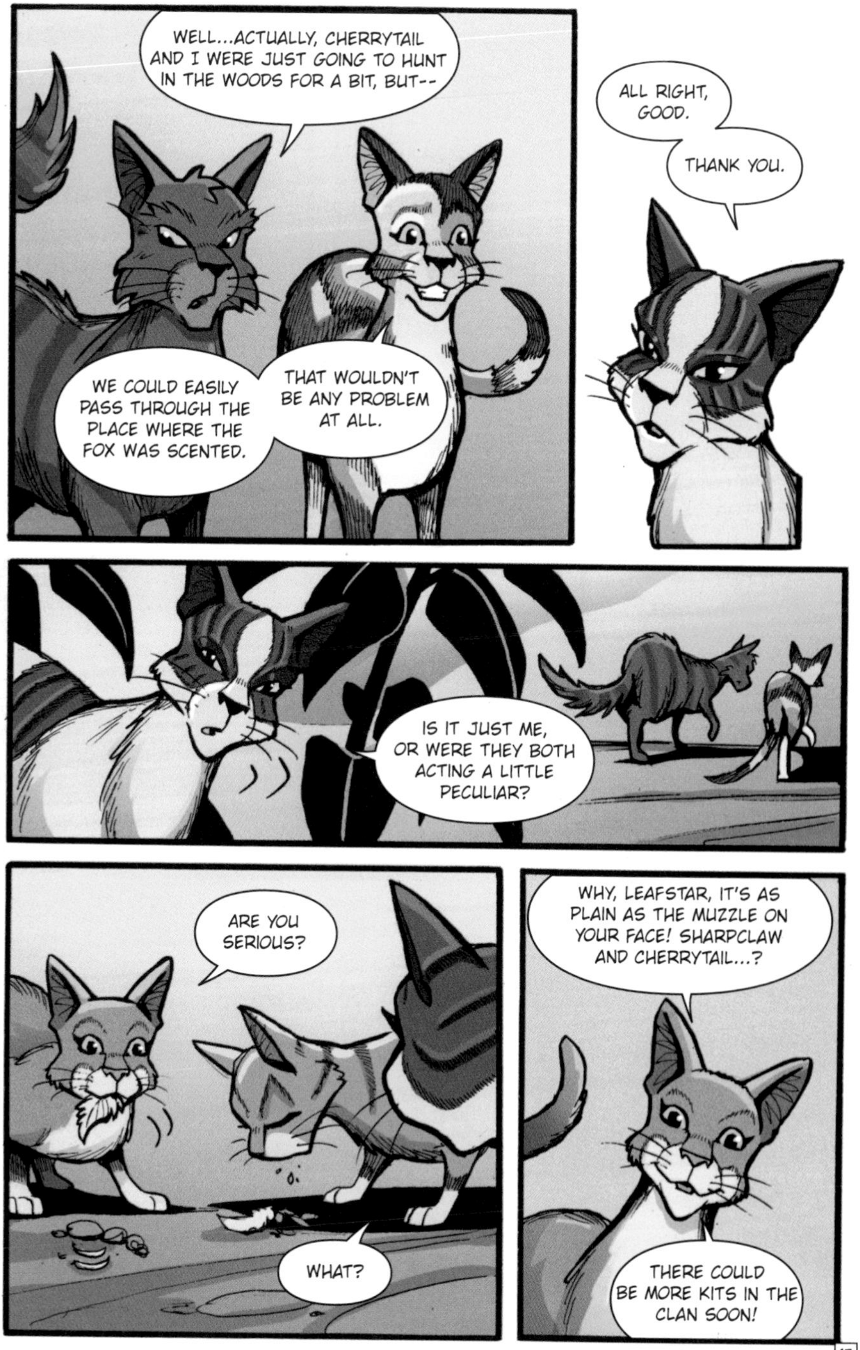

WELL...ACTUALLY, CHERRYTAIL AND I WERE JUST GOING TO HUNT IN THE WOODS FOR A BIT, BUT--
WE COULD EASILY PASS THROUGH THE PLACE WHERE THE FOX WAS SCENTED.
THAT WOULDN'T BE ANY PROBLEM AT ALL.
ALL RIGHT, GOOD.
THANK YOU.
IS IT JUST ME, OR WERE THEY BOTH ACTING A LITTLE PECULIAR?
ARE YOU SERIOUS?
WHAT?
WHY, LEAFSTAR, IT'S AS PLAIN AS THE MUZZLE ON YOUR FACE! SHARPCLAW AND CHERRYTAIL...?
THERE COULD BE MORE KITS IN THE CLAN SOON!

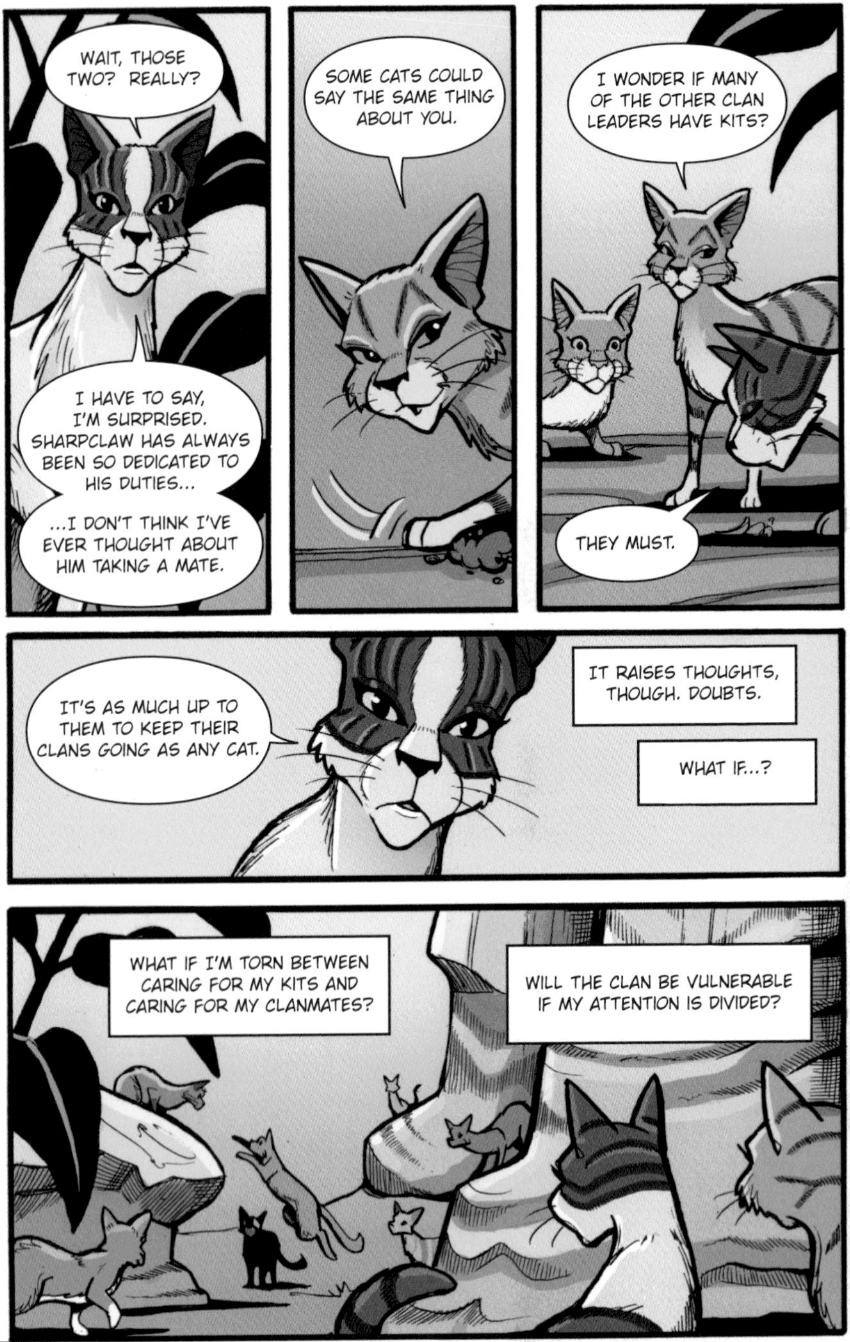
WAIT, THOSE TWO? REALLY?
I HAVE TO SAY, I'M SURPRISED. SHARPCLAW HAS ALWAYS BEEN SO DEDICATED TO HIS DUTIES...
...I DON'T THINK I'VE EVER THOUGHT ABOUT HIM TAKING A MATE.
SOME CATS COULD SAY THE SAME THING ABOUT YOU.
I WONDER IF MANY OF THE OTHER CLAN LEADERS HAVE KITS?
THEY MUST.
IT'S AS MUCH UP TO THEM TO KEEP THEIR CLANS GOING AS ANY CAT.
IT RAISES THOUGHTS, THOUGH. DOUBTS.
WHAT IF...?
WHAT IF I'M TORN BETWEEN CARING FOR MY KITS AND CARING FOR MY CLANMATES?
WILL THE CLAN BE VULNERABLE IF MY ATTENTION IS DIVIDED?

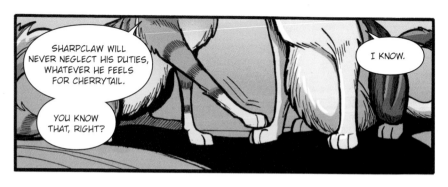

SHARPCLAW WILL NEVER NEGLECT HIS DUTIES, WHATEVER HE FEELS FOR CHERRYTAIL.

YOU KNOW THAT, RIGHT?

I KNOW.

NNN...NO...

WHERE ARE THEY?

WHERE ARE MY KITS? I'VE LOST THEM!

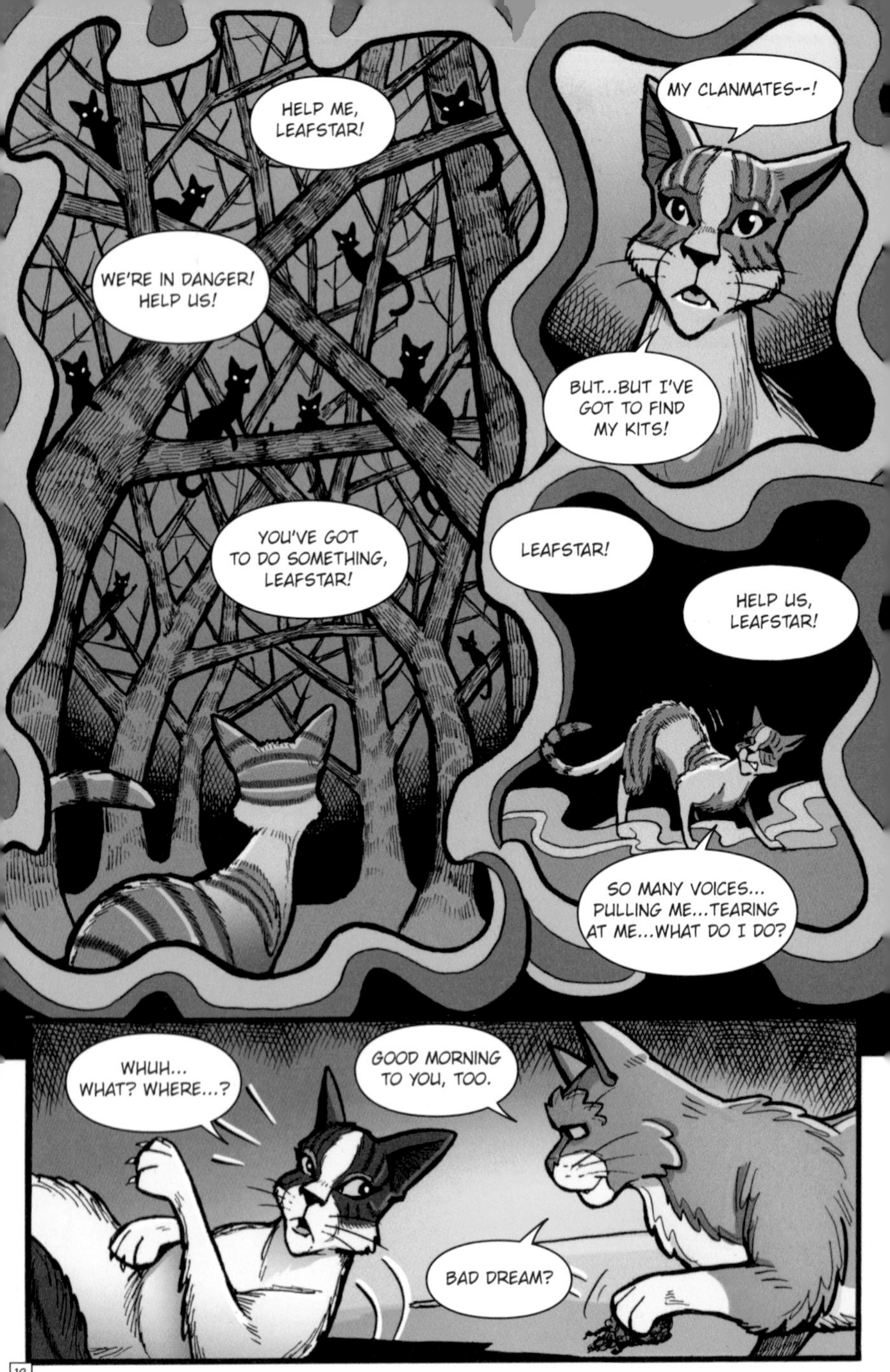
HELP ME, LEAFSTAR!
WE'RE IN DANGER! HELP US!
YOU'VE GOT TO DO SOMETHING, LEAFSTAR!
MY CLANMATES--!
BUT...BUT I'VE GOT TO FIND MY KITS!
LEAFSTAR!
HELP US, LEAFSTAR!
SO MANY VOICES... PULLING ME...TEARING AT ME...WHAT DO I DO?
WHUH... WHAT? WHERE...?
GOOD MORNING TO YOU, TOO.
BAD DREAM?

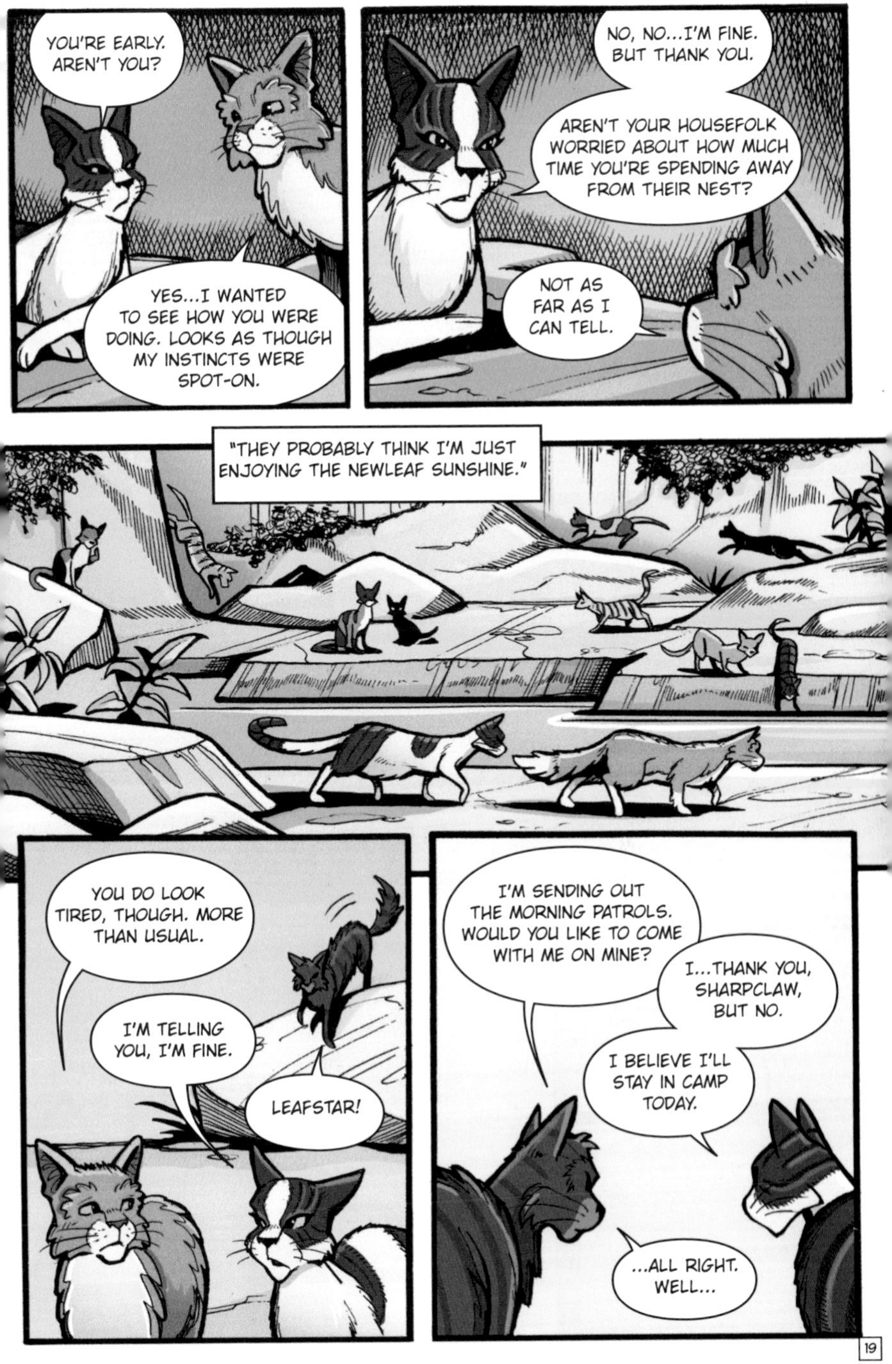

YOU'RE EARLY. AREN'T YOU?
YES...I WANTED TO SEE HOW YOU WERE DOING. LOOKS AS THOUGH MY INSTINCTS WERE SPOT-ON.
NO, NO...I'M FINE. BUT THANK YOU.
AREN'T YOUR HOUSEFOLK WORRIED ABOUT HOW MUCH TIME YOU'RE SPENDING AWAY FROM THEIR NEST?
NOT AS FAR AS I CAN TELL.
"THEY PROBABLY THINK I'M JUST ENJOYING THE NEWLEAF SUNSHINE."
YOU DO LOOK TIRED, THOUGH. MORE THAN USUAL.
I'M TELLING YOU, I'M FINE.
LEAFSTAR!
I'M SENDING OUT THE MORNING PATROLS. WOULD YOU LIKE TO COME WITH ME ON MINE?
I...THANK YOU, SHARPCLAW, BUT NO.
I BELIEVE I'LL STAY IN CAMP TODAY.
...ALL RIGHT. WELL...

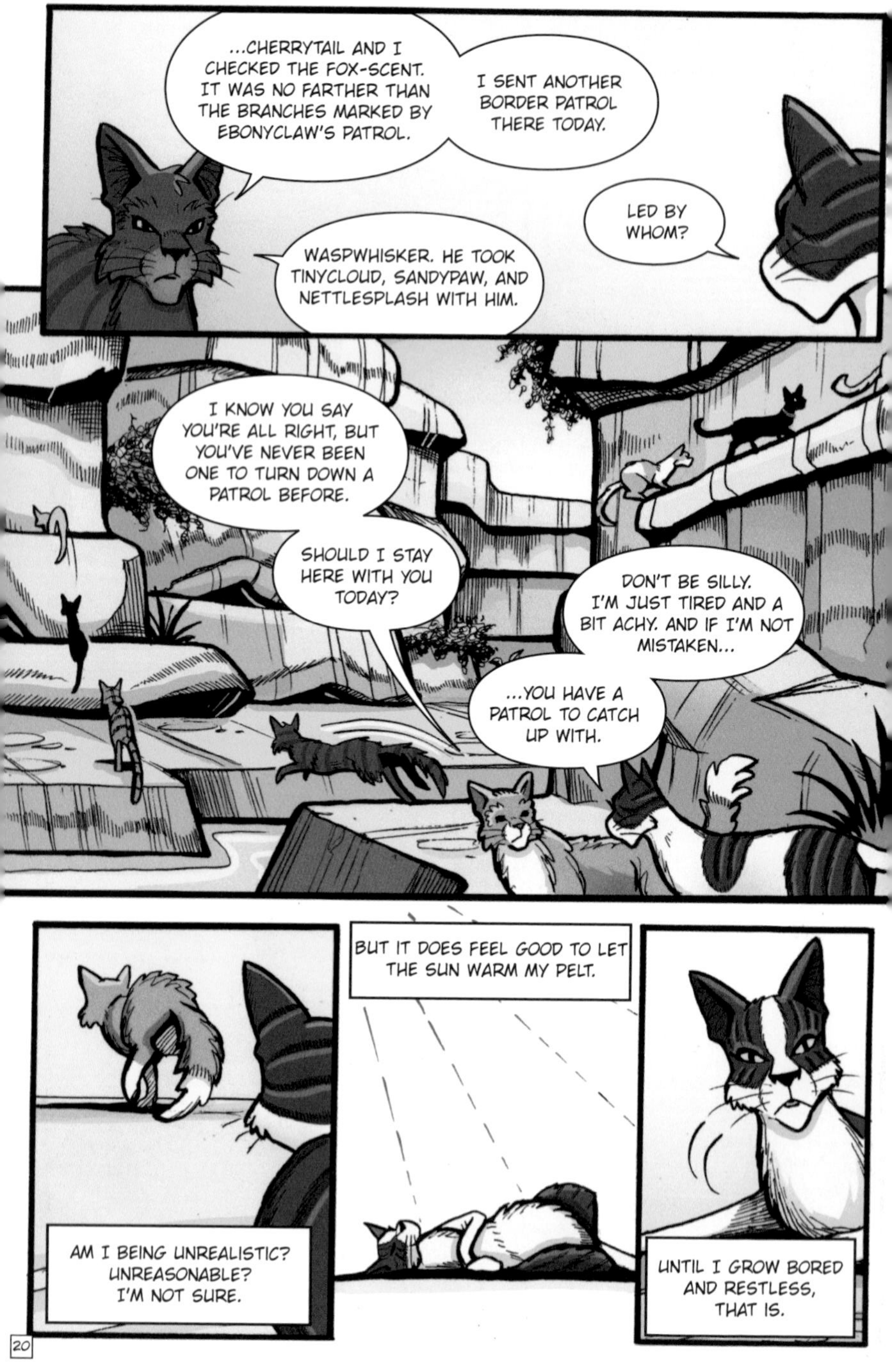
...CHERRYTAIL AND I CHECKED THE FOX-SCENT. IT WAS NO FARTHER THAN THE BRANCHES MARKED BY EBONYCLAW'S PATROL.
I SENT ANOTHER BORDER PATROL THERE TODAY.
LED BY WHOM?
WASPWHISKER. HE TOOK TINYCLOUD, SANDYPAW, AND NETTLESPLASH WITH HIM.
I KNOW YOU SAY YOU'RE ALL RIGHT, BUT YOU'VE NEVER BEEN ONE TO TURN DOWN A PATROL BEFORE.
SHOULD I STAY HERE WITH YOU TODAY?
DON'T BE SILLY. I'M JUST TIRED AND A BIT ACHY. AND IF I'M NOT MISTAKEN...
...YOU HAVE A PATROL TO CATCH UP WITH.
AM I BEING UNREALISTIC? UNREASONABLE? I'M NOT SURE.
BUT IT DOES FEEL GOOD TO LET THE SUN WARM MY PELT.
UNTIL I GROW BORED AND RESTLESS, THAT IS.

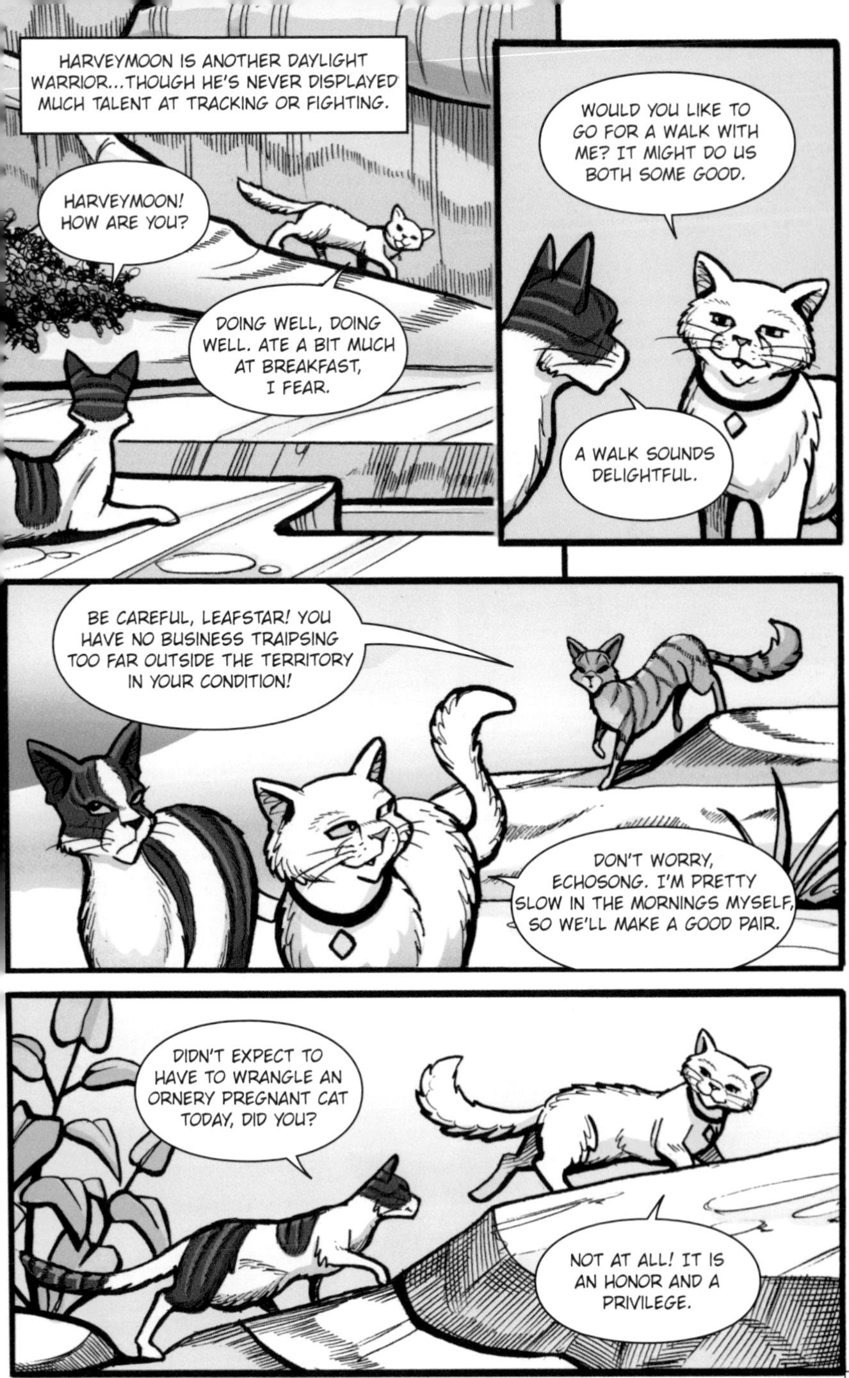
HARVEYMOON IS ANOTHER DAYLIGHT WARRIOR...THOUGH HE'S NEVER DISPLAYED MUCH TALENT AT TRACKING OR FIGHTING.
HARVEYMOON! HOW ARE YOU?
DOING WELL, DOING WELL. ATE A BIT MUCH AT BREAKFAST, I FEAR.
WOULD YOU LIKE TO GO FOR A WALK WITH ME? IT MIGHT DO US BOTH SOME GOOD.
A WALK SOUNDS DELIGHTFUL.
BE CAREFUL, LEAFSTAR! YOU HAVE NO BUSINESS TRAIPSING TOO FAR OUTSIDE THE TERRITORY IN YOUR CONDITION!
DON'T WORRY, ECHOSONG. I'M PRETTY SLOW IN THE MORNINGS MYSELF, SO WE'LL MAKE A GOOD PAIR.
DIDN'T EXPECT TO HAVE TO WRANGLE AN ORNERY PREGNANT CAT TODAY, DID YOU?
NOT AT ALL! IT IS AN HONOR AND A PRIVILEGE.

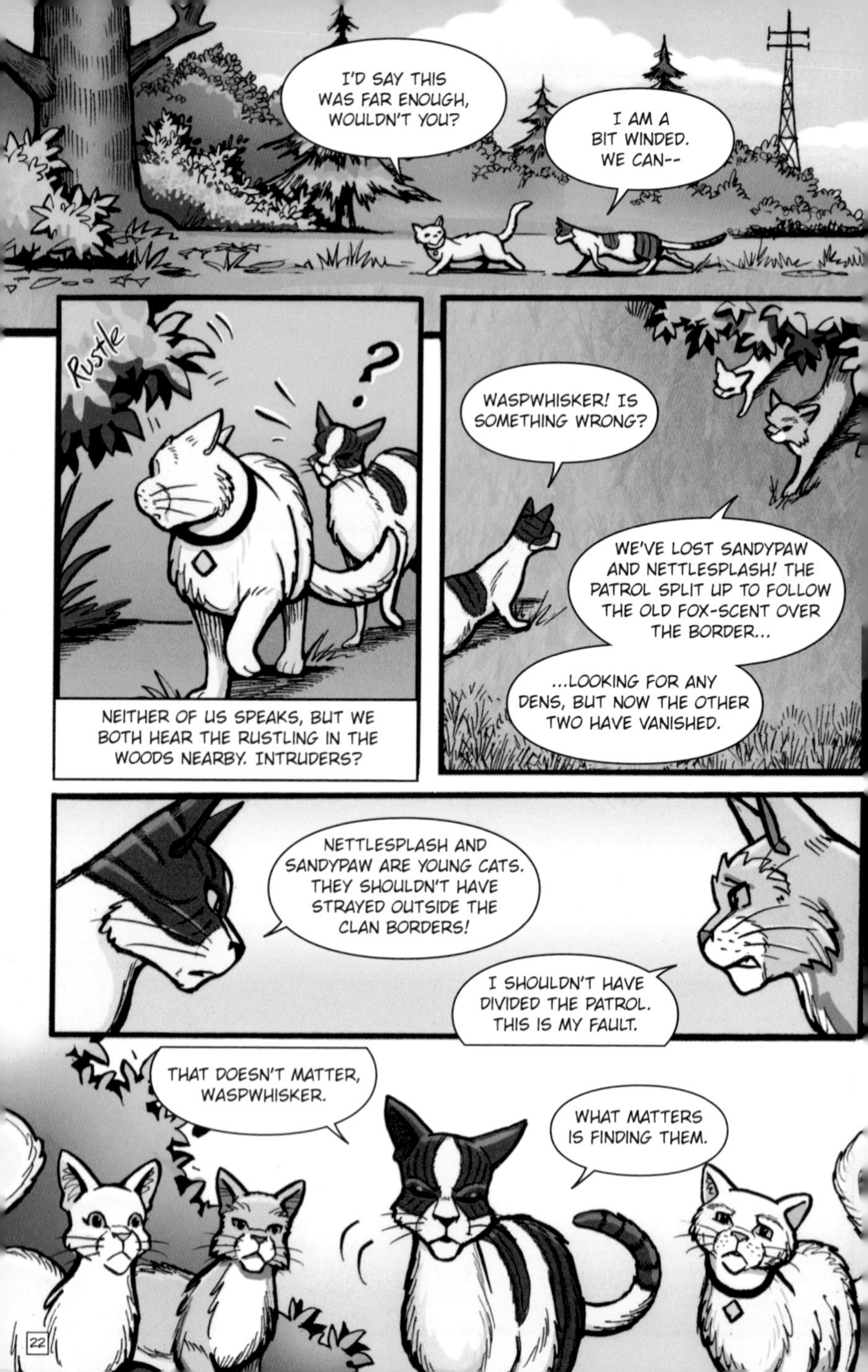
I'D SAY THIS WAS FAR ENOUGH, WOULDN'T YOU?
I AM A BIT WINDED. WE CAN--
Rustle
?
NEITHER OF US SPEAKS, BUT WE BOTH HEAR THE RUSTLING IN THE WOODS NEARBY. INTRUDERS?
WASPWHISKER! IS SOMETHING WRONG?
WE'VE LOST SANDYPAW AND NETTLESPLASH! THE PATROL SPLIT UP TO FOLLOW THE OLD FOX-SCENT OVER THE BORDER...
...LOOKING FOR ANY DENS, BUT NOW THE OTHER TWO HAVE VANISHED.
NETTLESPLASH AND SANDYPAW ARE YOUNG CATS. THEY SHOULDN'T HAVE STRAYED OUTSIDE THE CLAN BORDERS!
I SHOULDN'T HAVE DIVIDED THE PATROL. THIS IS MY FAULT.
THAT DOESN'T MATTER, WASPWHISKER.
WHAT MATTERS IS FINDING THEM.

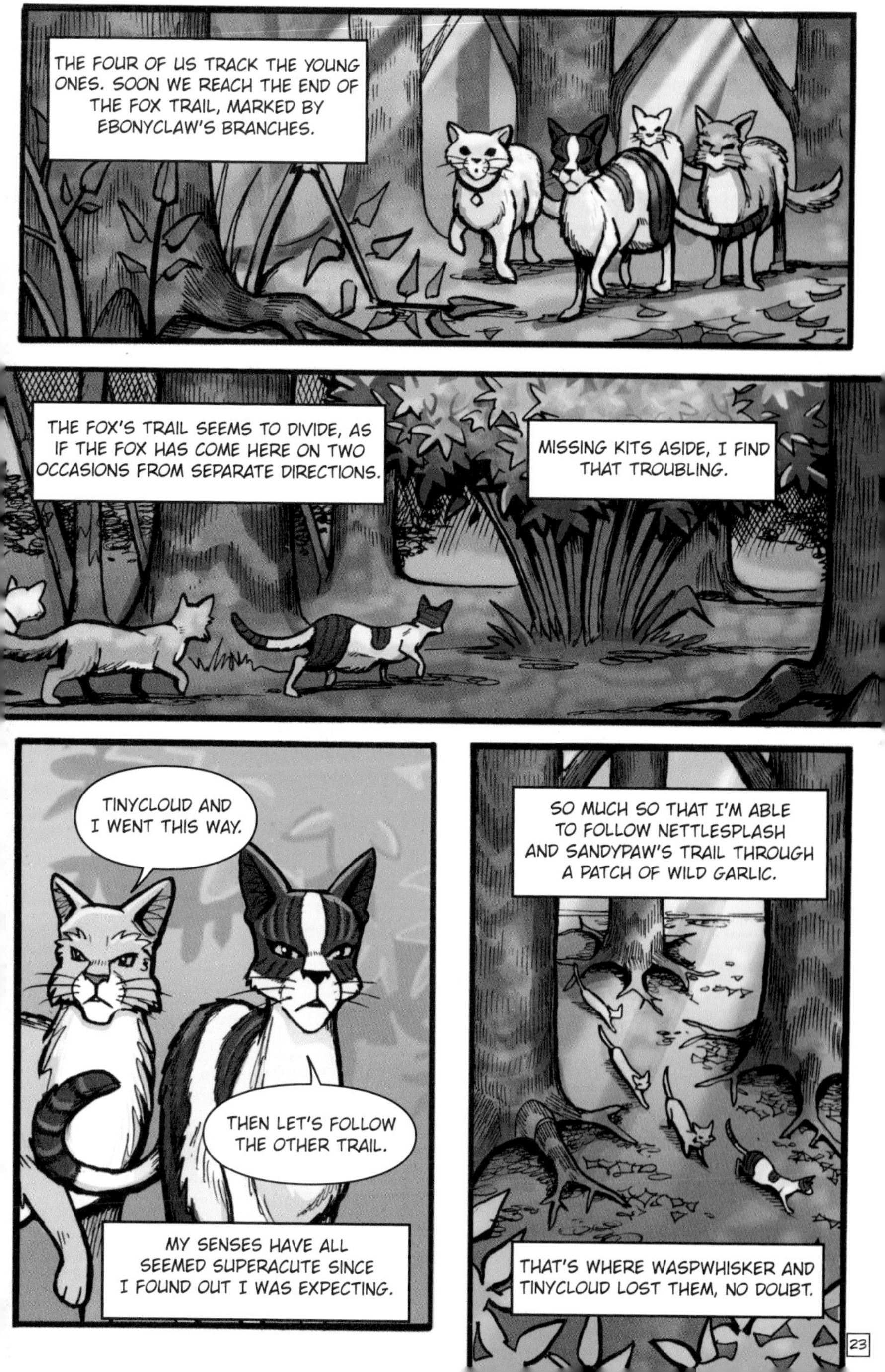
THE FOUR OF US TRACK THE YOUNG ONES. SOON WE REACH THE END OF THE FOX TRAIL, MARKED BY EBONYCLAW'S BRANCHES.
THE FOX'S TRAIL SEEMS TO DIVIDE, AS IF THE FOX HAS COME HERE ON TWO OCCASIONS FROM SEPARATE DIRECTIONS.
MISSING KITS ASIDE, I FIND THAT TROUBLING.
TINYCLOUD AND I WENT THIS WAY.
THEN LET'S FOLLOW THE OTHER TRAIL.
MY SENSES HAVE ALL SEEMED SUPERACUTE SINCE I FOUND OUT I WAS EXPECTING.
SO MUCH SO THAT I'M ABLE TO FOLLOW NETTLESPLASH AND SANDYPAW'S TRAIL THROUGH A PATCH OF WILD GARLIC.
THAT'S WHERE WASPWHISKER AND TINYCLOUD LOST THEM, NO DOUBT.

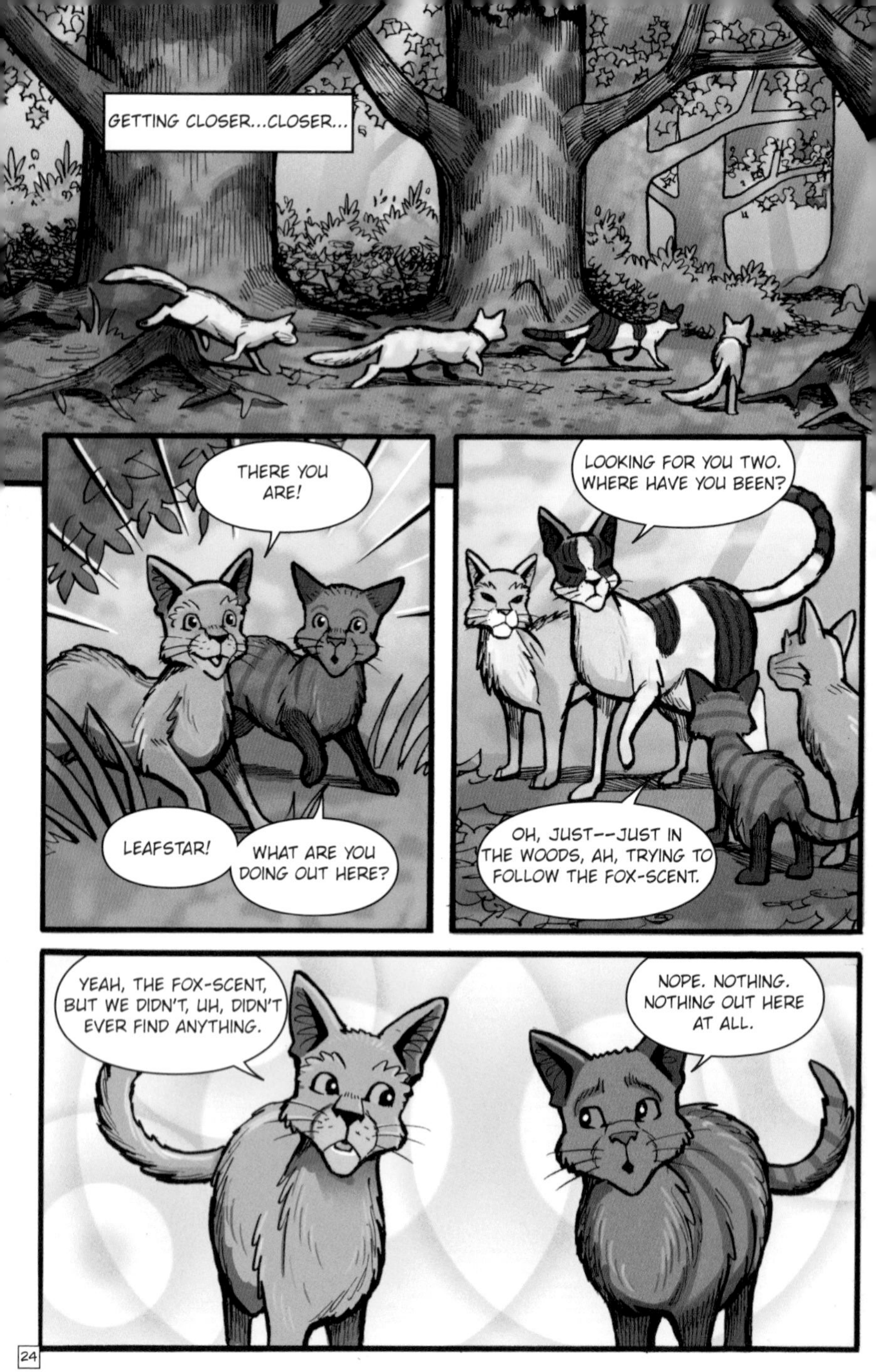
GETTING CLOSER...CLOSER...
THERE YOU ARE!
LEAFSTAR!
WHAT ARE YOU DOING OUT HERE?
LOOKING FOR YOU TWO. WHERE HAVE YOU BEEN?
OH, JUST--JUST IN THE WOODS, AH, TRYING TO FOLLOW THE FOX-SCENT.
YEAH, THE FOX-SCENT, BUT WE DIDN'T, UH, DIDN'T EVER FIND ANYTHING.
NOPE. NOTHING. NOTHING OUT HERE AT ALL.

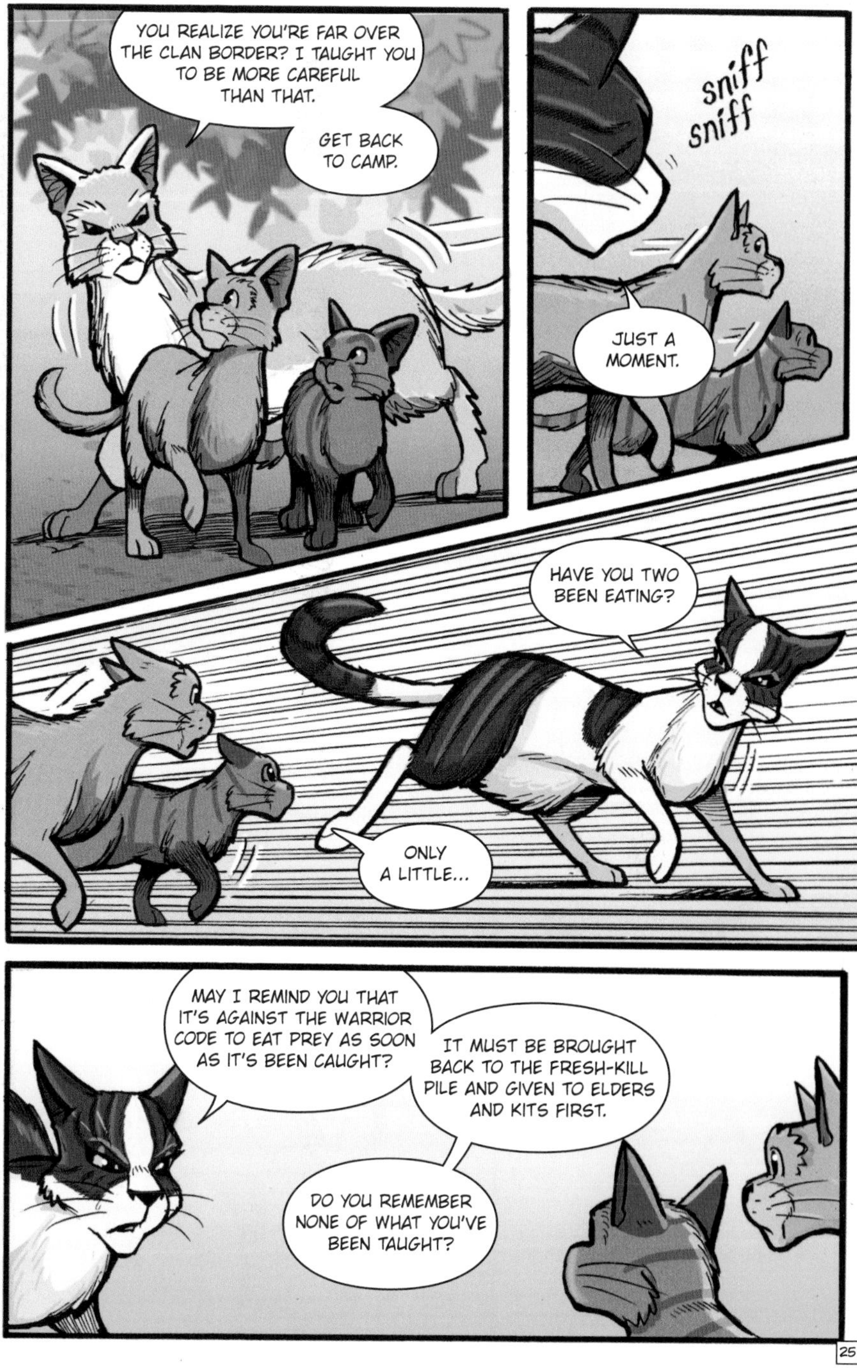

YOU REALIZE YOU'RE FAR OVER THE CLAN BORDER? I TAUGHT YOU TO BE MORE CAREFUL THAN THAT.
GET BACK TO CAMP.
sniff sniff
JUST A MOMENT.
HAVE YOU TWO BEEN EATING?
ONLY A LITTLE...
MAY I REMIND YOU THAT IT'S AGAINST THE WARRIOR CODE TO EAT PREY AS SOON AS IT'S BEEN CAUGHT?
IT MUST BE BROUGHT BACK TO THE FRESH-KILL PILE AND GIVEN TO ELDERS AND KITS FIRST.
DO YOU REMEMBER NONE OF WHAT YOU'VE BEEN TAUGHT?

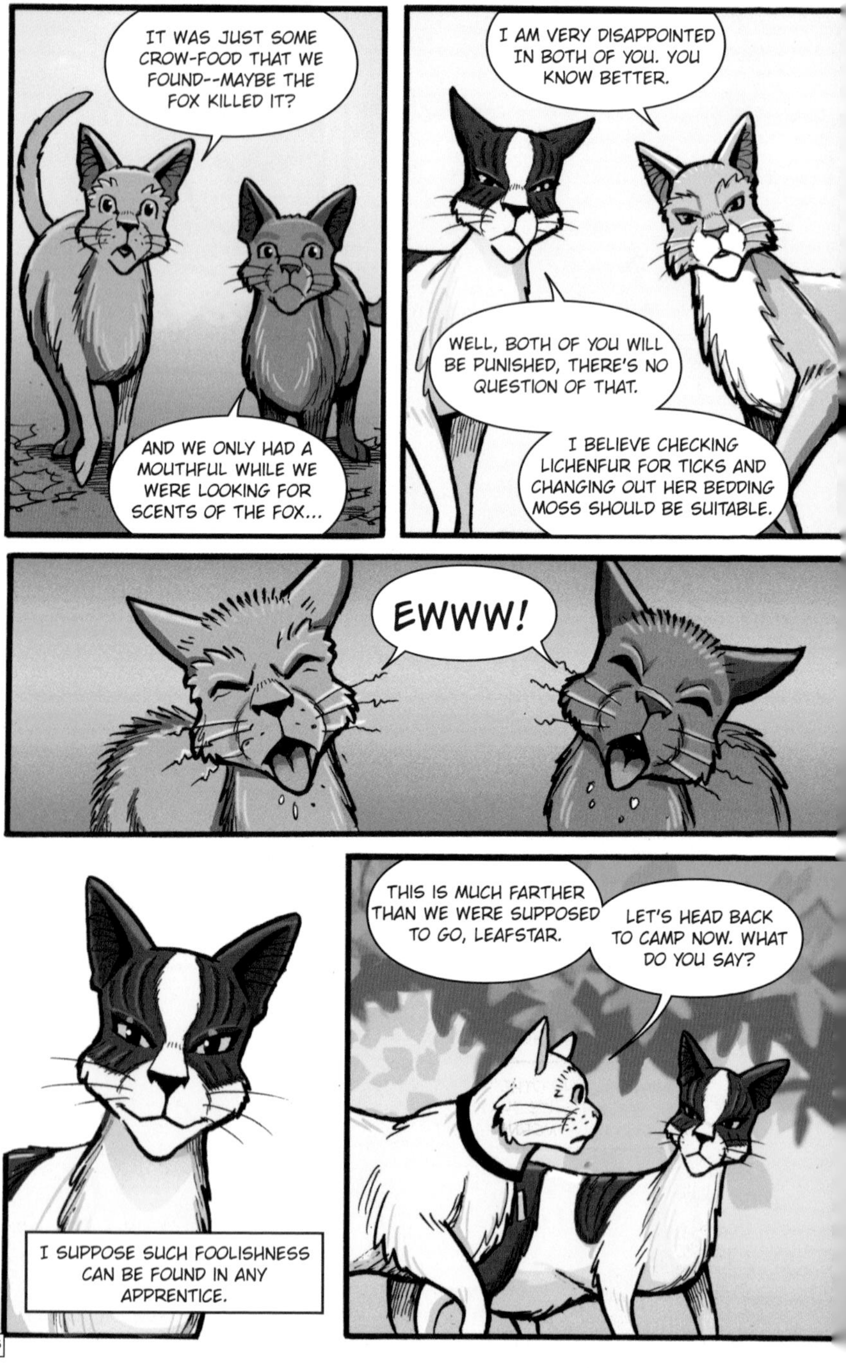
IT WAS JUST SOME CROW-FOOD THAT WE FOUND--MAYBE THE FOX KILLED IT?
AND WE ONLY HAD A MOUTHFUL WHILE WE WERE LOOKING FOR SCENTS OF THE FOX...
I AM VERY DISAPPOINTED IN BOTH OF YOU. YOU KNOW BETTER.
WELL, BOTH OF YOU WILL BE PUNISHED, THERE'S NO QUESTION OF THAT.
I BELIEVE CHECKING LICHENFUR FOR TICKS AND CHANGING OUT HER BEDDING MOSS SHOULD BE SUITABLE.
EWWW!
I SUPPOSE SUCH FOOLISHNESS CAN BE FOUND IN ANY APPRENTICE.
THIS IS MUCH FARTHER THAN WE WERE SUPPOSED TO GO, LEAFSTAR.
LET'S HEAD BACK TO CAMP NOW. WHAT DO YOU SAY?

BUT SOMETHING BOTHERS ME ABOUT THEIR STORY.

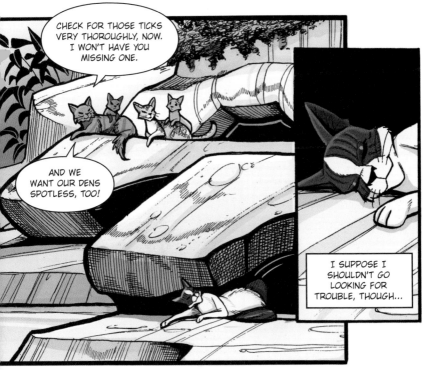

CHECK FOR THOSE TICKS VERY THOROUGHLY, NOW. I WON'T HAVE YOU MISSING ONE.

AND WE WANT OUR DENS SPOTLESS, TOO!

I SUPPOSE I SHOULDN'T GO LOOKING FOR TROUBLE, THOUGH...

...AND WITH NO OTHER DISTURBANCES, I SLEEP LATE THE FOLLOWING MORNING.

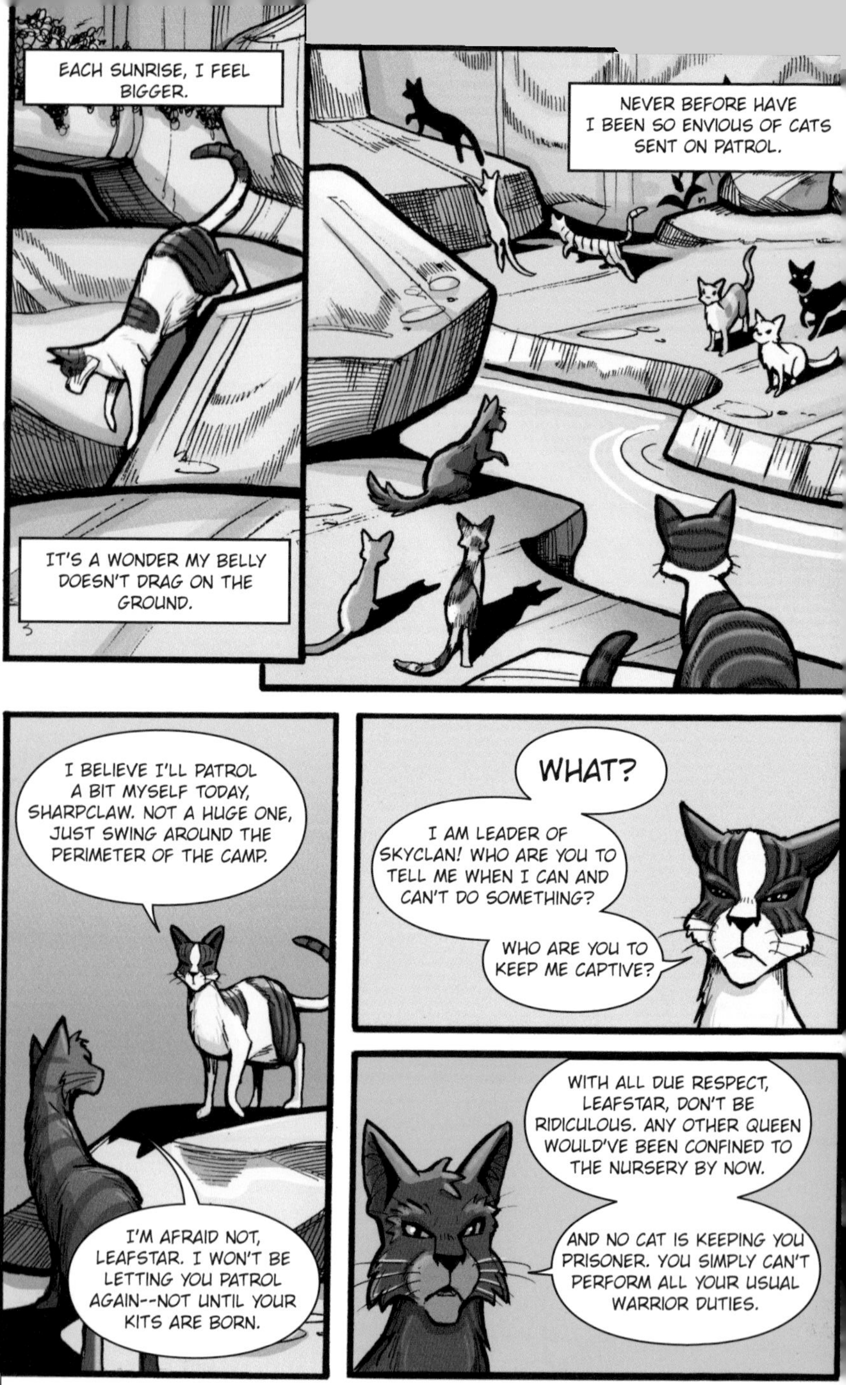
EACH SUNRISE, I FEEL BIGGER.
IT'S A WONDER MY BELLY DOESN'T DRAG ON THE GROUND.
NEVER BEFORE HAVE I BEEN SO ENVIOUS OF CATS SENT ON PATROL.
I BELIEVE I'LL PATROL A BIT MYSELF TODAY, SHARPCLAW. NOT A HUGE ONE, JUST SWING AROUND THE PERIMETER OF THE CAMP.
I'M AFRAID NOT, LEAFSTAR. I WON'T BE LETTING YOU PATROL AGAIN--NOT UNTIL YOUR KITS ARE BORN.
WHAT?
I AM LEADER OF SKYCLAN! WHO ARE YOU TO TELL ME WHEN I CAN AND CAN'T DO SOMETHING?
WHO ARE YOU TO KEEP ME CAPTIVE?
WITH ALL DUE RESPECT, LEAFSTAR, DON'T BE RIDICULOUS. ANY OTHER QUEEN WOULD'VE BEEN CONFINED TO THE NURSERY BY NOW.
AND NO CAT IS KEEPING YOU PRISONER. YOU SIMPLY CAN'T PERFORM ALL YOUR USUAL WARRIOR DUTIES.

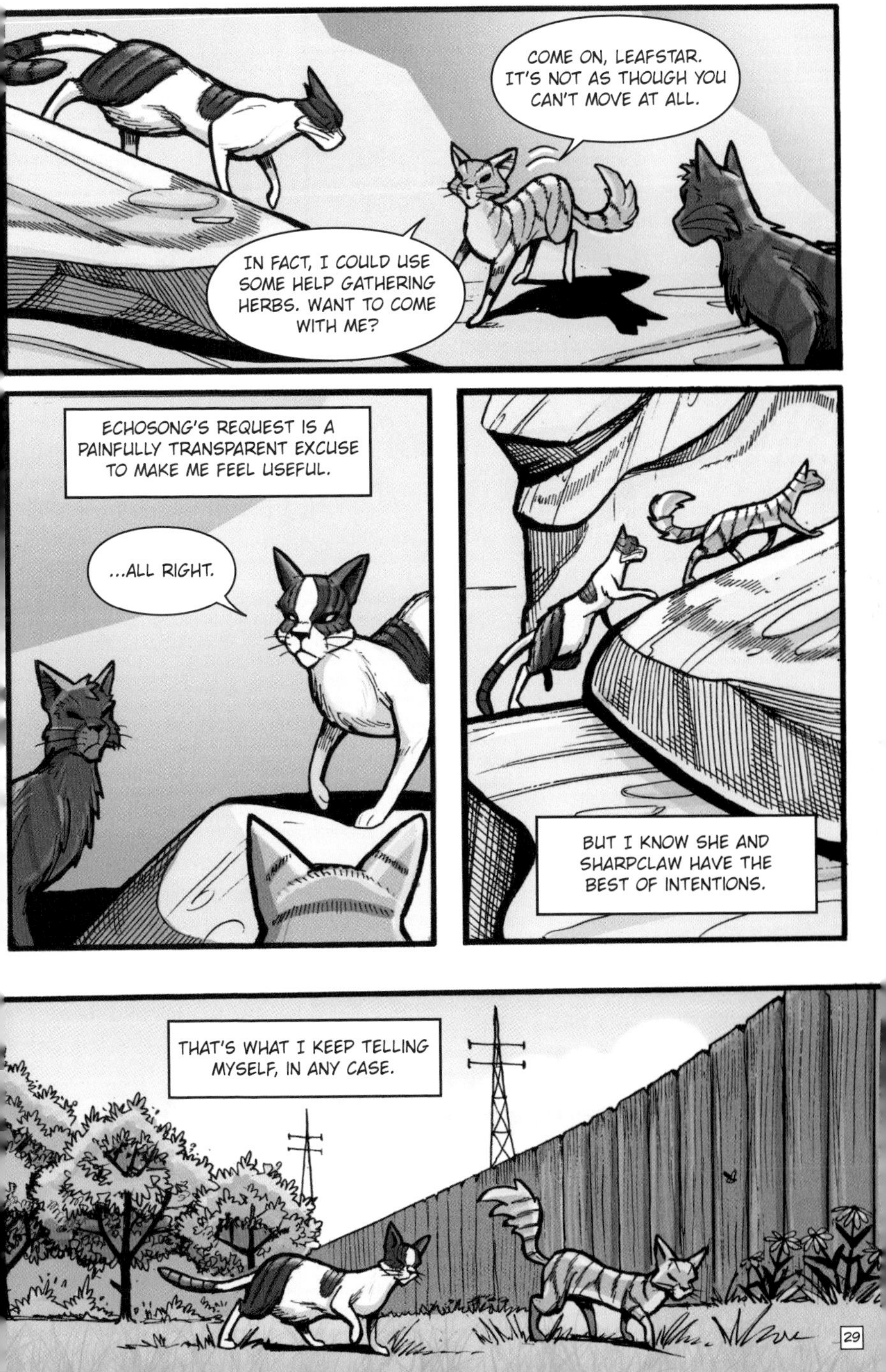
COME ON, LEAFSTAR. IT'S NOT AS THOUGH YOU CAN'T MOVE AT ALL.
IN FACT, I COULD USE SOME HELP GATHERING HERBS. WANT TO COME WITH ME?
ECHOSONG'S REQUEST IS A PAINFULLY TRANSPARENT EXCUSE TO MAKE ME FEEL USEFUL.
...ALL RIGHT.
BUT I KNOW SHE AND SHARPCLAW HAVE THE BEST OF INTENTIONS.
THAT'S WHAT I KEEP TELLING MYSELF, IN ANY CASE.

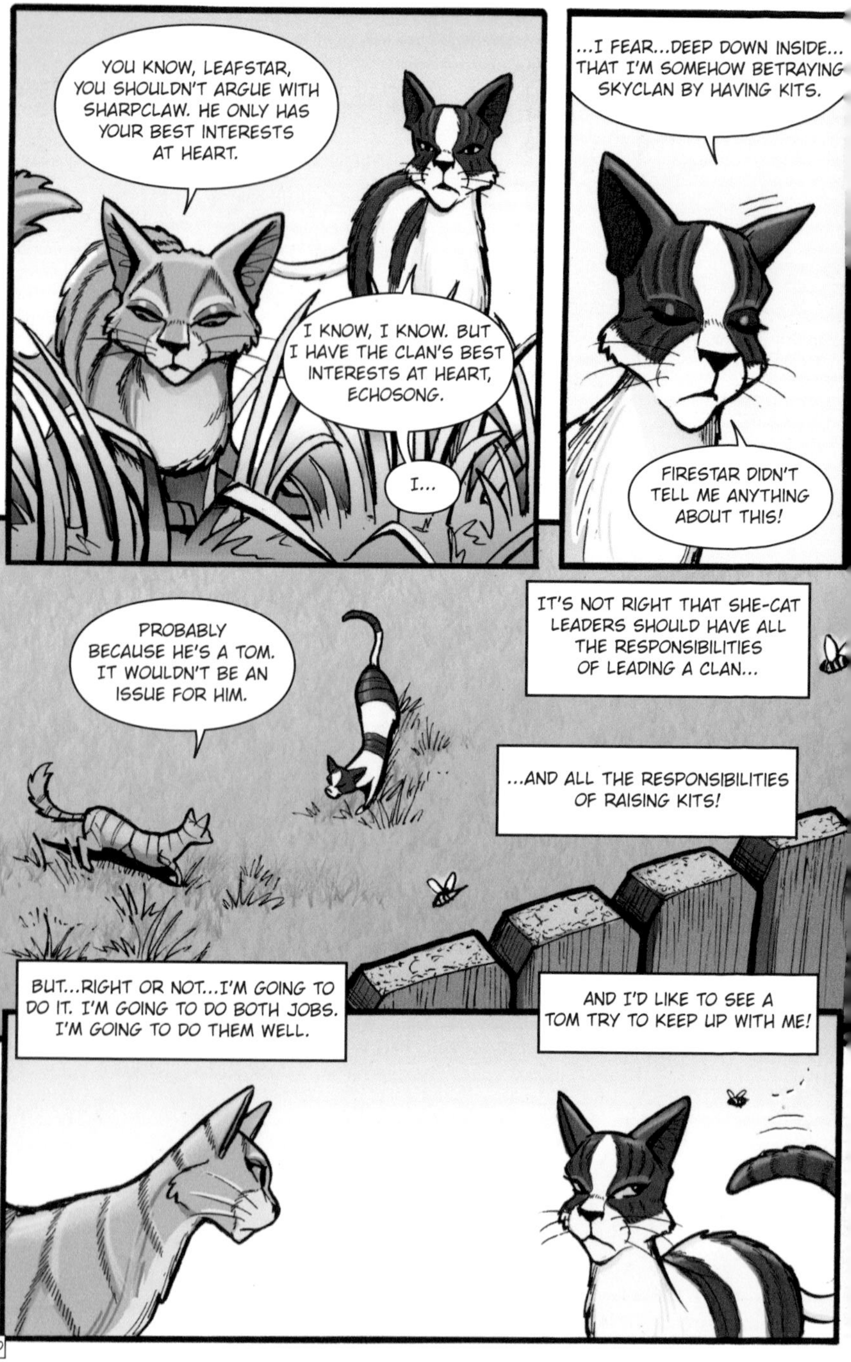

YOU KNOW, LEAFSTAR, YOU SHOULDN'T ARGUE WITH SHARPCLAW. HE ONLY HAS YOUR BEST INTERESTS AT HEART.
I KNOW, I KNOW. BUT I HAVE THE CLAN'S BEST INTERESTS AT HEART, ECHOSONG.
I...
...I FEAR...DEEP DOWN INSIDE... THAT I'M SOMEHOW BETRAYING SKYCLAN BY HAVING KITS.
FIRESTAR DIDN'T TELL ME ANYTHING ABOUT THIS!
PROBABLY BECAUSE HE'S A TOM. IT WOULDN'T BE AN ISSUE FOR HIM.
IT'S NOT RIGHT THAT SHE-CAT LEADERS SHOULD HAVE ALL THE RESPONSIBILITIES OF LEADING A CLAN...
...AND ALL THE RESPONSIBILITIES OF RAISING KITS!
BUT...RIGHT OR NOT...I'M GOING TO DO IT. I'M GOING TO DO BOTH JOBS. I'M GOING TO DO THEM WELL.
AND I'D LIKE TO SEE A TOM TRY TO KEEP UP WITH ME!

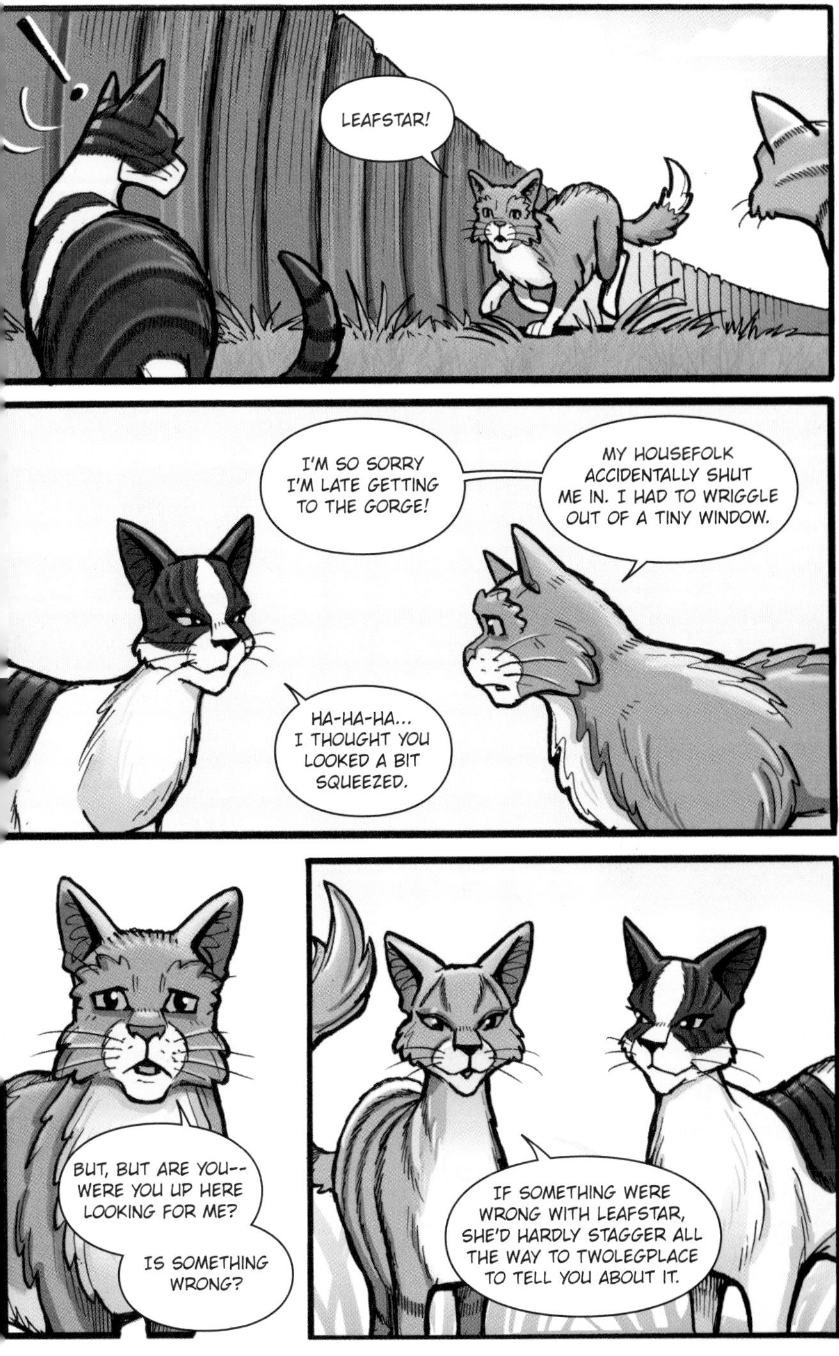
LEAFSTAR!
I'M SO SORRY I'M LATE GETTING TO THE GORGE!
MY HOUSEFOLK ACCIDENTALLY SHUT ME IN. I HAD TO WRIGGLE OUT OF A TINY WINDOW.
HA-HA-HA... I THOUGHT YOU LOOKED A BIT SQUEEZED.
BUT, BUT ARE YOU-- WERE YOU UP HERE LOOKING FOR ME?
IS SOMETHING WRONG?
IF SOMETHING WERE WRONG WITH LEAFSTAR, SHE'D HARDLY STAGGER ALL THE WAY TO TWOLEGPLACE TO TELL YOU ABOUT IT.

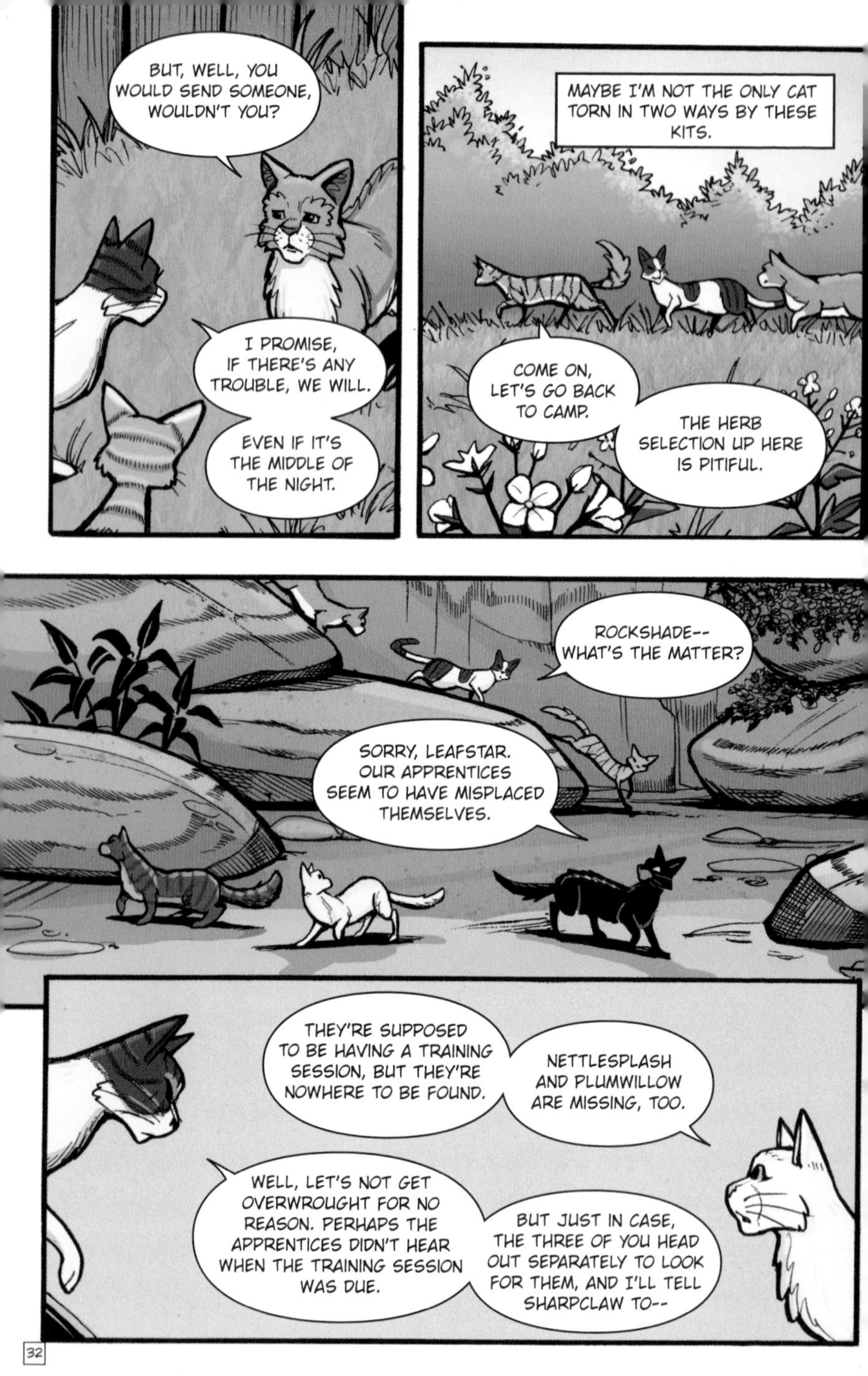
BUT, WELL, YOU WOULD SEND SOMEONE, WOULDN'T YOU?
I PROMISE, IF THERE'S ANY TROUBLE, WE WILL.
EVEN IF IT'S THE MIDDLE OF THE NIGHT.
MAYBE I'M NOT THE ONLY CAT TORN IN TWO WAYS BY THESE KITS.
COME ON, LET'S GO BACK TO CAMP.
THE HERB SELECTION UP HERE IS PITIFUL.
ROCKSHADE-- WHAT'S THE MATTER?
SORRY, LEAFSTAR. OUR APPRENTICES SEEM TO HAVE MISPLACED THEMSELVES.
THEY'RE SUPPOSED TO BE HAVING A TRAINING SESSION, BUT THEY'RE NOWHERE TO BE FOUND.
NETTLESPLASH AND PLUMWILLOW ARE MISSING, TOO.
WELL, LET'S NOT GET OVERWROUGHT FOR NO REASON. PERHAPS THE APPRENTICES DIDN'T HEAR WHEN THE TRAINING SESSION WAS DUE.
BUT JUST IN CASE, THE THREE OF YOU HEAD OUT SEPARATELY TO LOOK FOR THEM, AND I'LL TELL SHARPCLAW TO--

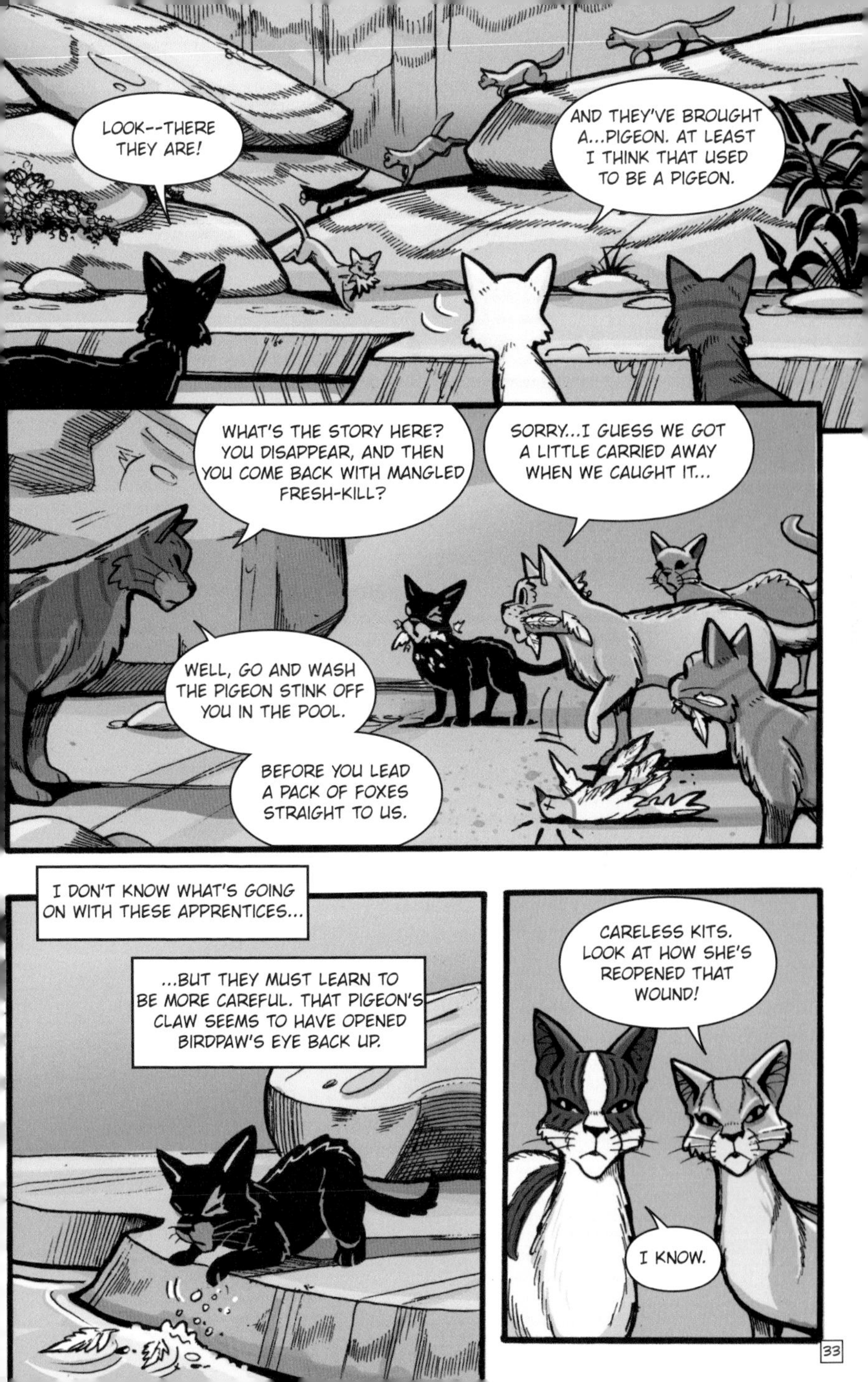
LOOK--THERE THEY ARE!
AND THEY'VE BROUGHT A...PIGEON. AT LEAST I THINK THAT USED TO BE A PIGEON.
WHAT'S THE STORY HERE? YOU DISAPPEAR, AND THEN YOU COME BACK WITH MANGLED FRESH-KILL?
SORRY...I GUESS WE GOT A LITTLE CARRIED AWAY WHEN WE CAUGHT IT...
WELL, GO AND WASH THE PIGEON STINK OFF YOU IN THE POOL.
BEFORE YOU LEAD A PACK OF FOXES STRAIGHT TO US.
I DON'T KNOW WHAT'S GOING ON WITH THESE APPRENTICES...
...BUT THEY MUST LEARN TO BE MORE CAREFUL. THAT PIGEON'S CLAW SEEMS TO HAVE OPENED BIRDPAW'S EYE BACK UP.
CARELESS KITS. LOOK AT HOW SHE'S REOPENED THAT WOUND!
I KNOW.

• • •

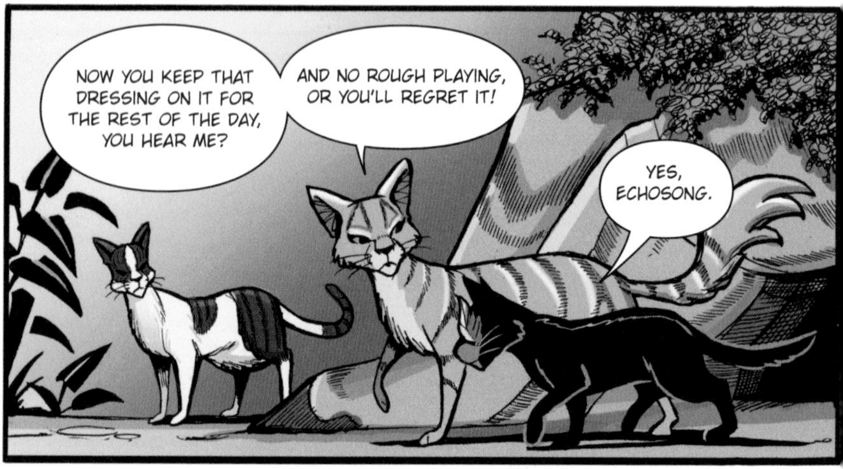
NOW YOU KEEP THAT DRESSING ON IT FOR THE REST OF THE DAY, YOU HEAR ME?
AND NO ROUGH PLAYING, OR YOU'LL REGRET IT!
YES, ECHOSONG.

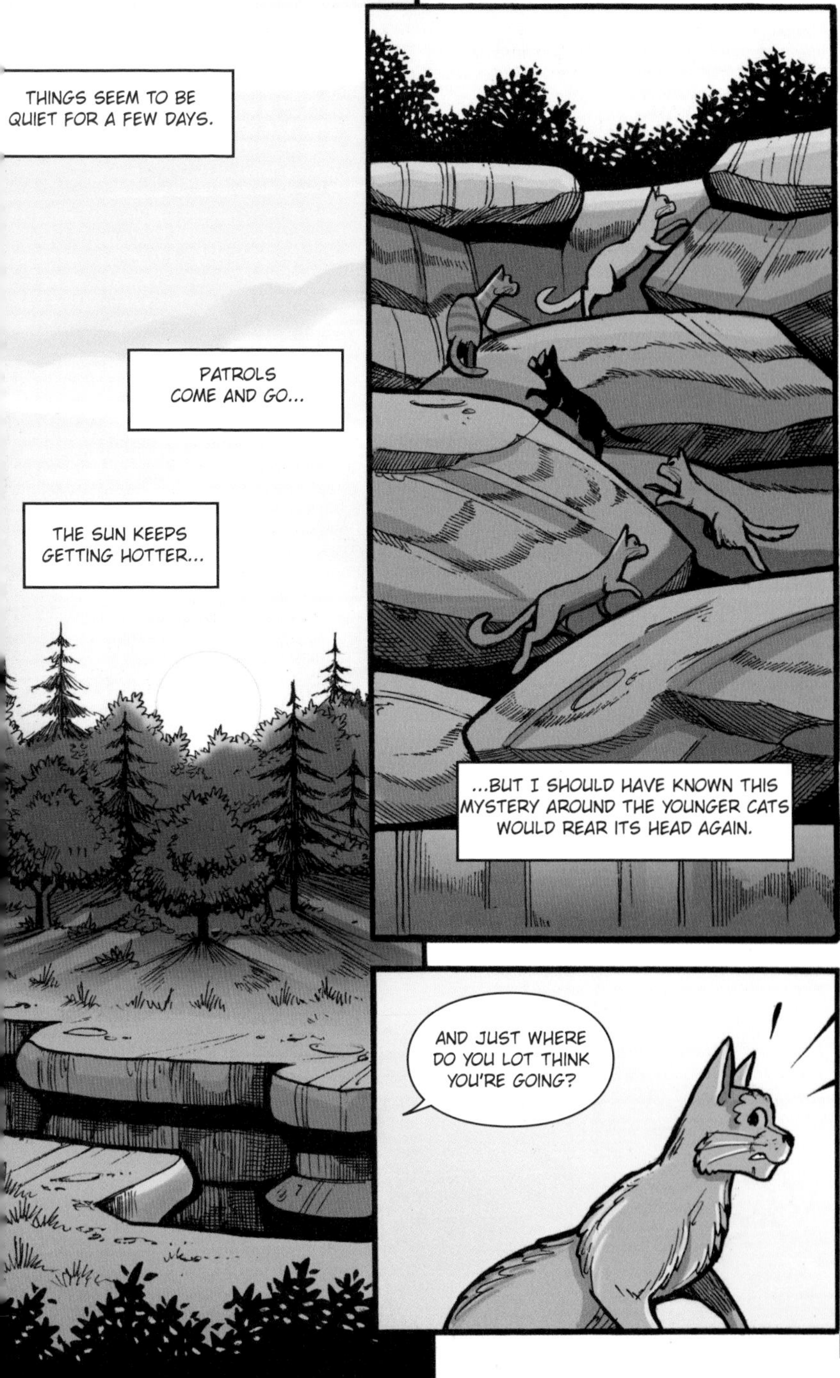
THINGS SEEM TO BE QUIET FOR A FEW DAYS.
PATROLS COME AND GO...
THE SUN KEEPS GETTING HOTTER...
...BUT I SHOULD HAVE KNOWN THIS MYSTERY AROUND THE YOUNGER CATS WOULD REAR ITS HEAD AGAIN.
AND JUST WHERE DO YOU LOT THINK YOU'RE GOING?

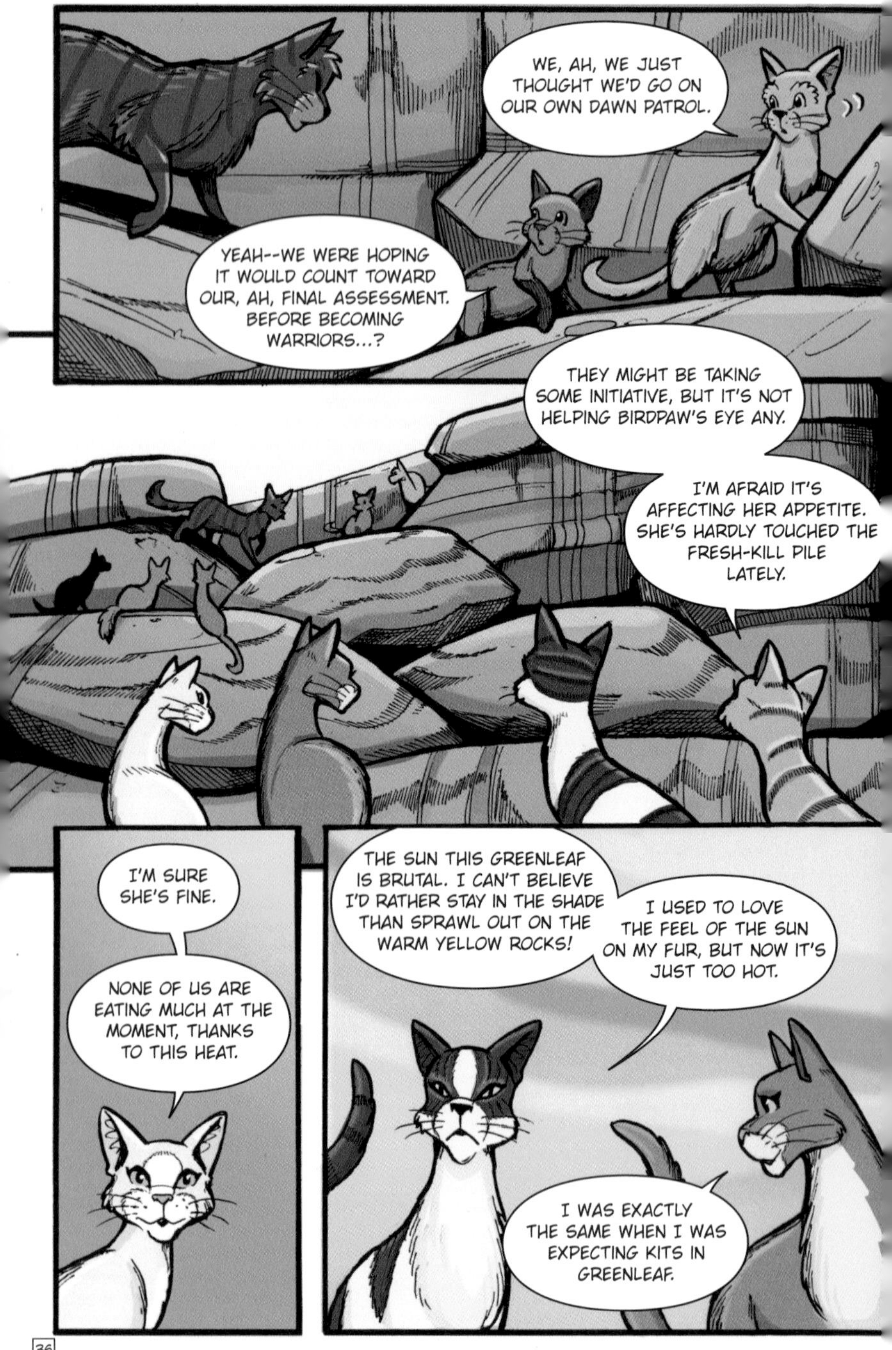
WE, AH, WE JUST THOUGHT WE'D GO ON OUR OWN DAWN PATROL.
YEAH--WE WERE HOPING IT WOULD COUNT TOWARD OUR, AH, FINAL ASSESSMENT. BEFORE BECOMING WARRIORS...?
THEY MIGHT BE TAKING SOME INITIATIVE, BUT IT'S NOT HELPING BIRDPAW'S EYE ANY.
I'M AFRAID IT'S AFFECTING HER APPETITE. SHE'S HARDLY TOUCHED THE FRESH-KILL PILE LATELY.
I'M SURE SHE'S FINE.
NONE OF US ARE EATING MUCH AT THE MOMENT, THANKS TO THIS HEAT.
THE SUN THIS GREENLEAF IS BRUTAL. I CAN'T BELIEVE I'D RATHER STAY IN THE SHADE THAN SPRAWL OUT ON THE WARM YELLOW ROCKS!
I USED TO LOVE THE FEEL OF THE SUN ON MY FUR, BUT NOW IT'S JUST TOO HOT.
I WAS EXACTLY THE SAME WHEN I WAS EXPECTING KITS IN GREENLEAF.

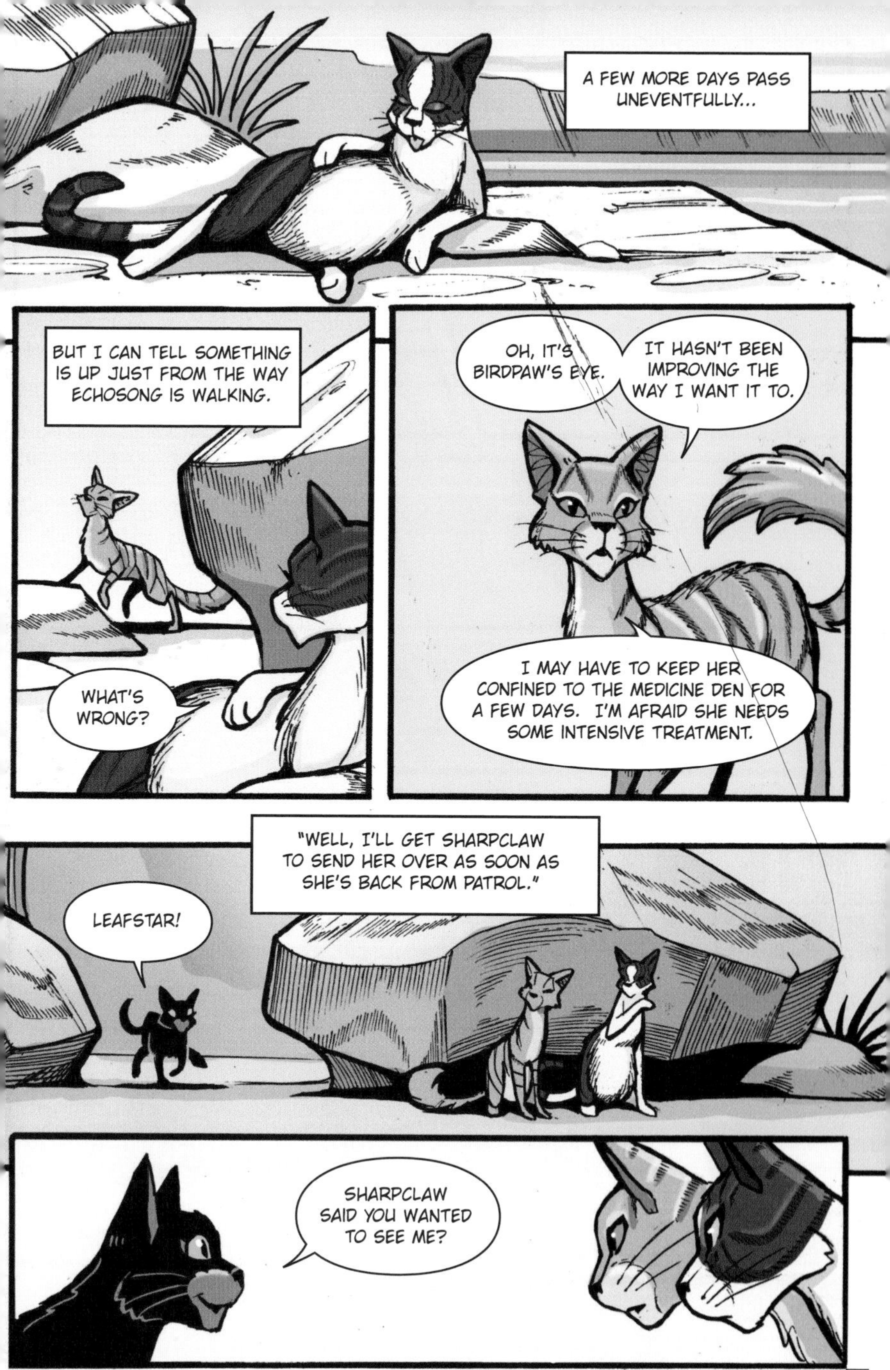
A FEW MORE DAYS PASS UNEVENTFULLY...
BUT I CAN TELL SOMETHING IS UP JUST FROM THE WAY ECHOSONG IS WALKING.
WHAT'S WRONG?
OH, IT'S BIRDPAW'S EYE.
IT HASN'T BEEN IMPROVING THE WAY I WANT IT TO.
I MAY HAVE TO KEEP HER CONFINED TO THE MEDICINE DEN FOR A FEW DAYS. I'M AFRAID SHE NEEDS SOME INTENSIVE TREATMENT.
"WELL, I'LL GET SHARPCLAW TO SEND HER OVER AS SOON AS SHE'S BACK FROM PATROL."
LEAFSTAR!
SHARPCLAW SAID YOU WANTED TO SEE ME?

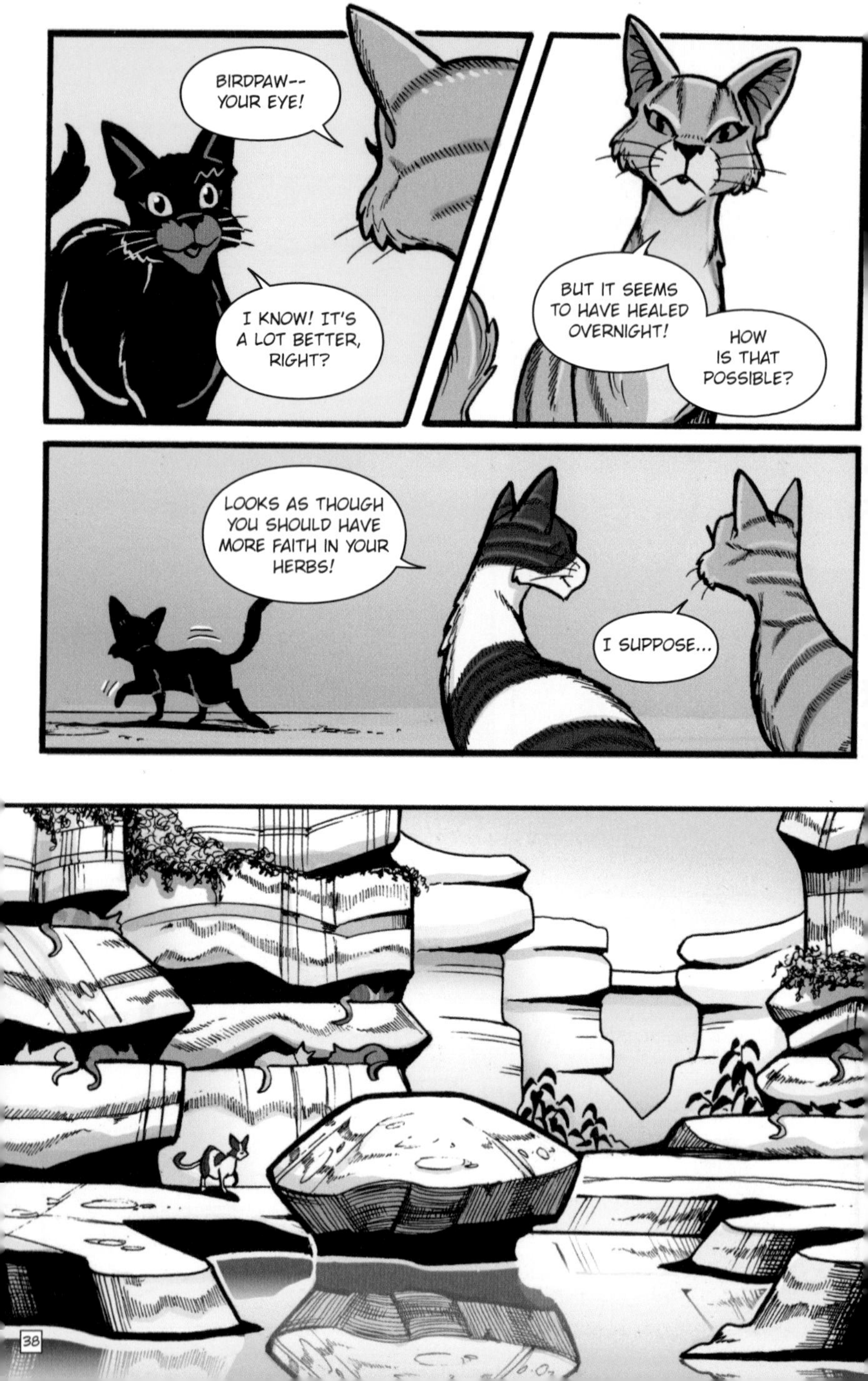
BIRDPAW-- YOUR EYE!
I KNOW! IT'S A LOT BETTER, RIGHT?
BUT IT SEEMS TO HAVE HEALED OVERNIGHT!
HOW IS THAT POSSIBLE?
LOOKS AS THOUGH YOU SHOULD HAVE MORE FAITH IN YOUR HERBS!
I SUPPOSE...

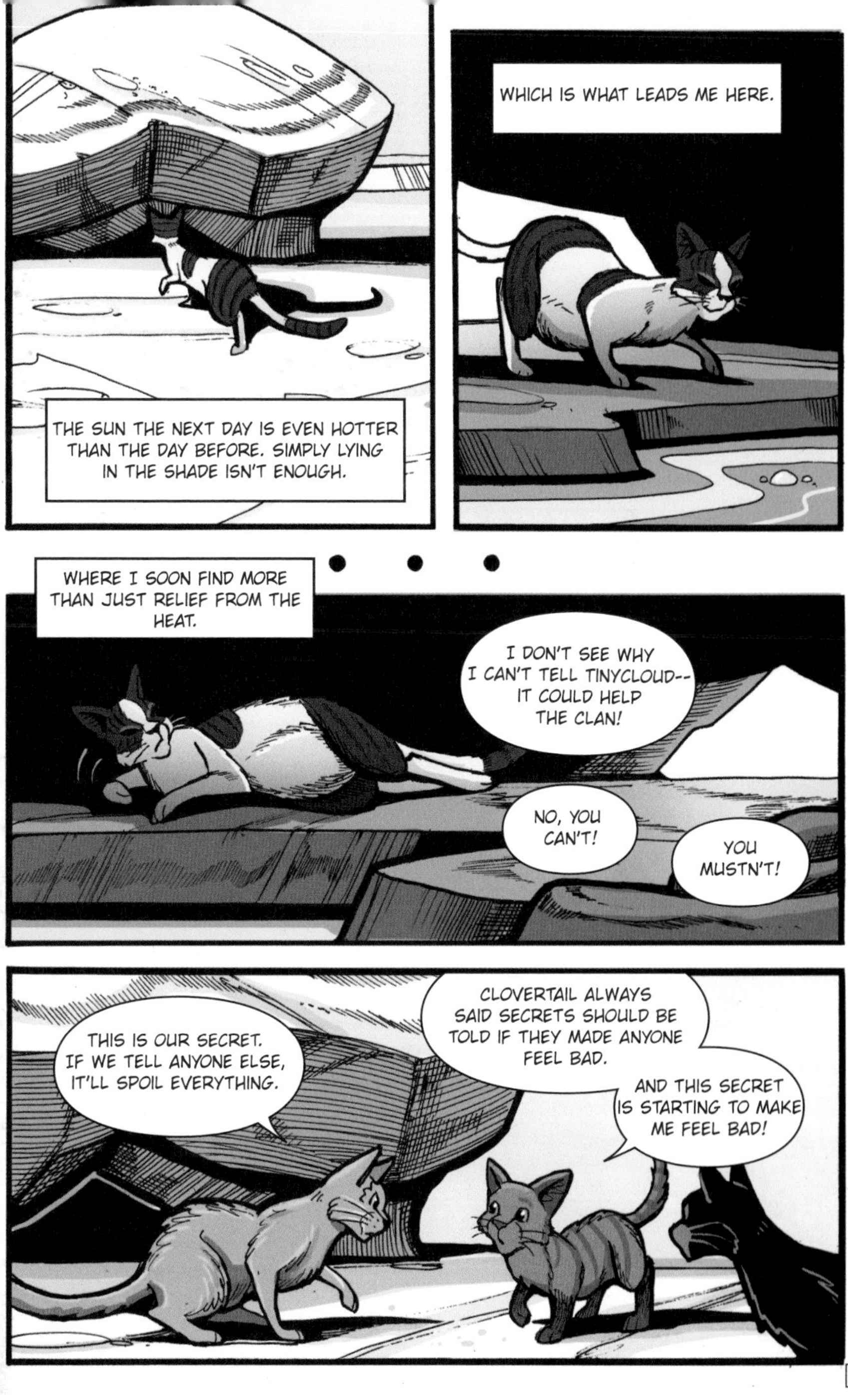
THE SUN THE NEXT DAY IS EVEN HOTTER THAN THE DAY BEFORE. SIMPLY LYING IN THE SHADE ISN'T ENOUGH.
WHICH IS WHAT LEADS ME HERE.
WHERE I SOON FIND MORE THAN JUST RELIEF FROM THE HEAT.
I DON'T SEE WHY I CAN'T TELL TINYCLOUD-- IT COULD HELP THE CLAN!
NO, YOU CAN'T!
YOU MUSTN'T!
THIS IS OUR SECRET. IF WE TELL ANYONE ELSE, IT'LL SPOIL EVERYTHING.
CLOVERTAIL ALWAYS SAID SECRETS SHOULD BE TOLD IF THEY MADE ANYONE FEEL BAD.
AND THIS SECRET IS STARTING TO MAKE ME FEEL BAD!

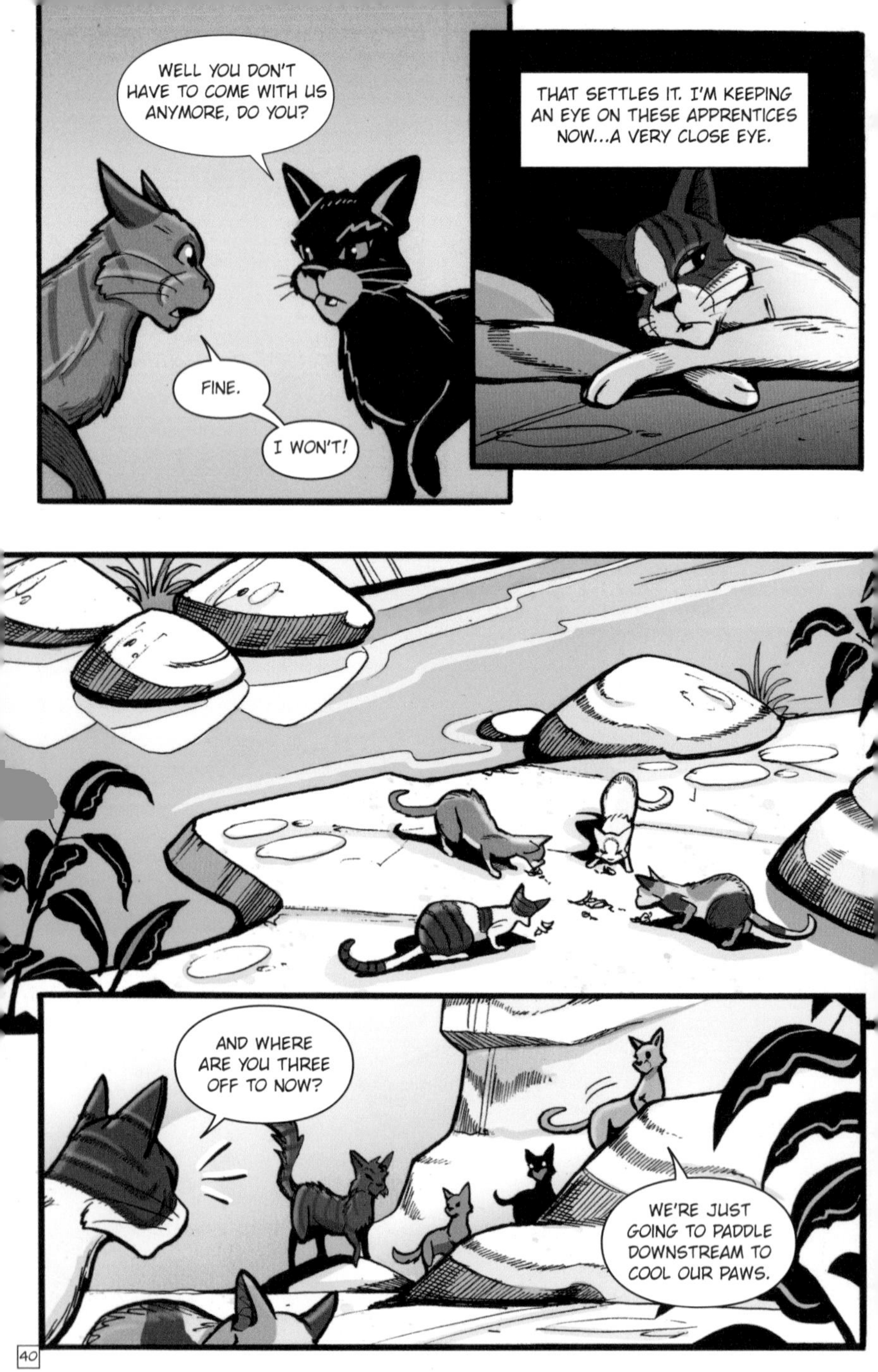
WELL YOU DON'T HAVE TO COME WITH US ANYMORE, DO YOU?
FINE.
I WON'T!
THAT SETTLES IT. I'M KEEPING AN EYE ON THESE APPRENTICES NOW...A VERY CLOSE EYE.
AND WHERE ARE YOU THREE OFF TO NOW?
WE'RE JUST GOING TO PADDLE DOWNSTREAM TO COOL OUR PAWS.

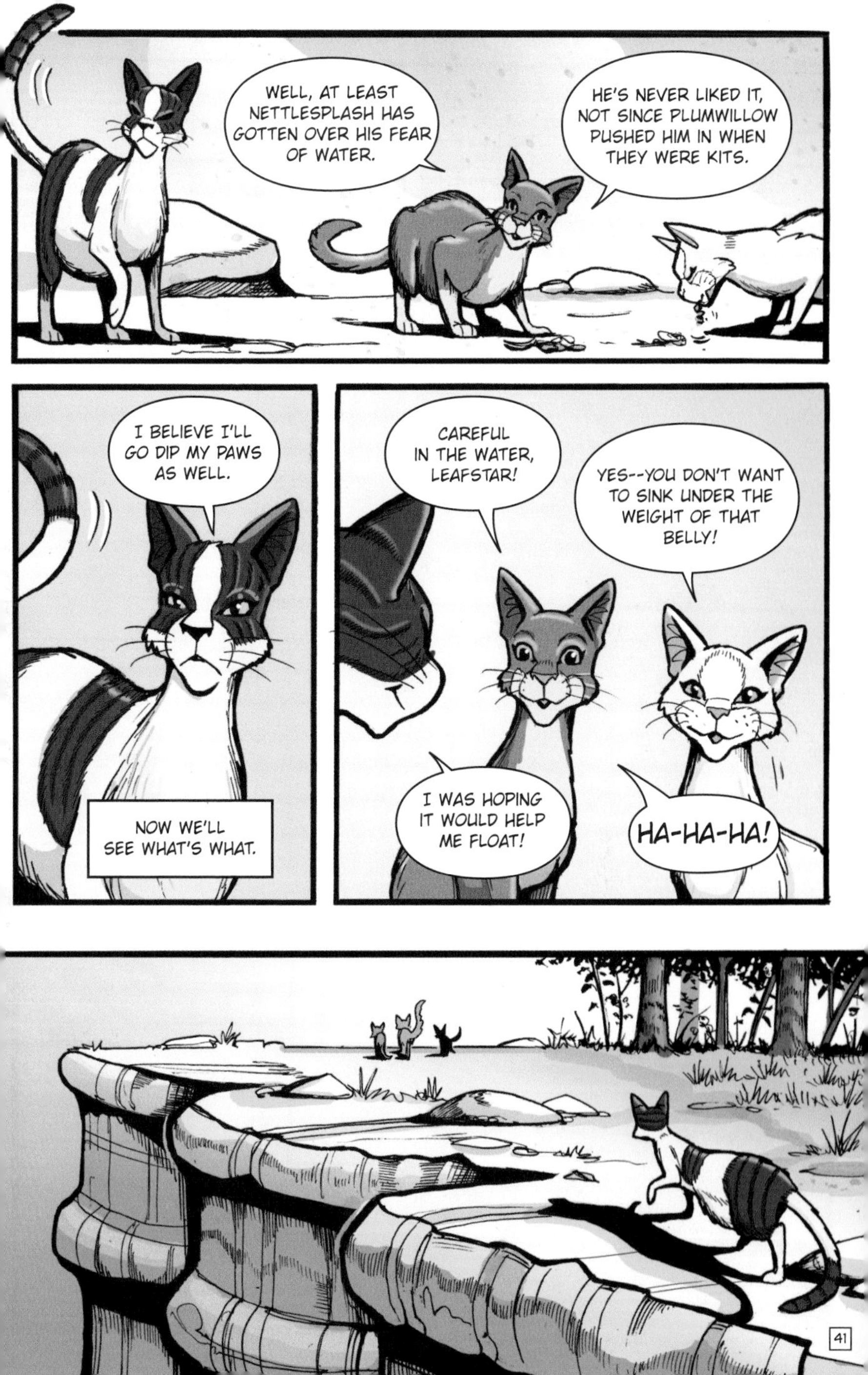
WELL, AT LEAST NETTLESPLASH HAS GOTTEN OVER HIS FEAR OF WATER.
HE'S NEVER LIKED IT, NOT SINCE PLUMWILLOW PUSHED HIM IN WHEN THEY WERE KITS.
I BELIEVE I'LL GO DIP MY PAWS AS WELL.
NOW WE'LL SEE WHAT'S WHAT.
CAREFUL IN THE WATER, LEAFSTAR!
YES--YOU DON'T WANT TO SINK UNDER THE WEIGHT OF THAT BELLY!
I WAS HOPING IT WOULD HELP ME FLOAT!
HA-HA-HA!

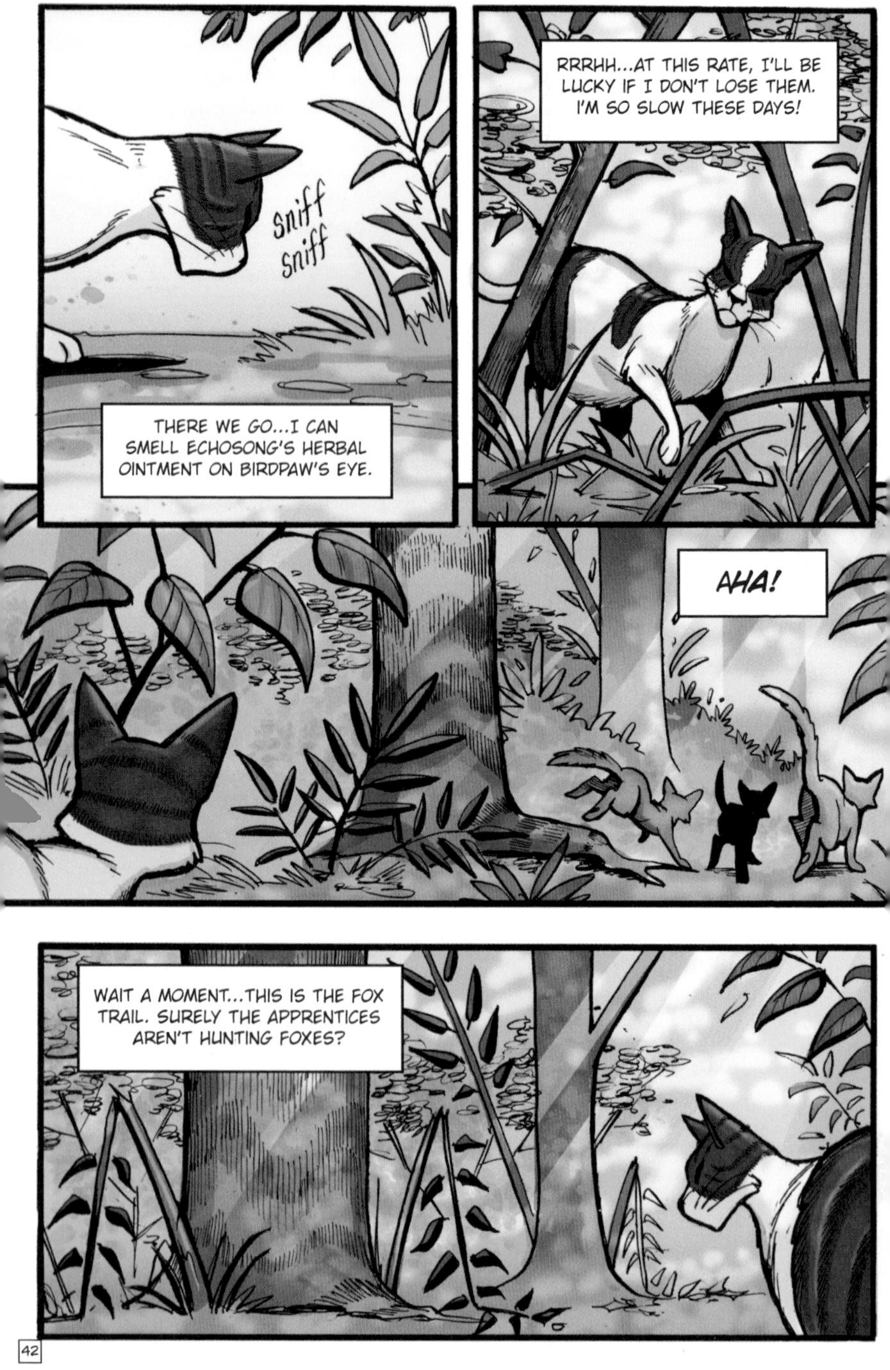
Sniff
Sniff
THERE WE GO...I CAN SMELL ECHOSONG'S HERBAL OINTMENT ON BIRDPAW'S EYE.
RRRHH...AT THIS RATE, I'LL BE LUCKY IF I DON'T LOSE THEM. I'M SO SLOW THESE DAYS!
AHA!
WAIT A MOMENT...THIS IS THE FOX TRAIL. SURELY THE APPRENTICES AREN'T HUNTING FOXES?

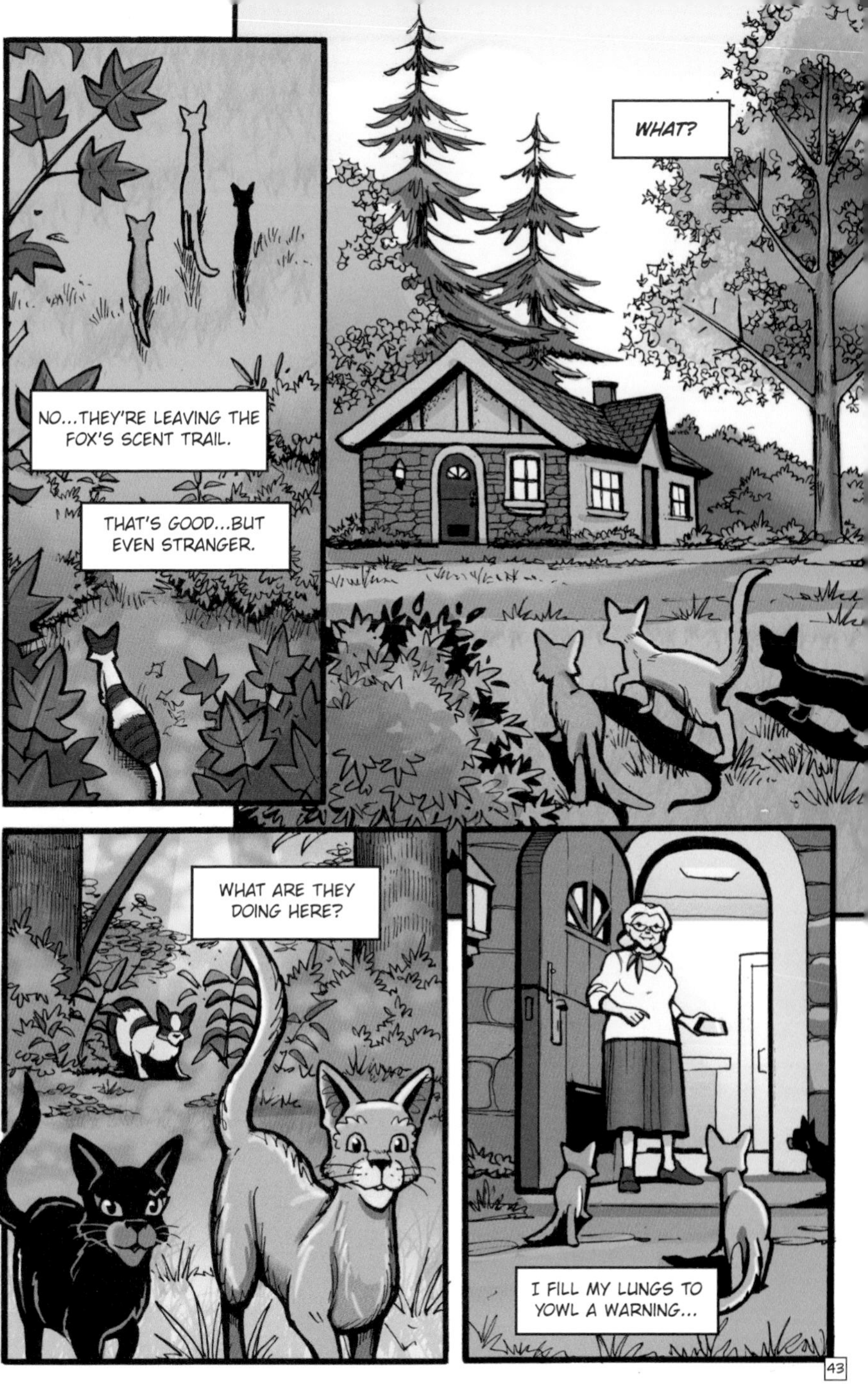
NO...THEY'RE LEAVING THE FOX'S SCENT TRAIL.
THAT'S GOOD...BUT EVEN STRANGER.
WHAT?
WHAT ARE THEY DOING HERE?
I FILL MY LUNGS TO YOWL A WARNING...

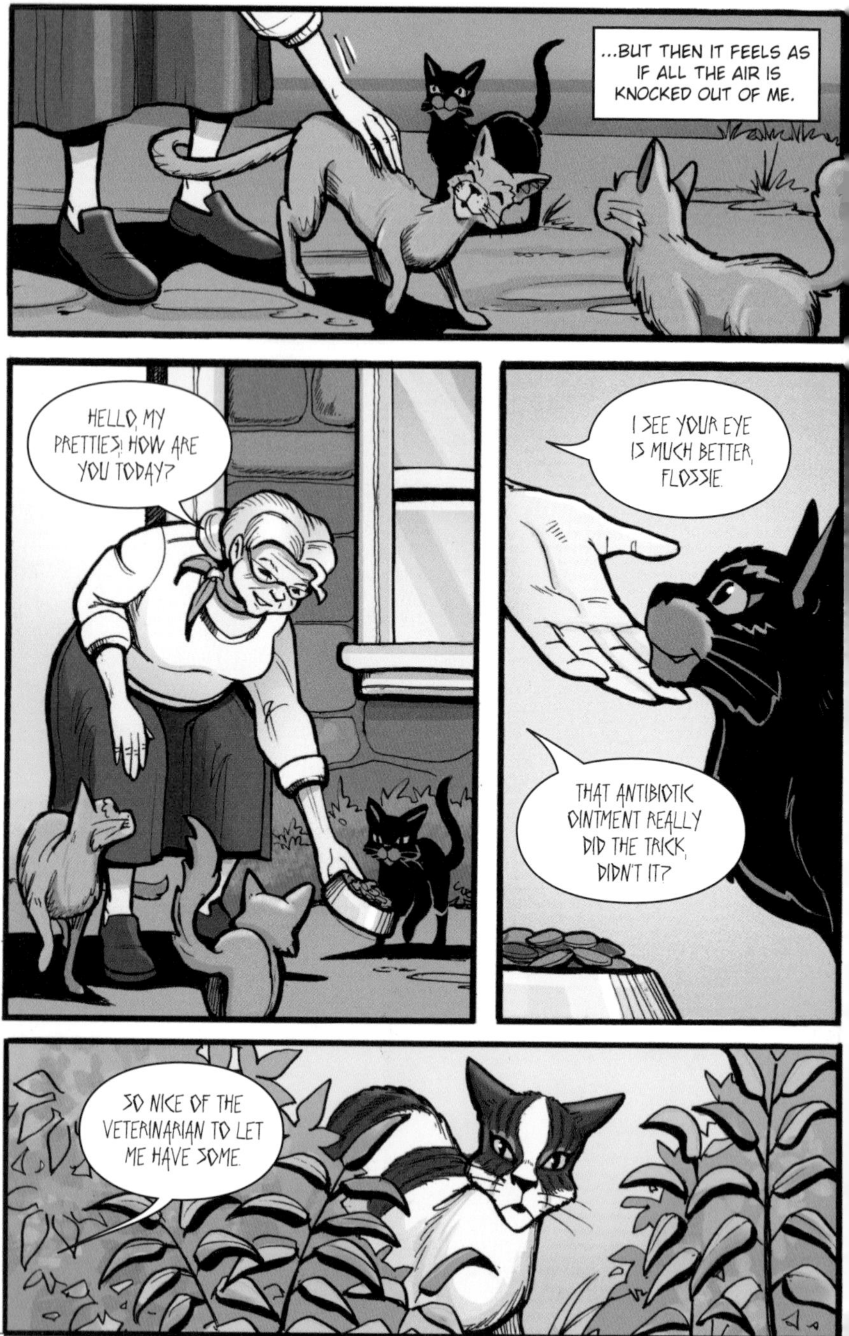
...BUT THEN IT FEELS AS IF ALL THE AIR IS KNOCKED OUT OF ME.
HELLO, MY PRETTIES! HOW ARE YOU TODAY?
I SEE YOUR EYE IS MUCH BETTER, FLOSSIE.
THAT ANTIBIOTIC OINTMENT REALLY DID THE TRICK, DIDN'T IT?
SO NICE OF THE VETERINARIAN TO LET ME HAVE SOME.

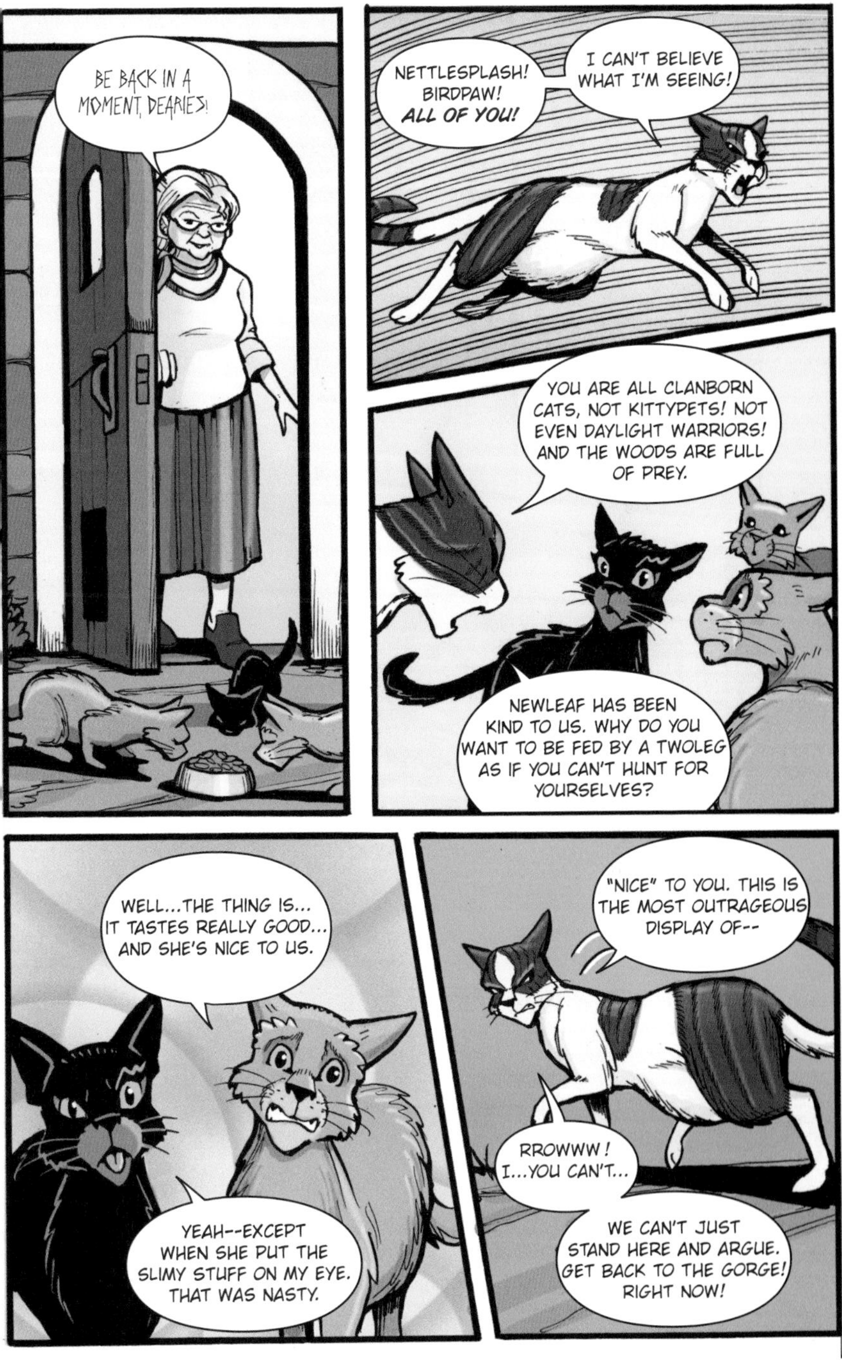
BE BACK IN A MOMENT, DEARIES!
NETTLESPLASH! BIRDPAW! ALL OF YOU!
I CAN'T BELIEVE WHAT I'M SEEING!
YOU ARE ALL CLANBORN CATS, NOT KITTYPETS! NOT EVEN DAYLIGHT WARRIORS! AND THE WOODS ARE FULL OF PREY.
NEWLEAF HAS BEEN KIND TO US. WHY DO YOU WANT TO BE FED BY A TWOLEG AS IF YOU CAN'T HUNT FOR YOURSELVES?
WELL...THE THING IS... IT TASTES REALLY GOOD... AND SHE'S NICE TO US.
YEAH--EXCEPT WHEN SHE PUT THE SLIMY STUFF ON MY EYE. THAT WAS NASTY.
"NICE" TO YOU. THIS IS THE MOST OUTRAGEOUS DISPLAY OF--
RROWWW! I...YOU CAN'T...
WE CAN'T JUST STAND HERE AND ARGUE. GET BACK TO THE GORGE! RIGHT NOW!

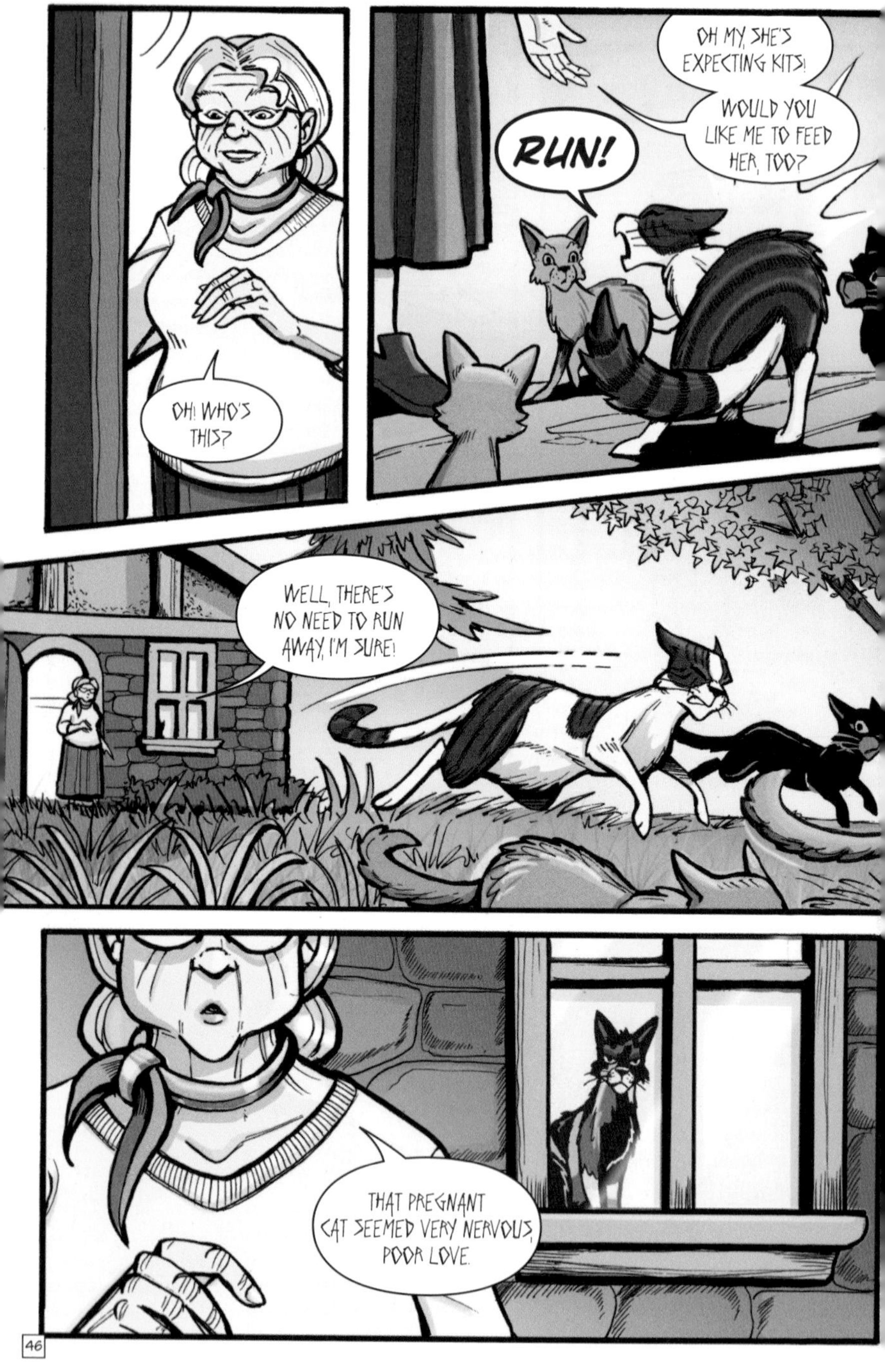
OH! WHO'S THIS?
RUN!
OH MY, SHE'S EXPECTING KITS!
WOULD YOU LIKE ME TO FEED HER, TOO?
WELL, THERE'S NO NEED TO RUN AWAY, I'M SURE!
THAT PREGNANT CAT SEEMED VERY NERVOUS, POOR LOVE.

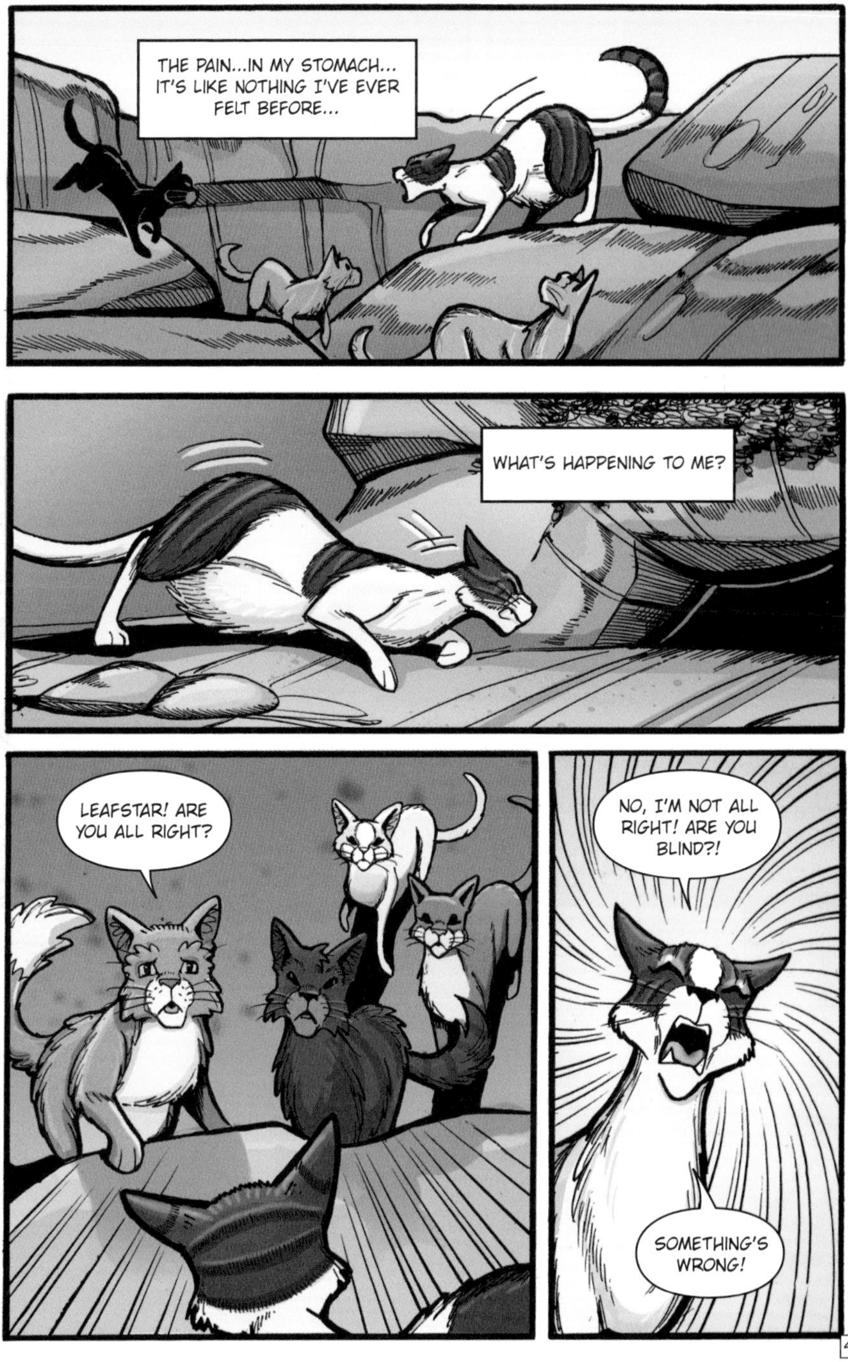
THE PAIN...IN MY STOMACH... IT'S LIKE NOTHING I'VE EVER FELT BEFORE...
WHAT'S HAPPENING TO ME?
LEAFSTAR! ARE YOU ALL RIGHT?
NO, I'M NOT ALL RIGHT! ARE YOU BLIND?!
SOMETHING'S WRONG!

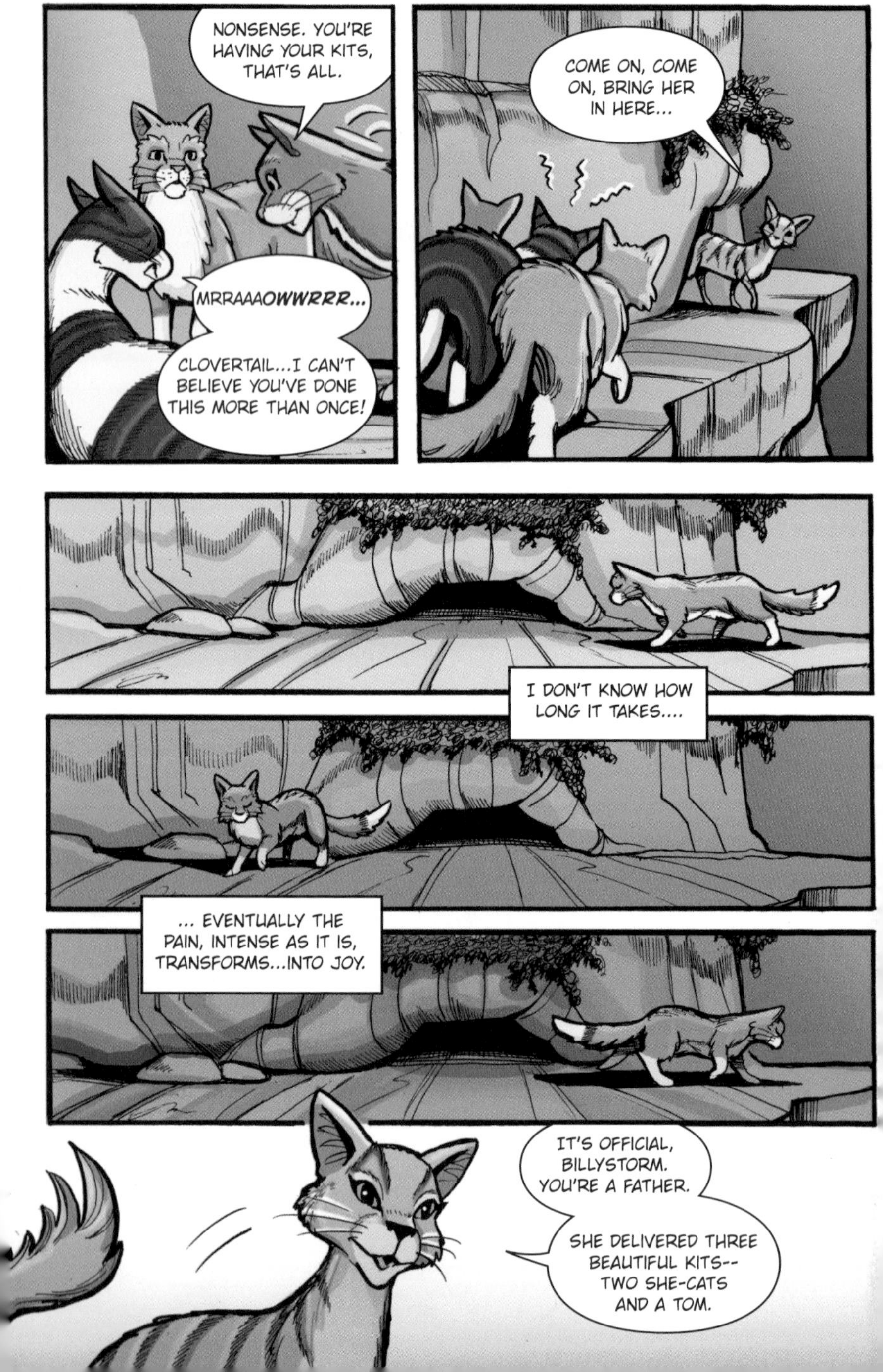
NONSENSE. YOU'RE HAVING YOUR KITS, THAT'S ALL.
MRRAAAOWWRRR...
CLOVERTAIL...I CAN'T BELIEVE YOU'VE DONE THIS MORE THAN ONCE!
COME ON, COME ON, BRING HER IN HERE...
I DON'T KNOW HOW LONG IT TAKES....
... EVENTUALLY THE PAIN, INTENSE AS IT IS, TRANSFORMS...INTO JOY.
IT'S OFFICIAL, BILLYSTORM. YOU'RE A FATHER.
SHE DELIVERED THREE BEAUTIFUL KITS-- TWO SHE-CATS AND A TOM.

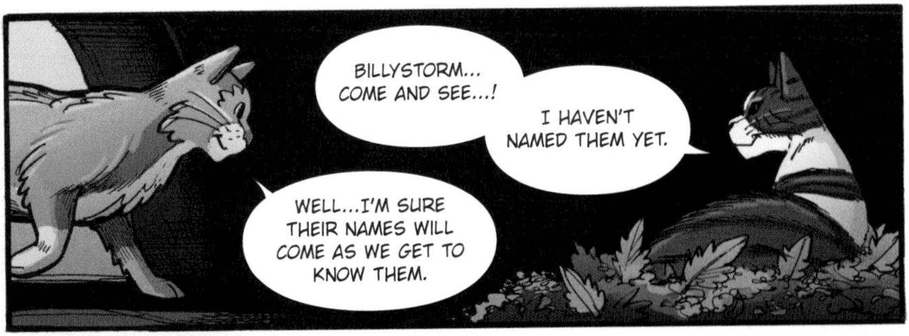
BILLYSTORM... COME AND SEE...!
I HAVEN'T NAMED THEM YET.
WELL...I'M SURE THEIR NAMES WILL COME AS WE GET TO KNOW THEM.

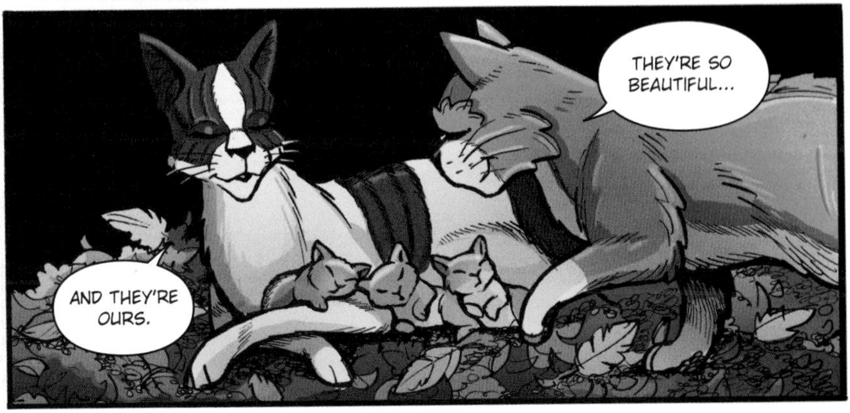
THEY'RE SO BEAUTIFUL...
AND THEY'RE OURS.

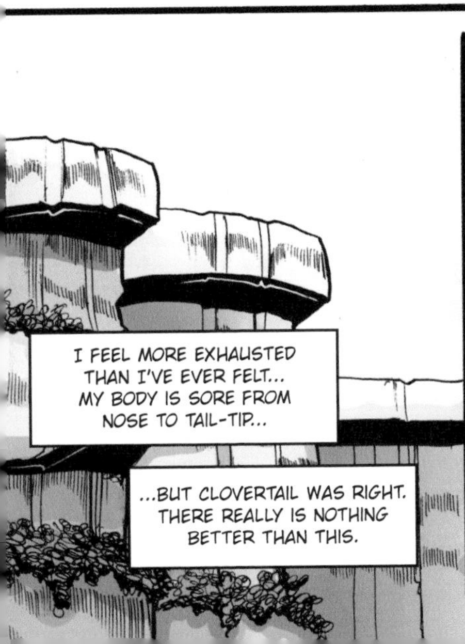
I FEEL MORE EXHAUSTED THAN I'VE EVER FELT... MY BODY IS SORE FROM NOSE TO TAIL-TIP...
...BUT CLOVERTAIL WAS RIGHT. THERE REALLY IS NOTHING BETTER THAN THIS.

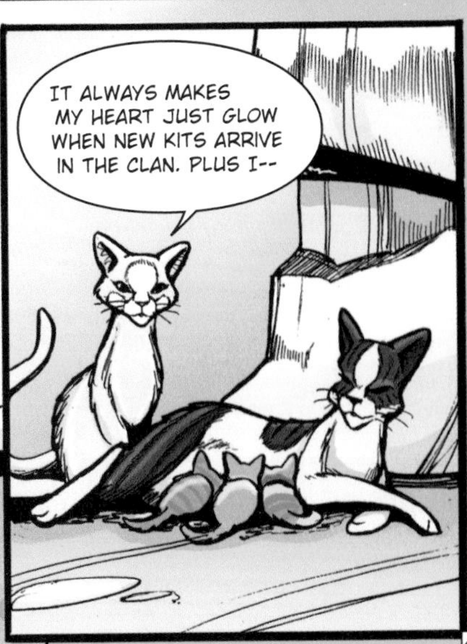
IT ALWAYS MAKES MY HEART JUST GLOW WHEN NEW KITS ARRIVE IN THE CLAN. PLUS I--

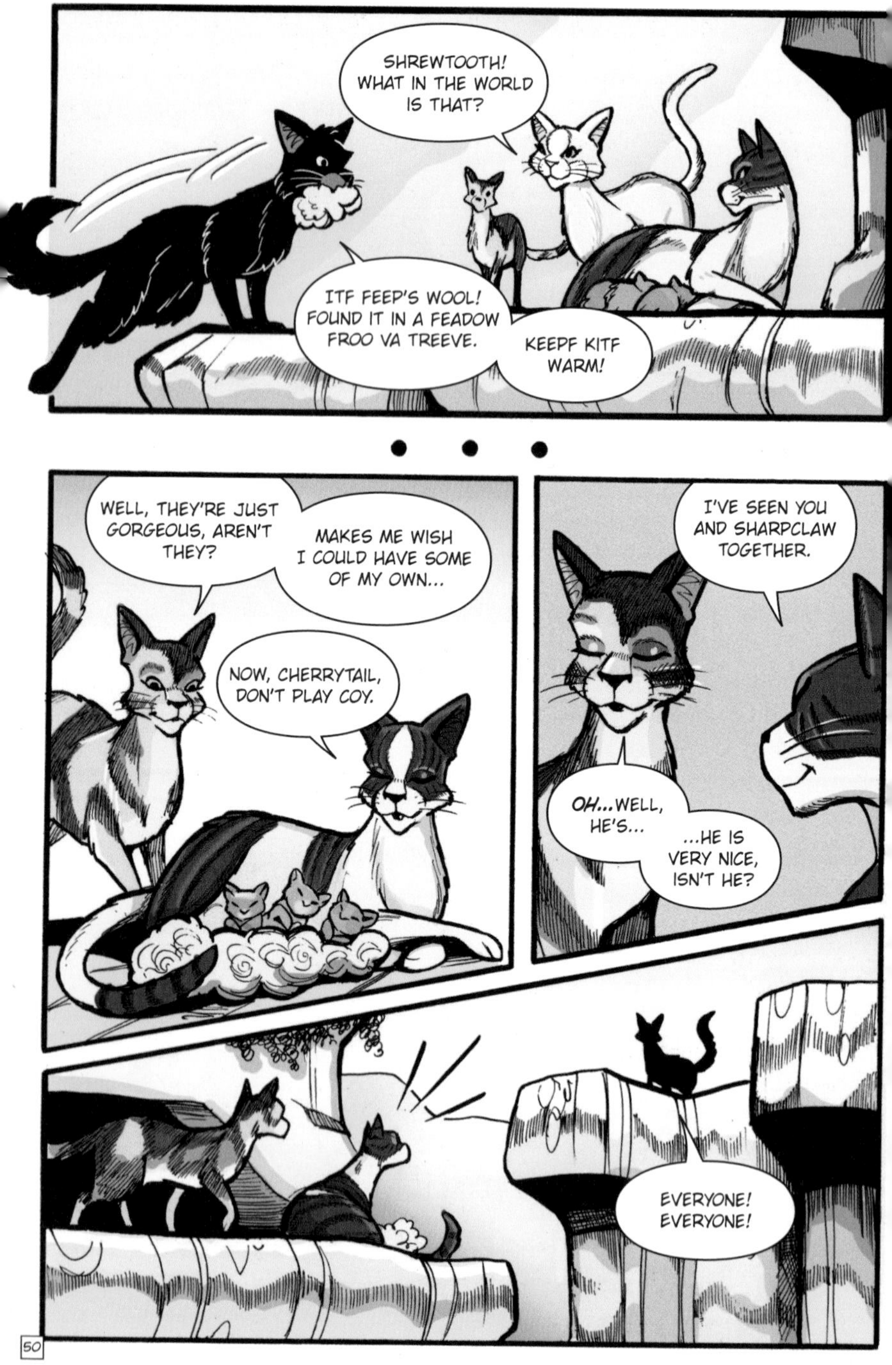
SHREWTOOTH! WHAT IN THE WORLD IS THAT?
ITF FEEP'S WOOL! FOUND IT IN A FEADOW FROO VA TREEVE.
KEEPF KITF WARM!
WELL, THEY'RE JUST GORGEOUS, AREN'T THEY?
MAKES ME WISH I COULD HAVE SOME OF MY OWN...
NOW, CHERRYTAIL, DON'T PLAY COY.
I'VE SEEN YOU AND SHARPCLAW TOGETHER.
*OH...*WELL, HE'S...
...HE IS VERY NICE, ISN'T HE?
EVERYONE! EVERYONE!

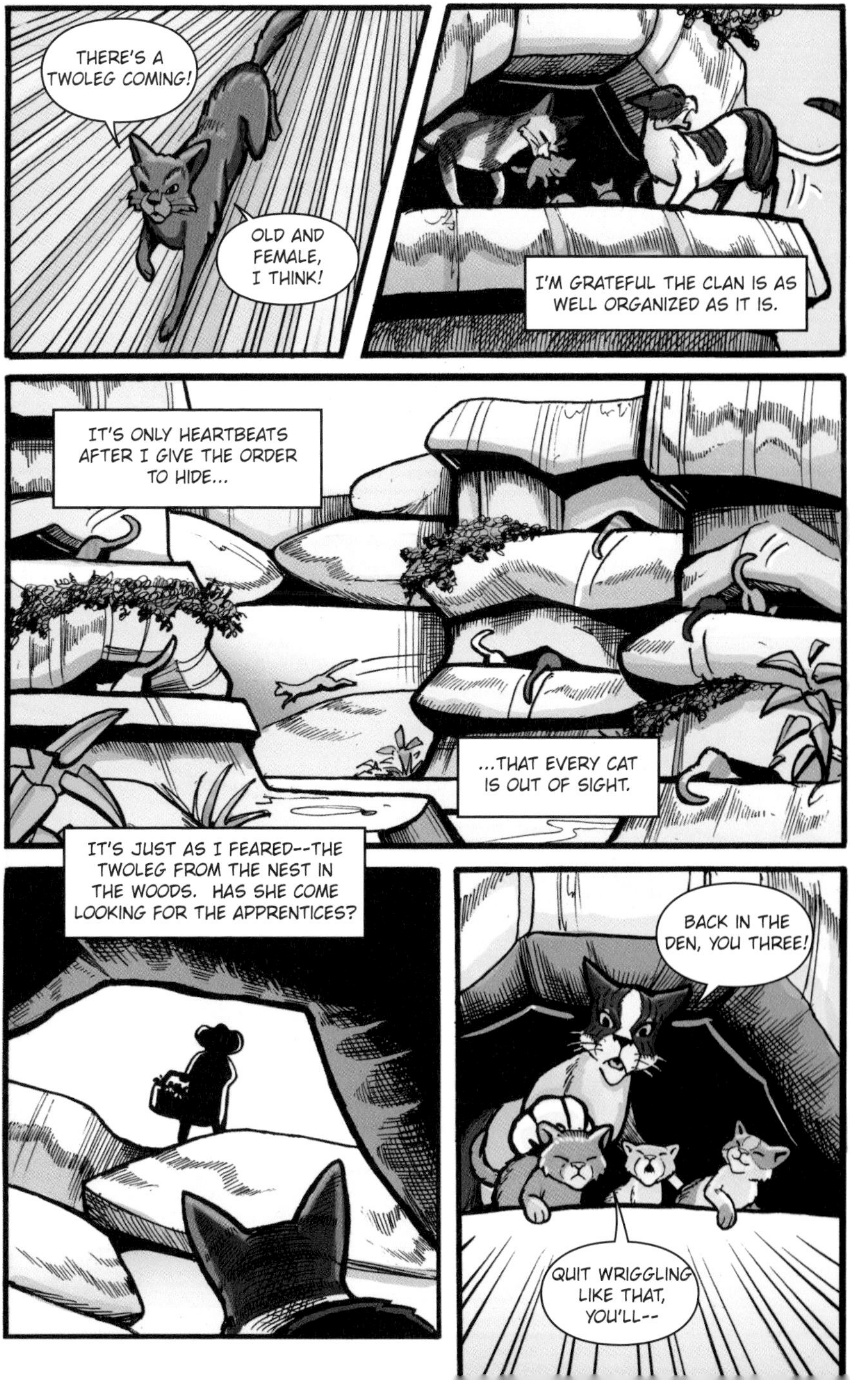
THERE'S A TWOLEG COMING!
OLD AND FEMALE, I THINK!
I'M GRATEFUL THE CLAN IS AS WELL ORGANIZED AS IT IS.
IT'S ONLY HEARTBEATS AFTER I GIVE THE ORDER TO HIDE...
...THAT EVERY CAT IS OUT OF SIGHT.
IT'S JUST AS I FEARED--THE TWOLEG FROM THE NEST IN THE WOODS. HAS SHE COME LOOKING FOR THE APPRENTICES?
BACK IN THE DEN, YOU THREE!
QUIT WRIGGLING LIKE THAT, YOU'LL--

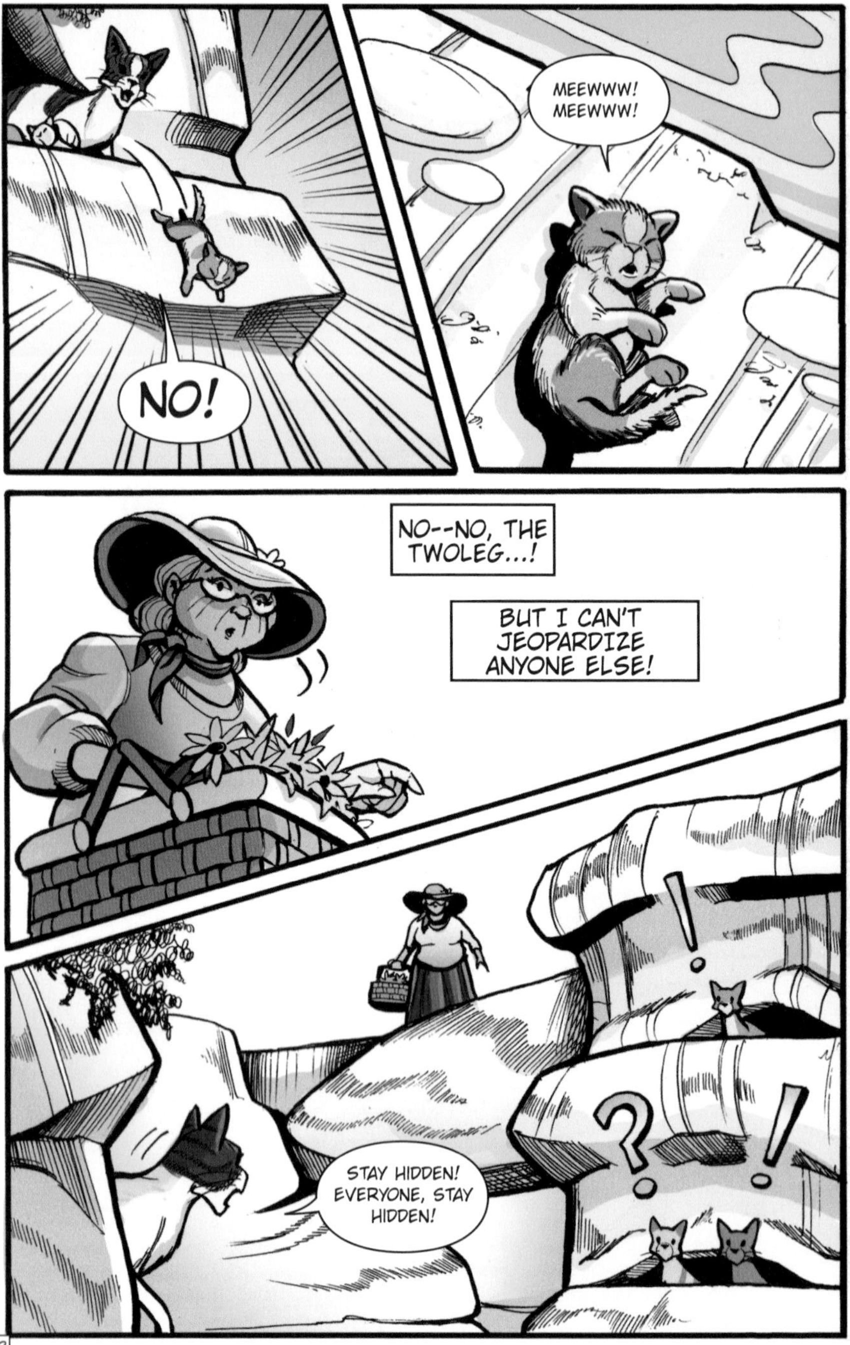
NO!
MEEWWW! MEEWWW!
NO--NO, THE TWOLEG...!
BUT I CAN'T JEOPARDIZE ANYONE ELSE!
!
STAY HIDDEN! EVERYONE, STAY HIDDEN!
?!

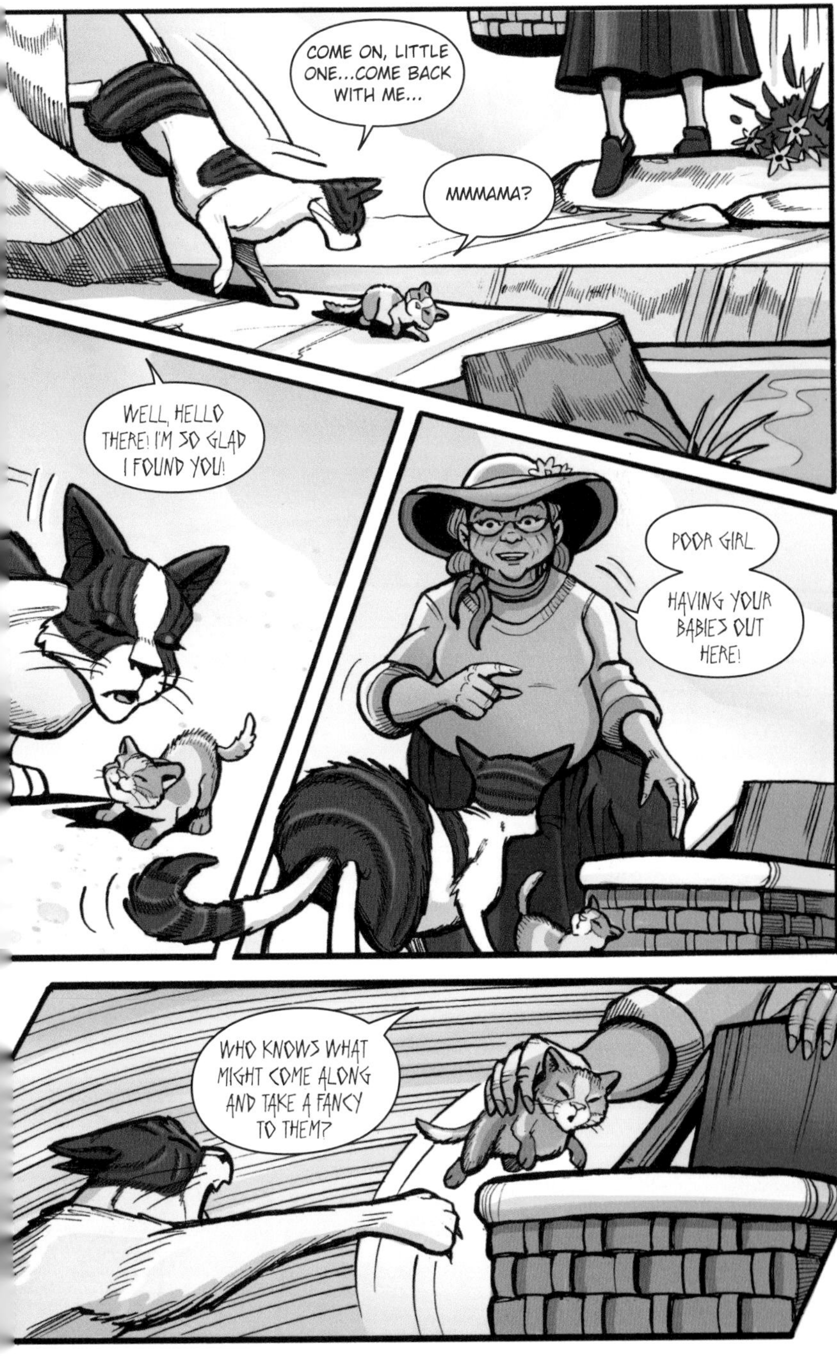

COME ON, LITTLE ONE...COME BACK WITH ME...
MMMAMA?
WELL, HELLO THERE! I'M SO GLAD I FOUND YOU!
POOR GIRL.
HAVING YOUR BABIES OUT HERE!
WHO KNOWS WHAT MIGHT COME ALONG AND TAKE A FANCY TO THEM?

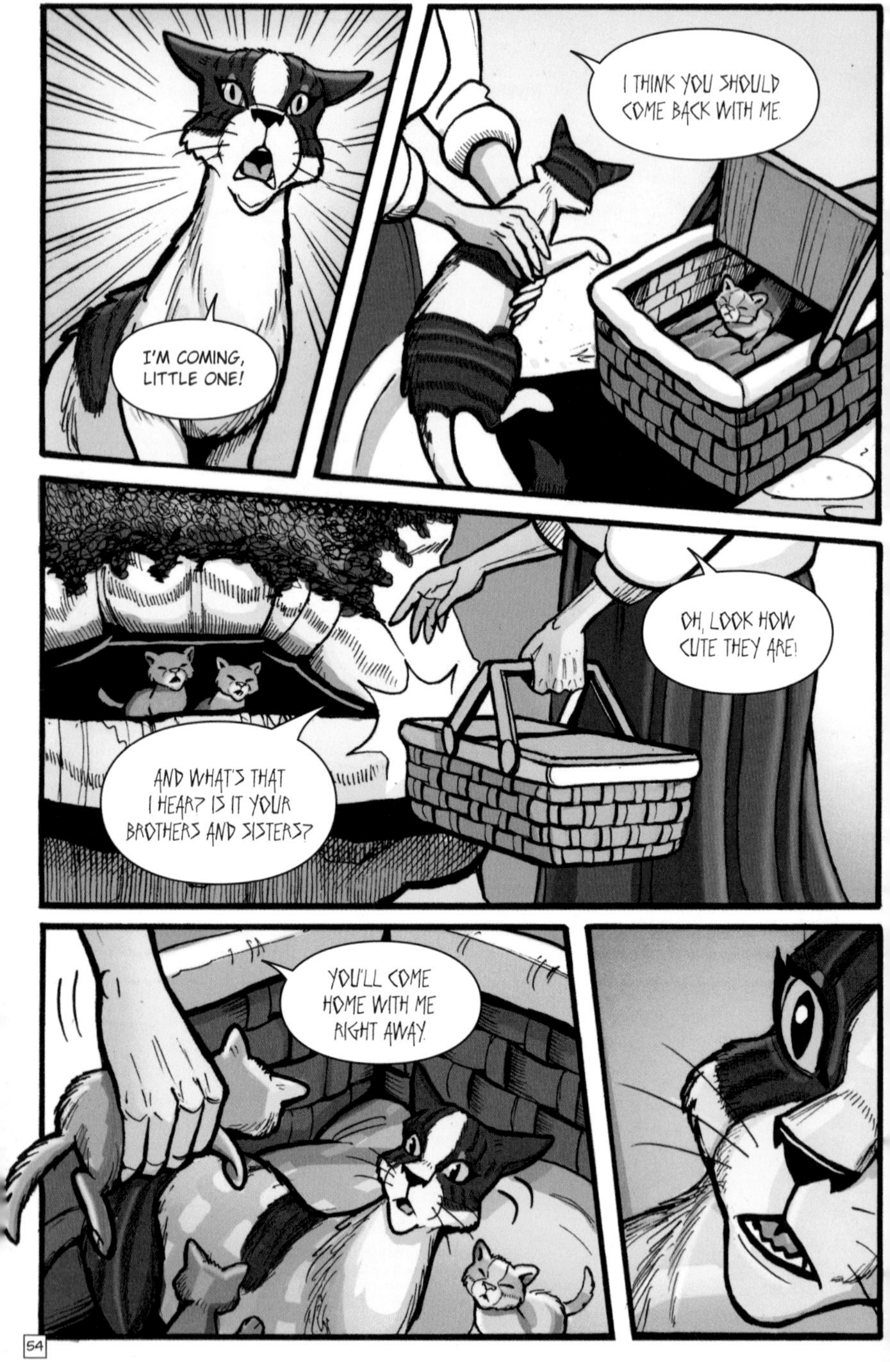
I'M COMING, LITTLE ONE!
I THINK YOU SHOULD COME BACK WITH ME.
OH, LOOK HOW CUTE THEY ARE!
AND WHAT'S THAT I HEAR? IS IT YOUR BROTHERS AND SISTERS?
YOU'LL COME HOME WITH ME RIGHT AWAY.

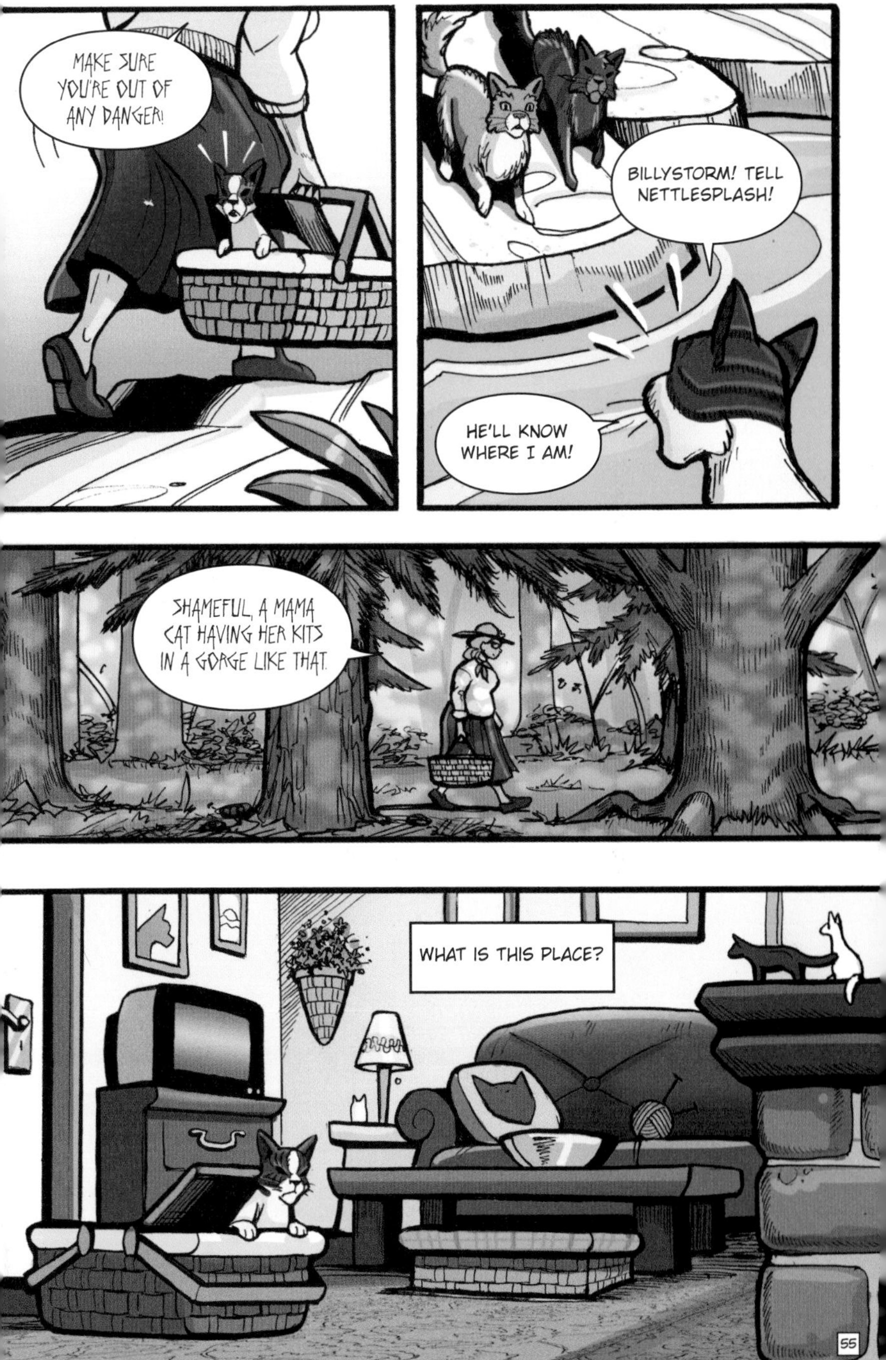
MAKE SURE YOU'RE OUT OF ANY DANGER!
BILLYSTORM! TELL NETTLESPLASH!
HE'LL KNOW WHERE I AM!
SHAMEFUL, A MAMA CAT HAVING HER KITS IN A GORGE LIKE THAT.
WHAT IS THIS PLACE?

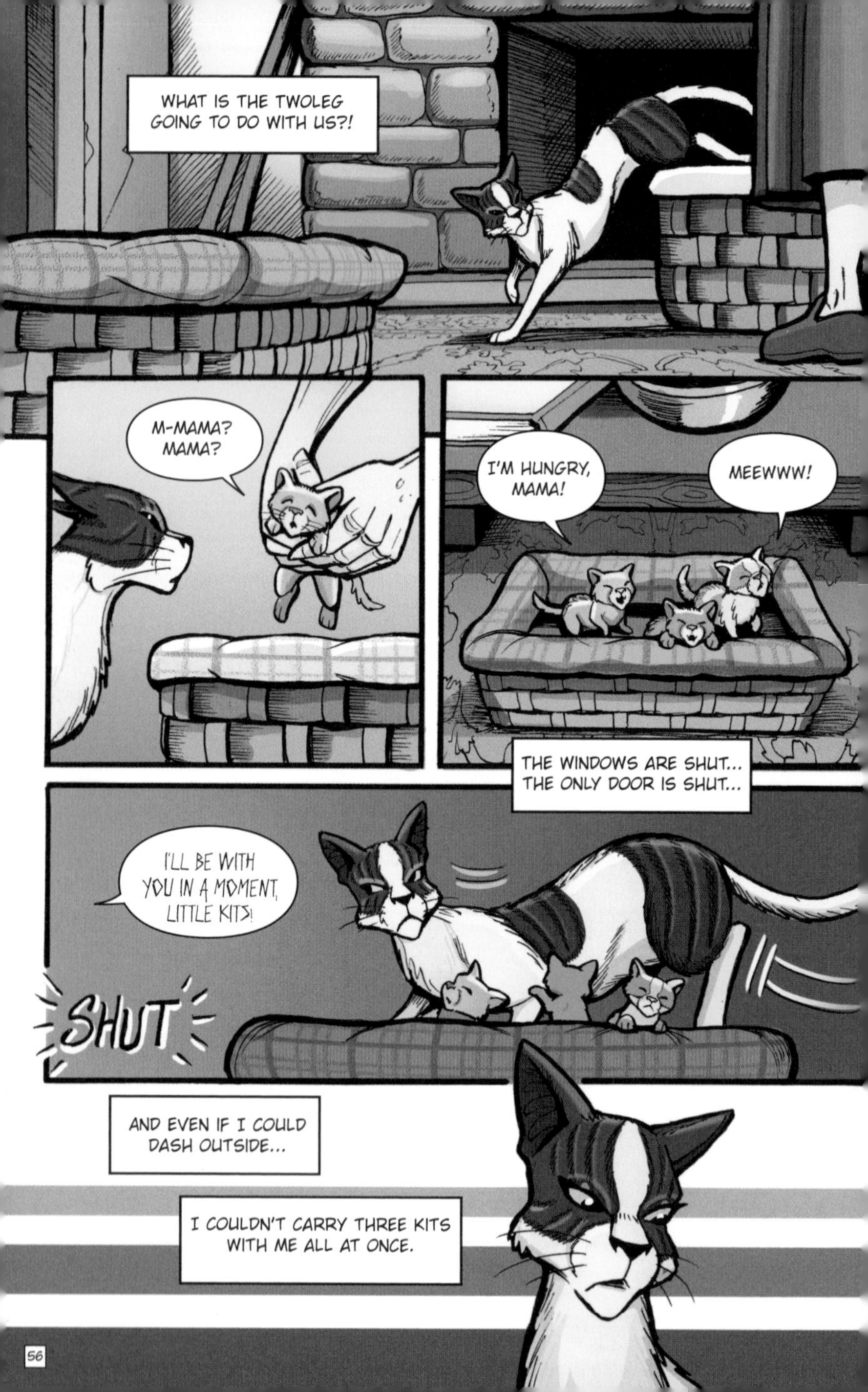
WHAT IS THE TWOLEG GOING TO DO WITH US?!
M-MAMA? MAMA?
I'M HUNGRY, MAMA!
MEEWWW!
THE WINDOWS ARE SHUT... THE ONLY DOOR IS SHUT...
I'LL BE WITH YOU IN A MOMENT, LITTLE KITS!
SHUT
AND EVEN IF I COULD DASH OUTSIDE...
I COULDN'T CARRY THREE KITS WITH ME ALL AT ONCE.

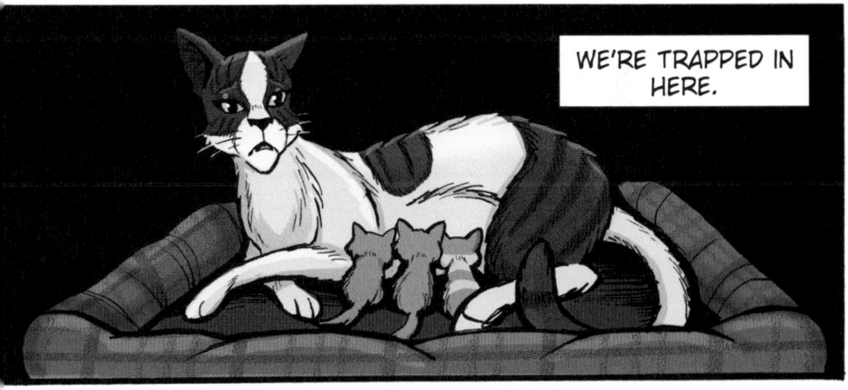
WE'RE TRAPPED IN HERE.

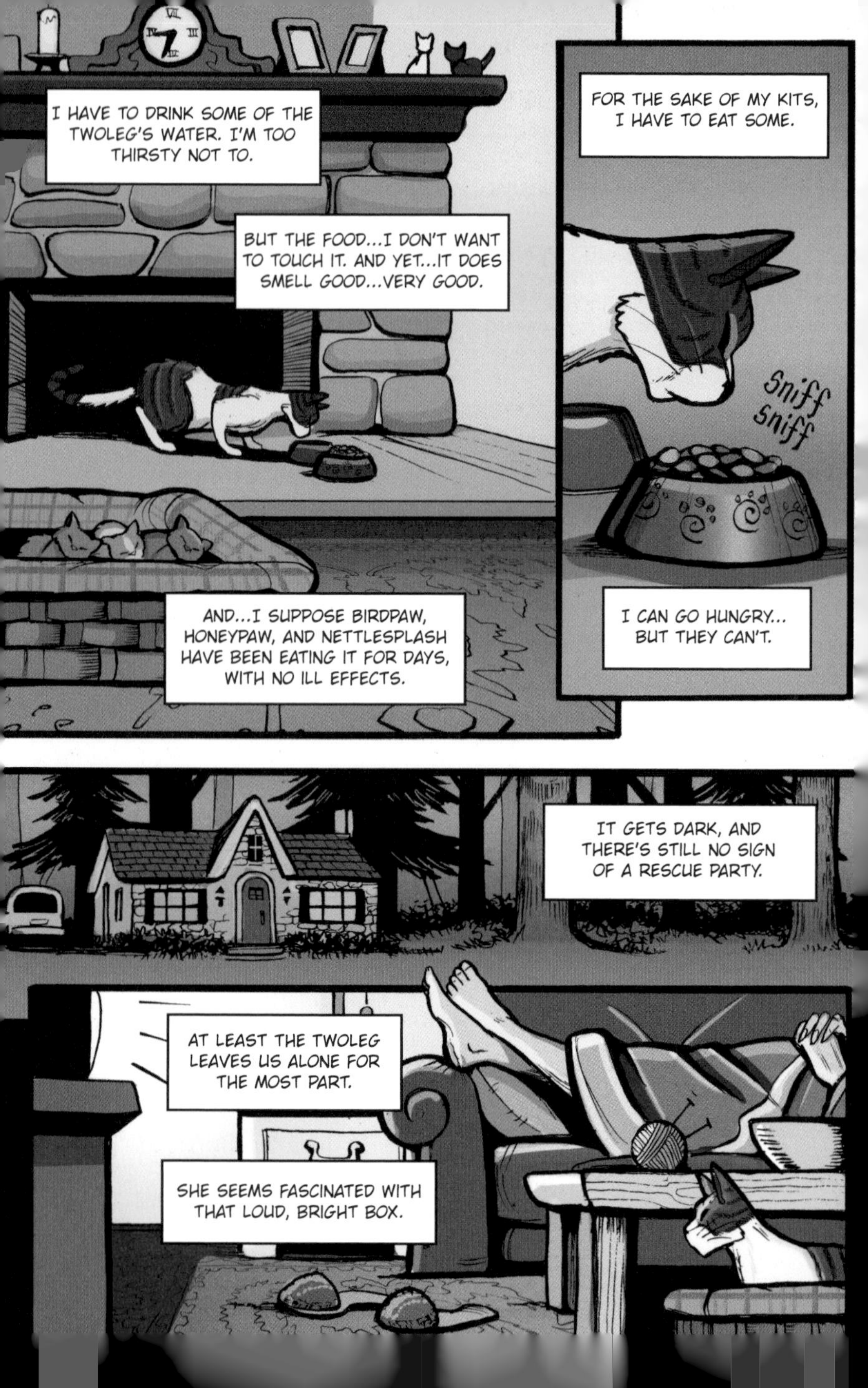
I HAVE TO DRINK SOME OF THE TWOLEG'S WATER. I'M TOO THIRSTY NOT TO.
BUT THE FOOD...I DON'T WANT TO TOUCH IT. AND YET...IT DOES SMELL GOOD...VERY GOOD.
AND...I SUPPOSE BIRDPAW, HONEYPAW, AND NETTLESPLASH HAVE BEEN EATING IT FOR DAYS, WITH NO ILL EFFECTS.
FOR THE SAKE OF MY KITS, I HAVE TO EAT SOME.
Sniff Sniff
I CAN GO HUNGRY... BUT THEY CAN'T.
IT GETS DARK, AND THERE'S STILL NO SIGN OF A RESCUE PARTY.
AT LEAST THE TWOLEG LEAVES US ALONE FOR THE MOST PART.
SHE SEEMS FASCINATED WITH THAT LOUD, BRIGHT BOX.

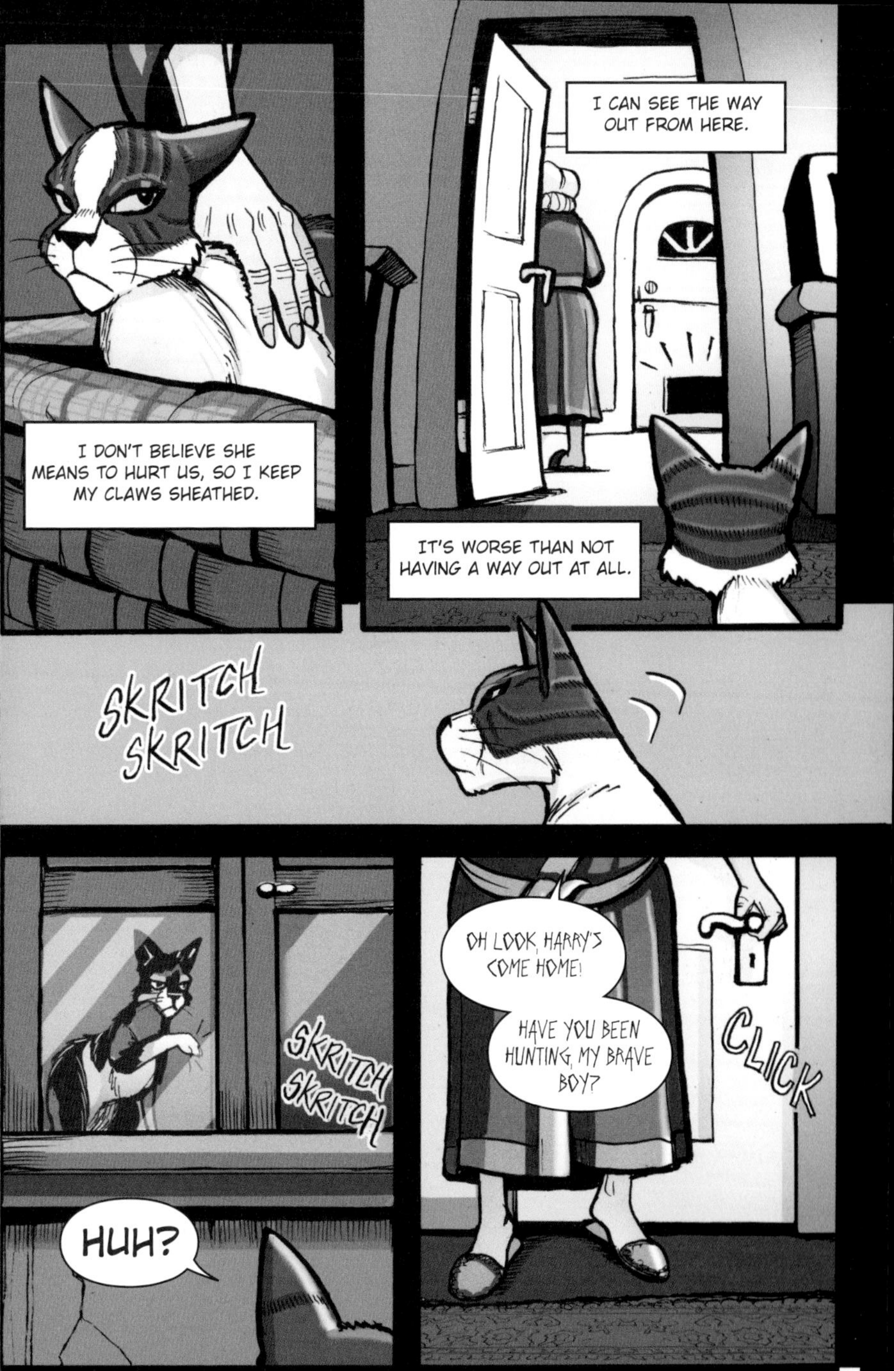
I DON'T BELIEVE SHE MEANS TO HURT US, SO I KEEP MY CLAWS SHEATHED.
I CAN SEE THE WAY OUT FROM HERE.
IT'S WORSE THAN NOT HAVING A WAY OUT AT ALL.
SKRITCH SKRITCH
SKRITCH SKRITCH
HUH?
OH LOOK, HARRY'S COME HOME!
HAVE YOU BEEN HUNTING, MY BRAVE BOY?
CLICK

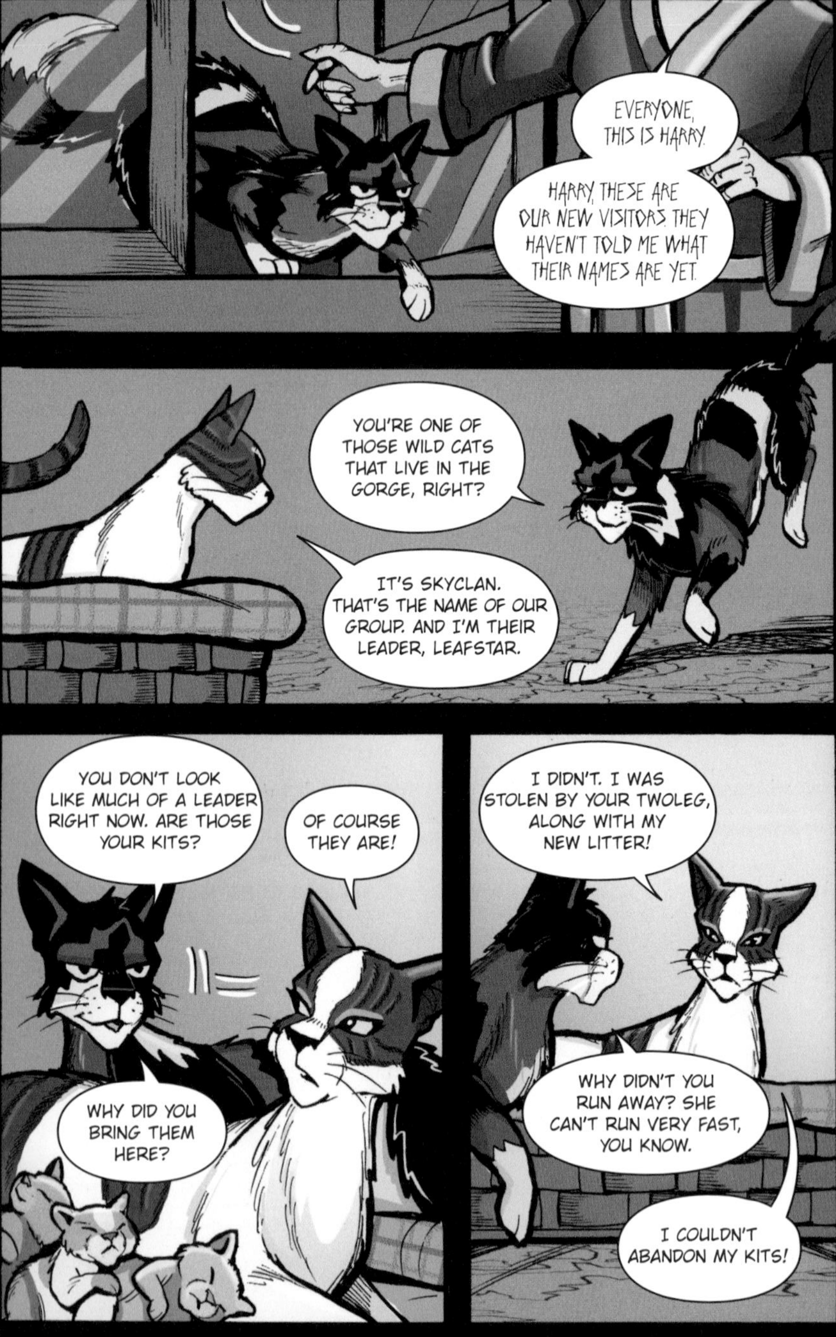
EVERYONE, THIS IS HARRY.
HARRY, THESE ARE OUR NEW VISITORS. THEY HAVEN'T TOLD ME WHAT THEIR NAMES ARE YET.
YOU'RE ONE OF THOSE WILD CATS THAT LIVE IN THE GORGE, RIGHT?
IT'S SKYCLAN. THAT'S THE NAME OF OUR GROUP. AND I'M THEIR LEADER, LEAFSTAR.
YOU DON'T LOOK LIKE MUCH OF A LEADER RIGHT NOW. ARE THOSE YOUR KITS?
OF COURSE THEY ARE!
WHY DID YOU BRING THEM HERE?
I DIDN'T. I WAS STOLEN BY YOUR TWOLEG, ALONG WITH MY NEW LITTER!
WHY DIDN'T YOU RUN AWAY? SHE CAN'T RUN VERY FAST, YOU KNOW.
I COULDN'T ABANDON MY KITS!

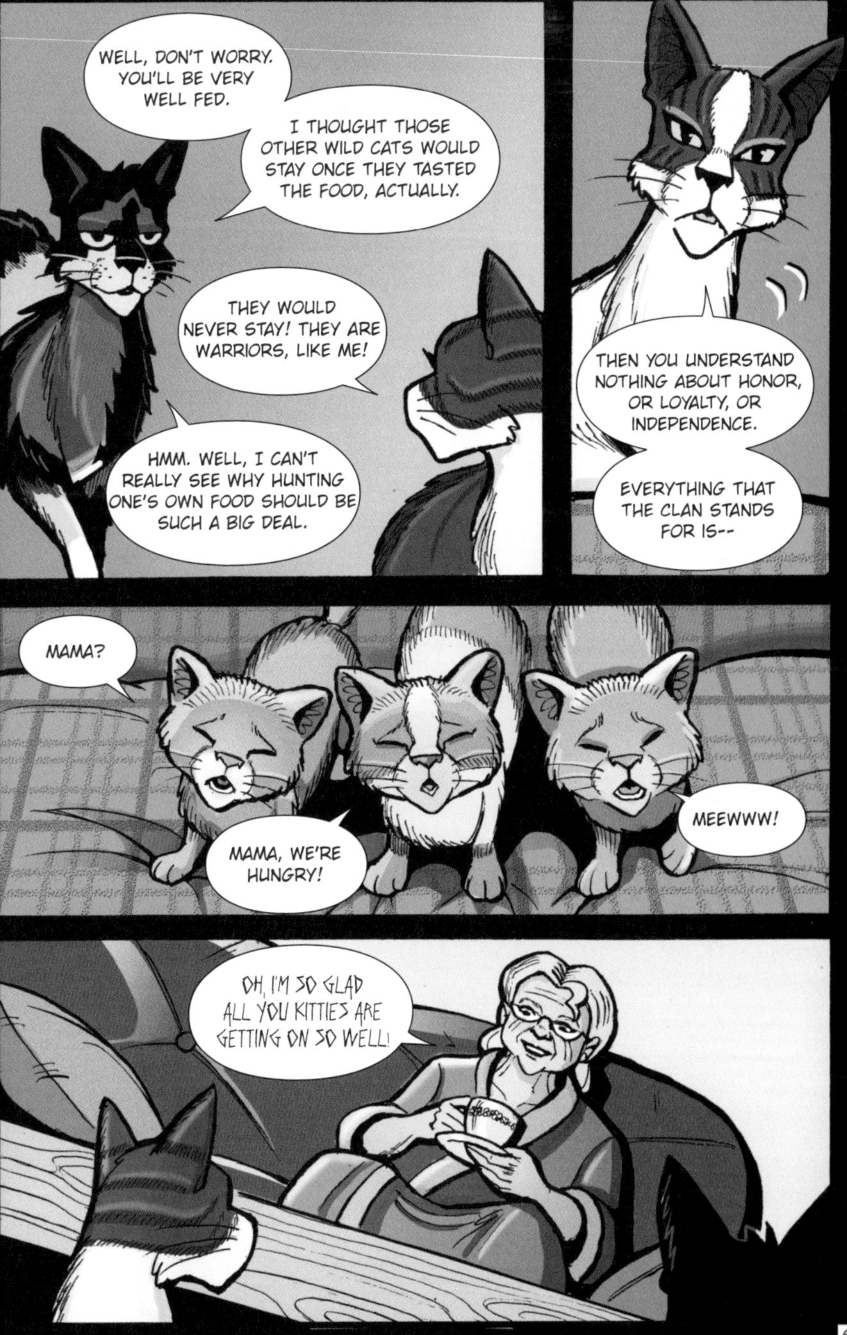
WELL, DON'T WORRY. YOU'LL BE VERY WELL FED.
I THOUGHT THOSE OTHER WILD CATS WOULD STAY ONCE THEY TASTED THE FOOD, ACTUALLY.
THEY WOULD NEVER STAY! THEY ARE WARRIORS, LIKE ME!
HMM. WELL, I CAN'T REALLY SEE WHY HUNTING ONE'S OWN FOOD SHOULD BE SUCH A BIG DEAL.
THEN YOU UNDERSTAND NOTHING ABOUT HONOR, OR LOYALTY, OR INDEPENDENCE.
EVERYTHING THAT THE CLAN STANDS FOR IS--
MAMA?
MAMA, WE'RE HUNGRY!
MEEWWW!
OH, I'M SO GLAD ALL YOU KITTIES ARE GETTING ON SO WELL!

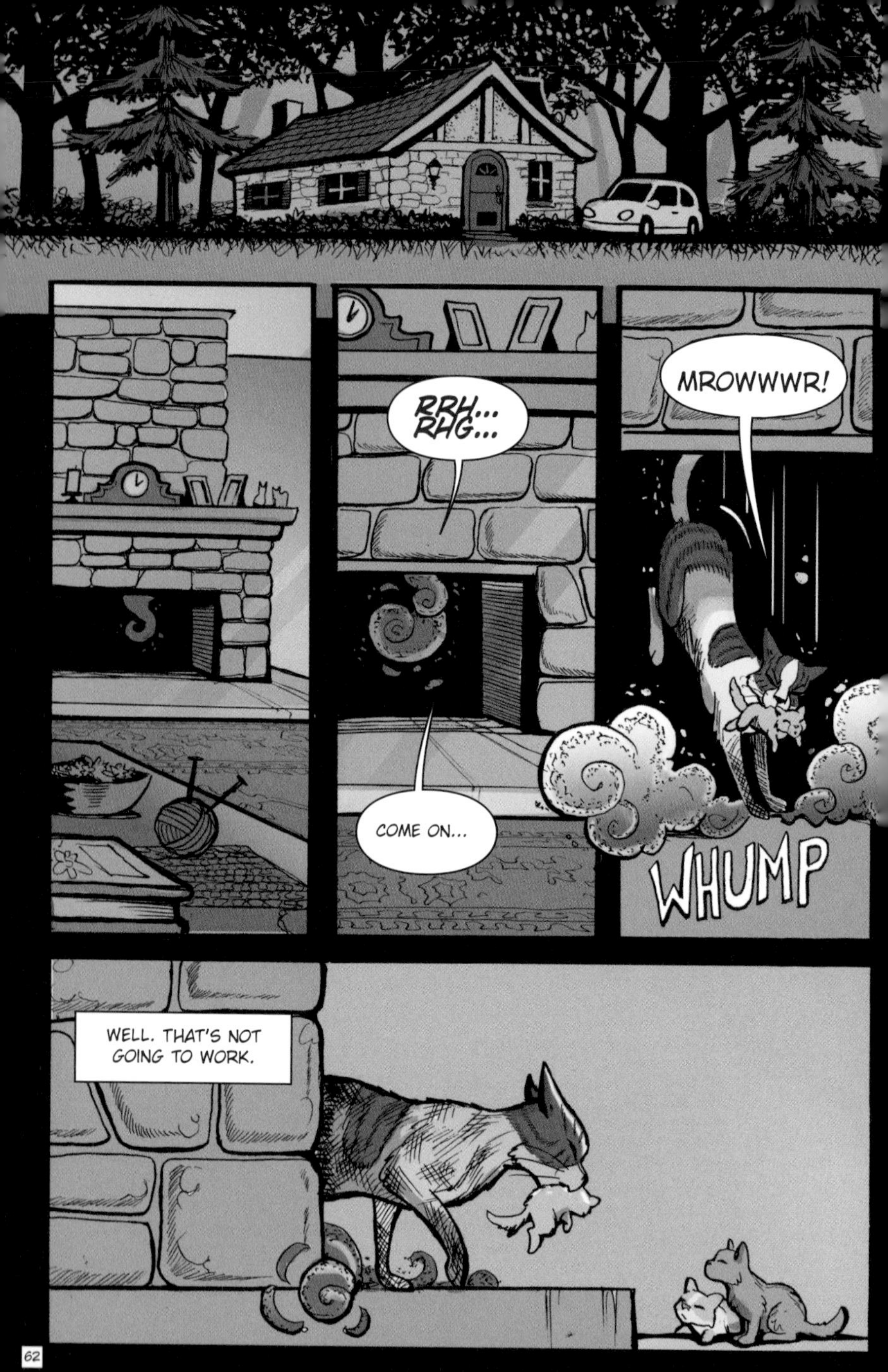
RRH... RHG...
COME ON...
MROWWWR!
WHUMP
WELL. THAT'S NOT GOING TO WORK.

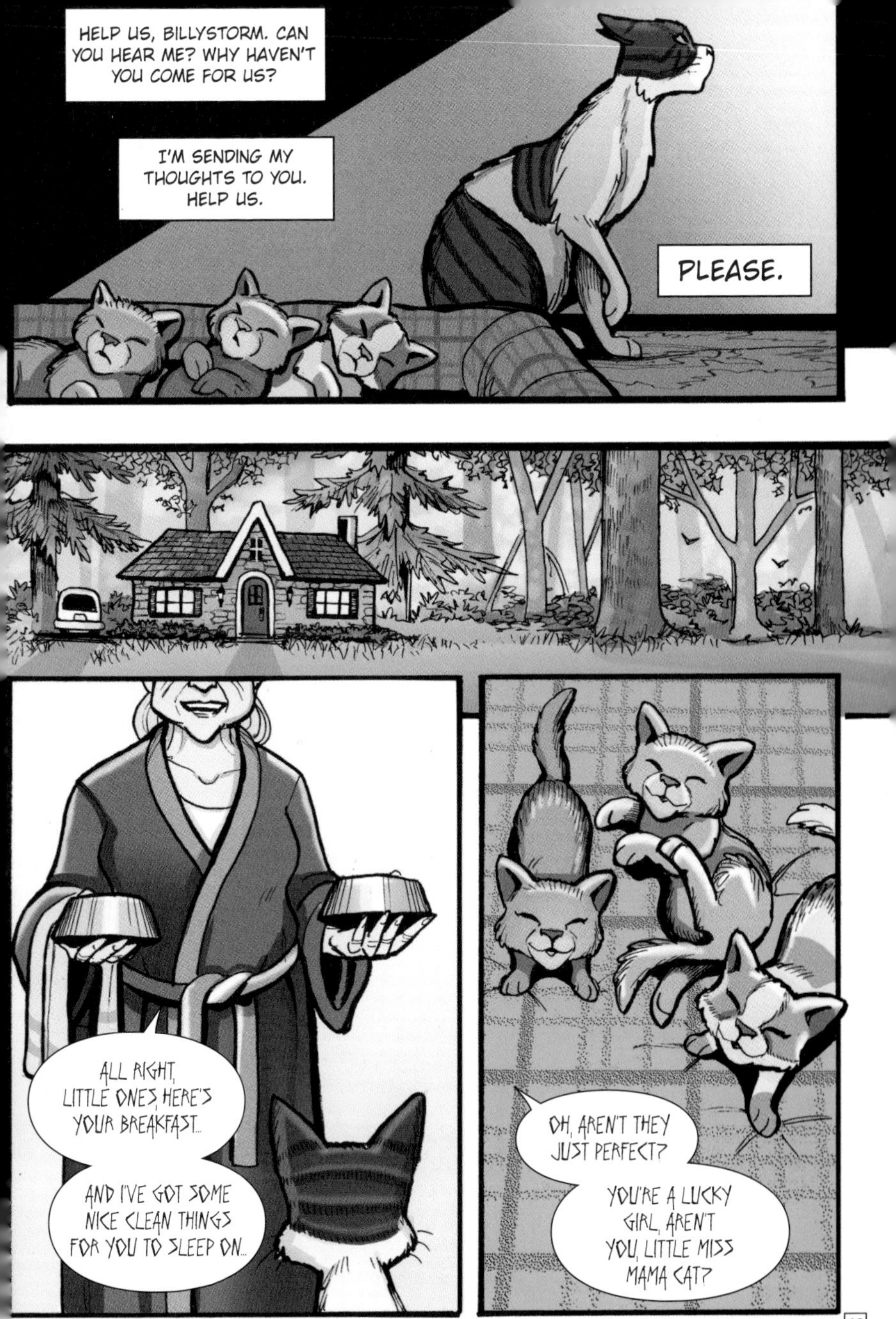
HELP US, BILLYSTORM. CAN YOU HEAR ME? WHY HAVEN'T YOU COME FOR US?
I'M SENDING MY THOUGHTS TO YOU. HELP US.
PLEASE.
ALL RIGHT, LITTLE ONES, HERE'S YOUR BREAKFAST...
AND I'VE GOT SOME NICE CLEAN THINGS FOR YOU TO SLEEP ON...
OH, AREN'T THEY JUST PERFECT?
YOU'RE A LUCKY GIRL, AREN'T YOU, LITTLE MISS MAMA CAT?

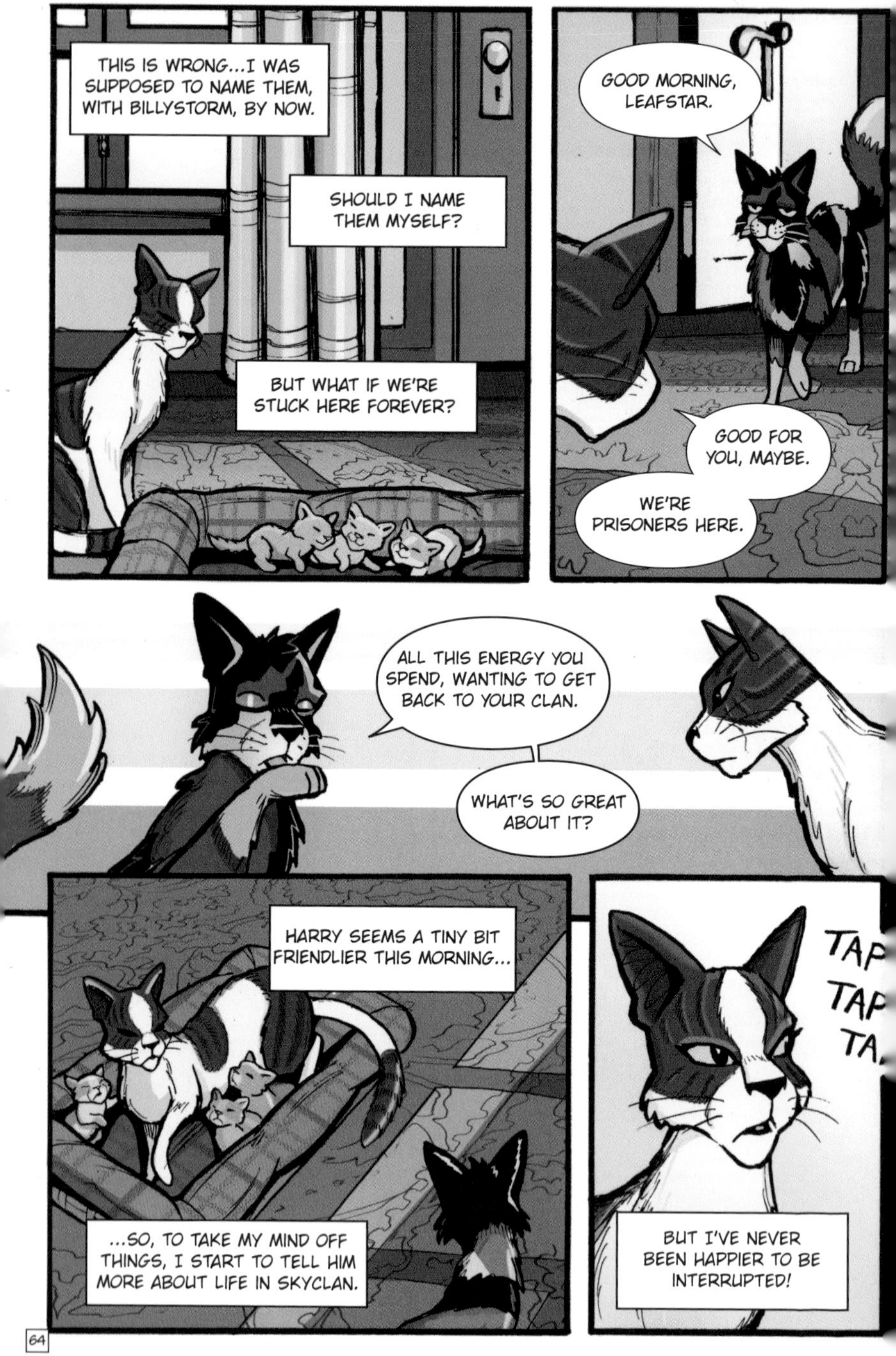
THIS IS WRONG...I WAS SUPPOSED TO NAME THEM, WITH BILLYSTORM, BY NOW.
SHOULD I NAME THEM MYSELF?
BUT WHAT IF WE'RE STUCK HERE FOREVER?
GOOD MORNING, LEAFSTAR.
GOOD FOR YOU, MAYBE.
WE'RE PRISONERS HERE.
ALL THIS ENERGY YOU SPEND, WANTING TO GET BACK TO YOUR CLAN.
WHAT'S SO GREAT ABOUT IT?
HARRY SEEMS A TINY BIT FRIENDLIER THIS MORNING...
...SO, TO TAKE MY MIND OFF THINGS, I START TO TELL HIM MORE ABOUT LIFE IN SKYCLAN.
TAP
TAP
TA
BUT I'VE NEVER BEEN HAPPIER TO BE INTERRUPTED!

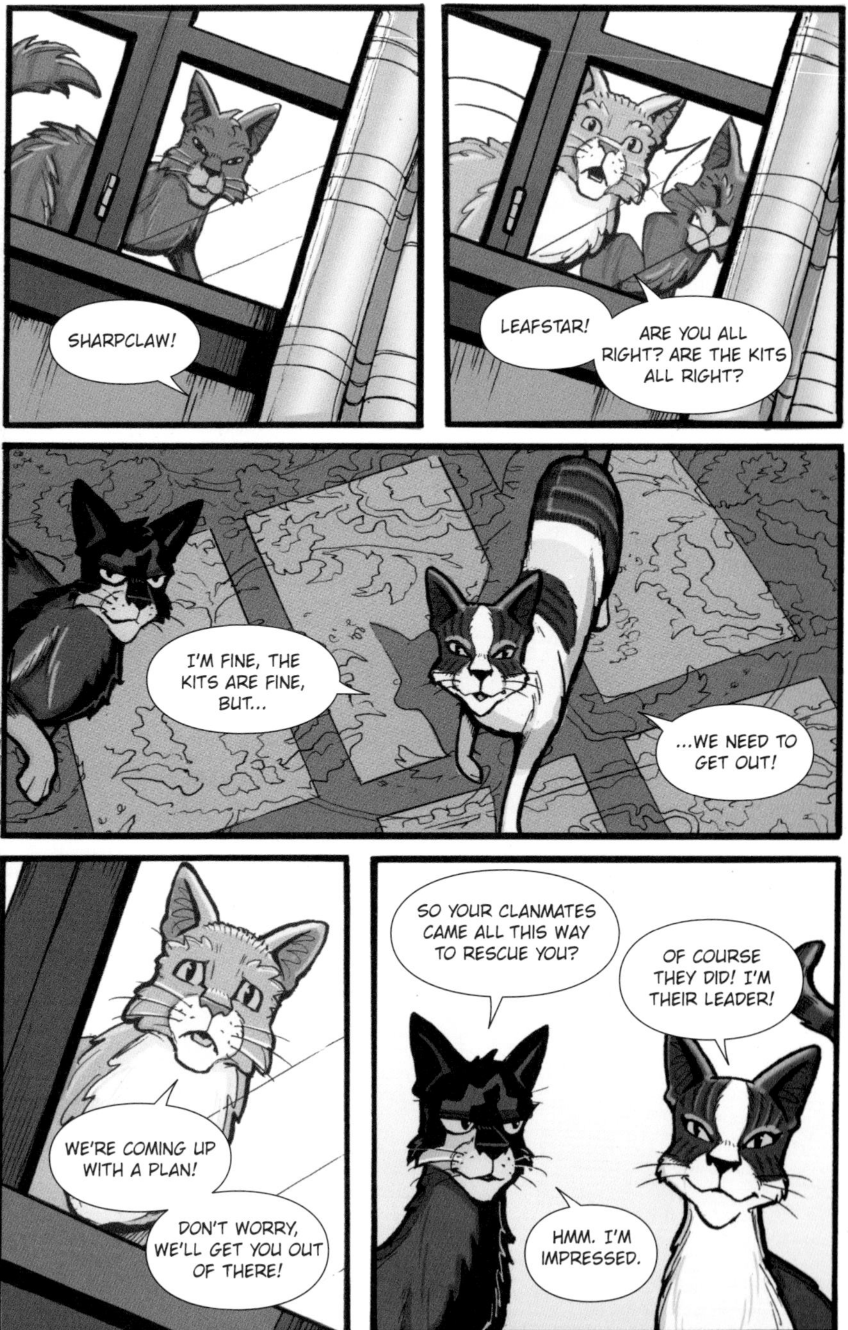
SHARPCLAW!
LEAFSTAR!
ARE YOU ALL RIGHT? ARE THE KITS ALL RIGHT?
I'M FINE, THE KITS ARE FINE, BUT...
...WE NEED TO GET OUT!
WE'RE COMING UP WITH A PLAN!
DON'T WORRY, WE'LL GET YOU OUT OF THERE!
SO YOUR CLANMATES CAME ALL THIS WAY TO RESCUE YOU?
OF COURSE THEY DID! I'M THEIR LEADER!
HMM. I'M IMPRESSED.

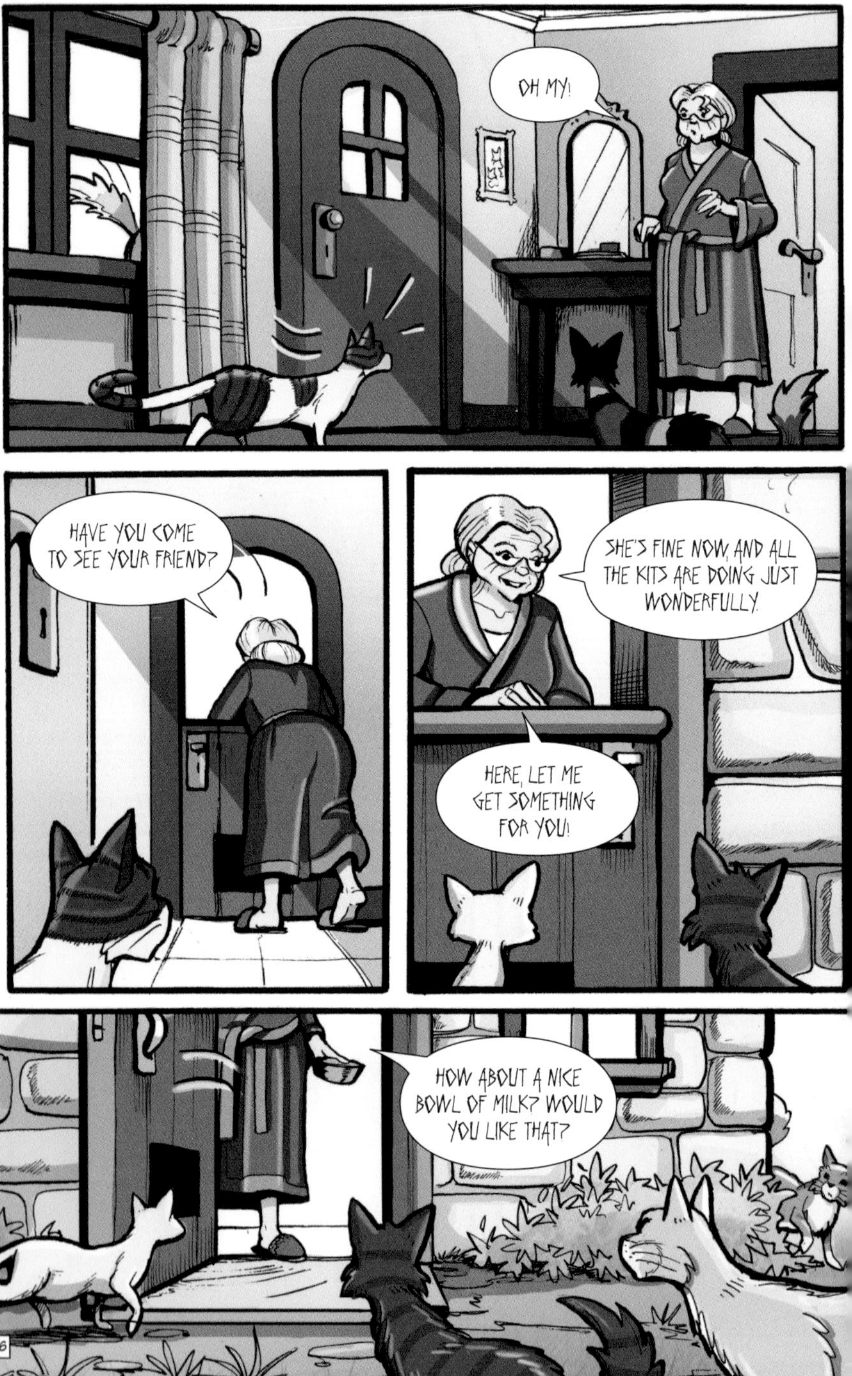
OH MY!
HAVE YOU COME TO SEE YOUR FRIEND?
SHE'S FINE NOW, AND ALL THE KITS ARE DOING JUST WONDERFULLY.
HERE, LET ME GET SOMETHING FOR YOU!
HOW ABOUT A NICE BOWL OF MILK? WOULD YOU LIKE THAT?

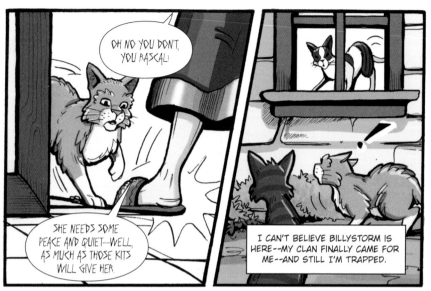

OH NO YOU DON'T, YOU RASCAL!

SHE NEEDS SOME PEACE AND QUIET--WELL, AS MUCH AS THOSE KITS WILL GIVE HER.

I CAN'T BELIEVE BILLYSTORM IS HERE--MY CLAN FINALLY CAME FOR ME--AND STILL I'M TRAPPED.

OH NO....SHARPCLAW!

SNIKT

DON'T HURT HER! SHARPCLAW, DO NOT HURT HER!

SHE MEANS NO HARM!

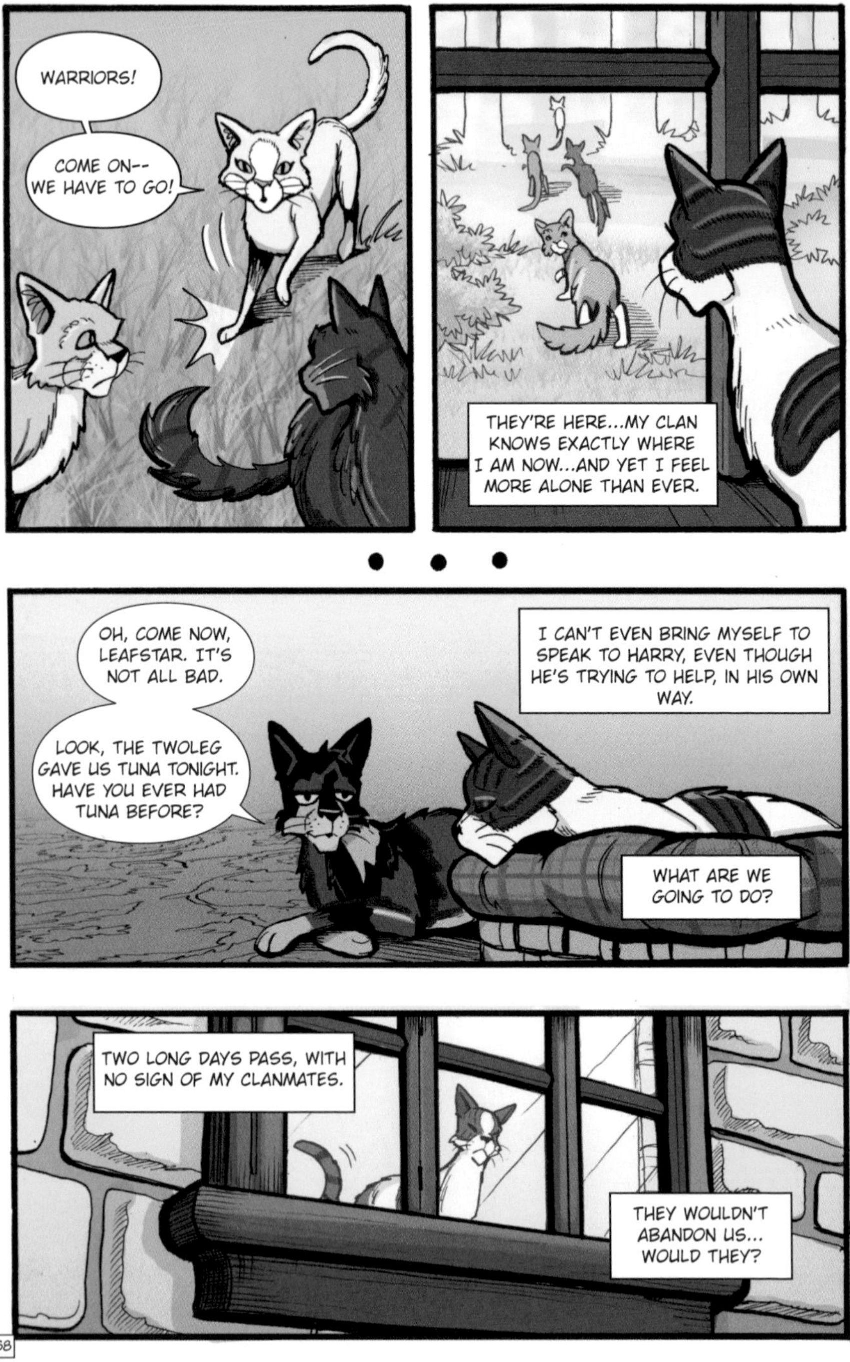
WARRIORS!
COME ON--
WE HAVE TO GO!
THEY'RE HERE...MY CLAN KNOWS EXACTLY WHERE I AM NOW...AND YET I FEEL MORE ALONE THAN EVER.
OH, COME NOW, LEAFSTAR. IT'S NOT ALL BAD.
LOOK, THE TWOLEG GAVE US TUNA TONIGHT. HAVE YOU EVER HAD TUNA BEFORE?
I CAN'T EVEN BRING MYSELF TO SPEAK TO HARRY, EVEN THOUGH HE'S TRYING TO HELP, IN HIS OWN WAY.
WHAT ARE WE GOING TO DO?
TWO LONG DAYS PASS, WITH NO SIGN OF MY CLANMATES.
THEY WOULDN'T ABANDON US... WOULD THEY?

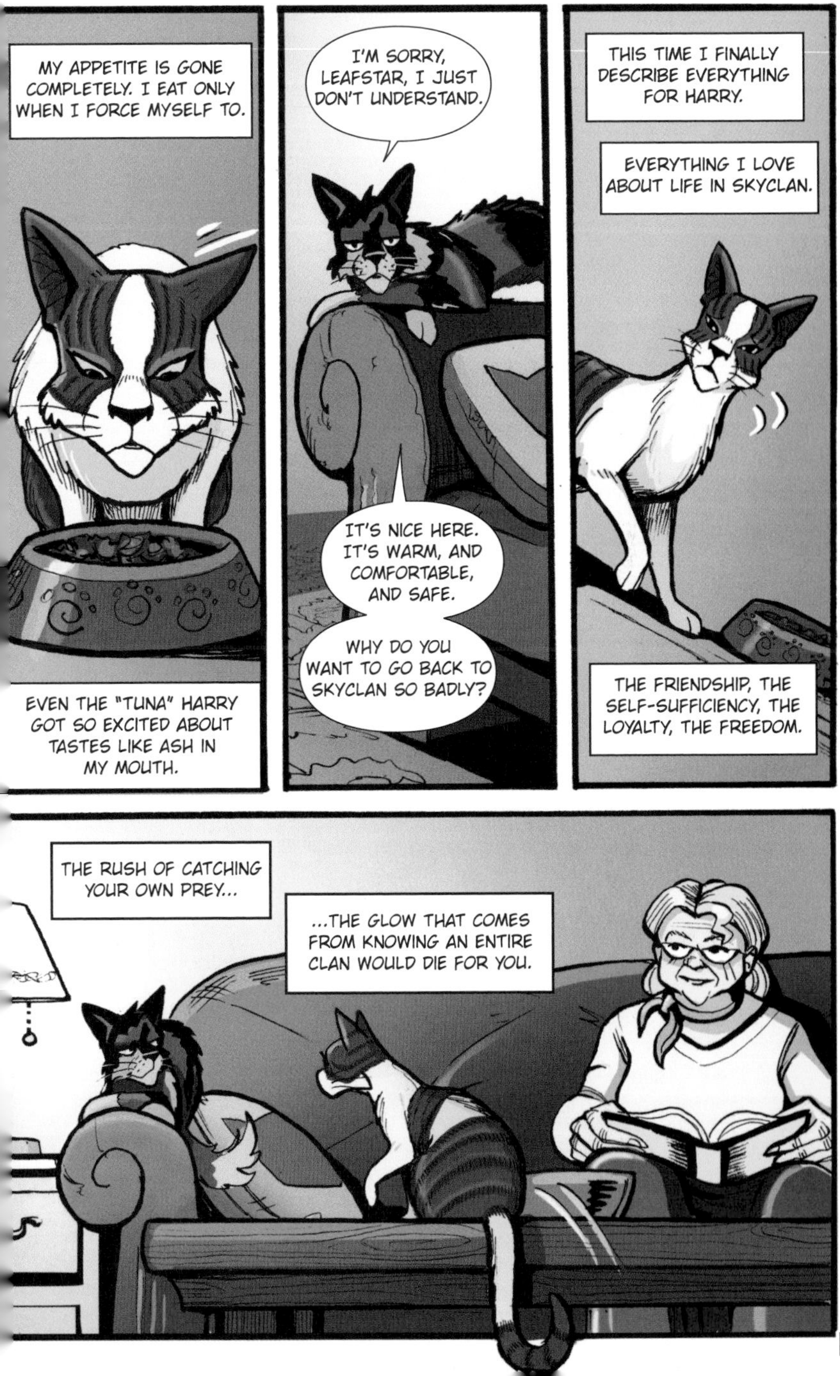
MY APPETITE IS GONE COMPLETELY. I EAT ONLY WHEN I FORCE MYSELF TO.
EVEN THE "TUNA" HARRY GOT SO EXCITED ABOUT TASTES LIKE ASH IN MY MOUTH.
I'M SORRY, LEAFSTAR, I JUST DON'T UNDERSTAND.
IT'S NICE HERE. IT'S WARM, AND COMFORTABLE, AND SAFE.
WHY DO YOU WANT TO GO BACK TO SKYCLAN SO BADLY?
THIS TIME I FINALLY DESCRIBE EVERYTHING FOR HARRY.
EVERYTHING I LOVE ABOUT LIFE IN SKYCLAN.
THE FRIENDSHIP, THE SELF-SUFFICIENCY, THE LOYALTY, THE FREEDOM.
THE RUSH OF CATCHING YOUR OWN PREY...
...THE GLOW THAT COMES FROM KNOWING AN ENTIRE CLAN WOULD DIE FOR YOU.

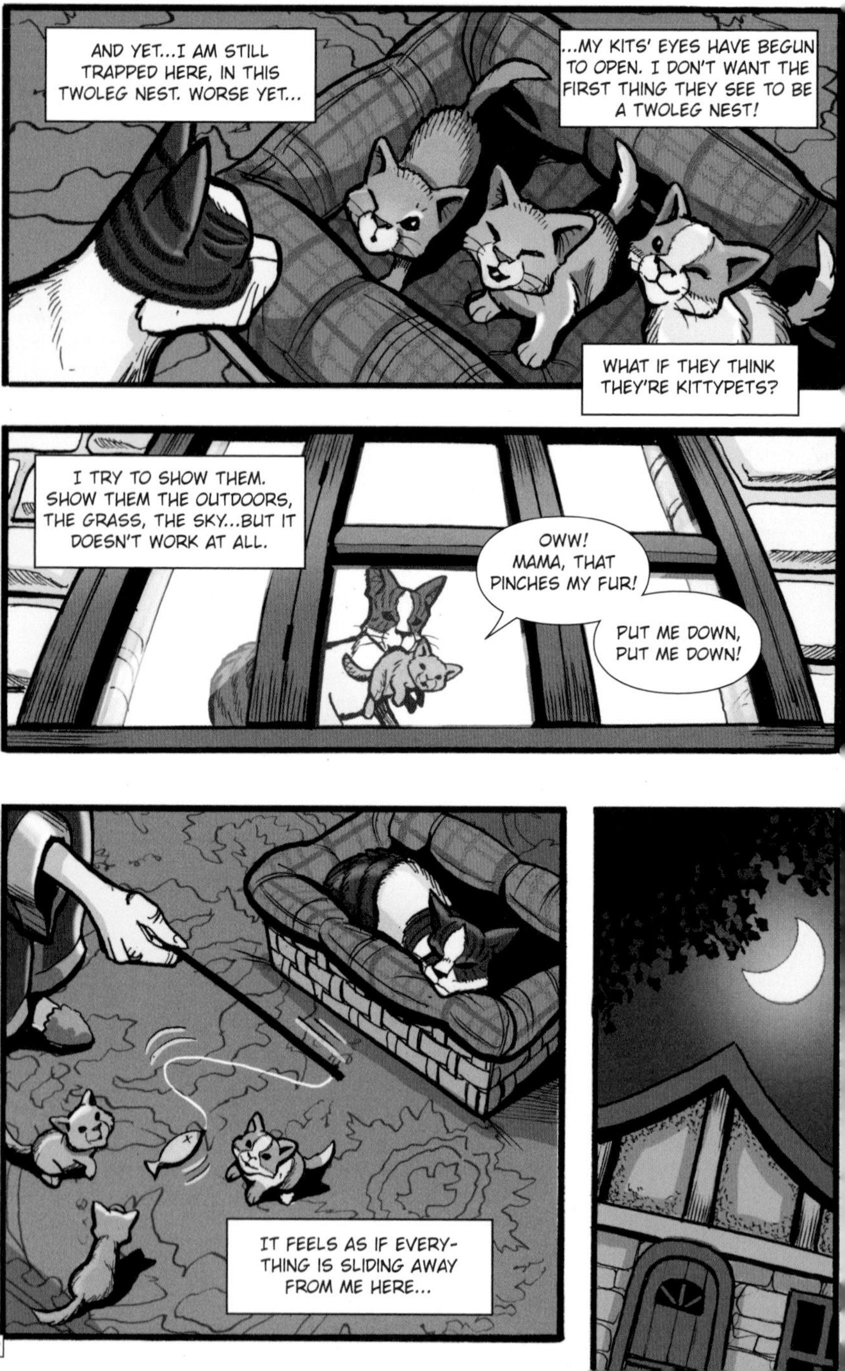
AND YET...I AM STILL TRAPPED HERE, IN THIS TWOLEG NEST. WORSE YET...
...MY KITS' EYES HAVE BEGUN TO OPEN. I DON'T WANT THE FIRST THING THEY SEE TO BE A TWOLEG NEST!
WHAT IF THEY THINK THEY'RE KITTYPETS?
I TRY TO SHOW THEM. SHOW THEM THE OUTDOORS, THE GRASS, THE SKY...BUT IT DOESN'T WORK AT ALL.
OWW! MAMA, THAT PINCHES MY FUR!
PUT ME DOWN, PUT ME DOWN!
IT FEELS AS IF EVERY-THING IS SLIDING AWAY FROM ME HERE...

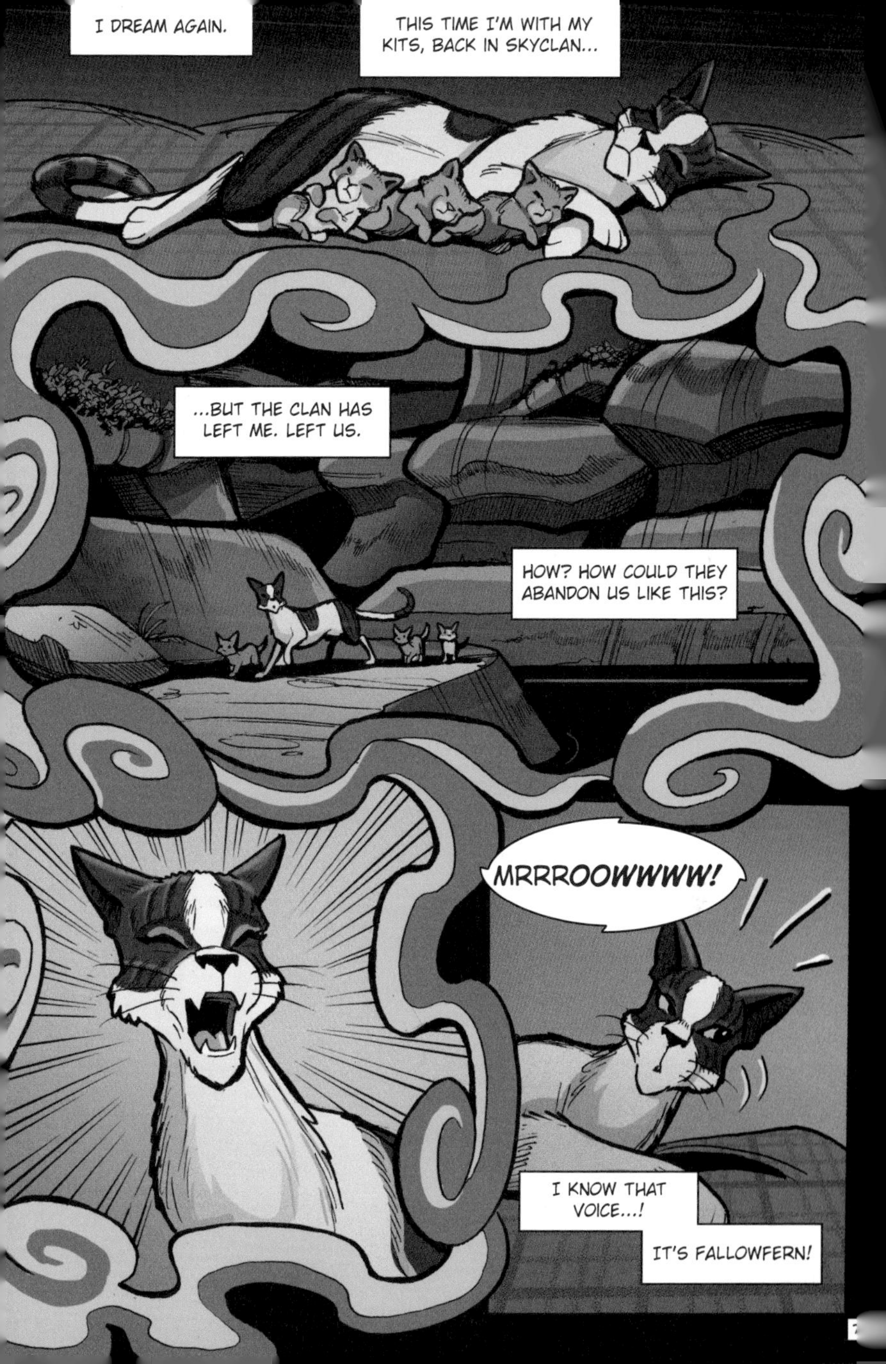
I DREAM AGAIN.
THIS TIME I'M WITH MY KITS, BACK IN SKYCLAN...
...BUT THE CLAN HAS LEFT ME. LEFT US.
HOW? HOW COULD THEY ABANDON US LIKE THIS?
MRRROOWWWW!
I KNOW THAT VOICE...!
IT'S FALLOWFERN!

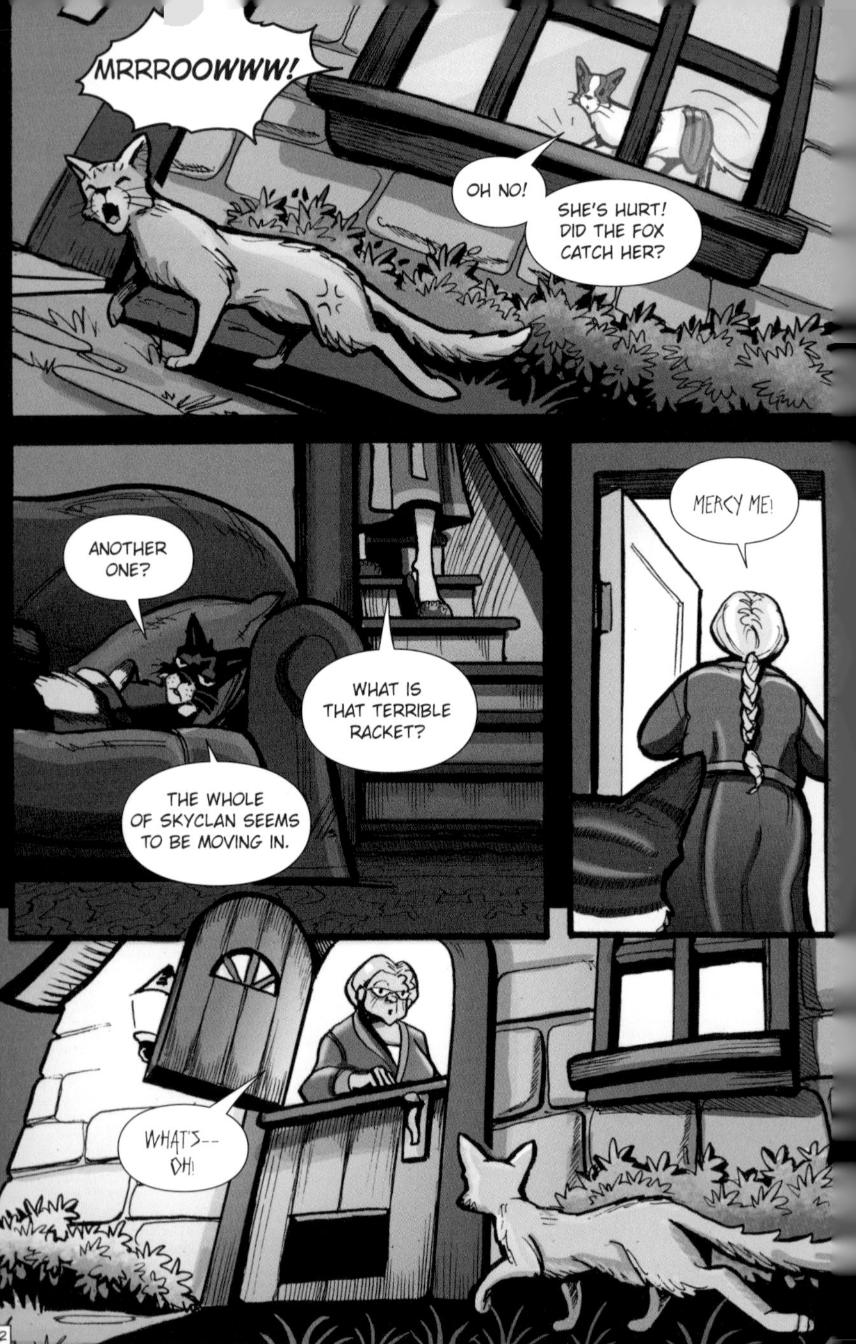

MRRROOWWW!
OH NO!
SHE'S HURT! DID THE FOX CATCH HER?
ANOTHER ONE?
WHAT IS THAT TERRIBLE RACKET?
THE WHOLE OF SKYCLAN SEEMS TO BE MOVING IN.
MERCY ME!
WHAT'S-- OH!

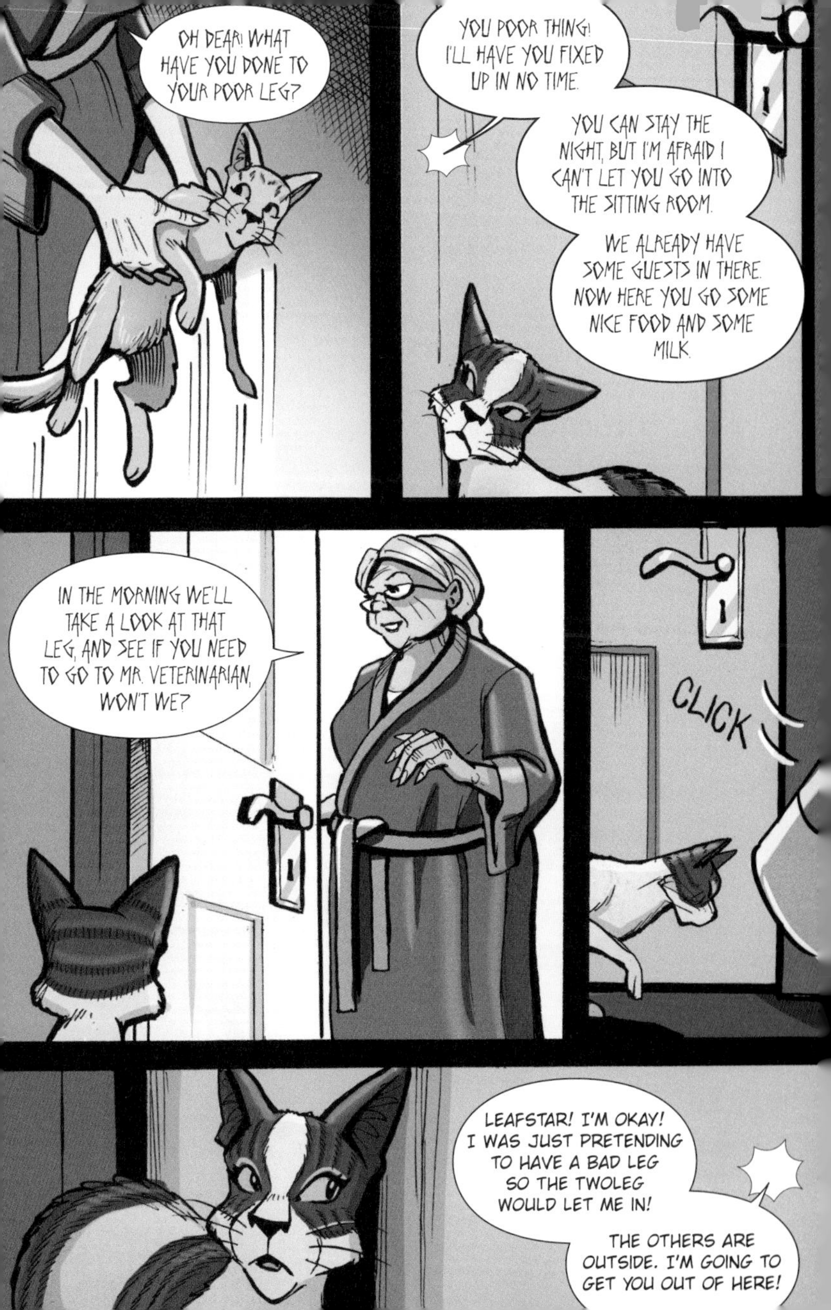
OH DEAR! WHAT HAVE YOU DONE TO YOUR POOR LEG?
YOU POOR THING! I'LL HAVE YOU FIXED UP IN NO TIME.
YOU CAN STAY THE NIGHT, BUT I'M AFRAID I CAN'T LET YOU GO INTO THE SITTING ROOM.
WE ALREADY HAVE SOME GUESTS IN THERE. NOW HERE YOU GO SOME NICE FOOD AND SOME MILK.
IN THE MORNING WE'LL TAKE A LOOK AT THAT LEG, AND SEE IF YOU NEED TO GO TO MR. VETERINARIAN, WON'T WE?
CLICK
LEAFSTAR! I'M OKAY! I WAS JUST PRETENDING TO HAVE A BAD LEG SO THE TWOLEG WOULD LET ME IN!
THE OTHERS ARE OUTSIDE. I'M GOING TO GET YOU OUT OF HERE!

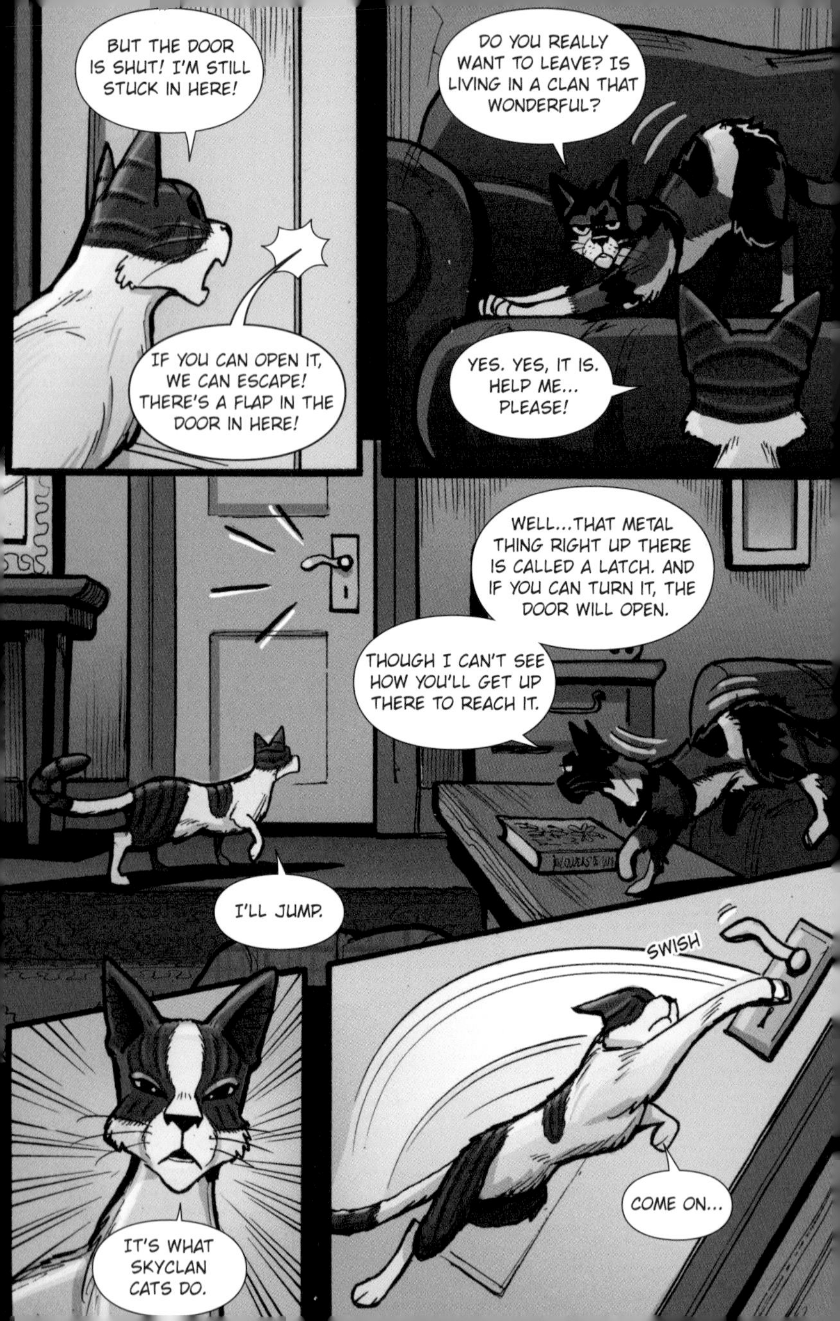
BUT THE DOOR IS SHUT! I'M STILL STUCK IN HERE!
IF YOU CAN OPEN IT, WE CAN ESCAPE! THERE'S A FLAP IN THE DOOR IN HERE!
DO YOU REALLY WANT TO LEAVE? IS LIVING IN A CLAN THAT WONDERFUL?
YES. YES, IT IS. HELP ME... PLEASE!
WELL...THAT METAL THING RIGHT UP THERE IS CALLED A LATCH. AND IF YOU CAN TURN IT, THE DOOR WILL OPEN.
THOUGH I CAN'T SEE HOW YOU'LL GET UP THERE TO REACH IT.
I'LL JUMP.
IT'S WHAT SKYCLAN CATS DO.
SWISH
COME ON...

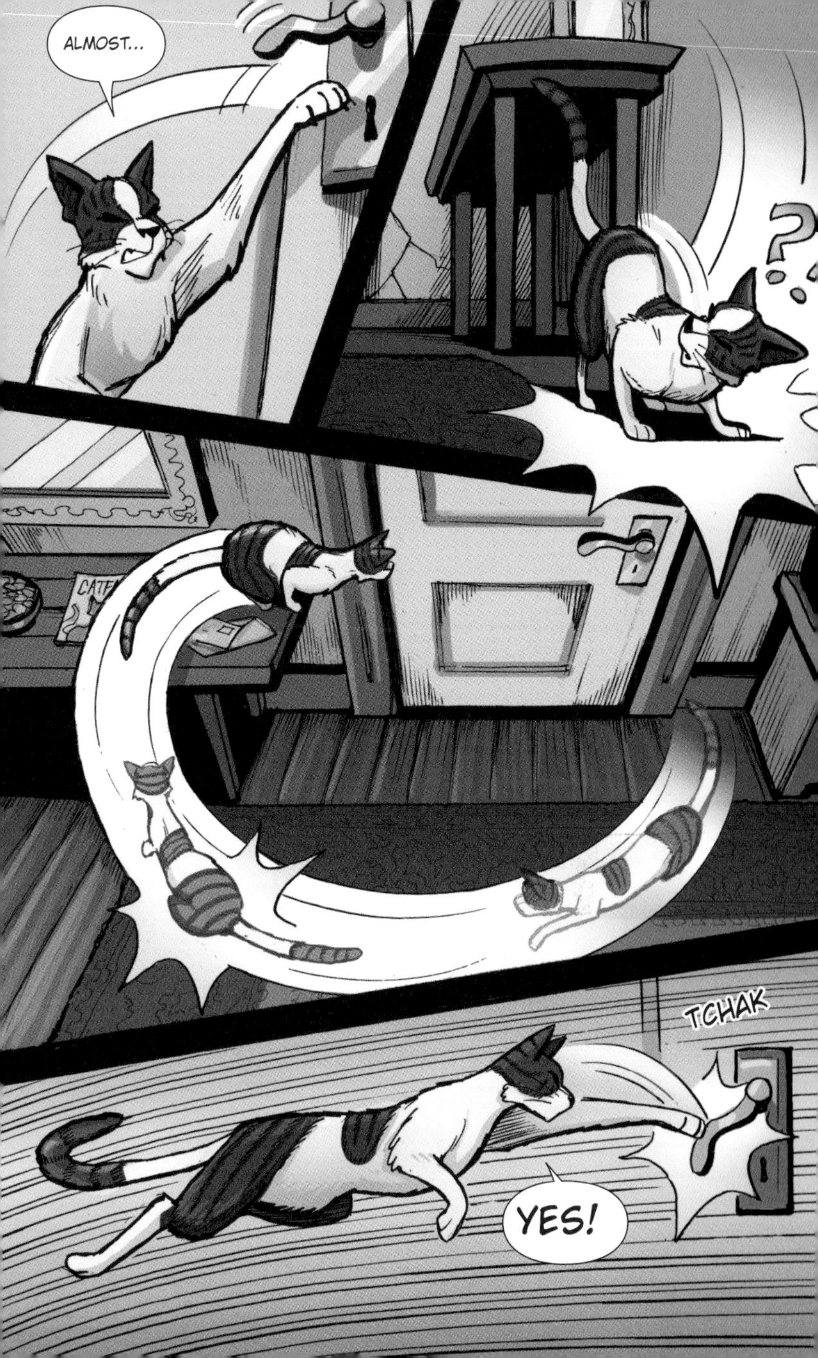
ALMOST...
?
TCHAK
YES!

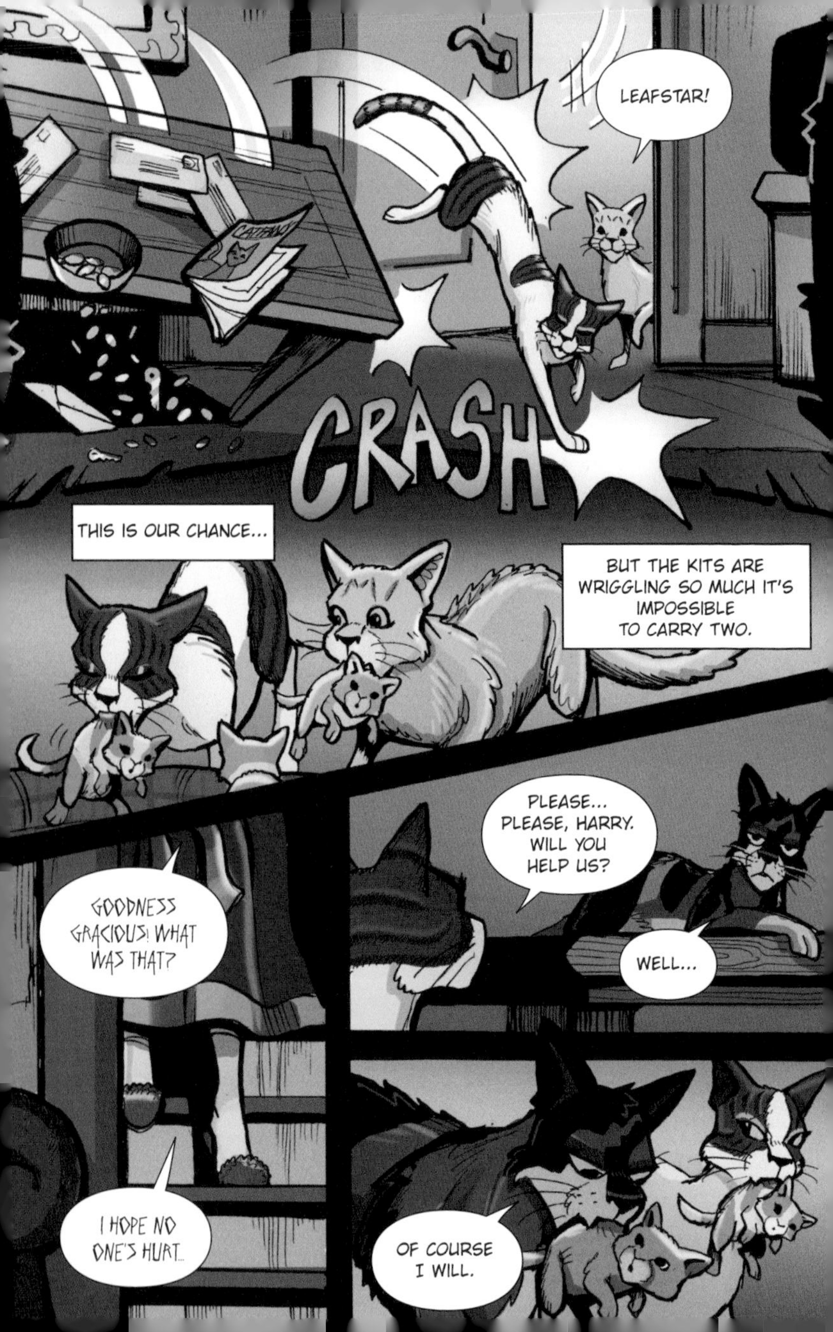
LEAFSTAR!
CRASH
THIS IS OUR CHANCE...
BUT THE KITS ARE WRIGGLING SO MUCH IT'S IMPOSSIBLE TO CARRY TWO.
GOODNESS GRACIOUS! WHAT WAS THAT?
I HOPE NO ONE'S HURT...
PLEASE... PLEASE, HARRY. WILL YOU HELP US?
WELL...
OF COURSE I WILL.

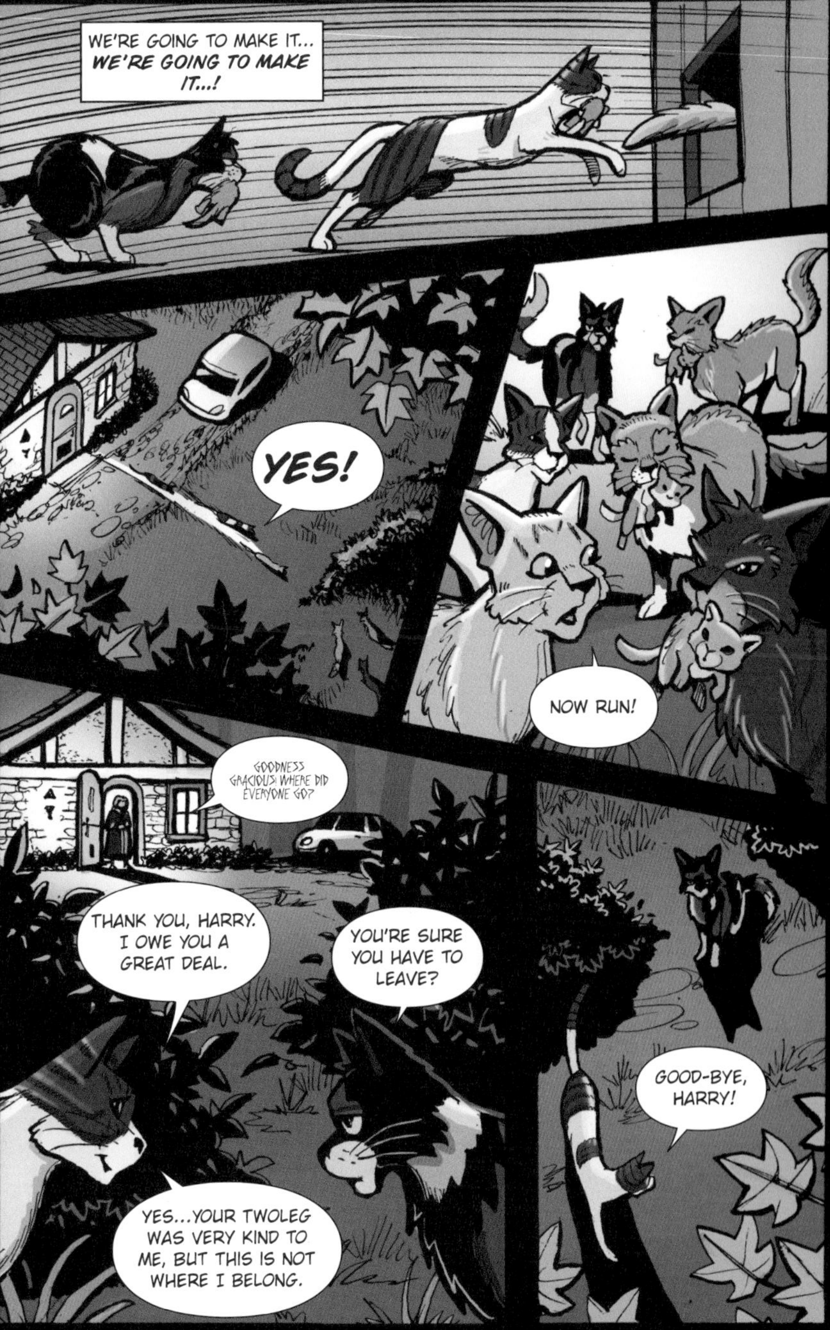

WE'RE GOING TO MAKE IT... *WE'RE GOING TO MAKE IT...!*
YES!
NOW RUN!
GOODNESS GRACIOUS! WHERE DID EVERYONE GO?
THANK YOU, HARRY. I OWE YOU A GREAT DEAL.
YOU'RE SURE YOU HAVE TO LEAVE?
YES...YOUR TWOLEG WAS VERY KIND TO ME, BUT THIS IS NOT WHERE I BELONG.
GOOD-BYE, HARRY!

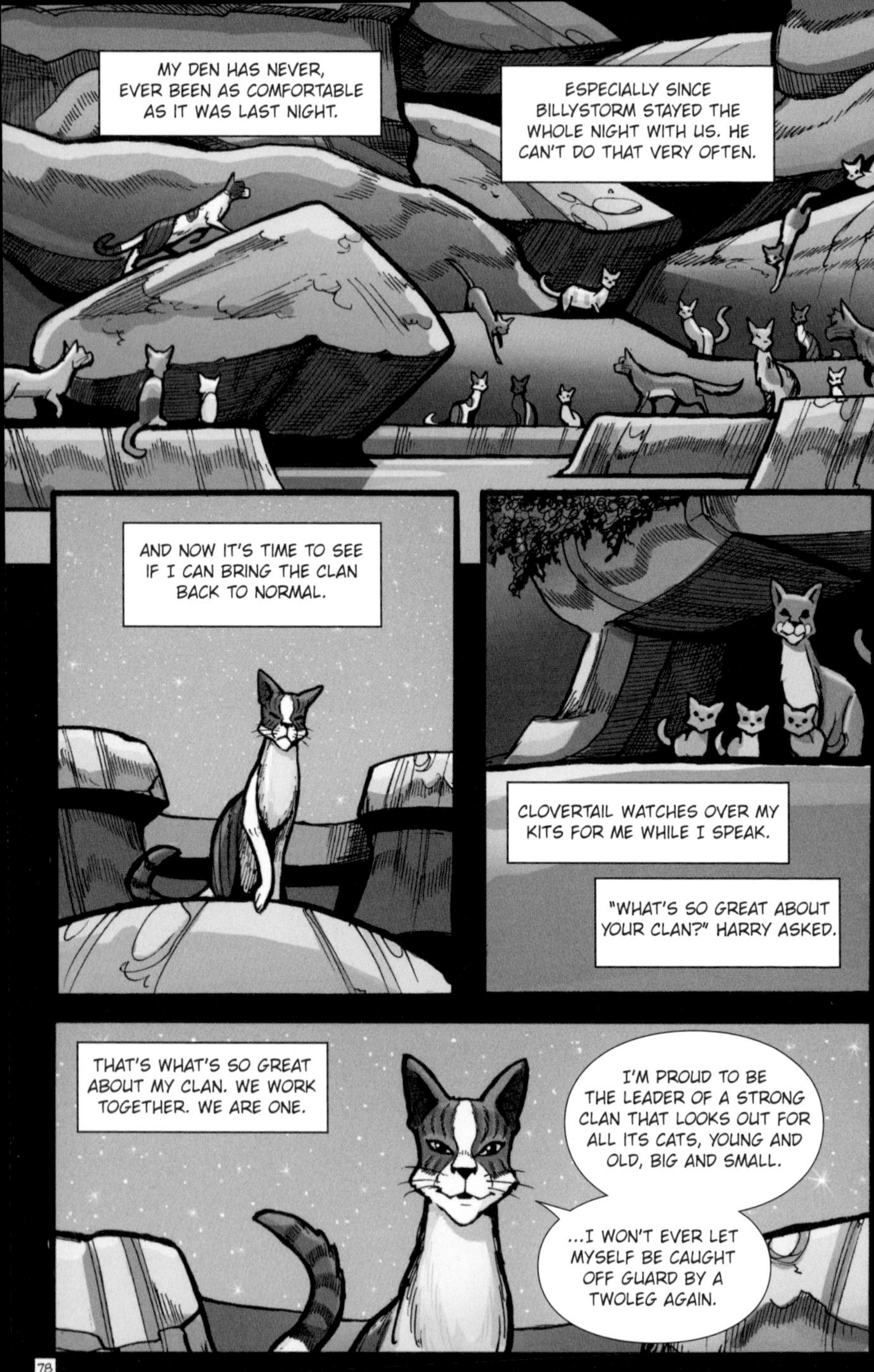
MY DEN HAS NEVER, EVER BEEN AS COMFORTABLE AS IT WAS LAST NIGHT.
ESPECIALLY SINCE BILLYSTORM STAYED THE WHOLE NIGHT WITH US. HE CAN'T DO THAT VERY OFTEN.
AND NOW IT'S TIME TO SEE IF I CAN BRING THE CLAN BACK TO NORMAL.
CLOVERTAIL WATCHES OVER MY KITS FOR ME WHILE I SPEAK.
"WHAT'S SO GREAT ABOUT YOUR CLAN?" HARRY ASKED.
THAT'S WHAT'S SO GREAT ABOUT MY CLAN. WE WORK TOGETHER. WE ARE ONE.
I'M PROUD TO BE THE LEADER OF A STRONG CLAN THAT LOOKS OUT FOR ALL ITS CATS, YOUNG AND OLD, BIG AND SMALL.
...I WON'T EVER LET MYSELF BE CAUGHT OFF GUARD BY A TWOLEG AGAIN.

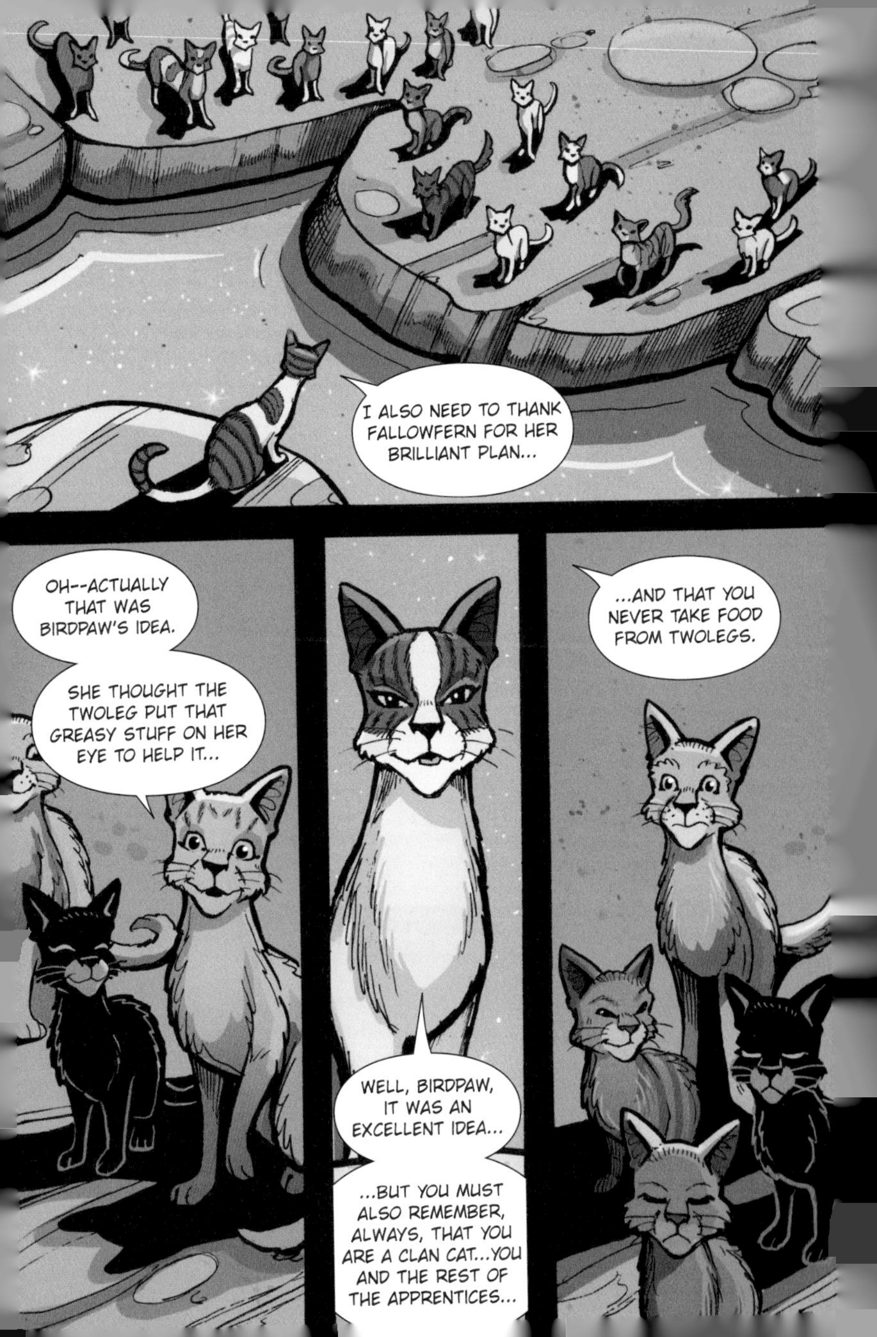
I ALSO NEED TO THANK FALLOWFERN FOR HER BRILLIANT PLAN...
OH--ACTUALLY THAT WAS BIRDPAW'S IDEA.
SHE THOUGHT THE TWOLEG PUT THAT GREASY STUFF ON HER EYE TO HELP IT...
WELL, BIRDPAW, IT WAS AN EXCELLENT IDEA...
...BUT YOU MUST ALSO REMEMBER, ALWAYS, THAT YOU ARE A CLAN CAT...YOU AND THE REST OF THE APPRENTICES...
...AND THAT YOU NEVER TAKE FOOD FROM TWOLEGS.

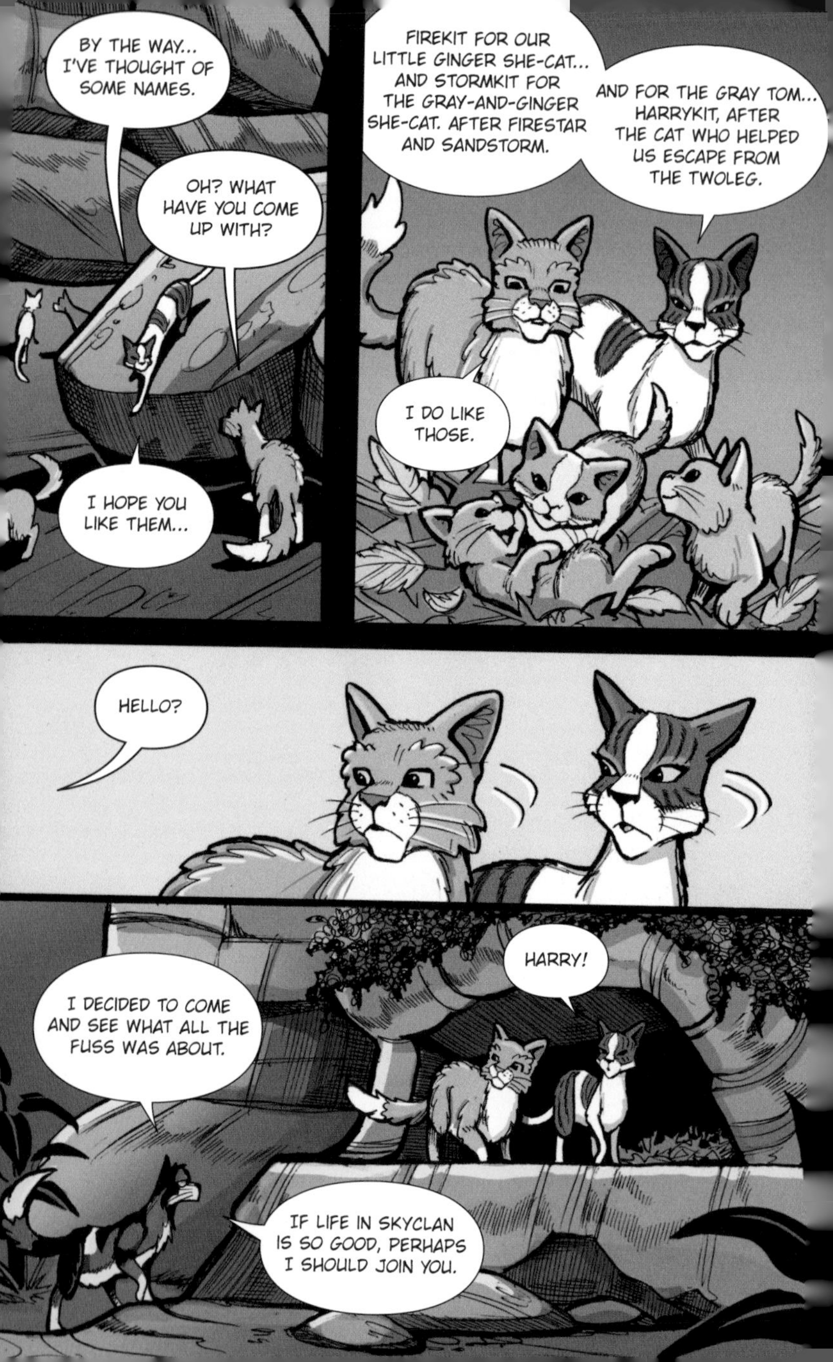
BY THE WAY... I'VE THOUGHT OF SOME NAMES.
OH? WHAT HAVE YOU COME UP WITH?
I HOPE YOU LIKE THEM...
FIREKIT FOR OUR LITTLE GINGER SHE-CAT... AND STORMKIT FOR THE GRAY-AND-GINGER SHE-CAT. AFTER FIRESTAR AND SANDSTORM.
AND FOR THE GRAY TOM... HARRYKIT, AFTER THE CAT WHO HELPED US ESCAPE FROM THE TWOLEG.
I DO LIKE THOSE.
HELLO?
I DECIDED TO COME AND SEE WHAT ALL THE FUSS WAS ABOUT.
HARRY!
IF LIFE IN SKYCLAN IS SO GOOD, PERHAPS I SHOULD JOIN YOU.

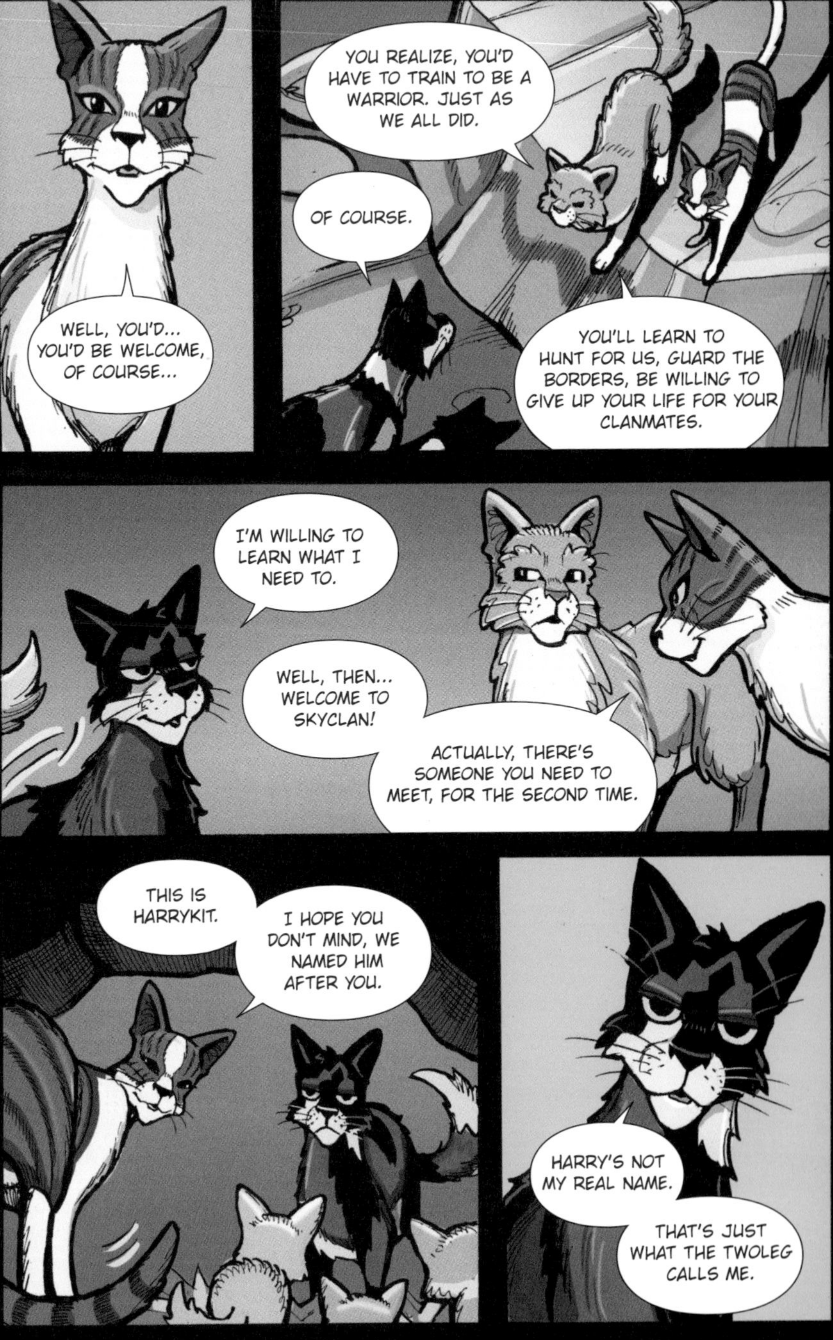
WELL, YOU'D... YOU'D BE WELCOME, OF COURSE...
YOU REALIZE, YOU'D HAVE TO TRAIN TO BE A WARRIOR. JUST AS WE ALL DID.
OF COURSE.
YOU'LL LEARN TO HUNT FOR US, GUARD THE BORDERS, BE WILLING TO GIVE UP YOUR LIFE FOR YOUR CLANMATES.
I'M WILLING TO LEARN WHAT I NEED TO.
WELL, THEN... WELCOME TO SKYCLAN!
ACTUALLY, THERE'S SOMEONE YOU NEED TO MEET, FOR THE SECOND TIME.
THIS IS HARRYKIT.
I HOPE YOU DON'T MIND, WE NAMED HIM AFTER YOU.
HARRY'S NOT MY REAL NAME.
THAT'S JUST WHAT THE TWOLEG CALLS ME.

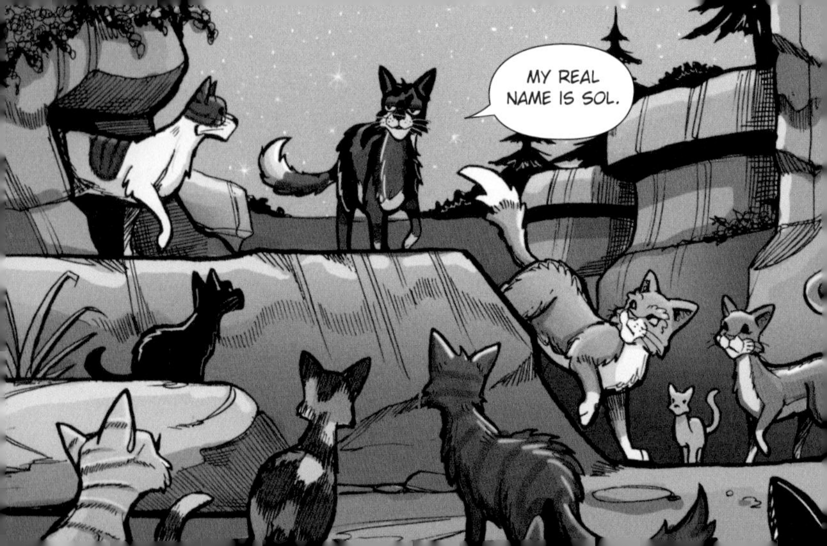
MY REAL NAME IS SOL.

WARRIORS

BEYOND THE
CODE

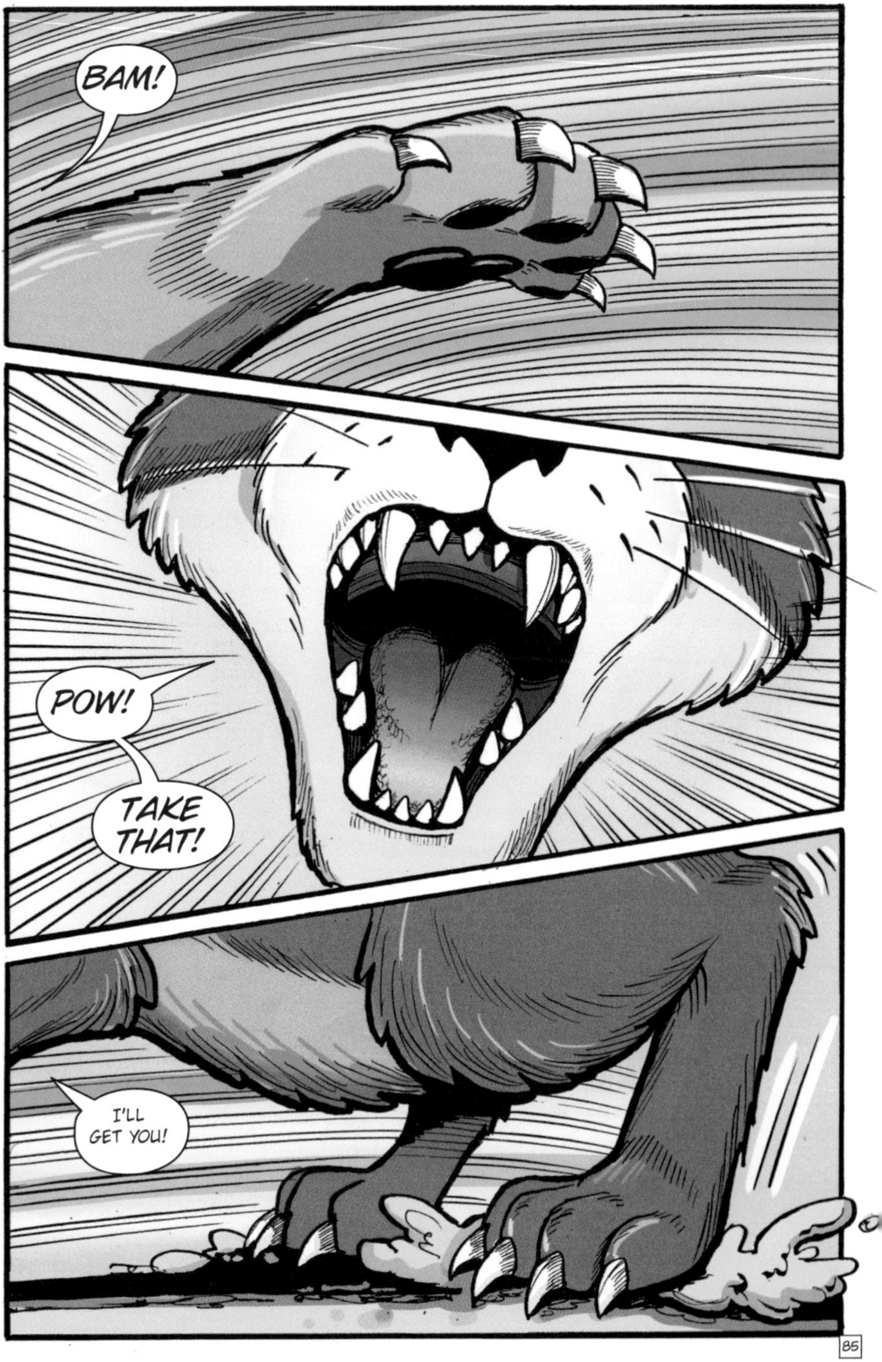
BAM!
POW!
TAKE THAT!
I'LL GET YOU!

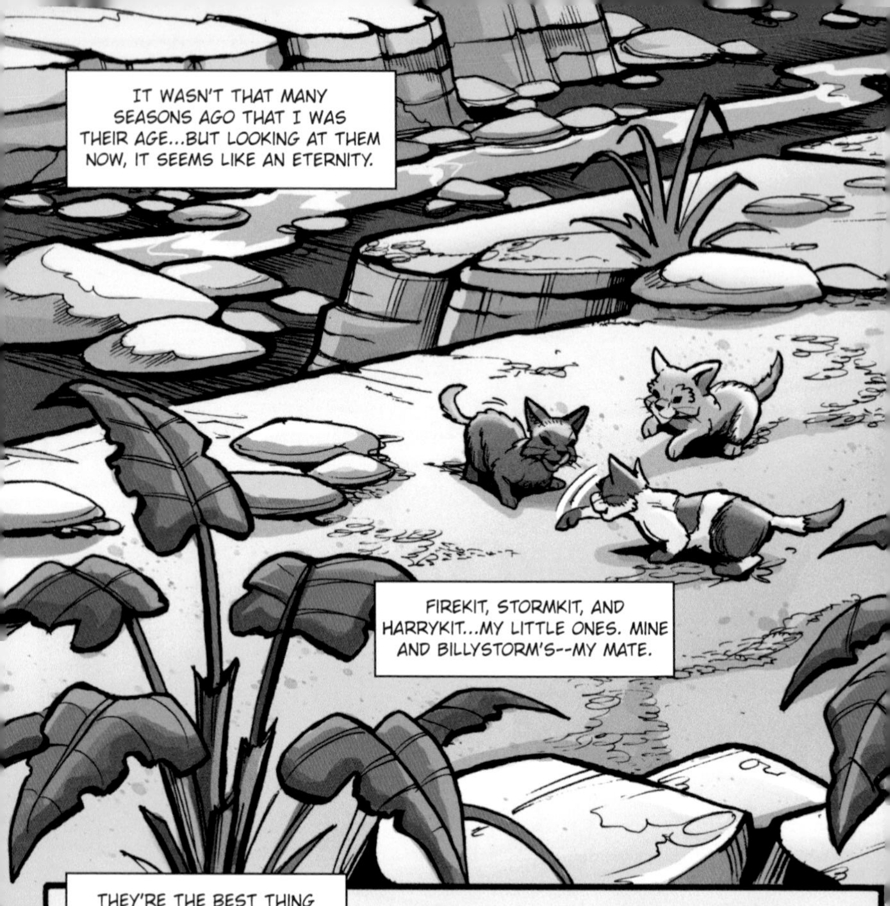
IT WASN'T THAT MANY SEASONS AGO THAT I WAS THEIR AGE...BUT LOOKING AT THEM NOW, IT SEEMS LIKE AN ETERNITY.
FIREKIT, STORMKIT, AND HARRYKIT...MY LITTLE ONES. MINE AND BILLYSTORM'S--MY MATE.

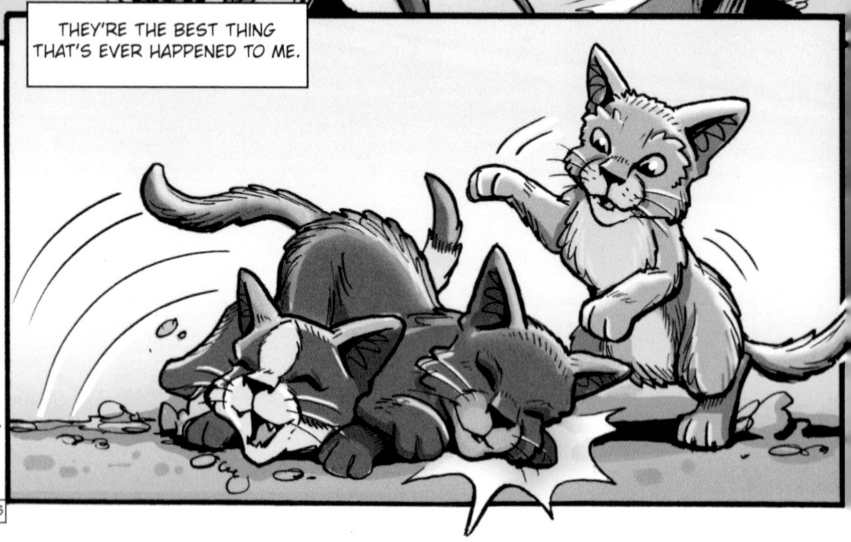
THEY'RE THE BEST THING THAT'S EVER HAPPENED TO ME.

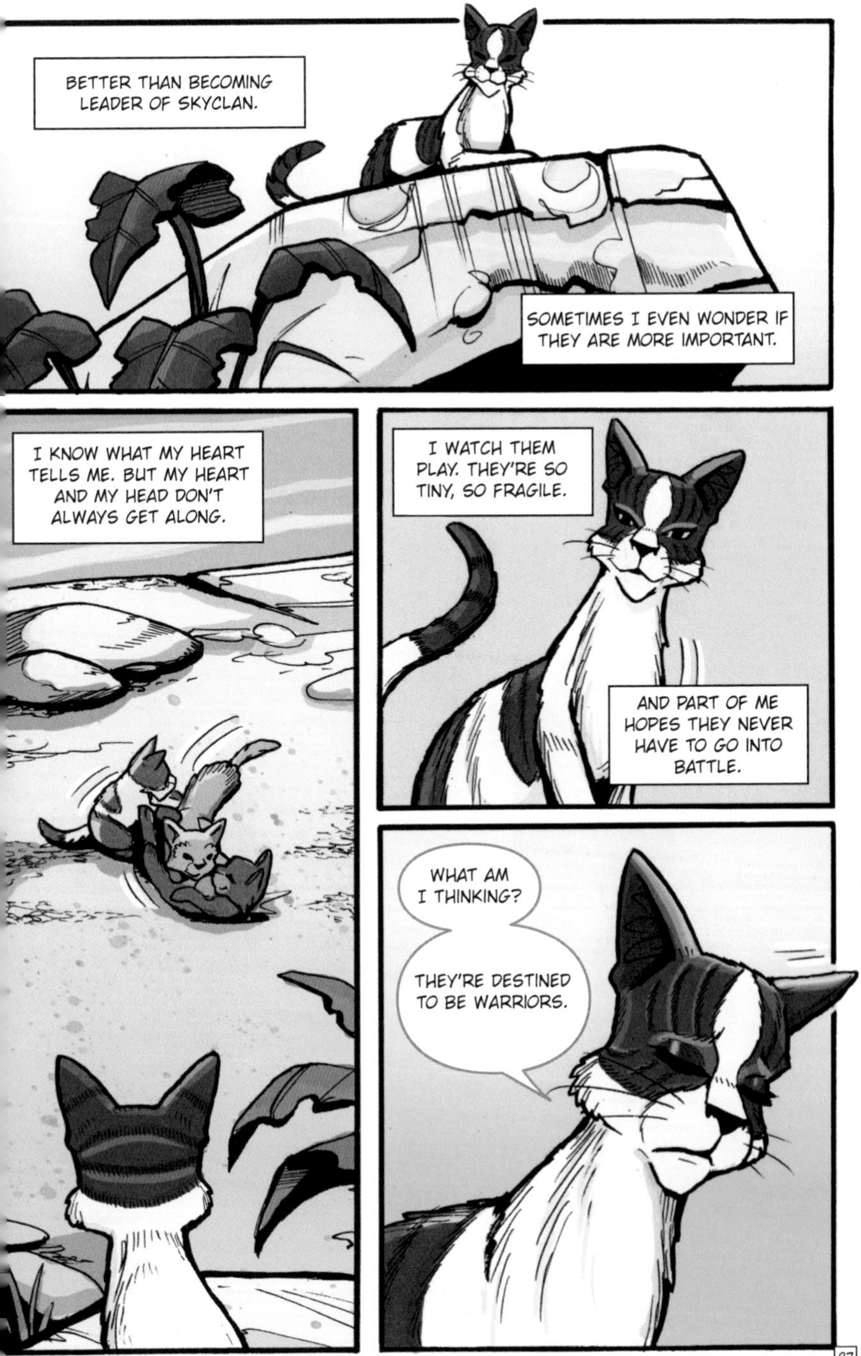
BETTER THAN BECOMING LEADER OF SKYCLAN.
SOMETIMES I EVEN WONDER IF THEY ARE MORE IMPORTANT.
I KNOW WHAT MY HEART TELLS ME. BUT MY HEART AND MY HEAD DON'T ALWAYS GET ALONG.
I WATCH THEM PLAY. THEY'RE SO TINY, SO FRAGILE.
AND PART OF ME HOPES THEY NEVER HAVE TO GO INTO BATTLE.
WHAT AM I THINKING?
THEY'RE DESTINED TO BE WARRIORS.

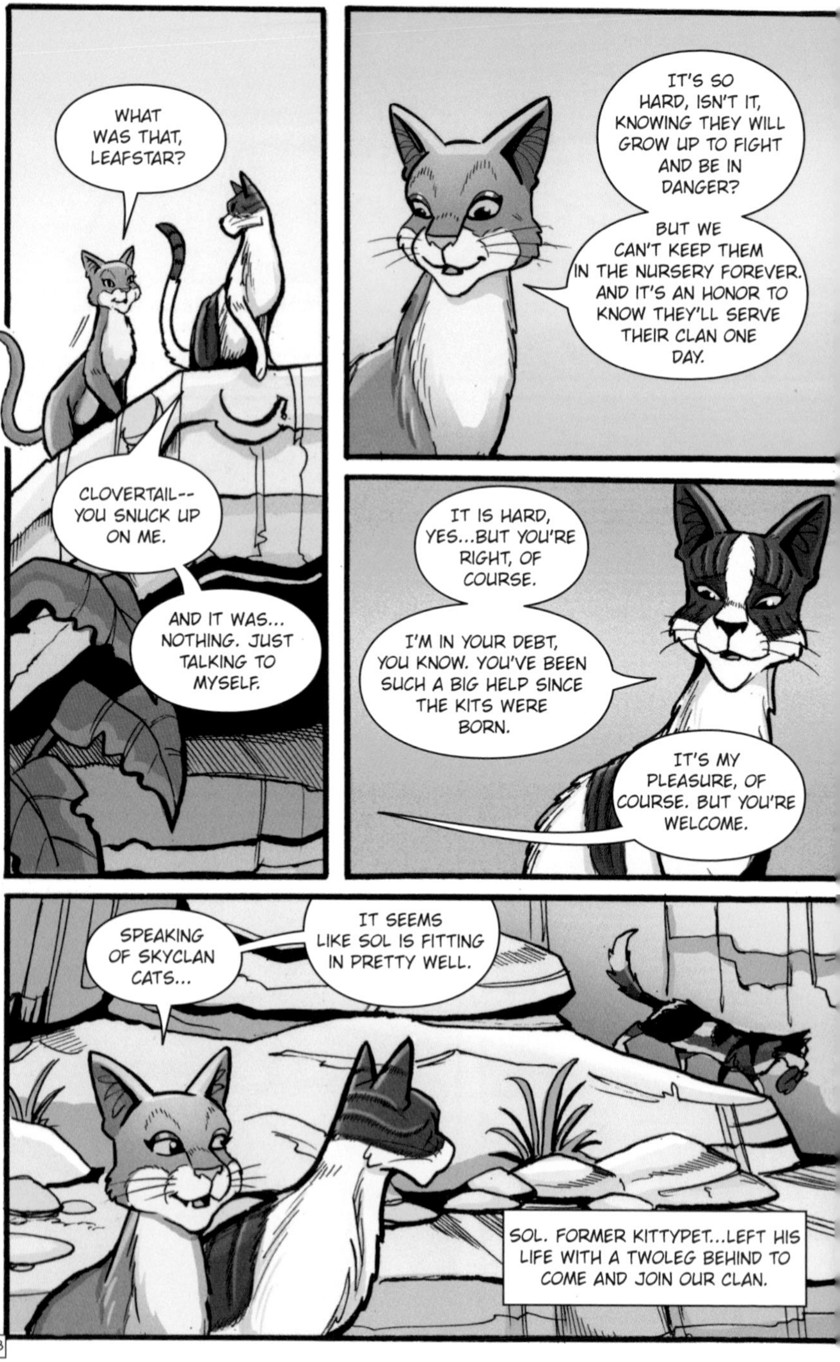
WHAT WAS THAT, LEAFSTAR?
CLOVERTAIL-- YOU SNUCK UP ON ME.
AND IT WAS... NOTHING. JUST TALKING TO MYSELF.
IT'S SO HARD, ISN'T IT, KNOWING THEY WILL GROW UP TO FIGHT AND BE IN DANGER?
BUT WE CAN'T KEEP THEM IN THE NURSERY FOREVER. AND IT'S AN HONOR TO KNOW THEY'LL SERVE THEIR CLAN ONE DAY.
IT IS HARD, YES...BUT YOU'RE RIGHT, OF COURSE.
I'M IN YOUR DEBT, YOU KNOW. YOU'VE BEEN SUCH A BIG HELP SINCE THE KITS WERE BORN.
IT'S MY PLEASURE, OF COURSE. BUT YOU'RE WELCOME.
SPEAKING OF SKYCLAN CATS...
IT SEEMS LIKE SOL IS FITTING IN PRETTY WELL.
SOL. FORMER KITTYPET...LEFT HIS LIFE WITH A TWOLEG BEHIND TO COME AND JOIN OUR CLAN.

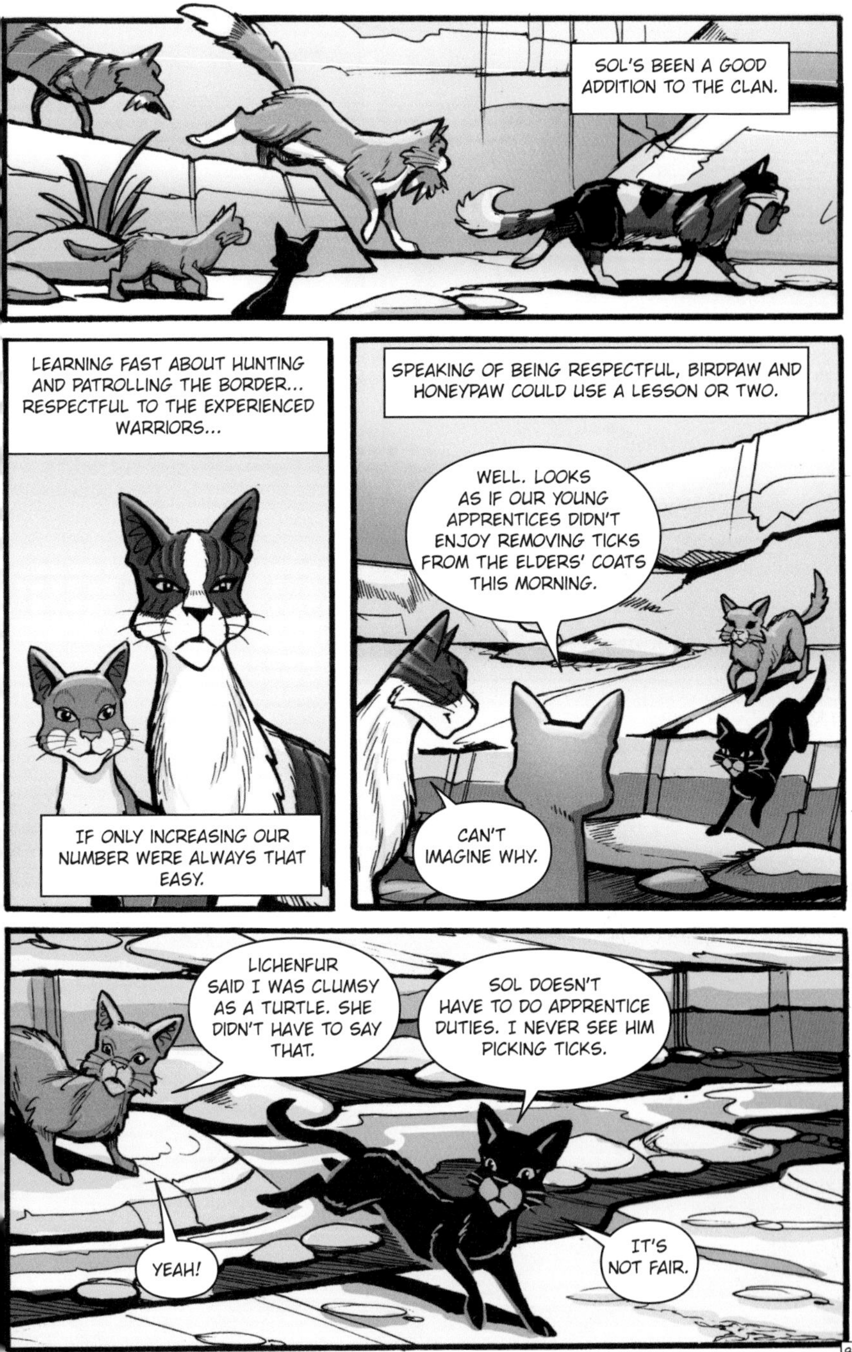
SOL'S BEEN A GOOD ADDITION TO THE CLAN.
LEARNING FAST ABOUT HUNTING AND PATROLLING THE BORDER... RESPECTFUL TO THE EXPERIENCED WARRIORS...
IF ONLY INCREASING OUR NUMBER WERE ALWAYS THAT EASY.
SPEAKING OF BEING RESPECTFUL, BIRDPAW AND HONEYPAW COULD USE A LESSON OR TWO.
WELL. LOOKS AS IF OUR YOUNG APPRENTICES DIDN'T ENJOY REMOVING TICKS FROM THE ELDERS' COATS THIS MORNING.
CAN'T IMAGINE WHY.
LICHENFUR SAID I WAS CLUMSY AS A TURTLE. SHE DIDN'T HAVE TO SAY THAT.
SOL DOESN'T HAVE TO DO APPRENTICE DUTIES. I NEVER SEE HIM PICKING TICKS.
YEAH!
IT'S NOT FAIR.

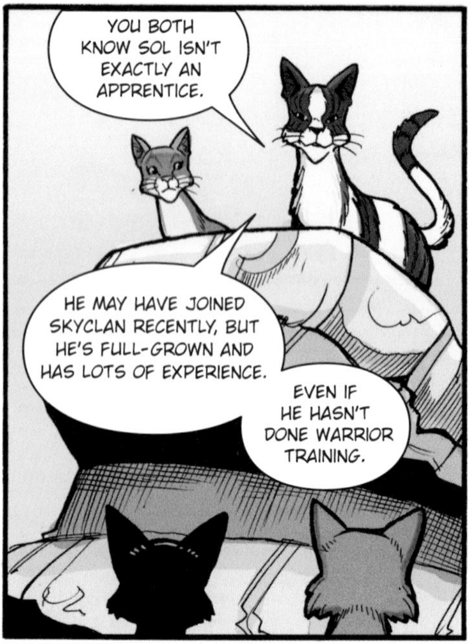
YOU BOTH KNOW SOL ISN'T EXACTLY AN APPRENTICE.
HE MAY HAVE JOINED SKYCLAN RECENTLY, BUT HE'S FULL-GROWN AND HAS LOTS OF EXPERIENCE.
EVEN IF HE HASN'T DONE WARRIOR TRAINING.

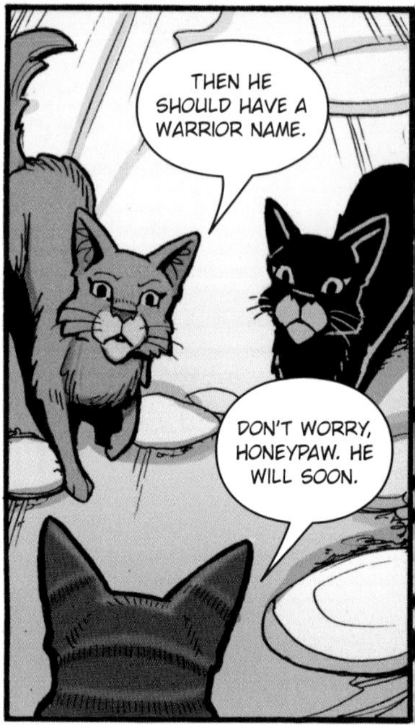
THEN HE SHOULD HAVE A WARRIOR NAME.
DON'T WORRY, HONEYPAW. HE WILL SOON.

IT'S BEEN HOT LATELY. VERY HOT. I DON'T KNOW THAT I CAN REMEMBER THE LAST TIME IT FELT LIKE THIS, FOR THIS LONG.

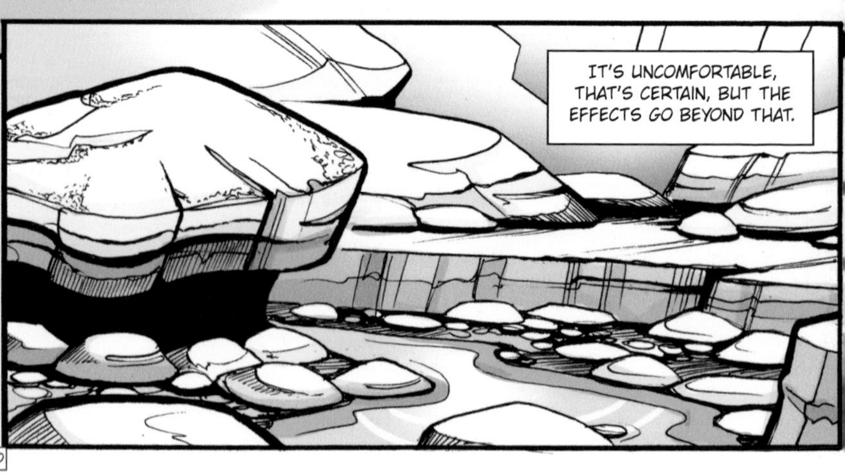
IT'S UNCOMFORTABLE, THAT'S CERTAIN, BUT THE EFFECTS GO BEYOND THAT.

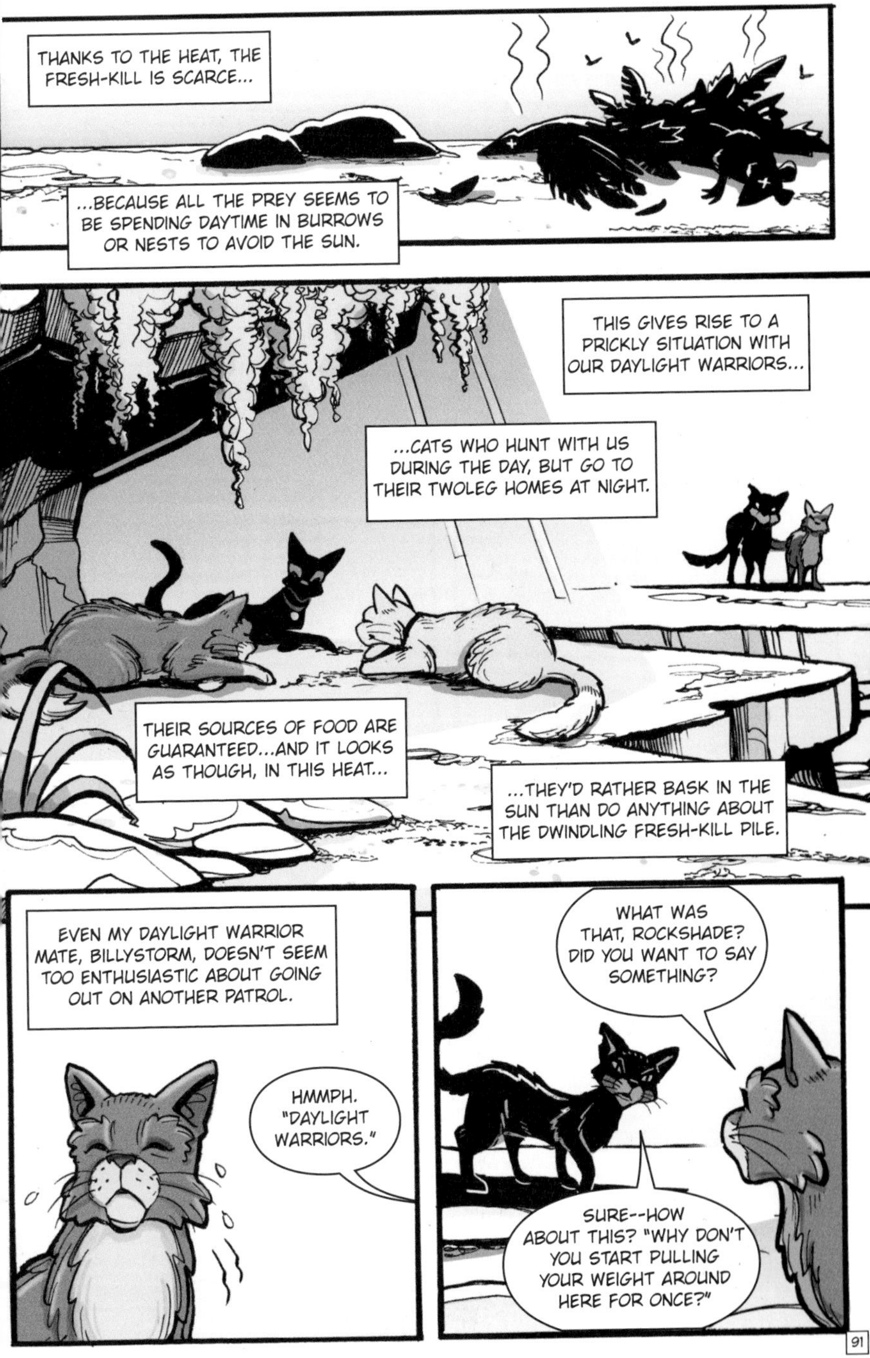
THANKS TO THE HEAT, THE FRESH-KILL IS SCARCE...
...BECAUSE ALL THE PREY SEEMS TO BE SPENDING DAYTIME IN BURROWS OR NESTS TO AVOID THE SUN.
THIS GIVES RISE TO A PRICKLY SITUATION WITH OUR DAYLIGHT WARRIORS...
...CATS WHO HUNT WITH US DURING THE DAY, BUT GO TO THEIR TWOLEG HOMES AT NIGHT.
THEIR SOURCES OF FOOD ARE GUARANTEED...AND IT LOOKS AS THOUGH, IN THIS HEAT...
...THEY'D RATHER BASK IN THE SUN THAN DO ANYTHING ABOUT THE DWINDLING FRESH-KILL PILE.
EVEN MY DAYLIGHT WARRIOR MATE, BILLYSTORM, DOESN'T SEEM TOO ENTHUSIASTIC ABOUT GOING OUT ON ANOTHER PATROL.
HMMPH. "DAYLIGHT WARRIORS."
WHAT WAS THAT, ROCKSHADE? DID YOU WANT TO SAY SOMETHING?
SURE--HOW ABOUT THIS? "WHY DON'T YOU START PULLING YOUR WEIGHT AROUND HERE FOR ONCE?"

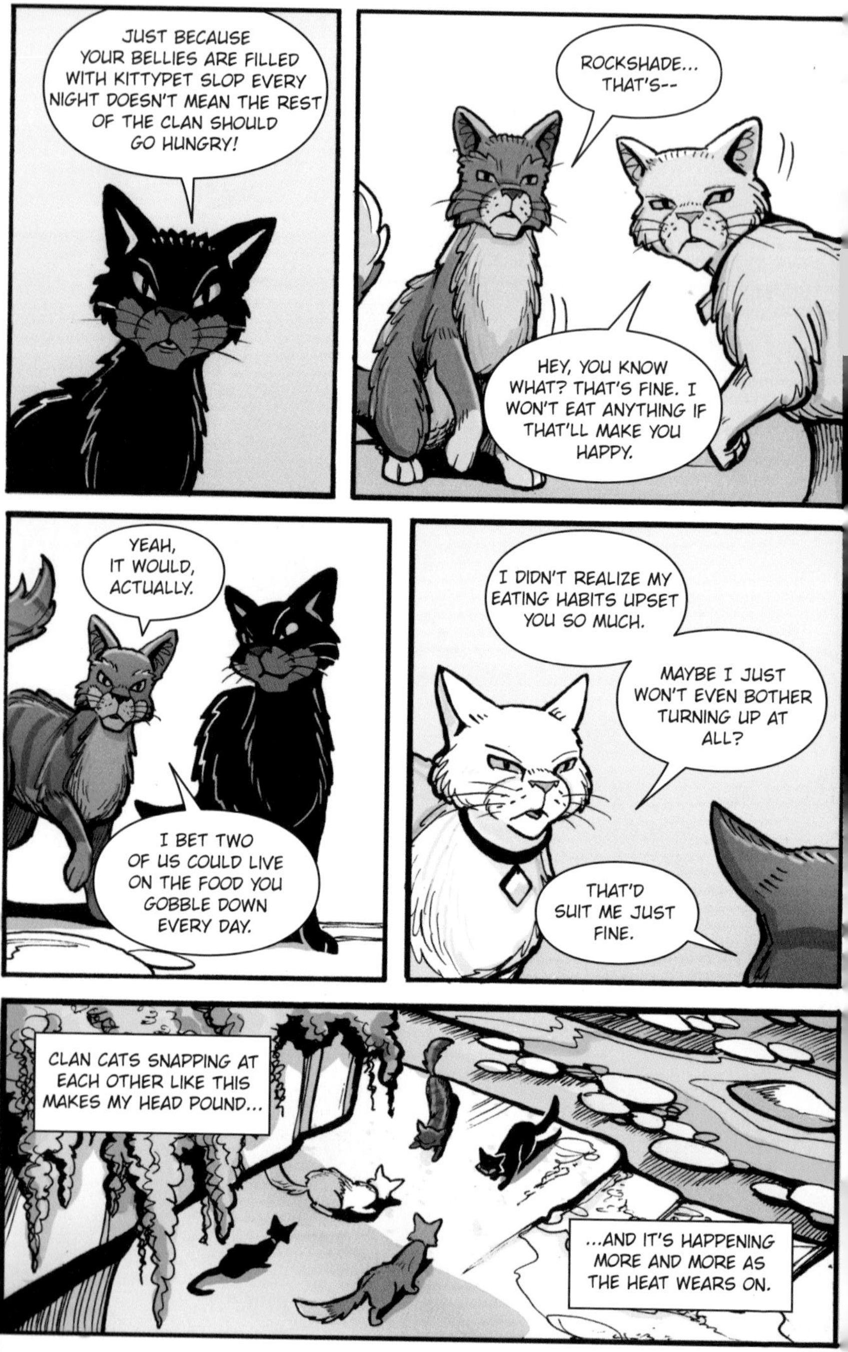
JUST BECAUSE YOUR BELLIES ARE FILLED WITH KITTYPET SLOP EVERY NIGHT DOESN'T MEAN THE REST OF THE CLAN SHOULD GO HUNGRY!
ROCKSHADE... THAT'S--
HEY, YOU KNOW WHAT? THAT'S FINE. I WON'T EAT ANYTHING IF THAT'LL MAKE YOU HAPPY.
YEAH, IT WOULD, ACTUALLY.
I BET TWO OF US COULD LIVE ON THE FOOD YOU GOBBLE DOWN EVERY DAY.
I DIDN'T REALIZE MY EATING HABITS UPSET YOU SO MUCH.
MAYBE I JUST WON'T EVEN BOTHER TURNING UP AT ALL?
THAT'D SUIT ME JUST FINE.
CLAN CATS SNAPPING AT EACH OTHER LIKE THIS MAKES MY HEAD POUND...
...AND IT'S HAPPENING MORE AND MORE AS THE HEAT WEARS ON.

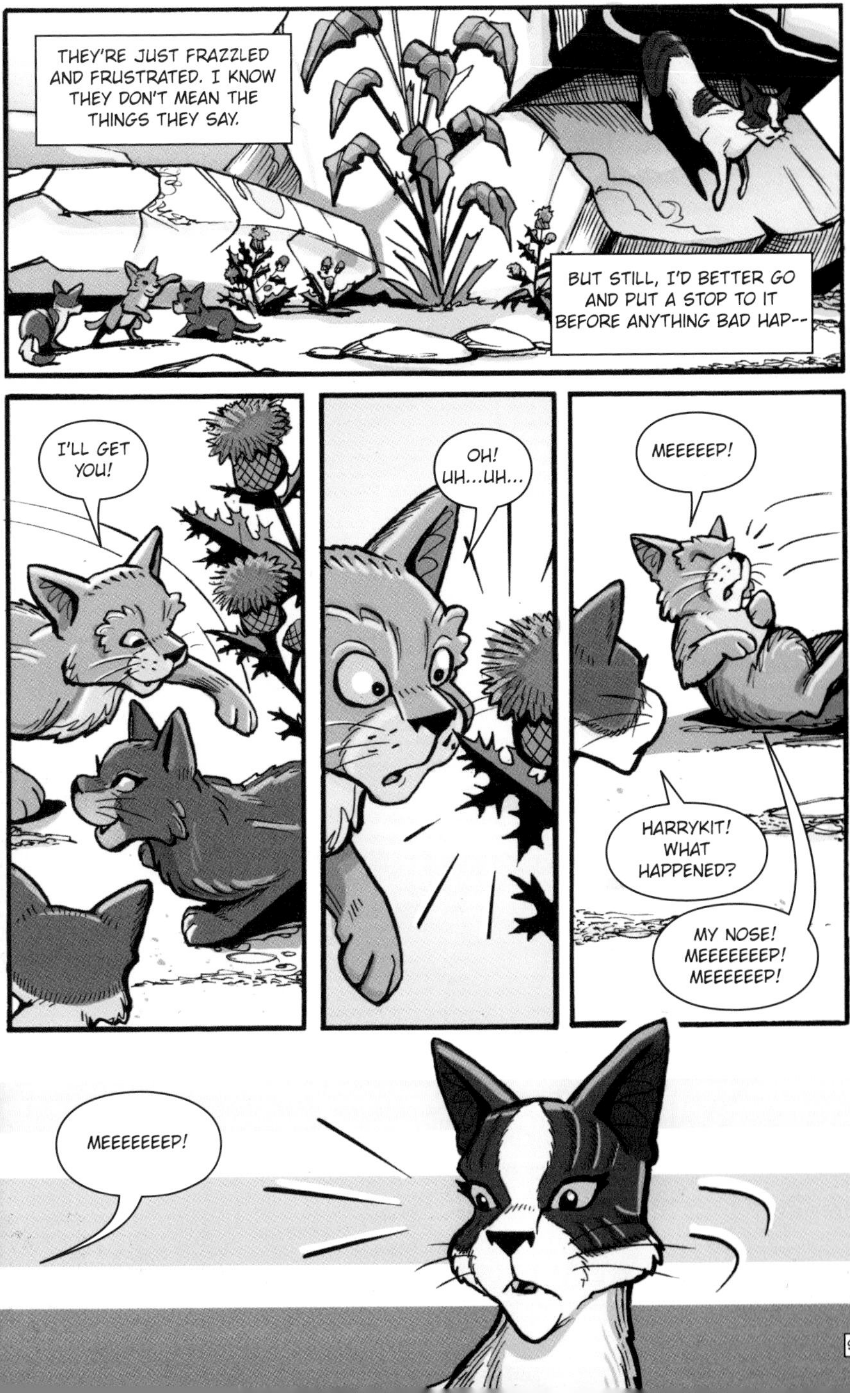
THEY'RE JUST FRAZZLED AND FRUSTRATED. I KNOW THEY DON'T MEAN THE THINGS THEY SAY.
BUT STILL, I'D BETTER GO AND PUT A STOP TO IT BEFORE ANYTHING BAD HAP--
I'LL GET YOU!
OH! UH...UH...
MEEEEEP!
HARRYKIT! WHAT HAPPENED?
MY NOSE! MEEEEEEEP! MEEEEEEP!
MEEEEEEEP!

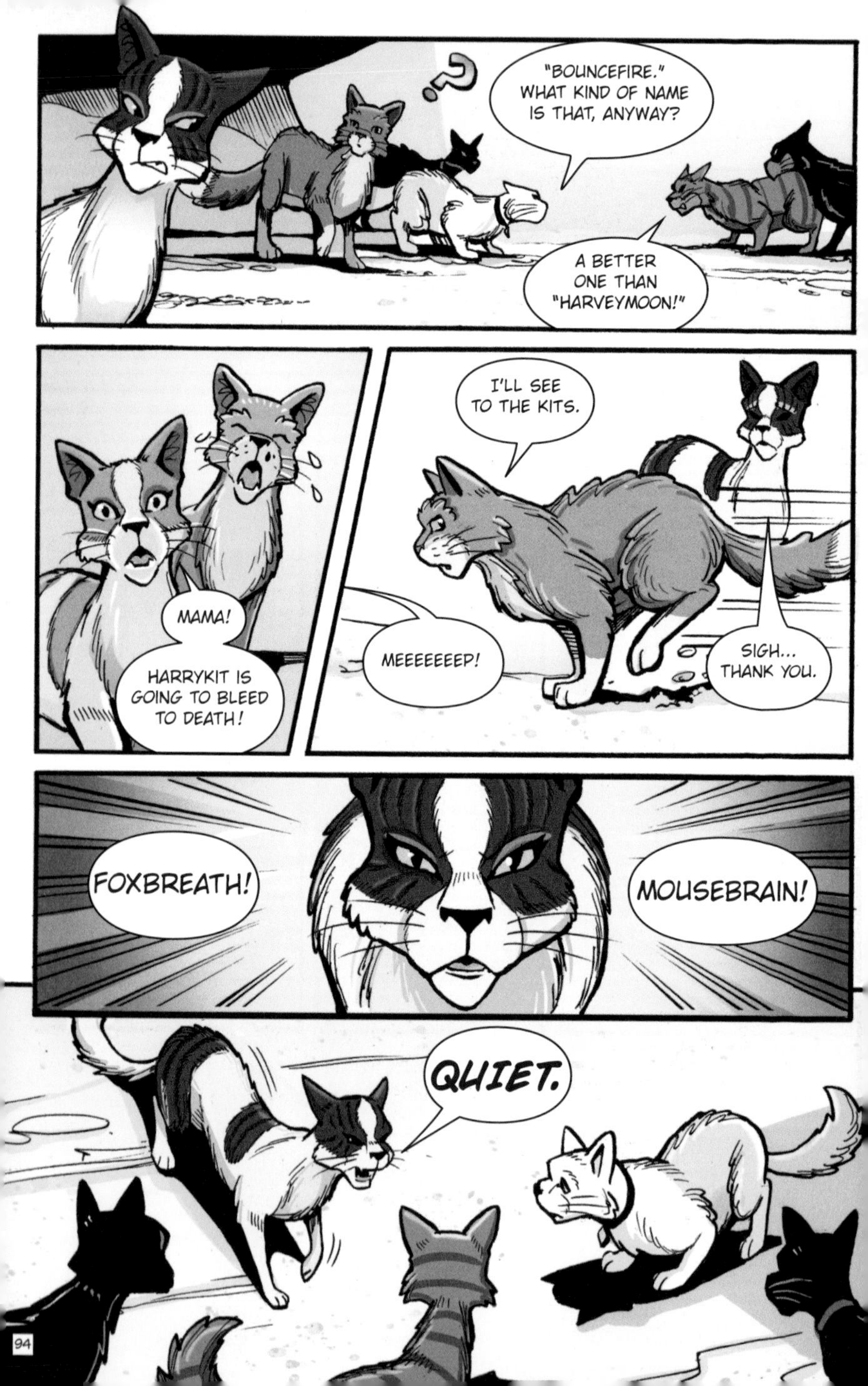
?
"BOUNCEFIRE." WHAT KIND OF NAME IS THAT, ANYWAY?
A BETTER ONE THAN "HARVEYMOON!"
MAMA!
HARRYKIT IS GOING TO BLEED TO DEATH!
I'LL SEE TO THE KITS.
MEEEEEEEP!
SIGH... THANK YOU.
FOXBREATH!
MOUSEBRAIN!
QUIET.

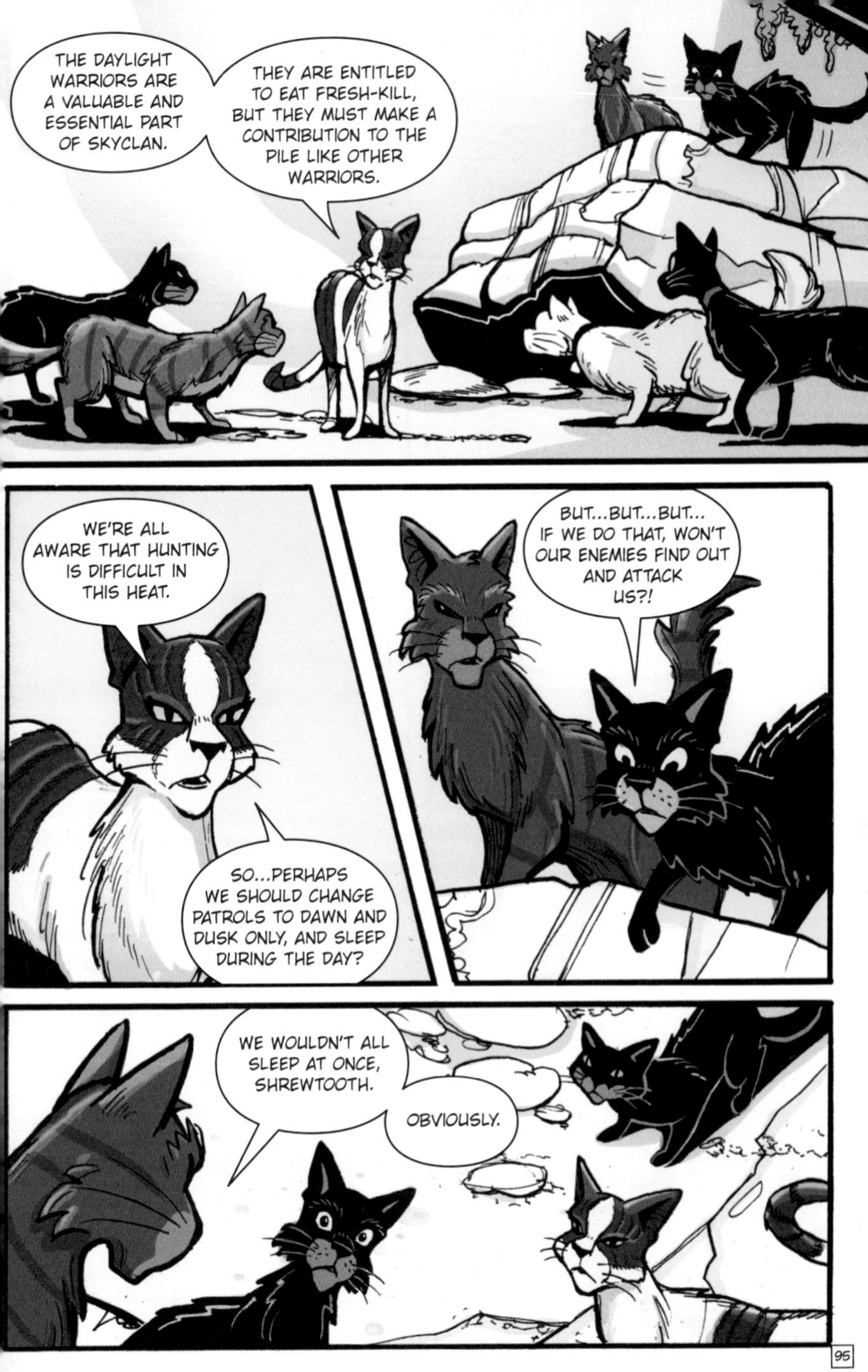
THE DAYLIGHT WARRIORS ARE A VALUABLE AND ESSENTIAL PART OF SKYCLAN.
THEY ARE ENTITLED TO EAT FRESH-KILL, BUT THEY MUST MAKE A CONTRIBUTION TO THE PILE LIKE OTHER WARRIORS.
WE'RE ALL AWARE THAT HUNTING IS DIFFICULT IN THIS HEAT.
SO...PERHAPS WE SHOULD CHANGE PATROLS TO DAWN AND DUSK ONLY, AND SLEEP DURING THE DAY?
BUT...BUT...BUT... IF WE DO THAT, WON'T OUR ENEMIES FIND OUT AND ATTACK US?!
WE WOULDN'T ALL SLEEP AT ONCE, SHREWTOOTH.
OBVIOUSLY.

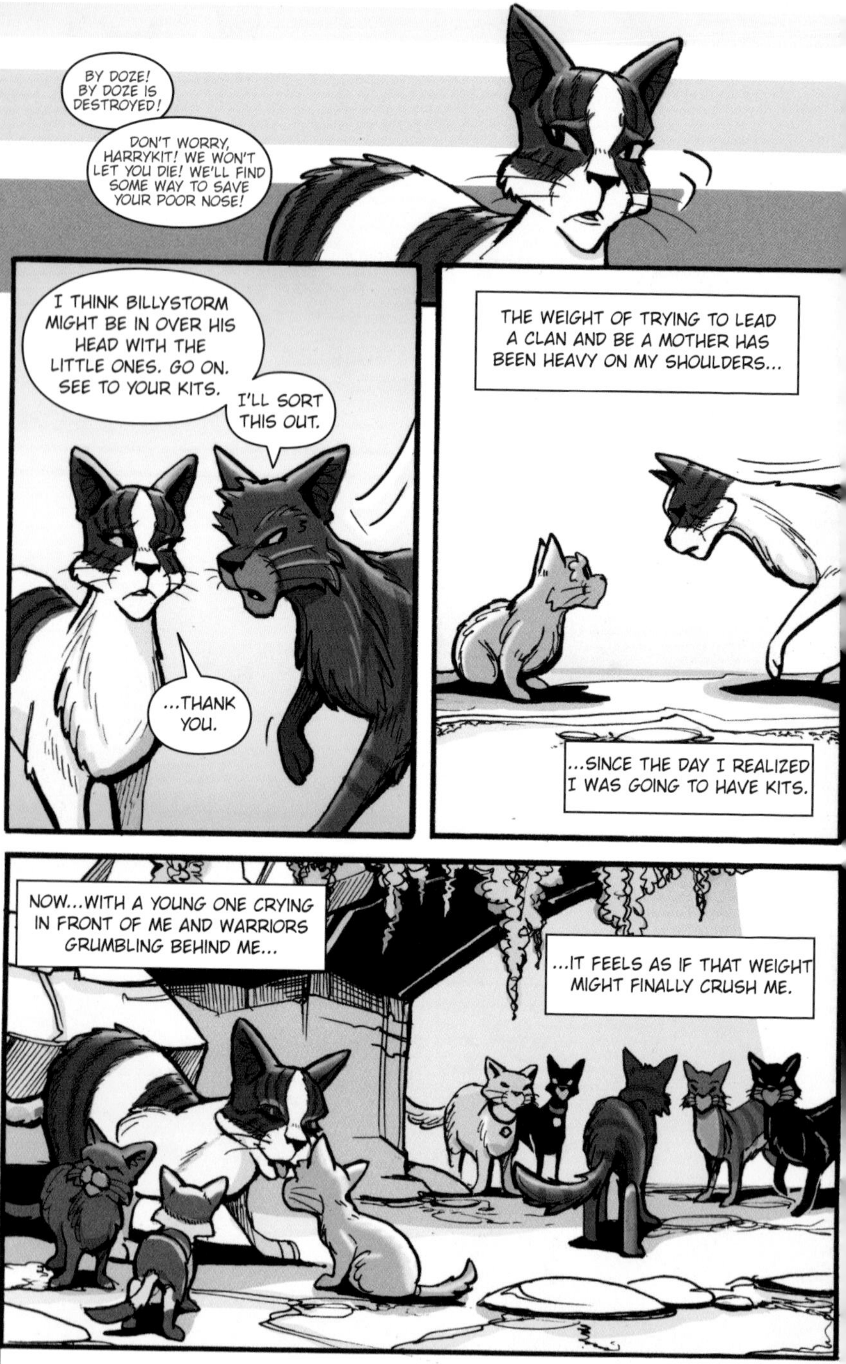
BY DOZE! BY DOZE IS DESTROYED!
DON'T WORRY, HARRYKIT! WE WON'T LET YOU DIE! WE'LL FIND SOME WAY TO SAVE YOUR POOR NOSE!
I THINK BILLYSTORM MIGHT BE IN OVER HIS HEAD WITH THE LITTLE ONES. GO ON. SEE TO YOUR KITS.
I'LL SORT THIS OUT.
...THANK YOU.
THE WEIGHT OF TRYING TO LEAD A CLAN AND BE A MOTHER HAS BEEN HEAVY ON MY SHOULDERS...
...SINCE THE DAY I REALIZED I WAS GOING TO HAVE KITS.
NOW...WITH A YOUNG ONE CRYING IN FRONT OF ME AND WARRIORS GRUMBLING BEHIND ME...
...IT FEELS AS IF THAT WEIGHT MIGHT FINALLY CRUSH ME.

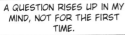

A QUESTION RISES UP IN MY MIND, NOT FOR THE FIRST TIME.

SHOULD CLAN LEADERS EVER HAVE KITS?

LEAFSTAR?

SOL--WHAT IS IT?

NOTHING, I... HERE. I THOUGHT THIS MIGHT HELP.

FOR THE LITTLE ONE, I MEAN.

THERE.

SOON YOU'LL BE GOOD AS NEW.

WOW...

YOU'VE GOT A TOUGH JOB. MANAGING THESE THREE AND ALL OF US. HOW DO YOU DO IT?

OH...IT JUST TAKES PATIENCE, IS ALL. PATIENCE, AND MUCH-APPRECIATED HELP FROM MY CLANMATES.

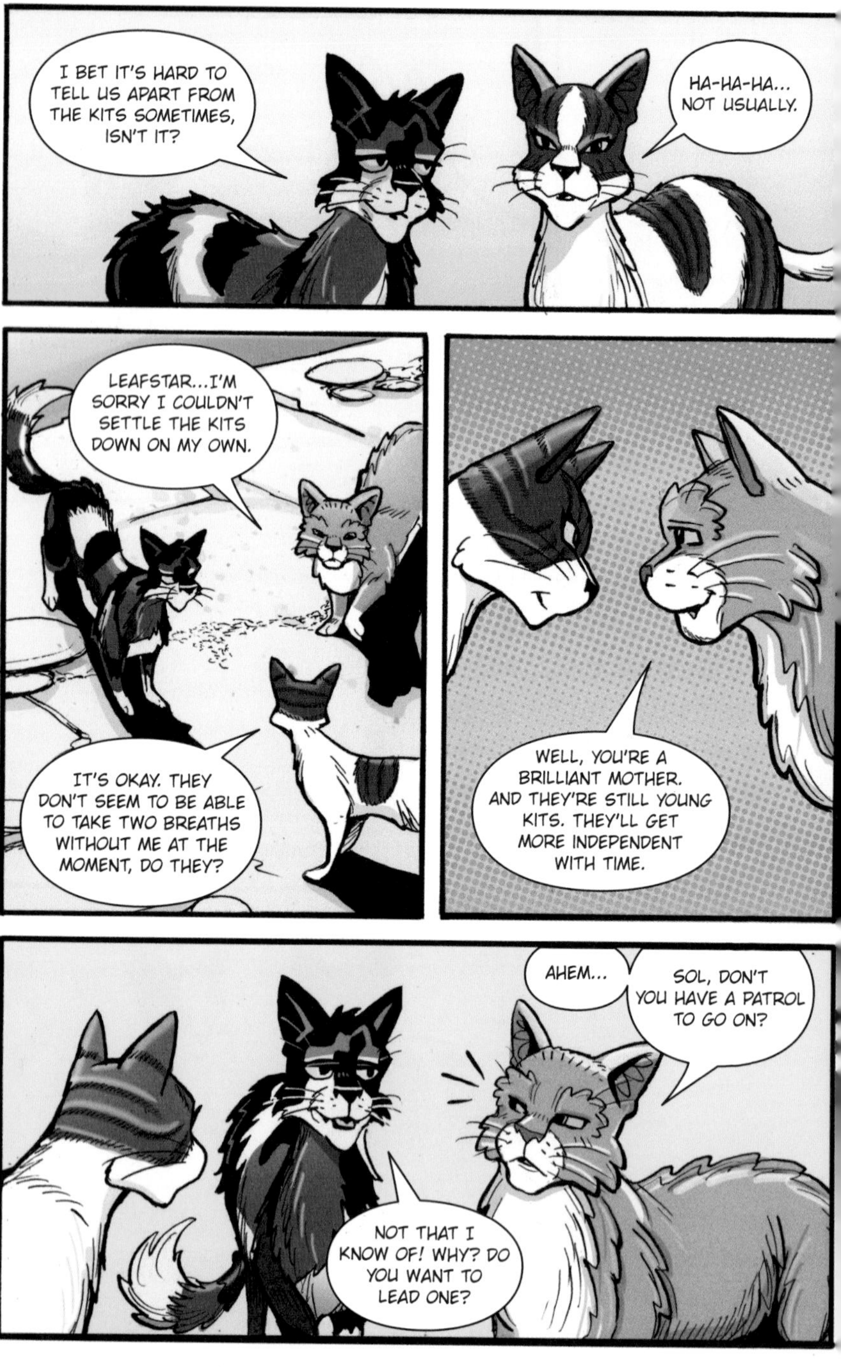
I BET IT'S HARD TO TELL US APART FROM THE KITS SOMETIMES, ISN'T IT?
HA-HA-HA... NOT USUALLY.
LEAFSTAR...I'M SORRY I COULDN'T SETTLE THE KITS DOWN ON MY OWN.
IT'S OKAY. THEY DON'T SEEM TO BE ABLE TO TAKE TWO BREATHS WITHOUT ME AT THE MOMENT, DO THEY?
WELL, YOU'RE A BRILLIANT MOTHER. AND THEY'RE STILL YOUNG KITS. THEY'LL GET MORE INDEPENDENT WITH TIME.
AHEM...
SOL, DON'T YOU HAVE A PATROL TO GO ON?
NOT THAT I KNOW OF! WHY? DO YOU WANT TO LEAD ONE?

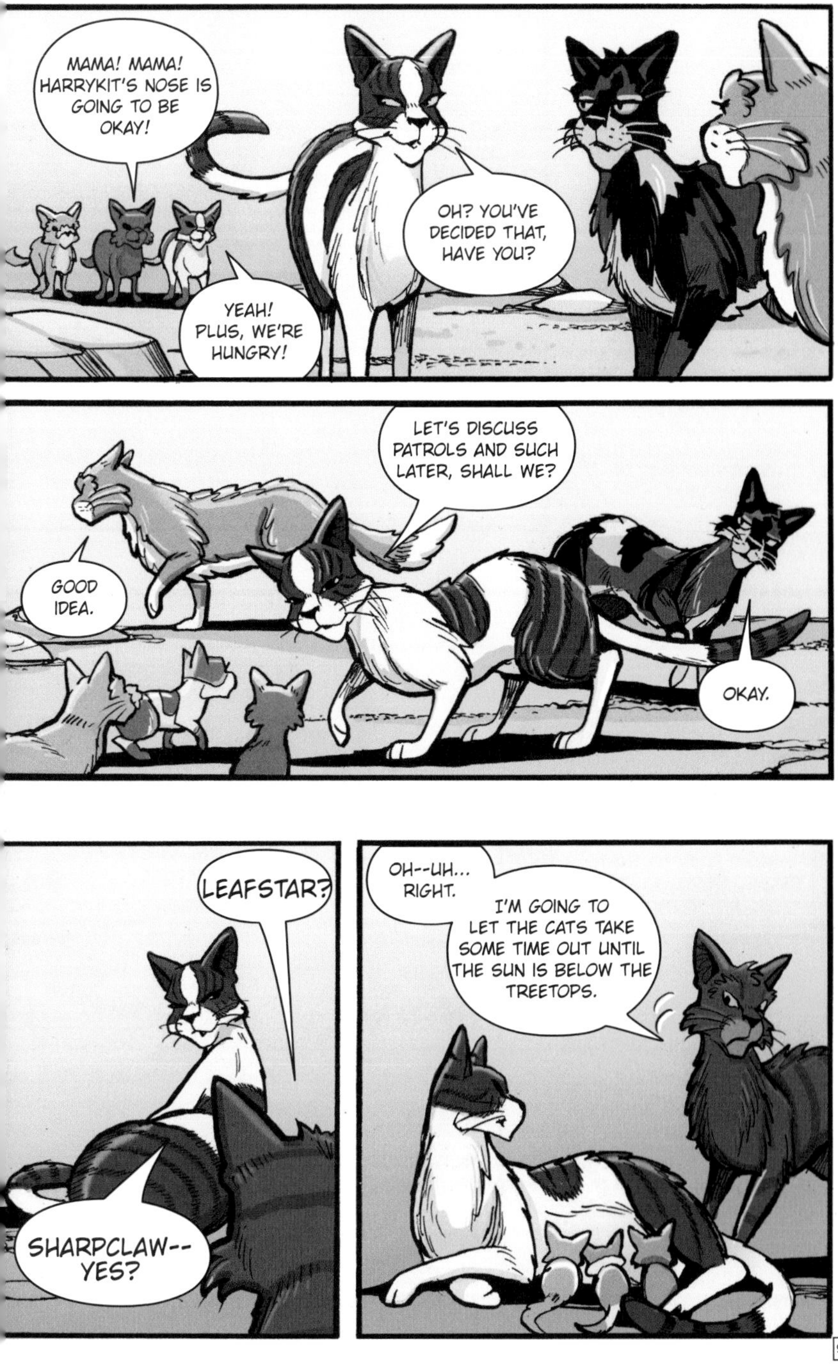
MAMA! MAMA! HARRYKIT'S NOSE IS GOING TO BE OKAY!
OH? YOU'VE DECIDED THAT, HAVE YOU?
YEAH! PLUS, WE'RE HUNGRY!
LET'S DISCUSS PATROLS AND SUCH LATER, SHALL WE?
GOOD IDEA.
OKAY.
LEAFSTAR?
SHARPCLAW--YES?
OH--UH... RIGHT.
I'M GOING TO LET THE CATS TAKE SOME TIME OUT UNTIL THE SUN IS BELOW THE TREETOPS.

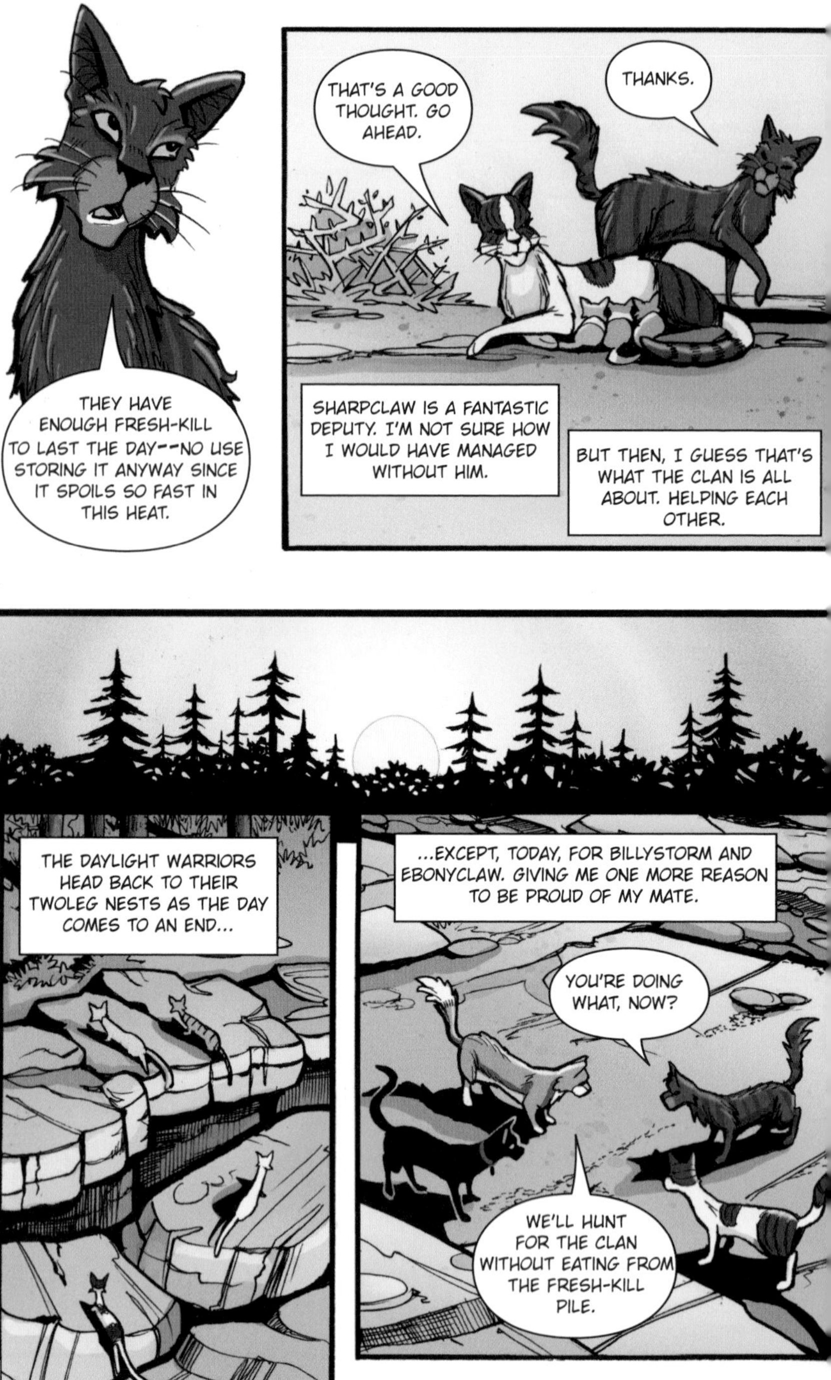
THEY HAVE ENOUGH FRESH-KILL TO LAST THE DAY--NO USE STORING IT ANYWAY SINCE IT SPOILS SO FAST IN THIS HEAT.
THAT'S A GOOD THOUGHT. GO AHEAD.
THANKS.
SHARPCLAW IS A FANTASTIC DEPUTY. I'M NOT SURE HOW I WOULD HAVE MANAGED WITHOUT HIM.
BUT THEN, I GUESS THAT'S WHAT THE CLAN IS ALL ABOUT. HELPING EACH OTHER.
THE DAYLIGHT WARRIORS HEAD BACK TO THEIR TWOLEG NESTS AS THE DAY COMES TO AN END...
...EXCEPT, TODAY, FOR BILLYSTORM AND EBONYCLAW. GIVING ME ONE MORE REASON TO BE PROUD OF MY MATE.
YOU'RE DOING WHAT, NOW?
WE'LL HUNT FOR THE CLAN WITHOUT EATING FROM THE FRESH-KILL PILE.

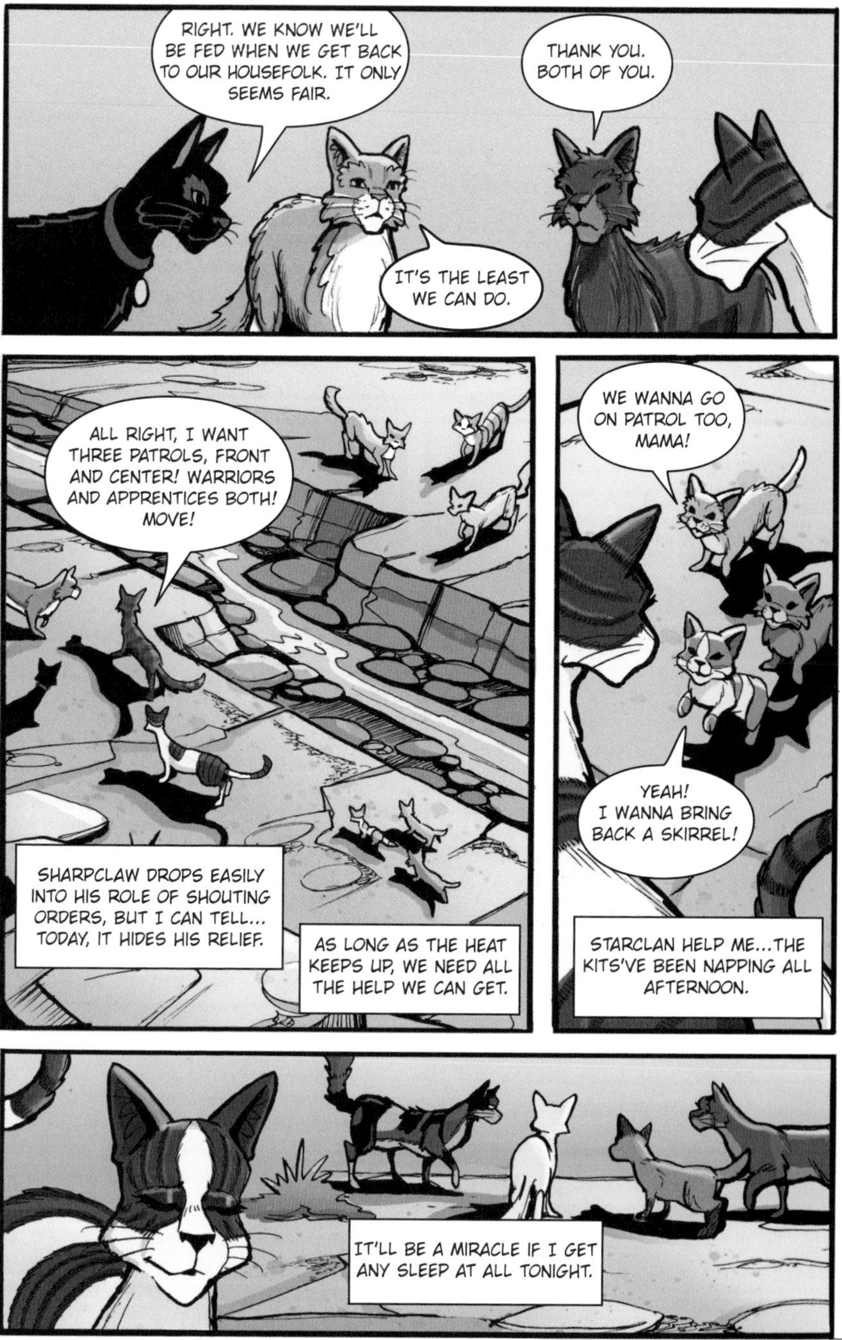
RIGHT. WE KNOW WE'LL BE FED WHEN WE GET BACK TO OUR HOUSEFOLK. IT ONLY SEEMS FAIR.
THANK YOU. BOTH OF YOU.
IT'S THE LEAST WE CAN DO.
ALL RIGHT, I WANT THREE PATROLS, FRONT AND CENTER! WARRIORS AND APPRENTICES BOTH! MOVE!
SHARPCLAW DROPS EASILY INTO HIS ROLE OF SHOUTING ORDERS, BUT I CAN TELL... TODAY, IT HIDES HIS RELIEF.
AS LONG AS THE HEAT KEEPS UP, WE NEED ALL THE HELP WE CAN GET.
WE WANNA GO ON PATROL TOO, MAMA!
YEAH! I WANNA BRING BACK A SKIRREL!
STARCLAN HELP ME...THE KITS'VE BEEN NAPPING ALL AFTERNOON.
IT'LL BE A MIRACLE IF I GET ANY SLEEP AT ALL TONIGHT.

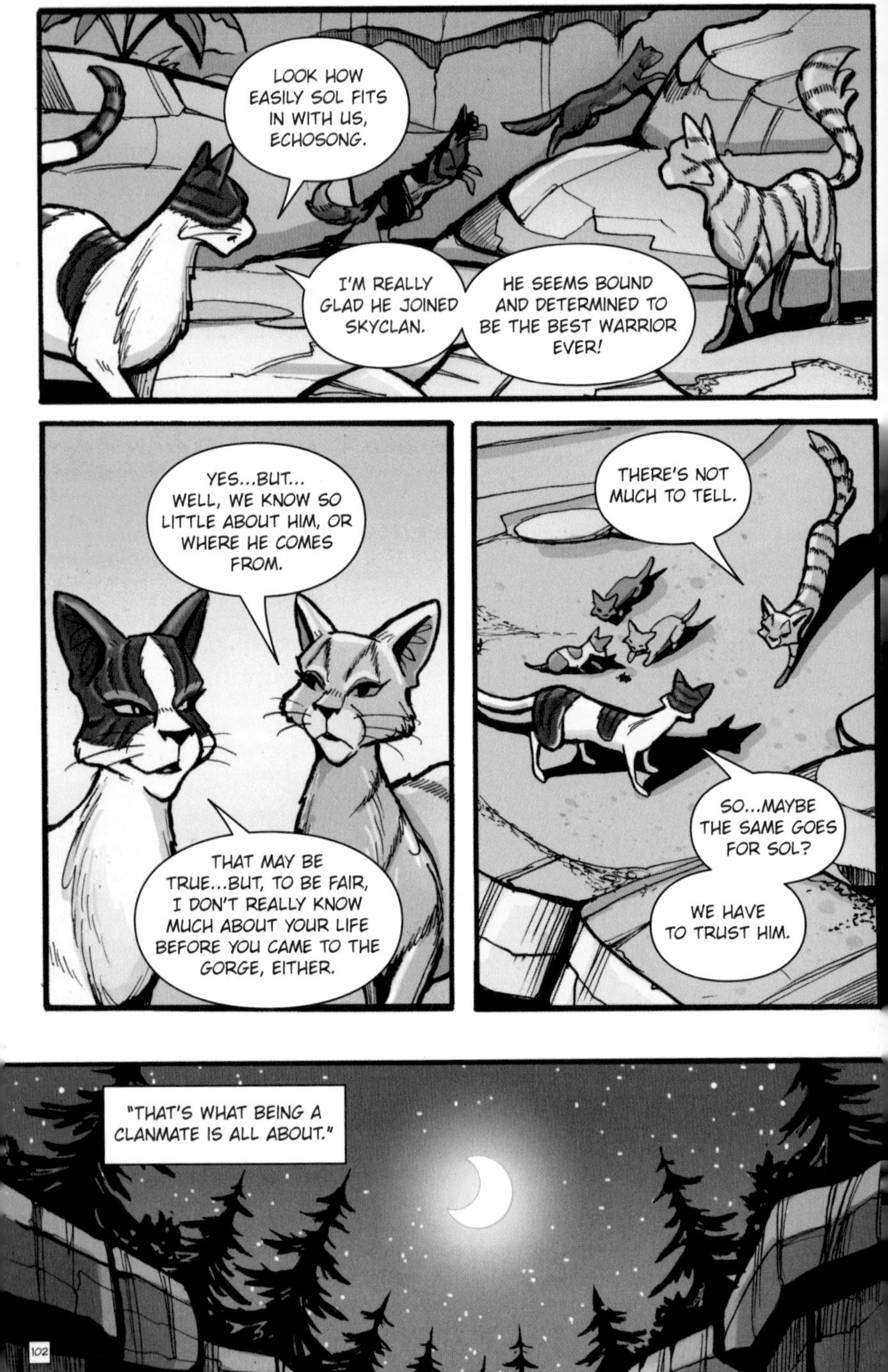
LOOK HOW EASILY SOL FITS IN WITH US, ECHOSONG.
I'M REALLY GLAD HE JOINED SKYCLAN.
HE SEEMS BOUND AND DETERMINED TO BE THE BEST WARRIOR EVER!
YES...BUT... WELL, WE KNOW SO LITTLE ABOUT HIM, OR WHERE HE COMES FROM.
THAT MAY BE TRUE...BUT, TO BE FAIR, I DON'T REALLY KNOW MUCH ABOUT YOUR LIFE BEFORE YOU CAME TO THE GORGE, EITHER.
THERE'S NOT MUCH TO TELL.
SO...MAYBE THE SAME GOES FOR SOL?
WE HAVE TO TRUST HIM.
"THAT'S WHAT BEING A CLANMATE IS ALL ABOUT."

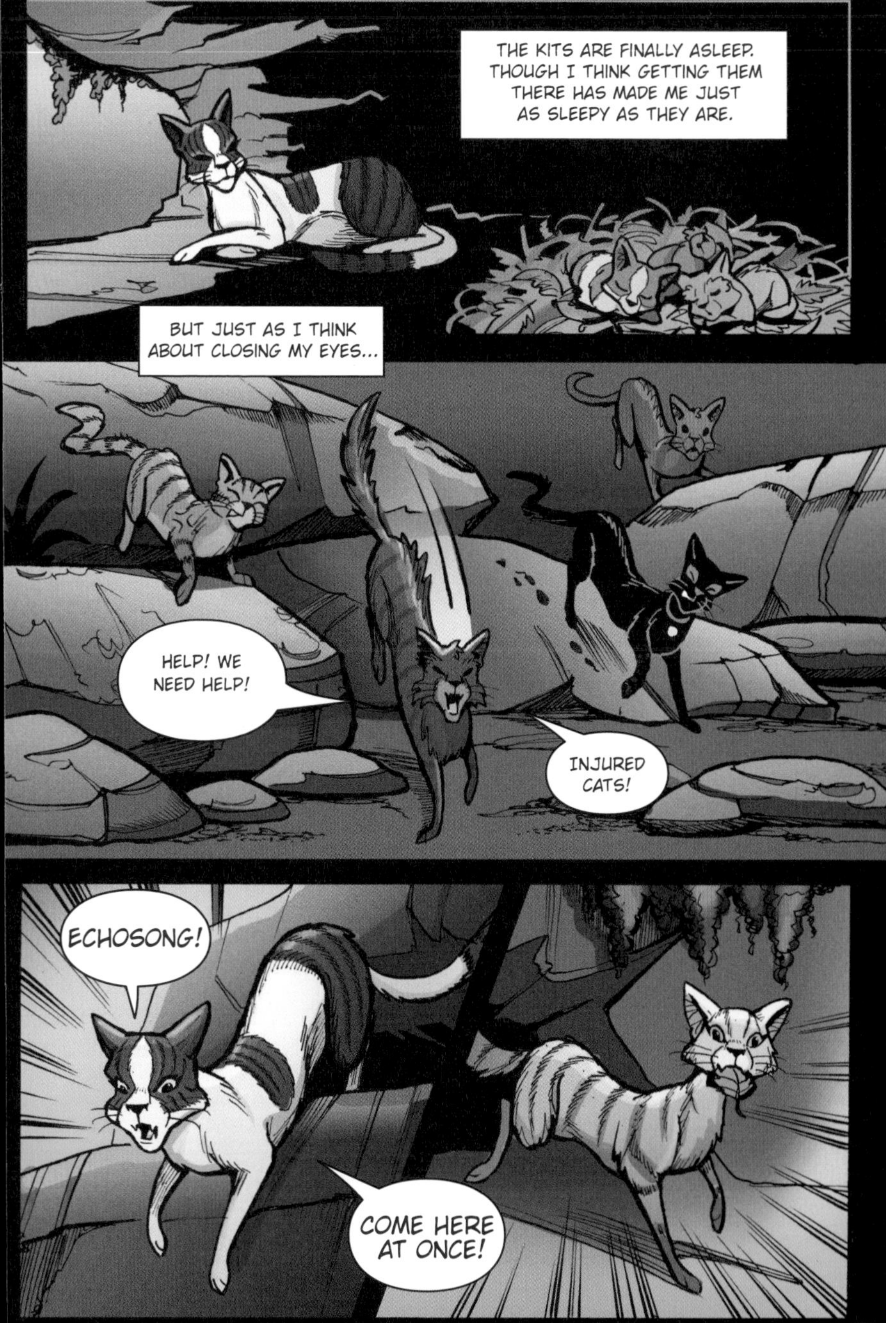
THE KITS ARE FINALLY ASLEEP. THOUGH I THINK GETTING THEM THERE HAS MADE ME JUST AS SLEEPY AS THEY ARE.
BUT JUST AS I THINK ABOUT CLOSING MY EYES...
HELP! WE NEED HELP!
INJURED CATS!
ECHOSONG!
COME HERE AT ONCE!

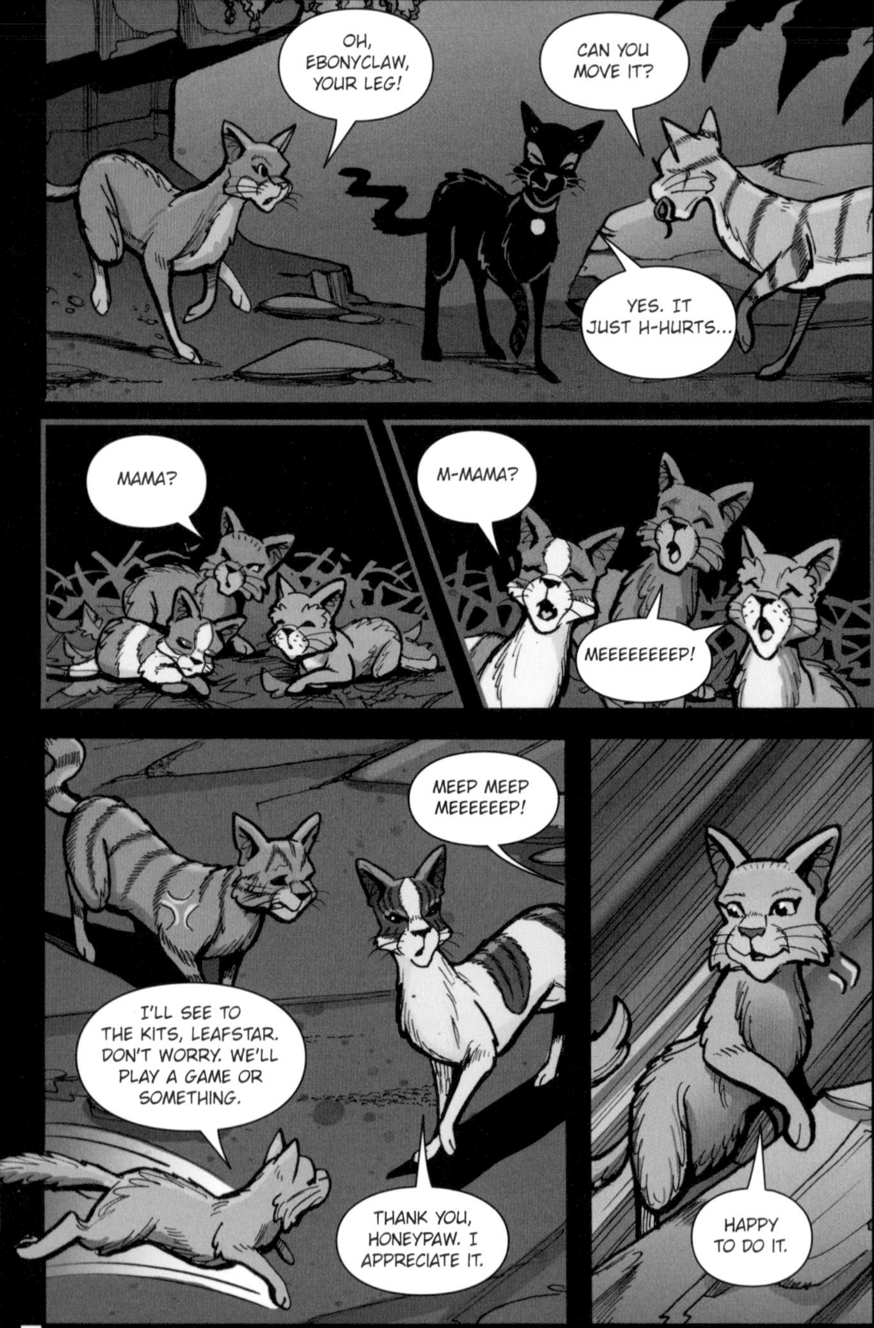
OH, EBONYCLAW, YOUR LEG!
CAN YOU MOVE IT?
YES. IT JUST H-HURTS...
MAMA?
M-MAMA?
MEEEEEEEEP!
MEEP MEEP MEEEEEEP!
I'LL SEE TO THE KITS, LEAFSTAR. DON'T WORRY. WE'LL PLAY A GAME OR SOMETHING.
THANK YOU, HONEYPAW. I APPRECIATE IT.
HAPPY TO DO IT.

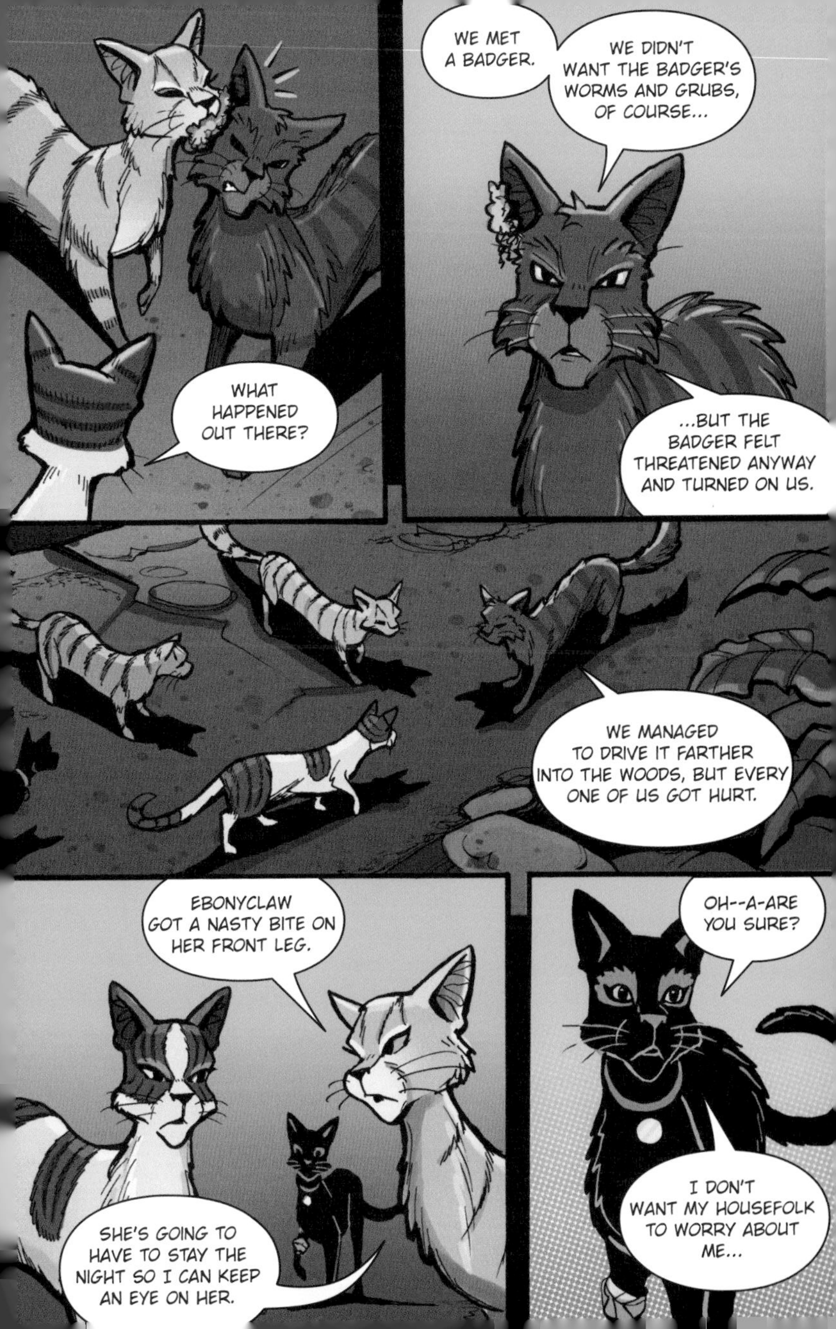
WHAT HAPPENED OUT THERE?
WE MET A BADGER.
WE DIDN'T WANT THE BADGER'S WORMS AND GRUBS, OF COURSE...
...BUT THE BADGER FELT THREATENED ANYWAY AND TURNED ON US.
WE MANAGED TO DRIVE IT FARTHER INTO THE WOODS, BUT EVERY ONE OF US GOT HURT.
EBONYCLAW GOT A NASTY BITE ON HER FRONT LEG.
SHE'S GOING TO HAVE TO STAY THE NIGHT SO I CAN KEEP AN EYE ON HER.
OH--A-ARE YOU SURE?
I DON'T WANT MY HOUSEFOLK TO WORRY ABOUT ME...

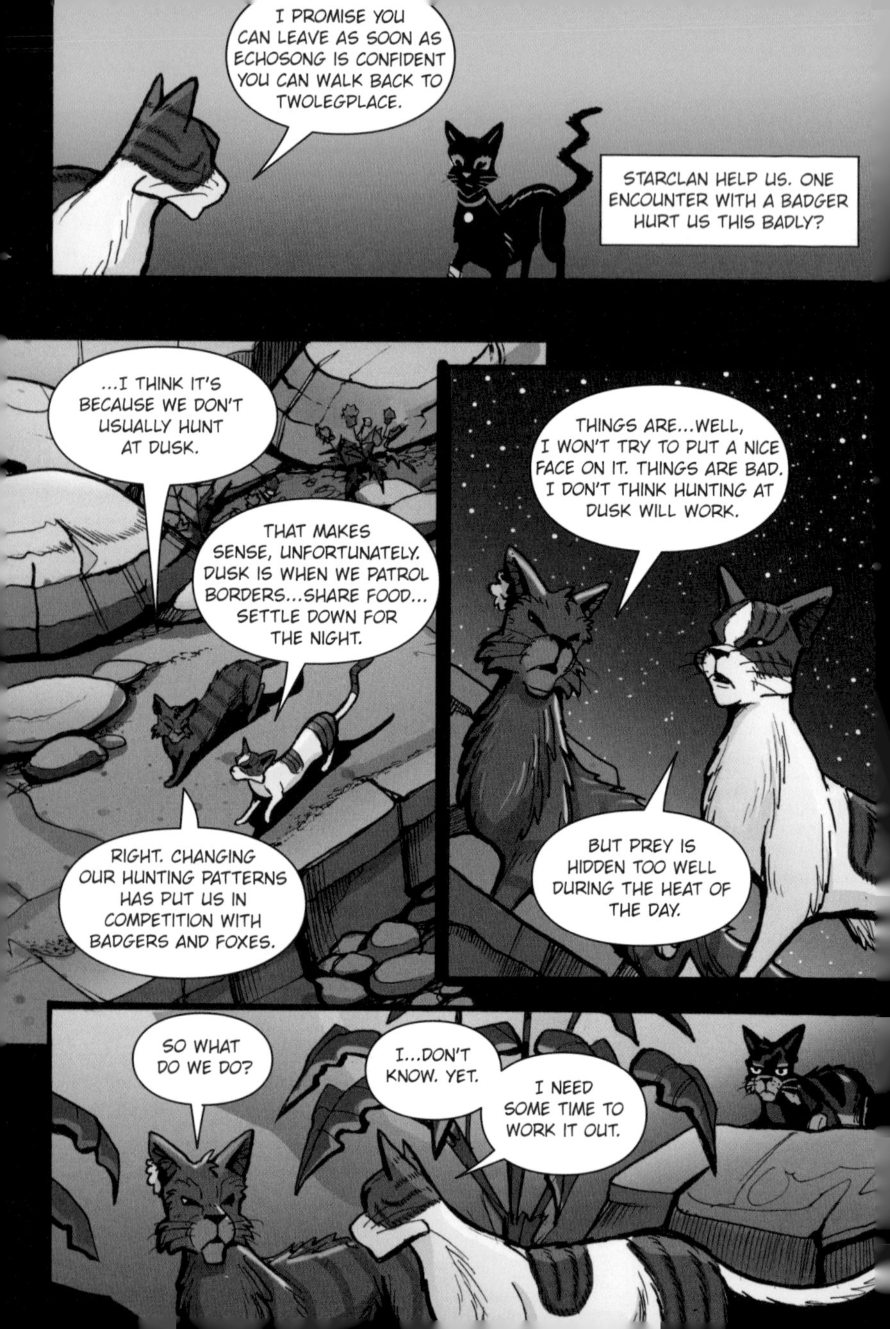
I PROMISE YOU CAN LEAVE AS SOON AS ECHOSONG IS CONFIDENT YOU CAN WALK BACK TO TWOLEGPLACE.
STARCLAN HELP US. ONE ENCOUNTER WITH A BADGER HURT US THIS BADLY?
...I THINK IT'S BECAUSE WE DON'T USUALLY HUNT AT DUSK.
THAT MAKES SENSE, UNFORTUNATELY. DUSK IS WHEN WE PATROL BORDERS...SHARE FOOD... SETTLE DOWN FOR THE NIGHT.
RIGHT. CHANGING OUR HUNTING PATTERNS HAS PUT US IN COMPETITION WITH BADGERS AND FOXES.
THINGS ARE...WELL, I WON'T TRY TO PUT A NICE FACE ON IT. THINGS ARE BAD. I DON'T THINK HUNTING AT DUSK WILL WORK.
BUT PREY IS HIDDEN TOO WELL DURING THE HEAT OF THE DAY.
SO WHAT DO WE DO?
I...DON'T KNOW. YET.
I NEED SOME TIME TO WORK IT OUT.

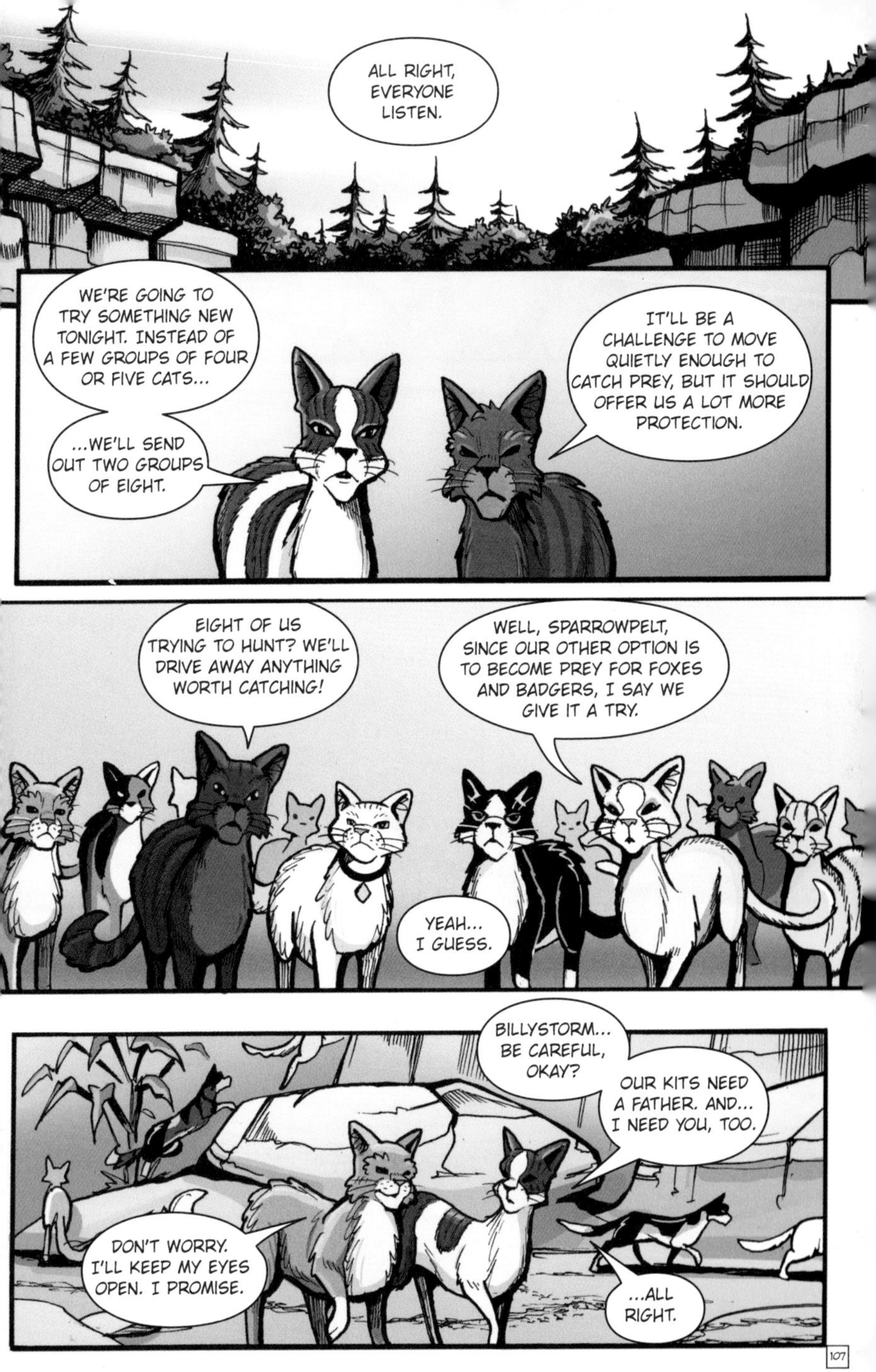
ALL RIGHT, EVERYONE LISTEN.
WE'RE GOING TO TRY SOMETHING NEW TONIGHT. INSTEAD OF A FEW GROUPS OF FOUR OR FIVE CATS...
...WE'LL SEND OUT TWO GROUPS OF EIGHT.
IT'LL BE A CHALLENGE TO MOVE QUIETLY ENOUGH TO CATCH PREY, BUT IT SHOULD OFFER US A LOT MORE PROTECTION.
EIGHT OF US TRYING TO HUNT? WE'LL DRIVE AWAY ANYTHING WORTH CATCHING!
WELL, SPARROWPELT, SINCE OUR OTHER OPTION IS TO BECOME PREY FOR FOXES AND BADGERS, I SAY WE GIVE IT A TRY.
YEAH... I GUESS.
BILLYSTORM... BE CAREFUL, OKAY?
OUR KITS NEED A FATHER. AND... I NEED YOU, TOO.
DON'T WORRY. I'LL KEEP MY EYES OPEN. I PROMISE.
...ALL RIGHT.

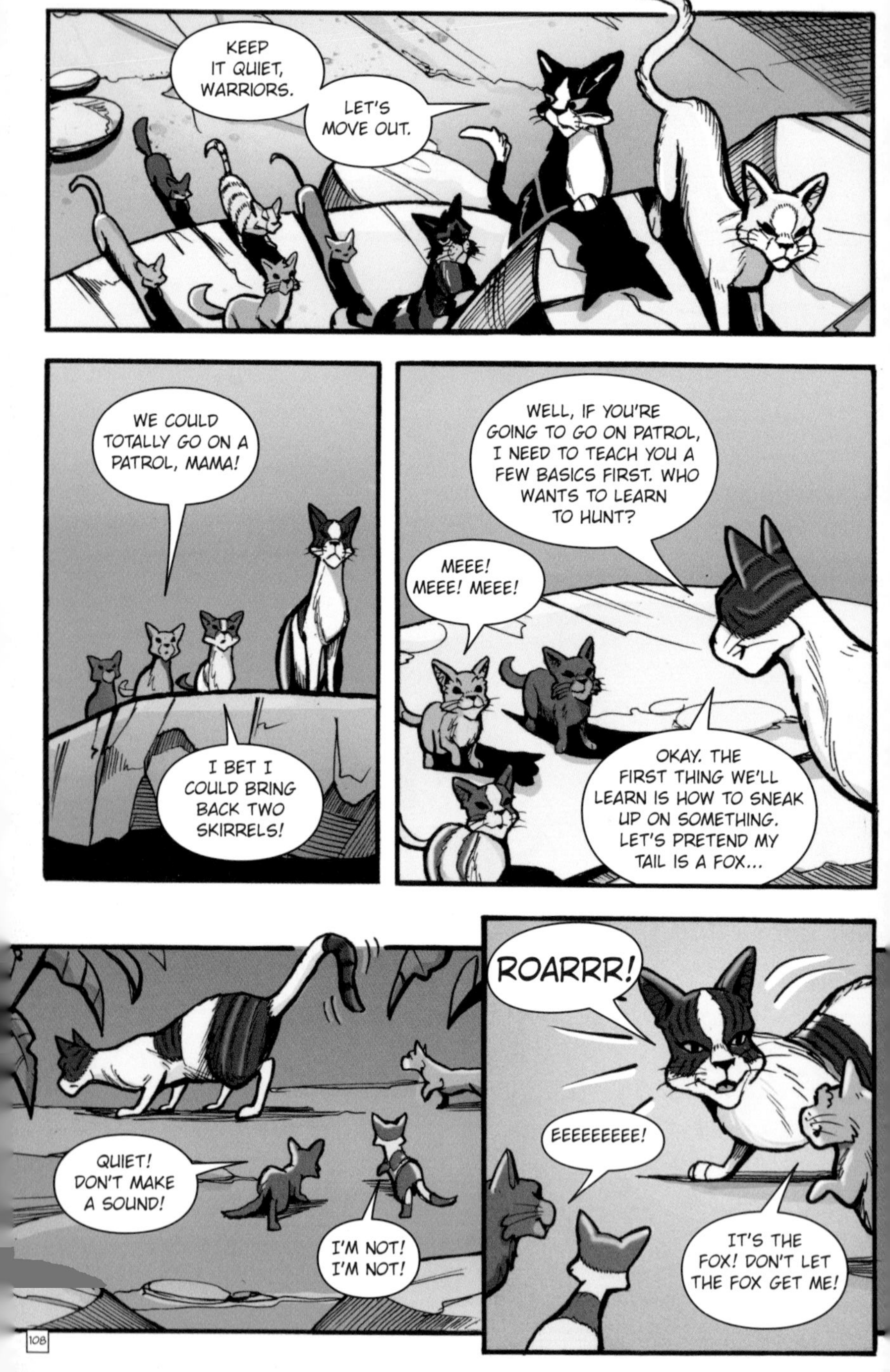
KEEP IT QUIET, WARRIORS.
LET'S MOVE OUT.
WE COULD TOTALLY GO ON A PATROL, MAMA!
I BET I COULD BRING BACK TWO SKIRRELS!
WELL, IF YOU'RE GOING TO GO ON PATROL, I NEED TO TEACH YOU A FEW BASICS FIRST. WHO WANTS TO LEARN TO HUNT?
MEEE! MEEE! MEEE!
OKAY. THE FIRST THING WE'LL LEARN IS HOW TO SNEAK UP ON SOMETHING. LET'S PRETEND MY TAIL IS A FOX...
QUIET! DON'T MAKE A SOUND!
I'M NOT! I'M NOT!
ROARRR!
EEEEEEEEE!
IT'S THE FOX! DON'T LET THE FOX GET ME!

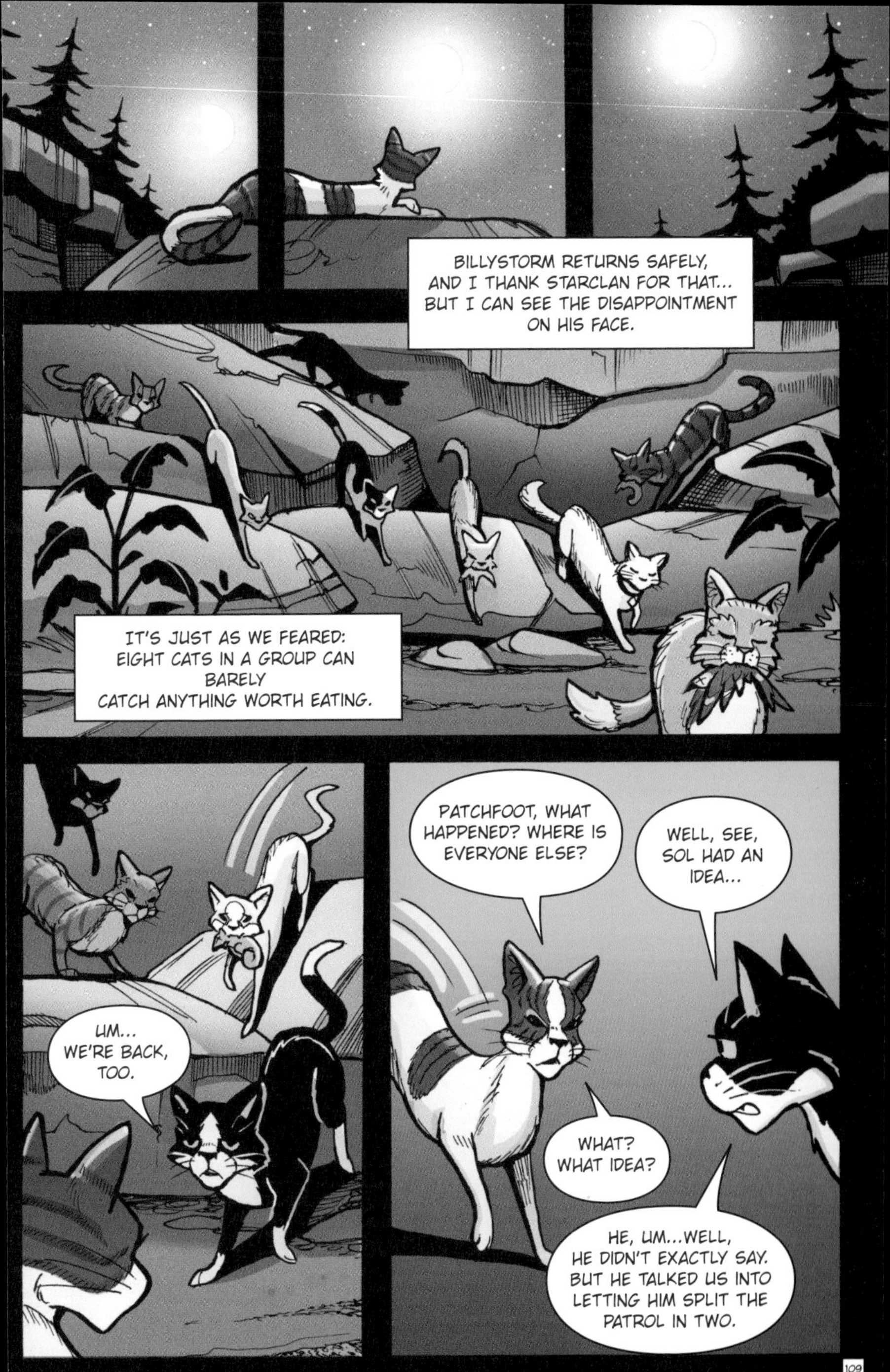
BILLYSTORM RETURNS SAFELY, AND I THANK STARCLAN FOR THAT... BUT I CAN SEE THE DISAPPOINTMENT ON HIS FACE.
IT'S JUST AS WE FEARED: EIGHT CATS IN A GROUP CAN BARELY CATCH ANYTHING WORTH EATING.
UM... WE'RE BACK, TOO.
PATCHFOOT, WHAT HAPPENED? WHERE IS EVERYONE ELSE?
WELL, SEE, SOL HAD AN IDEA...
WHAT? WHAT IDEA?
HE, UM...WELL, HE DIDN'T EXACTLY SAY. BUT HE TALKED US INTO LETTING HIM SPLIT THE PATROL IN TWO.

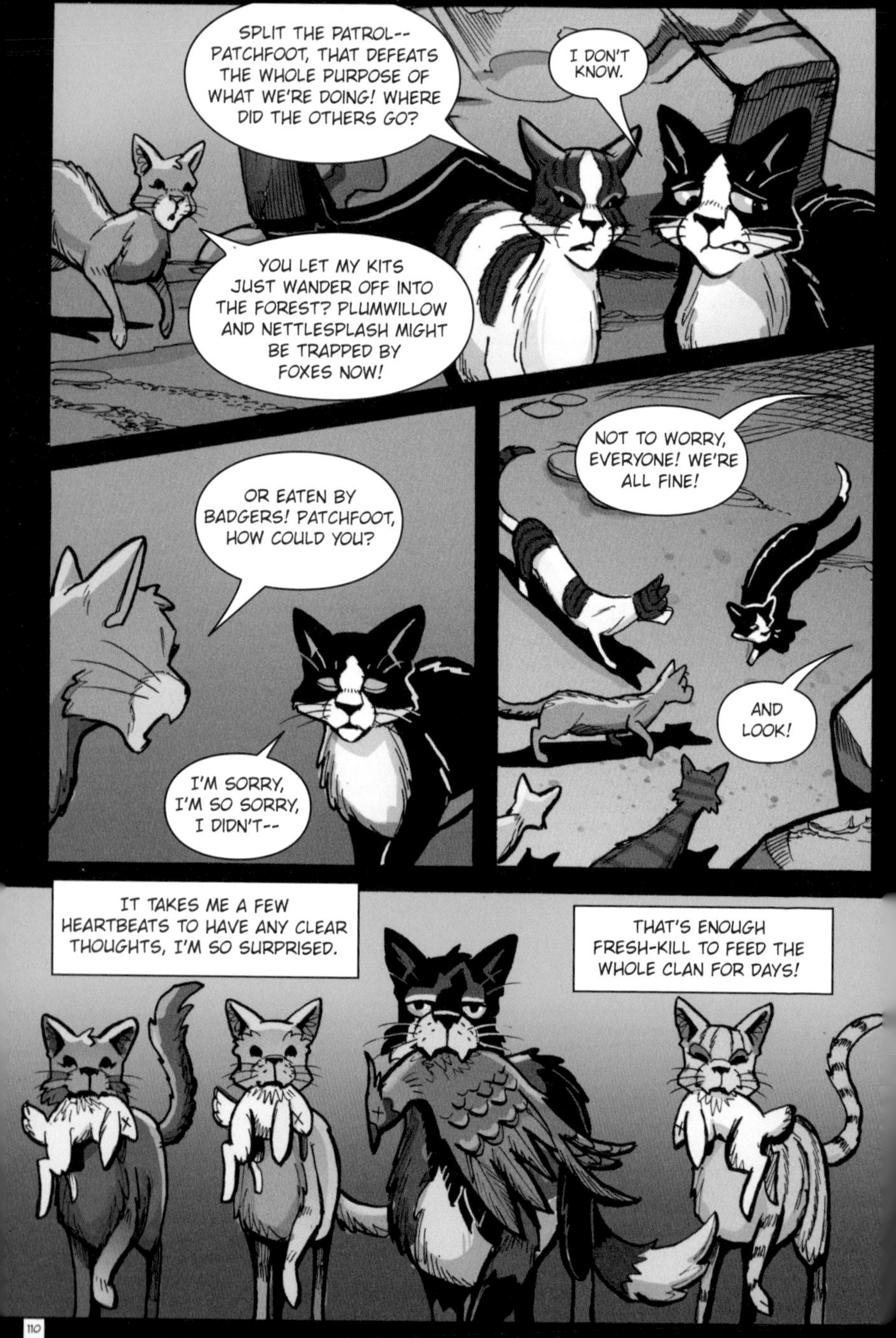
SPLIT THE PATROL-- PATCHFOOT, THAT DEFEATS THE WHOLE PURPOSE OF WHAT WE'RE DOING! WHERE DID THE OTHERS GO?
I DON'T KNOW.
YOU LET MY KITS JUST WANDER OFF INTO THE FOREST? PLUMWILLOW AND NETTLESPLASH MIGHT BE TRAPPED BY FOXES NOW!
OR EATEN BY BADGERS! PATCHFOOT, HOW COULD YOU?
I'M SORRY, I'M SO SORRY, I DIDN'T--
NOT TO WORRY, EVERYONE! WE'RE ALL FINE!
AND LOOK!
IT TAKES ME A FEW HEARTBEATS TO HAVE ANY CLEAR THOUGHTS, I'M SO SURPRISED.
THAT'S ENOUGH FRESH-KILL TO FEED THE WHOLE CLAN FOR DAYS!

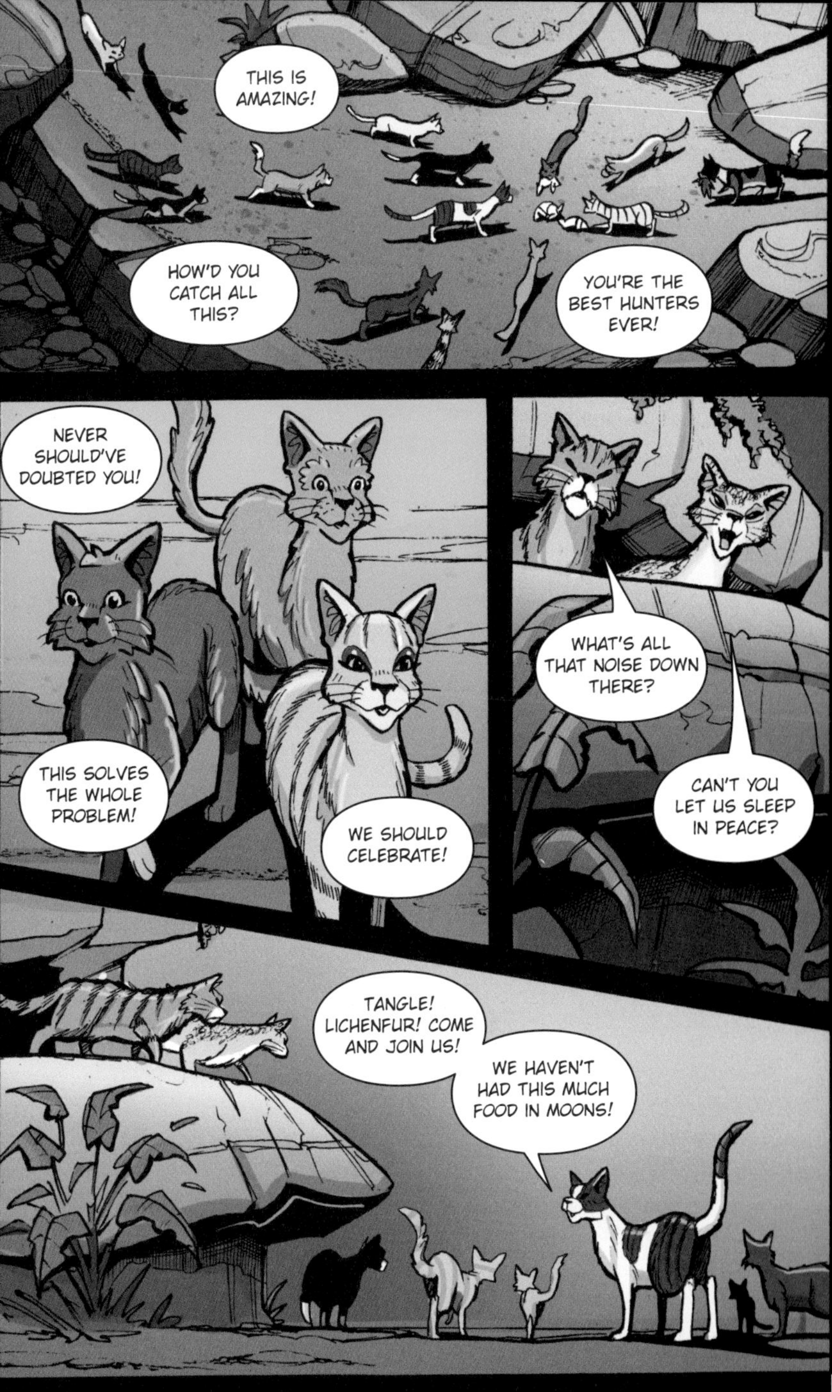
THIS IS AMAZING!
HOW'D YOU CATCH ALL THIS?
YOU'RE THE BEST HUNTERS EVER!
NEVER SHOULD'VE DOUBTED YOU!
THIS SOLVES THE WHOLE PROBLEM!
WE SHOULD CELEBRATE!
WHAT'S ALL THAT NOISE DOWN THERE?
CAN'T YOU LET US SLEEP IN PEACE?
TANGLE! LICHENFUR! COME AND JOIN US!
WE HAVEN'T HAD THIS MUCH FOOD IN MOONS!

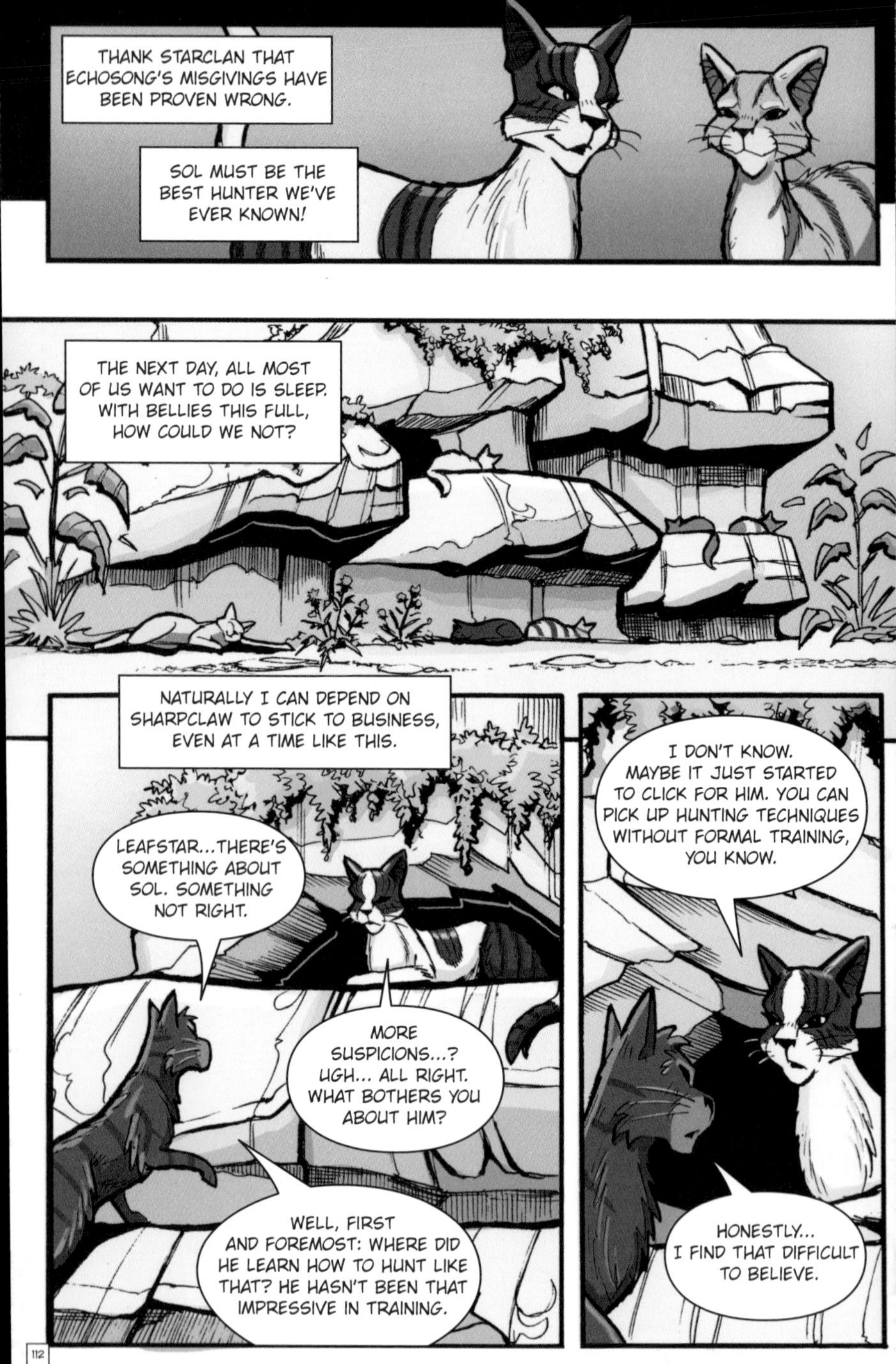
THANK STARCLAN THAT ECHOSONG'S MISGIVINGS HAVE BEEN PROVEN WRONG.
SOL MUST BE THE BEST HUNTER WE'VE EVER KNOWN!
THE NEXT DAY, ALL MOST OF US WANT TO DO IS SLEEP. WITH BELLIES THIS FULL, HOW COULD WE NOT?
NATURALLY I CAN DEPEND ON SHARPCLAW TO STICK TO BUSINESS, EVEN AT A TIME LIKE THIS.
LEAFSTAR...THERE'S SOMETHING ABOUT SOL. SOMETHING NOT RIGHT.
MORE SUSPICIONS...? UGH... ALL RIGHT. WHAT BOTHERS YOU ABOUT HIM?
WELL, FIRST AND FOREMOST: WHERE DID HE LEARN HOW TO HUNT LIKE THAT? HE HASN'T BEEN THAT IMPRESSIVE IN TRAINING.
I DON'T KNOW. MAYBE IT JUST STARTED TO CLICK FOR HIM. YOU CAN PICK UP HUNTING TECHNIQUES WITHOUT FORMAL TRAINING, YOU KNOW.
HONESTLY... I FIND THAT DIFFICULT TO BELIEVE.

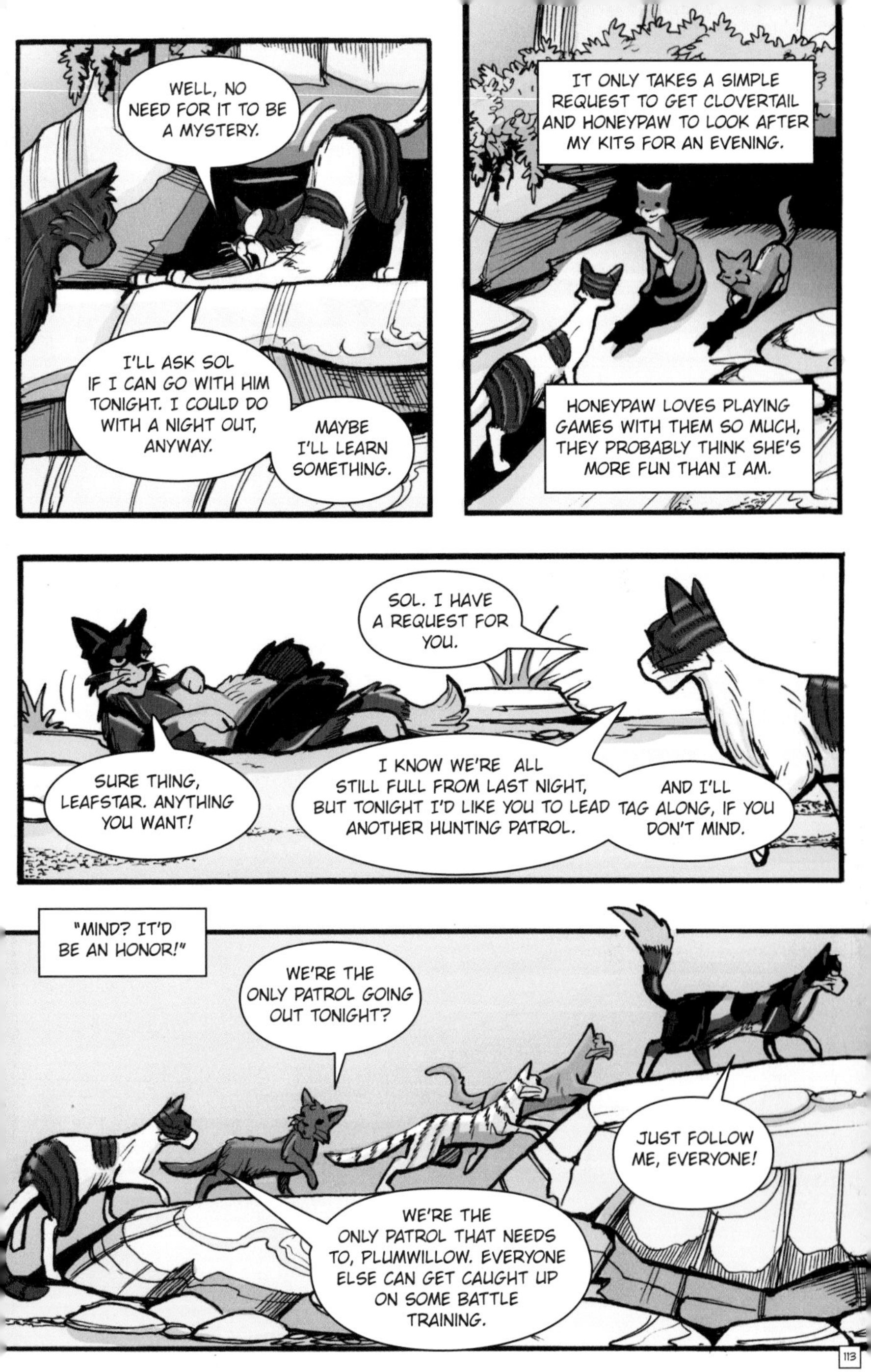
WELL, NO NEED FOR IT TO BE A MYSTERY.
I'LL ASK SOL IF I CAN GO WITH HIM TONIGHT. I COULD DO WITH A NIGHT OUT, ANYWAY.
MAYBE I'LL LEARN SOMETHING.
IT ONLY TAKES A SIMPLE REQUEST TO GET CLOVERTAIL AND HONEYPAW TO LOOK AFTER MY KITS FOR AN EVENING.
HONEYPAW LOVES PLAYING GAMES WITH THEM SO MUCH, THEY PROBABLY THINK SHE'S MORE FUN THAN I AM.
SOL. I HAVE A REQUEST FOR YOU.
SURE THING, LEAFSTAR. ANYTHING YOU WANT!
I KNOW WE'RE ALL STILL FULL FROM LAST NIGHT, BUT TONIGHT I'D LIKE YOU TO LEAD ANOTHER HUNTING PATROL.
AND I'LL TAG ALONG, IF YOU DON'T MIND.
"MIND? IT'D BE AN HONOR!"
WE'RE THE ONLY PATROL GOING OUT TONIGHT?
WE'RE THE ONLY PATROL THAT NEEDS TO, PLUMWILLOW. EVERYONE ELSE CAN GET CAUGHT UP ON SOME BATTLE TRAINING.
JUST FOLLOW ME, EVERYONE!

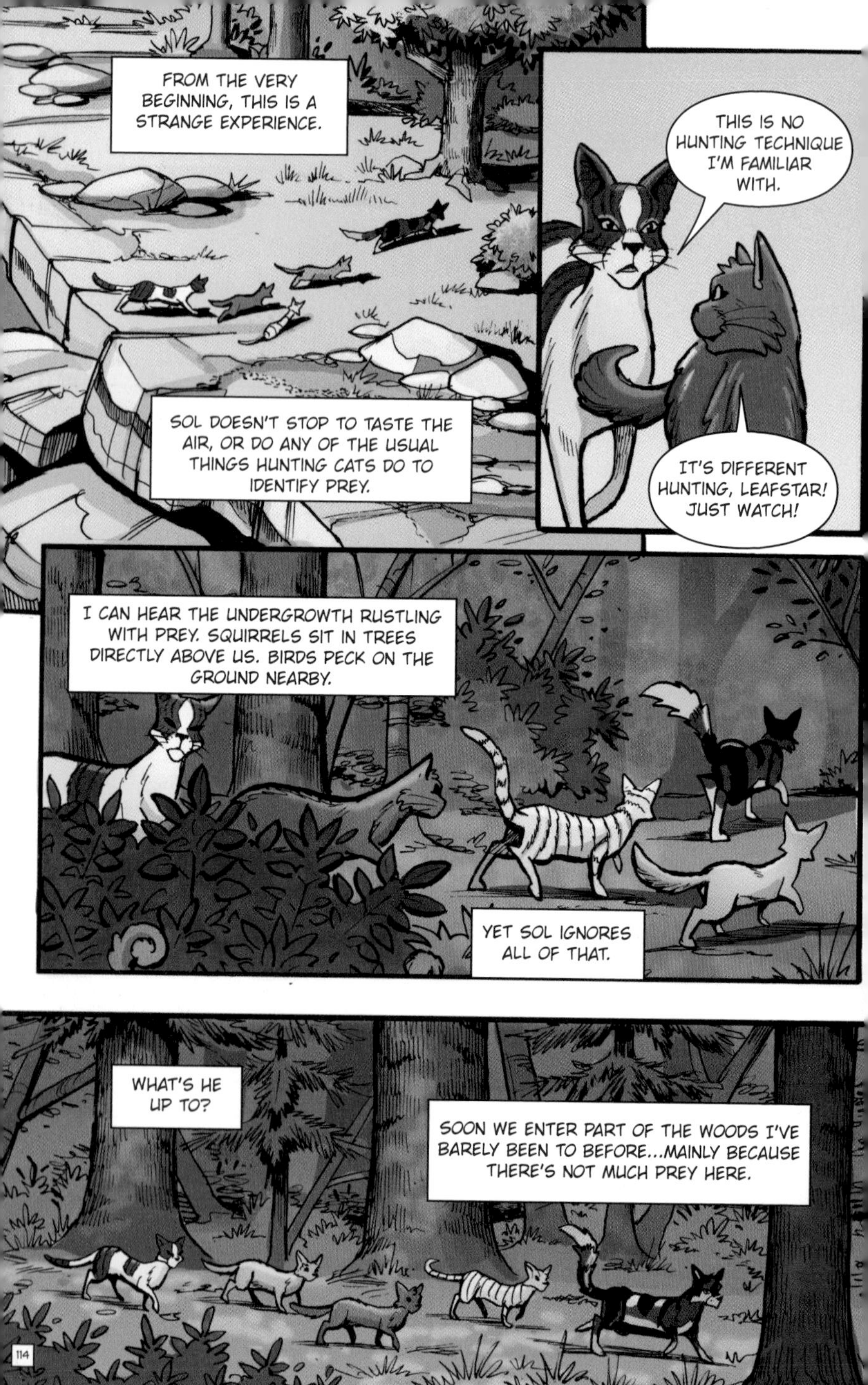
FROM THE VERY BEGINNING, THIS IS A STRANGE EXPERIENCE.
SOL DOESN'T STOP TO TASTE THE AIR, OR DO ANY OF THE USUAL THINGS HUNTING CATS DO TO IDENTIFY PREY.
THIS IS NO HUNTING TECHNIQUE I'M FAMILIAR WITH.
IT'S DIFFERENT HUNTING, LEAFSTAR! JUST WATCH!
I CAN HEAR THE UNDERGROWTH RUSTLING WITH PREY. SQUIRRELS SIT IN TREES DIRECTLY ABOVE US. BIRDS PECK ON THE GROUND NEARBY.
YET SOL IGNORES ALL OF THAT.
WHAT'S HE UP TO?
SOON WE ENTER PART OF THE WOODS I'VE BARELY BEEN TO BEFORE...MAINLY BECAUSE THERE'S NOT MUCH PREY HERE.

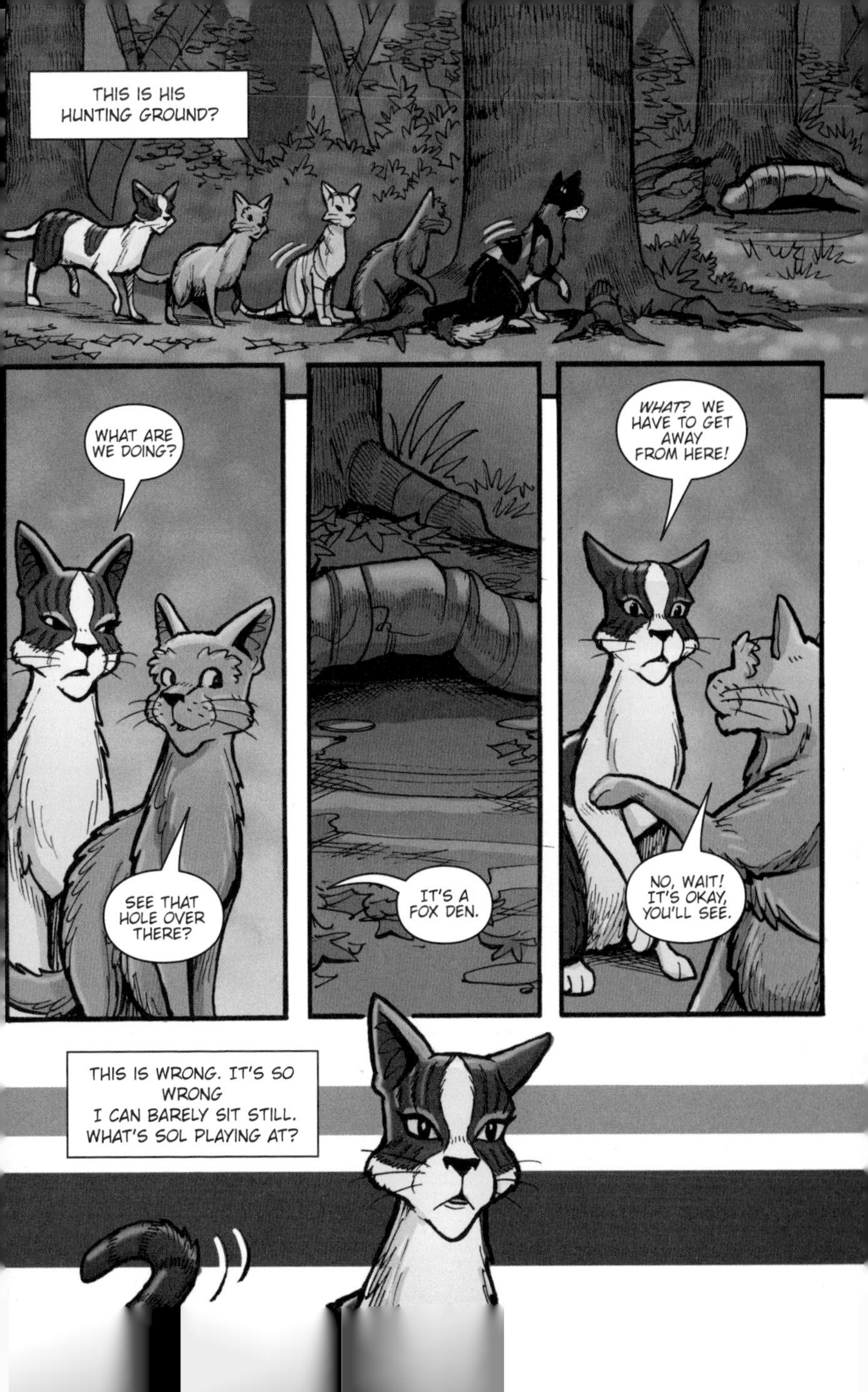
THIS IS HIS HUNTING GROUND?
WHAT ARE WE DOING?
SEE THAT HOLE OVER THERE?
IT'S A FOX DEN.
WHAT? WE HAVE TO GET AWAY FROM HERE!
NO, WAIT! IT'S OKAY, YOU'LL SEE.
THIS IS WRONG. IT'S SO WRONG I CAN BARELY SIT STILL. WHAT'S SOL PLAYING AT?

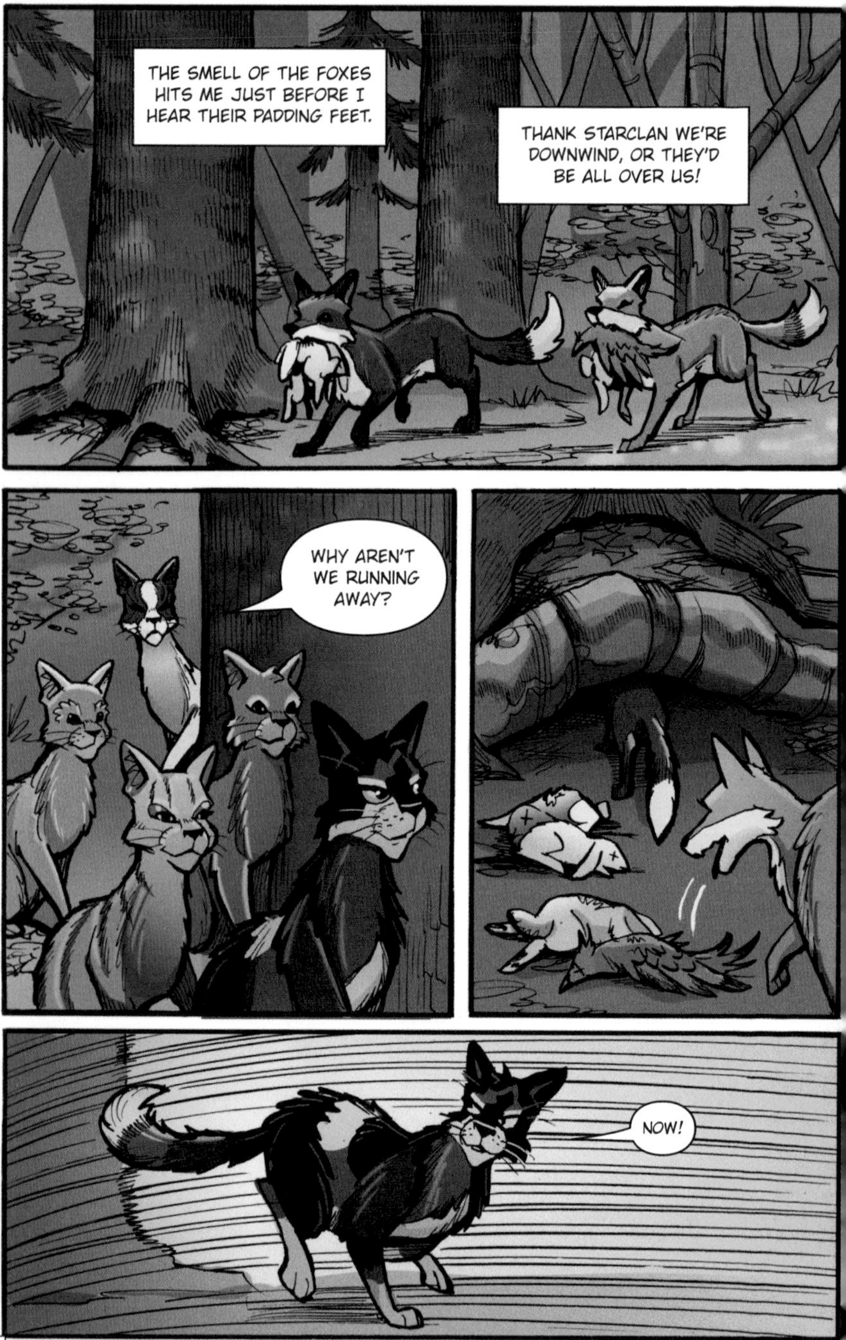
THE SMELL OF THE FOXES HITS ME JUST BEFORE I HEAR THEIR PADDING FEET.
THANK STARCLAN WE'RE DOWNWIND, OR THEY'D BE ALL OVER US!
WHY AREN'T WE RUNNING AWAY?
NOW!

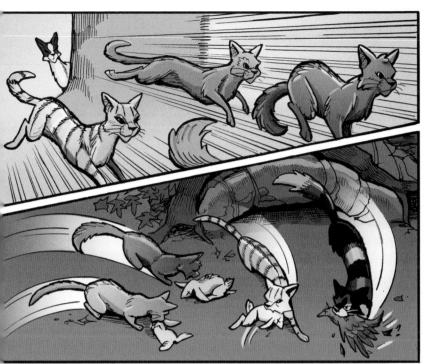

COME ON!

THE FOXES ARE BRINGING THEIR CUBS OUT OF THE DEN NOW... BRINGING THEM OUT TO FEED!

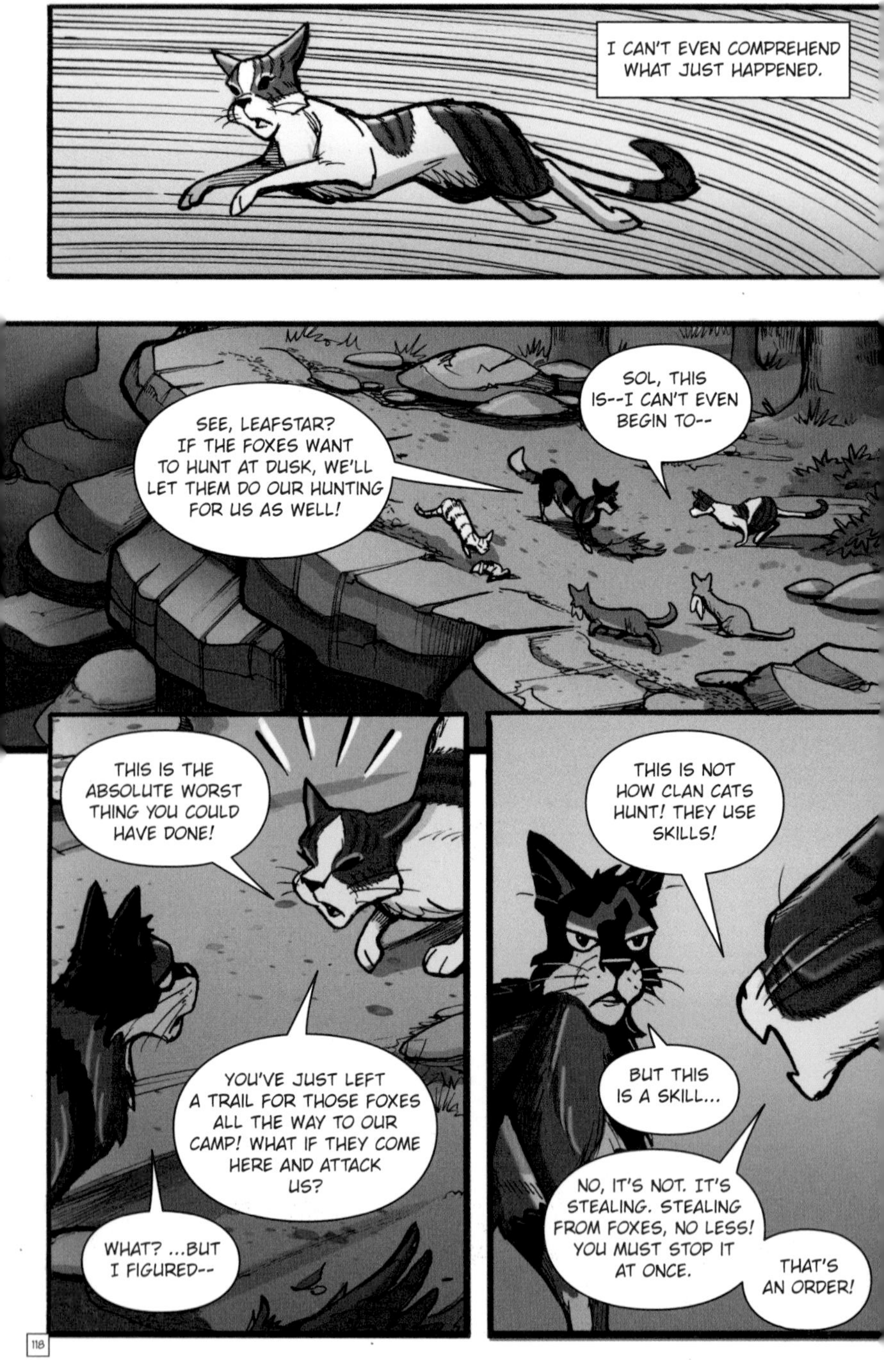

I CAN'T EVEN COMPREHEND WHAT JUST HAPPENED.
SEE, LEAFSTAR? IF THE FOXES WANT TO HUNT AT DUSK, WE'LL LET THEM DO OUR HUNTING FOR US AS WELL!
SOL, THIS IS--I CAN'T EVEN BEGIN TO--
THIS IS THE ABSOLUTE WORST THING YOU COULD HAVE DONE!
YOU'VE JUST LEFT A TRAIL FOR THOSE FOXES ALL THE WAY TO OUR CAMP! WHAT IF THEY COME HERE AND ATTACK US?
WHAT? ...BUT I FIGURED--
THIS IS NOT HOW CLAN CATS HUNT! THEY USE SKILLS!
BUT THIS IS A SKILL...
NO, IT'S NOT. IT'S STEALING. STEALING FROM FOXES, NO LESS! YOU MUST STOP IT AT ONCE.
THAT'S AN ORDER!

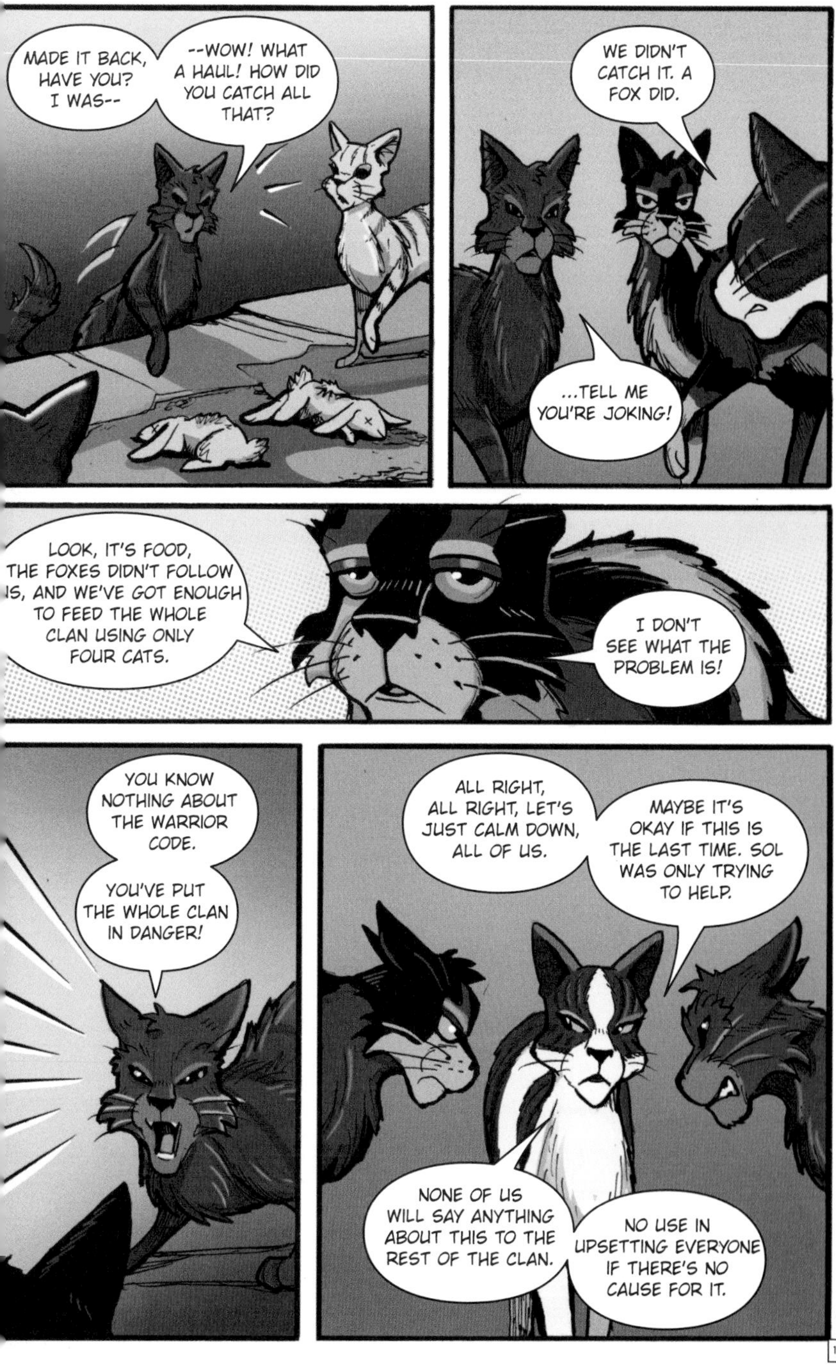
MADE IT BACK, HAVE YOU? I WAS--
--WOW! WHAT A HAUL! HOW DID YOU CATCH ALL THAT?
WE DIDN'T CATCH IT. A FOX DID.
...TELL ME YOU'RE JOKING!
LOOK, IT'S FOOD, THE FOXES DIDN'T FOLLOW US, AND WE'VE GOT ENOUGH TO FEED THE WHOLE CLAN USING ONLY FOUR CATS.
I DON'T SEE WHAT THE PROBLEM IS!
YOU KNOW NOTHING ABOUT THE WARRIOR CODE.
YOU'VE PUT THE WHOLE CLAN IN DANGER!
ALL RIGHT, ALL RIGHT, LET'S JUST CALM DOWN, ALL OF US.
MAYBE IT'S OKAY IF THIS IS THE LAST TIME. SOL WAS ONLY TRYING TO HELP.
NONE OF US WILL SAY ANYTHING ABOUT THIS TO THE REST OF THE CLAN.
NO USE IN UPSETTING EVERYONE IF THERE'S NO CAUSE FOR IT.

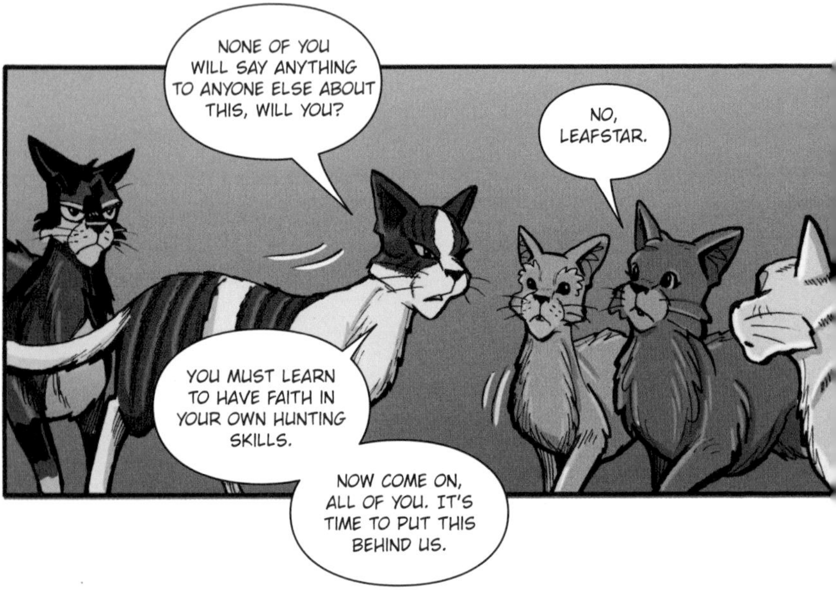
NONE OF YOU WILL SAY ANYTHING TO ANYONE ELSE ABOUT THIS, WILL YOU?
NO, LEAFSTAR.
YOU MUST LEARN TO HAVE FAITH IN YOUR OWN HUNTING SKILLS.
NOW COME ON, ALL OF YOU. IT'S TIME TO PUT THIS BEHIND US.

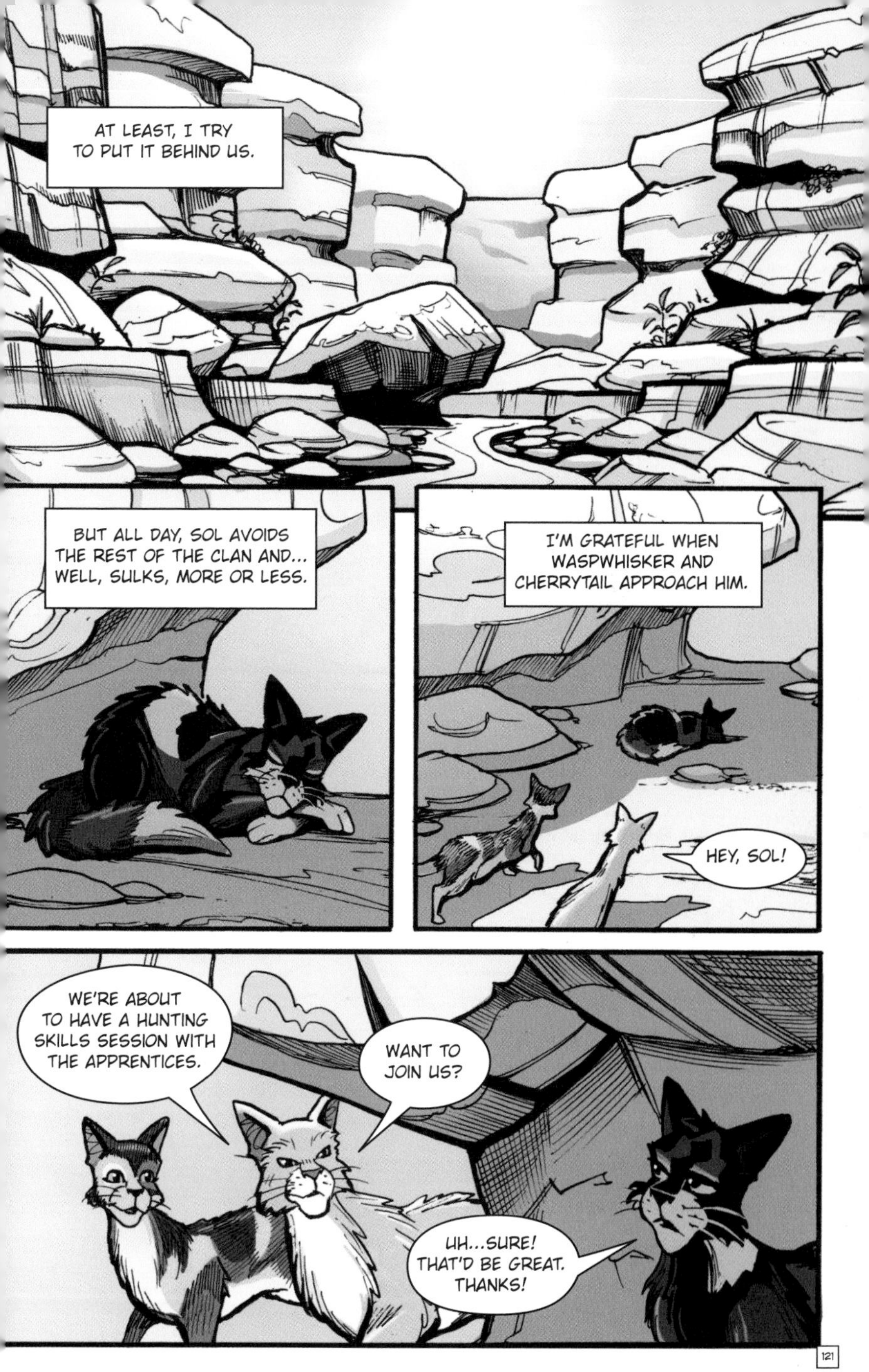
AT LEAST, I TRY TO PUT IT BEHIND US.
BUT ALL DAY, SOL AVOIDS THE REST OF THE CLAN AND... WELL, SULKS, MORE OR LESS.
I'M GRATEFUL WHEN WASPWHISKER AND CHERRYTAIL APPROACH HIM.
HEY, SOL!
WE'RE ABOUT TO HAVE A HUNTING SKILLS SESSION WITH THE APPRENTICES.
WANT TO JOIN US?
UH...SURE! THAT'D BE GREAT. THANKS!

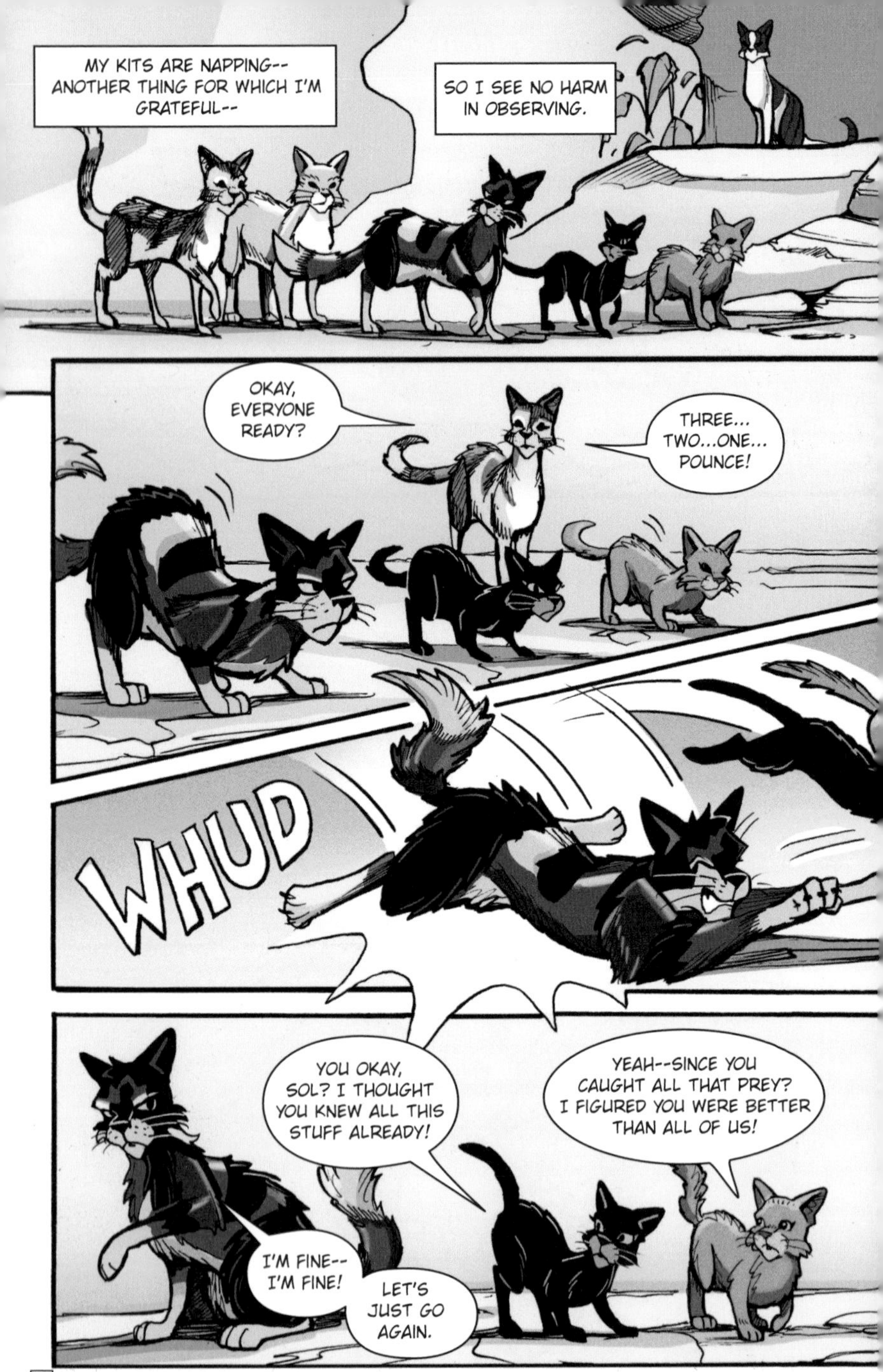
MY KITS ARE NAPPING-- ANOTHER THING FOR WHICH I'M GRATEFUL--
SO I SEE NO HARM IN OBSERVING.
OKAY, EVERYONE READY?
THREE... TWO...ONE... POUNCE!
WHUD
YOU OKAY, SOL? I THOUGHT YOU KNEW ALL THIS STUFF ALREADY!
YEAH--SINCE YOU CAUGHT ALL THAT PREY? I FIGURED YOU WERE BETTER THAN ALL OF US!
I'M FINE-- I'M FINE!
LET'S JUST GO AGAIN.

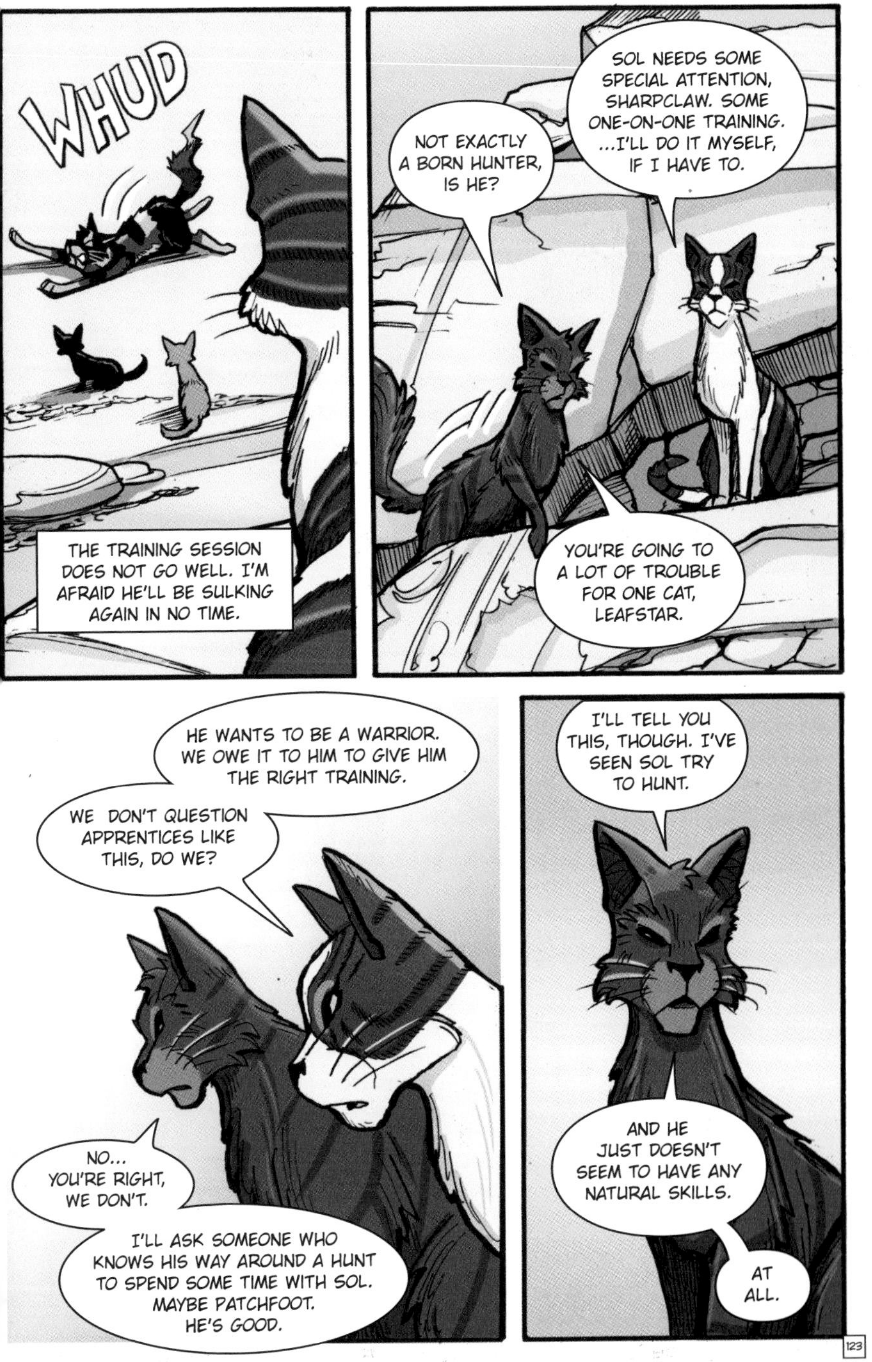
WHUD
THE TRAINING SESSION DOES NOT GO WELL. I'M AFRAID HE'LL BE SULKING AGAIN IN NO TIME.
NOT EXACTLY A BORN HUNTER, IS HE?
SOL NEEDS SOME SPECIAL ATTENTION, SHARPCLAW. SOME ONE-ON-ONE TRAINING. ...I'LL DO IT MYSELF, IF I HAVE TO.
YOU'RE GOING TO A LOT OF TROUBLE FOR ONE CAT, LEAFSTAR.
HE WANTS TO BE A WARRIOR. WE OWE IT TO HIM TO GIVE HIM THE RIGHT TRAINING.
WE DON'T QUESTION APPRENTICES LIKE THIS, DO WE?
NO... YOU'RE RIGHT, WE DON'T.
I'LL ASK SOMEONE WHO KNOWS HIS WAY AROUND A HUNT TO SPEND SOME TIME WITH SOL. MAYBE PATCHFOOT. HE'S GOOD.
I'LL TELL YOU THIS, THOUGH. I'VE SEEN SOL TRY TO HUNT.
AND HE JUST DOESN'T SEEM TO HAVE ANY NATURAL SKILLS.
AT ALL.

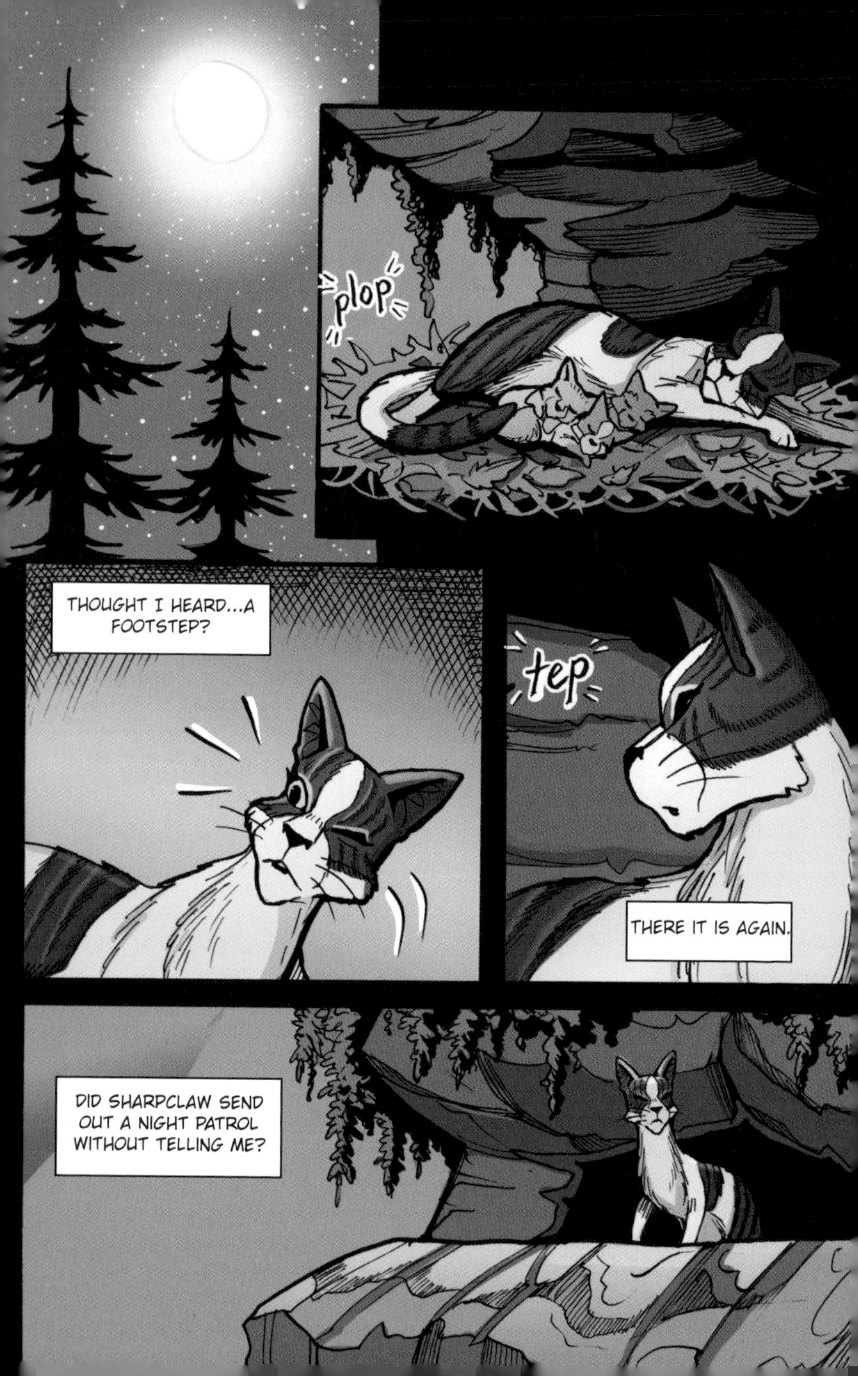
plop
THOUGHT I HEARD...A FOOTSTEP?
tep
THERE IT IS AGAIN.
DID SHARPCLAW SEND OUT A NIGHT PATROL WITHOUT TELLING ME?

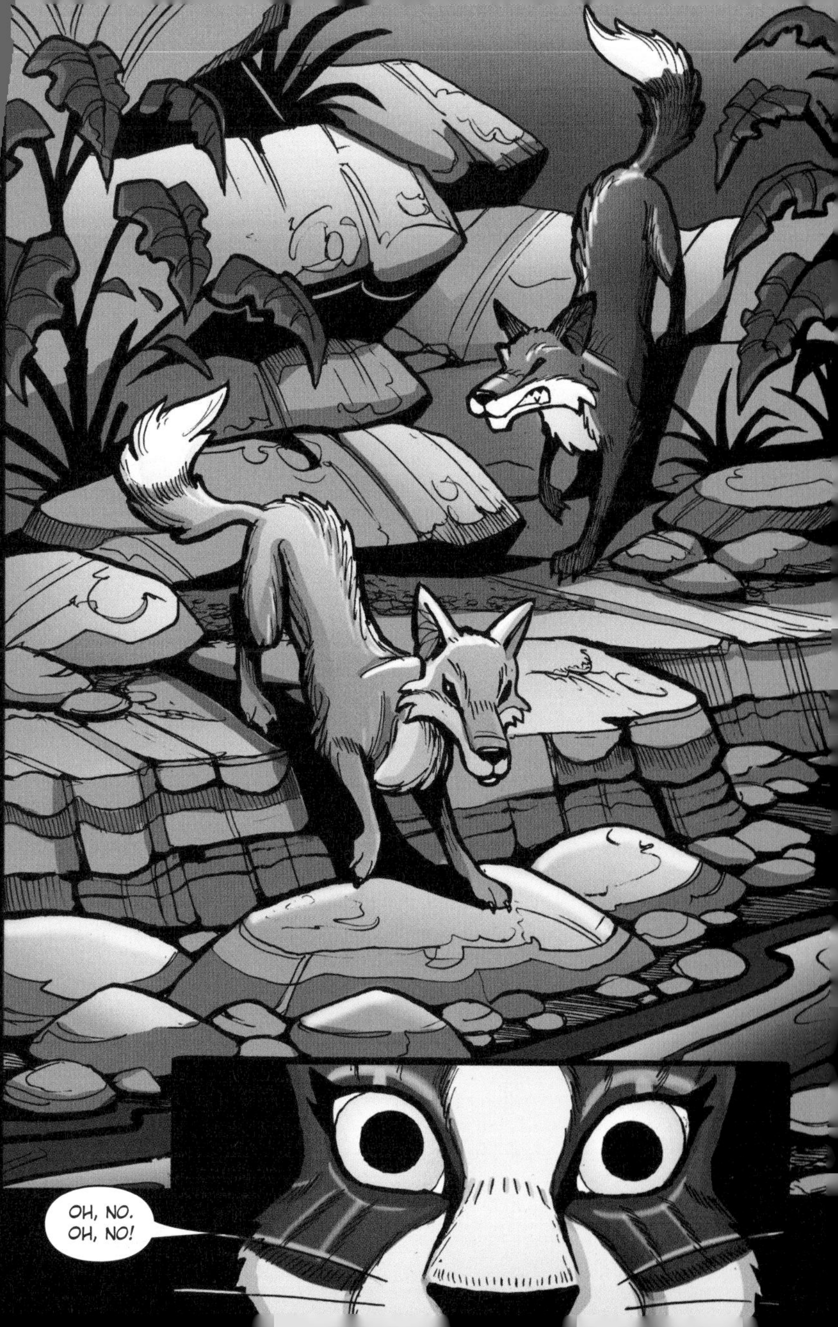
OH, NO.
OH, NO!

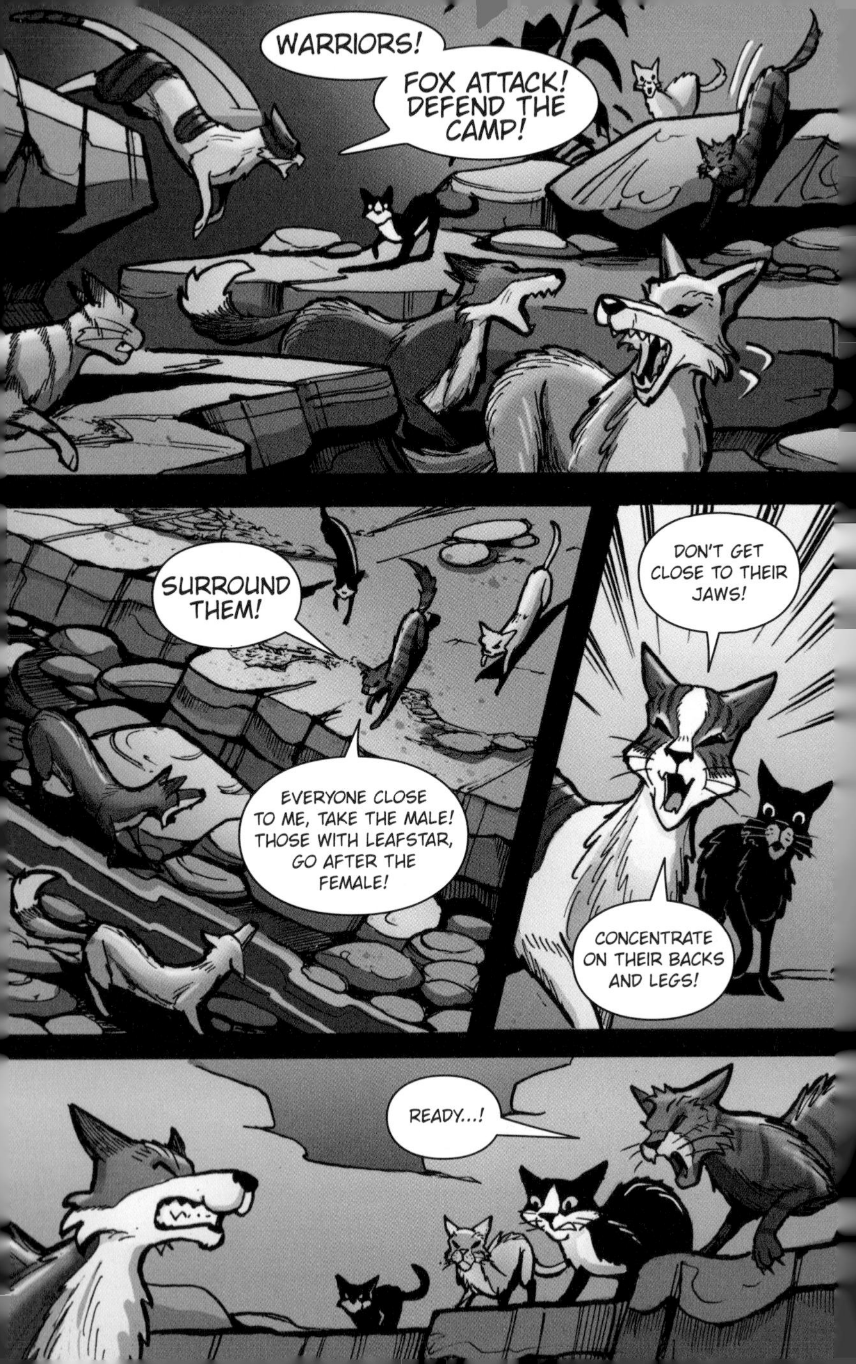
WARRIORS!
FOX ATTACK! DEFEND THE CAMP!
SURROUND THEM!
EVERYONE CLOSE TO ME, TAKE THE MALE! THOSE WITH LEAFSTAR, GO AFTER THE FEMALE!
DON'T GET CLOSE TO THEIR JAWS!
CONCENTRATE ON THEIR BACKS AND LEGS!
READY...!

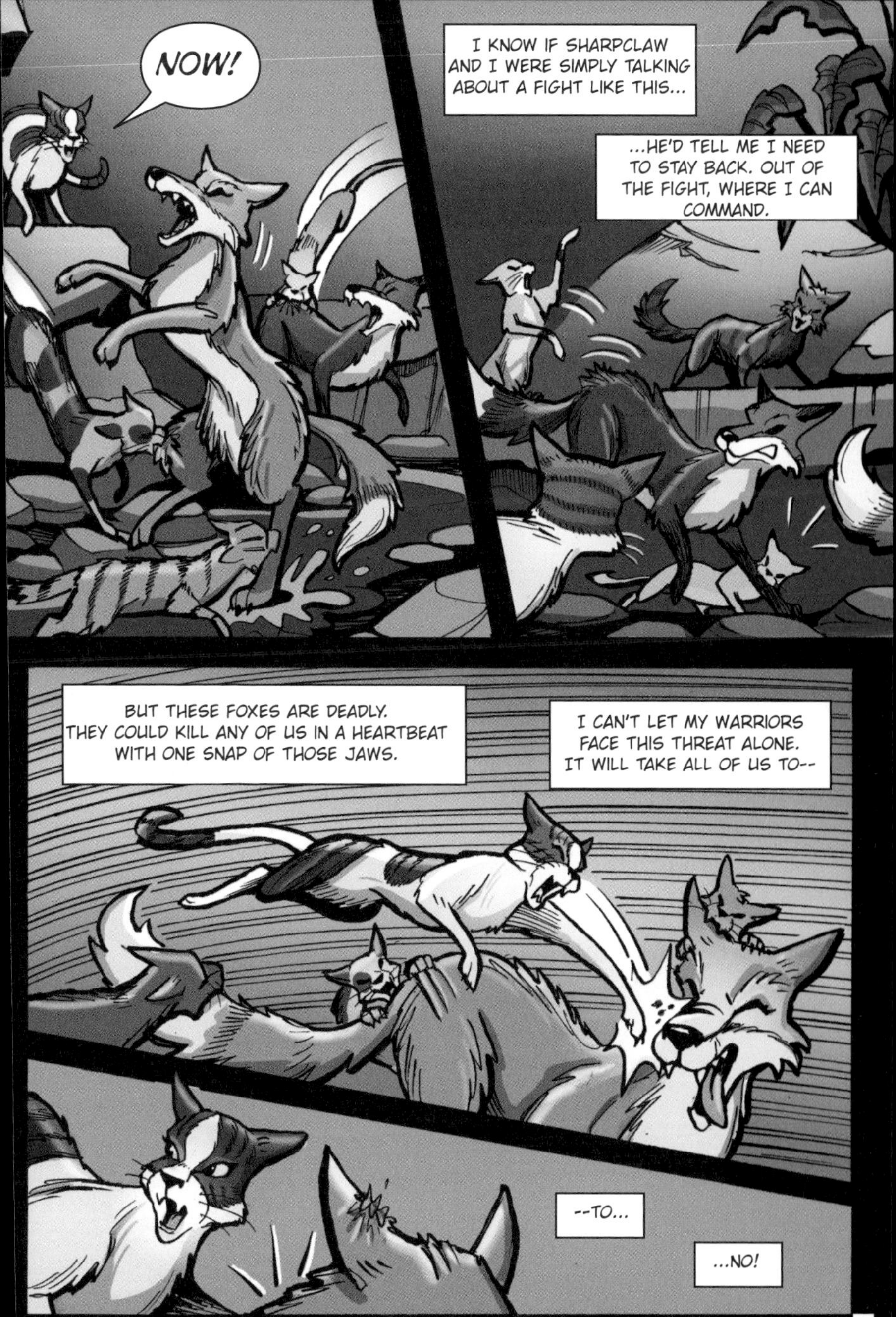
NOW!
I KNOW IF SHARPCLAW AND I WERE SIMPLY TALKING ABOUT A FIGHT LIKE THIS...
...HE'D TELL ME I NEED TO STAY BACK. OUT OF THE FIGHT, WHERE I CAN COMMAND.
BUT THESE FOXES ARE DEADLY. THEY COULD KILL ANY OF US IN A HEARTBEAT WITH ONE SNAP OF THOSE JAWS.
I CAN'T LET MY WARRIORS FACE THIS THREAT ALONE. IT WILL TAKE ALL OF US TO--
--TO...
...NO!

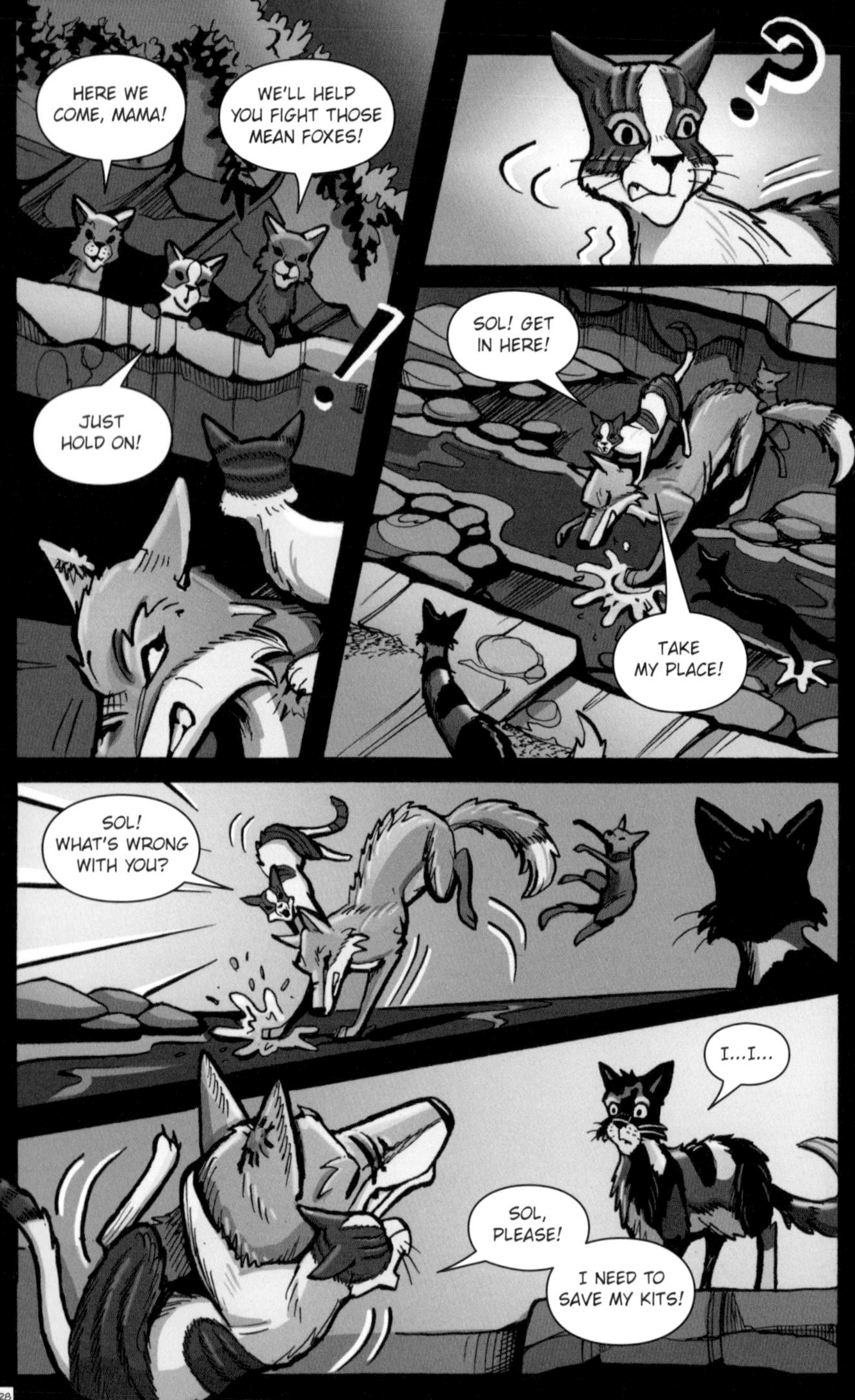
HERE WE COME, MAMA!
WE'LL HELP YOU FIGHT THOSE MEAN FOXES!
JUST HOLD ON!
SOL! GET IN HERE!
TAKE MY PLACE!
SOL! WHAT'S WRONG WITH YOU?
I...I...
SOL, PLEASE!
I NEED TO SAVE MY KITS!

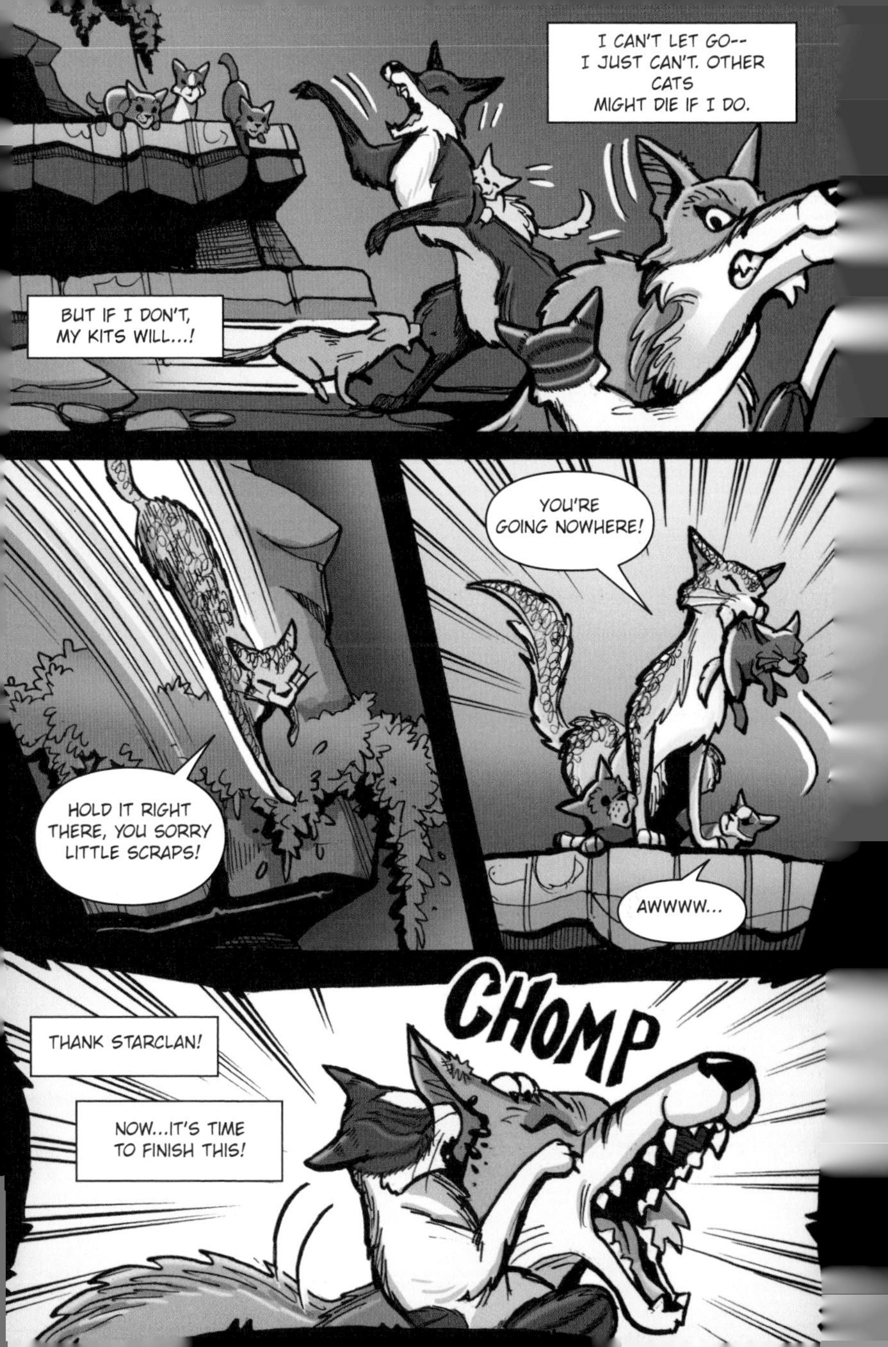
I CAN'T LET GO--
I JUST CAN'T. OTHER CATS MIGHT DIE IF I DO.
BUT IF I DON'T, MY KITS WILL...!
HOLD IT RIGHT THERE, YOU SORRY LITTLE SCRAPS!
YOU'RE GOING NOWHERE!
AWWWW...
CHOMP
THANK STARCLAN!
NOW...IT'S TIME TO FINISH THIS!

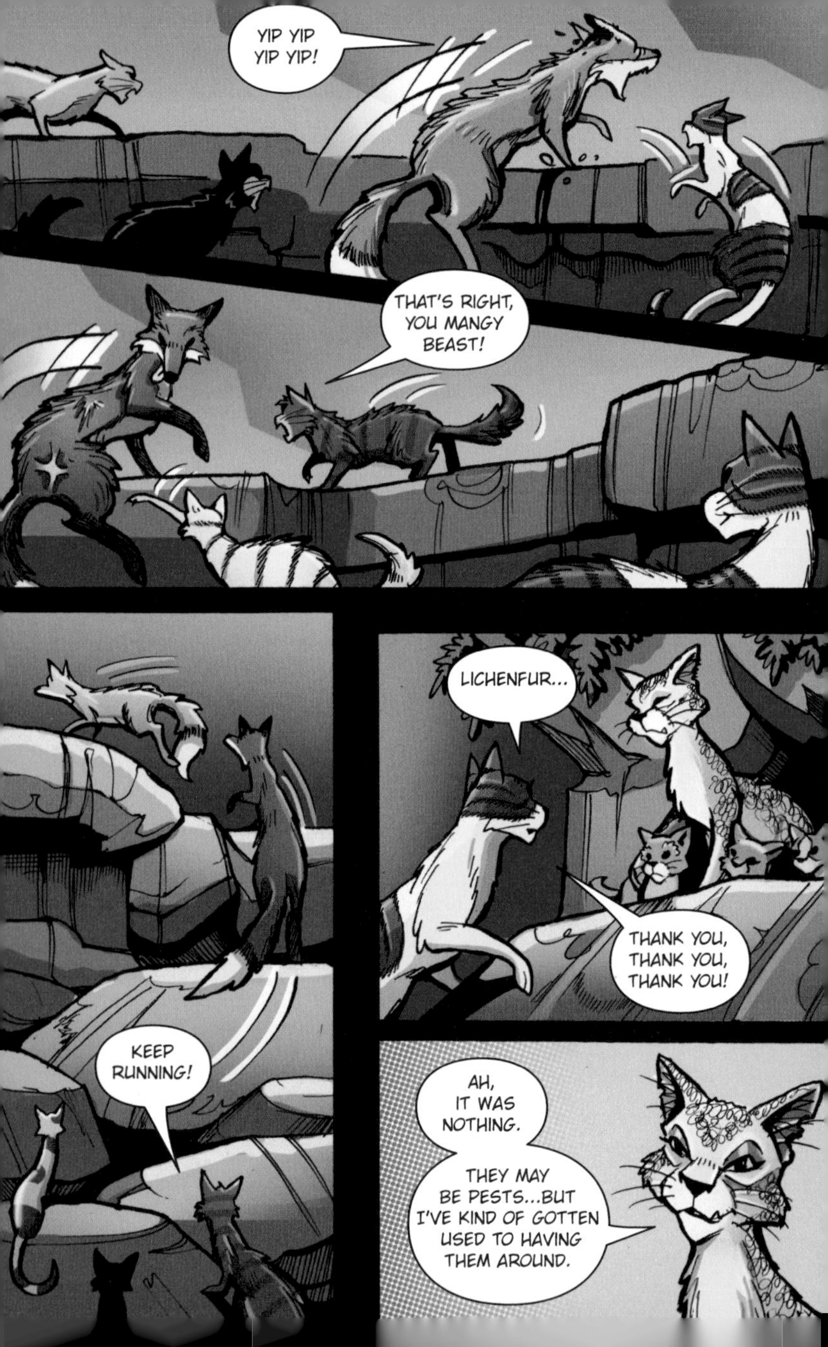
YIP YIP YIP YIP!
THAT'S RIGHT, YOU MANGY BEAST!
KEEP RUNNING!
LICHENFUR...
THANK YOU, THANK YOU, THANK YOU!
AH, IT WAS NOTHING.
THEY MAY BE PESTS...BUT I'VE KIND OF GOTTEN USED TO HAVING THEM AROUND.

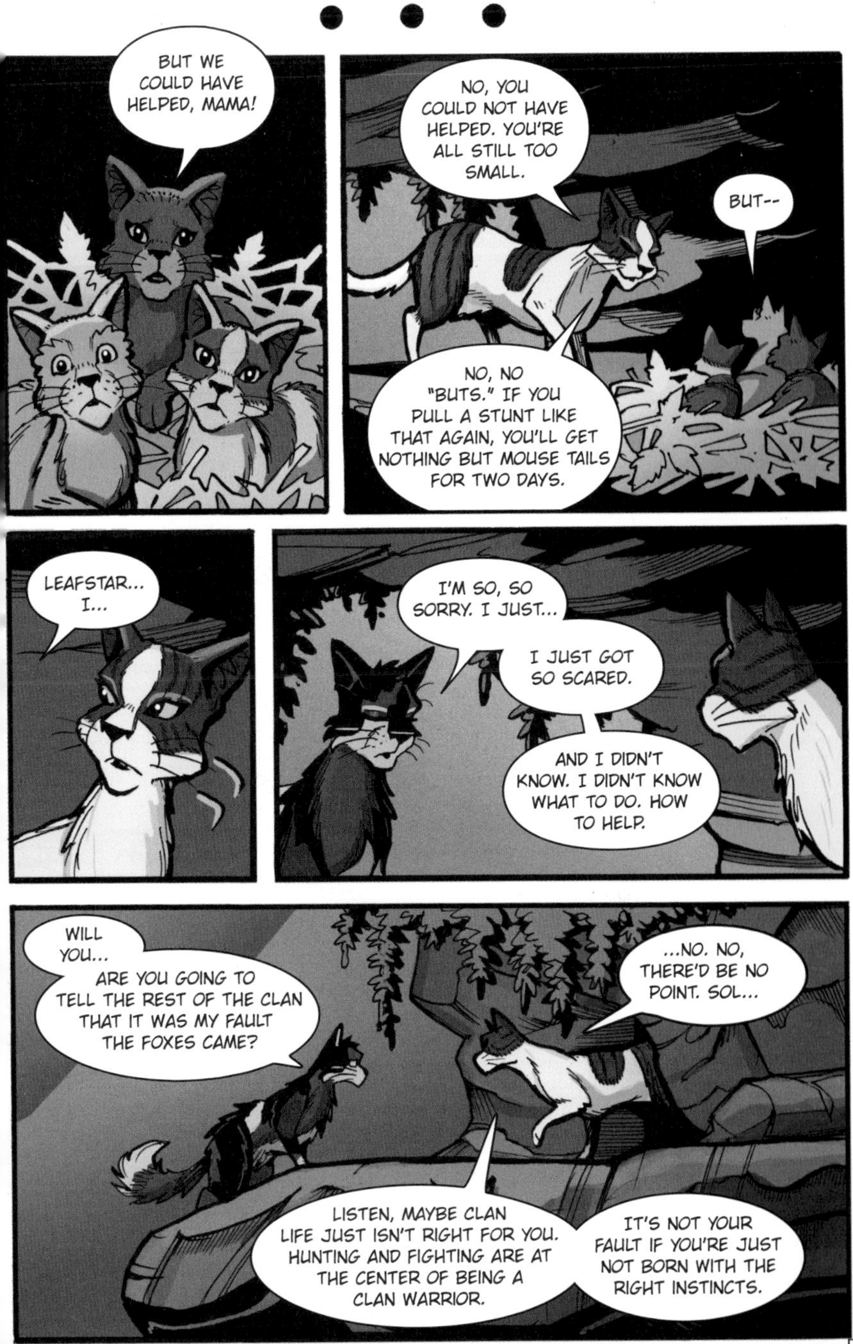
BUT WE COULD HAVE HELPED, MAMA!
NO, YOU COULD NOT HAVE HELPED. YOU'RE ALL STILL TOO SMALL.
BUT--
NO, NO "BUTS." IF YOU PULL A STUNT LIKE THAT AGAIN, YOU'LL GET NOTHING BUT MOUSE TAILS FOR TWO DAYS.
LEAFSTAR... I...
I'M SO, SO SORRY. I JUST...
I JUST GOT SO SCARED.
AND I DIDN'T KNOW. I DIDN'T KNOW WHAT TO DO. HOW TO HELP.
WILL YOU... ARE YOU GOING TO TELL THE REST OF THE CLAN THAT IT WAS MY FAULT THE FOXES CAME?
...NO. NO, THERE'D BE NO POINT. SOL...
LISTEN, MAYBE CLAN LIFE JUST ISN'T RIGHT FOR YOU. HUNTING AND FIGHTING ARE AT THE CENTER OF BEING A CLAN WARRIOR.
IT'S NOT YOUR FAULT IF YOU'RE JUST NOT BORN WITH THE RIGHT INSTINCTS.

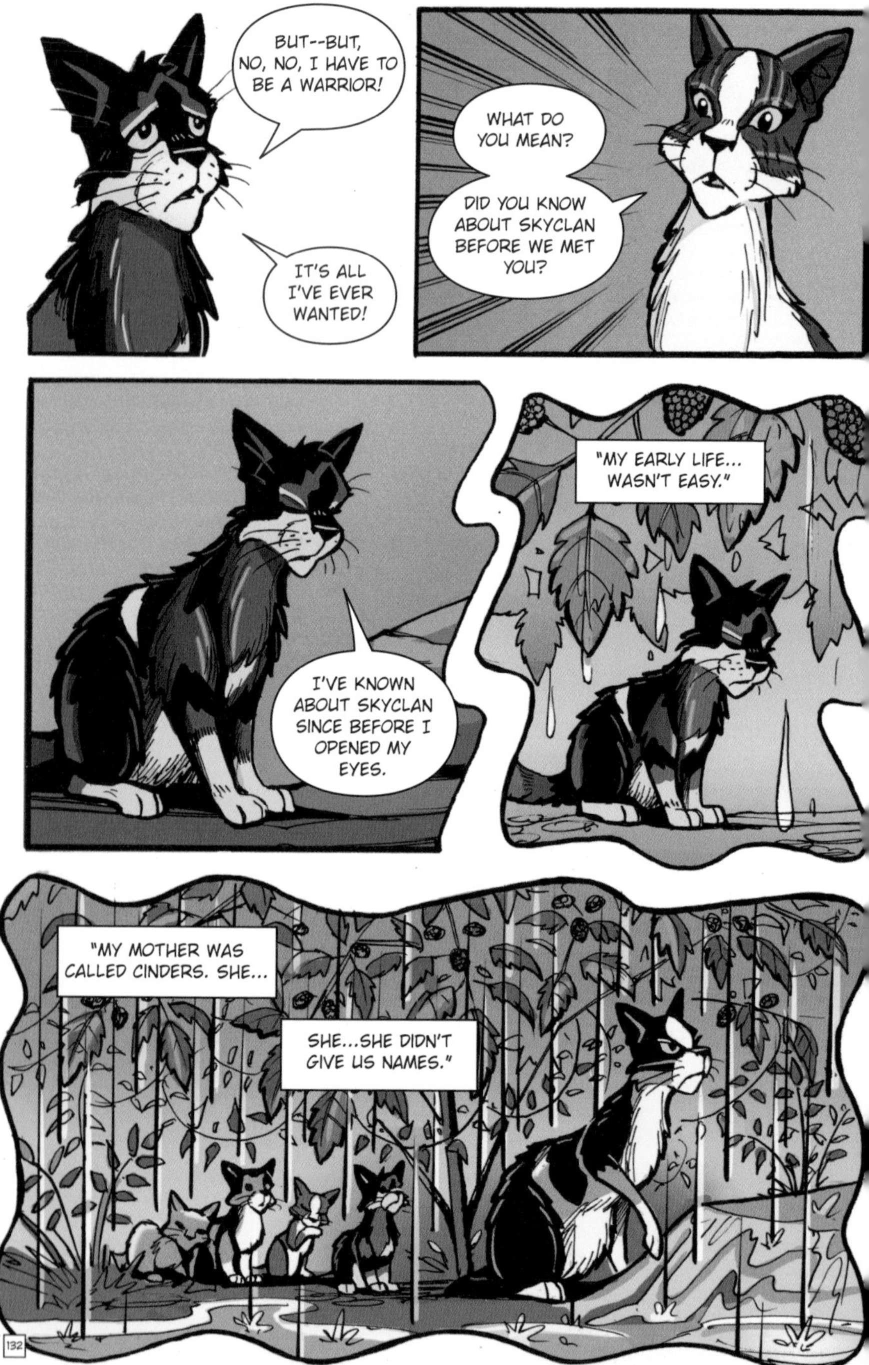
BUT--BUT, NO, NO, I HAVE TO BE A WARRIOR!
IT'S ALL I'VE EVER WANTED!
WHAT DO YOU MEAN?
DID YOU KNOW ABOUT SKYCLAN BEFORE WE MET YOU?
I'VE KNOWN ABOUT SKYCLAN SINCE BEFORE I OPENED MY EYES.
"MY EARLY LIFE... WASN'T EASY."
"MY MOTHER WAS CALLED CINDERS. SHE...
SHE...SHE DIDN'T GIVE US NAMES."

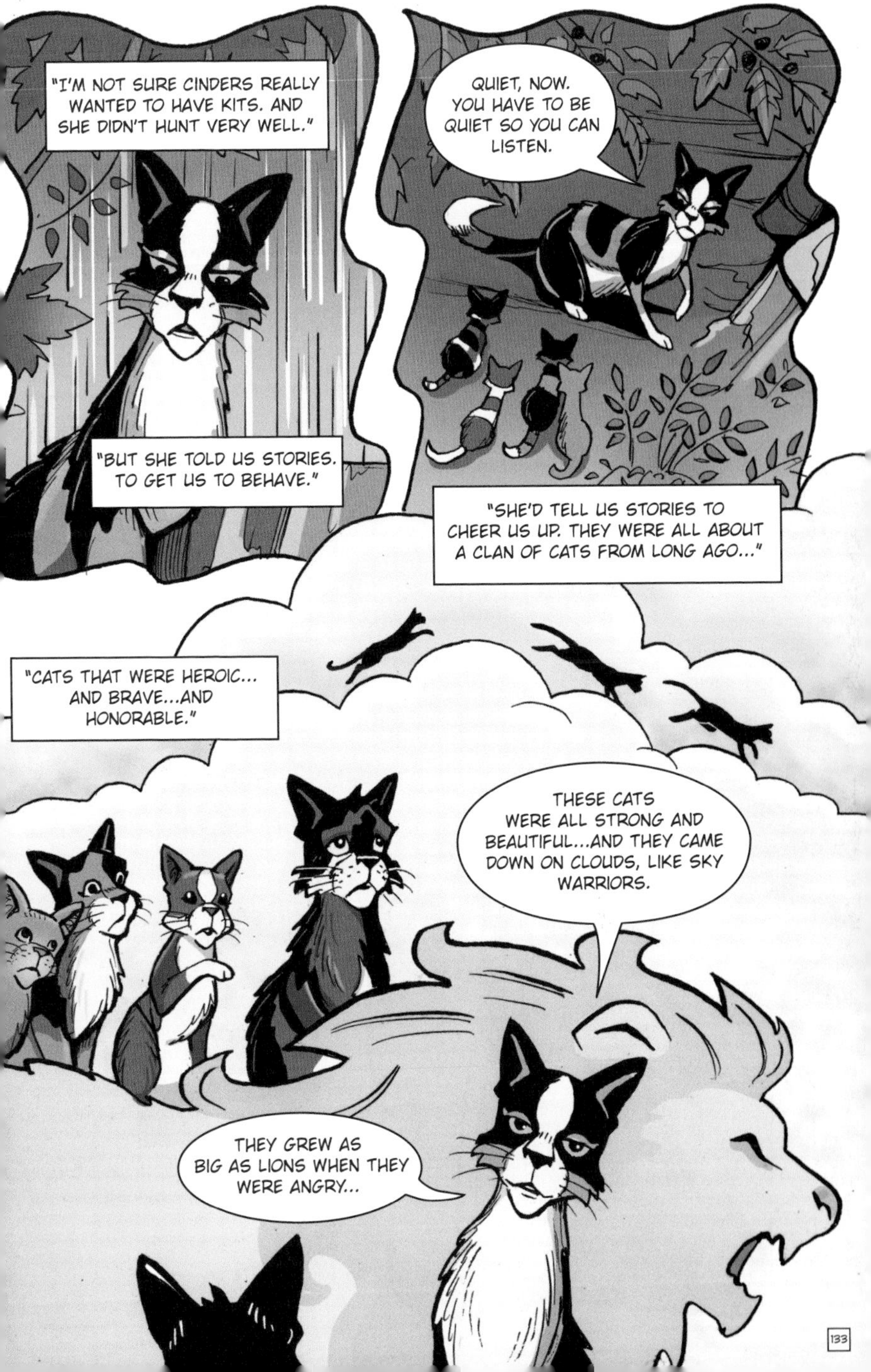
"I'M NOT SURE CINDERS REALLY WANTED TO HAVE KITS. AND SHE DIDN'T HUNT VERY WELL."
"BUT SHE TOLD US STORIES. TO GET US TO BEHAVE."
QUIET, NOW. YOU HAVE TO BE QUIET SO YOU CAN LISTEN.
"SHE'D TELL US STORIES TO CHEER US UP. THEY WERE ALL ABOUT A CLAN OF CATS FROM LONG AGO..."
"CATS THAT WERE HEROIC... AND BRAVE...AND HONORABLE."
THESE CATS WERE ALL STRONG AND BEAUTIFUL...AND THEY CAME DOWN ON CLOUDS, LIKE SKY WARRIORS.
THEY GREW AS BIG AS LIONS WHEN THEY WERE ANGRY...

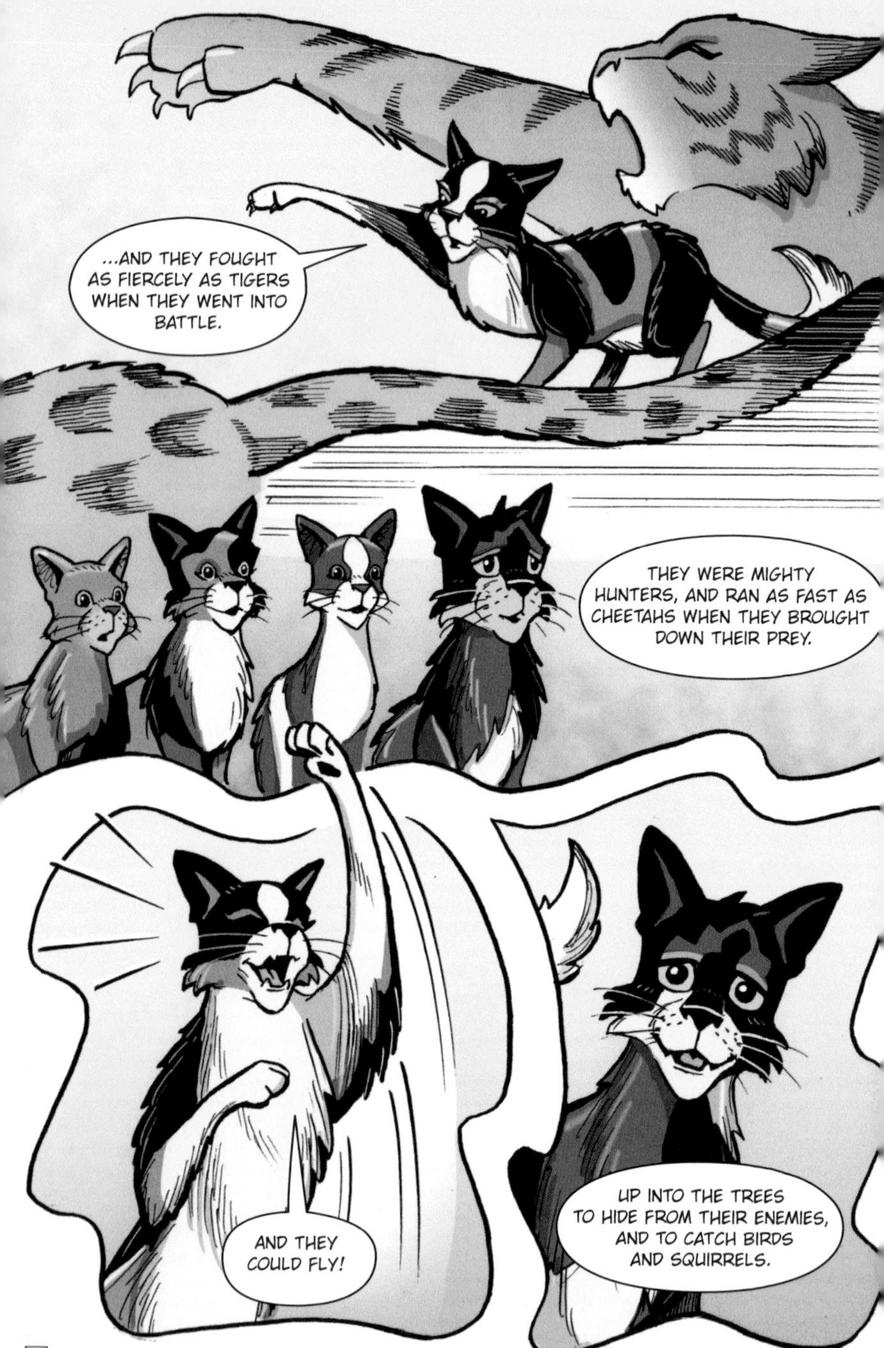
...AND THEY FOUGHT AS FIERCELY AS TIGERS WHEN THEY WENT INTO BATTLE.
THEY WERE MIGHTY HUNTERS, AND RAN AS FAST AS CHEETAHS WHEN THEY BROUGHT DOWN THEIR PREY.
AND THEY COULD FLY!
UP INTO THE TREES TO HIDE FROM THEIR ENEMIES, AND TO CATCH BIRDS AND SQUIRRELS.

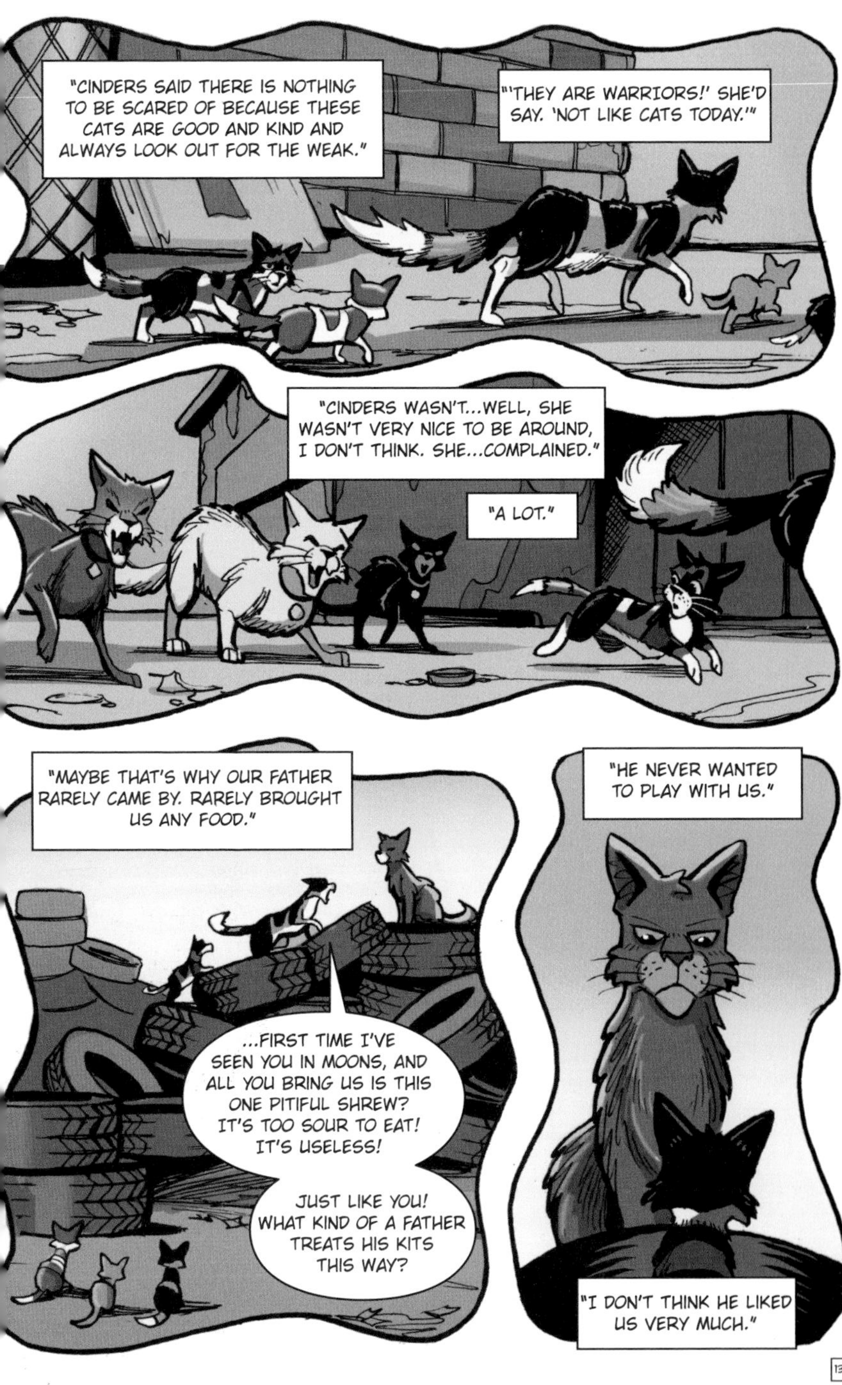
"CINDERS SAID THERE IS NOTHING TO BE SCARED OF BECAUSE THESE CATS ARE GOOD AND KIND AND ALWAYS LOOK OUT FOR THE WEAK."
"'THEY ARE WARRIORS!' SHE'D SAY. 'NOT LIKE CATS TODAY.'"
"CINDERS WASN'T...WELL, SHE WASN'T VERY NICE TO BE AROUND, I DON'T THINK. SHE...COMPLAINED."
"A LOT."
"MAYBE THAT'S WHY OUR FATHER RARELY CAME BY. RARELY BROUGHT US ANY FOOD."
...FIRST TIME I'VE SEEN YOU IN MOONS, AND ALL YOU BRING US IS THIS ONE PITIFUL SHREW? IT'S TOO SOUR TO EAT! IT'S USELESS!
JUST LIKE YOU! WHAT KIND OF A FATHER TREATS HIS KITS THIS WAY?
"HE NEVER WANTED TO PLAY WITH US."
"I DON'T THINK HE LIKED US VERY MUCH."

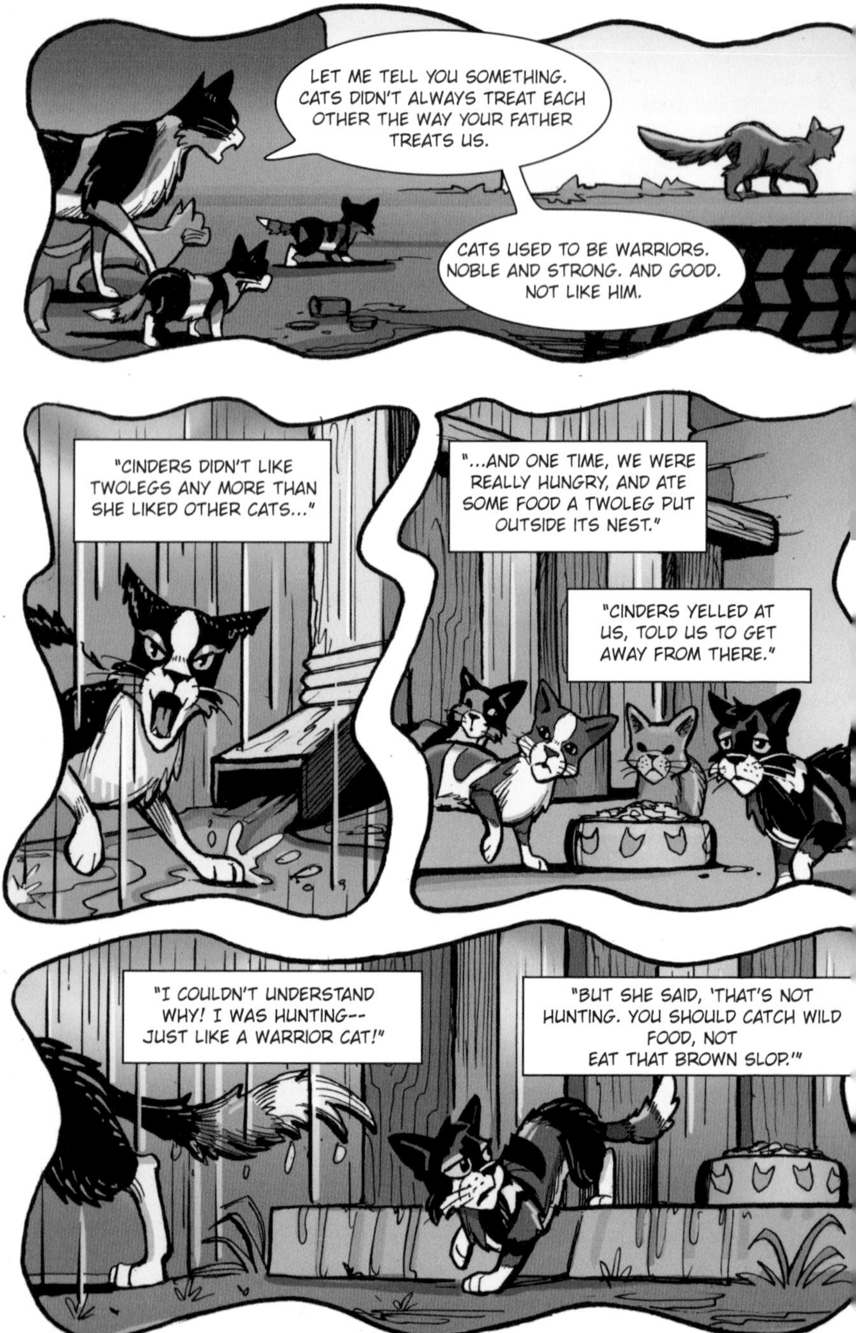
LET ME TELL YOU SOMETHING. CATS DIDN'T ALWAYS TREAT EACH OTHER THE WAY YOUR FATHER TREATS US.
CATS USED TO BE WARRIORS. NOBLE AND STRONG. AND GOOD. NOT LIKE HIM.
"CINDERS DIDN'T LIKE TWOLEGS ANY MORE THAN SHE LIKED OTHER CATS..."
"...AND ONE TIME, WE WERE REALLY HUNGRY, AND ATE SOME FOOD A TWOLEG PUT OUTSIDE ITS NEST."
"CINDERS YELLED AT US, TOLD US TO GET AWAY FROM THERE."
"I COULDN'T UNDERSTAND WHY! I WAS HUNTING-- JUST LIKE A WARRIOR CAT!"
"BUT SHE SAID, 'THAT'S NOT HUNTING. YOU SHOULD CATCH WILD FOOD, NOT EAT THAT BROWN SLOP.'"

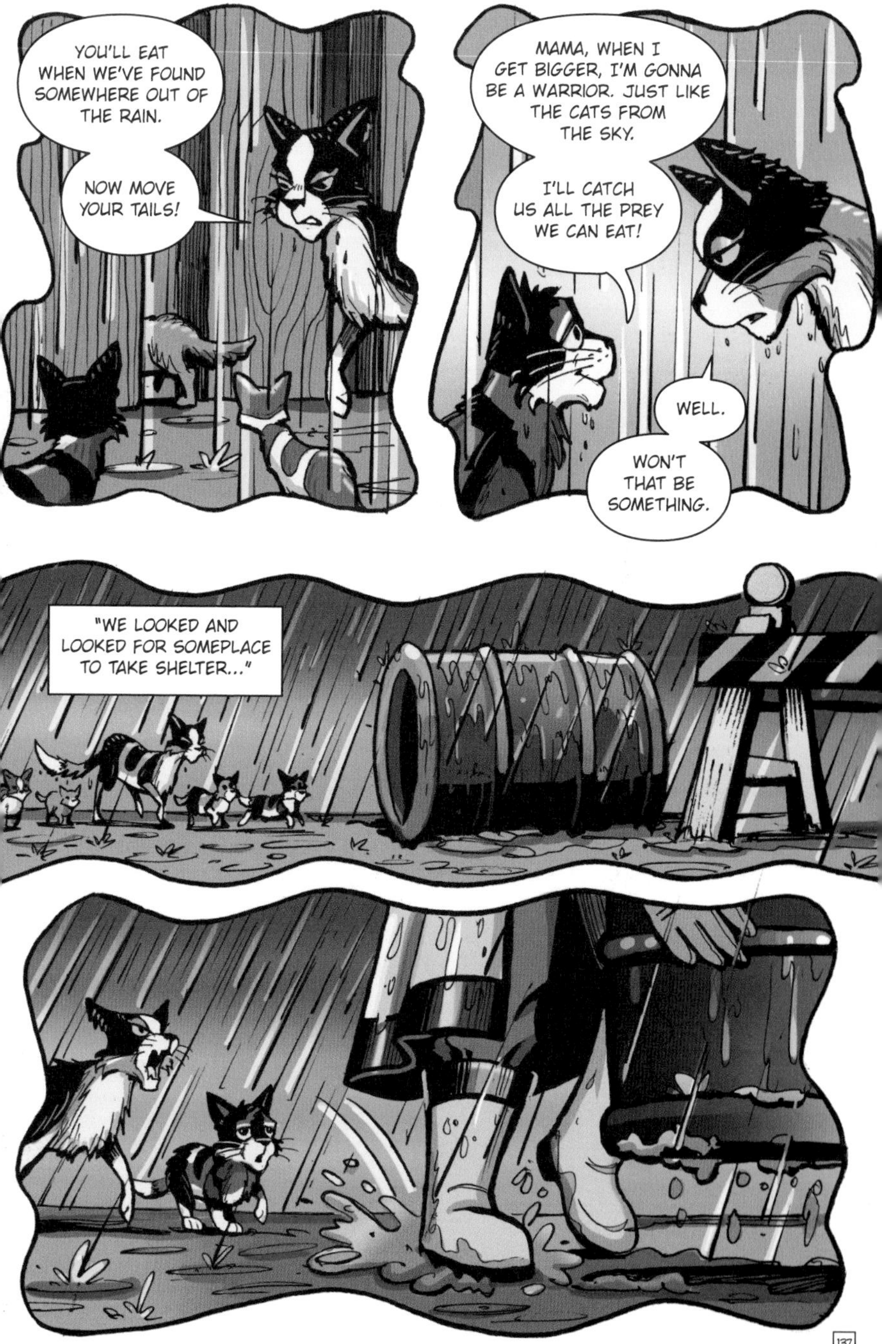
YOU'LL EAT WHEN WE'VE FOUND SOMEWHERE OUT OF THE RAIN.
NOW MOVE YOUR TAILS!
MAMA, WHEN I GET BIGGER, I'M GONNA BE A WARRIOR. JUST LIKE THE CATS FROM THE SKY.
I'LL CATCH US ALL THE PREY WE CAN EAT!
WELL.
WON'T THAT BE SOMETHING.
"WE LOOKED AND LOOKED FOR SOMEPLACE TO TAKE SHELTER..."

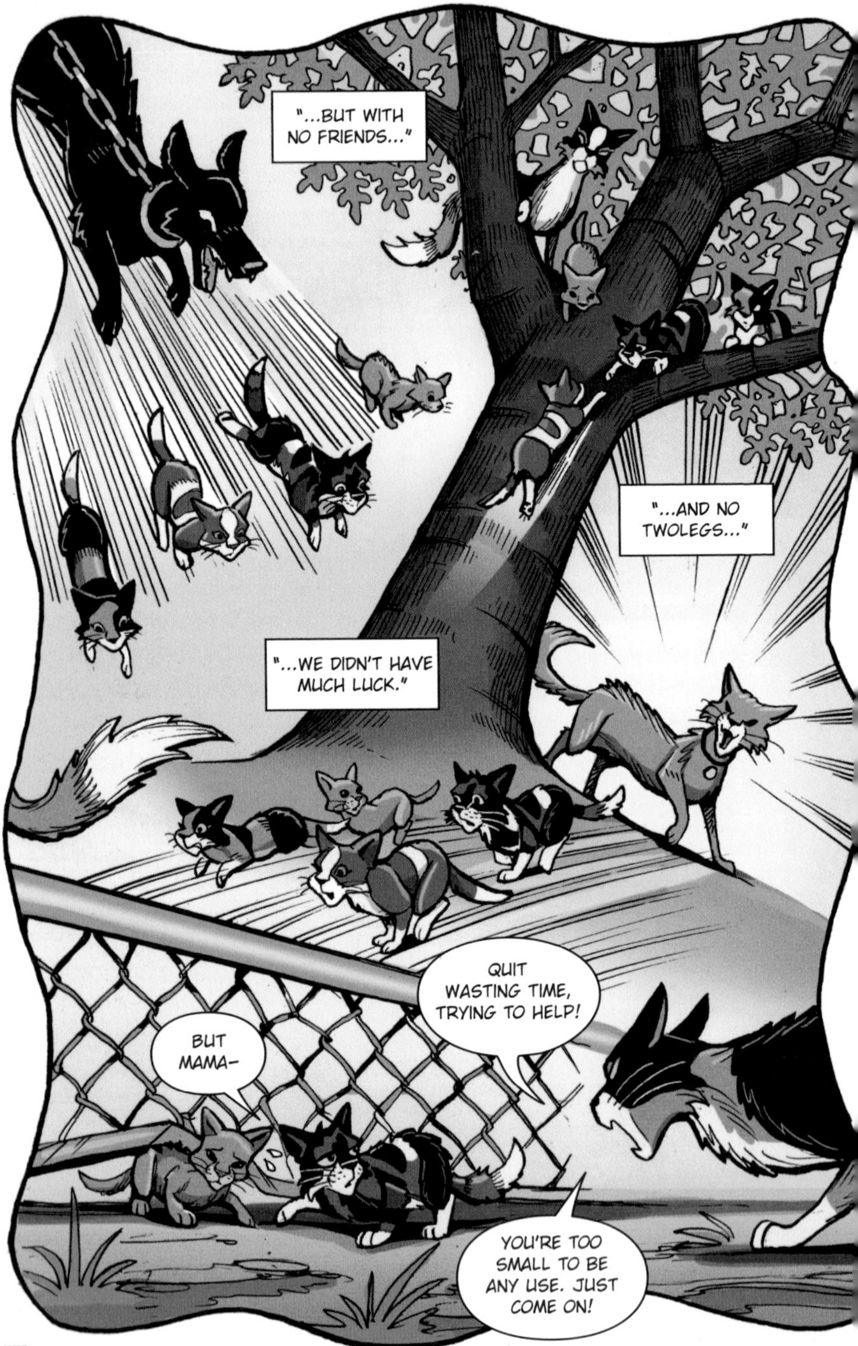
"...BUT WITH NO FRIENDS..."
"...AND NO TWOLEGS..."
"...WE DIDN'T HAVE MUCH LUCK."
QUIT WASTING TIME, TRYING TO HELP!
BUT MAMA-
YOU'RE TOO SMALL TO BE ANY USE. JUST COME ON!

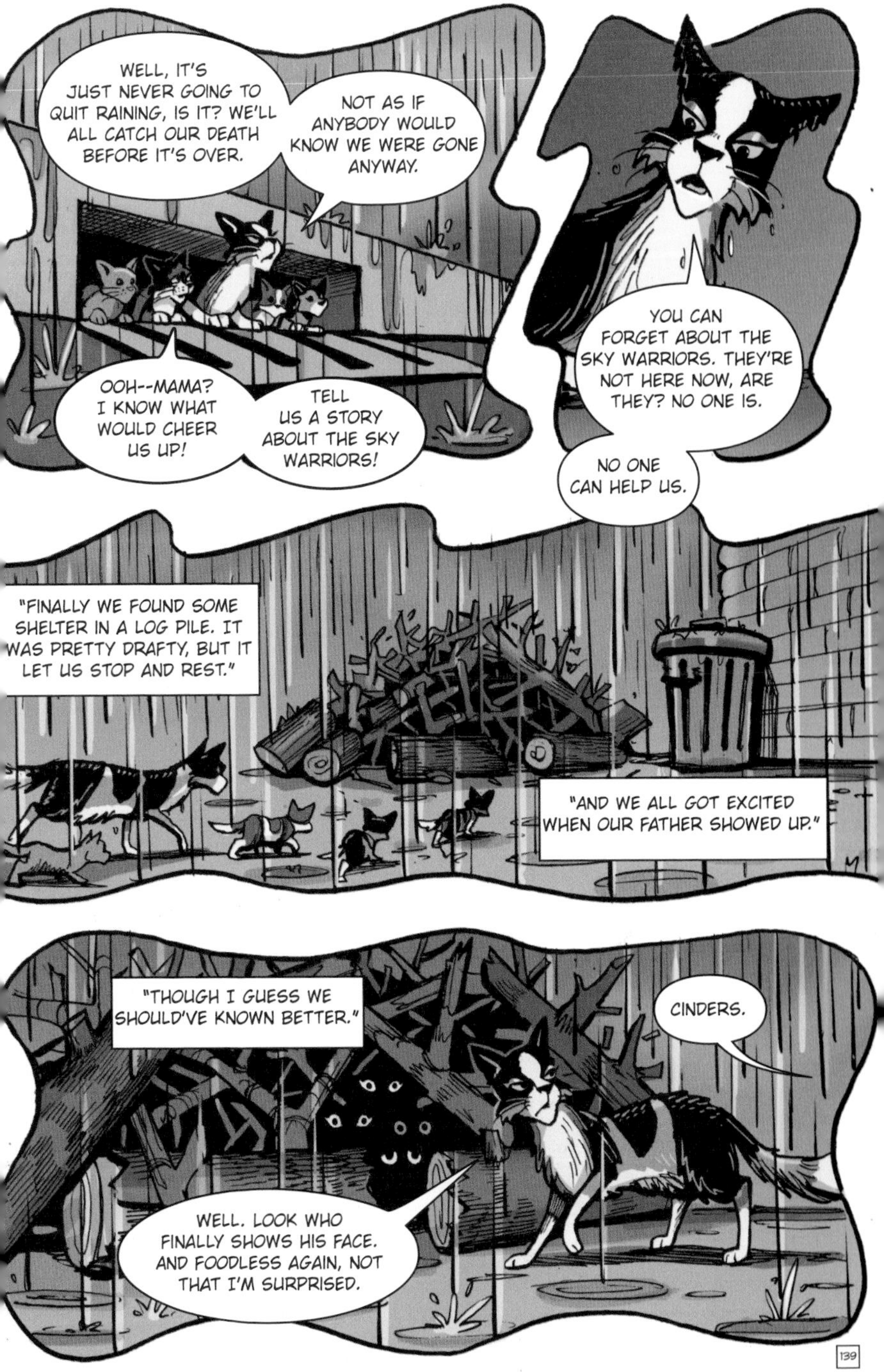

WELL, IT'S JUST NEVER GOING TO QUIT RAINING, IS IT? WE'LL ALL CATCH OUR DEATH BEFORE IT'S OVER.
NOT AS IF ANYBODY WOULD KNOW WE WERE GONE ANYWAY.
OOH--MAMA? I KNOW WHAT WOULD CHEER US UP!
TELL US A STORY ABOUT THE SKY WARRIORS!
YOU CAN FORGET ABOUT THE SKY WARRIORS. THEY'RE NOT HERE NOW, ARE THEY? NO ONE IS.
NO ONE CAN HELP US.
"FINALLY WE FOUND SOME SHELTER IN A LOG PILE. IT WAS PRETTY DRAFTY, BUT IT LET US STOP AND REST."
"AND WE ALL GOT EXCITED WHEN OUR FATHER SHOWED UP."
"THOUGH I GUESS WE SHOULD'VE KNOWN BETTER."
CINDERS.
WELL. LOOK WHO FINALLY SHOWS HIS FACE. AND FOODLESS AGAIN, NOT THAT I'M SURPRISED.

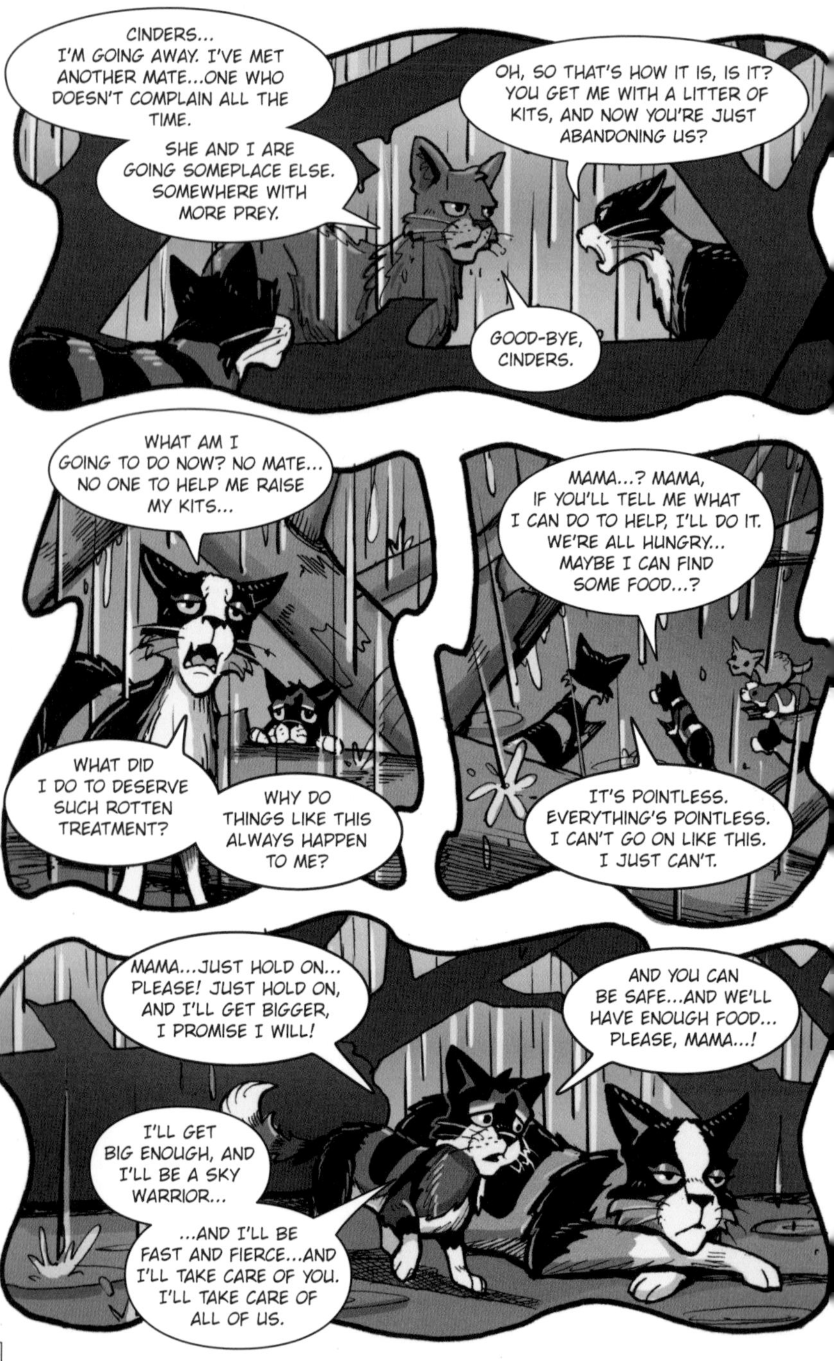
CINDERS... I'M GOING AWAY. I'VE MET ANOTHER MATE...ONE WHO DOESN'T COMPLAIN ALL THE TIME.
SHE AND I ARE GOING SOMEPLACE ELSE. SOMEWHERE WITH MORE PREY.
OH, SO THAT'S HOW IT IS, IS IT? YOU GET ME WITH A LITTER OF KITS, AND NOW YOU'RE JUST ABANDONING US?
GOOD-BYE, CINDERS.
WHAT AM I GOING TO DO NOW? NO MATE... NO ONE TO HELP ME RAISE MY KITS...
WHAT DID I DO TO DESERVE SUCH ROTTEN TREATMENT?
WHY DO THINGS LIKE THIS ALWAYS HAPPEN TO ME?
MAMA...? MAMA, IF YOU'LL TELL ME WHAT I CAN DO TO HELP, I'LL DO IT. WE'RE ALL HUNGRY... MAYBE I CAN FIND SOME FOOD...?
IT'S POINTLESS. EVERYTHING'S POINTLESS. I CAN'T GO ON LIKE THIS. I JUST CAN'T.
MAMA...JUST HOLD ON... PLEASE! JUST HOLD ON, AND I'LL GET BIGGER, I PROMISE I WILL!
AND YOU CAN BE SAFE...AND WE'LL HAVE ENOUGH FOOD... PLEASE, MAMA...!
I'LL GET BIG ENOUGH, AND I'LL BE A SKY WARRIOR...
...AND I'LL BE FAST AND FIERCE...AND I'LL TAKE CARE OF YOU. I'LL TAKE CARE OF ALL OF US.

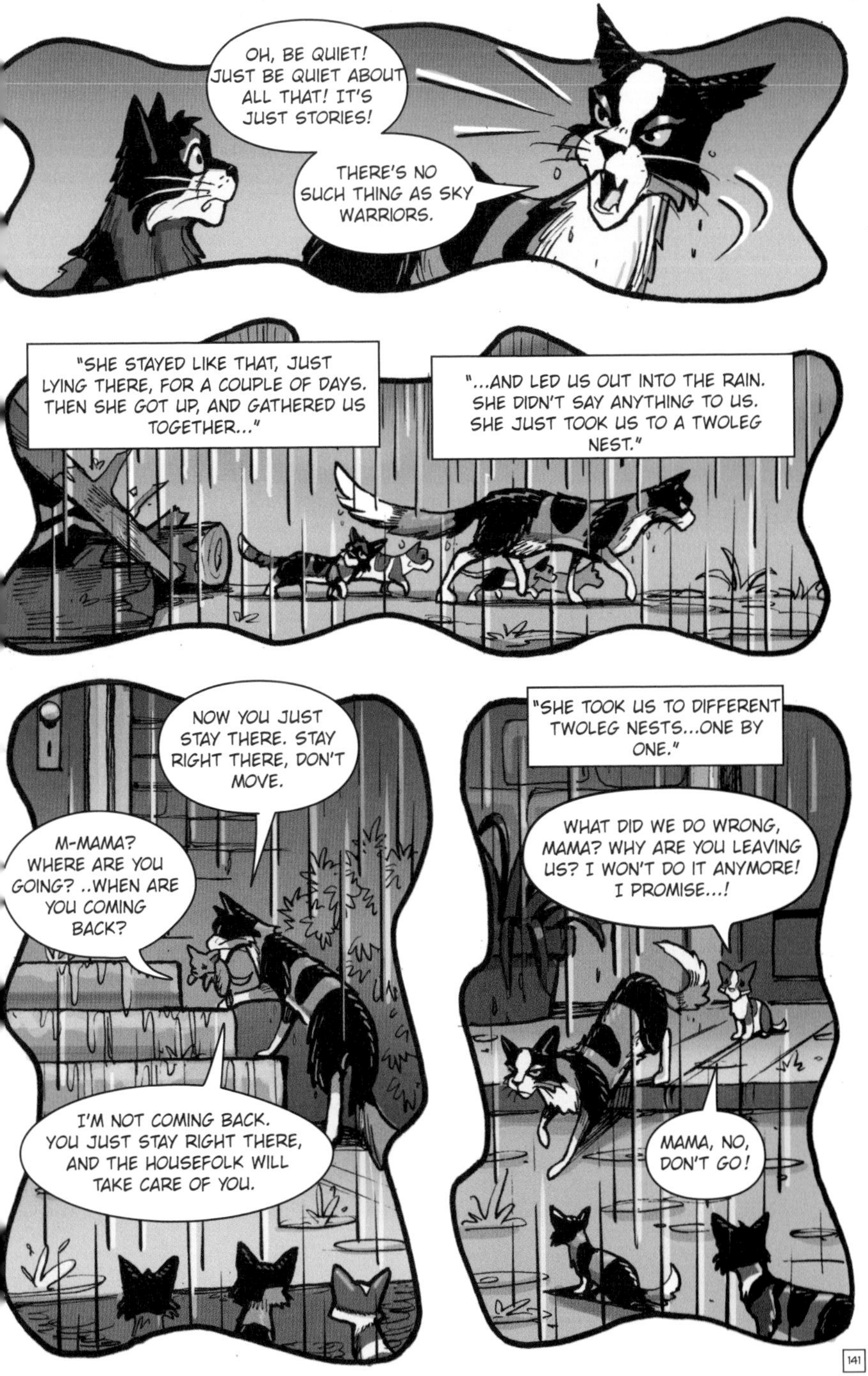

OH, BE QUIET! JUST BE QUIET ABOUT ALL THAT! IT'S JUST STORIES!
THERE'S NO SUCH THING AS SKY WARRIORS.
"SHE STAYED LIKE THAT, JUST LYING THERE, FOR A COUPLE OF DAYS. THEN SHE GOT UP, AND GATHERED US TOGETHER..."
"...AND LED US OUT INTO THE RAIN. SHE DIDN'T SAY ANYTHING TO US. SHE JUST TOOK US TO A TWOLEG NEST."
NOW YOU JUST STAY THERE. STAY RIGHT THERE, DON'T MOVE.
M-MAMA? WHERE ARE YOU GOING? ..WHEN ARE YOU COMING BACK?
I'M NOT COMING BACK. YOU JUST STAY RIGHT THERE, AND THE HOUSEFOLK WILL TAKE CARE OF YOU.
"SHE TOOK US TO DIFFERENT TWOLEG NESTS...ONE BY ONE."
WHAT DID WE DO WRONG, MAMA? WHY ARE YOU LEAVING US? I WON'T DO IT ANYMORE! I PROMISE...!
MAMA, NO, DON'T GO!

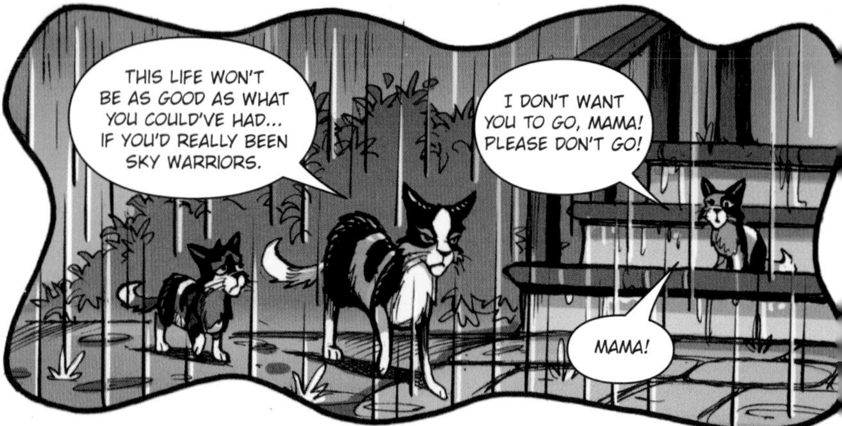
THIS LIFE WON'T BE AS GOOD AS WHAT YOU COULD'VE HAD... IF YOU'D REALLY BEEN SKY WARRIORS.
I DON'T WANT YOU TO GO, MAMA! PLEASE DON'T GO!
MAMA!

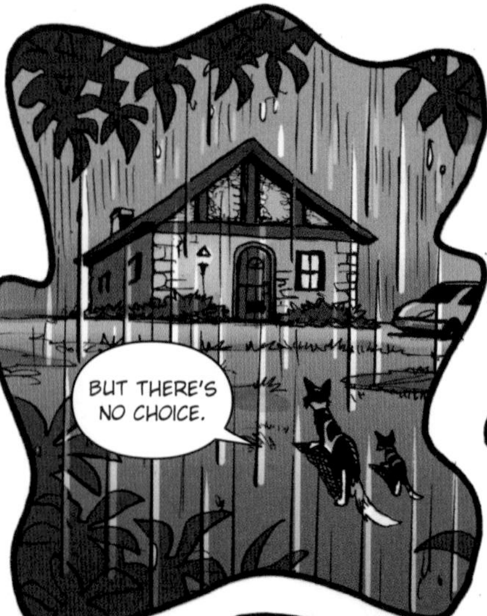
BUT THERE'S NO CHOICE.

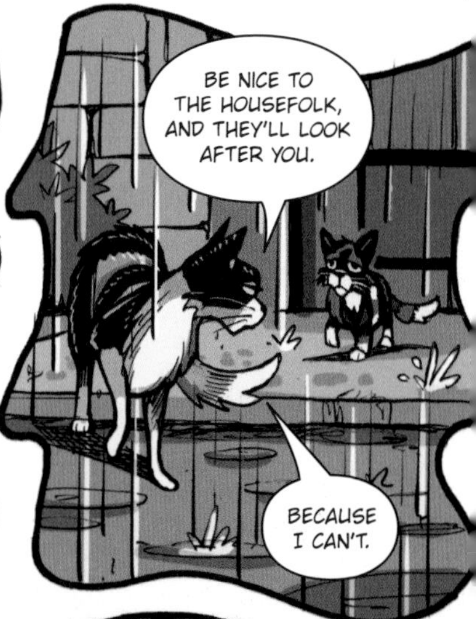
BE NICE TO THE HOUSEFOLK, AND THEY'LL LOOK AFTER YOU.
BECAUSE I CAN'T.

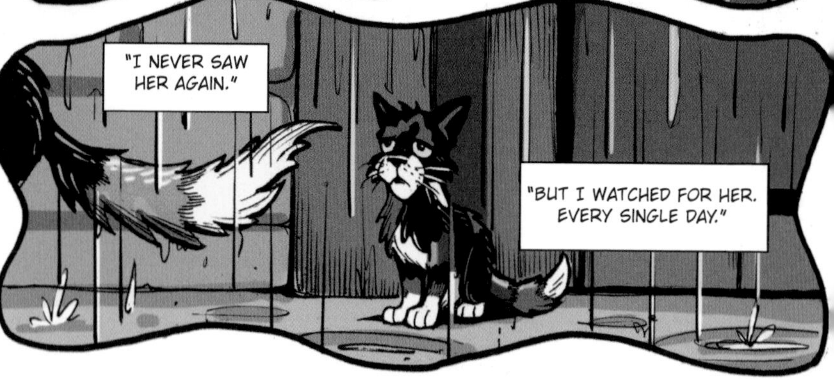
"I NEVER SAW HER AGAIN."
"BUT I WATCHED FOR HER. EVERY SINGLE DAY."

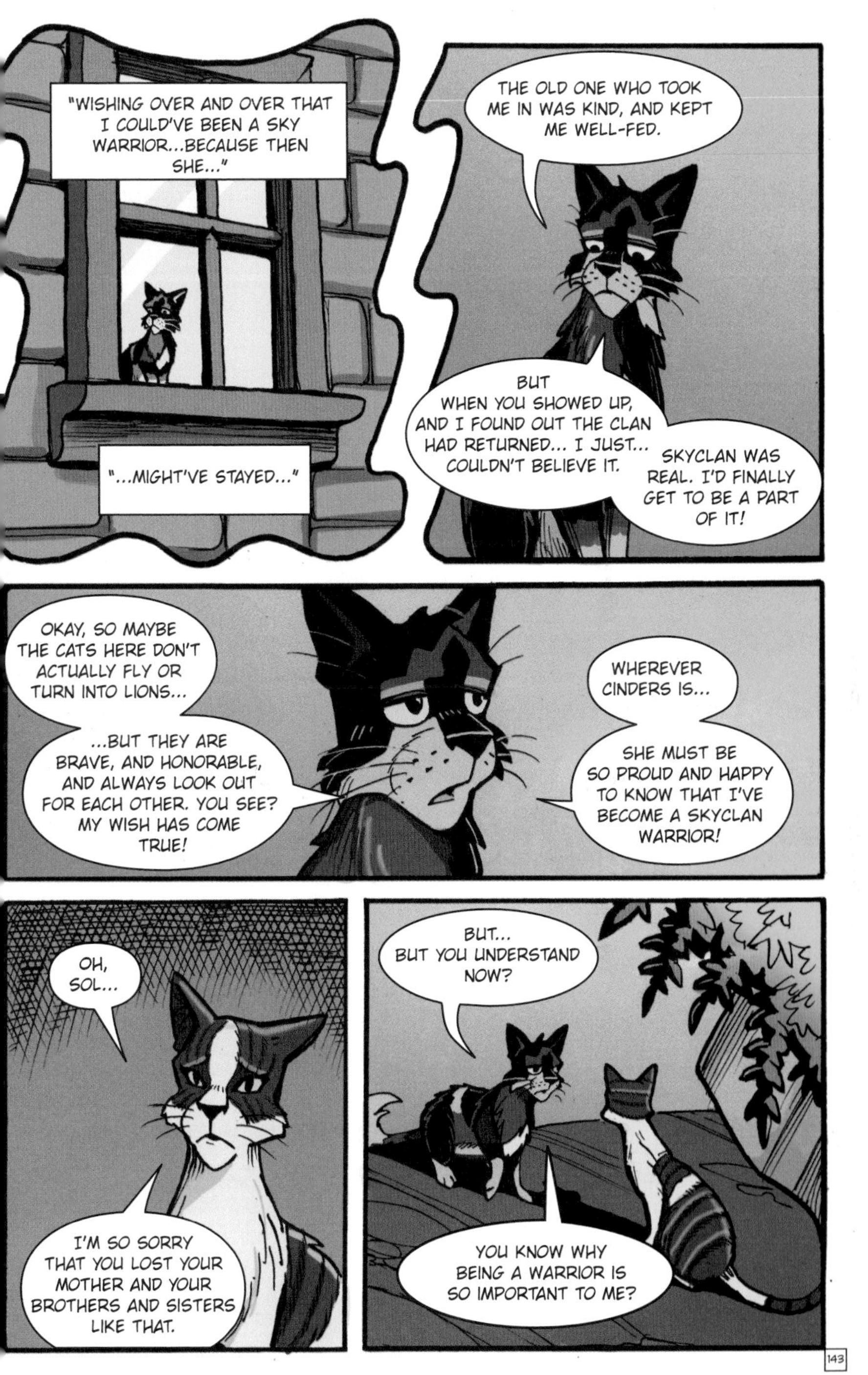
"WISHING OVER AND OVER THAT I COULD'VE BEEN A SKY WARRIOR...BECAUSE THEN SHE..."
"...MIGHT'VE STAYED..."
THE OLD ONE WHO TOOK ME IN WAS KIND, AND KEPT ME WELL-FED.
BUT WHEN YOU SHOWED UP, AND I FOUND OUT THE CLAN HAD RETURNED... I JUST... COULDN'T BELIEVE IT.
SKYCLAN WAS REAL. I'D FINALLY GET TO BE A PART OF IT!
OKAY, SO MAYBE THE CATS HERE DON'T ACTUALLY FLY OR TURN INTO LIONS...
...BUT THEY ARE BRAVE, AND HONORABLE, AND ALWAYS LOOK OUT FOR EACH OTHER. YOU SEE? MY WISH HAS COME TRUE!
WHEREVER CINDERS IS...
SHE MUST BE SO PROUD AND HAPPY TO KNOW THAT I'VE BECOME A SKYCLAN WARRIOR!
OH, SOL...
I'M SO SORRY THAT YOU LOST YOUR MOTHER AND YOUR BROTHERS AND SISTERS LIKE THAT.
BUT... BUT YOU UNDERSTAND NOW?
YOU KNOW WHY BEING A WARRIOR IS SO IMPORTANT TO ME?

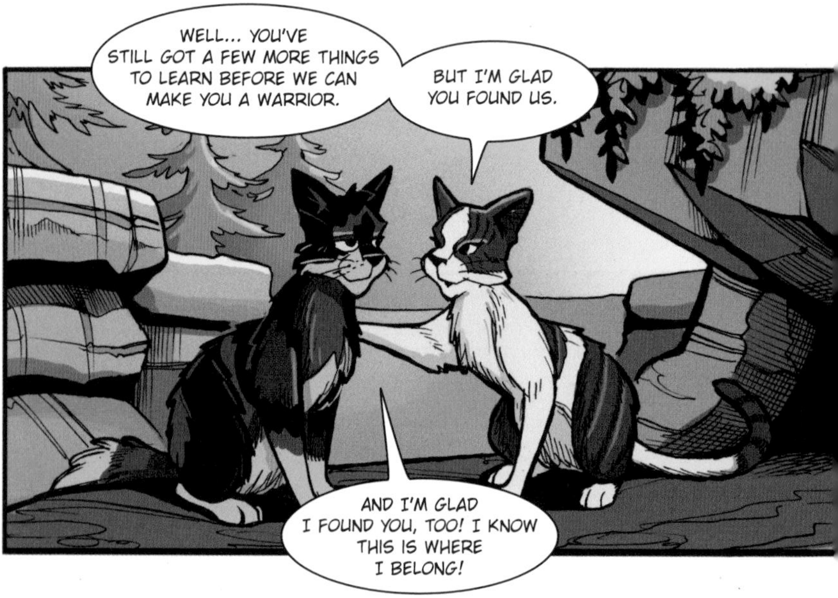
WELL... YOU'VE STILL GOT A FEW MORE THINGS TO LEARN BEFORE WE CAN MAKE YOU A WARRIOR.
BUT I'M GLAD YOU FOUND US.
AND I'M GLAD I FOUND YOU, TOO! I KNOW THIS IS WHERE I BELONG!

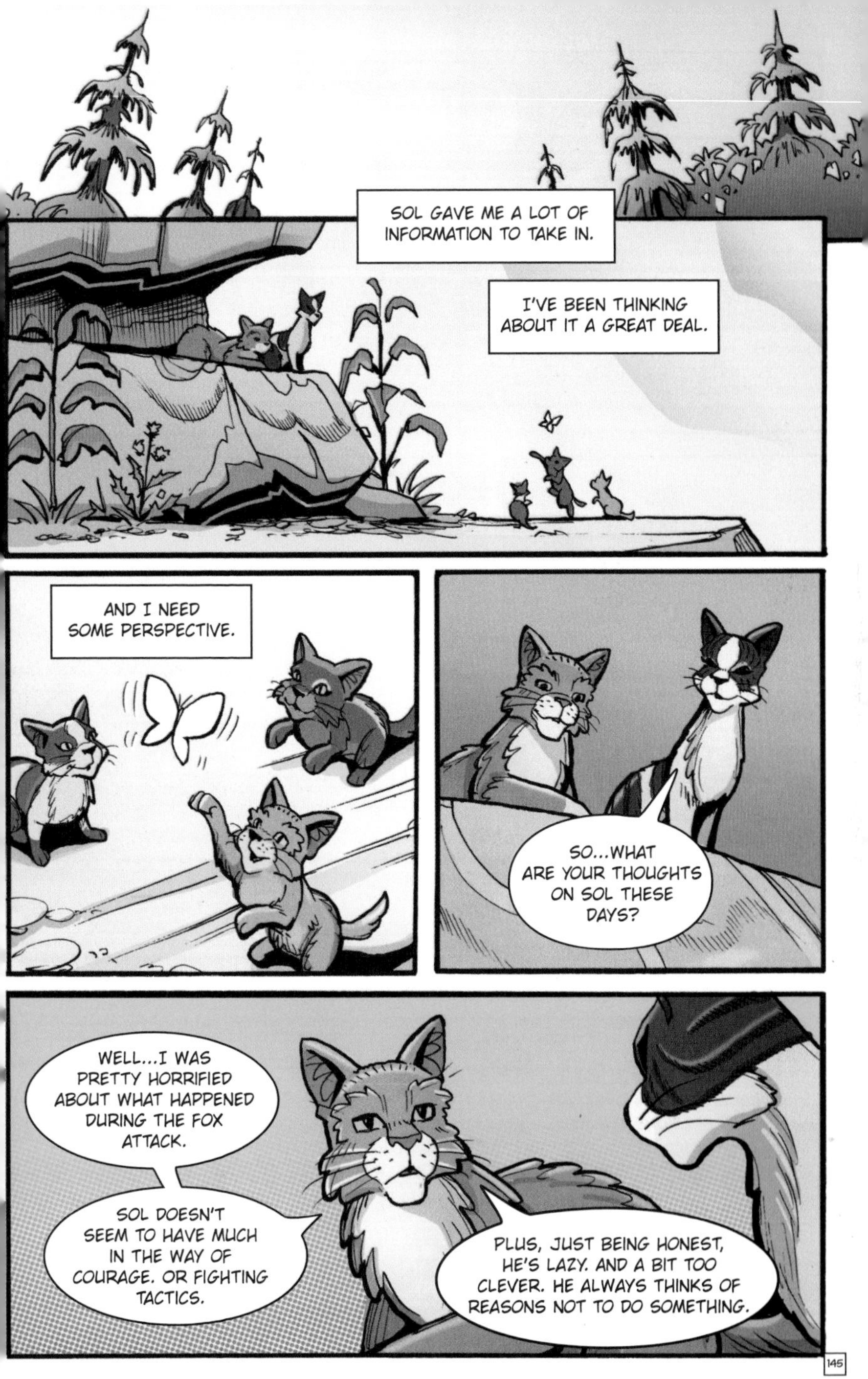
SOL GAVE ME A LOT OF INFORMATION TO TAKE IN.
I'VE BEEN THINKING ABOUT IT A GREAT DEAL.
AND I NEED SOME PERSPECTIVE.
SO...WHAT ARE YOUR THOUGHTS ON SOL THESE DAYS?
WELL...I WAS PRETTY HORRIFIED ABOUT WHAT HAPPENED DURING THE FOX ATTACK.
SOL DOESN'T SEEM TO HAVE MUCH IN THE WAY OF COURAGE. OR FIGHTING TACTICS.
PLUS, JUST BEING HONEST, HE'S LAZY. AND A BIT TOO CLEVER. HE ALWAYS THINKS OF REASONS NOT TO DO SOMETHING.

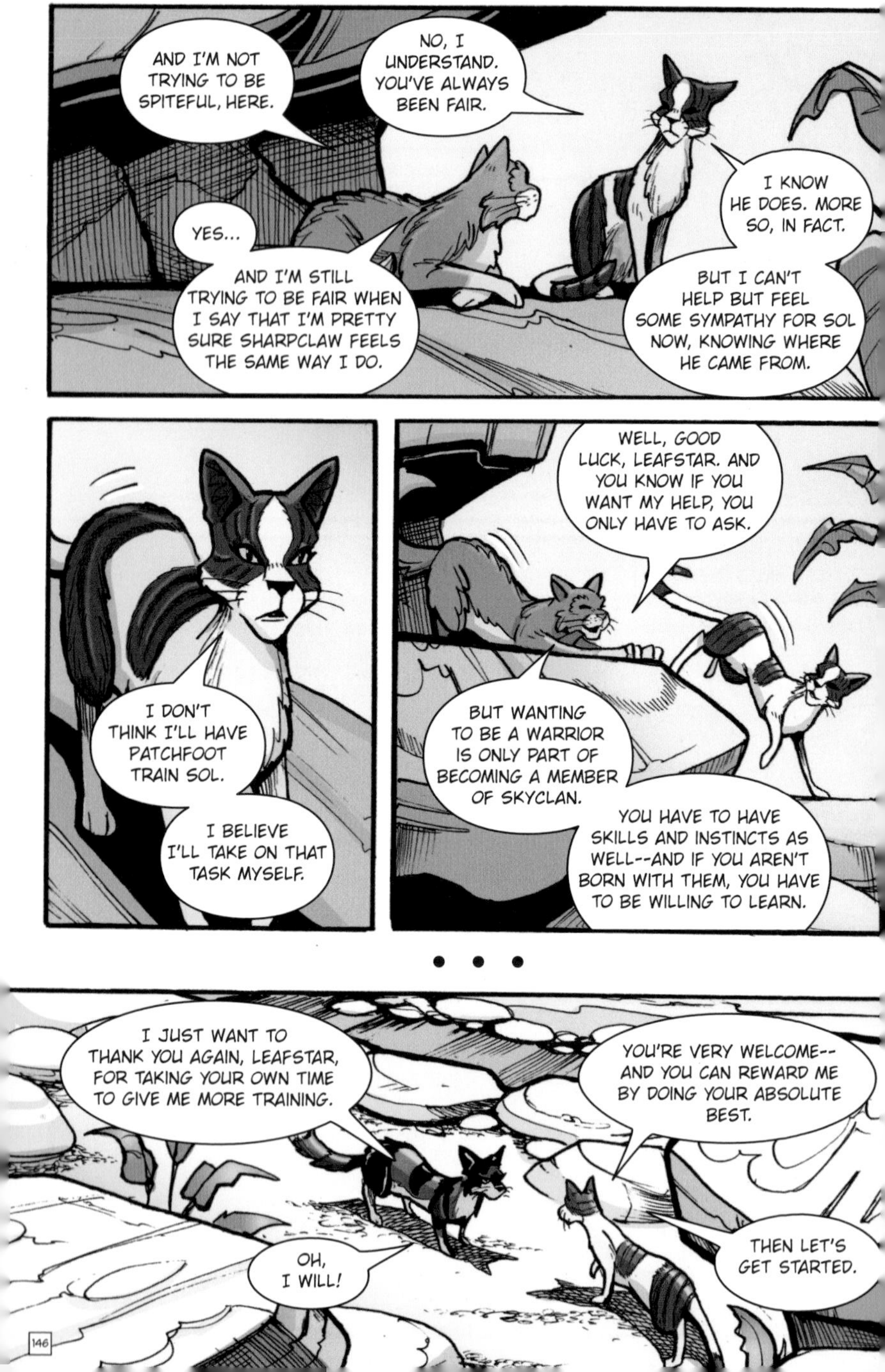
AND I'M NOT TRYING TO BE SPITEFUL, HERE.
NO, I UNDERSTAND. YOU'VE ALWAYS BEEN FAIR.
YES...
AND I'M STILL TRYING TO BE FAIR WHEN I SAY THAT I'M PRETTY SURE SHARPCLAW FEELS THE SAME WAY I DO.
I KNOW HE DOES. MORE SO, IN FACT.
BUT I CAN'T HELP BUT FEEL SOME SYMPATHY FOR SOL NOW, KNOWING WHERE HE CAME FROM.
I DON'T THINK I'LL HAVE PATCHFOOT TRAIN SOL.
I BELIEVE I'LL TAKE ON THAT TASK MYSELF.
WELL, GOOD LUCK, LEAFSTAR. AND YOU KNOW IF YOU WANT MY HELP, YOU ONLY HAVE TO ASK.
BUT WANTING TO BE A WARRIOR IS ONLY PART OF BECOMING A MEMBER OF SKYCLAN.
YOU HAVE TO HAVE SKILLS AND INSTINCTS AS WELL--AND IF YOU AREN'T BORN WITH THEM, YOU HAVE TO BE WILLING TO LEARN.
I JUST WANT TO THANK YOU AGAIN, LEAFSTAR, FOR TAKING YOUR OWN TIME TO GIVE ME MORE TRAINING.
YOU'RE VERY WELCOME--AND YOU CAN REWARD ME BY DOING YOUR ABSOLUTE BEST.
OH, I WILL!
THEN LET'S GET STARTED.

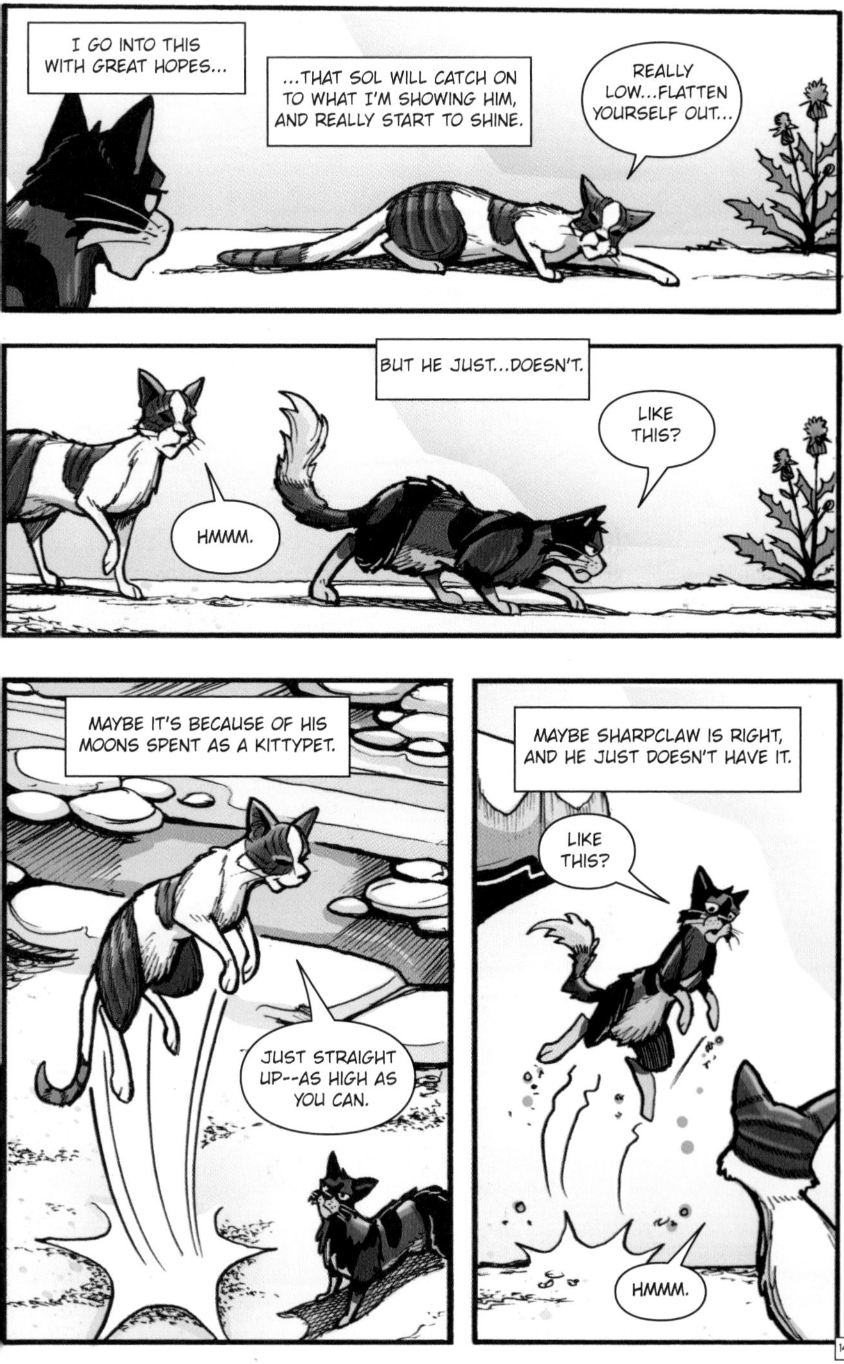
I GO INTO THIS WITH GREAT HOPES...
...THAT SOL WILL CATCH ON TO WHAT I'M SHOWING HIM, AND REALLY START TO SHINE.
REALLY LOW...FLATTEN YOURSELF OUT...
BUT HE JUST...DOESN'T.
HMMM.
LIKE THIS?
MAYBE IT'S BECAUSE OF HIS MOONS SPENT AS A KITTYPET.
JUST STRAIGHT UP--AS HIGH AS YOU CAN.
MAYBE SHARPCLAW IS RIGHT, AND HE JUST DOESN'T HAVE IT.
LIKE THIS?
HMMM.

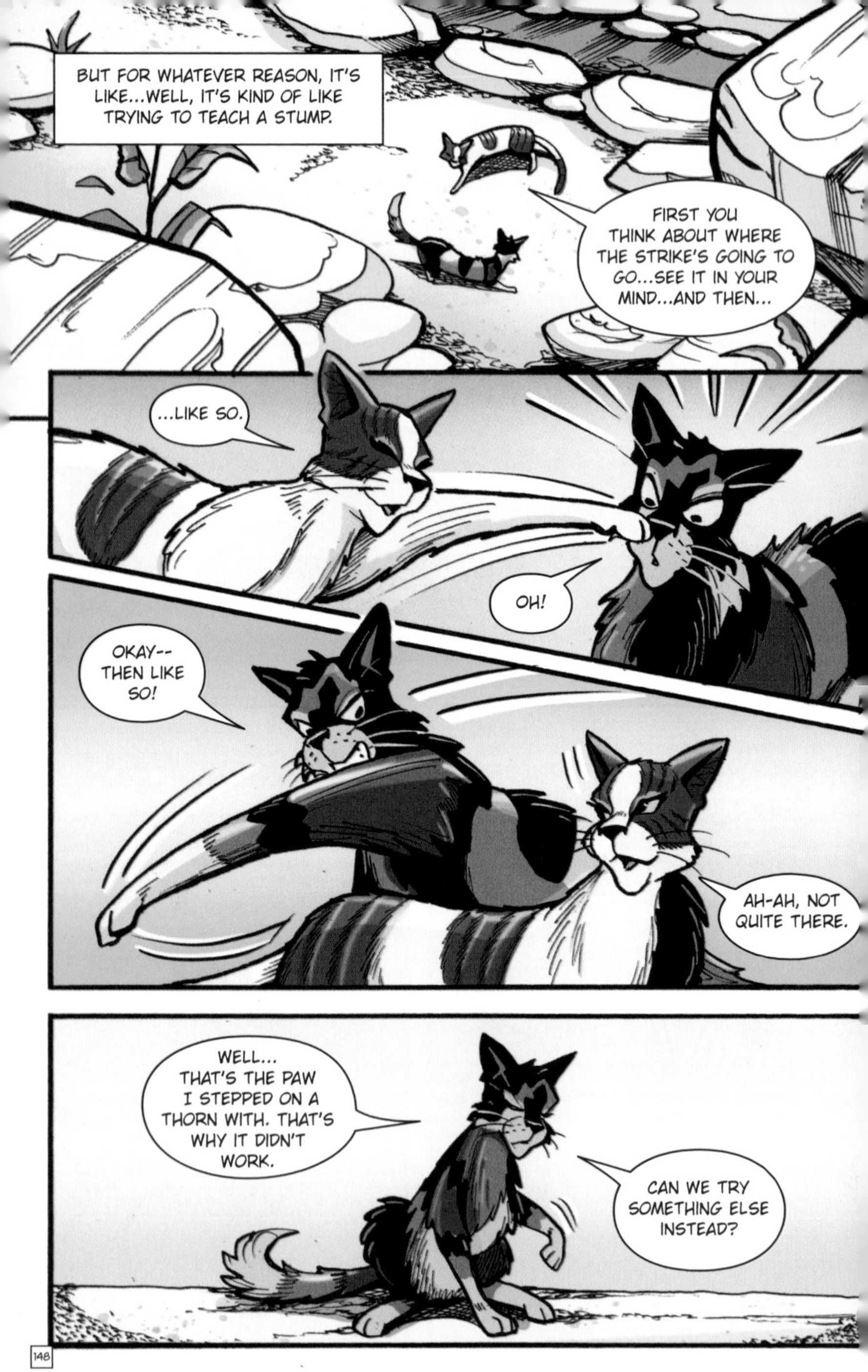
BUT FOR WHATEVER REASON, IT'S LIKE...WELL, IT'S KIND OF LIKE TRYING TO TEACH A STUMP.
FIRST YOU THINK ABOUT WHERE THE STRIKE'S GOING TO GO...SEE IT IN YOUR MIND...AND THEN...
...LIKE SO.
OH!
OKAY--THEN LIKE SO!
AH-AH, NOT QUITE THERE.
WELL... THAT'S THE PAW I STEPPED ON A THORN WITH. THAT'S WHY IT DIDN'T WORK.
CAN WE TRY SOMETHING ELSE INSTEAD?

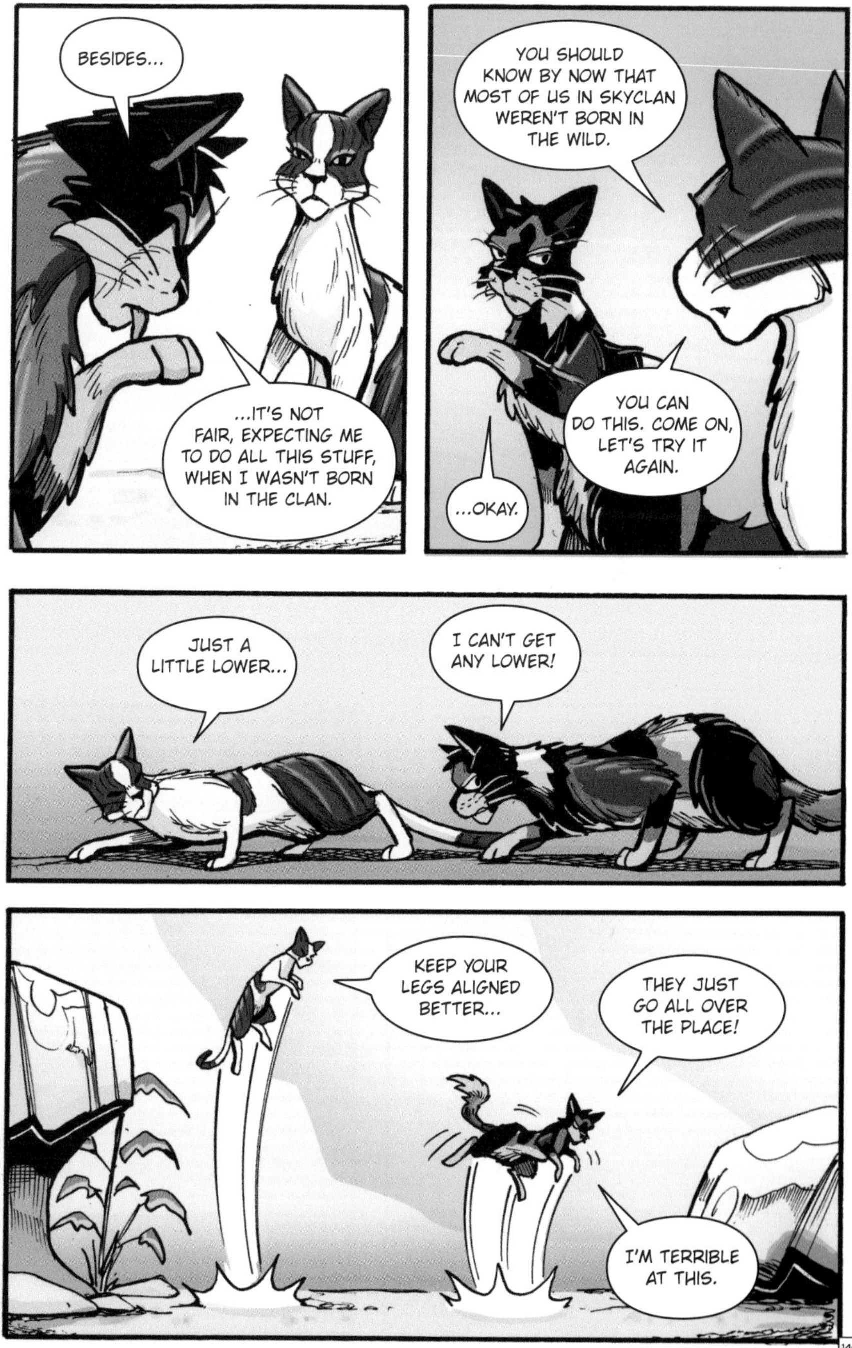
BESIDES...
...IT'S NOT FAIR, EXPECTING ME TO DO ALL THIS STUFF, WHEN I WASN'T BORN IN THE CLAN.
YOU SHOULD KNOW BY NOW THAT MOST OF US IN SKYCLAN WEREN'T BORN IN THE WILD.
YOU CAN DO THIS. COME ON, LET'S TRY IT AGAIN.
...OKAY.
JUST A LITTLE LOWER...
I CAN'T GET ANY LOWER!
KEEP YOUR LEGS ALIGNED BETTER...
THEY JUST GO ALL OVER THE PLACE!
I'M TERRIBLE AT THIS.

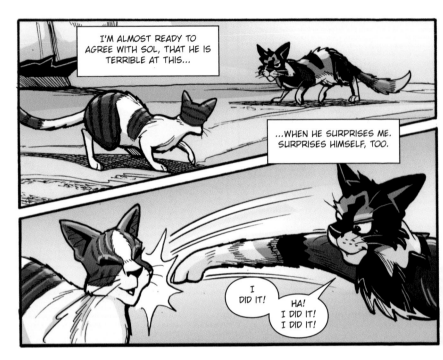

I'M ALMOST READY TO AGREE WITH SOL, THAT HE IS TERRIBLE AT THIS...

...WHEN HE SURPRISES ME. SURPRISES HIMSELF, TOO.

I DID IT!

HA! I DID IT! I DID IT!

A LITTLE BIT OF SUCCESS PROVES TO BE A TURNING POINT OF SORTS FOR SOL. WE START IN ON EVASION TECHNIQUES...

...AND HE DOESN'T DO HALF BAD.

THEN WE TRY THE SAME THING I TAUGHT MY KITS...

SNEAKING UP ON SOMETHING SOUNDLESSLY...

...AND AGAIN, HE'S SURPRISINGLY DECENT AT IT.

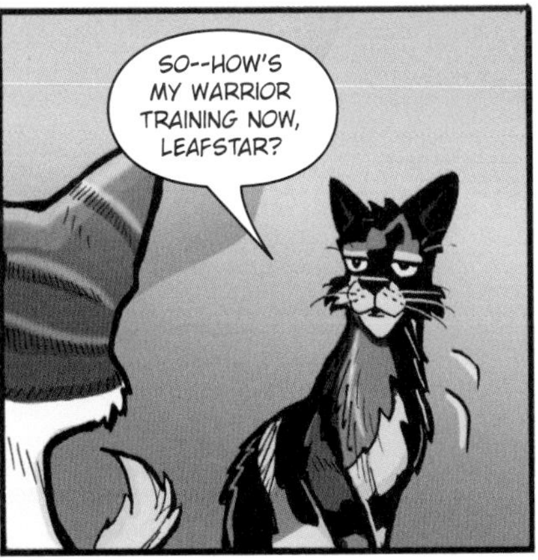
SO--HOW'S MY WARRIOR TRAINING NOW, LEAFSTAR?

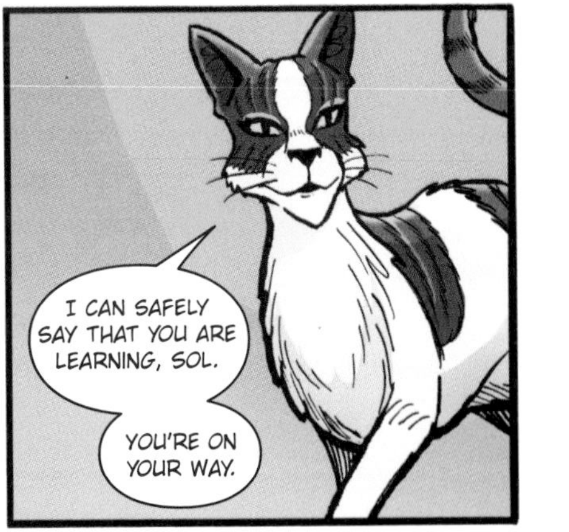
I CAN SAFELY SAY THAT YOU ARE LEARNING, SOL.
YOU'RE ON YOUR WAY.

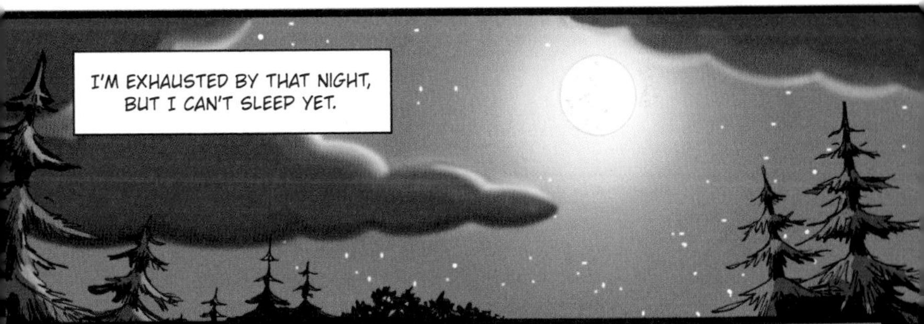
I'M EXHAUSTED BY THAT NIGHT, BUT I CAN'T SLEEP YET.

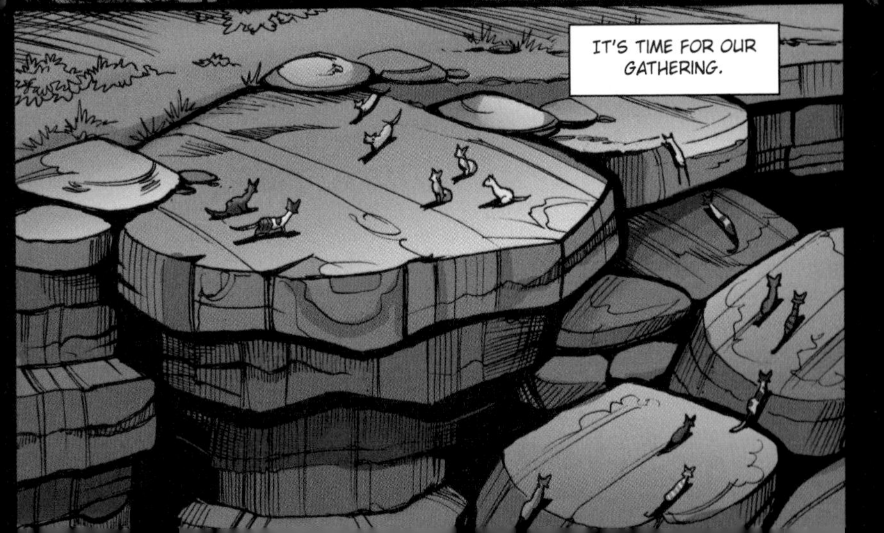
IT'S TIME FOR OUR GATHERING.

A LOT HAS HAPPENED SINCE OUR LAST ONE.

BUT I'M HOPING TO KEEP THINGS FOCUSED ON MOVING FORWARD TONIGHT...

...RATHER THAN LOOKING BACK.

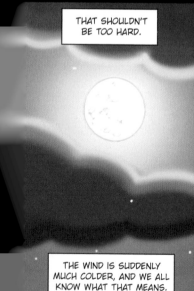

THAT SHOULDN'T BE TOO HARD.

THE WIND IS SUDDENLY MUCH COLDER, AND WE ALL KNOW WHAT THAT MEANS.

⋛ SNFF SNFF ⋚ RAIN'S ON THE WAY.

GOOD.

WE COULD SURE USE SOME!

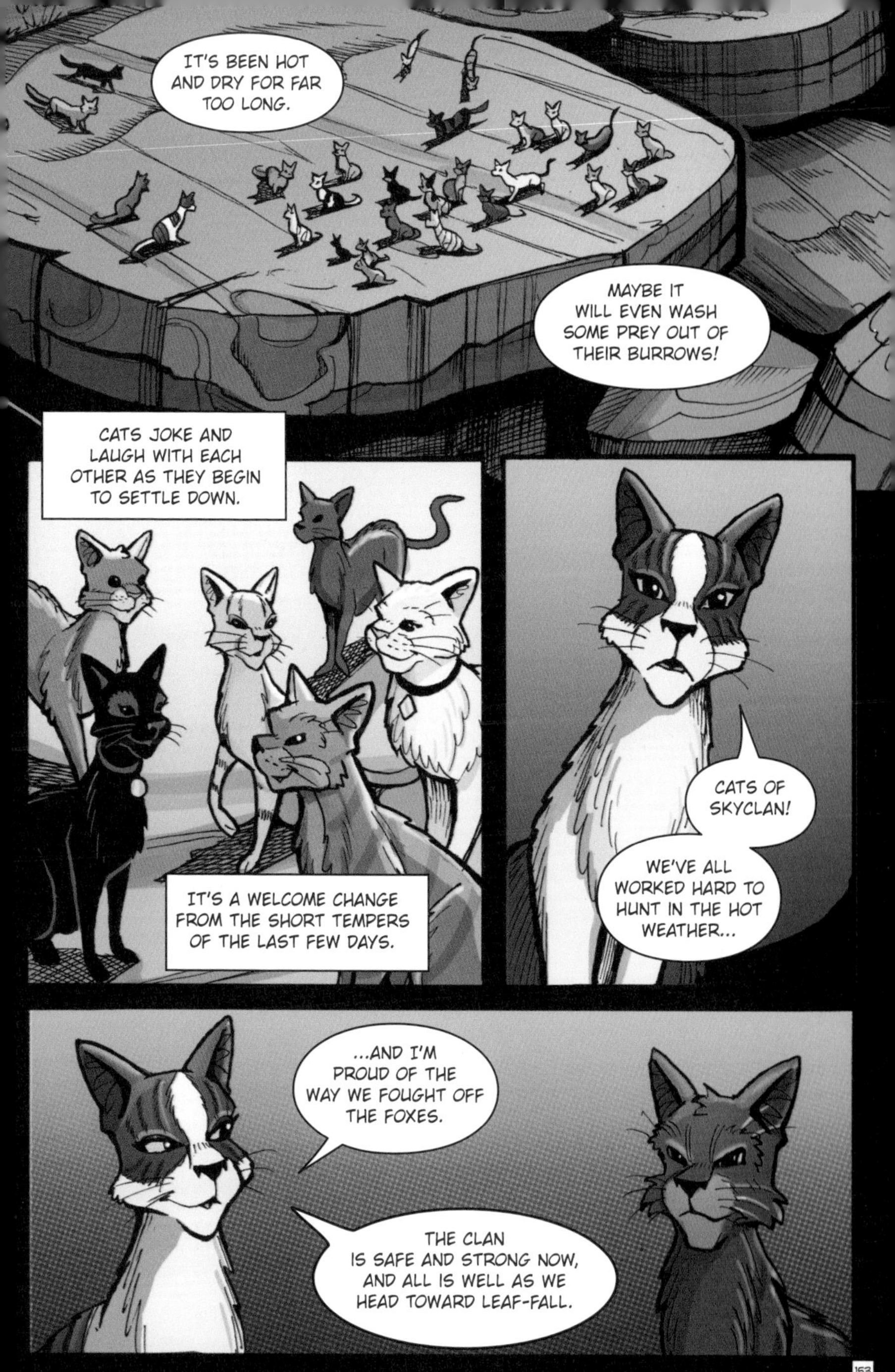
IT'S BEEN HOT AND DRY FOR FAR TOO LONG.
MAYBE IT WILL EVEN WASH SOME PREY OUT OF THEIR BURROWS!
CATS JOKE AND LAUGH WITH EACH OTHER AS THEY BEGIN TO SETTLE DOWN.
IT'S A WELCOME CHANGE FROM THE SHORT TEMPERS OF THE LAST FEW DAYS.
CATS OF SKYCLAN!
WE'VE ALL WORKED HARD TO HUNT IN THE HOT WEATHER...
...AND I'M PROUD OF THE WAY WE FOUGHT OFF THE FOXES.
THE CLAN IS SAFE AND STRONG NOW, AND ALL IS WELL AS WE HEAD TOWARD LEAF-FALL.

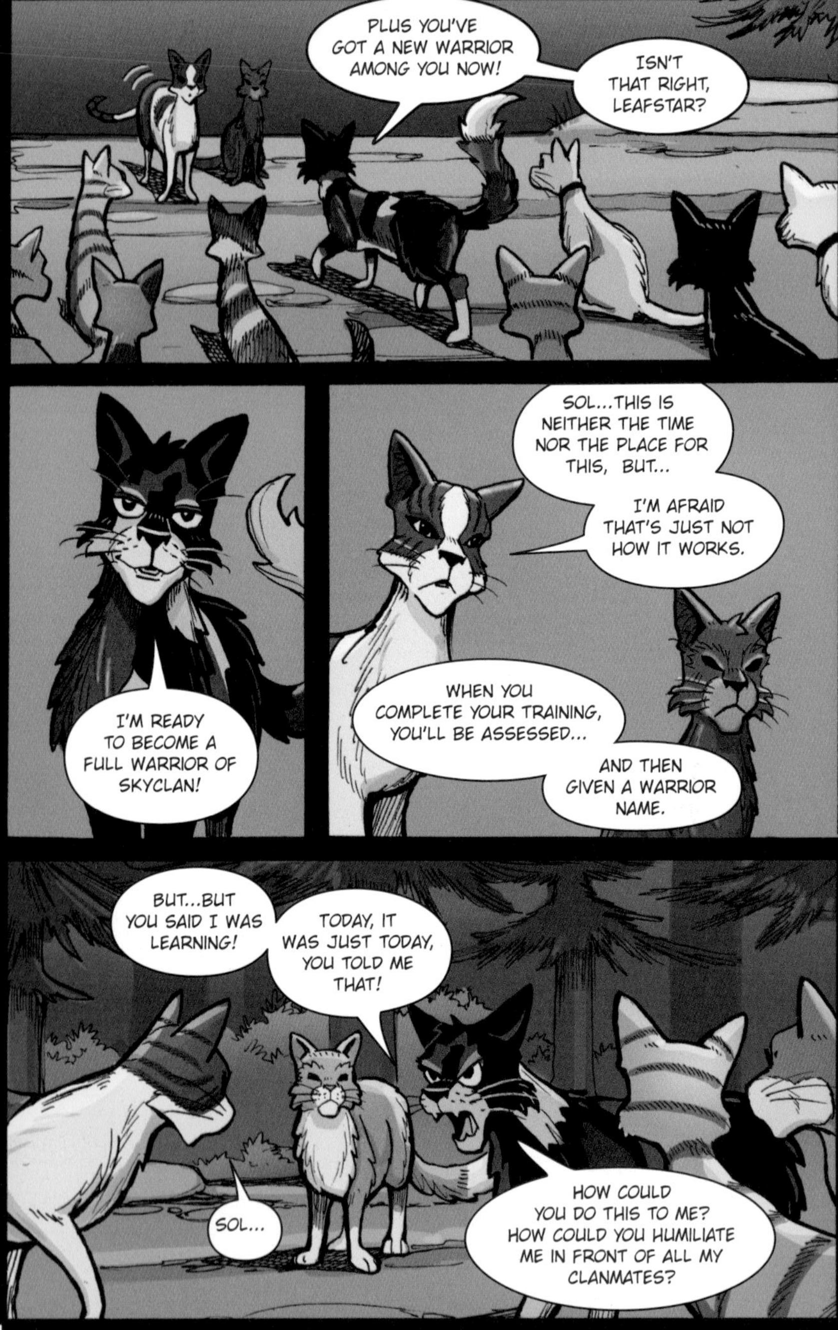
PLUS YOU'VE GOT A NEW WARRIOR AMONG YOU NOW!
ISN'T THAT RIGHT, LEAFSTAR?
I'M READY TO BECOME A FULL WARRIOR OF SKYCLAN!
SOL...THIS IS NEITHER THE TIME NOR THE PLACE FOR THIS, BUT...
I'M AFRAID THAT'S JUST NOT HOW IT WORKS.
WHEN YOU COMPLETE YOUR TRAINING, YOU'LL BE ASSESSED...
AND THEN GIVEN A WARRIOR NAME.
BUT...BUT YOU SAID I WAS LEARNING!
TODAY, IT WAS JUST TODAY, YOU TOLD ME THAT!
SOL...
HOW COULD YOU DO THIS TO ME? HOW COULD YOU HUMILIATE ME IN FRONT OF ALL MY CLANMATES?

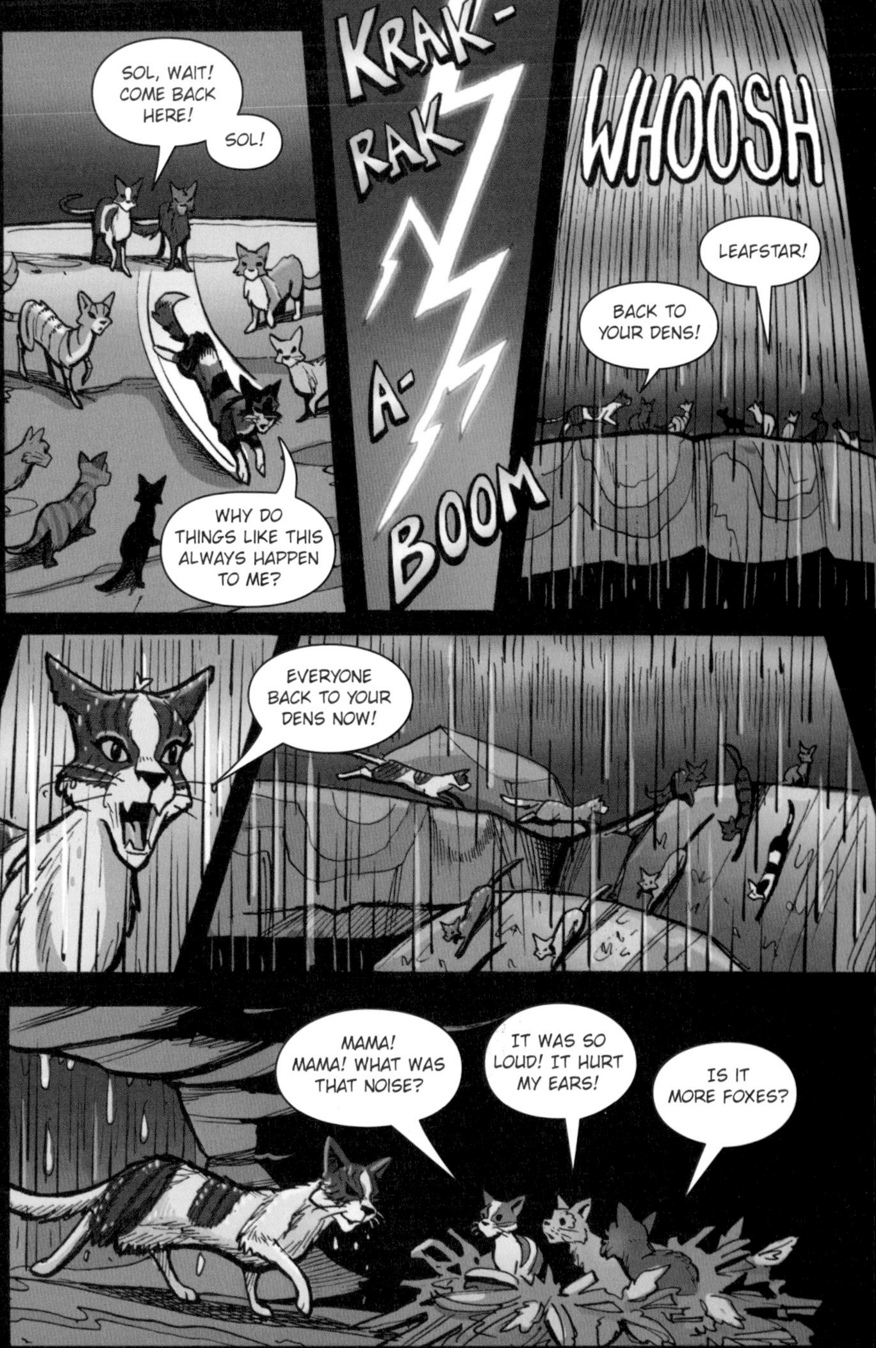
SOL, WAIT! COME BACK HERE!
SOL!
WHY DO THINGS LIKE THIS ALWAYS HAPPEN TO ME?
KRAK-RAK A-BOOM
WHOOSH
LEAFSTAR!
BACK TO YOUR DENS!
EVERYONE BACK TO YOUR DENS NOW!
MAMA! MAMA! WHAT WAS THAT NOISE?
IT WAS SO LOUD! IT HURT MY EARS!
IS IT MORE FOXES?

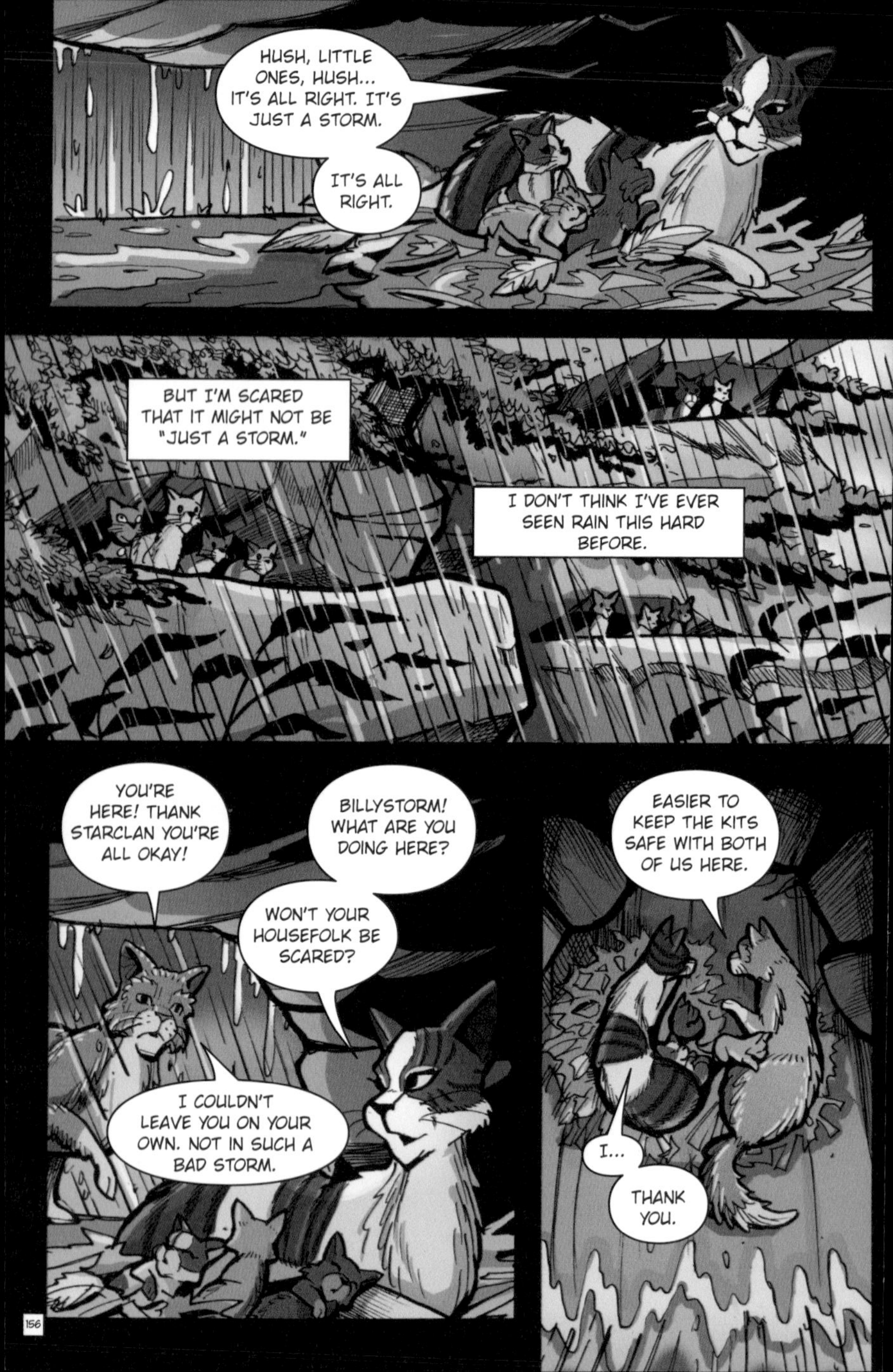
HUSH, LITTLE ONES, HUSH... IT'S ALL RIGHT. IT'S JUST A STORM.
IT'S ALL RIGHT.
BUT I'M SCARED THAT IT MIGHT NOT BE "JUST A STORM."
I DON'T THINK I'VE EVER SEEN RAIN THIS HARD BEFORE.
YOU'RE HERE! THANK STARCLAN YOU'RE ALL OKAY!
BILLYSTORM! WHAT ARE YOU DOING HERE?
WON'T YOUR HOUSEFOLK BE SCARED?
I COULDN'T LEAVE YOU ON YOUR OWN. NOT IN SUCH A BAD STORM.
EASIER TO KEEP THE KITS SAFE WITH BOTH OF US HERE.
I...
THANK YOU.

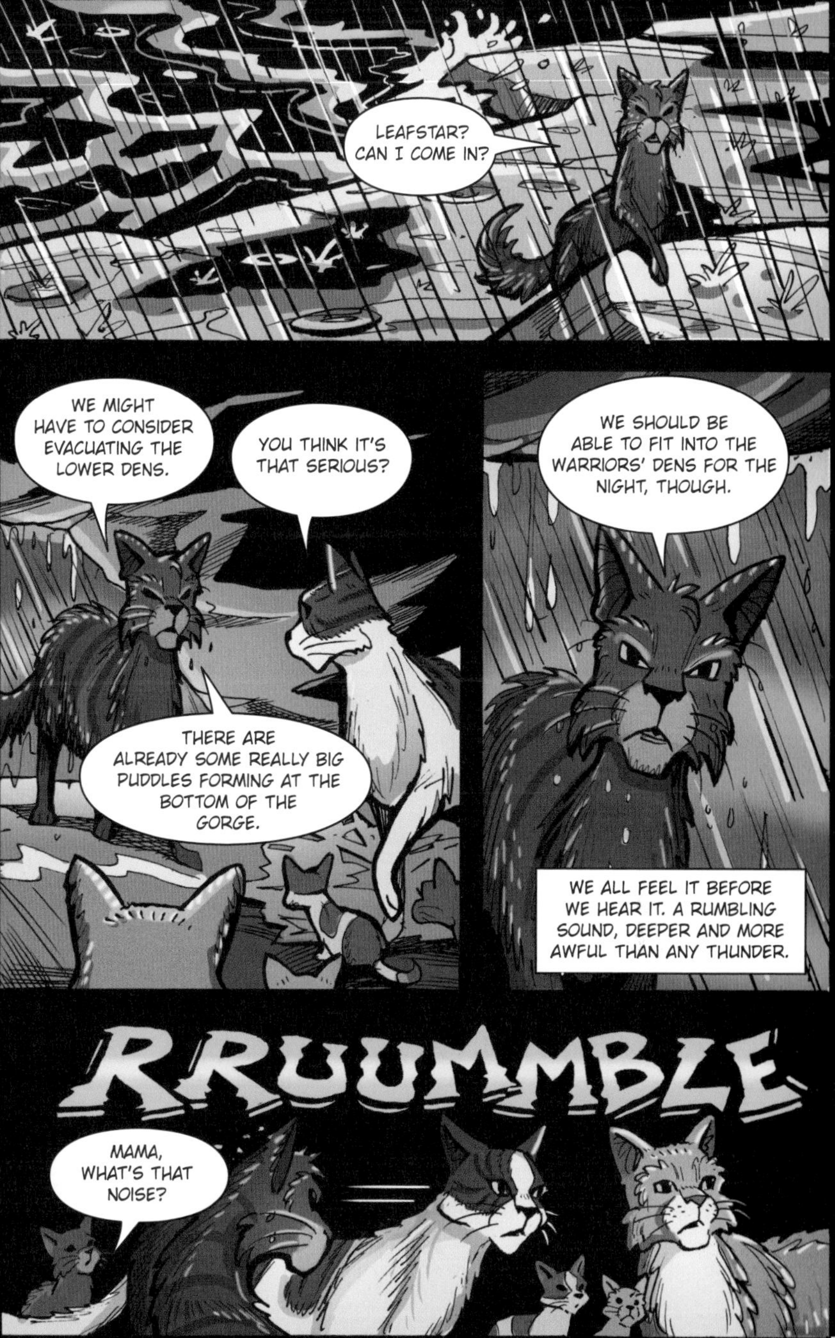
LEAFSTAR? CAN I COME IN?
WE MIGHT HAVE TO CONSIDER EVACUATING THE LOWER DENS.
YOU THINK IT'S THAT SERIOUS?
THERE ARE ALREADY SOME REALLY BIG PUDDLES FORMING AT THE BOTTOM OF THE GORGE.
WE SHOULD BE ABLE TO FIT INTO THE WARRIORS' DENS FOR THE NIGHT, THOUGH.
WE ALL FEEL IT BEFORE WE HEAR IT. A RUMBLING SOUND, DEEPER AND MORE AWFUL THAN ANY THUNDER.
RRUUMMBLE
MAMA, WHAT'S THAT NOISE?

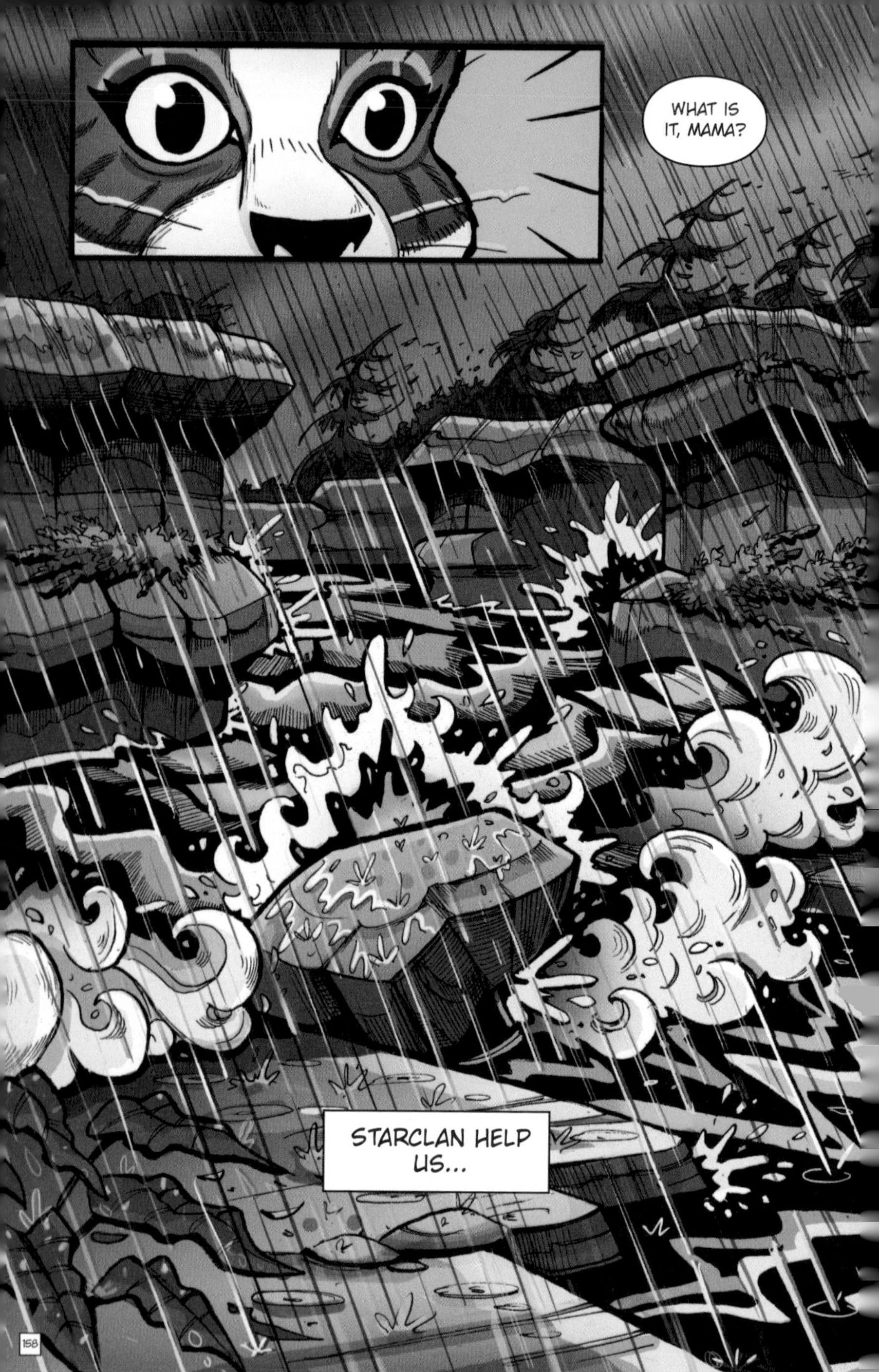
WHAT IS IT, MAMA?
STARCLAN HELP US...

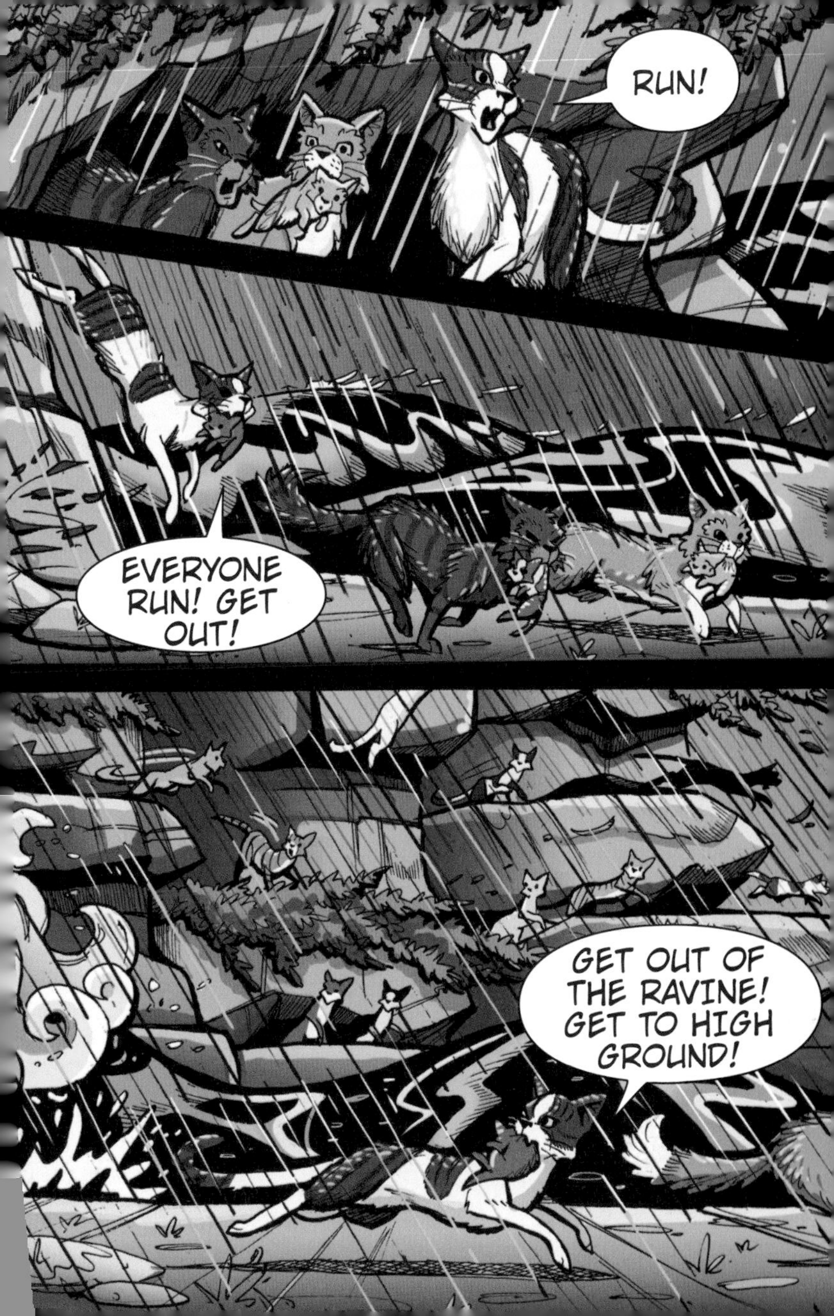
RUN!
EVERYONE RUN! GET OUT!
GET OUT OF THE RAVINE! GET TO HIGH GROUND!

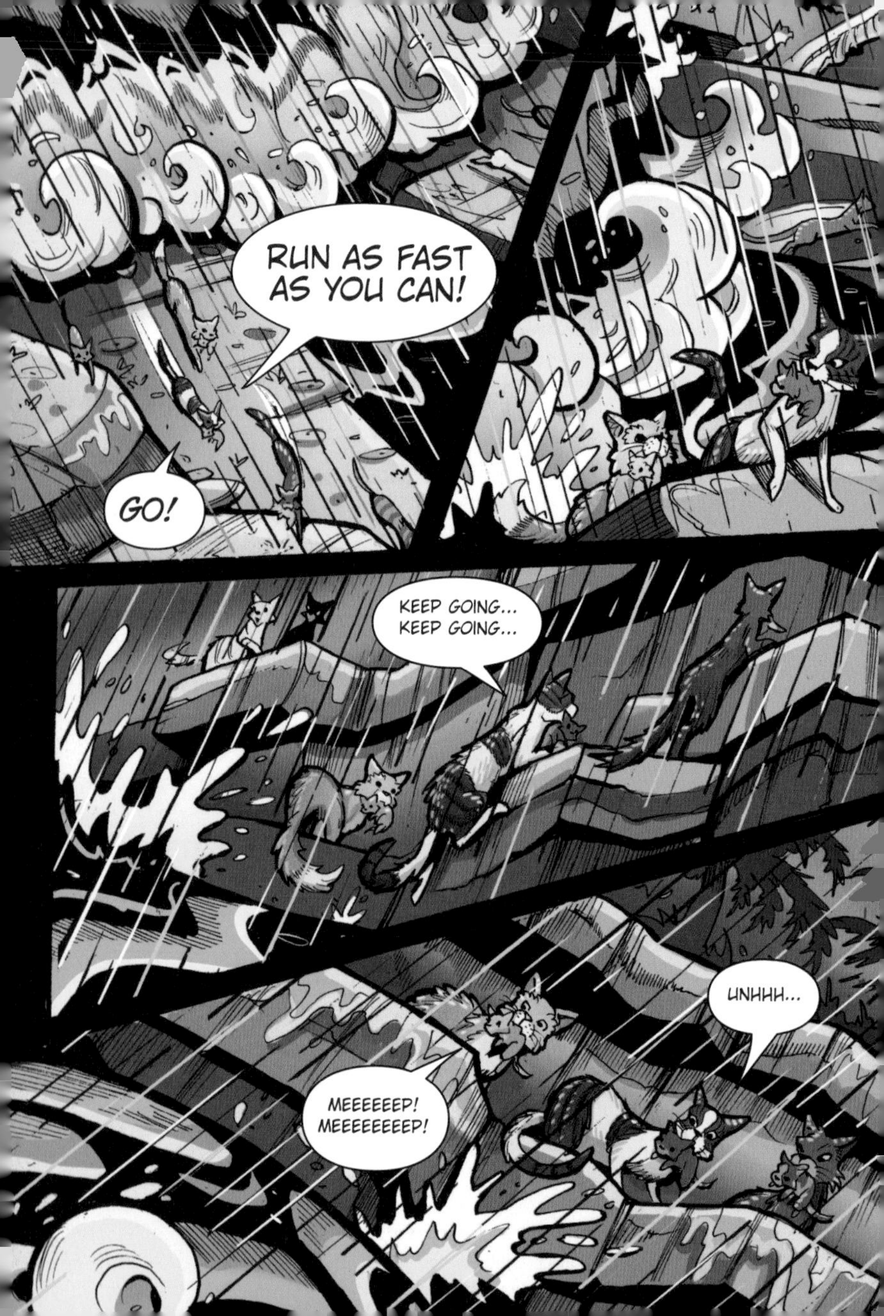
RUN AS FAST AS YOU CAN!
GO!
KEEP GOING... KEEP GOING...
MEEEEEEP! MEEEEEEEEP!
UNHHH...

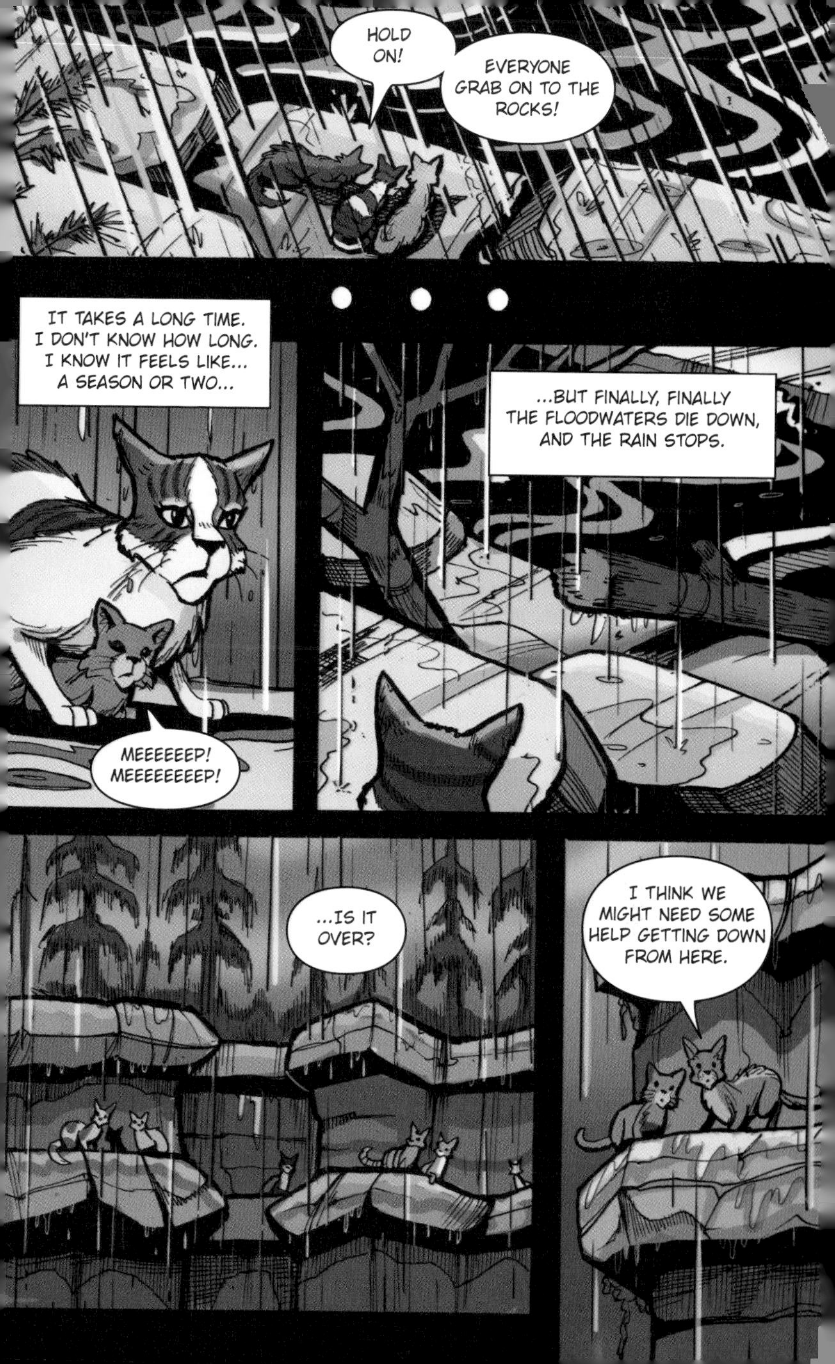
HOLD ON!
EVERYONE GRAB ON TO THE ROCKS!
IT TAKES A LONG TIME. I DON'T KNOW HOW LONG. I KNOW IT FEELS LIKE... A SEASON OR TWO...
MEEEEEEP! MEEEEEEEP!
...BUT FINALLY, FINALLY THE FLOODWATERS DIE DOWN, AND THE RAIN STOPS.
...IS IT OVER?
I THINK WE MIGHT NEED SOME HELP GETTING DOWN FROM HERE.

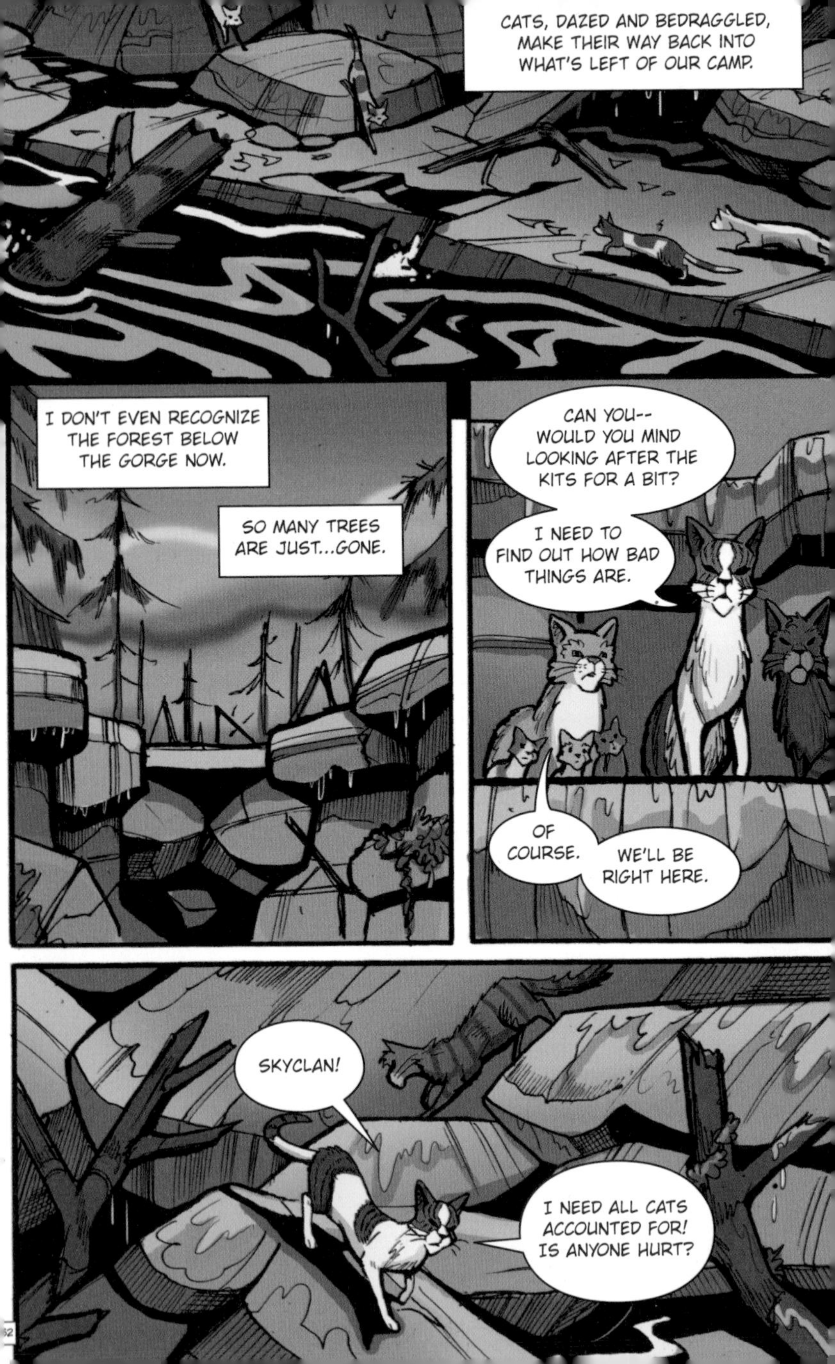

CATS, DAZED AND BEDRAGGLED, MAKE THEIR WAY BACK INTO WHAT'S LEFT OF OUR CAMP.
I DON'T EVEN RECOGNIZE THE FOREST BELOW THE GORGE NOW.
SO MANY TREES ARE JUST...GONE.
CAN YOU-- WOULD YOU MIND LOOKING AFTER THE KITS FOR A BIT?
I NEED TO FIND OUT HOW BAD THINGS ARE.
OF COURSE.
WE'LL BE RIGHT HERE.
SKYCLAN!
I NEED ALL CATS ACCOUNTED FOR! IS ANYONE HURT?

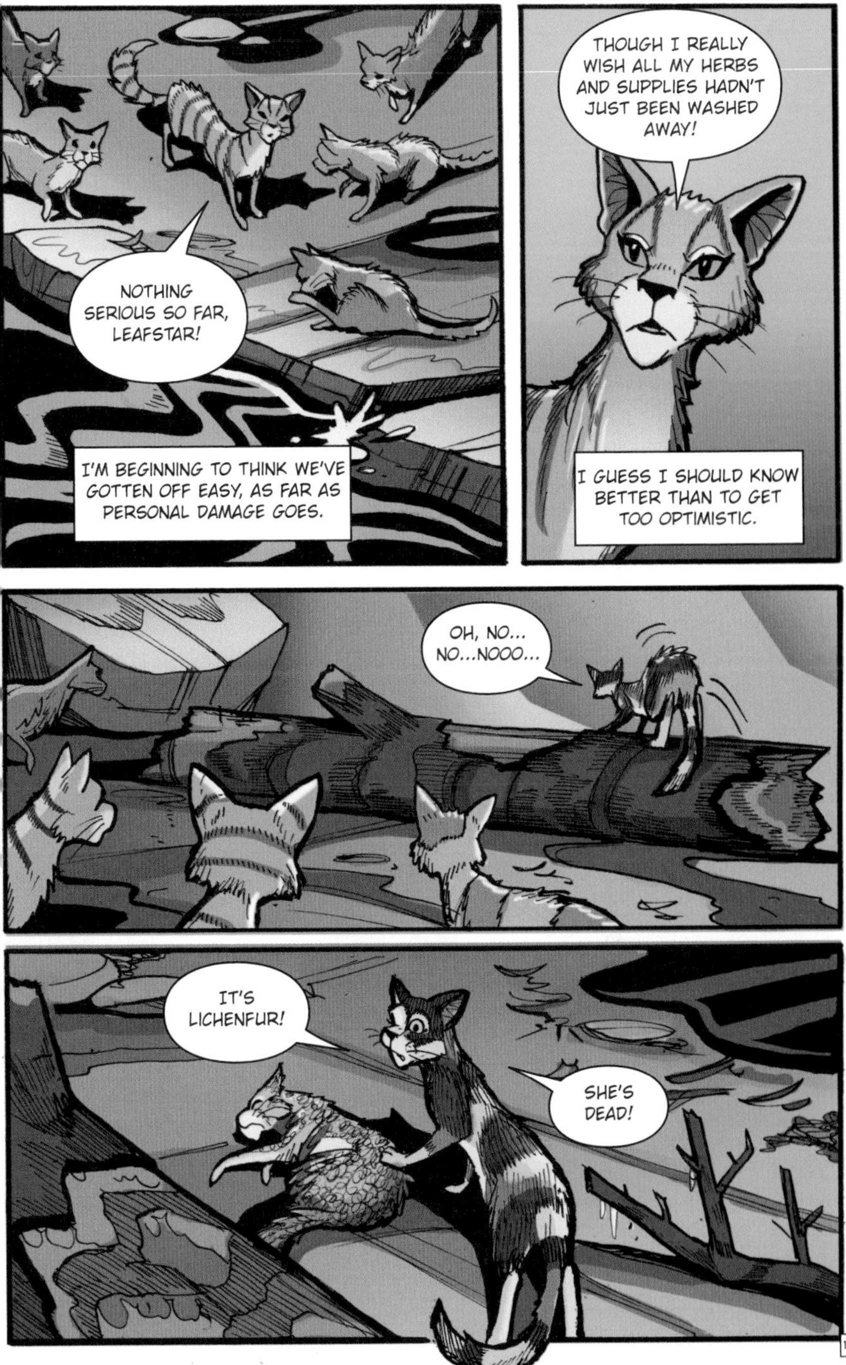
NOTHING SERIOUS SO FAR, LEAFSTAR!
I'M BEGINNING TO THINK WE'VE GOTTEN OFF EASY, AS FAR AS PERSONAL DAMAGE GOES.
THOUGH I REALLY WISH ALL MY HERBS AND SUPPLIES HADN'T JUST BEEN WASHED AWAY!
I GUESS I SHOULD KNOW BETTER THAN TO GET TOO OPTIMISTIC.
OH, NO... NO...NOOO...
IT'S LICHENFUR!
SHE'S DEAD!

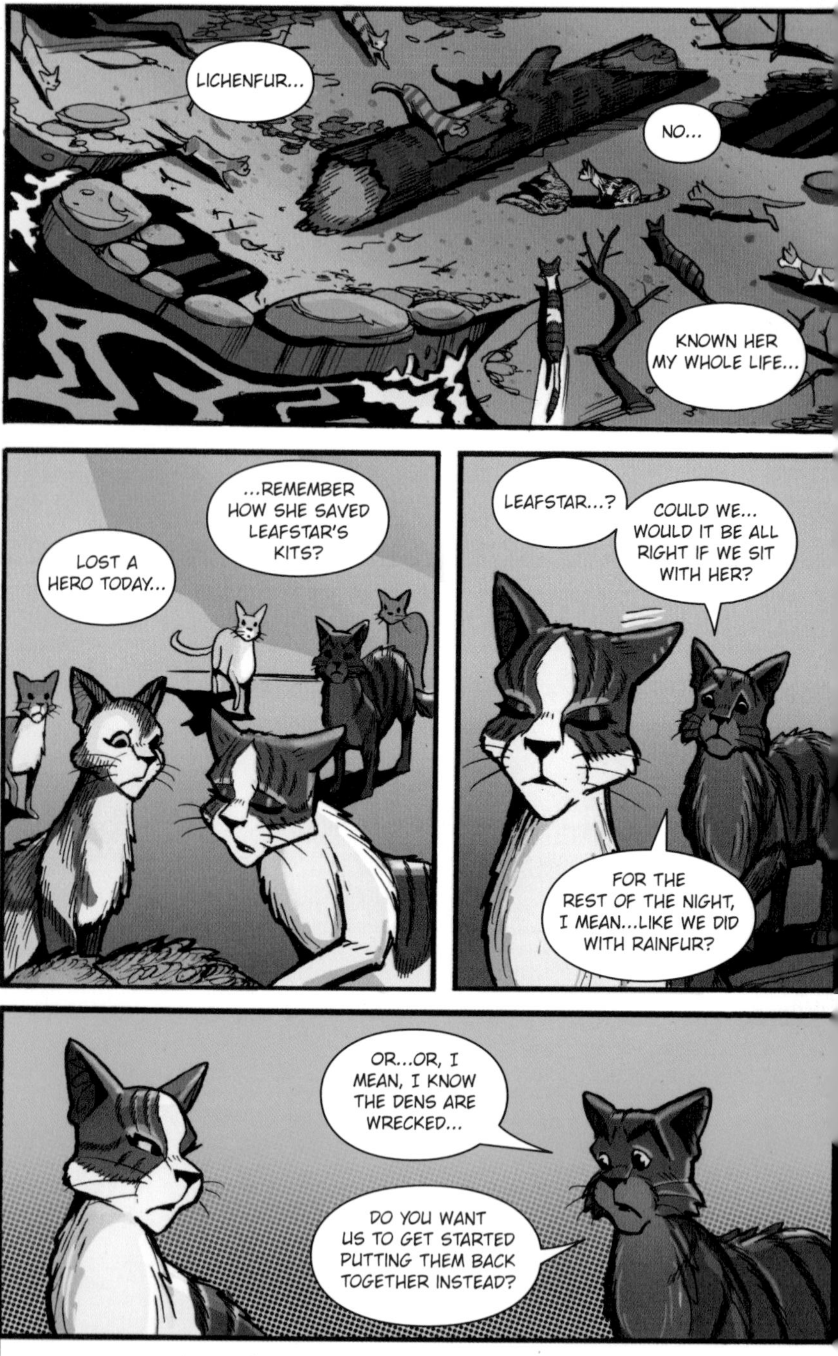
LICHENFUR...
NO...
KNOWN HER MY WHOLE LIFE...
LOST A HERO TODAY...
...REMEMBER HOW SHE SAVED LEAFSTAR'S KITS?
LEAFSTAR...?
COULD WE... WOULD IT BE ALL RIGHT IF WE SIT WITH HER?
FOR THE REST OF THE NIGHT, I MEAN...LIKE WE DID WITH RAINFUR?
OR...OR, I MEAN, I KNOW THE DENS ARE WRECKED...
DO YOU WANT US TO GET STARTED PUTTING THEM BACK TOGETHER INSTEAD?

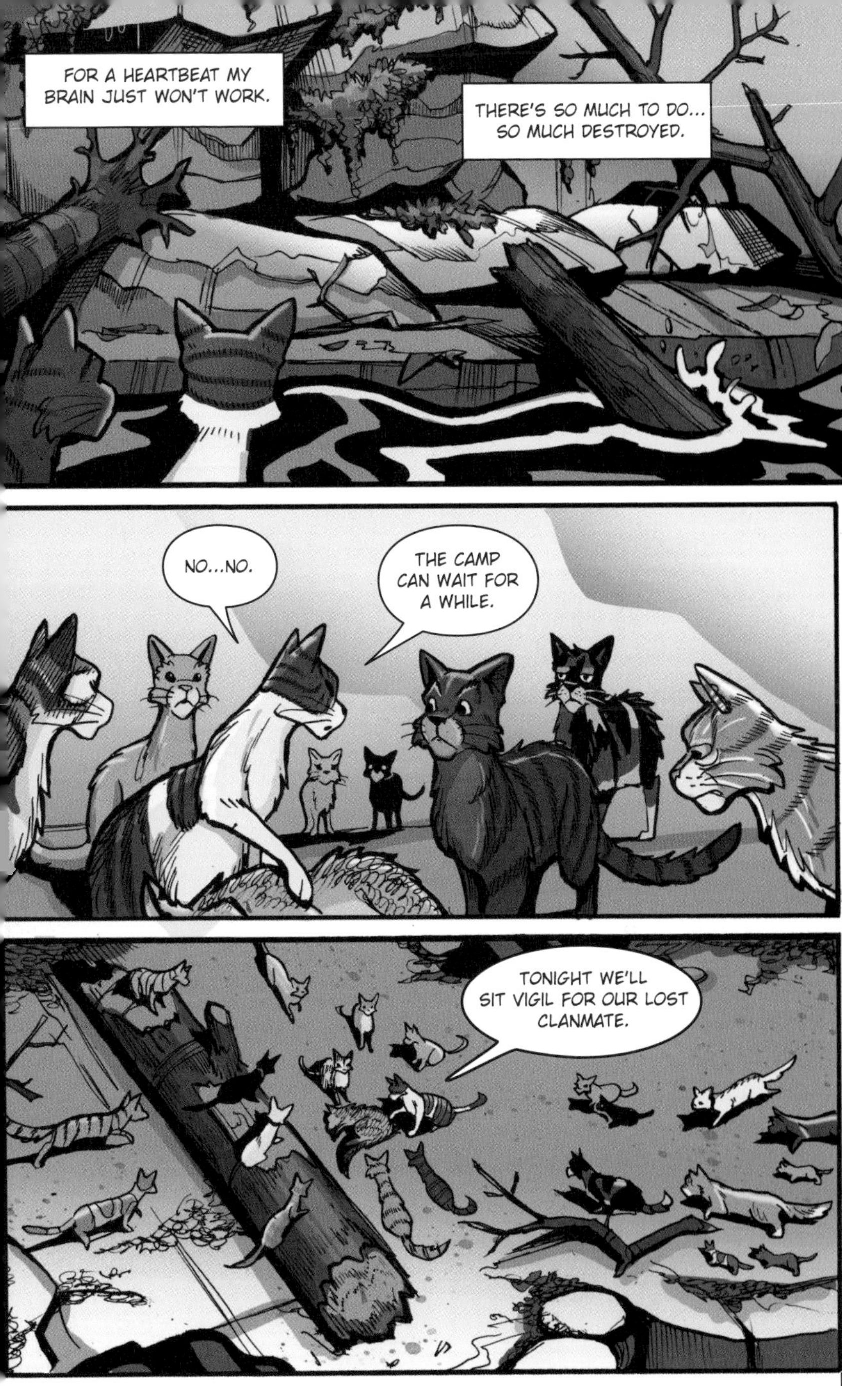
FOR A HEARTBEAT MY BRAIN JUST WON'T WORK.
THERE'S SO MUCH TO DO... SO MUCH DESTROYED.
NO...NO.
THE CAMP CAN WAIT FOR A WHILE.
TONIGHT WE'LL SIT VIGIL FOR OUR LOST CLANMATE.

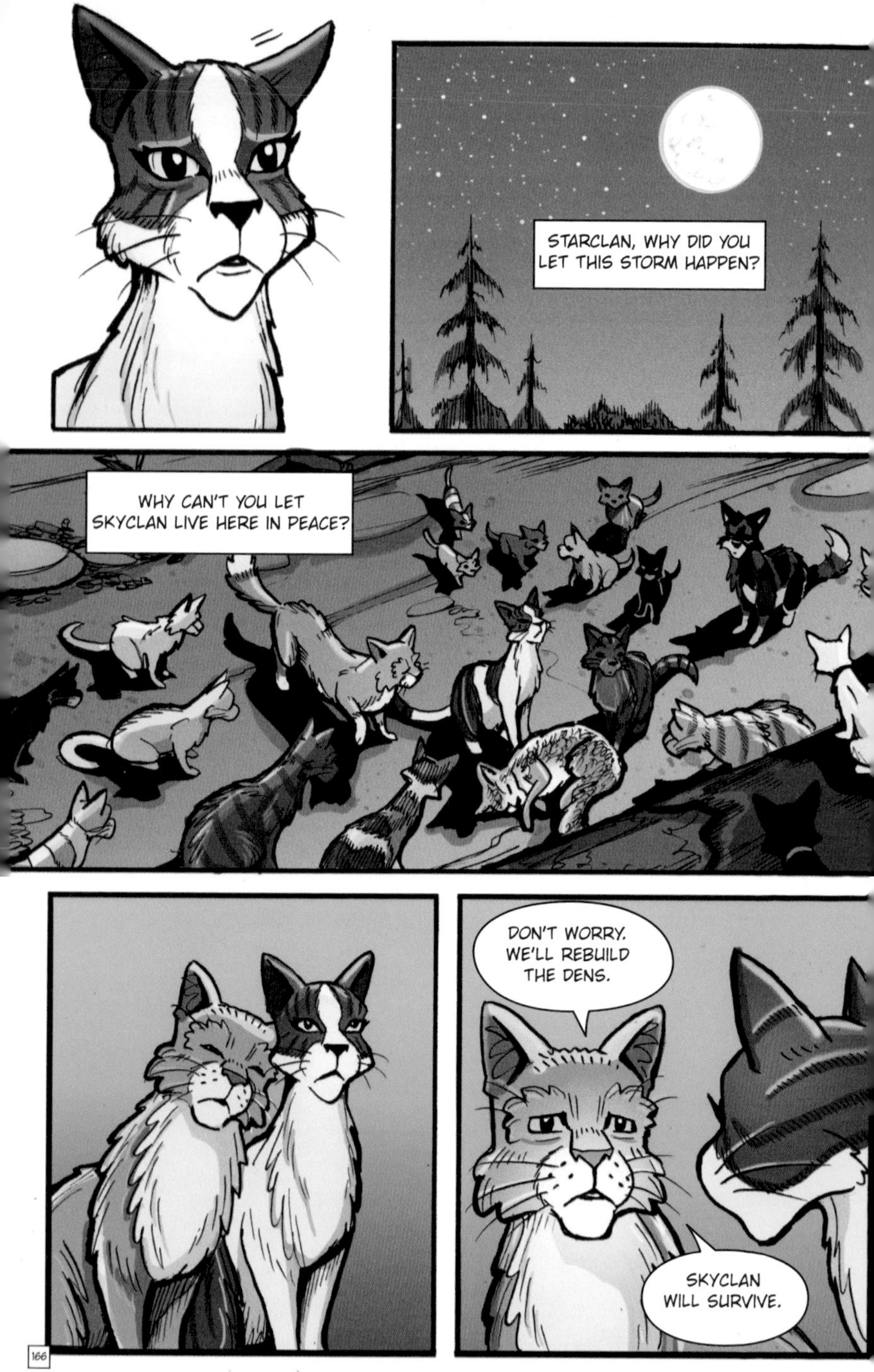
STARCLAN, WHY DID YOU LET THIS STORM HAPPEN?
WHY CAN'T YOU LET SKYCLAN LIVE HERE IN PEACE?
DON'T WORRY. WE'LL REBUILD THE DENS.
SKYCLAN WILL SURVIVE.

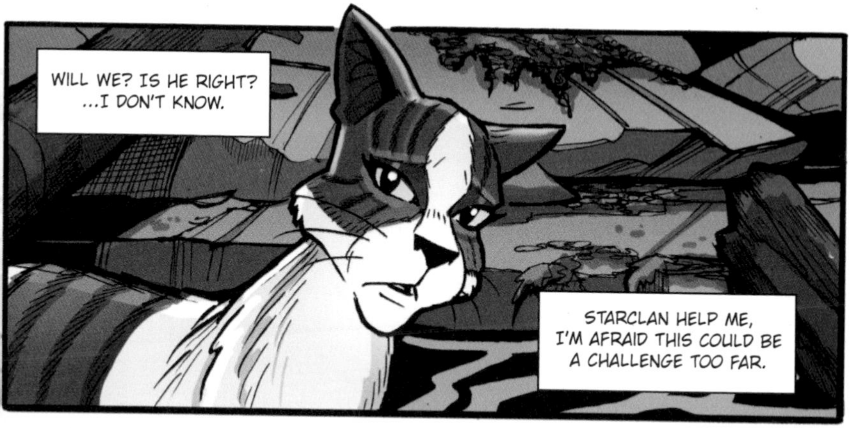
WILL WE? IS HE RIGHT? ...I DON'T KNOW.
STARCLAN HELP ME, I'M AFRAID THIS COULD BE A CHALLENGE TOO FAR.

WARRIORS

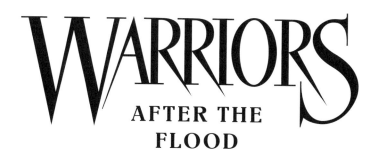

AFTER THE FLOOD

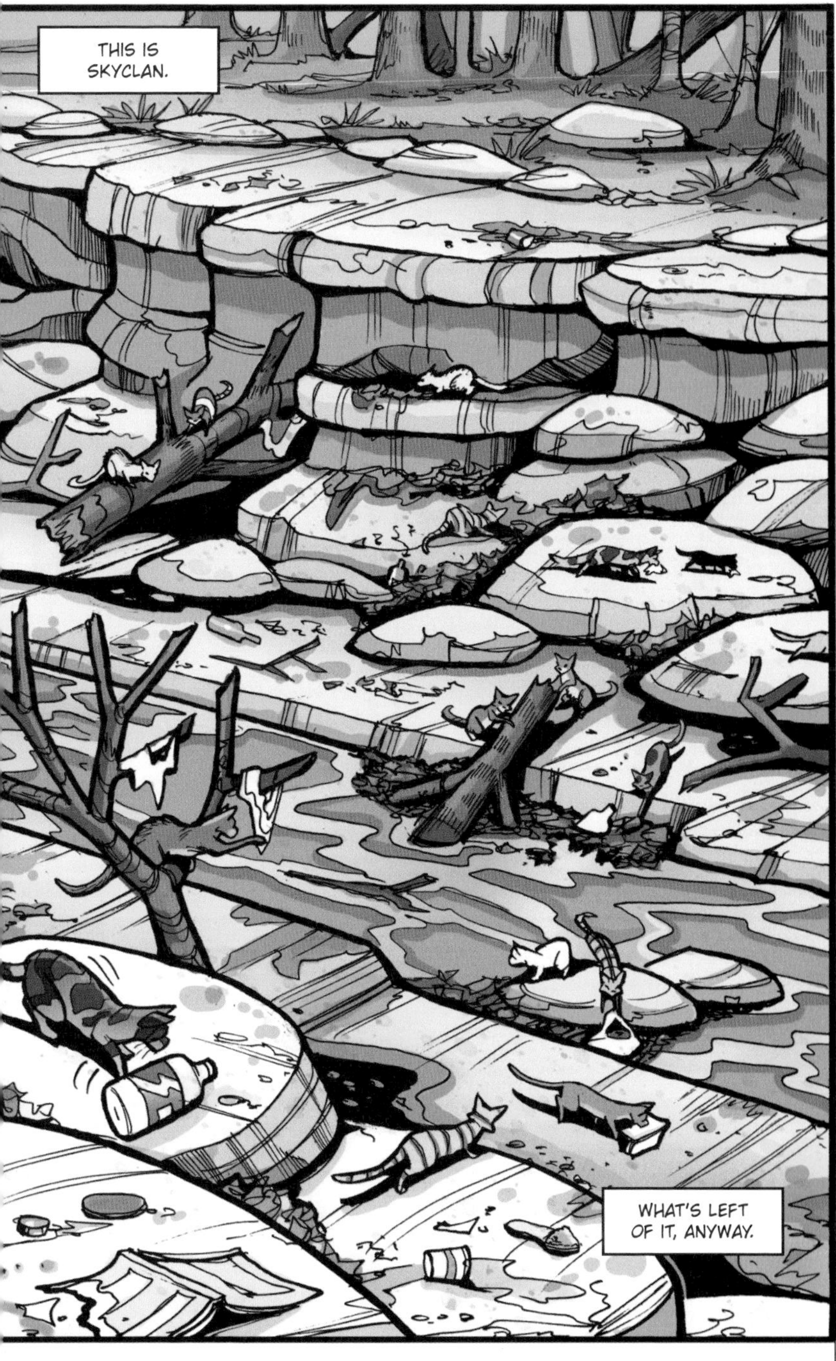
THIS IS SKYCLAN.
WHAT'S LEFT OF IT, ANYWAY.

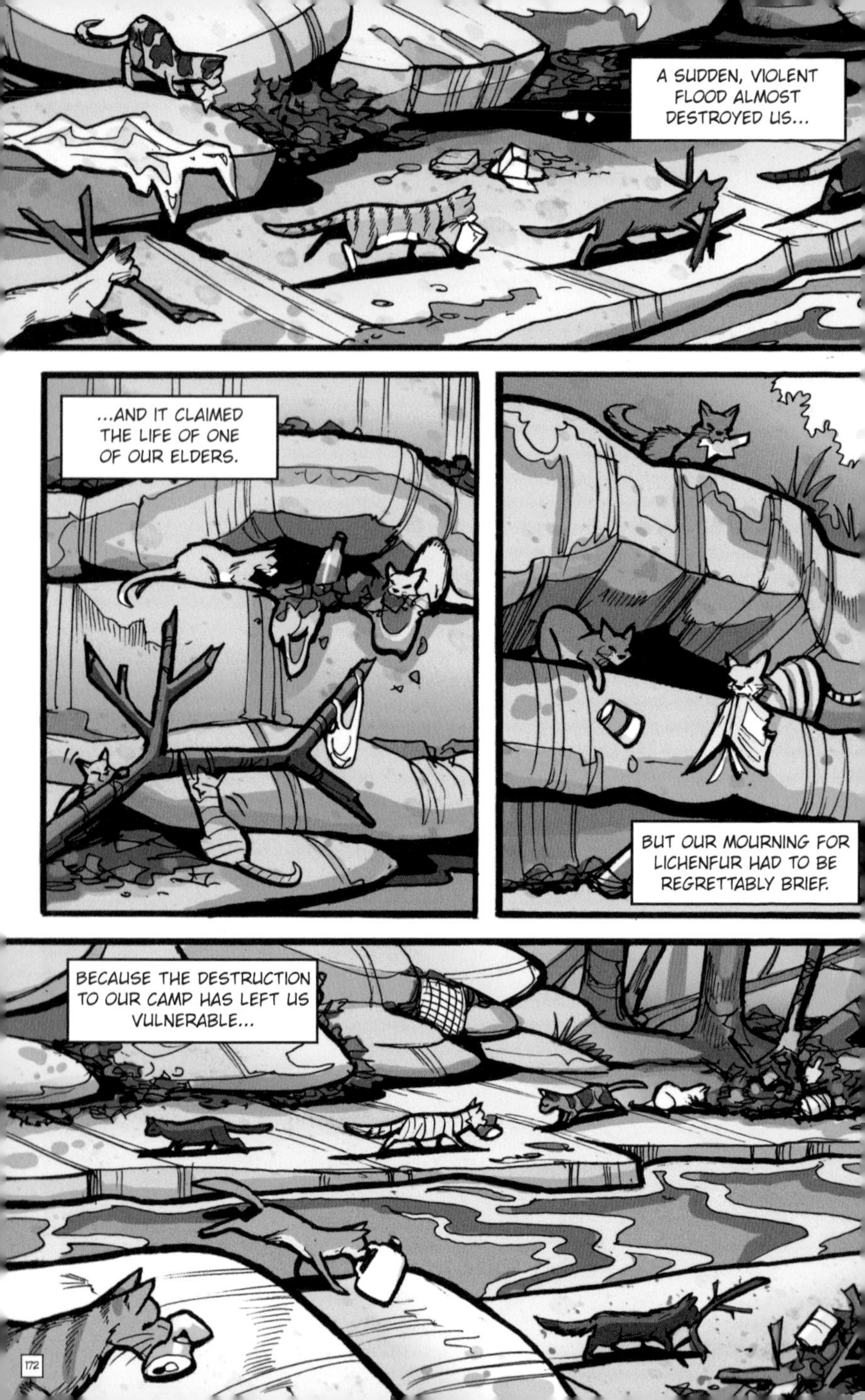
A SUDDEN, VIOLENT FLOOD ALMOST DESTROYED US...
...AND IT CLAIMED THE LIFE OF ONE OF OUR ELDERS.
BUT OUR MOURNING FOR LICHENFUR HAD TO BE REGRETTABLY BRIEF.
BECAUSE THE DESTRUCTION TO OUR CAMP HAS LEFT US VULNERABLE...

...OPEN TO ATTACKS FROM RATS...FOXES... ROGUE CATS...

...EVEN TWOLEGS.

NOT THAT OUTSIDE THREATS ARE OUR ONLY TROUBLES.

JUST AS DANGEROUS TO THE CLAN IS A LACK OF CLEAN WATER TO DRINK.

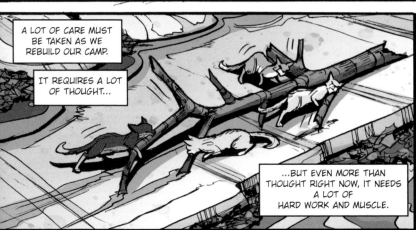

A LOT OF CARE MUST BE TAKEN AS WE REBUILD OUR CAMP.

IT REQUIRES A LOT OF THOUGHT...

...BUT EVEN MORE THAN THOUGHT RIGHT NOW, IT NEEDS A LOT OF HARD WORK AND MUSCLE.

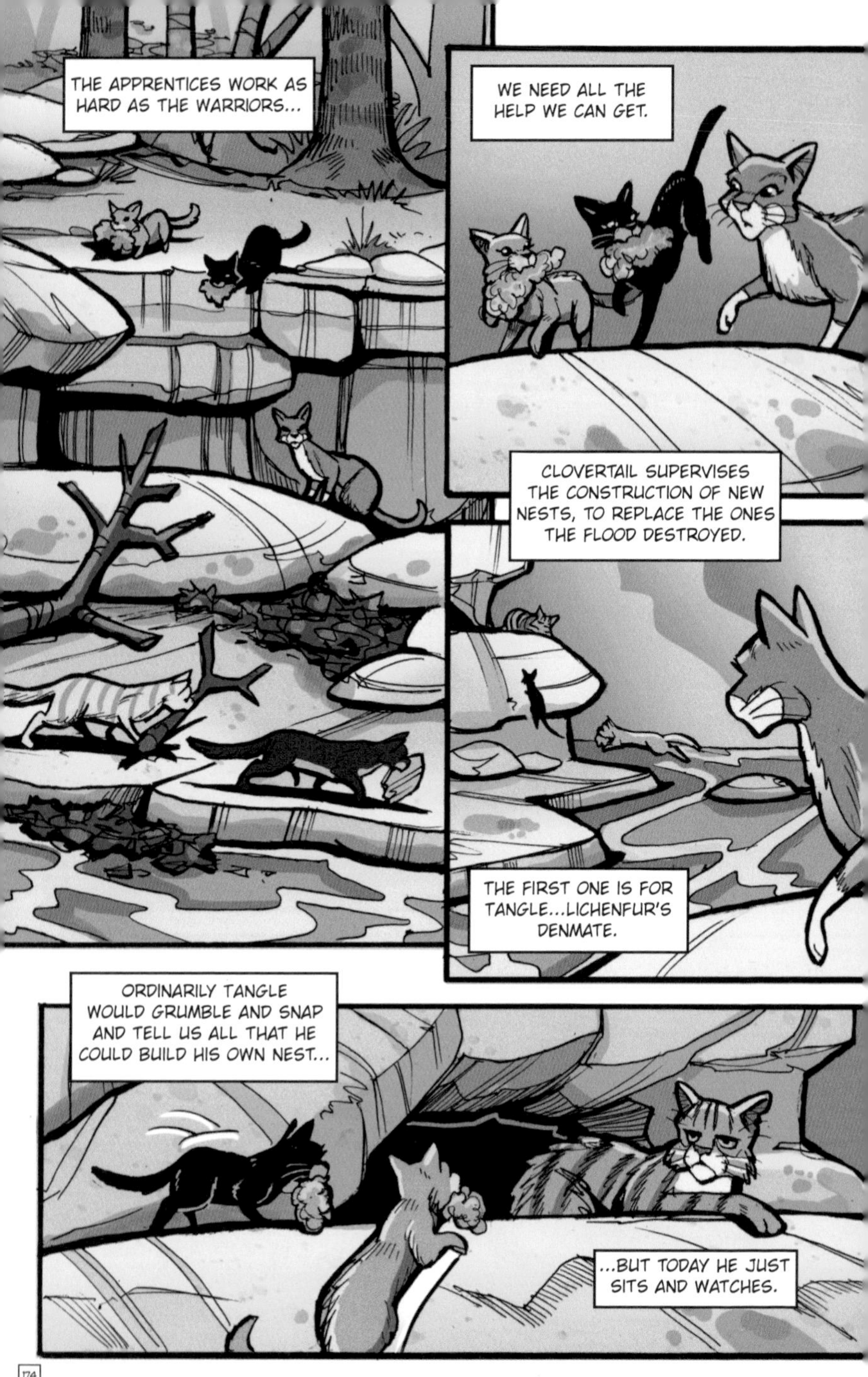
THE APPRENTICES WORK AS HARD AS THE WARRIORS...
WE NEED ALL THE HELP WE CAN GET.
CLOVERTAIL SUPERVISES THE CONSTRUCTION OF NEW NESTS, TO REPLACE THE ONES THE FLOOD DESTROYED.
THE FIRST ONE IS FOR TANGLE...LICHENFUR'S DENMATE.
ORDINARILY TANGLE WOULD GRUMBLE AND SNAP AND TELL US ALL THAT HE COULD BUILD HIS OWN NEST...
...BUT TODAY HE JUST SITS AND WATCHES.

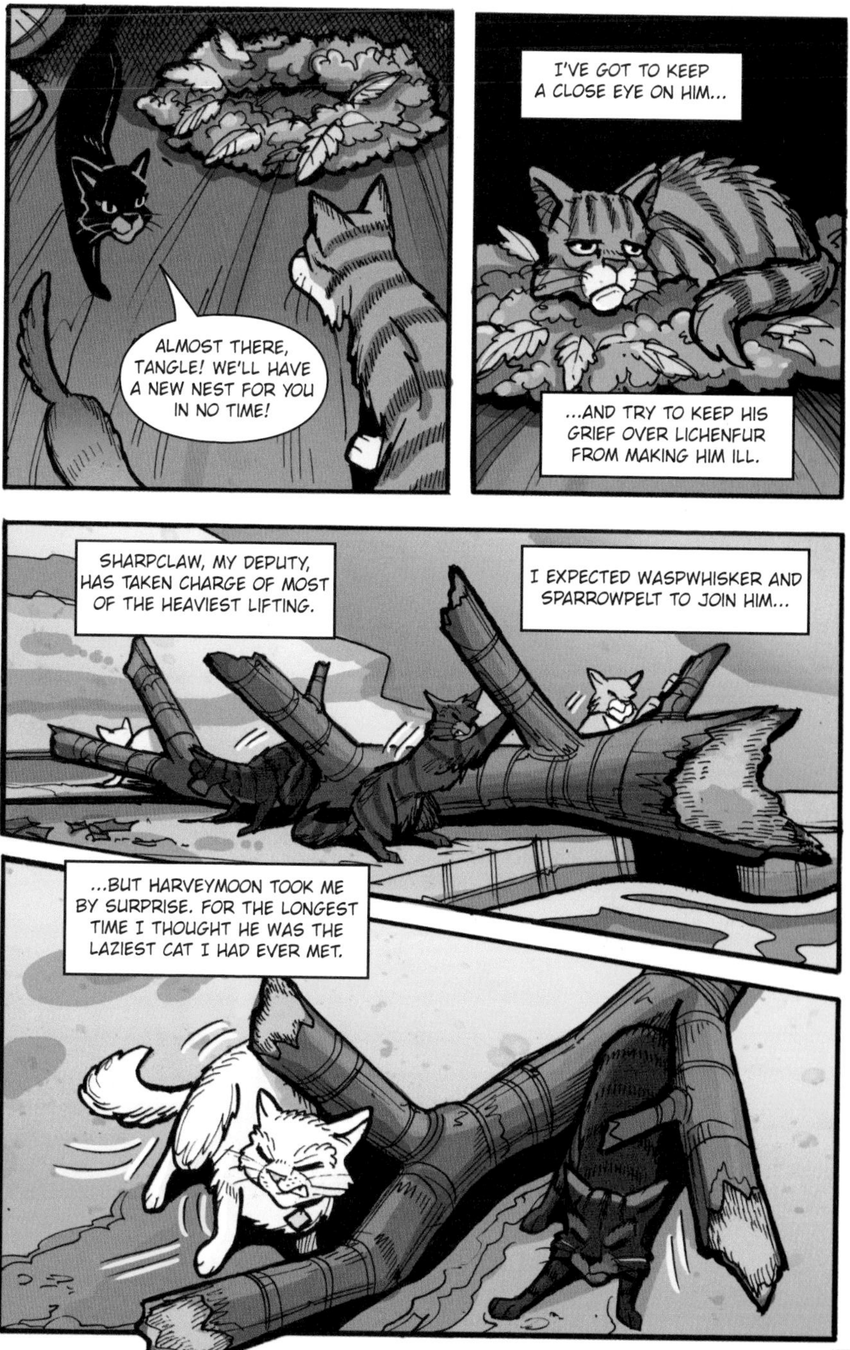
ALMOST THERE, TANGLE! WE'LL HAVE A NEW NEST FOR YOU IN NO TIME!
I'VE GOT TO KEEP A CLOSE EYE ON HIM...
...AND TRY TO KEEP HIS GRIEF OVER LICHENFUR FROM MAKING HIM ILL.
SHARPCLAW, MY DEPUTY, HAS TAKEN CHARGE OF MOST OF THE HEAVIEST LIFTING.
I EXPECTED WASPWHISKER AND SPARROWPELT TO JOIN HIM...
...BUT HARVEYMOON TOOK ME BY SURPRISE. FOR THE LONGEST TIME I THOUGHT HE WAS THE LAZIEST CAT I HAD EVER MET.

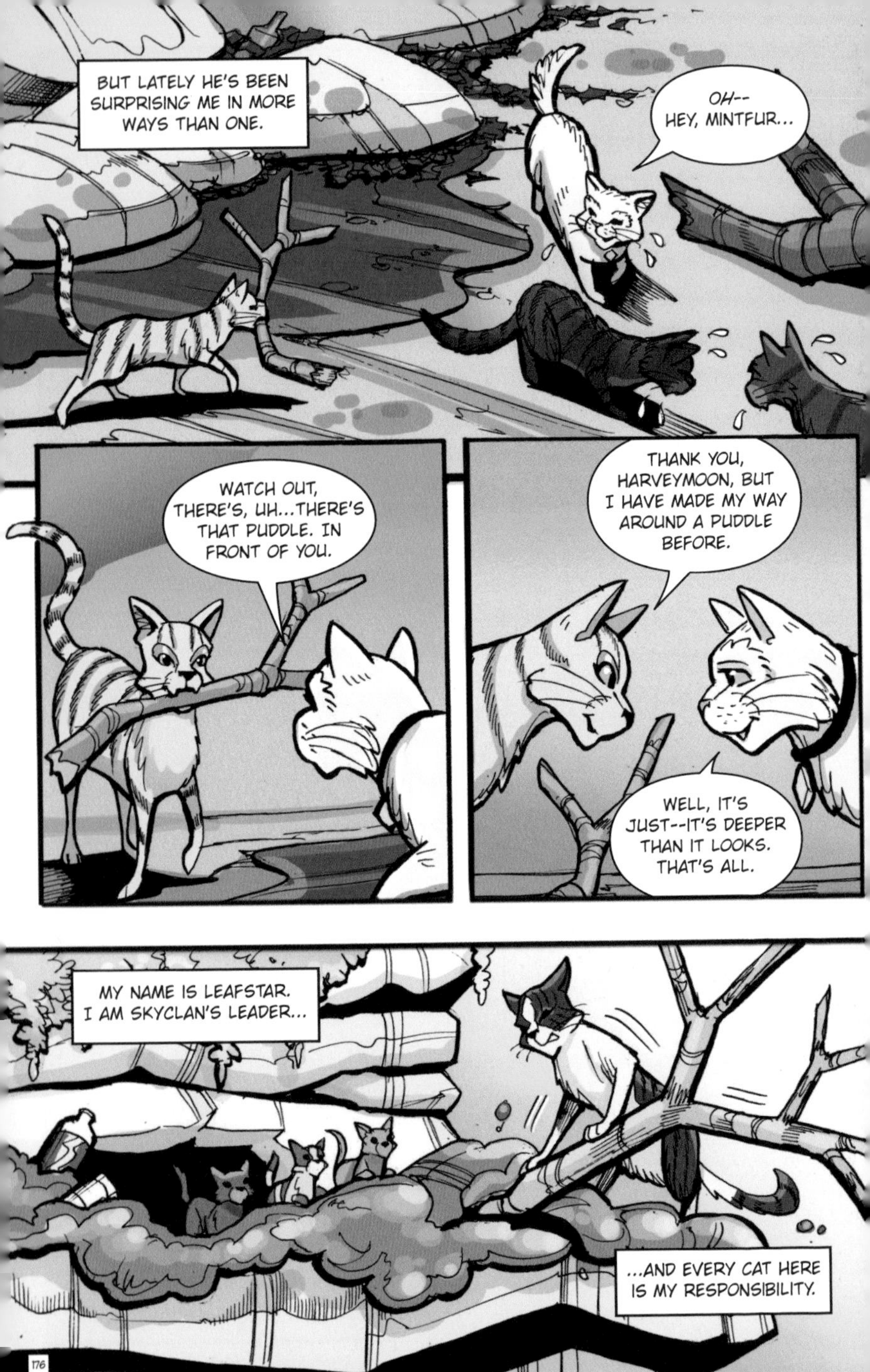

BUT LATELY HE'S BEEN SURPRISING ME IN MORE WAYS THAN ONE.
OH-- HEY, MINTFUR...
WATCH OUT, THERE'S, UH...THERE'S THAT PUDDLE. IN FRONT OF YOU.
THANK YOU, HARVEYMOON, BUT I HAVE MADE MY WAY AROUND A PUDDLE BEFORE.
WELL, IT'S JUST--IT'S DEEPER THAN IT LOOKS. THAT'S ALL.
MY NAME IS LEAFSTAR. I AM SKYCLAN'S LEADER...
...AND EVERY CAT HERE IS MY RESPONSIBILITY.

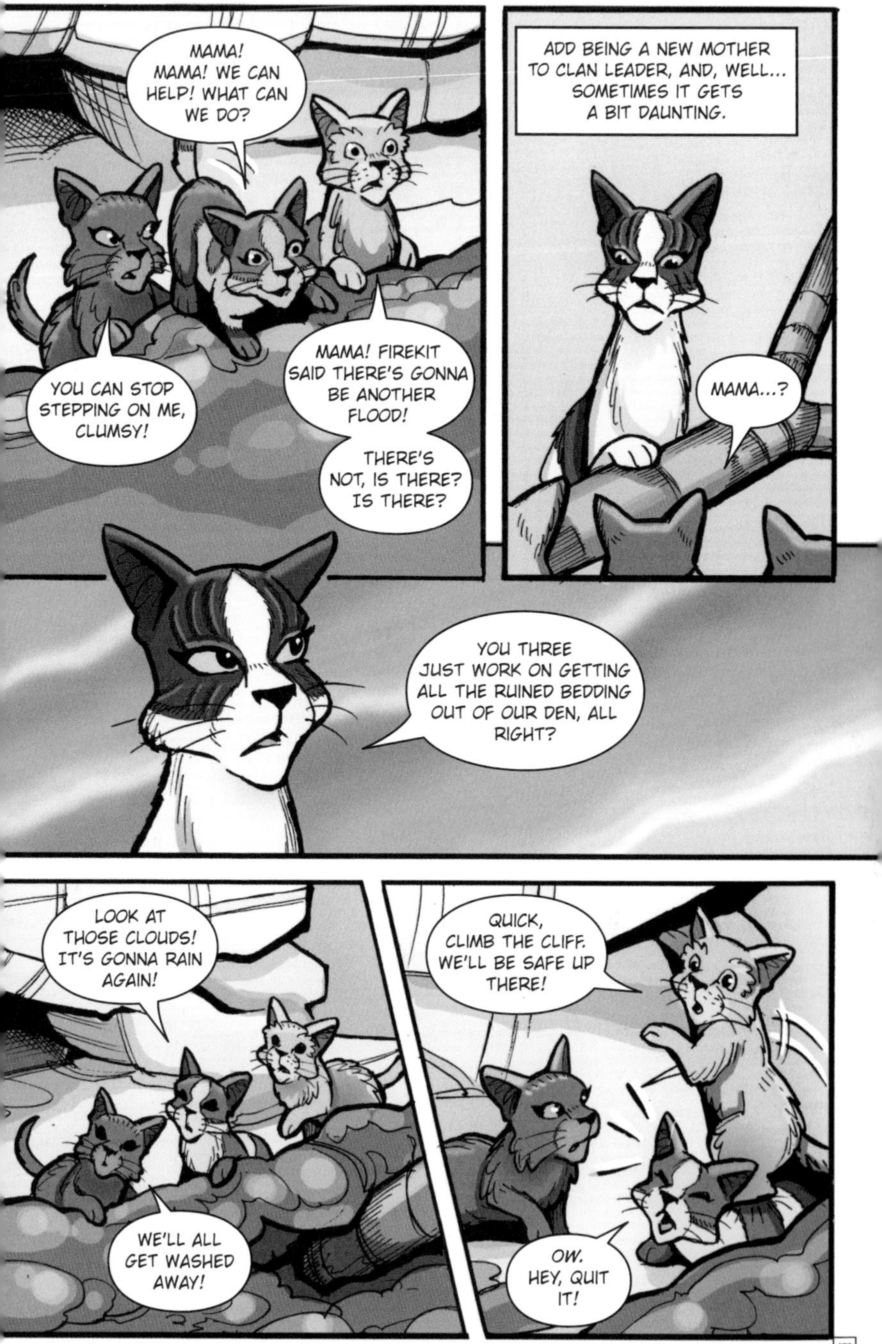
MAMA! MAMA! WE CAN HELP! WHAT CAN WE DO?
YOU CAN STOP STEPPING ON ME, CLUMSY!
MAMA! FIREKIT SAID THERE'S GONNA BE ANOTHER FLOOD!
THERE'S NOT, IS THERE? IS THERE?
ADD BEING A NEW MOTHER TO CLAN LEADER, AND, WELL... SOMETIMES IT GETS A BIT DAUNTING.
MAMA...?
YOU THREE JUST WORK ON GETTING ALL THE RUINED BEDDING OUT OF OUR DEN, ALL RIGHT?
LOOK AT THOSE CLOUDS! IT'S GONNA RAIN AGAIN!
WE'LL ALL GET WASHED AWAY!
QUICK, CLIMB THE CLIFF. WE'LL BE SAFE UP THERE!
OW. HEY, QUIT IT!

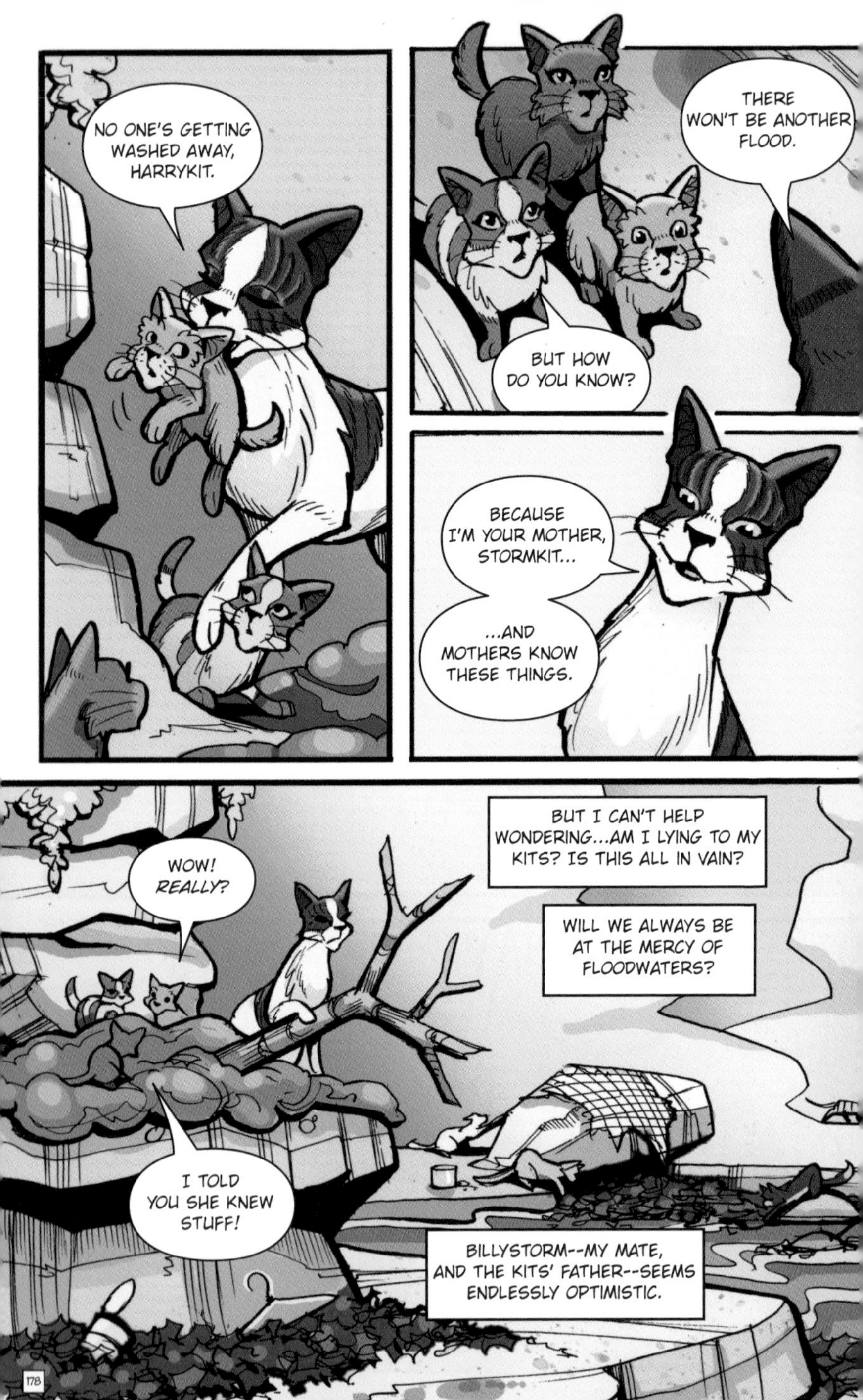
NO ONE'S GETTING WASHED AWAY, HARRYKIT.
THERE WON'T BE ANOTHER FLOOD.
BUT HOW DO YOU KNOW?
BECAUSE I'M YOUR MOTHER, STORMKIT...
...AND MOTHERS KNOW THESE THINGS.
WOW! *REALLY?*
BUT I CAN'T HELP WONDERING...AM I LYING TO MY KITS? IS THIS ALL IN VAIN?
WILL WE ALWAYS BE AT THE MERCY OF FLOODWATERS?
I TOLD YOU SHE KNEW STUFF!
BILLYSTORM--MY MATE, AND THE KITS' FATHER--SEEMS ENDLESSLY OPTIMISTIC.

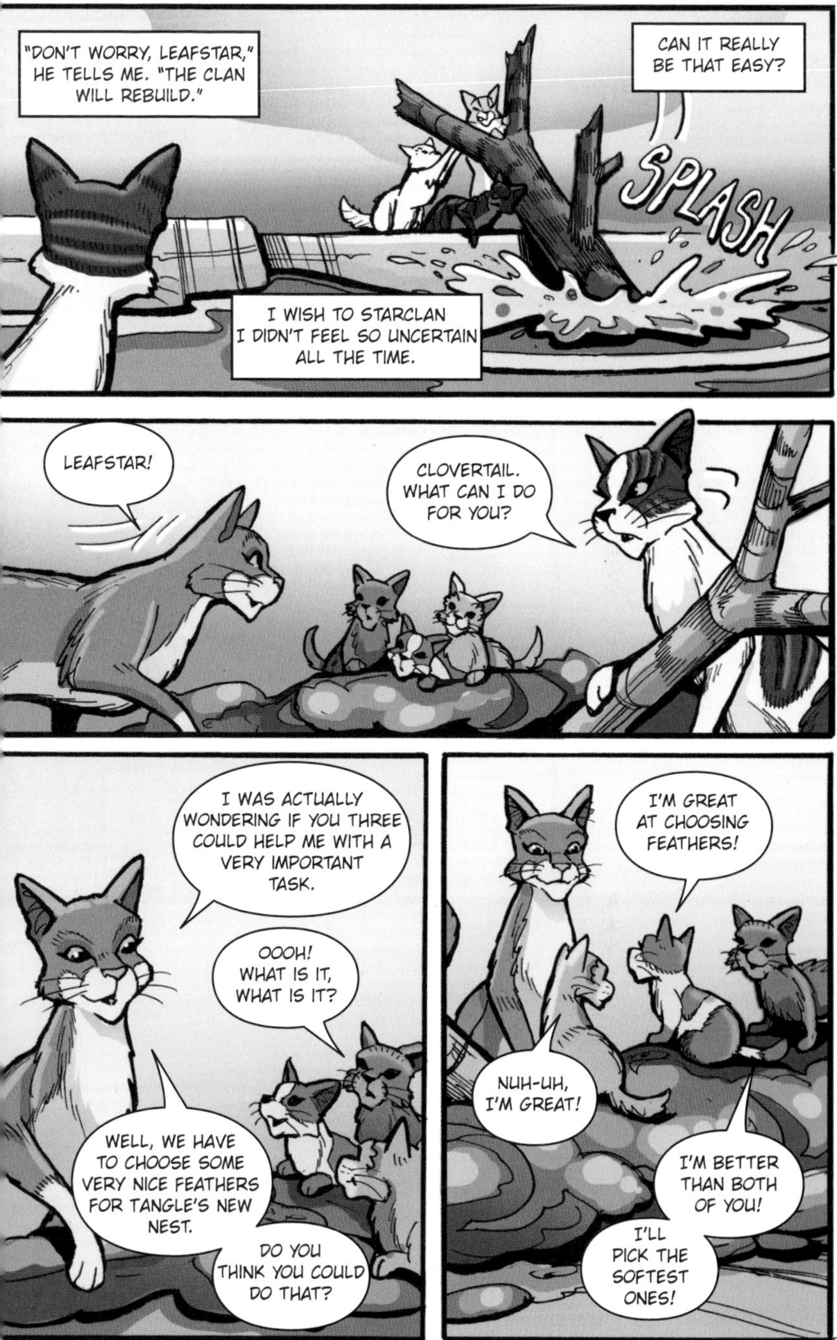
"DON'T WORRY, LEAFSTAR," HE TELLS ME. "THE CLAN WILL REBUILD."
CAN IT REALLY BE THAT EASY?
SPLASH
I WISH TO STARCLAN I DIDN'T FEEL SO UNCERTAIN ALL THE TIME.
LEAFSTAR!
CLOVERTAIL. WHAT CAN I DO FOR YOU?
I WAS ACTUALLY WONDERING IF YOU THREE COULD HELP ME WITH A VERY IMPORTANT TASK.
OOOH! WHAT IS IT, WHAT IS IT?
WELL, WE HAVE TO CHOOSE SOME VERY NICE FEATHERS FOR TANGLE'S NEW NEST.
DO YOU THINK YOU COULD DO THAT?
I'M GREAT AT CHOOSING FEATHERS!
NUH-UH, I'M GREAT!
I'M BETTER THAN BOTH OF YOU!
I'LL PICK THE SOFTEST ONES!

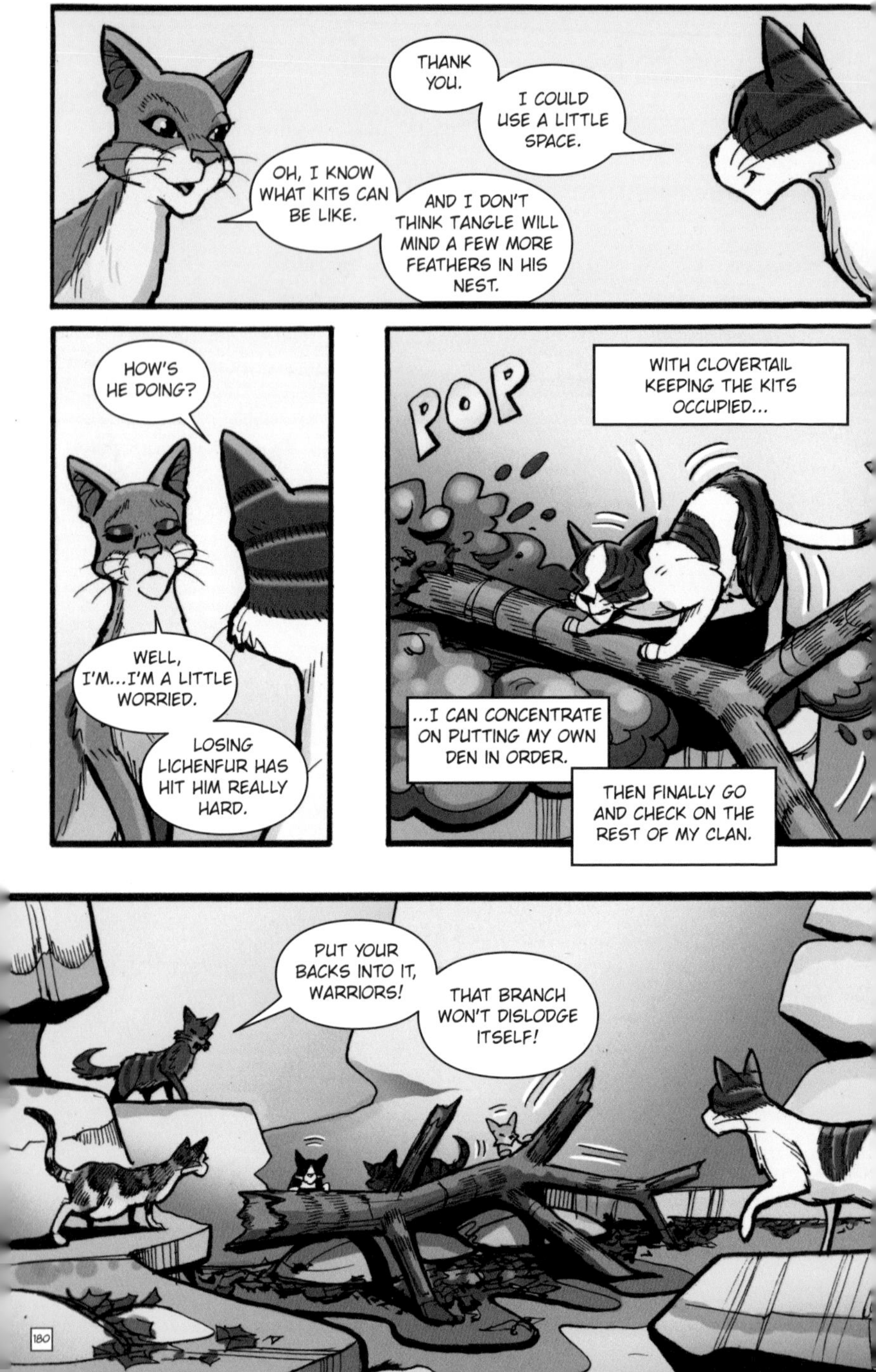
THANK YOU.
I COULD USE A LITTLE SPACE.
OH, I KNOW WHAT KITS CAN BE LIKE.
AND I DON'T THINK TANGLE WILL MIND A FEW MORE FEATHERS IN HIS NEST.
HOW'S HE DOING?
WELL, I'M...I'M A LITTLE WORRIED.
LOSING LICHENFUR HAS HIT HIM REALLY HARD.
POP
WITH CLOVERTAIL KEEPING THE KITS OCCUPIED...
...I CAN CONCENTRATE ON PUTTING MY OWN DEN IN ORDER.
THEN FINALLY GO AND CHECK ON THE REST OF MY CLAN.
PUT YOUR BACKS INTO IT, WARRIORS!
THAT BRANCH WON'T DISLODGE ITSELF!

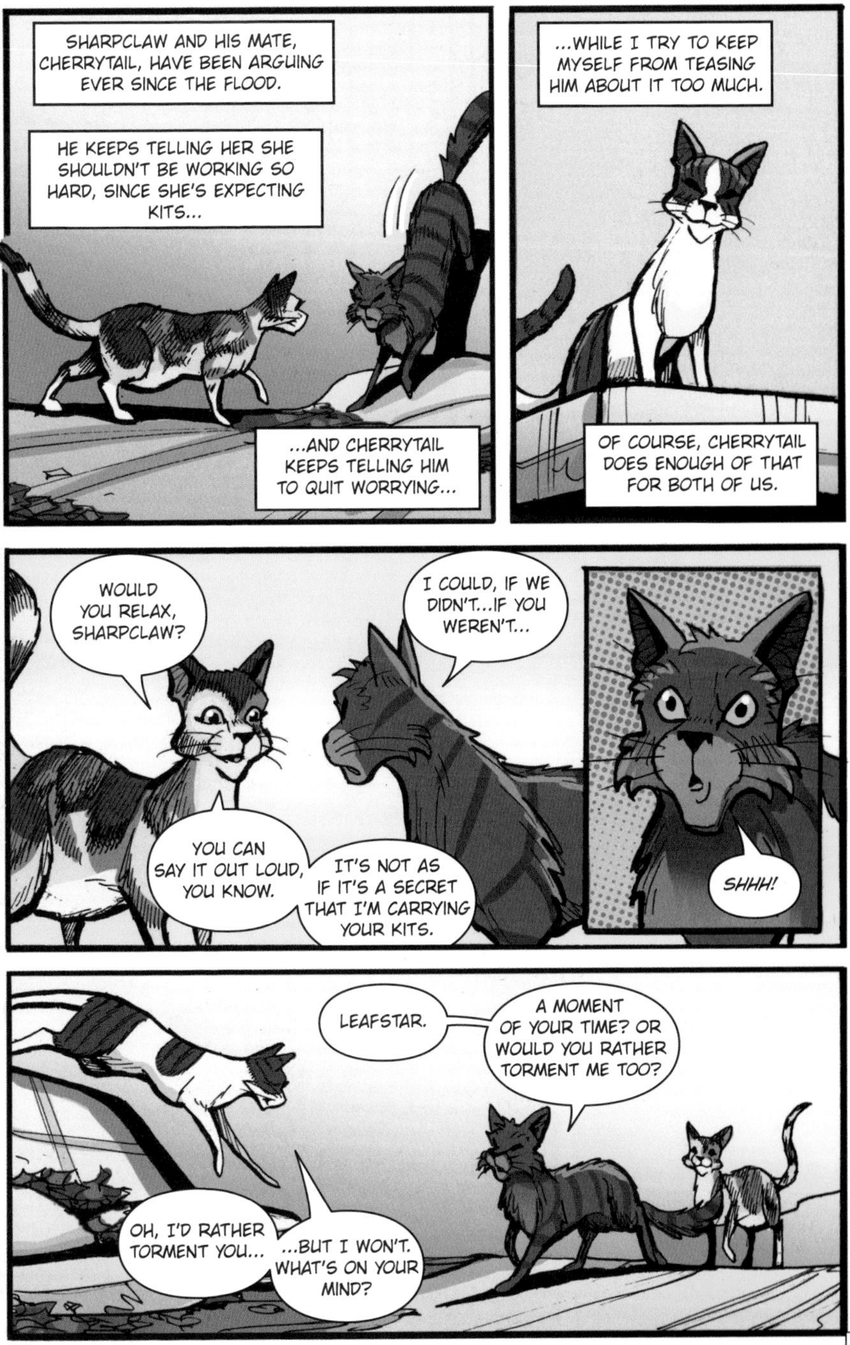
SHARPCLAW AND HIS MATE, CHERRYTAIL, HAVE BEEN ARGUING EVER SINCE THE FLOOD.
HE KEEPS TELLING HER SHE SHOULDN'T BE WORKING SO HARD, SINCE SHE'S EXPECTING KITS...
...AND CHERRYTAIL KEEPS TELLING HIM TO QUIT WORRYING...
...WHILE I TRY TO KEEP MYSELF FROM TEASING HIM ABOUT IT TOO MUCH.
OF COURSE, CHERRYTAIL DOES ENOUGH OF THAT FOR BOTH OF US.
WOULD YOU RELAX, SHARPCLAW?
I COULD, IF WE DIDN'T...IF YOU WEREN'T...
YOU CAN SAY IT OUT LOUD, YOU KNOW.
IT'S NOT AS IF IT'S A SECRET THAT I'M CARRYING YOUR KITS.
SHHH!
LEAFSTAR.
A MOMENT OF YOUR TIME? OR WOULD YOU RATHER TORMENT ME TOO?
OH, I'D RATHER TORMENT YOU...
...BUT I WON'T. WHAT'S ON YOUR MIND?

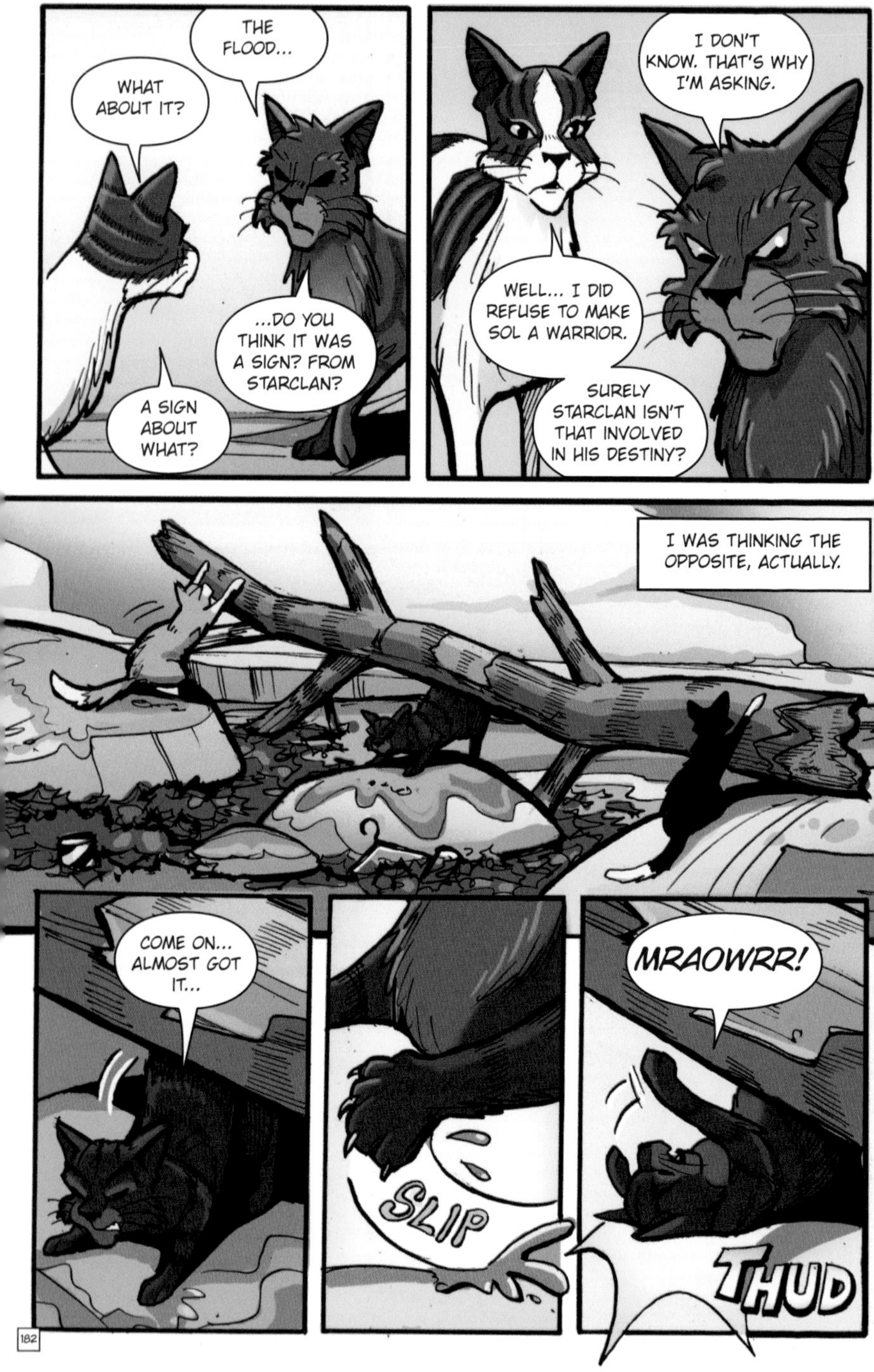
THE FLOOD...
WHAT ABOUT IT?
...DO YOU THINK IT WAS A SIGN? FROM STARCLAN?
A SIGN ABOUT WHAT?
I DON'T KNOW. THAT'S WHY I'M ASKING.
WELL... I DID REFUSE TO MAKE SOL A WARRIOR.
SURELY STARCLAN ISN'T THAT INVOLVED IN HIS DESTINY?
I WAS THINKING THE OPPOSITE, ACTUALLY.
COME ON... ALMOST GOT IT...
SLIP
MRAOWRR!
THUD

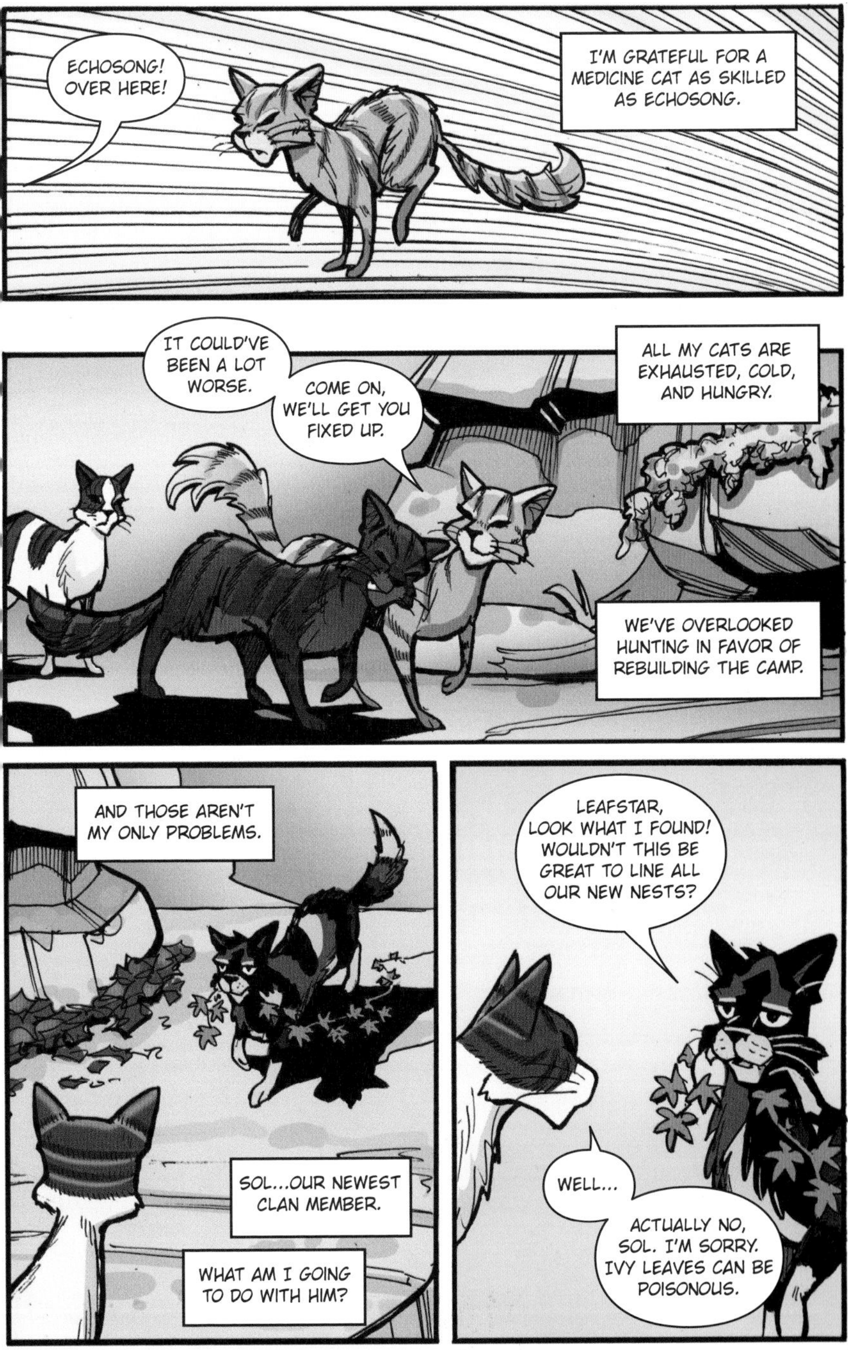
ECHOSONG! OVER HERE!
I'M GRATEFUL FOR A MEDICINE CAT AS SKILLED AS ECHOSONG.
IT COULD'VE BEEN A LOT WORSE.
COME ON, WE'LL GET YOU FIXED UP.
ALL MY CATS ARE EXHAUSTED, COLD, AND HUNGRY.
WE'VE OVERLOOKED HUNTING IN FAVOR OF REBUILDING THE CAMP.
AND THOSE AREN'T MY ONLY PROBLEMS.
SOL...OUR NEWEST CLAN MEMBER.
WHAT AM I GOING TO DO WITH HIM?
LEAFSTAR, LOOK WHAT I FOUND! WOULDN'T THIS BE GREAT TO LINE ALL OUR NEW NESTS?
WELL...
ACTUALLY NO, SOL. I'M SORRY. IVY LEAVES CAN BE POISONOUS.

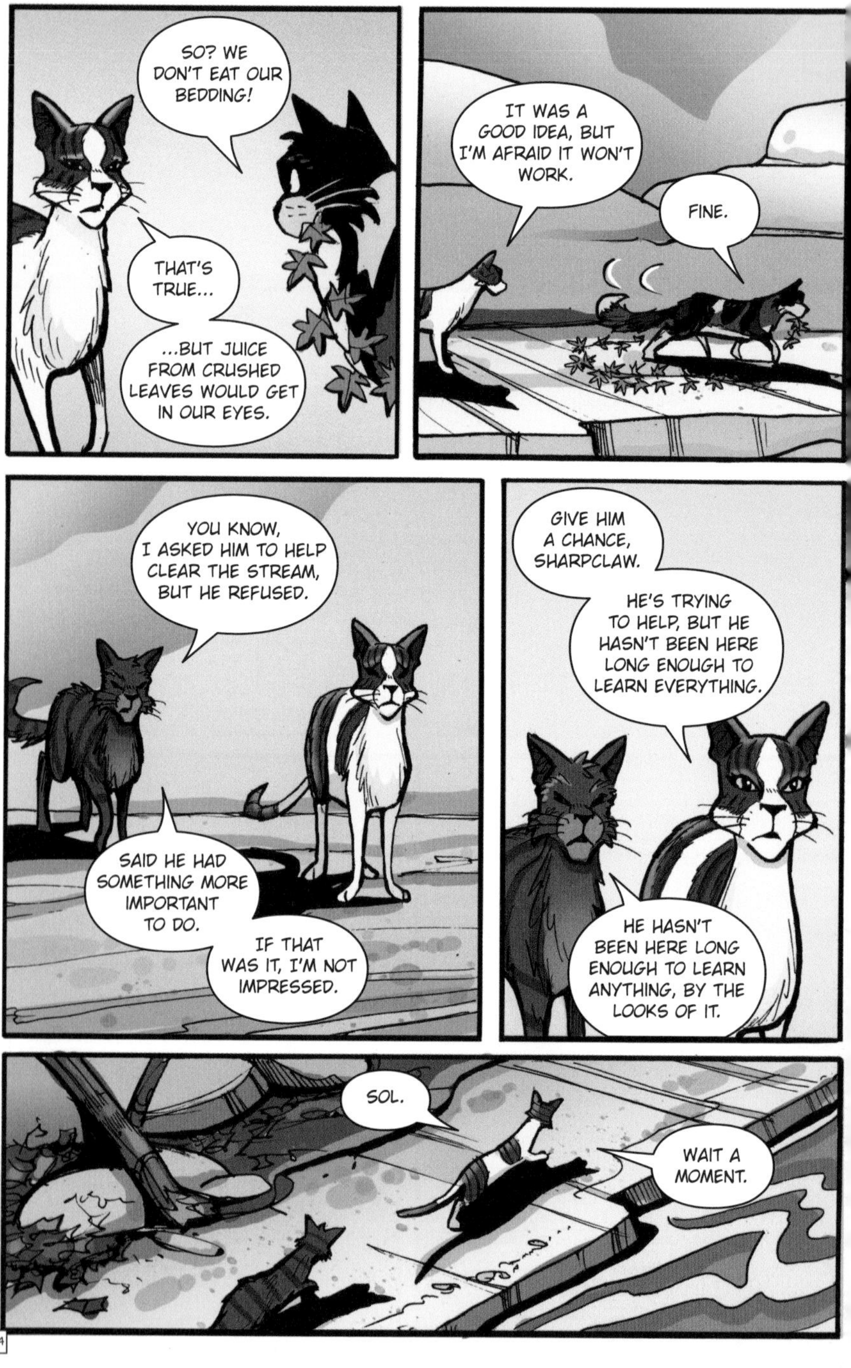
SO? WE DON'T EAT OUR BEDDING!
THAT'S TRUE...
...BUT JUICE FROM CRUSHED LEAVES WOULD GET IN OUR EYES.
IT WAS A GOOD IDEA, BUT I'M AFRAID IT WON'T WORK.
FINE.
YOU KNOW, I ASKED HIM TO HELP CLEAR THE STREAM, BUT HE REFUSED.
SAID HE HAD SOMETHING MORE IMPORTANT TO DO.
IF THAT WAS IT, I'M NOT IMPRESSED.
GIVE HIM A CHANCE, SHARPCLAW.
HE'S TRYING TO HELP, BUT HE HASN'T BEEN HERE LONG ENOUGH TO LEARN EVERYTHING.
HE HASN'T BEEN HERE LONG ENOUGH TO LEARN ANYTHING, BY THE LOOKS OF IT.
SOL.
WAIT A MOMENT.

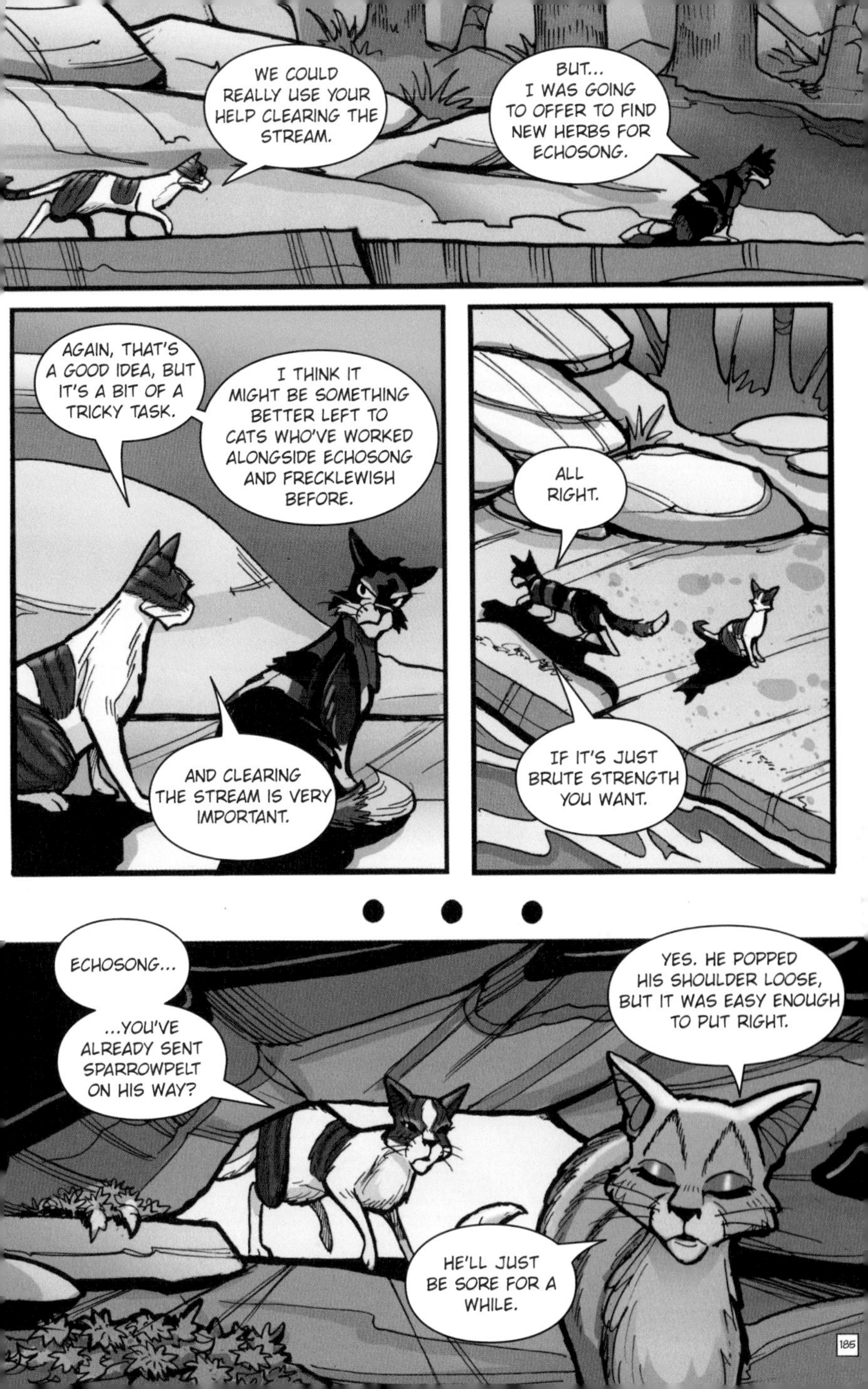
WE COULD REALLY USE YOUR HELP CLEARING THE STREAM.
BUT... I WAS GOING TO OFFER TO FIND NEW HERBS FOR ECHOSONG.
AGAIN, THAT'S A GOOD IDEA, BUT IT'S A BIT OF A TRICKY TASK.
I THINK IT MIGHT BE SOMETHING BETTER LEFT TO CATS WHO'VE WORKED ALONGSIDE ECHOSONG AND FRECKLEWISH BEFORE.
AND CLEARING THE STREAM IS VERY IMPORTANT.
ALL RIGHT.
IF IT'S JUST BRUTE STRENGTH YOU WANT.
ECHOSONG...
...YOU'VE ALREADY SENT SPARROWPELT ON HIS WAY?
YES. HE POPPED HIS SHOULDER LOOSE, BUT IT WAS EASY ENOUGH TO PUT RIGHT.
HE'LL JUST BE SORE FOR A WHILE.

UGH... THESE HERBS ARE SOGGY.

LISTEN, I WANTED TO ASK YOU... HAS STARCLAN TOLD YOU ANYTHING?

ABOUT THE FLOOD, I MEAN?

I'M AFRAID NOT. PLUS, HONESTLY, I'VE BEEN TOO BUSY TO ASK.

THE FLOOD WAS JUST ONE OF THOSE THINGS.

WHAT THINGS?

THE THINGS THAT REMIND US JUST HOW VULNERABLE WE ARE.

I DON'T SAY ANYTHING TO ECHOSONG...OR ANYONE ELSE, FOR THAT MATTER...

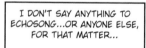

...BUT I FEEL A PANG OF FEAR.

WHAT IF THE SPECTER OF ANOTHER FLOOD SENDS SOME OF MY CLANMATES BACK TO THEIR OLD LIVES...

...AS LONERS OR KITTYPETS?

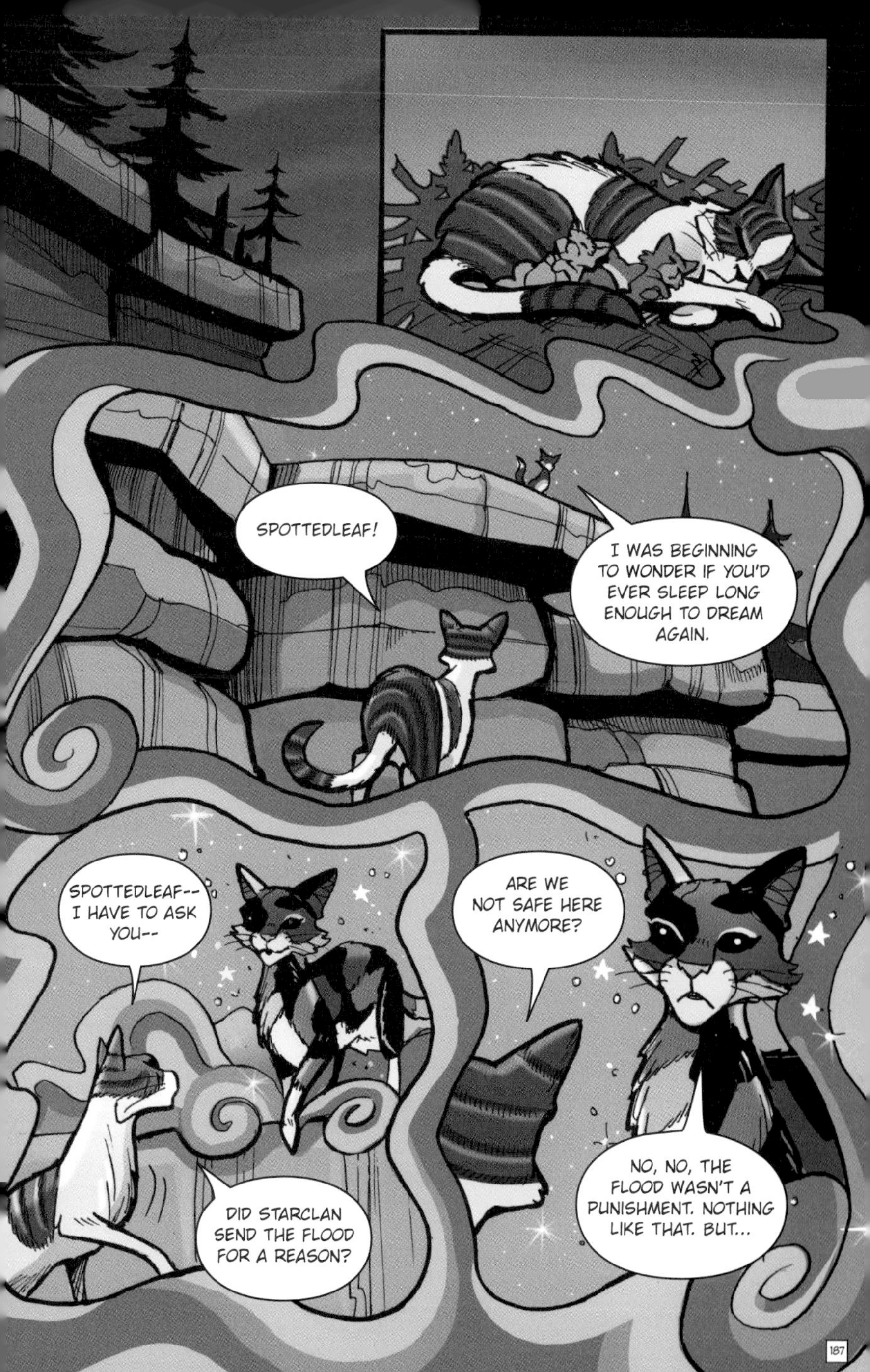
SPOTTEDLEAF!
I WAS BEGINNING TO WONDER IF YOU'D EVER SLEEP LONG ENOUGH TO DREAM AGAIN.
SPOTTEDLEAF-- I HAVE TO ASK YOU--
DID STARCLAN SEND THE FLOOD FOR A REASON?
ARE WE NOT SAFE HERE ANYMORE?
NO, NO, THE FLOOD WASN'T A PUNISHMENT. NOTHING LIKE THAT. BUT...

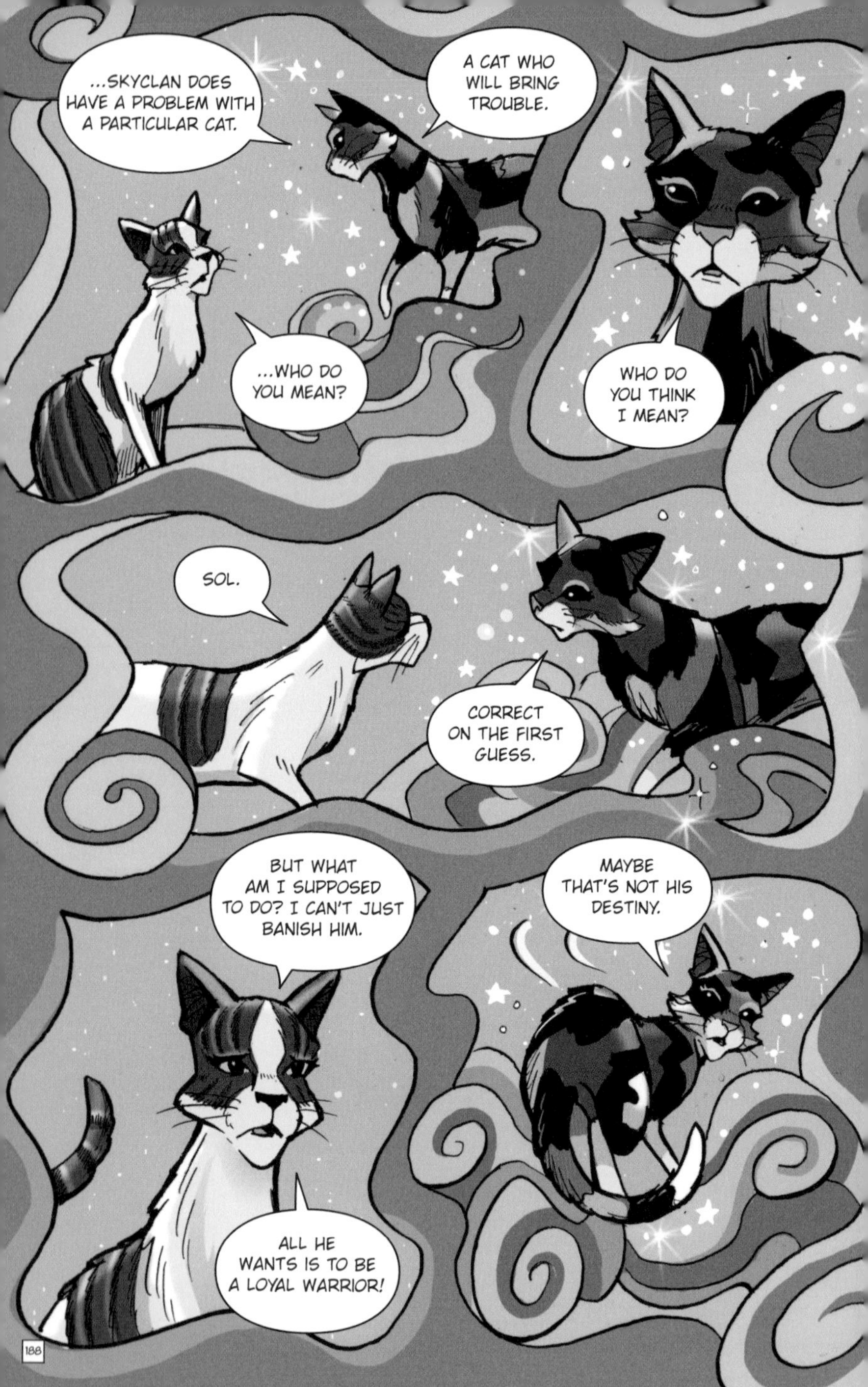
...SKYCLAN DOES HAVE A PROBLEM WITH A PARTICULAR CAT.
A CAT WHO WILL BRING TROUBLE.
...WHO DO YOU MEAN?
WHO DO YOU THINK I MEAN?
SOL.
CORRECT ON THE FIRST GUESS.
BUT WHAT AM I SUPPOSED TO DO? I CAN'T JUST BANISH HIM.
ALL HE WANTS IS TO BE A LOYAL WARRIOR!
MAYBE THAT'S NOT HIS DESTINY.

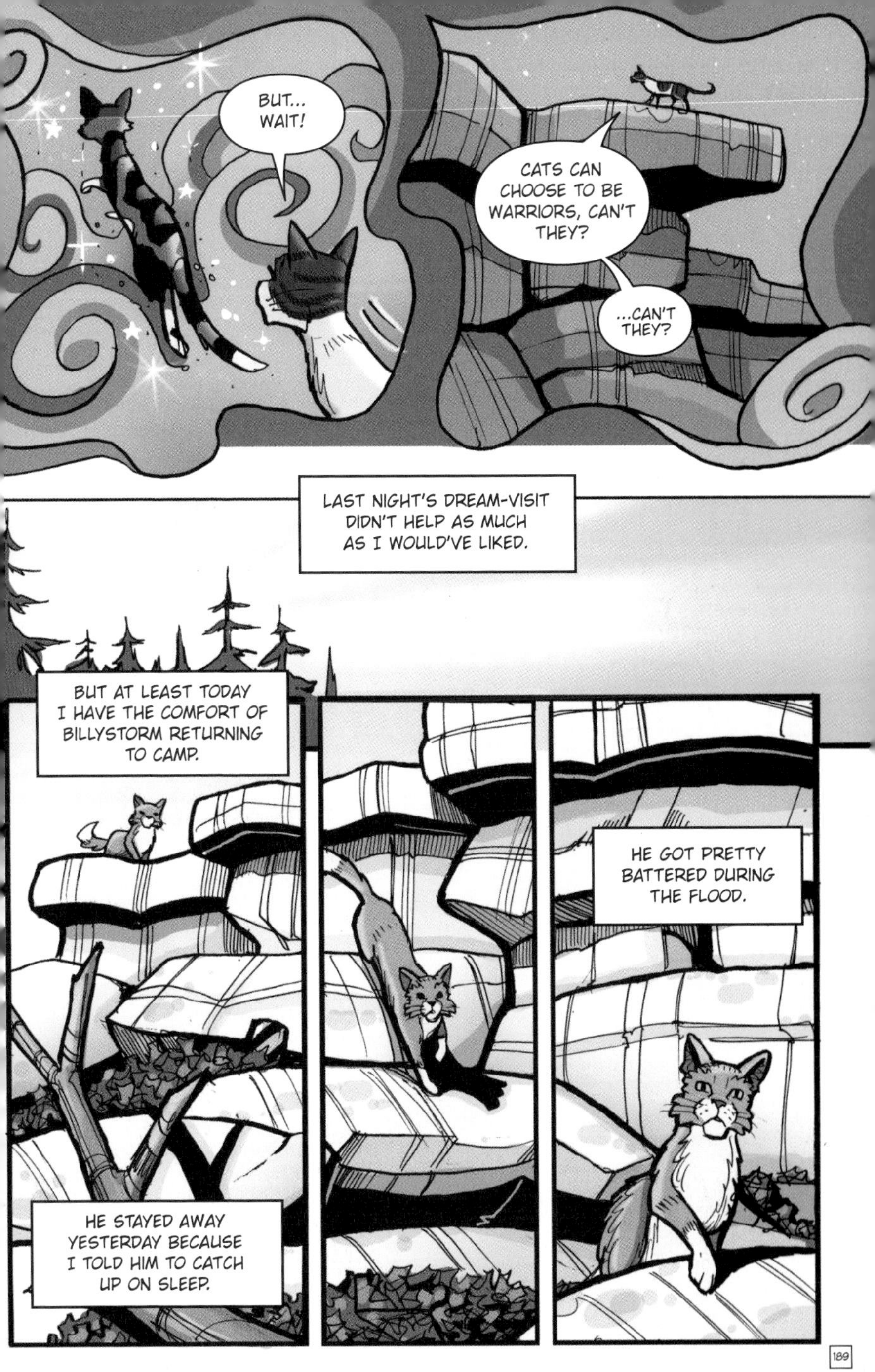
BUT... WAIT!
CATS CAN CHOOSE TO BE WARRIORS, CAN'T THEY?
...CAN'T THEY?
LAST NIGHT'S DREAM-VISIT DIDN'T HELP AS MUCH AS I WOULD'VE LIKED.
BUT AT LEAST TODAY I HAVE THE COMFORT OF BILLYSTORM RETURNING TO CAMP.
HE STAYED AWAY YESTERDAY BECAUSE I TOLD HIM TO CATCH UP ON SLEEP.
HE GOT PRETTY BATTERED DURING THE FLOOD.

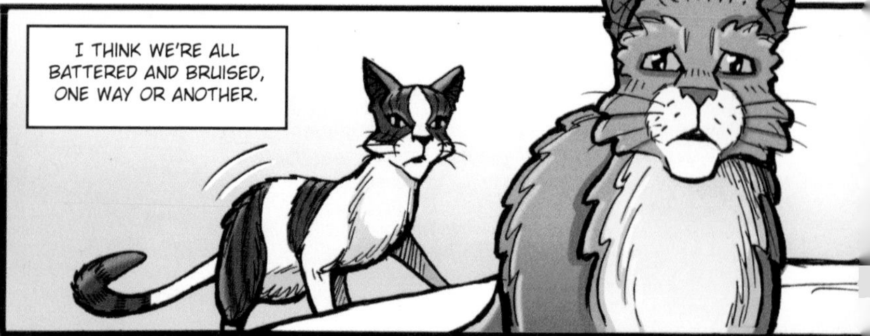
I THINK WE'RE ALL BATTERED AND BRUISED, ONE WAY OR ANOTHER.

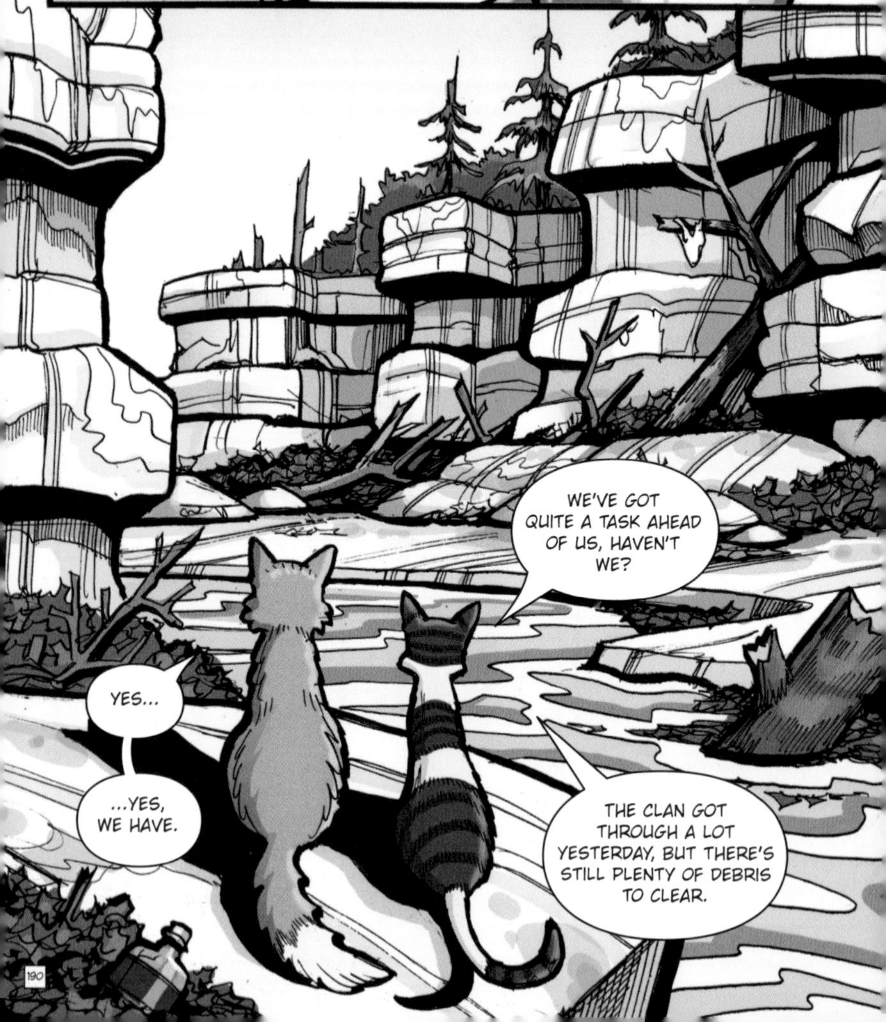
WE'VE GOT QUITE A TASK AHEAD OF US, HAVEN'T WE?
YES...
...YES, WE HAVE.
THE CLAN GOT THROUGH A LOT YESTERDAY, BUT THERE'S STILL PLENTY OF DEBRIS TO CLEAR.

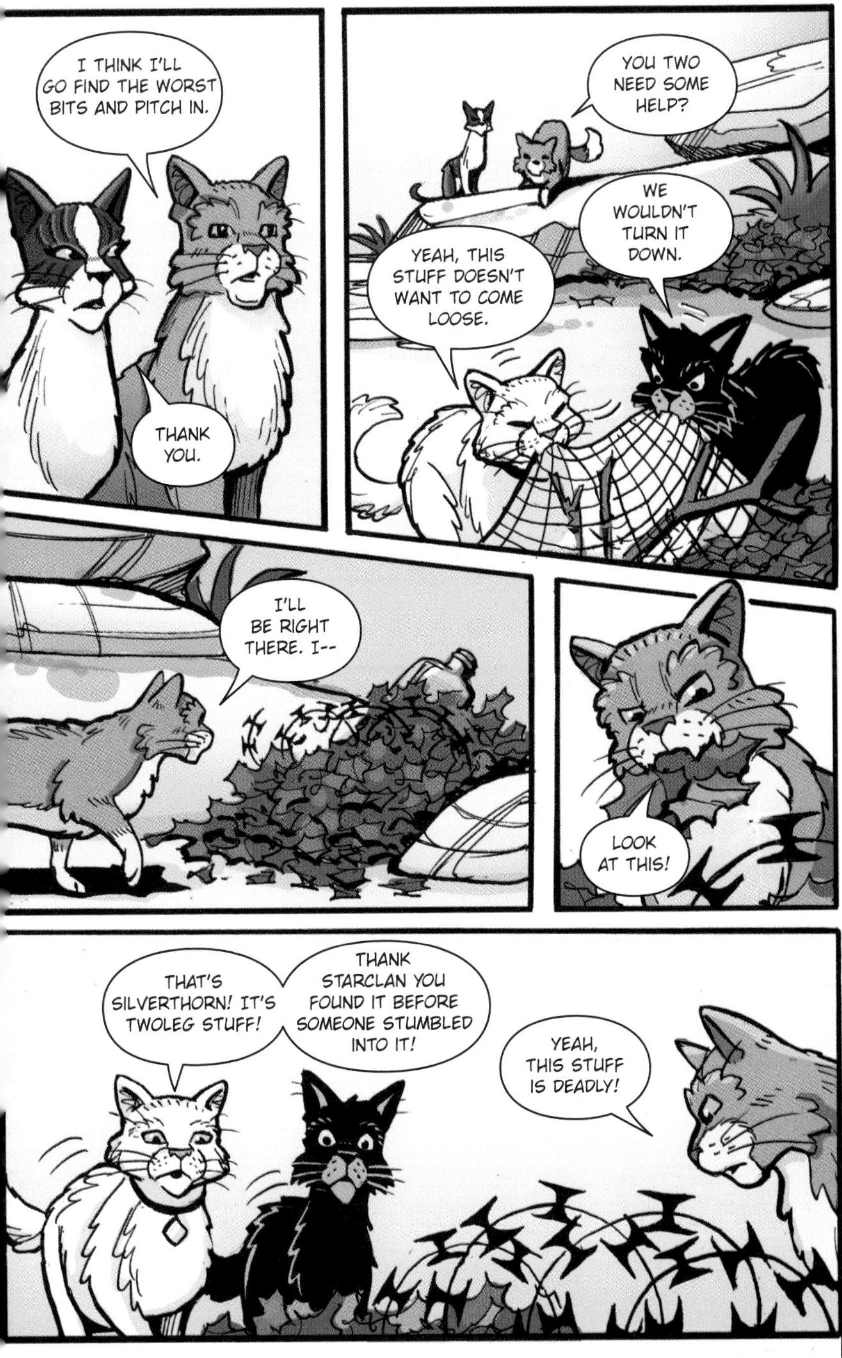
I THINK I'LL GO FIND THE WORST BITS AND PITCH IN.
THANK YOU.
YOU TWO NEED SOME HELP?
YEAH, THIS STUFF DOESN'T WANT TO COME LOOSE.
WE WOULDN'T TURN IT DOWN.
I'LL BE RIGHT THERE. I--
LOOK AT THIS!
THAT'S SILVERTHORN! IT'S TWOLEG STUFF!
THANK STARCLAN YOU FOUND IT BEFORE SOMEONE STUMBLED INTO IT!
YEAH, THIS STUFF IS DEADLY!

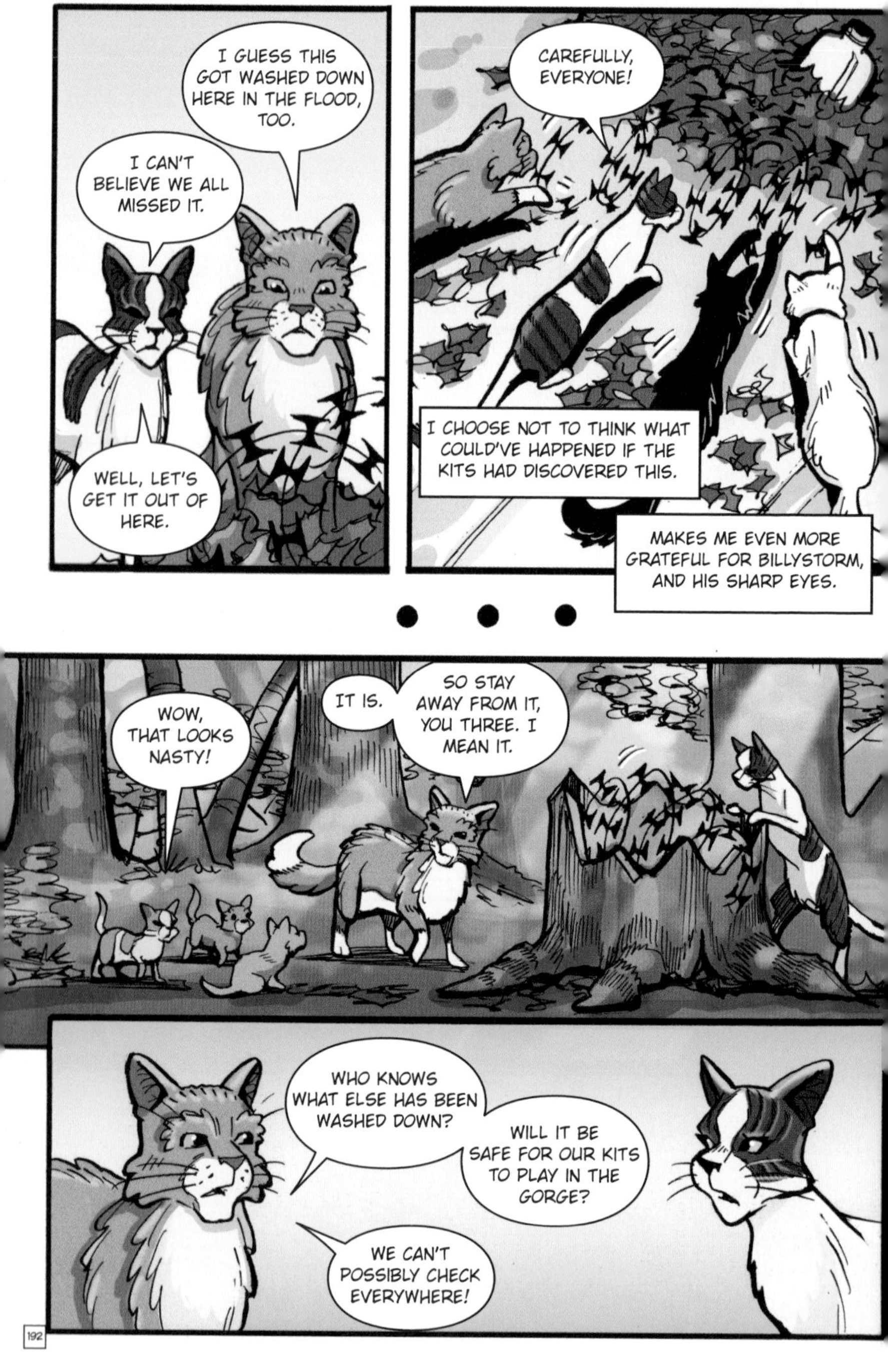
I CAN'T BELIEVE WE ALL MISSED IT.
I GUESS THIS GOT WASHED DOWN HERE IN THE FLOOD, TOO.
WELL, LET'S GET IT OUT OF HERE.
CAREFULLY, EVERYONE!
I CHOOSE NOT TO THINK WHAT COULD'VE HAPPENED IF THE KITS HAD DISCOVERED THIS.
MAKES ME EVEN MORE GRATEFUL FOR BILLYSTORM, AND HIS SHARP EYES.
WOW, THAT LOOKS NASTY!
IT IS.
SO STAY AWAY FROM IT, YOU THREE. I MEAN IT.
WHO KNOWS WHAT ELSE HAS BEEN WASHED DOWN?
WILL IT BE SAFE FOR OUR KITS TO PLAY IN THE GORGE?
WE CAN'T POSSIBLY CHECK EVERYWHERE!

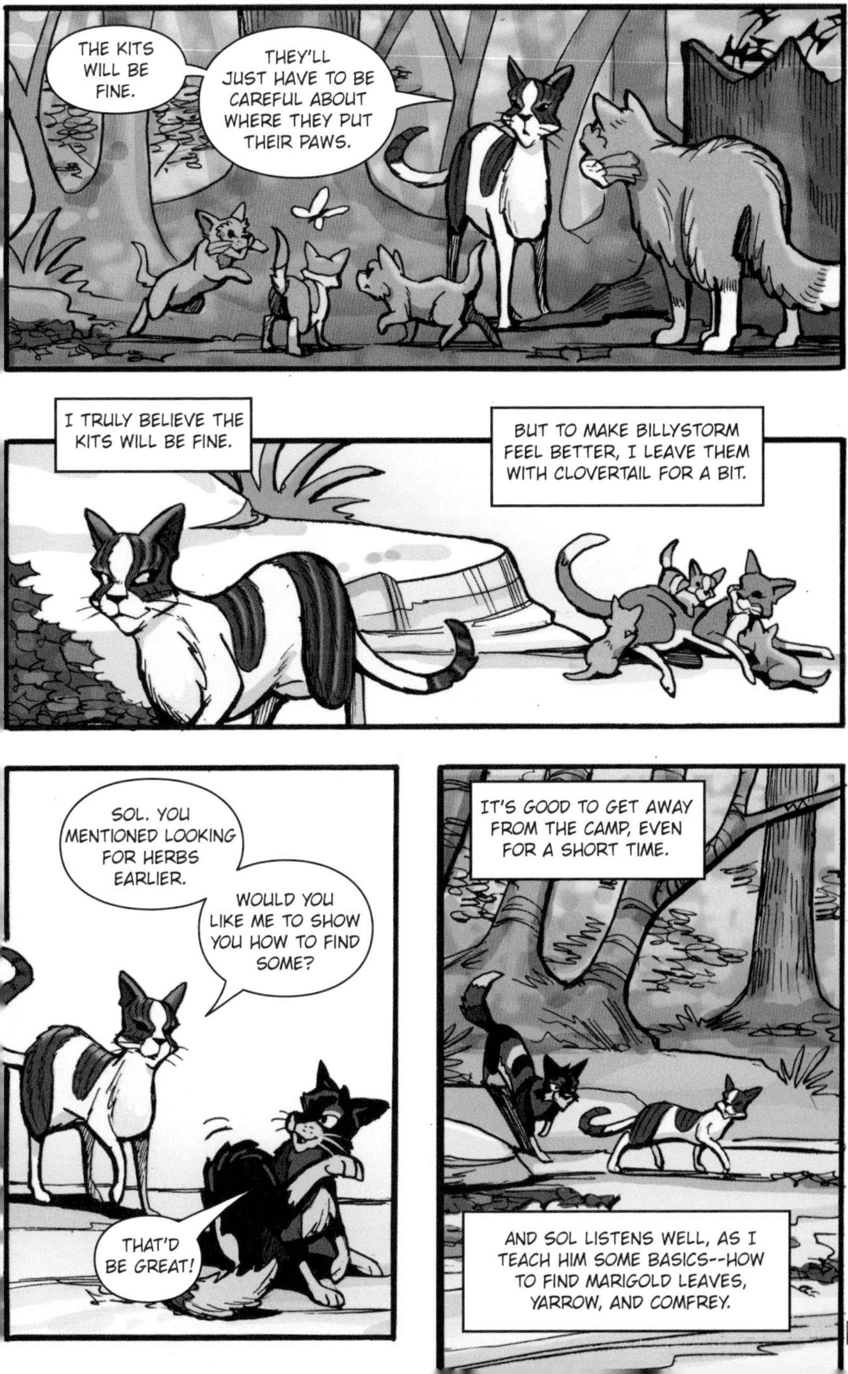
THE KITS WILL BE FINE.
THEY'LL JUST HAVE TO BE CAREFUL ABOUT WHERE THEY PUT THEIR PAWS.
I TRULY BELIEVE THE KITS WILL BE FINE.
BUT TO MAKE BILLYSTORM FEEL BETTER, I LEAVE THEM WITH CLOVERTAIL FOR A BIT.
SOL. YOU MENTIONED LOOKING FOR HERBS EARLIER.
WOULD YOU LIKE ME TO SHOW YOU HOW TO FIND SOME?
THAT'D BE GREAT!
IT'S GOOD TO GET AWAY FROM THE CAMP, EVEN FOR A SHORT TIME.
AND SOL LISTENS WELL, AS I TEACH HIM SOME BASICS--HOW TO FIND MARIGOLD LEAVES, YARROW, AND COMFREY.

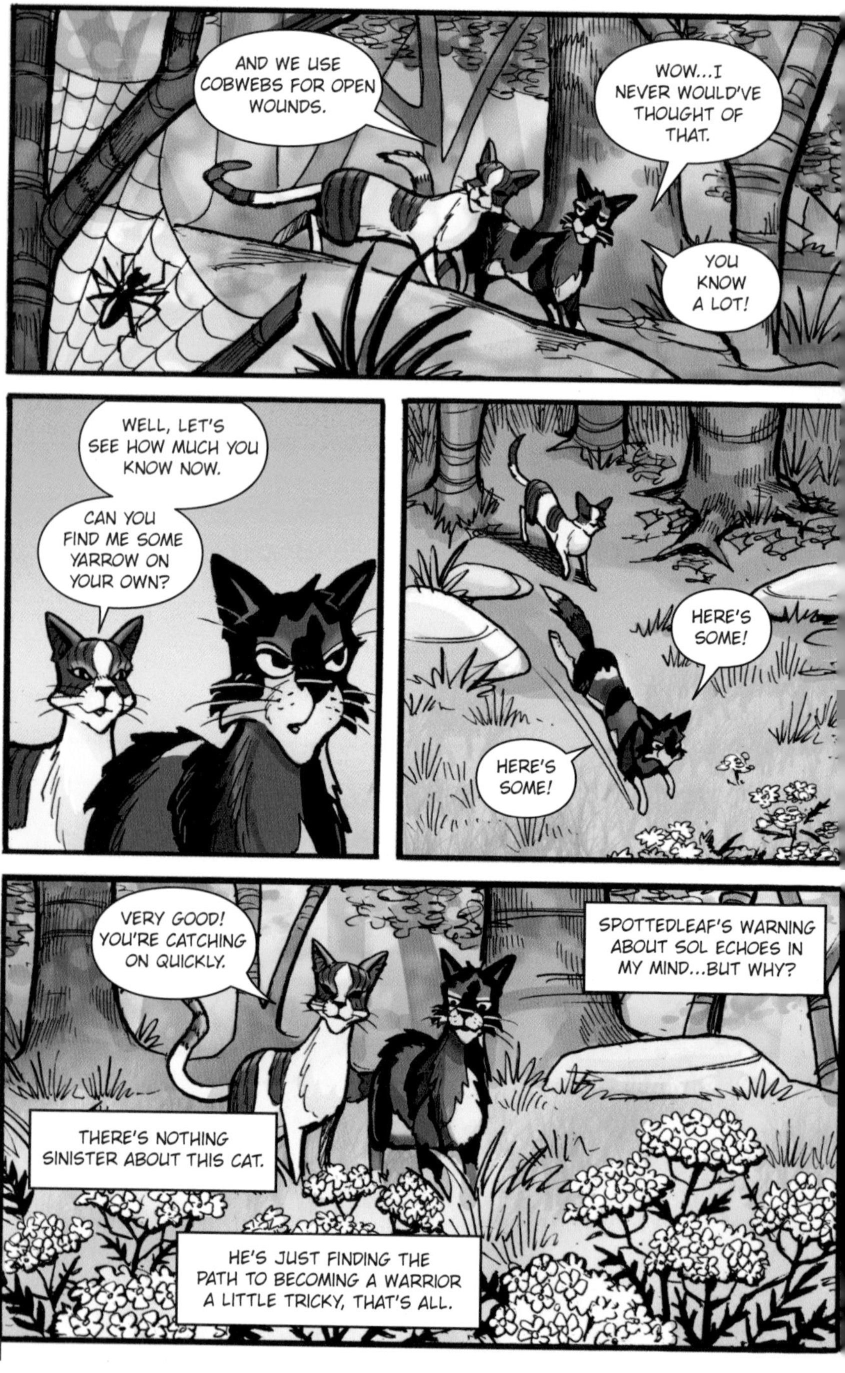
AND WE USE COBWEBS FOR OPEN WOUNDS.
WOW...I NEVER WOULD'VE THOUGHT OF THAT.
YOU KNOW A LOT!
WELL, LET'S SEE HOW MUCH YOU KNOW NOW.
CAN YOU FIND ME SOME YARROW ON YOUR OWN?
HERE'S SOME!
HERE'S SOME!
VERY GOOD! YOU'RE CATCHING ON QUICKLY.
SPOTTEDLEAF'S WARNING ABOUT SOL ECHOES IN MY MIND...BUT WHY?
THERE'S NOTHING SINISTER ABOUT THIS CAT.
HE'S JUST FINDING THE PATH TO BECOMING A WARRIOR A LITTLE TRICKY, THAT'S ALL.

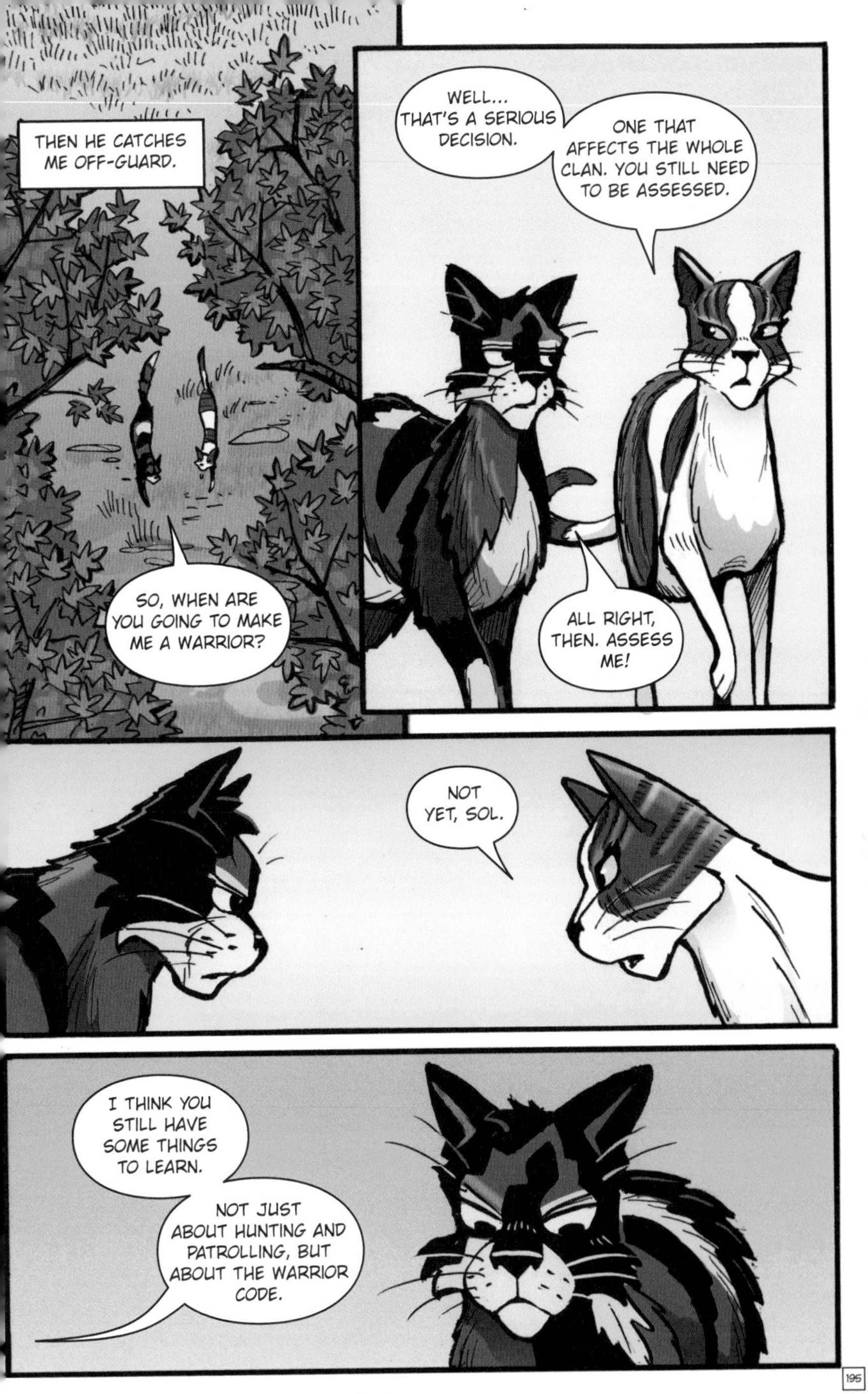

THEN HE CATCHES ME OFF-GUARD.
SO, WHEN ARE YOU GOING TO MAKE ME A WARRIOR?
WELL... THAT'S A SERIOUS DECISION.
ONE THAT AFFECTS THE WHOLE CLAN. YOU STILL NEED TO BE ASSESSED.
ALL RIGHT, THEN. ASSESS ME!
NOT YET, SOL.
I THINK YOU STILL HAVE SOME THINGS TO LEARN.
NOT JUST ABOUT HUNTING AND PATROLLING, BUT ABOUT THE WARRIOR CODE.

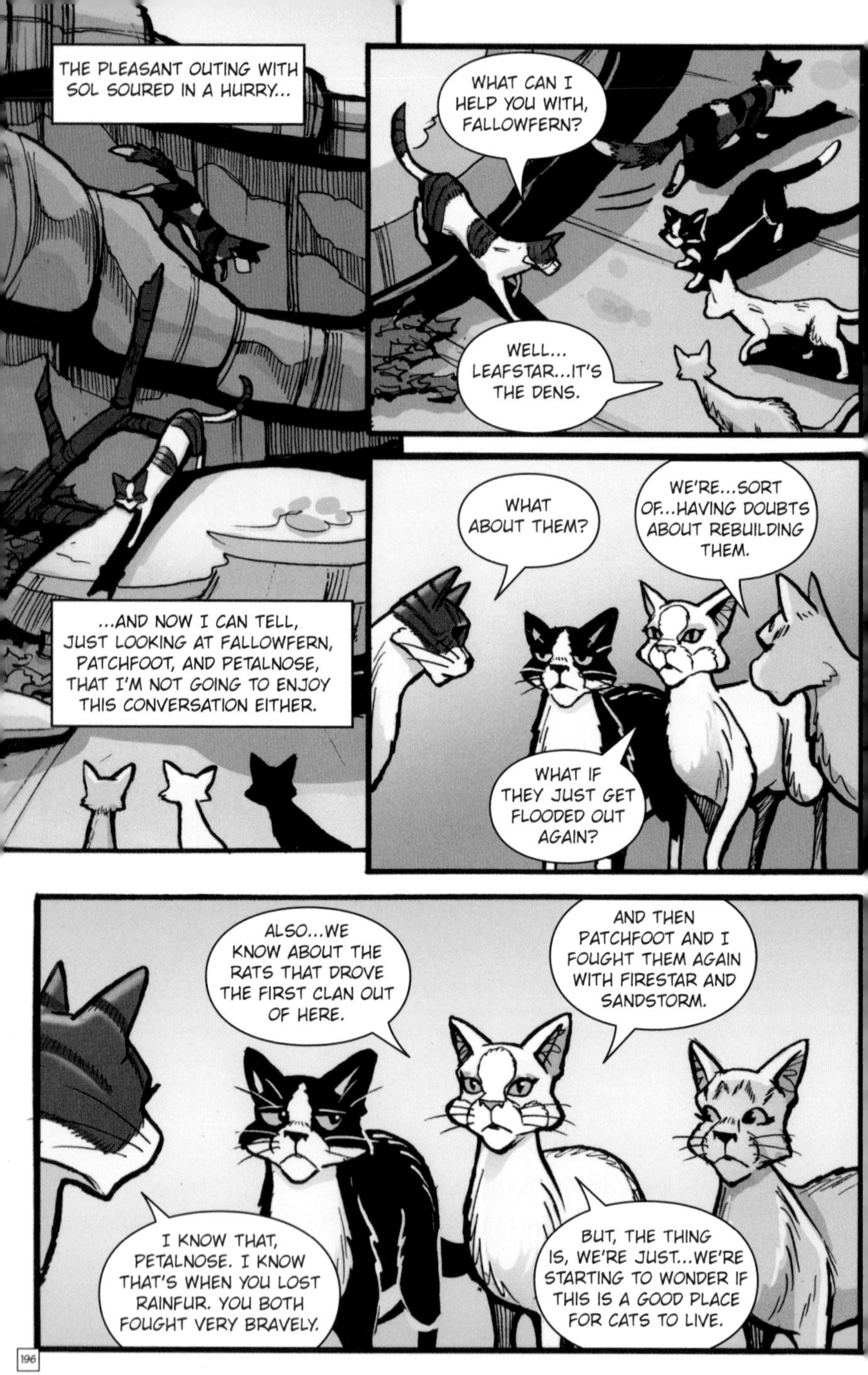
THE PLEASANT OUTING WITH SOL SOURED IN A HURRY...
...AND NOW I CAN TELL, JUST LOOKING AT FALLOWFERN, PATCHFOOT, AND PETALNOSE, THAT I'M NOT GOING TO ENJOY THIS CONVERSATION EITHER.
WHAT CAN I HELP YOU WITH, FALLOWFERN?
WELL... LEAFSTAR...IT'S THE DENS.
WHAT ABOUT THEM?
WE'RE...SORT OF...HAVING DOUBTS ABOUT REBUILDING THEM.
WHAT IF THEY JUST GET FLOODED OUT AGAIN?
ALSO...WE KNOW ABOUT THE RATS THAT DROVE THE FIRST CLAN OUT OF HERE.
AND THEN PATCHFOOT AND I FOUGHT THEM AGAIN WITH FIRESTAR AND SANDSTORM.
I KNOW THAT, PETALNOSE. I KNOW THAT'S WHEN YOU LOST RAINFUR. YOU BOTH FOUGHT VERY BRAVELY.
BUT, THE THING IS, WE'RE JUST...WE'RE STARTING TO WONDER IF THIS IS A GOOD PLACE FOR CATS TO LIVE.

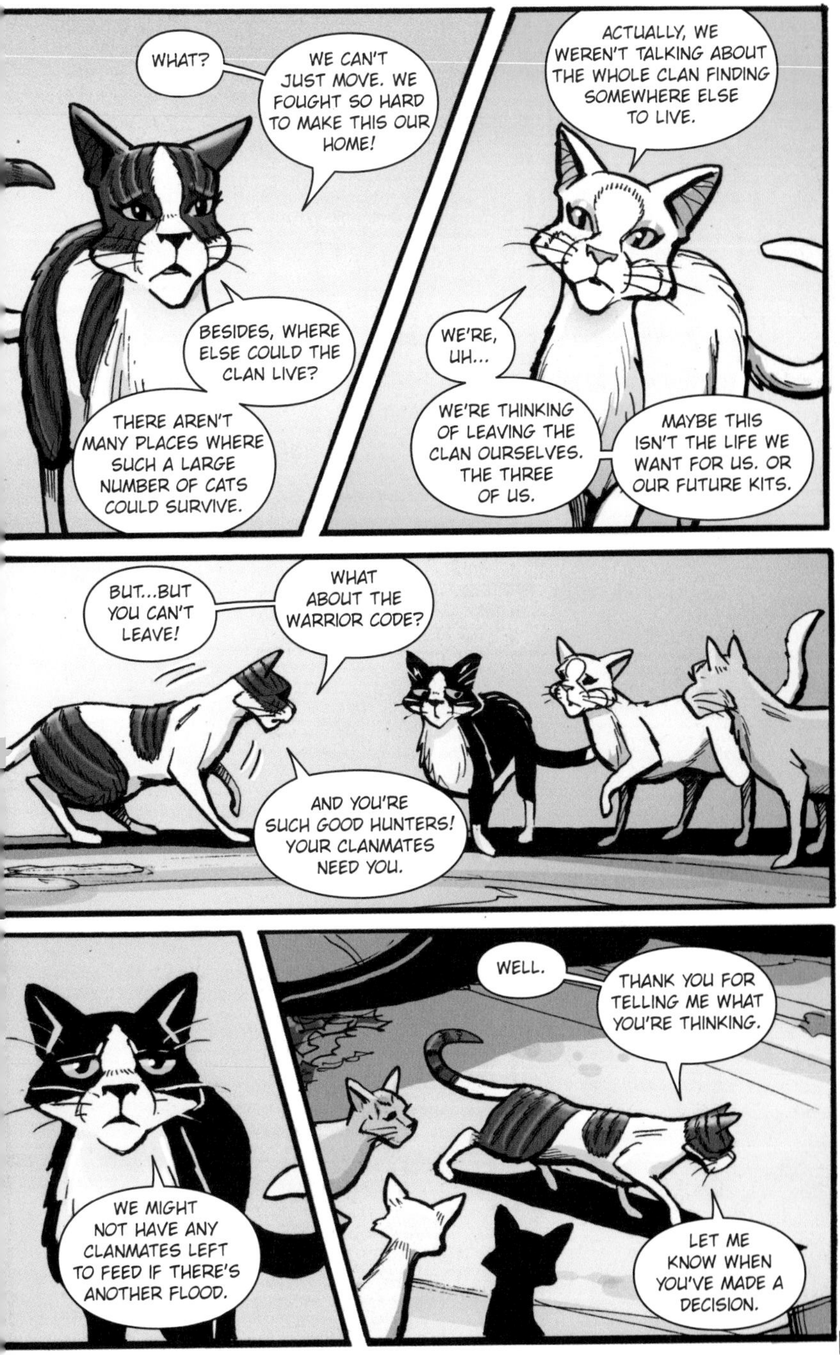
WHAT?
WE CAN'T JUST MOVE. WE FOUGHT SO HARD TO MAKE THIS OUR HOME!
BESIDES, WHERE ELSE COULD THE CLAN LIVE?
THERE AREN'T MANY PLACES WHERE SUCH A LARGE NUMBER OF CATS COULD SURVIVE.
ACTUALLY, WE WEREN'T TALKING ABOUT THE WHOLE CLAN FINDING SOMEWHERE ELSE TO LIVE.
WE'RE, UH...
WE'RE THINKING OF LEAVING THE CLAN OURSELVES. THE THREE OF US.
MAYBE THIS ISN'T THE LIFE WE WANT FOR US. OR OUR FUTURE KITS.
BUT...BUT YOU CAN'T LEAVE!
WHAT ABOUT THE WARRIOR CODE?
AND YOU'RE SUCH GOOD HUNTERS! YOUR CLANMATES NEED YOU.
WE MIGHT NOT HAVE ANY CLANMATES LEFT TO FEED IF THERE'S ANOTHER FLOOD.
WELL.
THANK YOU FOR TELLING ME WHAT YOU'RE THINKING.
LET ME KNOW WHEN YOU'VE MADE A DECISION.

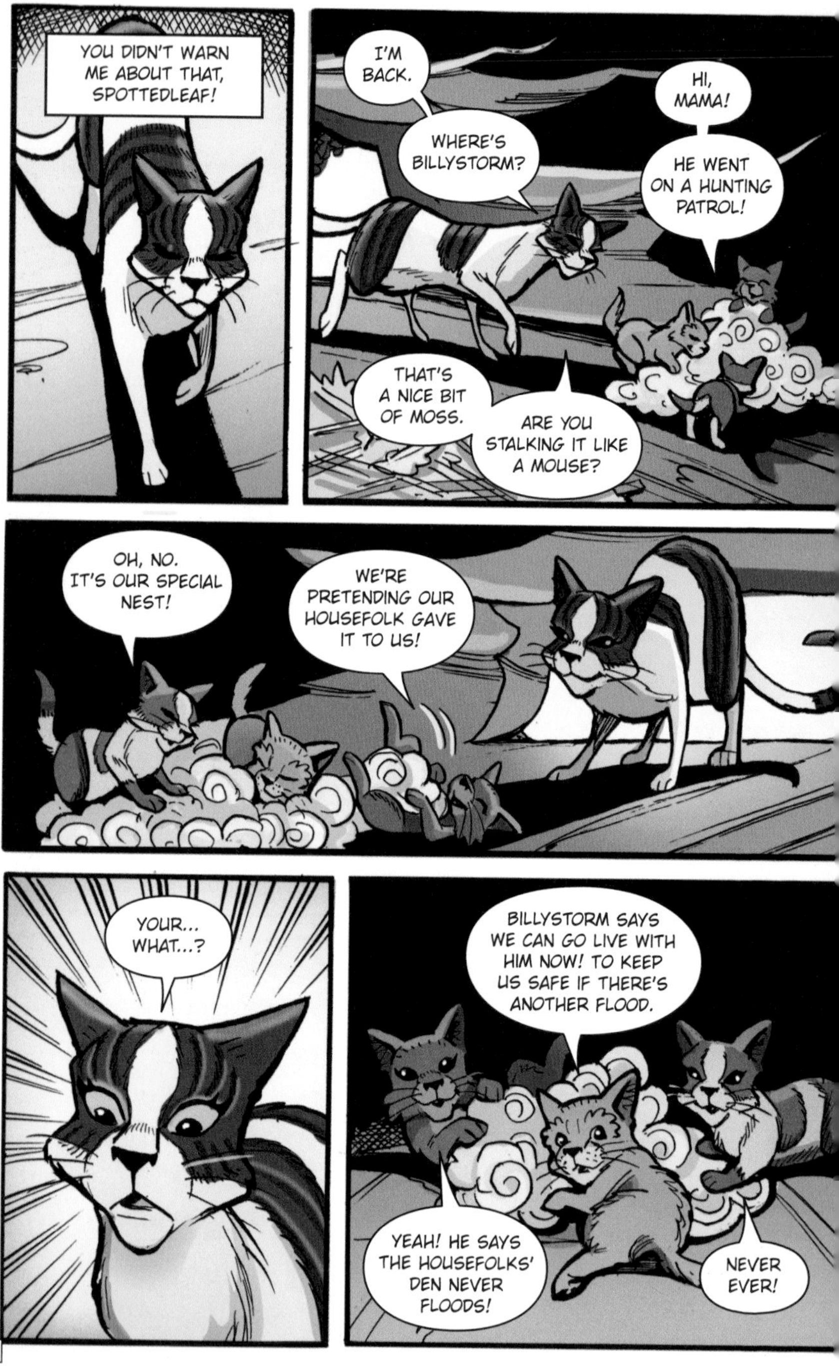
YOU DIDN'T WARN ME ABOUT THAT, SPOTTEDLEAF!
I'M BACK.
WHERE'S BILLYSTORM?
HI, MAMA!
HE WENT ON A HUNTING PATROL!
THAT'S A NICE BIT OF MOSS.
ARE YOU STALKING IT LIKE A MOUSE?
OH, NO. IT'S OUR SPECIAL NEST!
WE'RE PRETENDING OUR HOUSEFOLK GAVE IT TO US!
YOUR... WHAT...?
BILLYSTORM SAYS WE CAN GO LIVE WITH HIM NOW! TO KEEP US SAFE IF THERE'S ANOTHER FLOOD.
YEAH! HE SAYS THE HOUSEFOLKS' DEN NEVER FLOODS!
NEVER EVER!

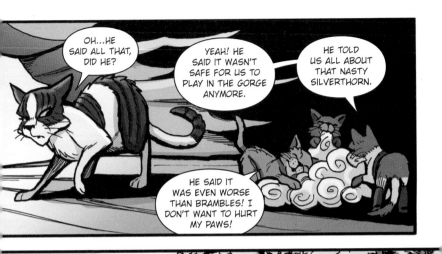

OH...HE SAID ALL THAT, DID HE?

YEAH! HE SAID IT WASN'T SAFE FOR US TO PLAY IN THE GORGE ANYMORE.

HE TOLD US ALL ABOUT THAT NASTY SILVERTHORN.

HE SAID IT WAS EVEN WORSE THAN BRAMBLES! I DON'T WANT TO HURT MY PAWS!

I DON'T TRUST MYSELF TO SPEAK. NOT YET.

BETTER TO WAIT.

AND...*THINK* ABOUT THIS.

UH-OH.

THUD

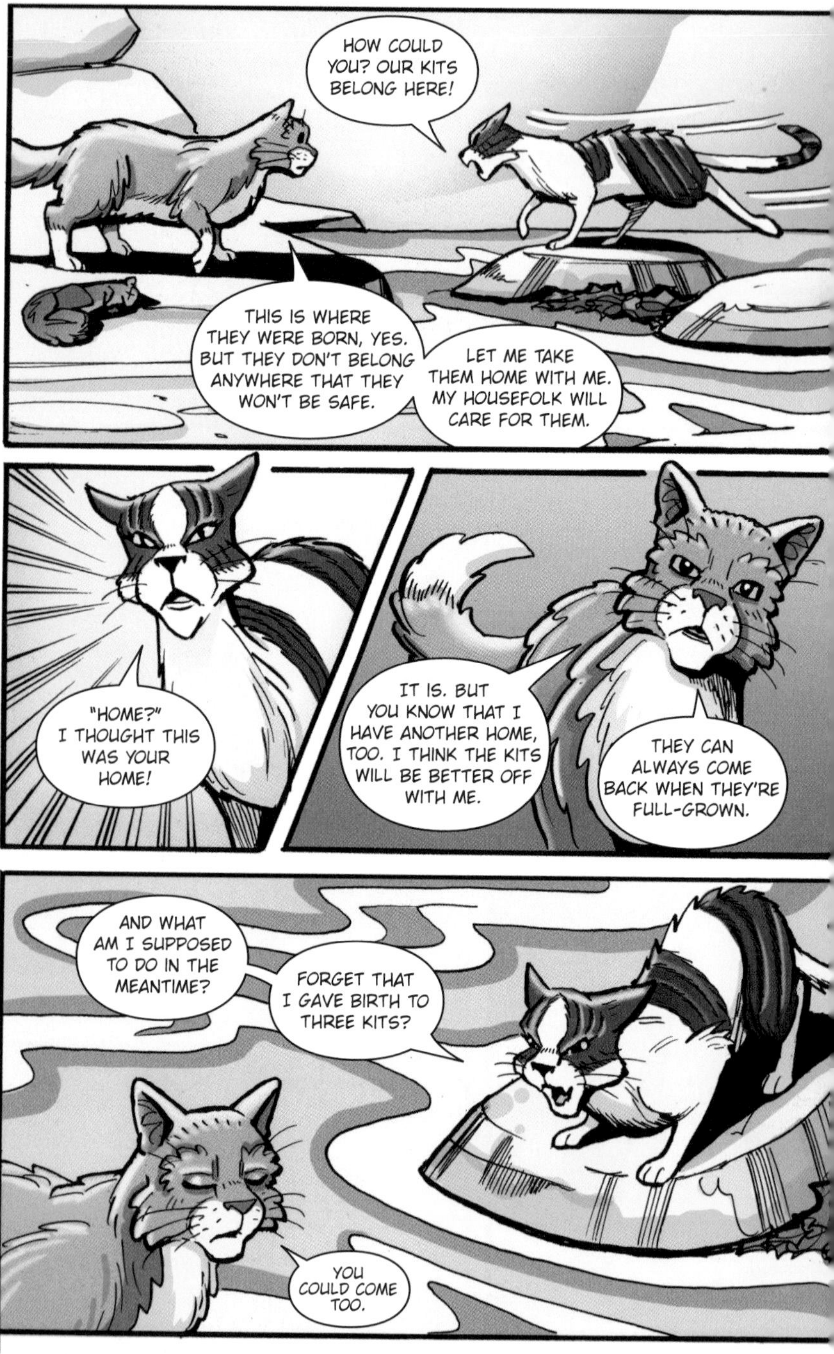
HOW COULD YOU? OUR KITS BELONG HERE!
THIS IS WHERE THEY WERE BORN, YES. BUT THEY DON'T BELONG ANYWHERE THAT THEY WON'T BE SAFE.
LET ME TAKE THEM HOME WITH ME. MY HOUSEFOLK WILL CARE FOR THEM.
"HOME?" I THOUGHT THIS WAS YOUR HOME!
IT IS. BUT YOU KNOW THAT I HAVE ANOTHER HOME, TOO. I THINK THE KITS WILL BE BETTER OFF WITH ME.
THEY CAN ALWAYS COME BACK WHEN THEY'RE FULL-GROWN.
AND WHAT AM I SUPPOSED TO DO IN THE MEANTIME?
FORGET THAT I GAVE BIRTH TO THREE KITS?
YOU COULD COME TOO.

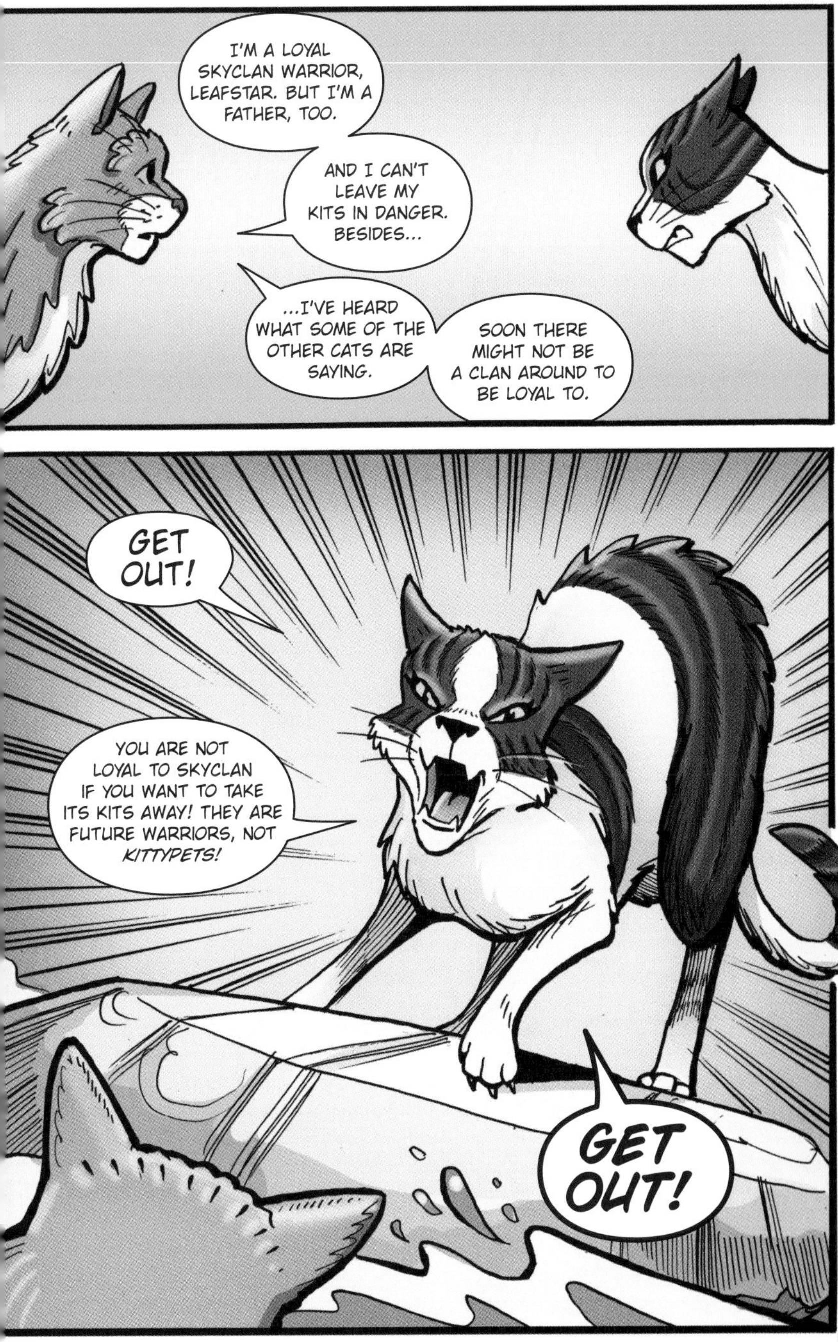
I'M A LOYAL SKYCLAN WARRIOR, LEAFSTAR. BUT I'M A FATHER, TOO.
AND I CAN'T LEAVE MY KITS IN DANGER. BESIDES...
...I'VE HEARD WHAT SOME OF THE OTHER CATS ARE SAYING.
SOON THERE MIGHT NOT BE A CLAN AROUND TO BE LOYAL TO.
GET OUT!
YOU ARE NOT LOYAL TO SKYCLAN IF YOU WANT TO TAKE ITS KITS AWAY! THEY ARE FUTURE WARRIORS, NOT *KITTYPETS!*
GET OUT!

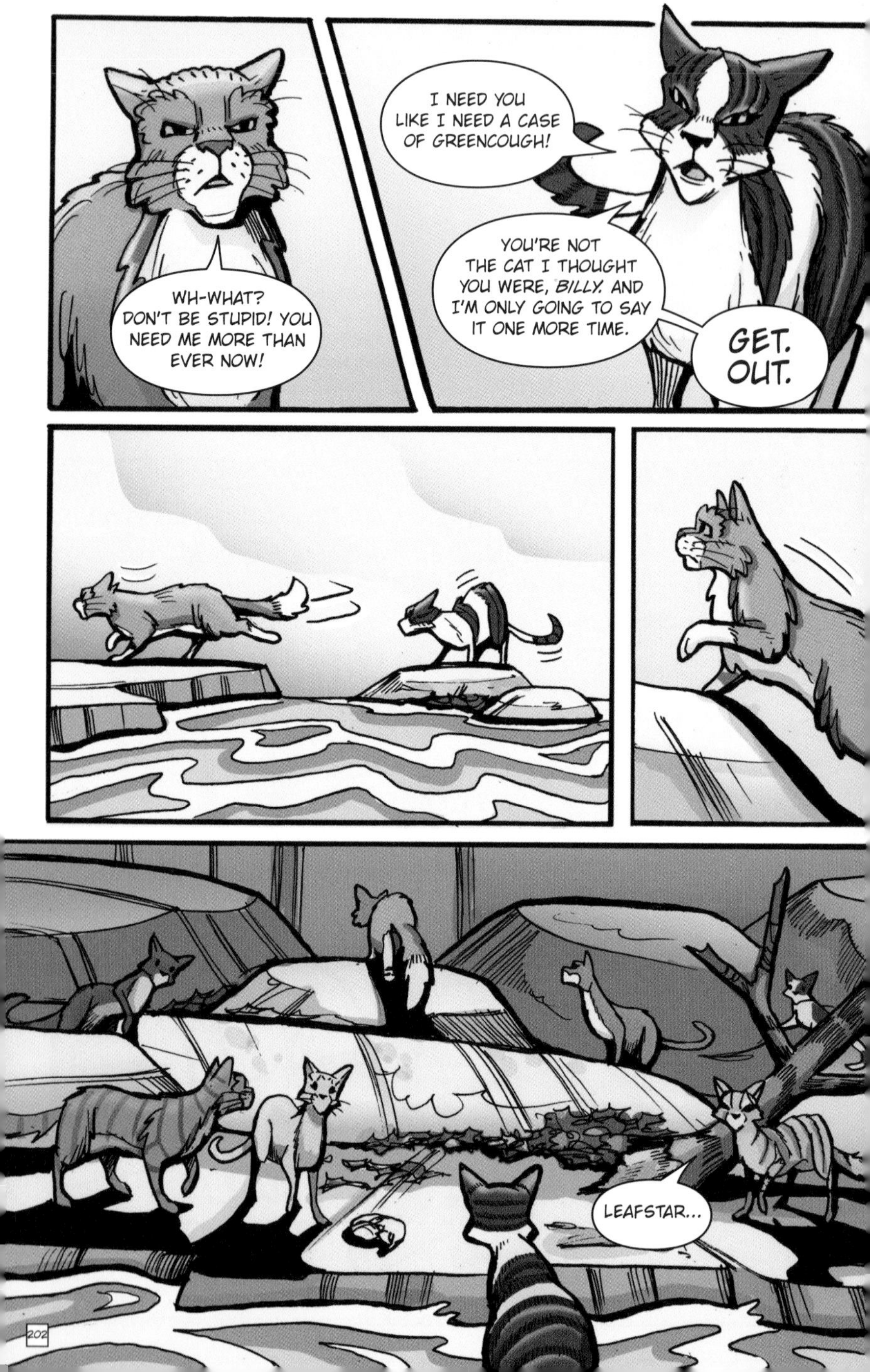
WH-WHAT? DON'T BE STUPID! YOU NEED ME MORE THAN EVER NOW!
I NEED YOU LIKE I NEED A CASE OF GREENCOUGH!
YOU'RE NOT THE CAT I THOUGHT YOU WERE, *BILLY*. AND I'M ONLY GOING TO SAY IT ONE MORE TIME.
GET. OUT.
LEAFSTAR...

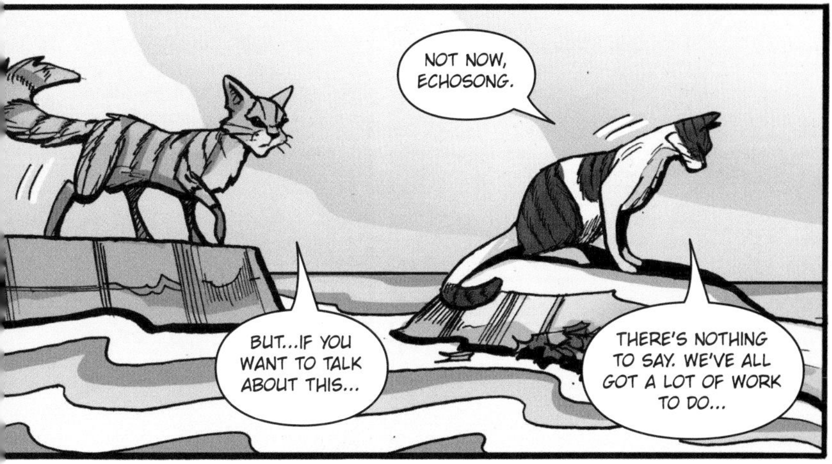
NOT NOW, ECHOSONG.
BUT...IF YOU WANT TO TALK ABOUT THIS...
THERE'S NOTHING TO SAY. WE'VE ALL GOT A LOT OF WORK TO DO...

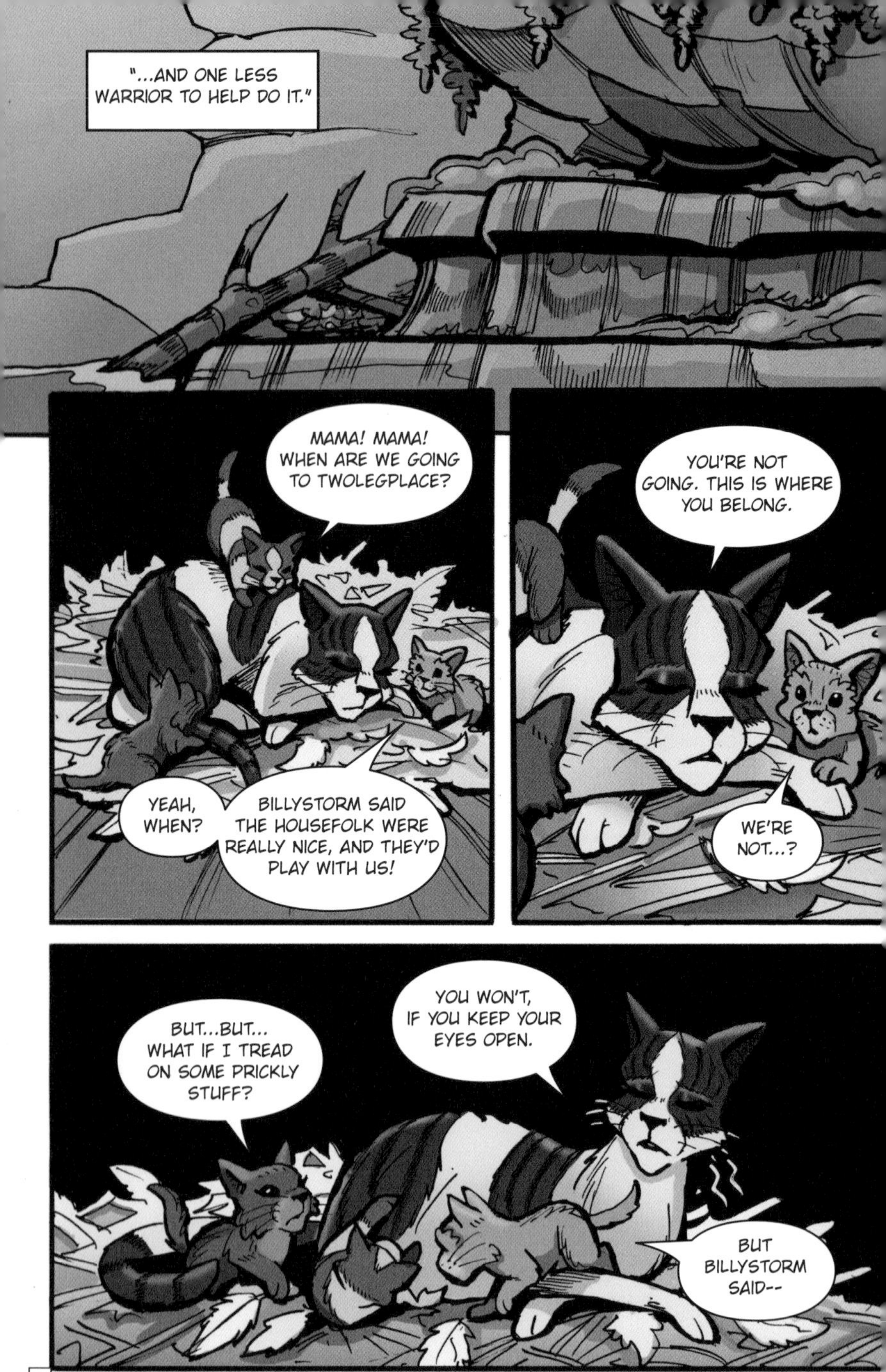
"...AND ONE LESS WARRIOR TO HELP DO IT."
MAMA! MAMA! WHEN ARE WE GOING TO TWOLEGPLACE?
YEAH, WHEN?
BILLYSTORM SAID THE HOUSEFOLK WERE REALLY NICE, AND THEY'D PLAY WITH US!
YOU'RE NOT GOING. THIS IS WHERE YOU BELONG.
WE'RE NOT...?
BUT...BUT... WHAT IF I TREAD ON SOME PRICKLY STUFF?
YOU WON'T, IF YOU KEEP YOUR EYES OPEN.
BUT BILLYSTORM SAID--

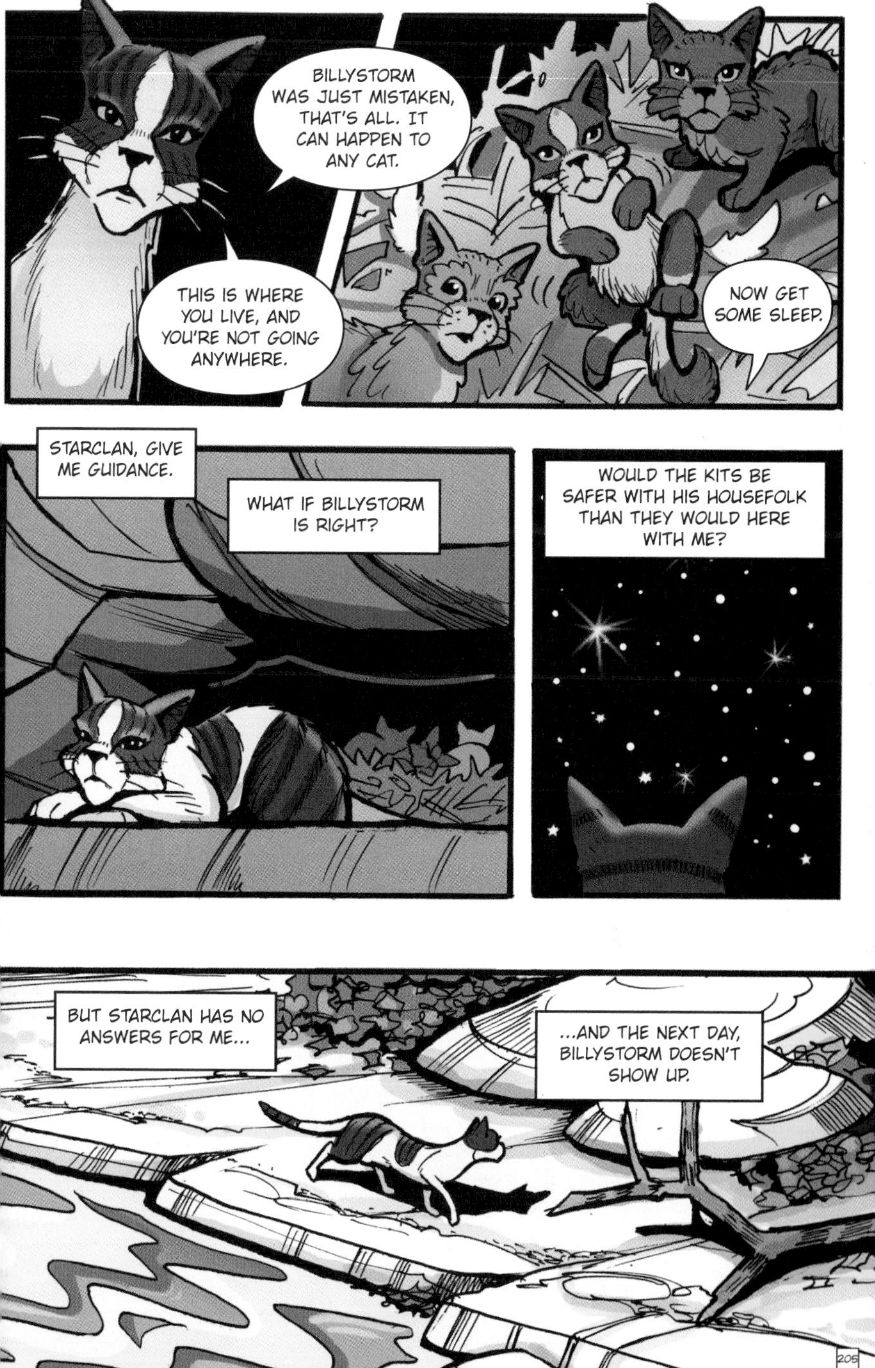
BILLYSTORM WAS JUST MISTAKEN, THAT'S ALL. IT CAN HAPPEN TO ANY CAT.
THIS IS WHERE YOU LIVE, AND YOU'RE NOT GOING ANYWHERE.
NOW GET SOME SLEEP.
STARCLAN, GIVE ME GUIDANCE.
WHAT IF BILLYSTORM IS RIGHT?
WOULD THE KITS BE SAFER WITH HIS HOUSEFOLK THAN THEY WOULD HERE WITH ME?
BUT STARCLAN HAS NO ANSWERS FOR ME...
...AND THE NEXT DAY, BILLYSTORM DOESN'T SHOW UP.

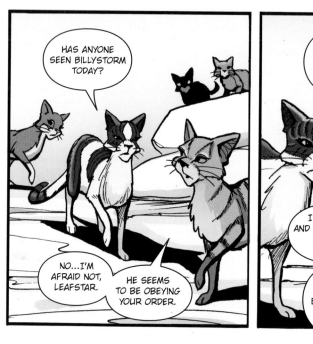

HAS ANYONE SEEN BILLYSTORM TODAY?

NO...I'M AFRAID NOT, LEAFSTAR.

HE SEEMS TO BE OBEYING YOUR ORDER.

I HATE THIS. PUTTING MY PERSONAL PROBLEMS ON DISPLAY FOR THE WHOLE CLAN. IT'S HUMILIATING.

I UNDERSTAND. AND I DON'T MEAN TO ADD TO YOUR STRESS...

...BUT...HAVE YOU THOUGHT ABOUT CONSIDERING WHETHER BILLYSTORM MIGHT HAVE HAD A POINT? ABOUT THE KITS' SAFETY?

IF ECHOSONG ONLY KNEW HOW MUCH I'D CONSIDERED THAT.

IF I DON'T DO SOMETHING ELSE...SOMETHING PRODUCTIVE...I'LL GO INSANE.

SOL!

HOW WOULD YOU LIKE TO GET ASSESSED TODAY?

ARE YOU SERIOUS? OF COURSE!

GOOD. COME WITH ME.

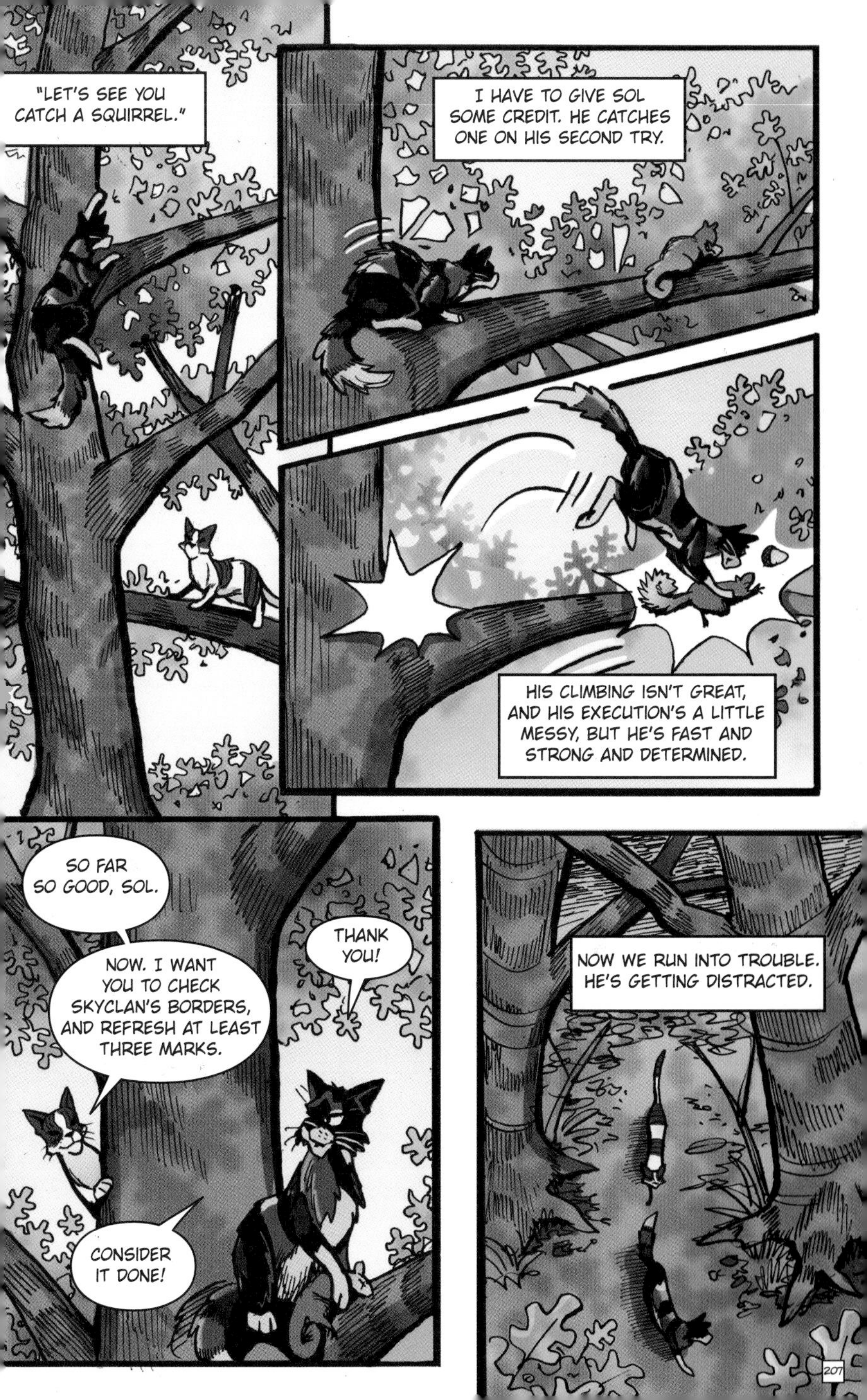
"LET'S SEE YOU CATCH A SQUIRREL."
I HAVE TO GIVE SOL SOME CREDIT. HE CATCHES ONE ON HIS SECOND TRY.
HIS CLIMBING ISN'T GREAT, AND HIS EXECUTION'S A LITTLE MESSY, BUT HE'S FAST AND STRONG AND DETERMINED.
SO FAR SO GOOD, SOL.
NOW. I WANT YOU TO CHECK SKYCLAN'S BORDERS, AND REFRESH AT LEAST THREE MARKS.
THANK YOU!
CONSIDER IT DONE!
NOW WE RUN INTO TROUBLE. HE'S GETTING DISTRACTED.

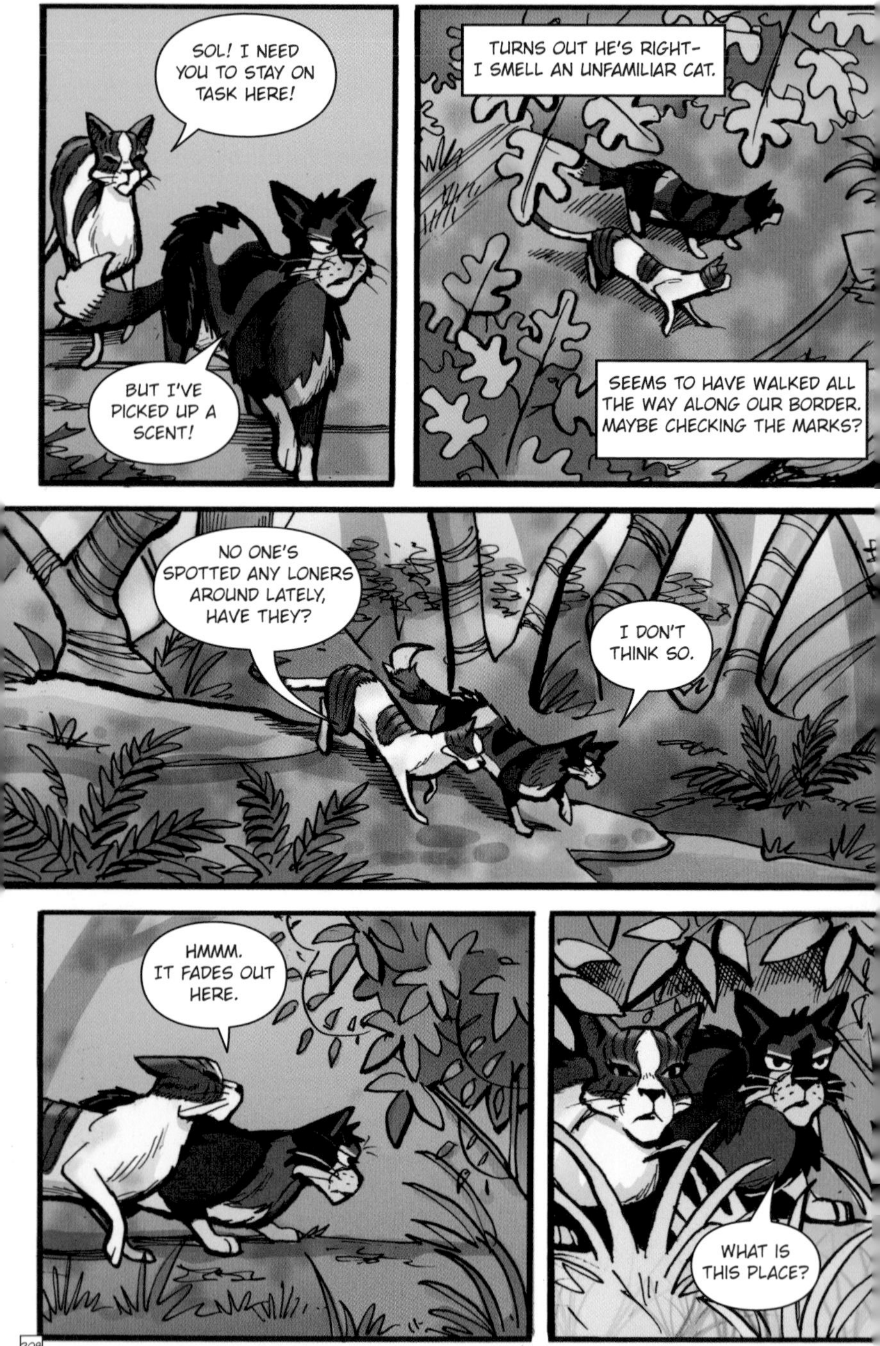
SOL! I NEED YOU TO STAY ON TASK HERE!
BUT I'VE PICKED UP A SCENT!
TURNS OUT HE'S RIGHT- I SMELL AN UNFAMILIAR CAT.
SEEMS TO HAVE WALKED ALL THE WAY ALONG OUR BORDER. MAYBE CHECKING THE MARKS?
NO ONE'S SPOTTED ANY LONERS AROUND LATELY, HAVE THEY?
I DON'T THINK SO.
HMMM. IT FADES OUT HERE.
WHAT IS THIS PLACE?

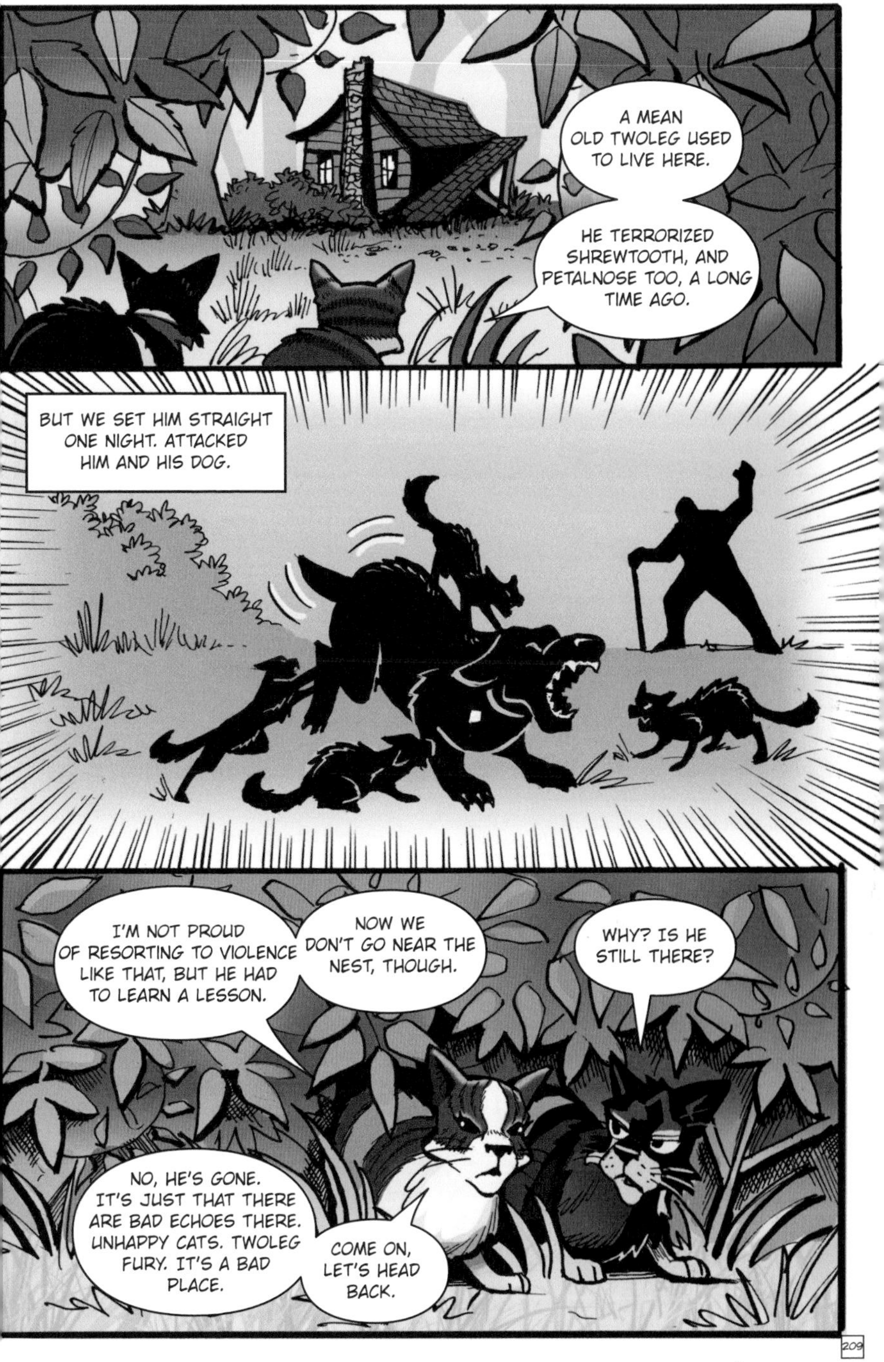
A MEAN OLD TWOLEG USED TO LIVE HERE.
HE TERRORIZED SHREWTOOTH, AND PETALNOSE TOO, A LONG TIME AGO.
BUT WE SET HIM STRAIGHT ONE NIGHT. ATTACKED HIM AND HIS DOG.
I'M NOT PROUD OF RESORTING TO VIOLENCE LIKE THAT, BUT HE HAD TO LEARN A LESSON.
NOW WE DON'T GO NEAR THE NEST, THOUGH.
WHY? IS HE STILL THERE?
NO, HE'S GONE. IT'S JUST THAT THERE ARE BAD ECHOES THERE. UNHAPPY CATS. TWOLEG FURY. IT'S A BAD PLACE.
COME ON, LET'S HEAD BACK.

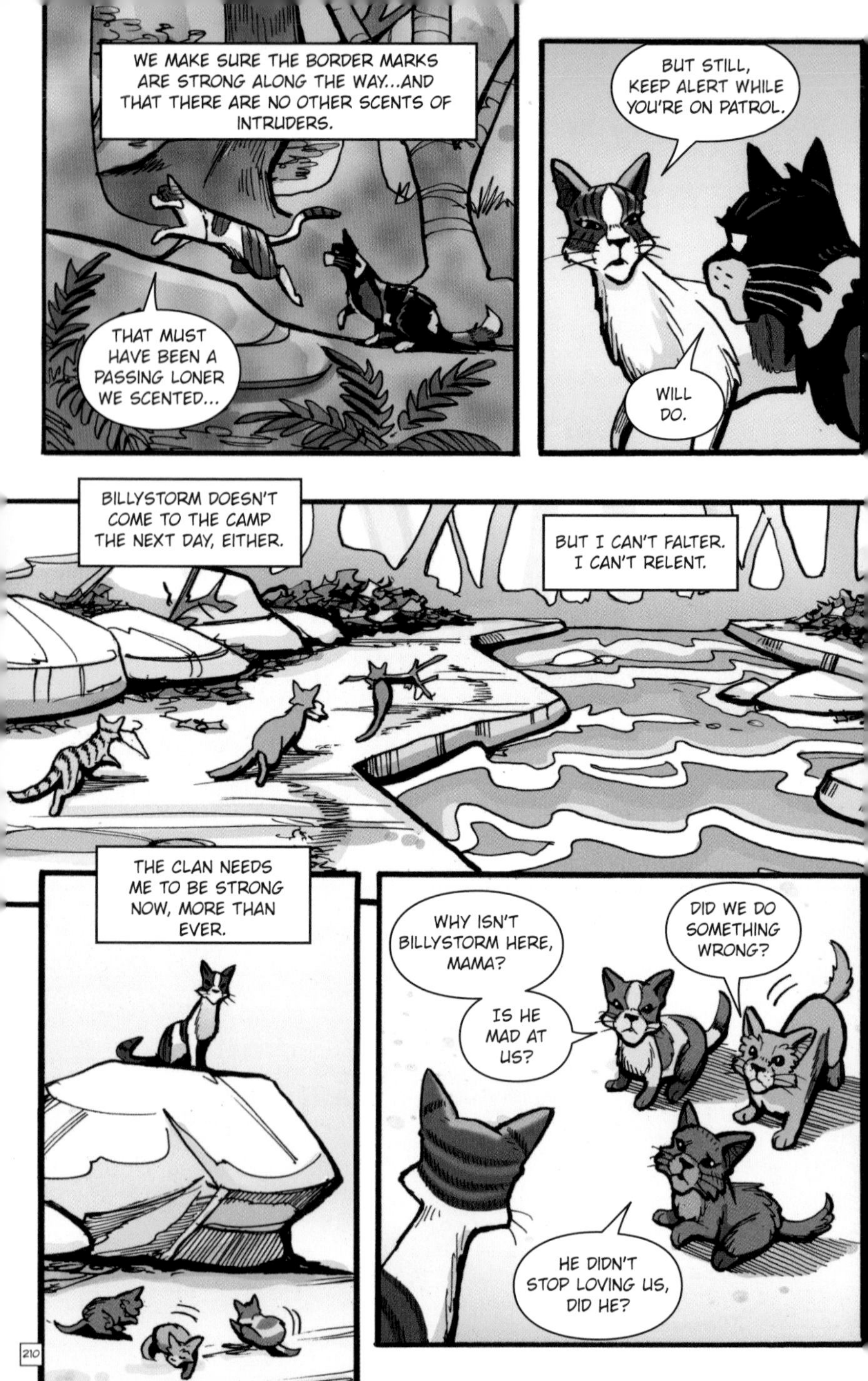
WE MAKE SURE THE BORDER MARKS ARE STRONG ALONG THE WAY...AND THAT THERE ARE NO OTHER SCENTS OF INTRUDERS.
THAT MUST HAVE BEEN A PASSING LONER WE SCENTED...
BUT STILL, KEEP ALERT WHILE YOU'RE ON PATROL.
WILL DO.
BILLYSTORM DOESN'T COME TO THE CAMP THE NEXT DAY, EITHER.
BUT I CAN'T FALTER. I CAN'T RELENT.
THE CLAN NEEDS ME TO BE STRONG NOW, MORE THAN EVER.
WHY ISN'T BILLYSTORM HERE, MAMA?
IS HE MAD AT US?
DID WE DO SOMETHING WRONG?
HE DIDN'T STOP LOVING US, DID HE?

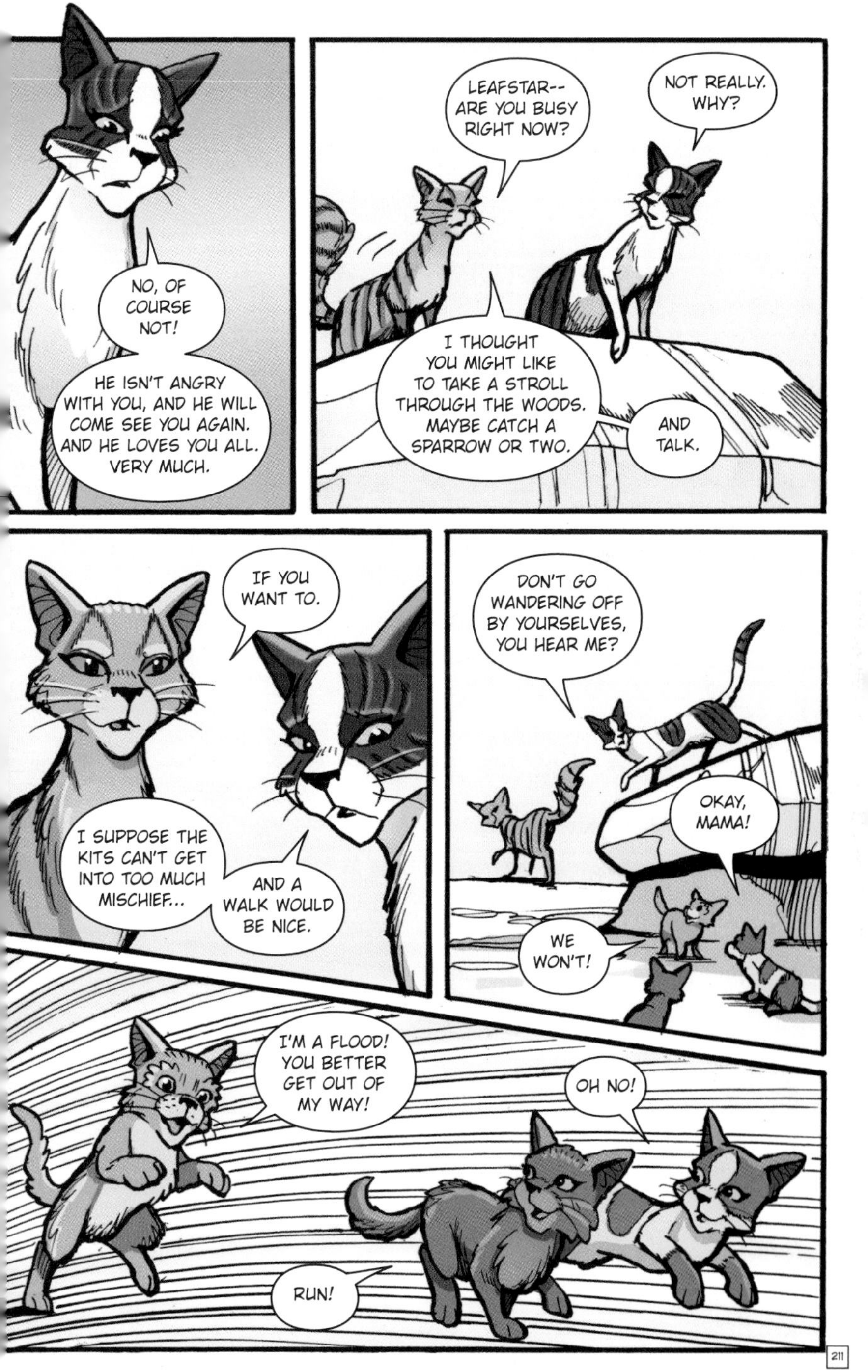
NO, OF COURSE NOT!
HE ISN'T ANGRY WITH YOU, AND HE WILL COME SEE YOU AGAIN. AND HE LOVES YOU ALL. VERY MUCH.
LEAFSTAR-- ARE YOU BUSY RIGHT NOW?
NOT REALLY. WHY?
I THOUGHT YOU MIGHT LIKE TO TAKE A STROLL THROUGH THE WOODS. MAYBE CATCH A SPARROW OR TWO.
AND TALK.
IF YOU WANT TO.
I SUPPOSE THE KITS CAN'T GET INTO TOO MUCH MISCHIEF...
AND A WALK WOULD BE NICE.
DON'T GO WANDERING OFF BY YOURSELVES, YOU HEAR ME?
OKAY, MAMA!
WE WON'T!
I'M A FLOOD! YOU BETTER GET OUT OF MY WAY!
OH NO!
RUN!

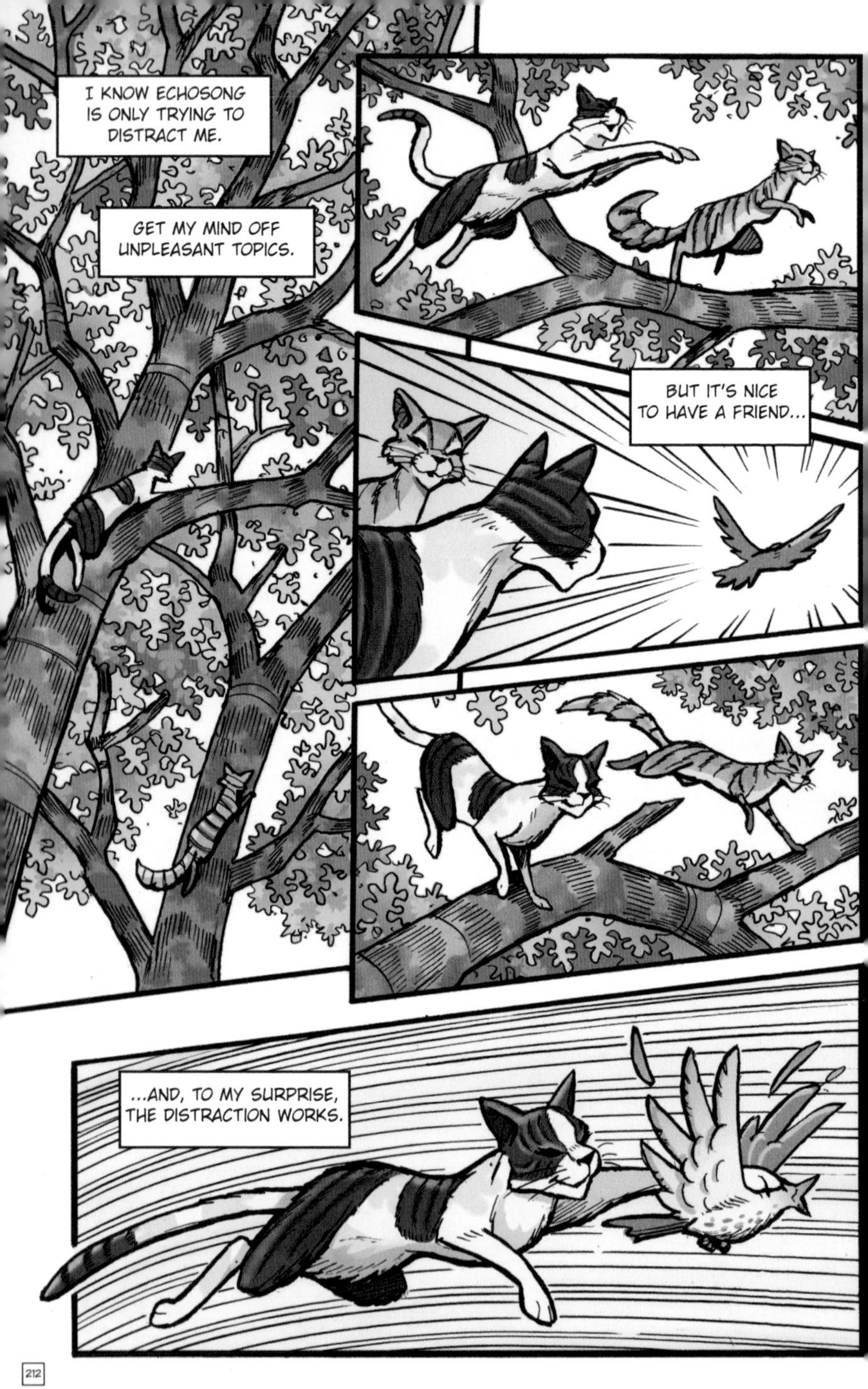
I KNOW ECHOSONG IS ONLY TRYING TO DISTRACT ME.
GET MY MIND OFF UNPLEASANT TOPICS.
BUT IT'S NICE TO HAVE A FRIEND...
...AND, TO MY SURPRISE, THE DISTRACTION WORKS.

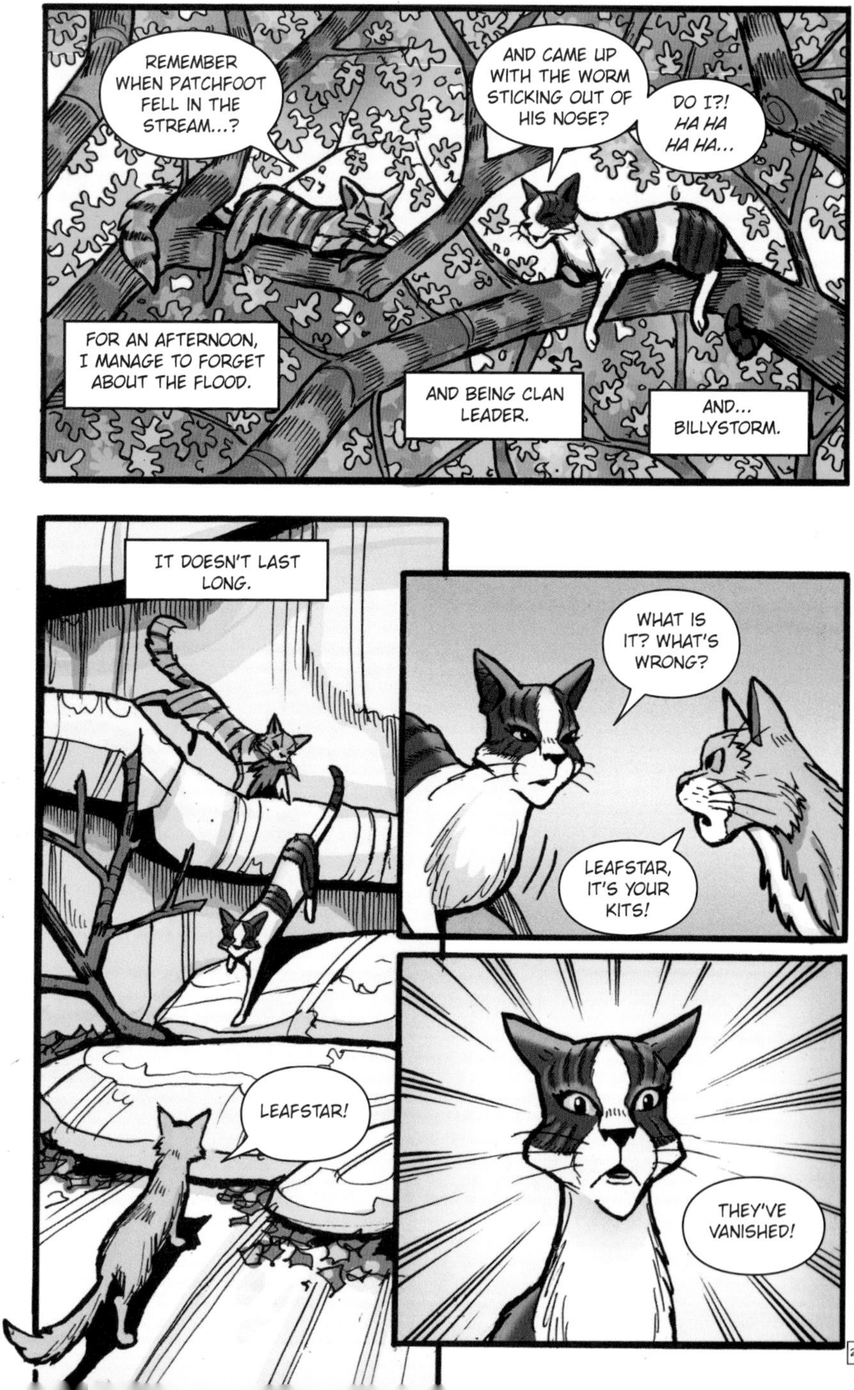
REMEMBER WHEN PATCHFOOT FELL IN THE STREAM...?
AND CAME UP WITH THE WORM STICKING OUT OF HIS NOSE?
DO I?! HA HA HA HA...
FOR AN AFTERNOON, I MANAGE TO FORGET ABOUT THE FLOOD.
AND BEING CLAN LEADER.
AND... BILLYSTORM.
IT DOESN'T LAST LONG.
LEAFSTAR!
WHAT IS IT? WHAT'S WRONG?
LEAFSTAR, IT'S YOUR KITS!
THEY'VE VANISHED!

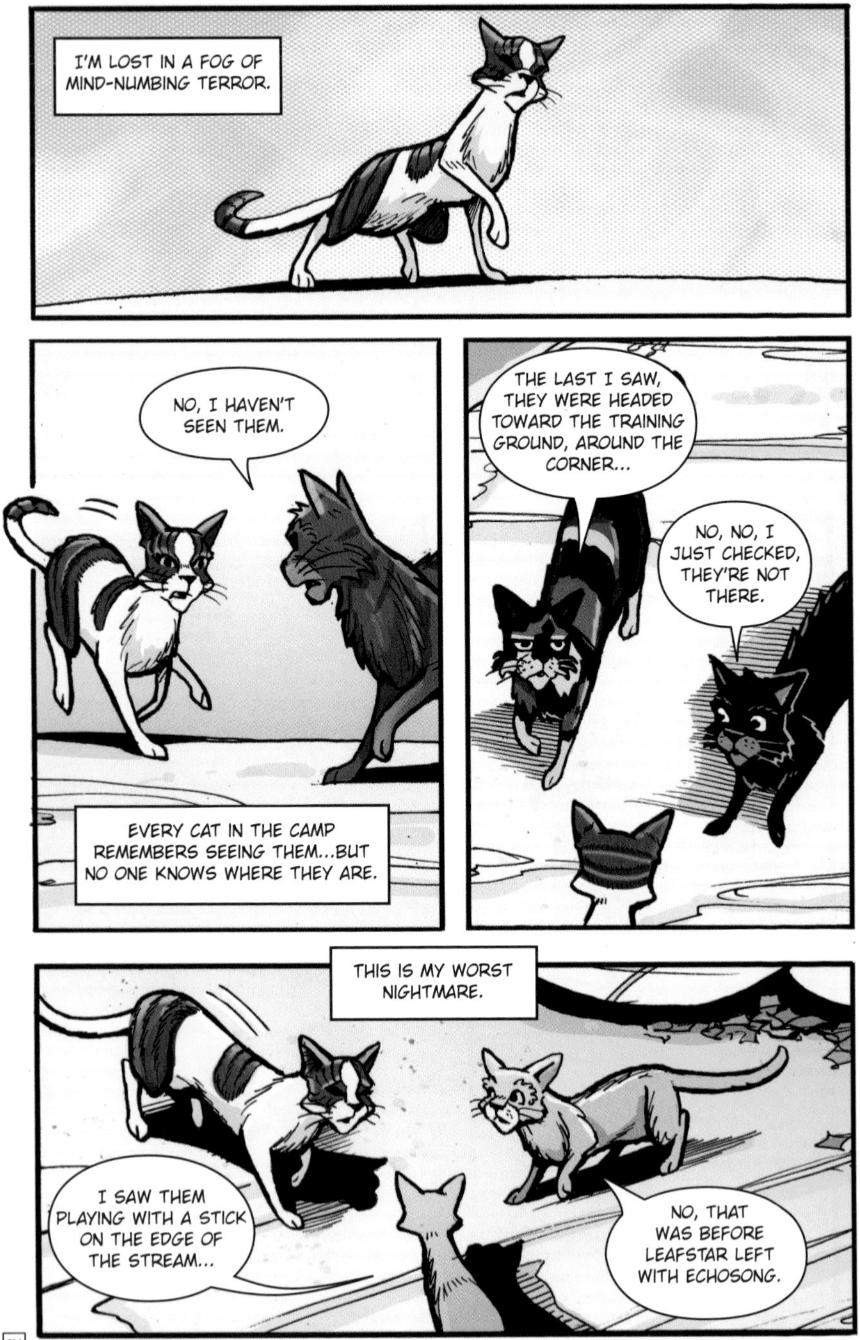
I'M LOST IN A FOG OF MIND-NUMBING TERROR.
NO, I HAVEN'T SEEN THEM.
EVERY CAT IN THE CAMP REMEMBERS SEEING THEM...BUT NO ONE KNOWS WHERE THEY ARE.
THE LAST I SAW, THEY WERE HEADED TOWARD THE TRAINING GROUND, AROUND THE CORNER...
NO, NO, I JUST CHECKED, THEY'RE NOT THERE.
THIS IS MY WORST NIGHTMARE.
I SAW THEM PLAYING WITH A STICK ON THE EDGE OF THE STREAM...
NO, THAT WAS BEFORE LEAFSTAR LEFT WITH ECHOSONG.

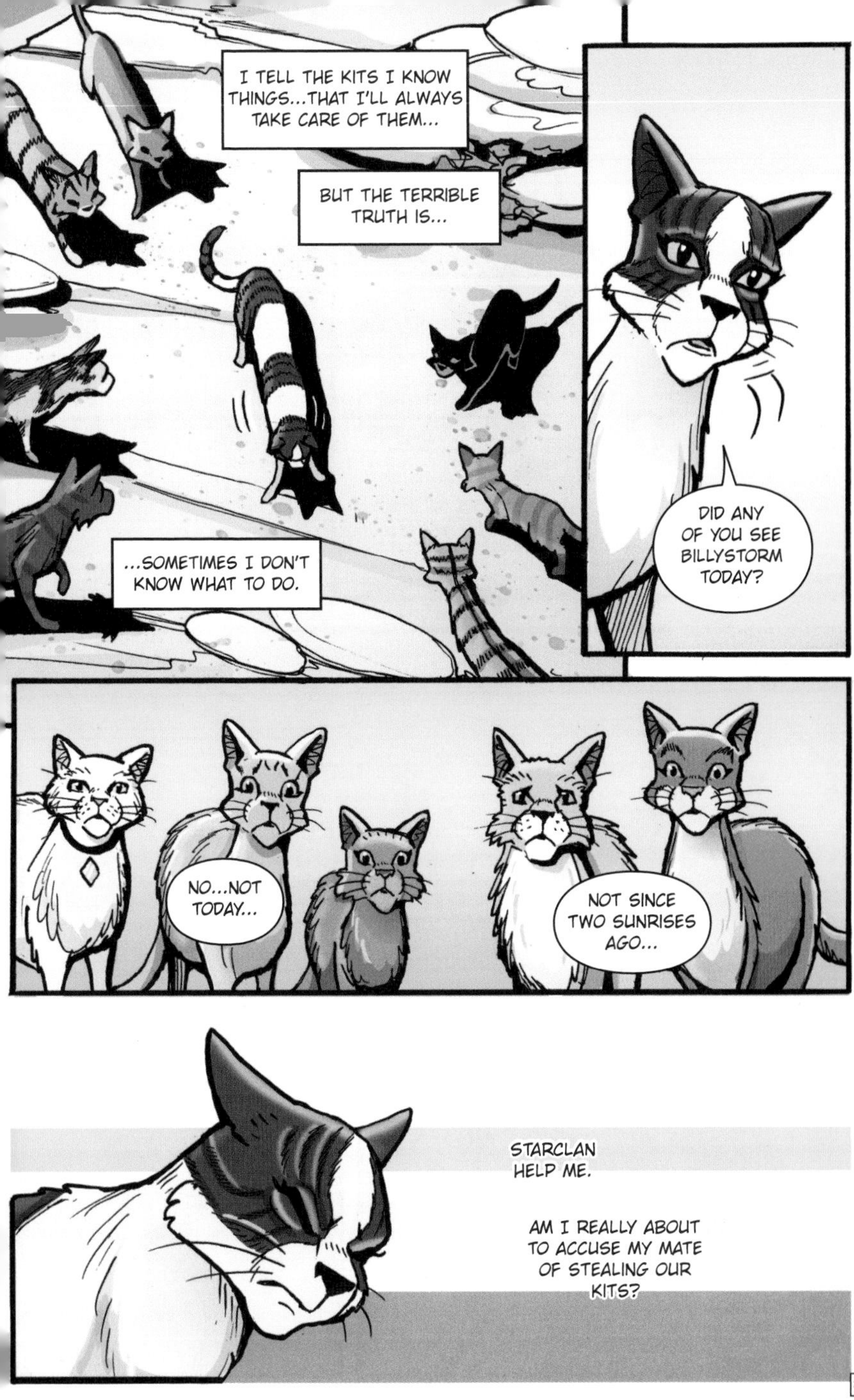
I TELL THE KITS I KNOW THINGS...THAT I'LL ALWAYS TAKE CARE OF THEM...
BUT THE TERRIBLE TRUTH IS...
...SOMETIMES I DON'T KNOW WHAT TO DO.
DID ANY OF YOU SEE BILLYSTORM TODAY?
NO...NOT TODAY...
NOT SINCE TWO SUNRISES AGO...
STARCLAN HELP ME.
AM I REALLY ABOUT TO ACCUSE MY MATE OF STEALING OUR KITS?

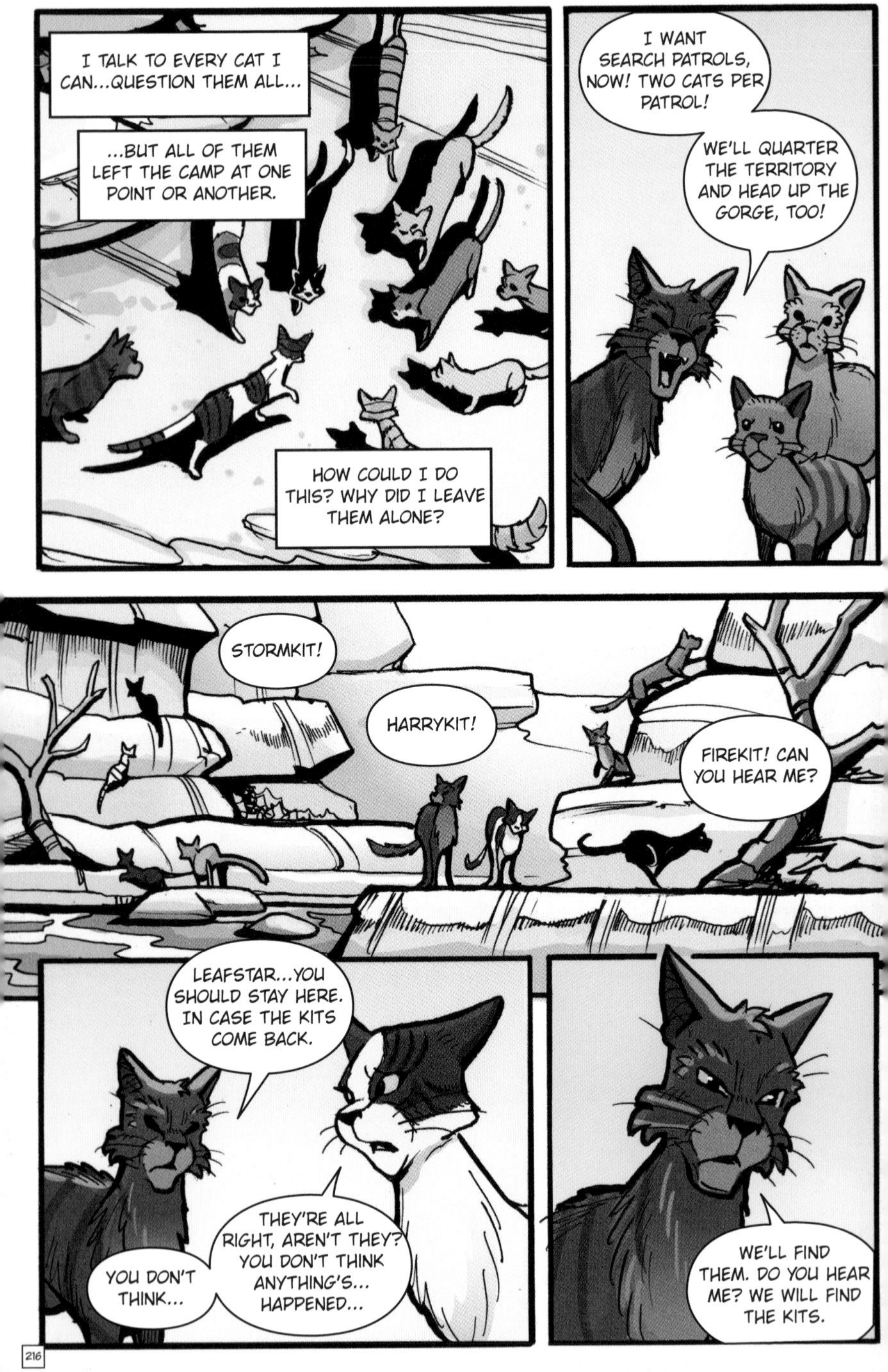
I TALK TO EVERY CAT I CAN...QUESTION THEM ALL...
...BUT ALL OF THEM LEFT THE CAMP AT ONE POINT OR ANOTHER.
HOW COULD I DO THIS? WHY DID I LEAVE THEM ALONE?
I WANT SEARCH PATROLS, NOW! TWO CATS PER PATROL!
WE'LL QUARTER THE TERRITORY AND HEAD UP THE GORGE, TOO!
STORMKIT!
HARRYKIT!
FIREKIT! CAN YOU HEAR ME?
LEAFSTAR...YOU SHOULD STAY HERE. IN CASE THE KITS COME BACK.
YOU DON'T THINK...
THEY'RE ALL RIGHT, AREN'T THEY? YOU DON'T THINK ANYTHING'S... HAPPENED...
WE'LL FIND THEM. DO YOU HEAR ME? WE WILL FIND THE KITS.

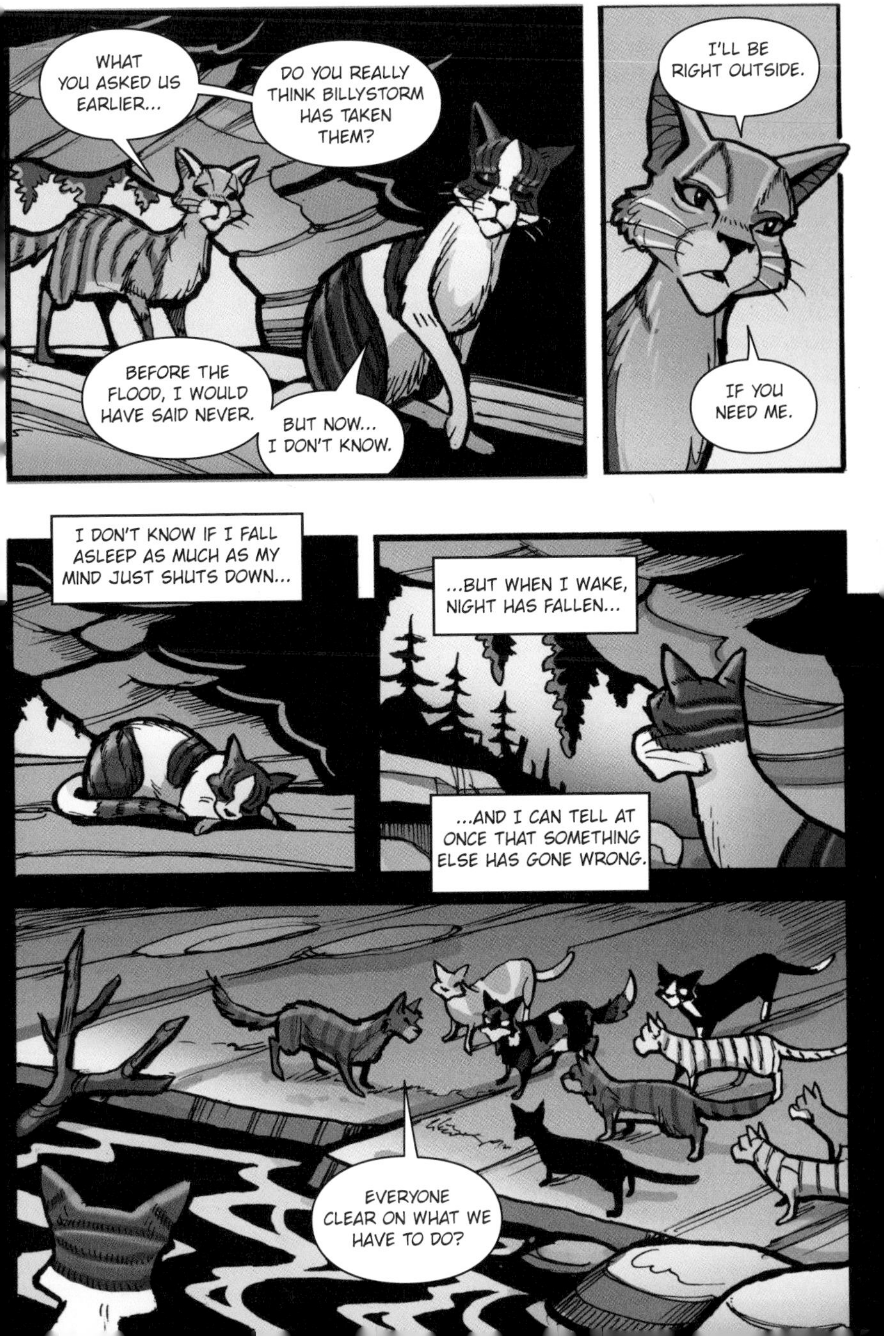
WHAT YOU ASKED US EARLIER...
DO YOU REALLY THINK BILLYSTORM HAS TAKEN THEM?
BEFORE THE FLOOD, I WOULD HAVE SAID NEVER.
BUT NOW... I DON'T KNOW.
I'LL BE RIGHT OUTSIDE.
IF YOU NEED ME.
I DON'T KNOW IF I FALL ASLEEP AS MUCH AS MY MIND JUST SHUTS DOWN...
...BUT WHEN I WAKE, NIGHT HAS FALLEN...
...AND I CAN TELL AT ONCE THAT SOMETHING ELSE HAS GONE WRONG.
EVERYONE CLEAR ON WHAT WE HAVE TO DO?

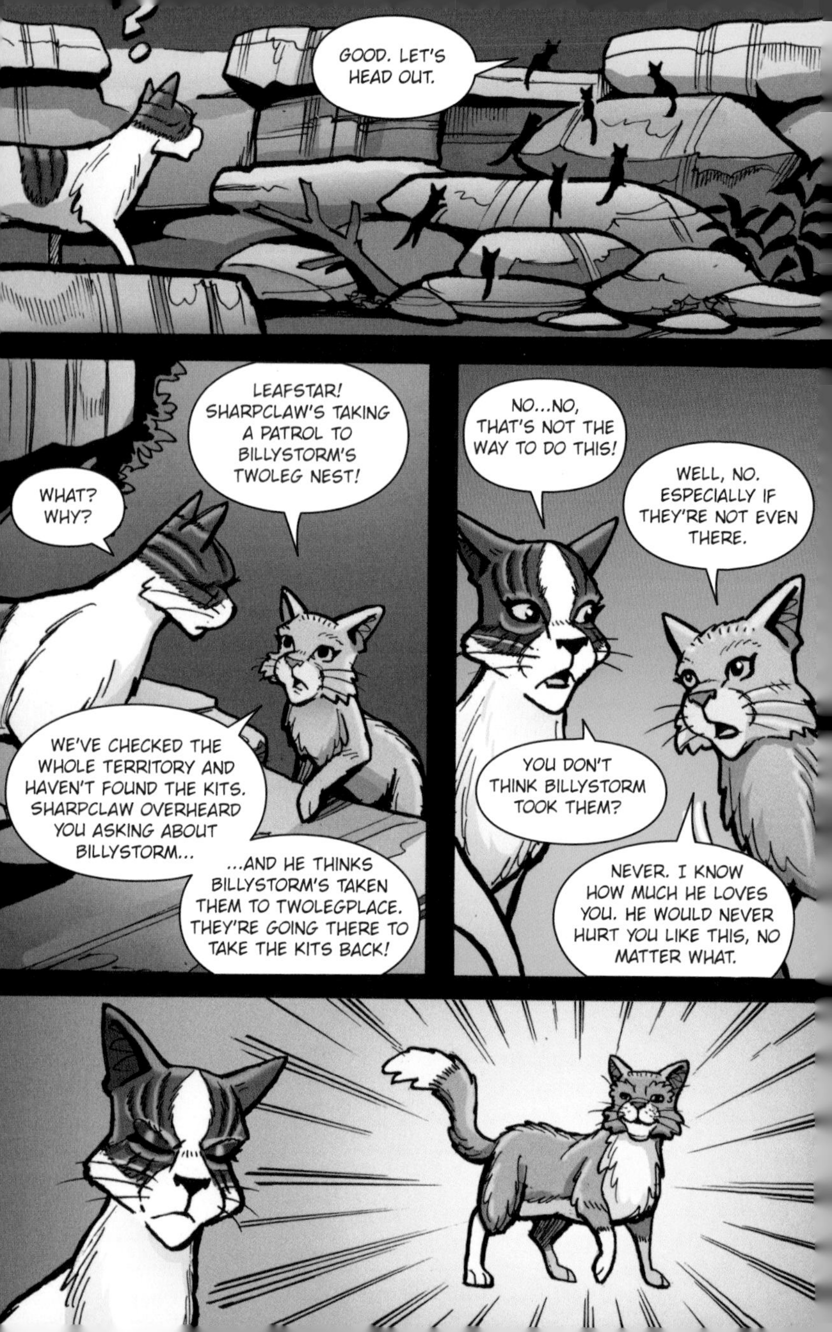

GOOD. LET'S HEAD OUT.
WHAT? WHY?
LEAFSTAR! SHARPCLAW'S TAKING A PATROL TO BILLYSTORM'S TWOLEG NEST!
WE'VE CHECKED THE WHOLE TERRITORY AND HAVEN'T FOUND THE KITS. SHARPCLAW OVERHEARD YOU ASKING ABOUT BILLYSTORM...
...AND HE THINKS BILLYSTORM'S TAKEN THEM TO TWOLEGPLACE. THEY'RE GOING THERE TO TAKE THE KITS BACK!
NO...NO, THAT'S NOT THE WAY TO DO THIS!
WELL, NO. ESPECIALLY IF THEY'RE NOT EVEN THERE.
YOU DON'T THINK BILLYSTORM TOOK THEM?
NEVER. I KNOW HOW MUCH HE LOVES YOU. HE WOULD NEVER HURT YOU LIKE THIS, NO MATTER WHAT.

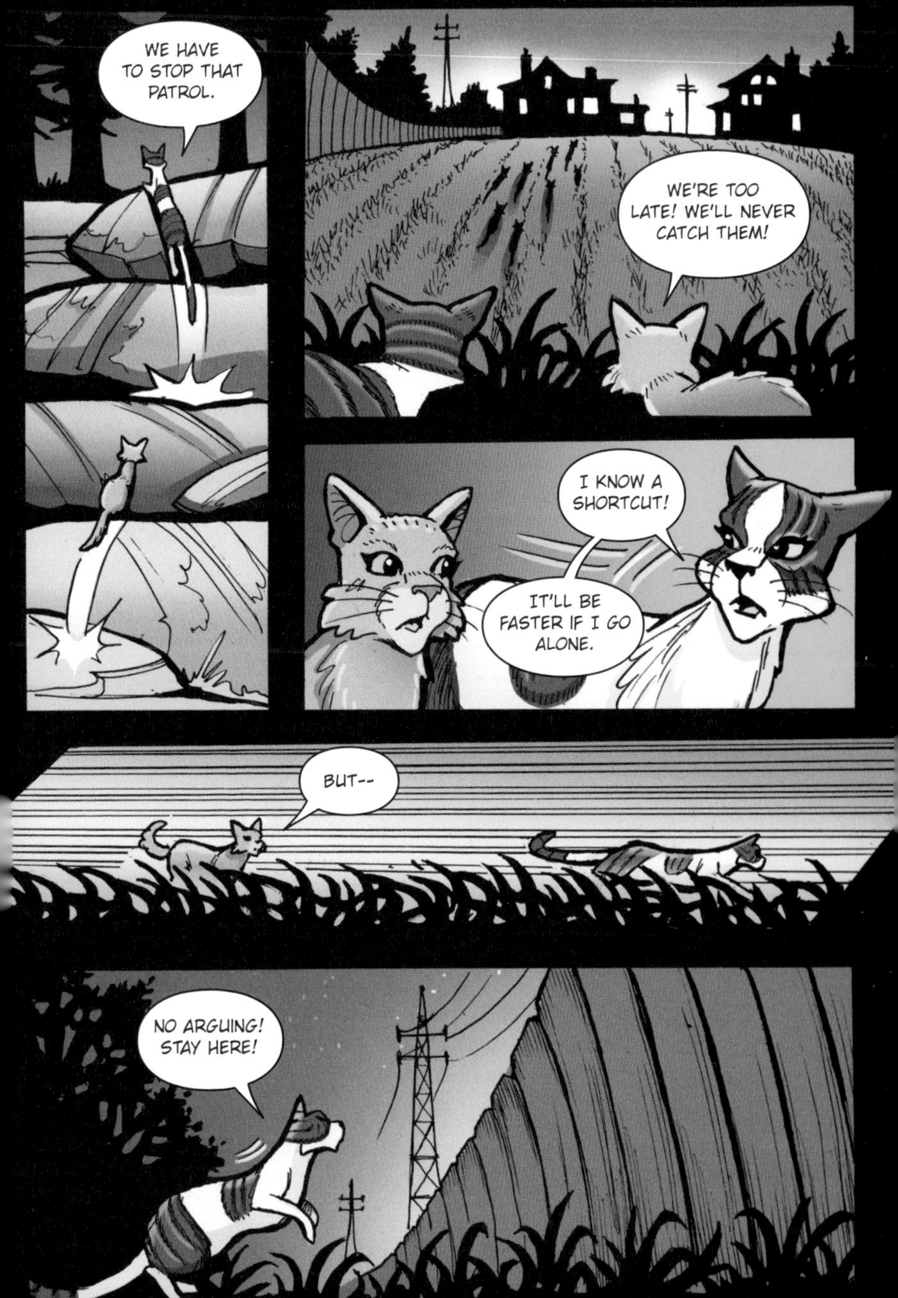
WE HAVE TO STOP THAT PATROL.
WE'RE TOO LATE! WE'LL NEVER CATCH THEM!
I KNOW A SHORTCUT!
IT'LL BE FASTER IF I GO ALONE.
BUT--
NO ARGUING! STAY HERE!

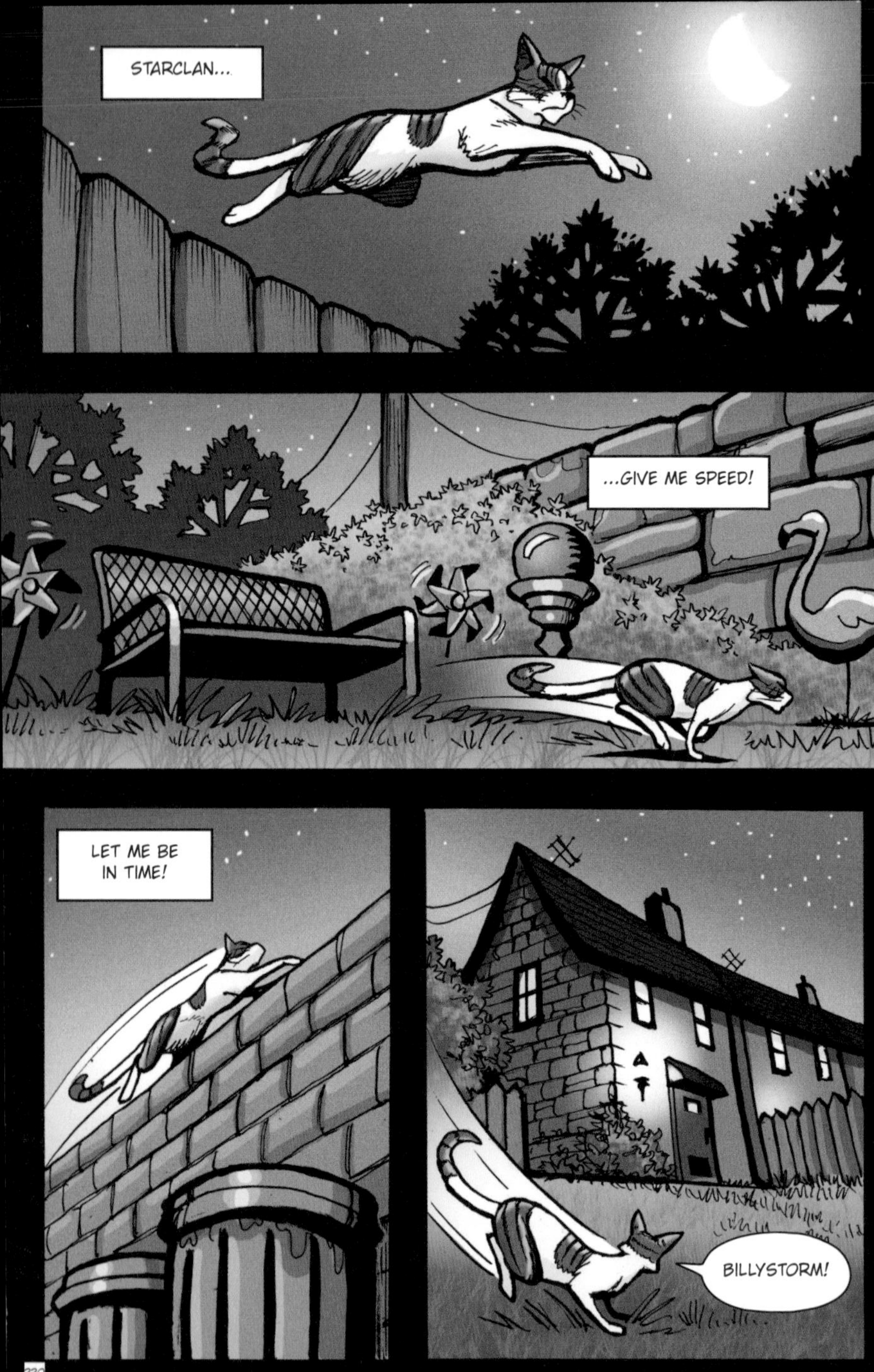
STARCLAN...
...GIVE ME SPEED!
LET ME BE IN TIME!
BILLYSTORM!

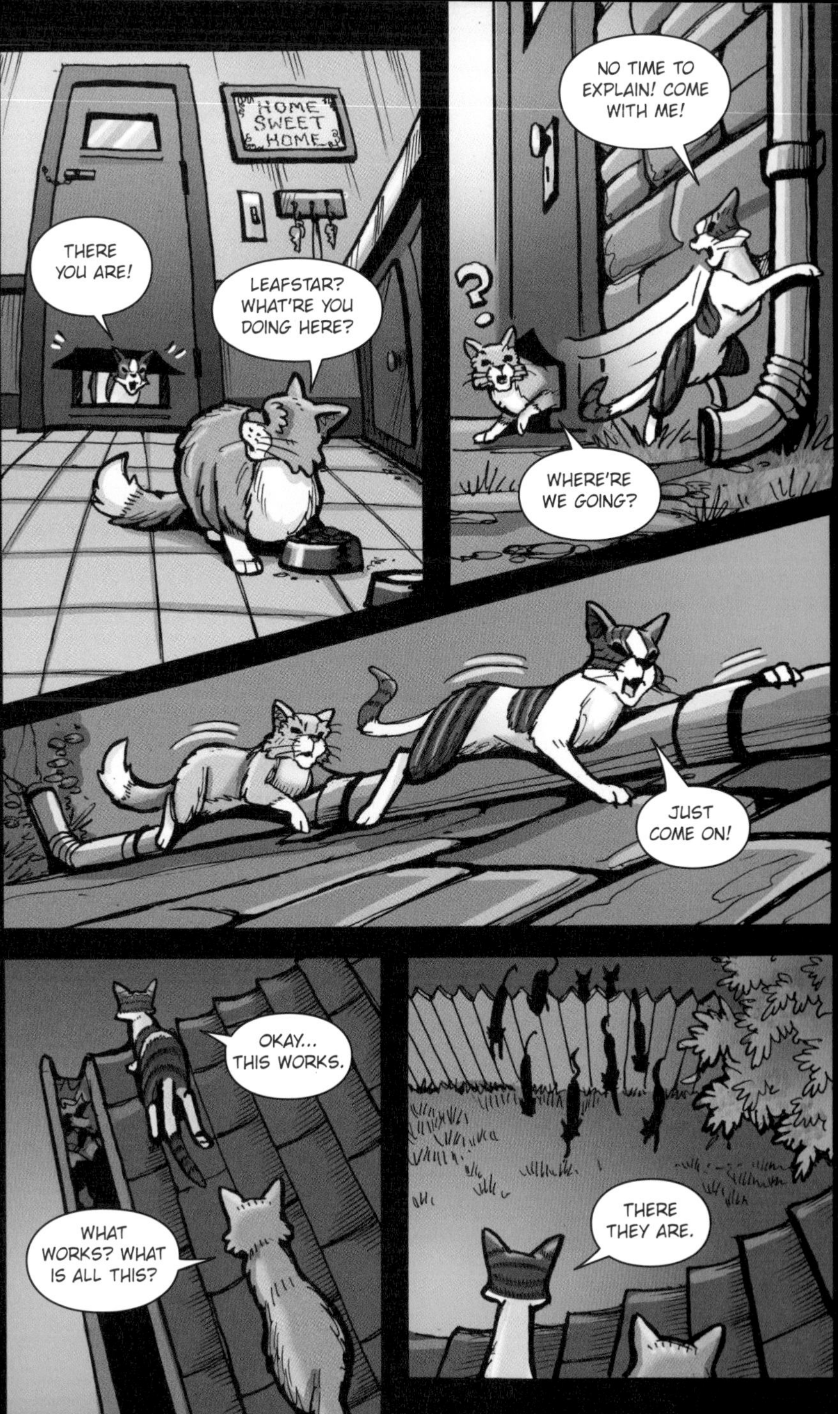
HOME SWEET HOME
THERE YOU ARE!
LEAFSTAR? WHAT'RE YOU DOING HERE?
?
NO TIME TO EXPLAIN! COME WITH ME!
WHERE'RE WE GOING?
JUST COME ON!
OKAY... THIS WORKS.
WHAT WORKS? WHAT IS ALL THIS?
THERE THEY ARE.

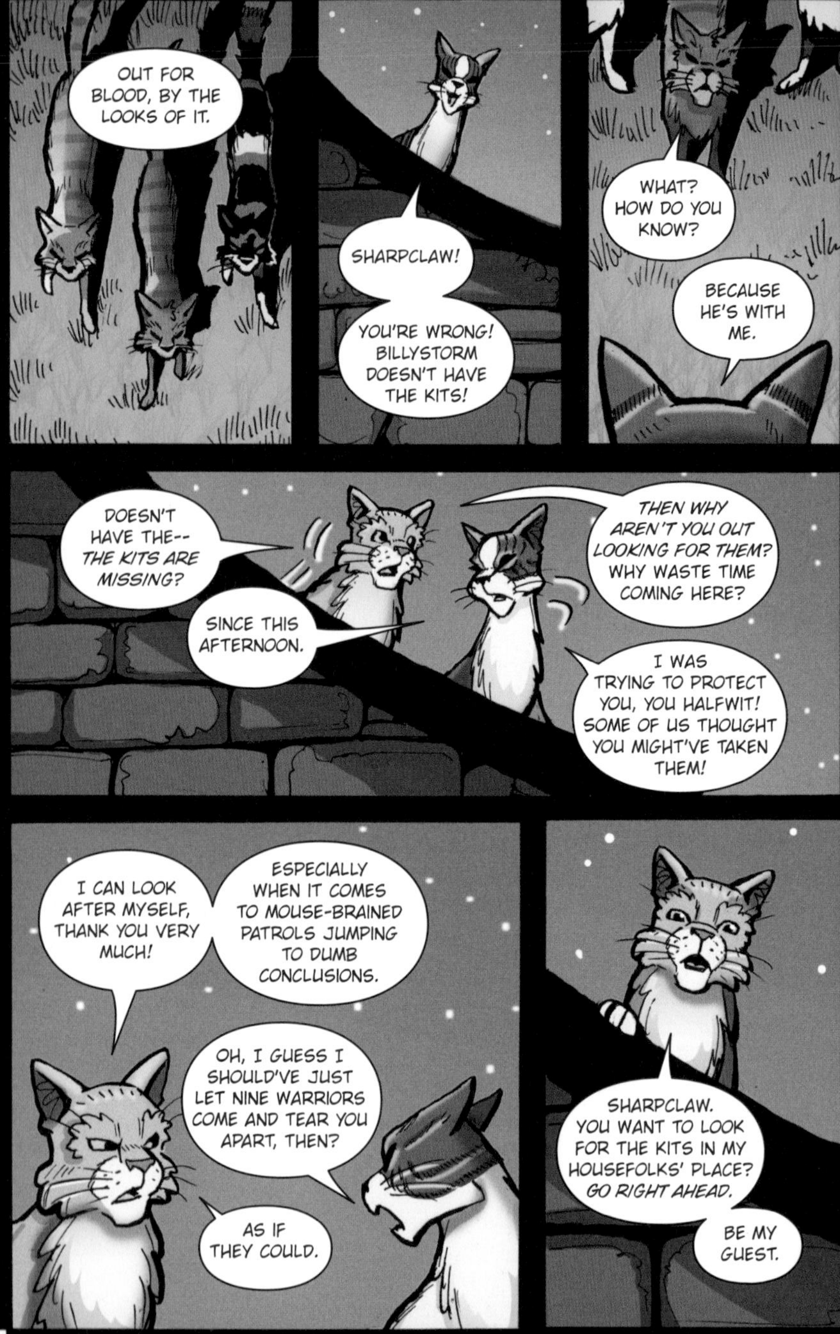
OUT FOR BLOOD, BY THE LOOKS OF IT.
SHARPCLAW!
YOU'RE WRONG! BILLYSTORM DOESN'T HAVE THE KITS!
WHAT? HOW DO YOU KNOW?
BECAUSE HE'S WITH ME.
DOESN'T HAVE THE-- *THE KITS ARE MISSING?*
SINCE THIS AFTERNOON.
THEN WHY AREN'T YOU OUT LOOKING FOR THEM? WHY WASTE TIME COMING HERE?
I WAS TRYING TO PROTECT YOU, YOU HALFWIT! SOME OF US THOUGHT YOU MIGHT'VE TAKEN THEM!
I CAN LOOK AFTER MYSELF, THANK YOU VERY MUCH!
ESPECIALLY WHEN IT COMES TO MOUSE-BRAINED PATROLS JUMPING TO DUMB CONCLUSIONS.
OH, I GUESS I SHOULD'VE JUST LET NINE WARRIORS COME AND TEAR YOU APART, THEN?
AS IF THEY COULD.
SHARPCLAW. YOU WANT TO LOOK FOR THE KITS IN MY HOUSEFOLKS' PLACE? *GO RIGHT AHEAD.*
BE MY GUEST.

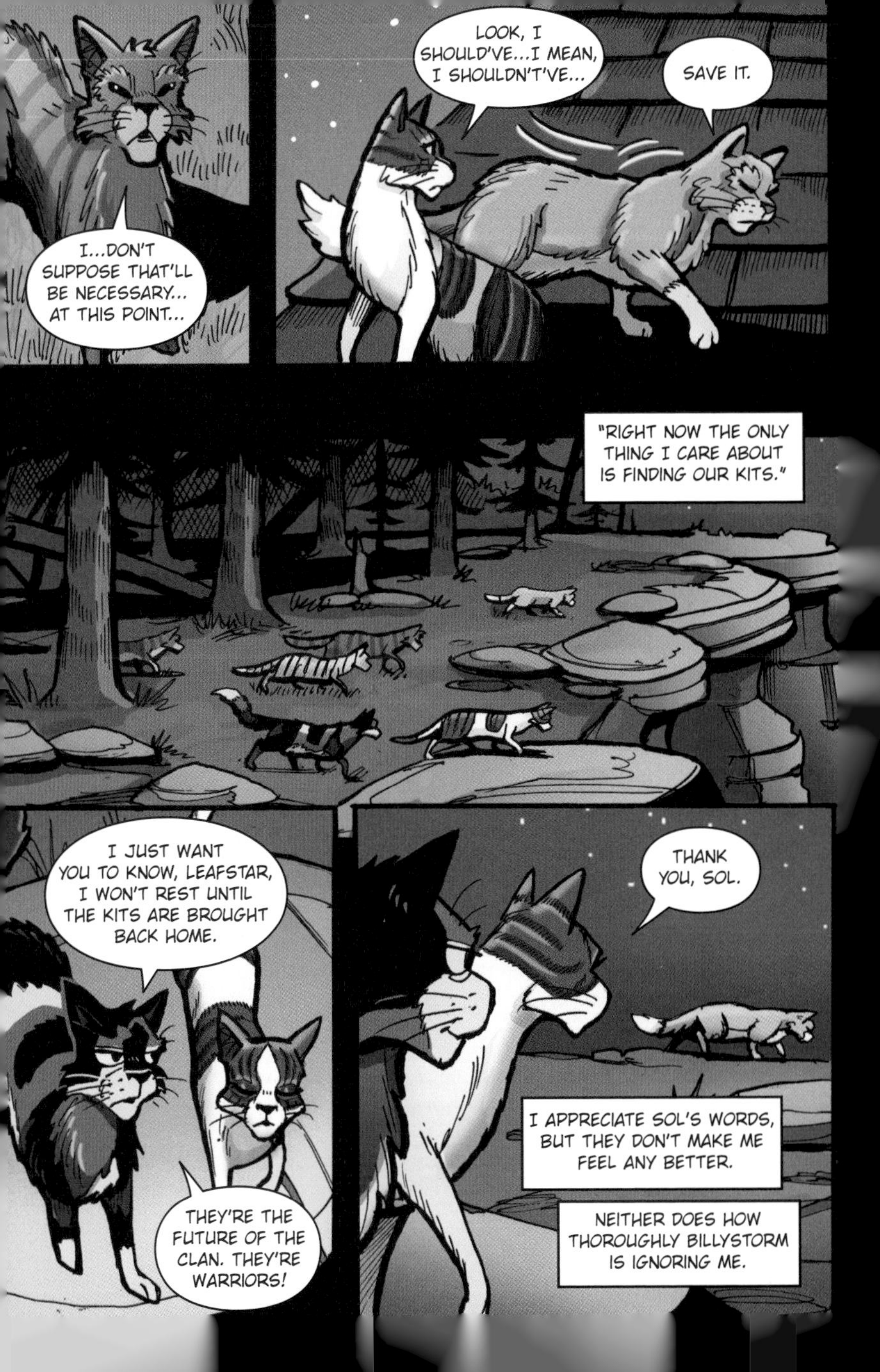
I…DON'T SUPPOSE THAT'LL BE NECESSARY… AT THIS POINT…
LOOK, I SHOULD'VE…I MEAN, I SHOULDN'T'VE…
SAVE IT.
"RIGHT NOW THE ONLY THING I CARE ABOUT IS FINDING OUR KITS."
I JUST WANT YOU TO KNOW, LEAFSTAR, I WON'T REST UNTIL THE KITS ARE BROUGHT BACK HOME.
THEY'RE THE FUTURE OF THE CLAN. THEY'RE WARRIORS!
THANK YOU, SOL.
I APPRECIATE SOL'S WORDS, BUT THEY DON'T MAKE ME FEEL ANY BETTER.
NEITHER DOES HOW THOROUGHLY BILLYSTORM IS IGNORING ME.

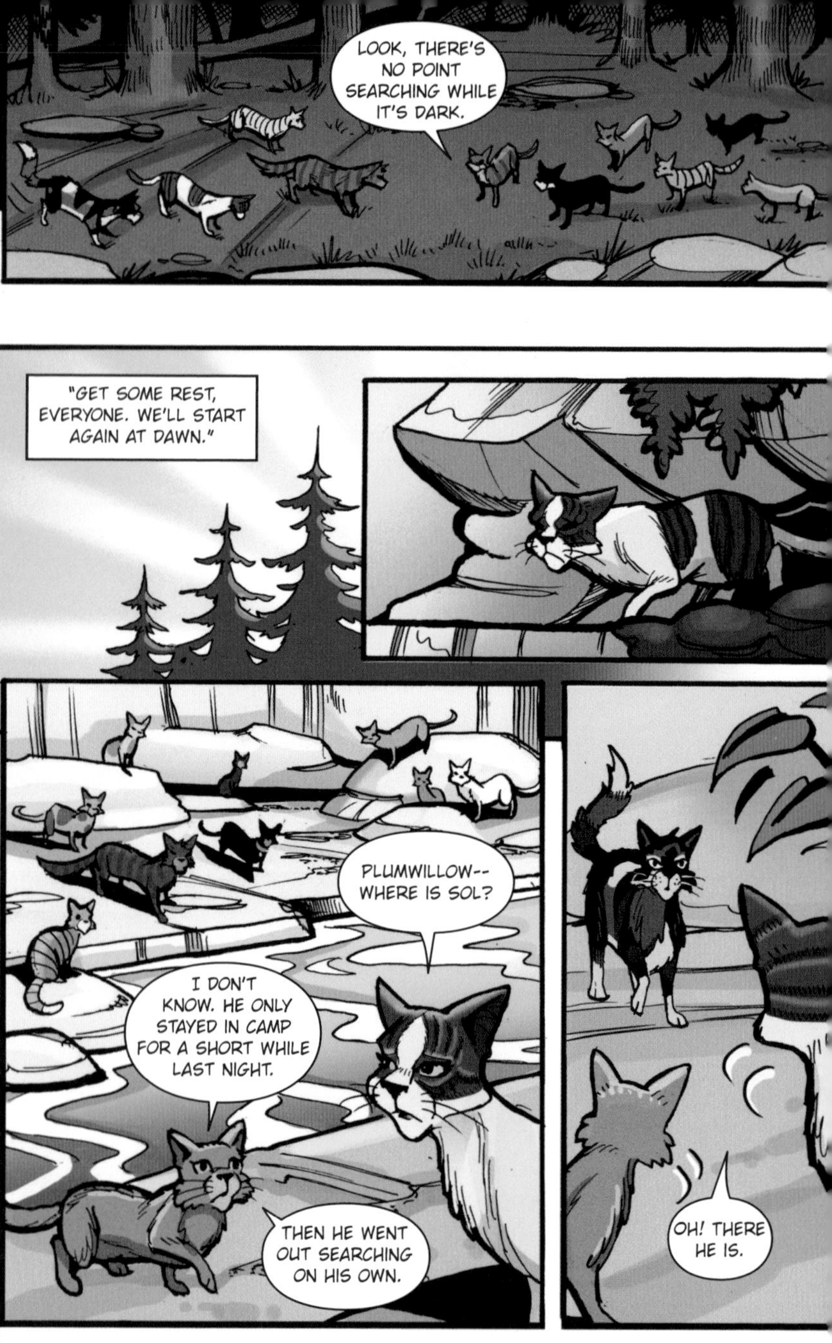
LOOK, THERE'S NO POINT SEARCHING WHILE IT'S DARK.
"GET SOME REST, EVERYONE. WE'LL START AGAIN AT DAWN."
PLUMWILLOW-- WHERE IS SOL?
I DON'T KNOW. HE ONLY STAYED IN CAMP FOR A SHORT WHILE LAST NIGHT.
THEN HE WENT OUT SEARCHING ON HIS OWN.
OH! THERE HE IS.

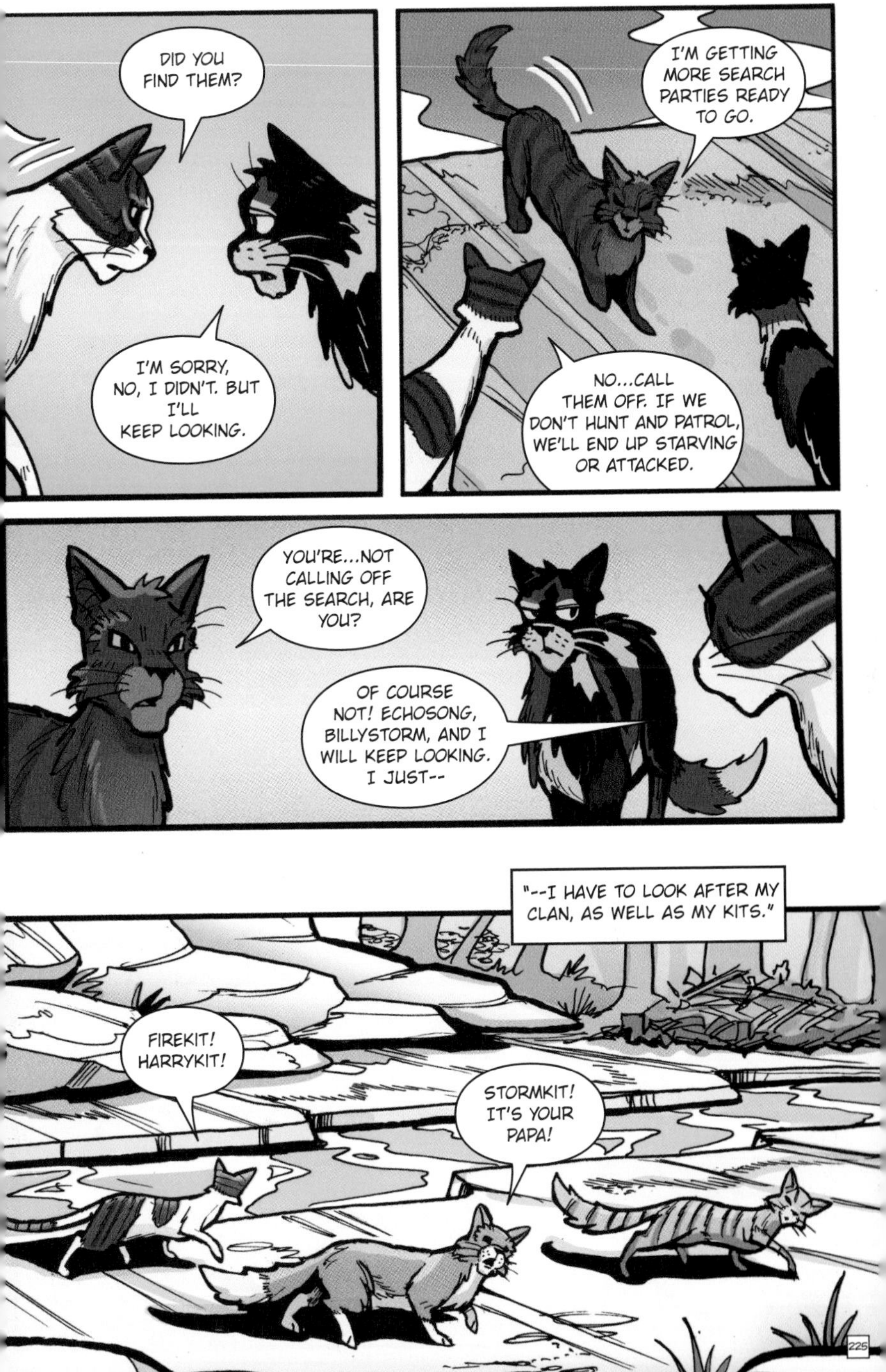
DID YOU FIND THEM?
I'M SORRY, NO, I DIDN'T. BUT I'LL KEEP LOOKING.
I'M GETTING MORE SEARCH PARTIES READY TO GO.
NO...CALL THEM OFF. IF WE DON'T HUNT AND PATROL, WE'LL END UP STARVING OR ATTACKED.
YOU'RE...NOT CALLING OFF THE SEARCH, ARE YOU?
OF COURSE NOT! ECHOSONG, BILLYSTORM, AND I WILL KEEP LOOKING. I JUST--
"--I HAVE TO LOOK AFTER MY CLAN, AS WELL AS MY KITS."
FIREKIT! HARRYKIT!
STORMKIT! IT'S YOUR PAPA!

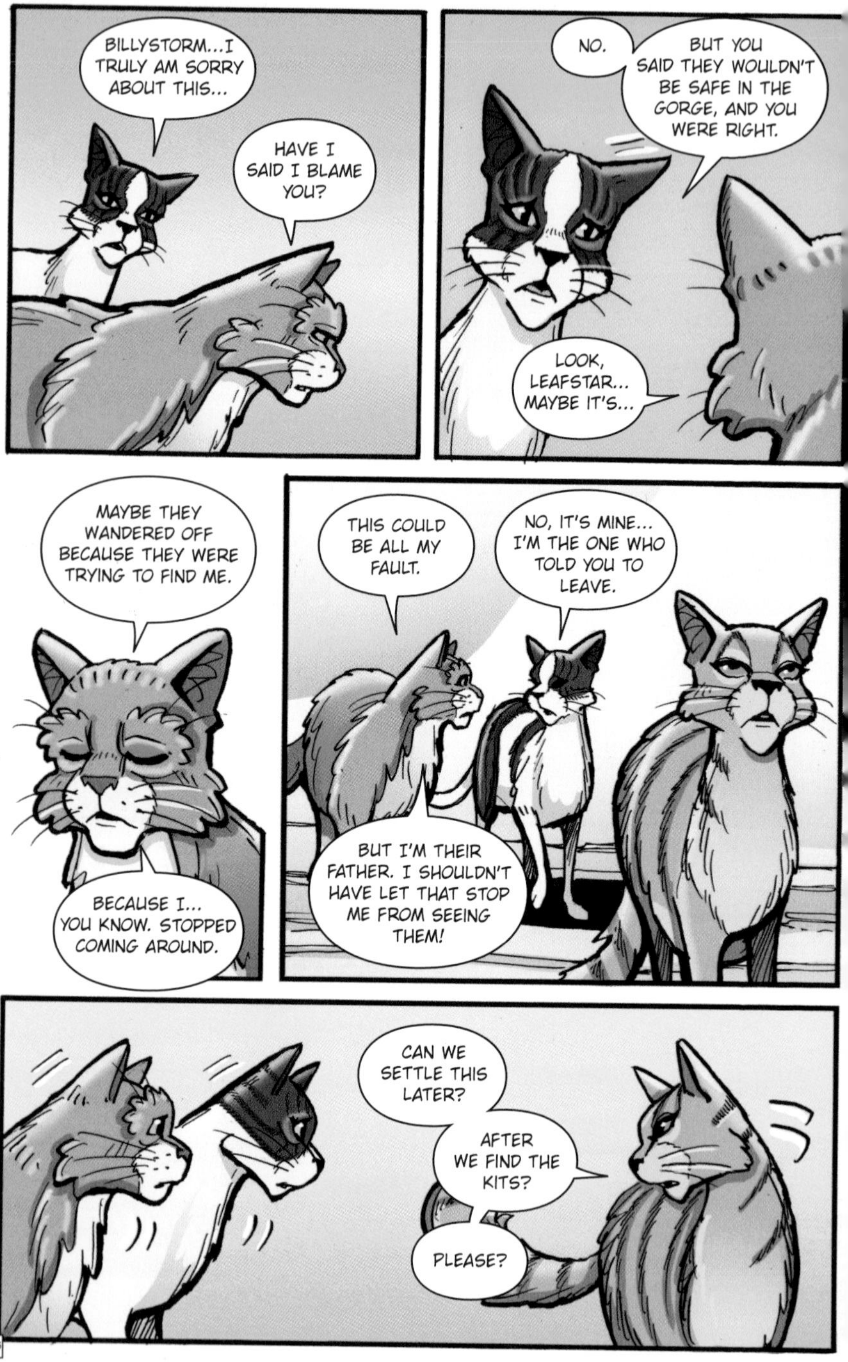
BILLYSTORM...I TRULY AM SORRY ABOUT THIS...
HAVE I SAID I BLAME YOU?
NO.
BUT YOU SAID THEY WOULDN'T BE SAFE IN THE GORGE, AND YOU WERE RIGHT.
LOOK, LEAFSTAR... MAYBE IT'S...
MAYBE THEY WANDERED OFF BECAUSE THEY WERE TRYING TO FIND ME.
BECAUSE I... YOU KNOW. STOPPED COMING AROUND.
THIS COULD BE ALL MY FAULT.
NO, IT'S MINE... I'M THE ONE WHO TOLD YOU TO LEAVE.
BUT I'M THEIR FATHER. I SHOULDN'T HAVE LET THAT STOP ME FROM SEEING THEM!
CAN WE SETTLE THIS LATER?
AFTER WE FIND THE KITS?
PLEASE?

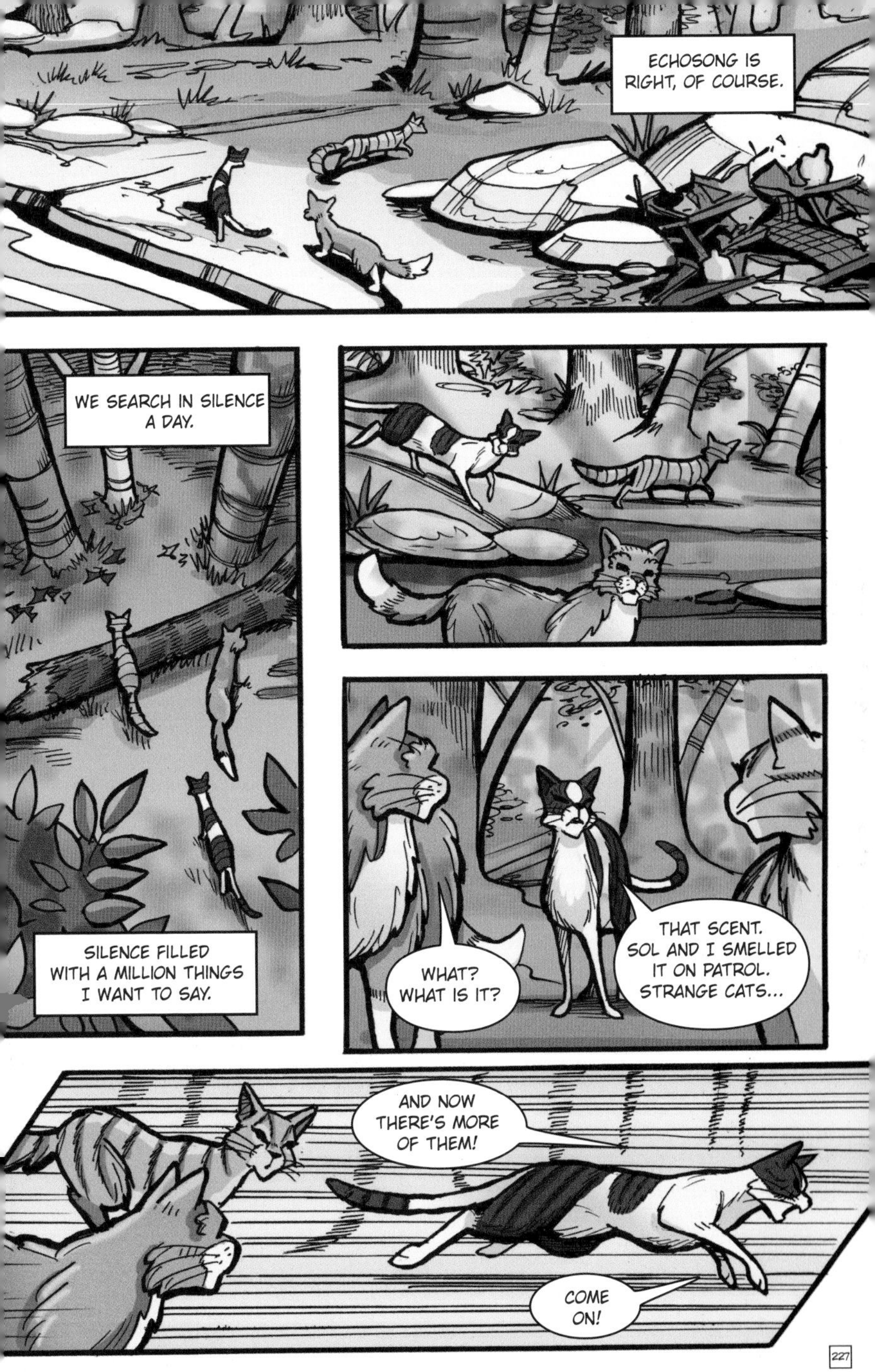
ECHOSONG IS RIGHT, OF COURSE.
WE SEARCH IN SILENCE A DAY.
SILENCE FILLED WITH A MILLION THINGS I WANT TO SAY.
WHAT? WHAT IS IT?
THAT SCENT. SOL AND I SMELLED IT ON PATROL. STRANGE CATS...
AND NOW THERE'S MORE OF THEM!
COME ON!

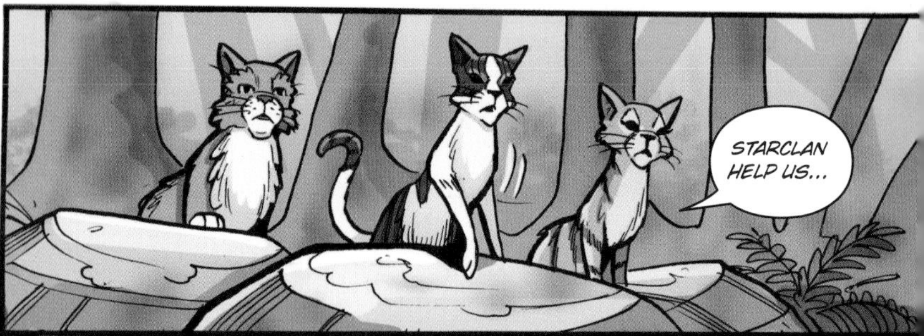
STARCLAN HELP US...

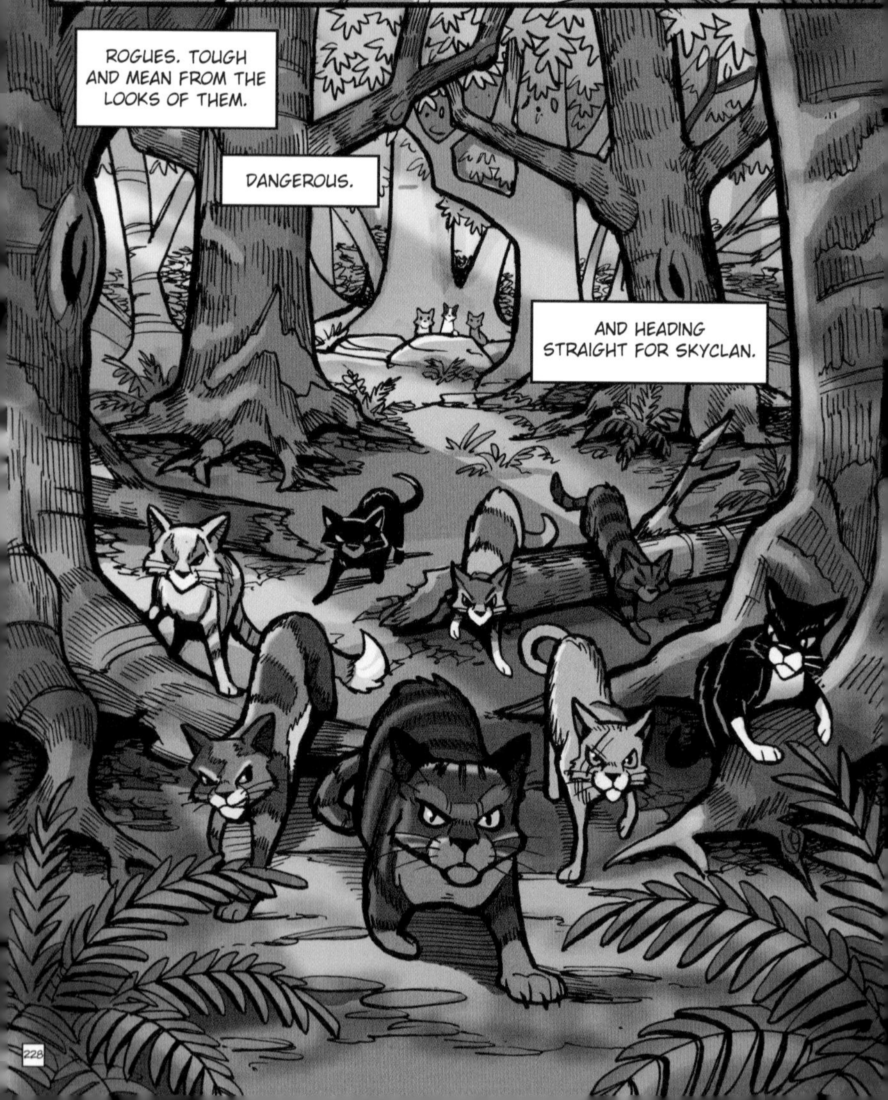
ROGUES. TOUGH AND MEAN FROM THE LOOKS OF THEM.
DANGEROUS.
AND HEADING STRAIGHT FOR SKYCLAN.

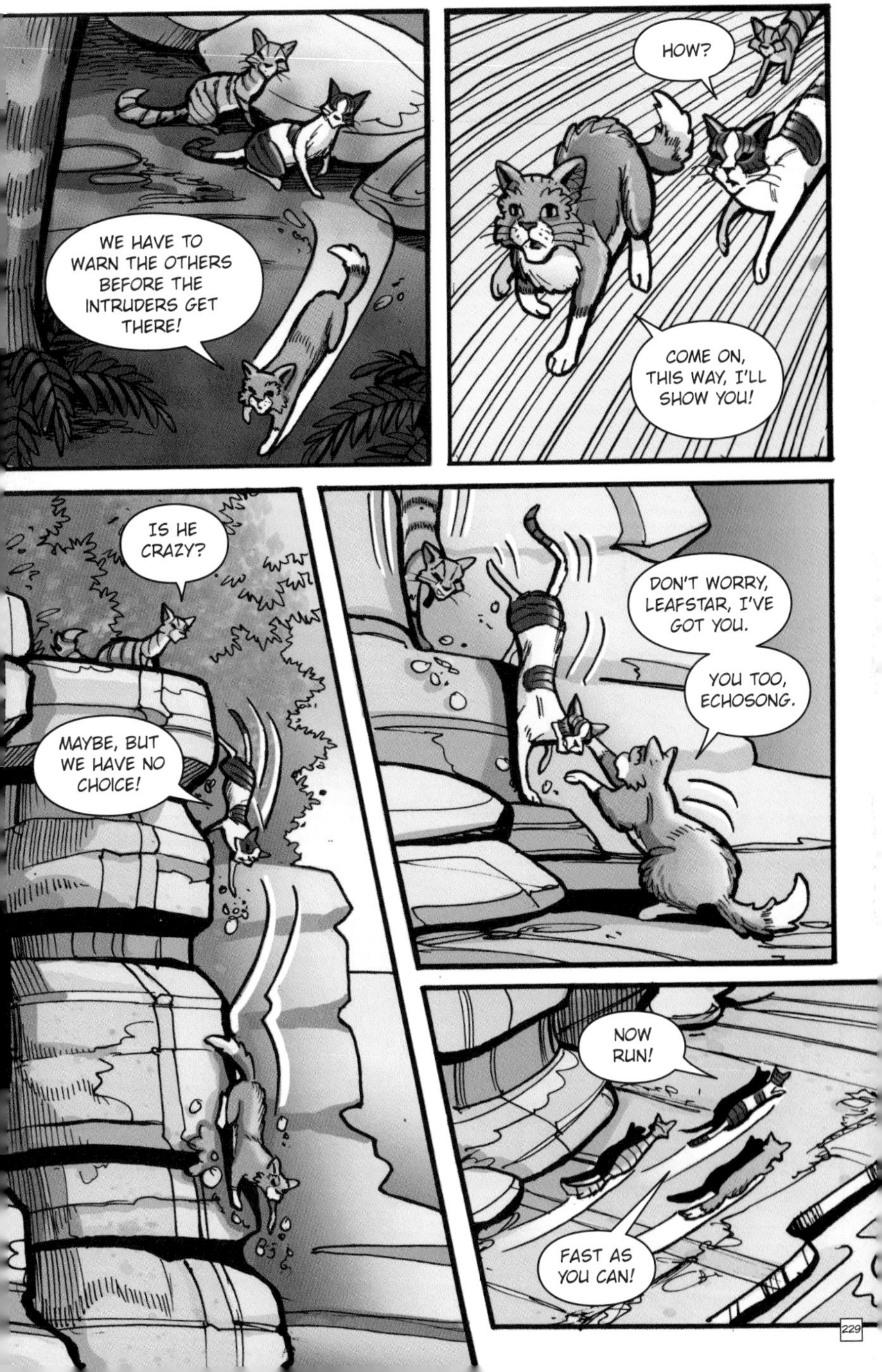
WE HAVE TO WARN THE OTHERS BEFORE THE INTRUDERS GET THERE!
HOW?
COME ON, THIS WAY, I'LL SHOW YOU!
IS HE CRAZY?
MAYBE, BUT WE HAVE NO CHOICE!
DON'T WORRY, LEAFSTAR, I'VE GOT YOU.
YOU TOO, ECHOSONG.
NOW RUN!
FAST AS YOU CAN!

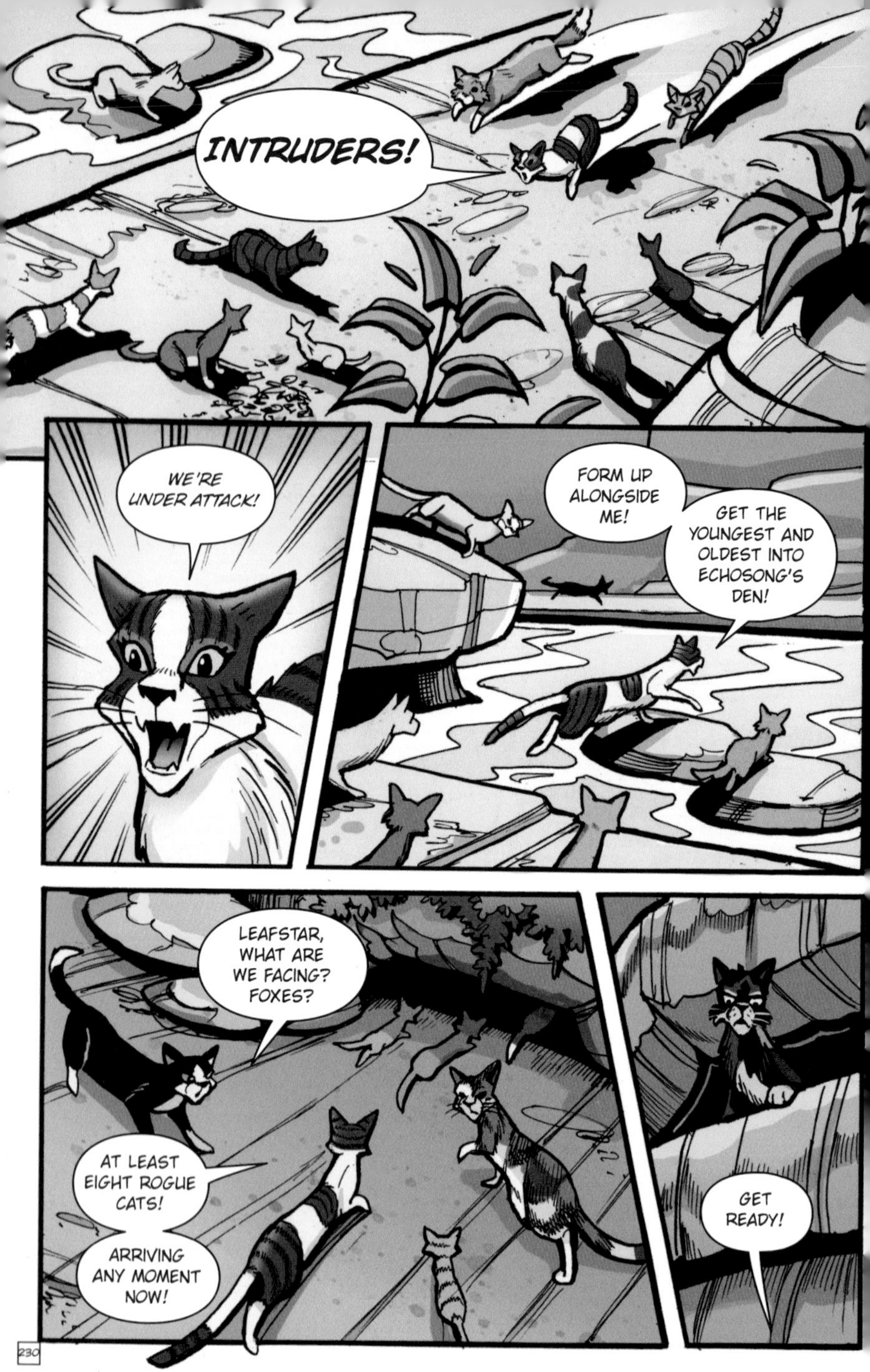
INTRUDERS!
WE'RE UNDER ATTACK!
FORM UP ALONGSIDE ME!
GET THE YOUNGEST AND OLDEST INTO ECHOSONG'S DEN!
LEAFSTAR, WHAT ARE WE FACING? FOXES?
AT LEAST EIGHT ROGUE CATS!
ARRIVING ANY MOMENT NOW!
GET READY!

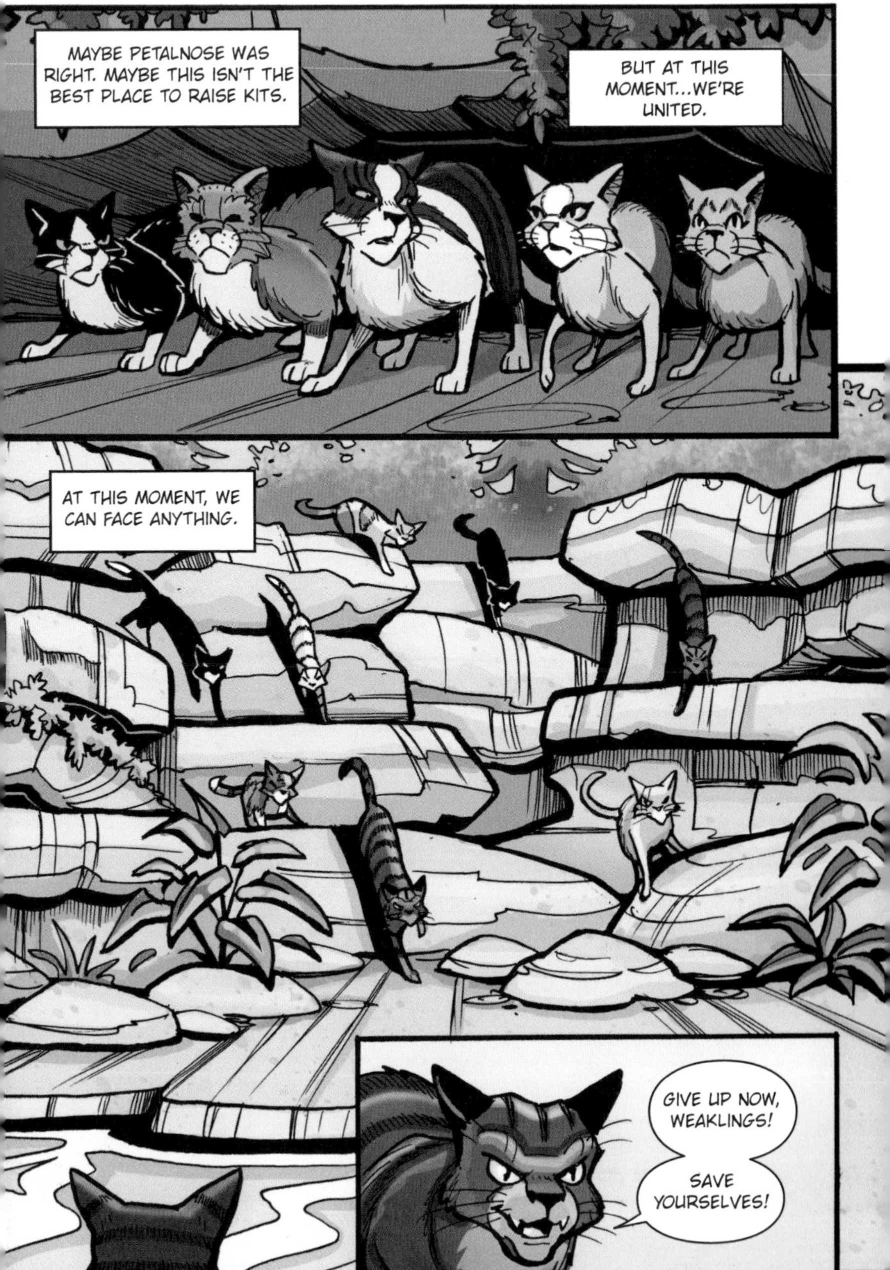
MAYBE PETALNOSE WAS RIGHT. MAYBE THIS ISN'T THE BEST PLACE TO RAISE KITS.
BUT AT THIS MOMENT...WE'RE UNITED.
AT THIS MOMENT, WE CAN FACE ANYTHING.
GIVE UP NOW, WEAKLINGS!
SAVE YOURSELVES!

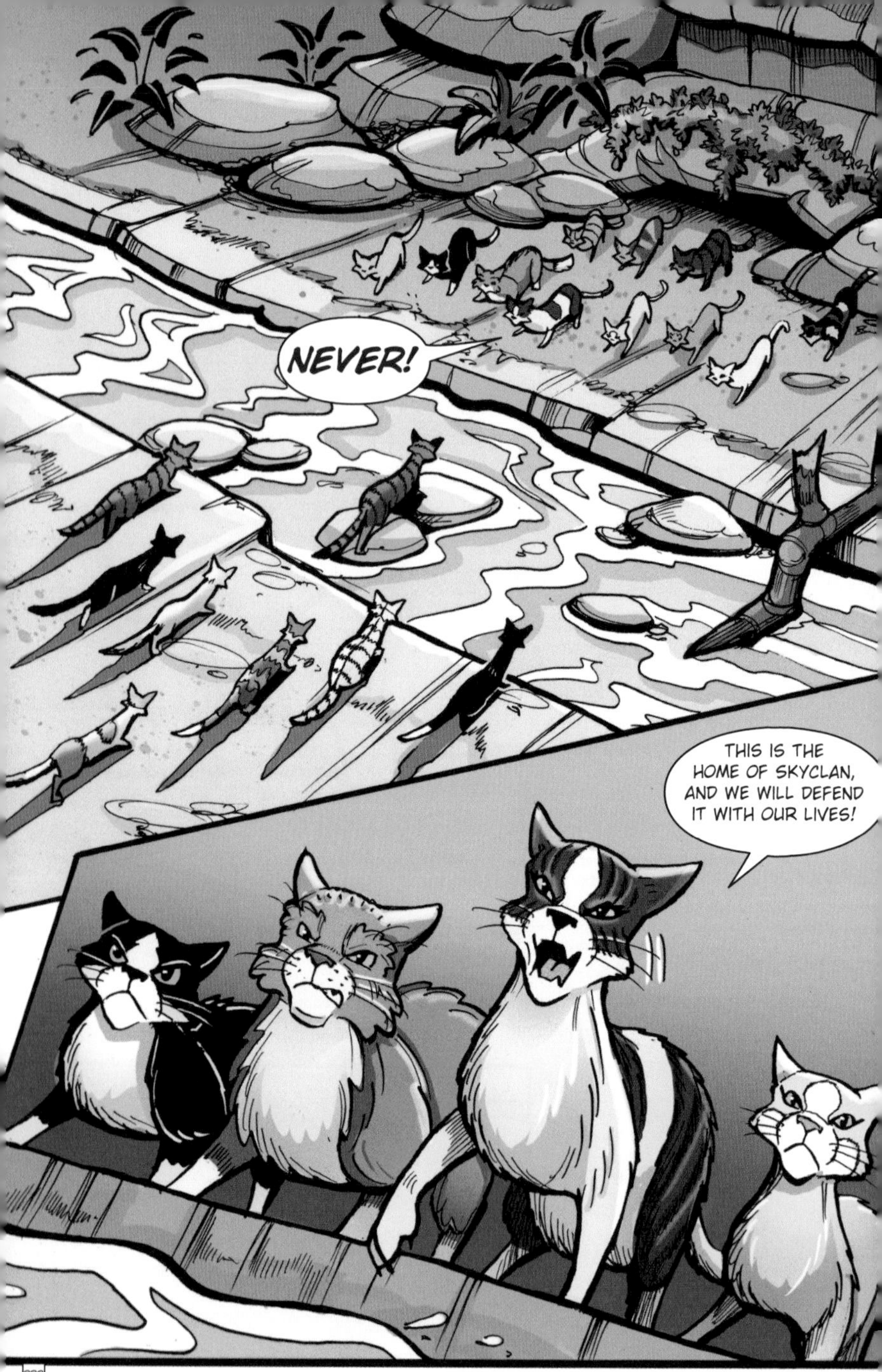
NEVER!
THIS IS THE HOME OF SKYCLAN, AND WE WILL DEFEND IT WITH OUR LIVES!

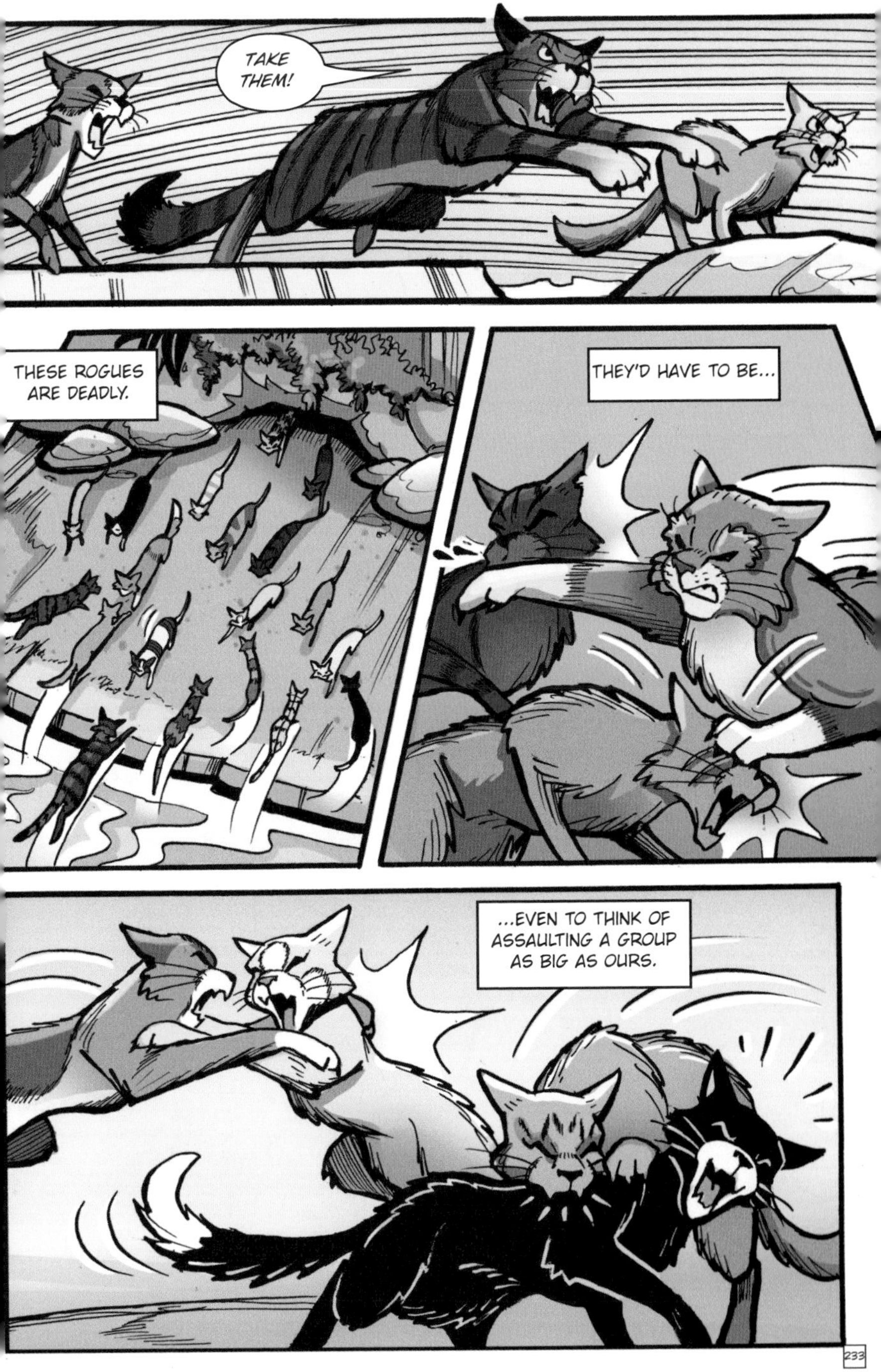
TAKE THEM!
THESE ROGUES ARE DEADLY.
THEY'D HAVE TO BE...
...EVEN TO THINK OF ASSAULTING A GROUP AS BIG AS OURS.

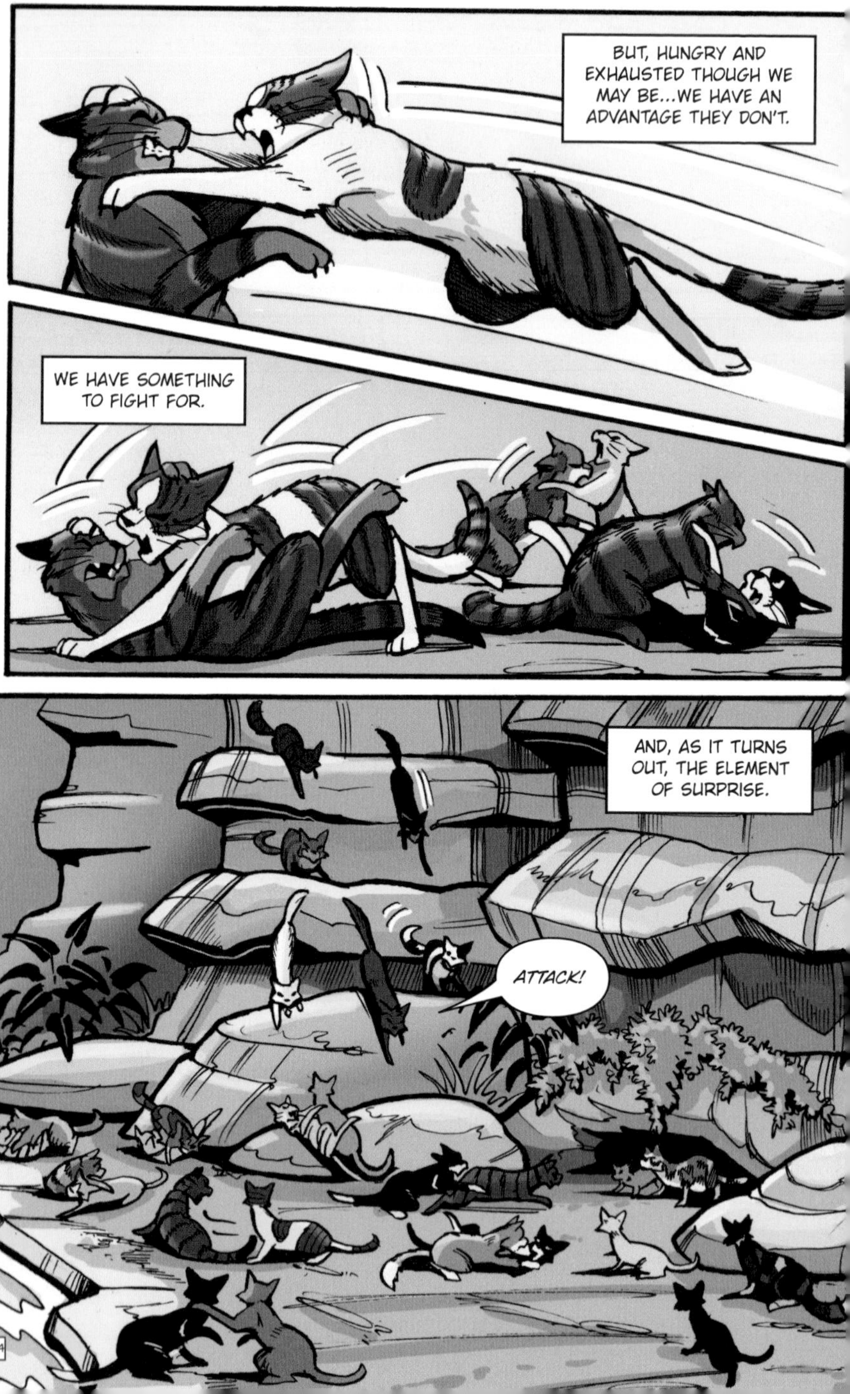
BUT, HUNGRY AND EXHAUSTED THOUGH WE MAY BE...WE HAVE AN ADVANTAGE THEY DON'T.
WE HAVE SOMETHING TO FIGHT FOR.
AND, AS IT TURNS OUT, THE ELEMENT OF SURPRISE.
ATTACK!

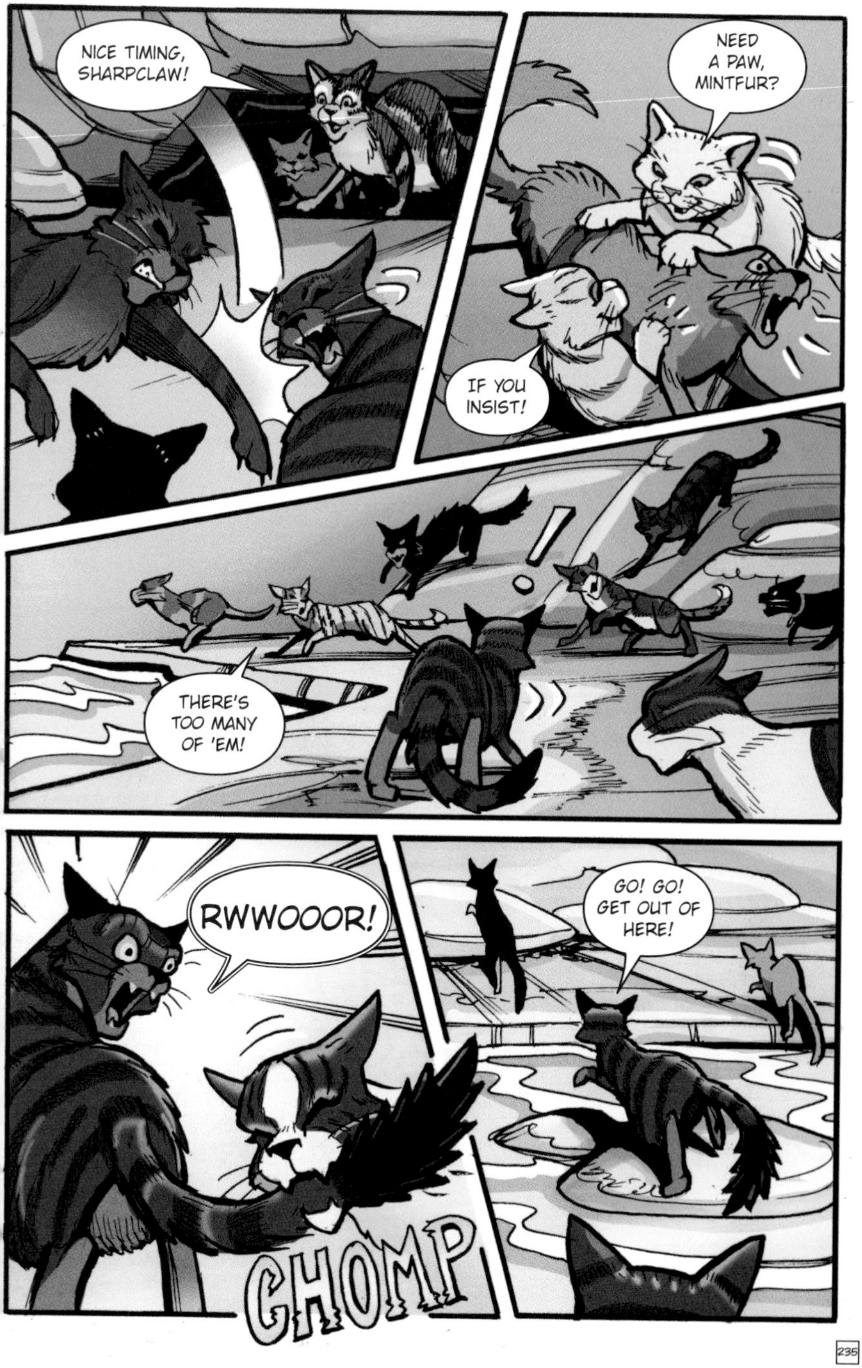
NICE TIMING, SHARPCLAW!
NEED A PAW, MINTFUR?
IF YOU INSIST!
!
THERE'S TOO MANY OF 'EM!
!
RWWOOOR!
CHOMP
GO! GO! GET OUT OF HERE!

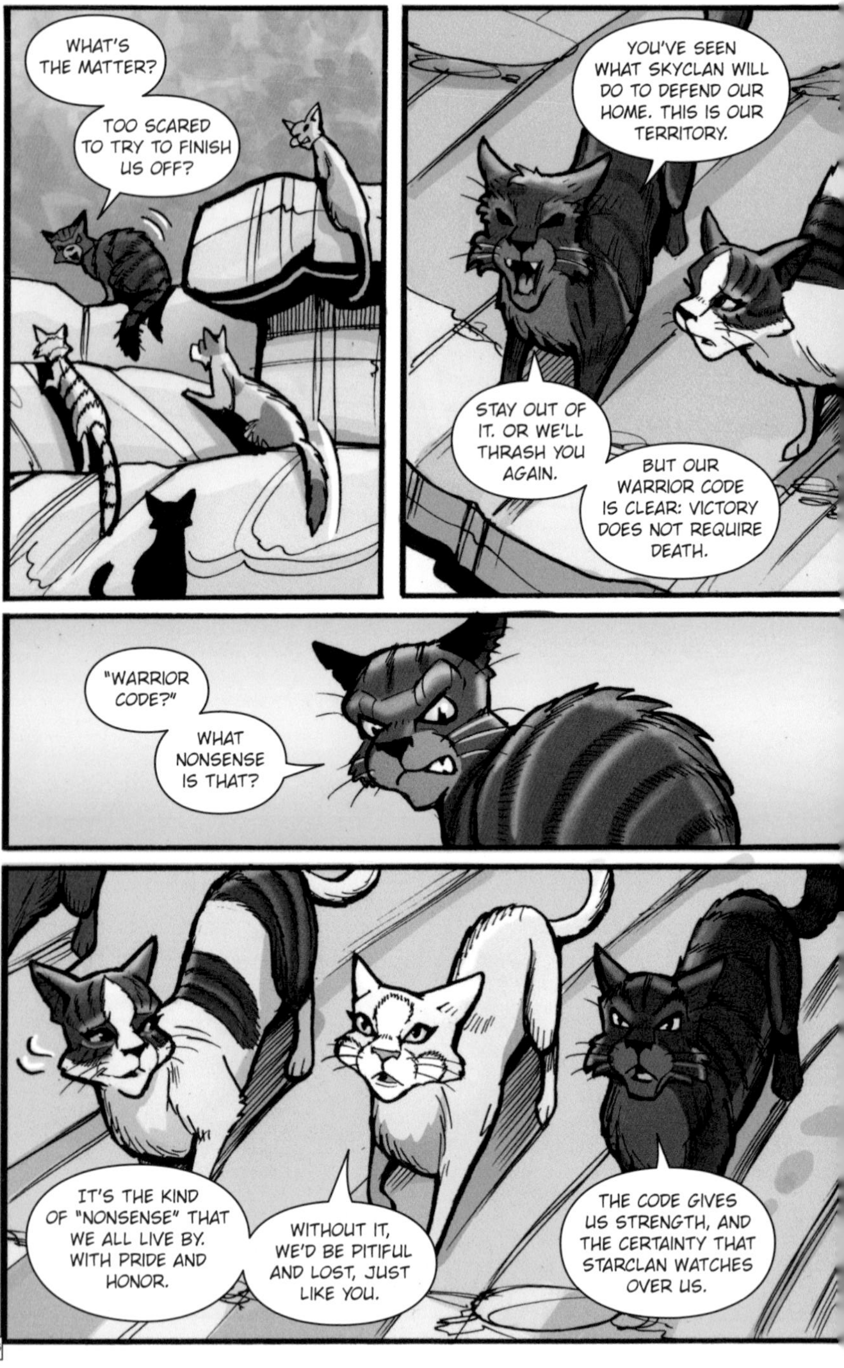
WHAT'S THE MATTER?
TOO SCARED TO TRY TO FINISH US OFF?
YOU'VE SEEN WHAT SKYCLAN WILL DO TO DEFEND OUR HOME. THIS IS OUR TERRITORY.
STAY OUT OF IT. OR WE'LL THRASH YOU AGAIN.
BUT OUR WARRIOR CODE IS CLEAR: VICTORY DOES NOT REQUIRE DEATH.
"WARRIOR CODE?"
WHAT NONSENSE IS THAT?
IT'S THE KIND OF "NONSENSE" THAT WE ALL LIVE BY. WITH PRIDE AND HONOR.
WITHOUT IT, WE'D BE PITIFUL AND LOST, JUST LIKE YOU.
THE CODE GIVES US STRENGTH, AND THE CERTAINTY THAT STARCLAN WATCHES OVER US.

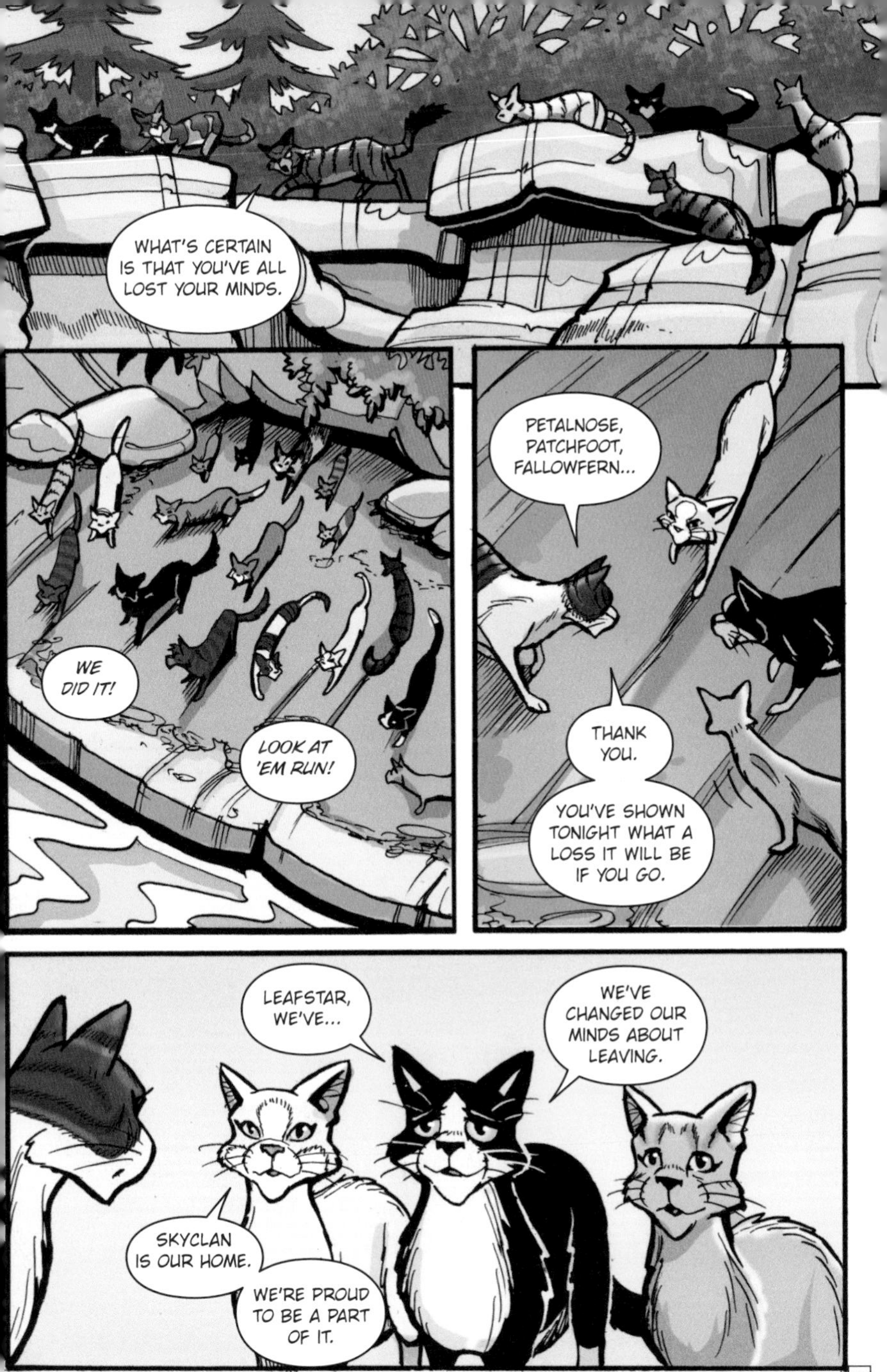
WHAT'S CERTAIN IS THAT YOU'VE ALL LOST YOUR MINDS.
WE DID IT!
LOOK AT 'EM RUN!
PETALNOSE, PATCHFOOT, FALLOWFERN...
THANK YOU.
YOU'VE SHOWN TONIGHT WHAT A LOSS IT WILL BE IF YOU GO.
LEAFSTAR, WE'VE...
WE'VE CHANGED OUR MINDS ABOUT LEAVING.
SKYCLAN IS OUR HOME.
WE'RE PROUD TO BE A PART OF IT.

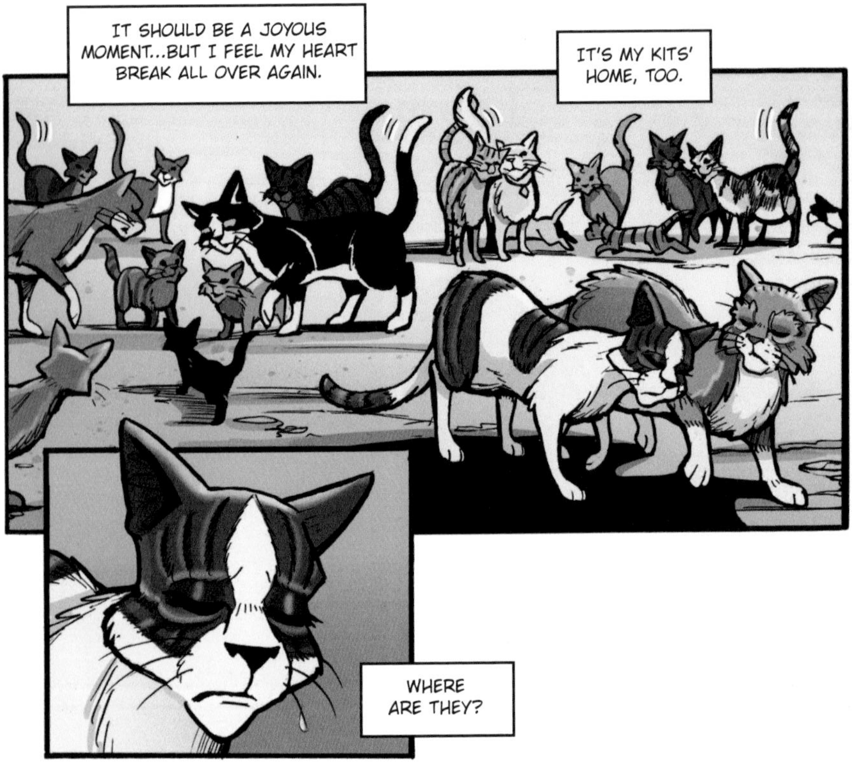
IT SHOULD BE A JOYOUS MOMENT...BUT I FEEL MY HEART BREAK ALL OVER AGAIN.
IT'S MY KITS' HOME, TOO.
WHERE ARE THEY?

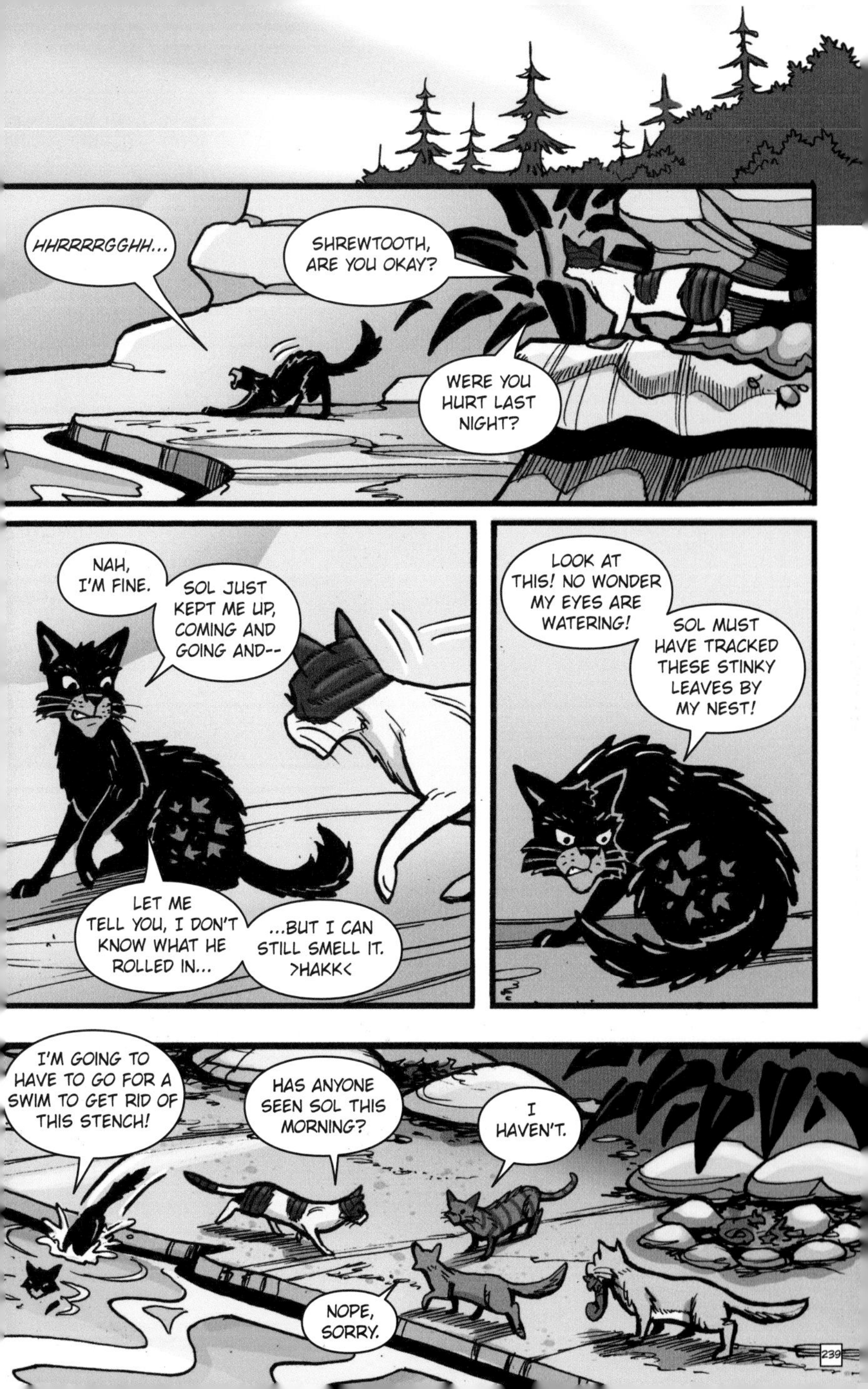
HHRRRRGGHH...
SHREWTOOTH, ARE YOU OKAY?
WERE YOU HURT LAST NIGHT?
NAH, I'M FINE.
SOL JUST KEPT ME UP, COMING AND GOING AND--
LET ME TELL YOU, I DON'T KNOW WHAT HE ROLLED IN...
...BUT I CAN STILL SMELL IT. >HAKK<
LOOK AT THIS! NO WONDER MY EYES ARE WATERING!
SOL MUST HAVE TRACKED THESE STINKY LEAVES BY MY NEST!
I'M GOING TO HAVE TO GO FOR A SWIM TO GET RID OF THIS STENCH!
HAS ANYONE SEEN SOL THIS MORNING?
I HAVEN'T.
NOPE, SORRY.

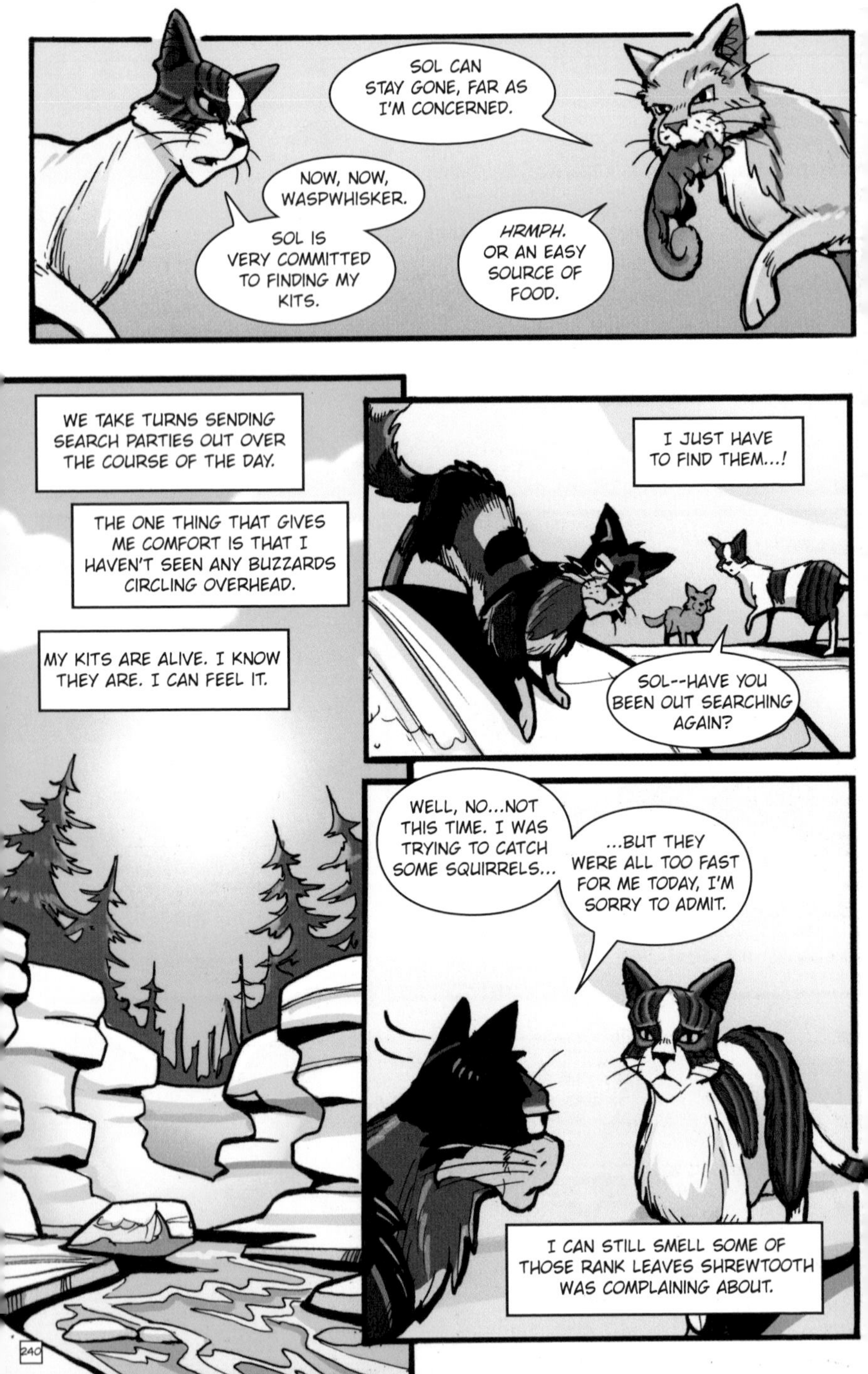
SOL CAN STAY GONE, FAR AS I'M CONCERNED.
NOW, NOW, WASPWHISKER.
SOL IS VERY COMMITTED TO FINDING MY KITS.
HRMPH. OR AN EASY SOURCE OF FOOD.
WE TAKE TURNS SENDING SEARCH PARTIES OUT OVER THE COURSE OF THE DAY.
THE ONE THING THAT GIVES ME COMFORT IS THAT I HAVEN'T SEEN ANY BUZZARDS CIRCLING OVERHEAD.
MY KITS ARE ALIVE. I KNOW THEY ARE. I CAN FEEL IT.
I JUST HAVE TO FIND THEM...!
SOL--HAVE YOU BEEN OUT SEARCHING AGAIN?
WELL, NO...NOT THIS TIME. I WAS TRYING TO CATCH SOME SQUIRRELS...
...BUT THEY WERE ALL TOO FAST FOR ME TODAY, I'M SORRY TO ADMIT.
I CAN STILL SMELL SOME OF THOSE RANK LEAVES SHREWTOOTH WAS COMPLAINING ABOUT.

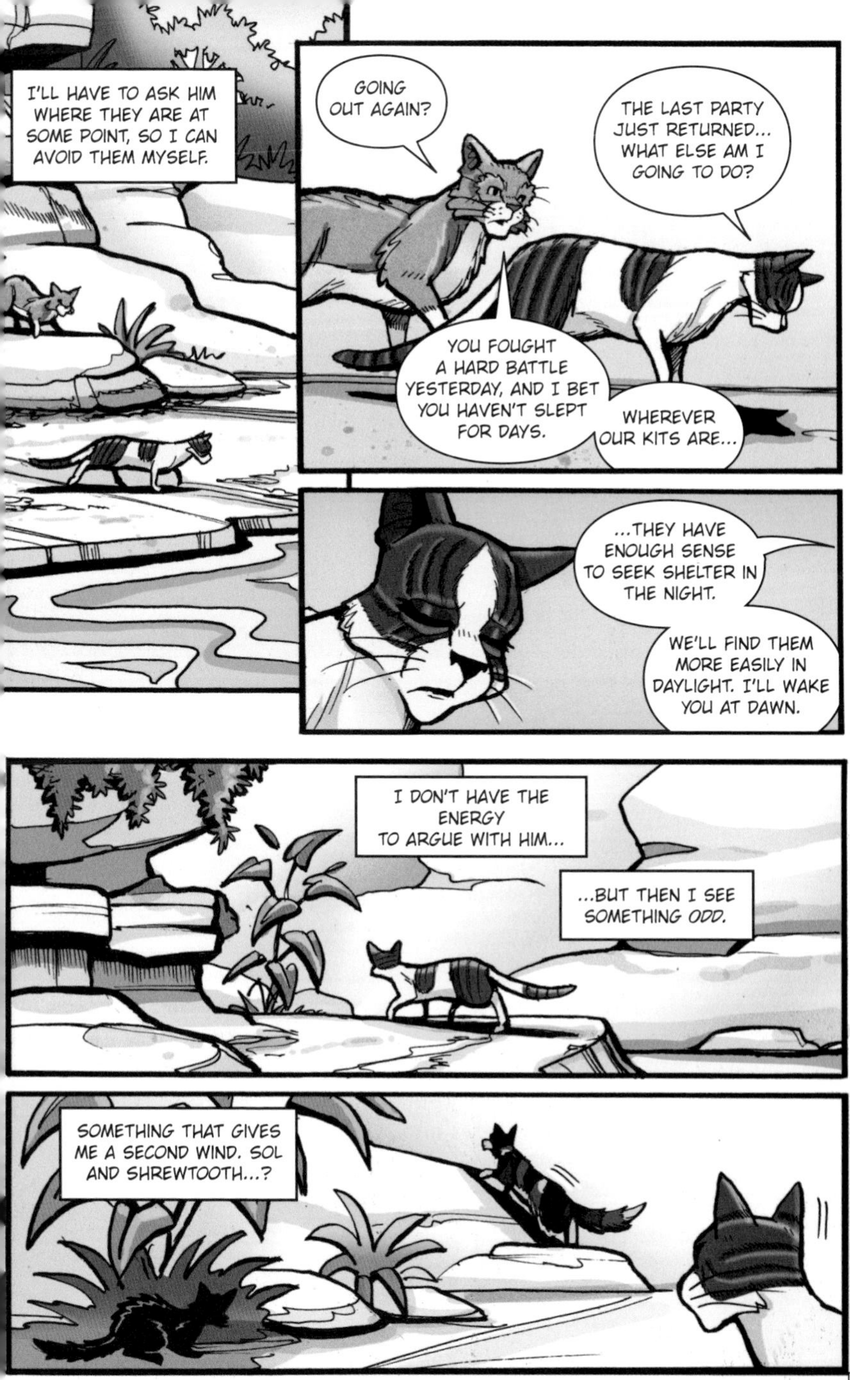
I'LL HAVE TO ASK HIM WHERE THEY ARE AT SOME POINT, SO I CAN AVOID THEM MYSELF.
GOING OUT AGAIN?
THE LAST PARTY JUST RETURNED... WHAT ELSE AM I GOING TO DO?
YOU FOUGHT A HARD BATTLE YESTERDAY, AND I BET YOU HAVEN'T SLEPT FOR DAYS.
WHEREVER OUR KITS ARE...
...THEY HAVE ENOUGH SENSE TO SEEK SHELTER IN THE NIGHT.
WE'LL FIND THEM MORE EASILY IN DAYLIGHT. I'LL WAKE YOU AT DAWN.
I DON'T HAVE THE ENERGY TO ARGUE WITH HIM...
...BUT THEN I SEE SOMETHING *ODD.*
SOMETHING THAT GIVES ME A SECOND WIND. SOL AND SHREWTOOTH...?

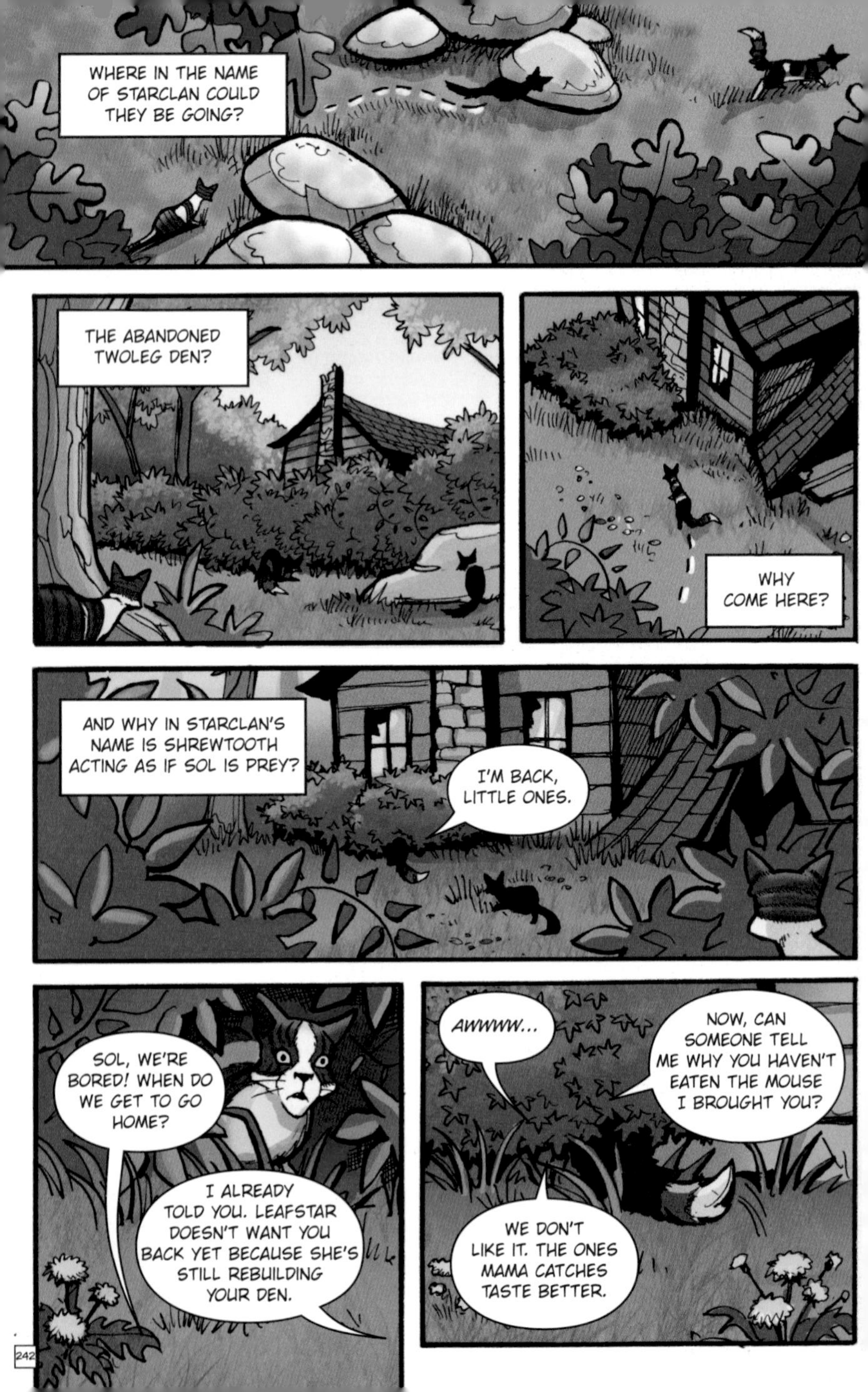
WHERE IN THE NAME OF STARCLAN COULD THEY BE GOING?
THE ABANDONED TWOLEG DEN?
WHY COME HERE?
AND WHY IN STARCLAN'S NAME IS SHREWTOOTH ACTING AS IF SOL IS PREY?
I'M BACK, LITTLE ONES.
SOL, WE'RE BORED! WHEN DO WE GET TO GO HOME?
I ALREADY TOLD YOU. LEAFSTAR DOESN'T WANT YOU BACK YET BECAUSE SHE'S STILL REBUILDING YOUR DEN.
AWWWW...
NOW, CAN SOMEONE TELL ME WHY YOU HAVEN'T EATEN THE MOUSE I BROUGHT YOU?
WE DON'T LIKE IT. THE ONES MAMA CATCHES TASTE BETTER.

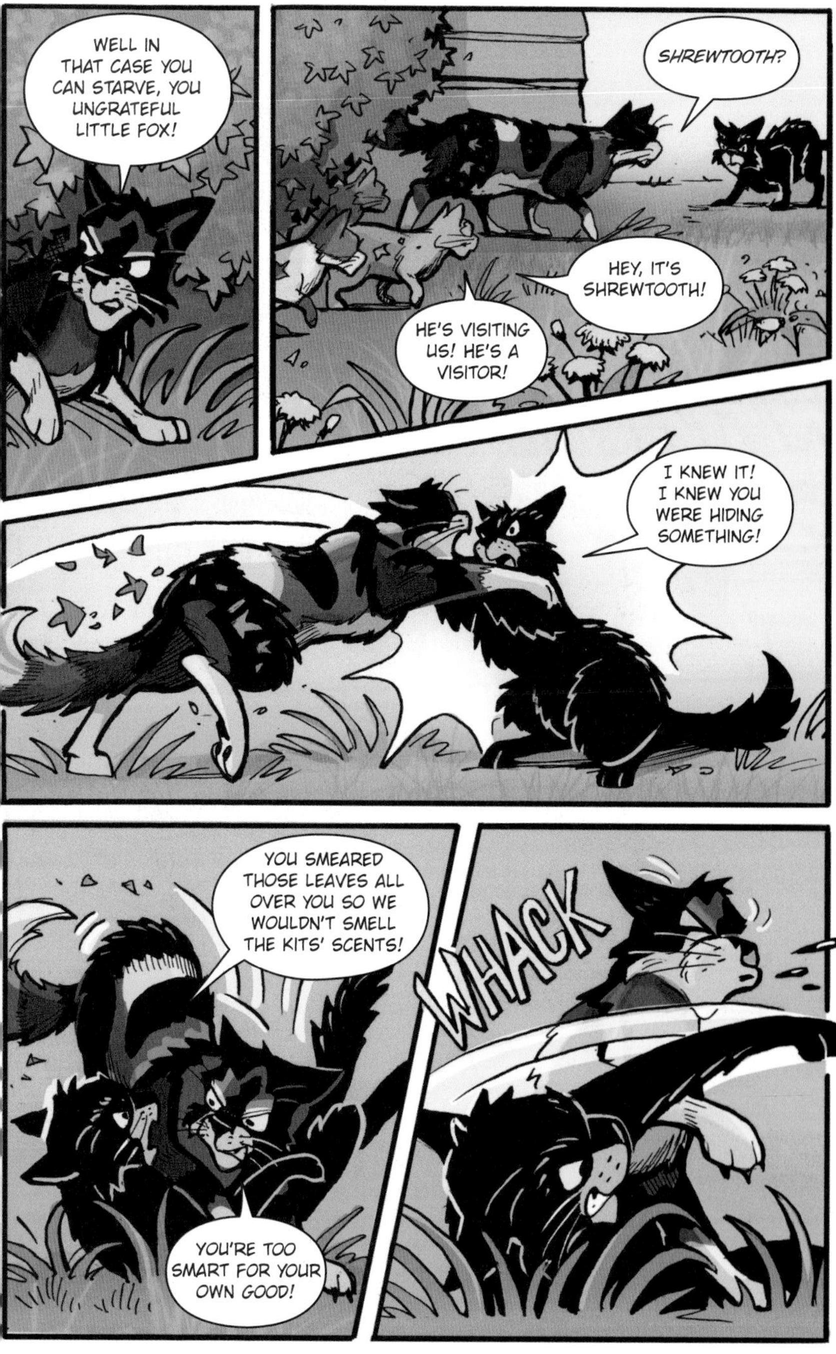
WELL IN THAT CASE YOU CAN STARVE, YOU UNGRATEFUL LITTLE FOX!
SHREWTOOTH?
HEY, IT'S SHREWTOOTH!
HE'S VISITING US! HE'S A VISITOR!
I KNEW IT! I KNEW YOU WERE HIDING SOMETHING!
YOU SMEARED THOSE LEAVES ALL OVER YOU SO WE WOULDN'T SMELL THE KITS' SCENTS!
YOU'RE TOO SMART FOR YOUR OWN GOOD!
WHACK

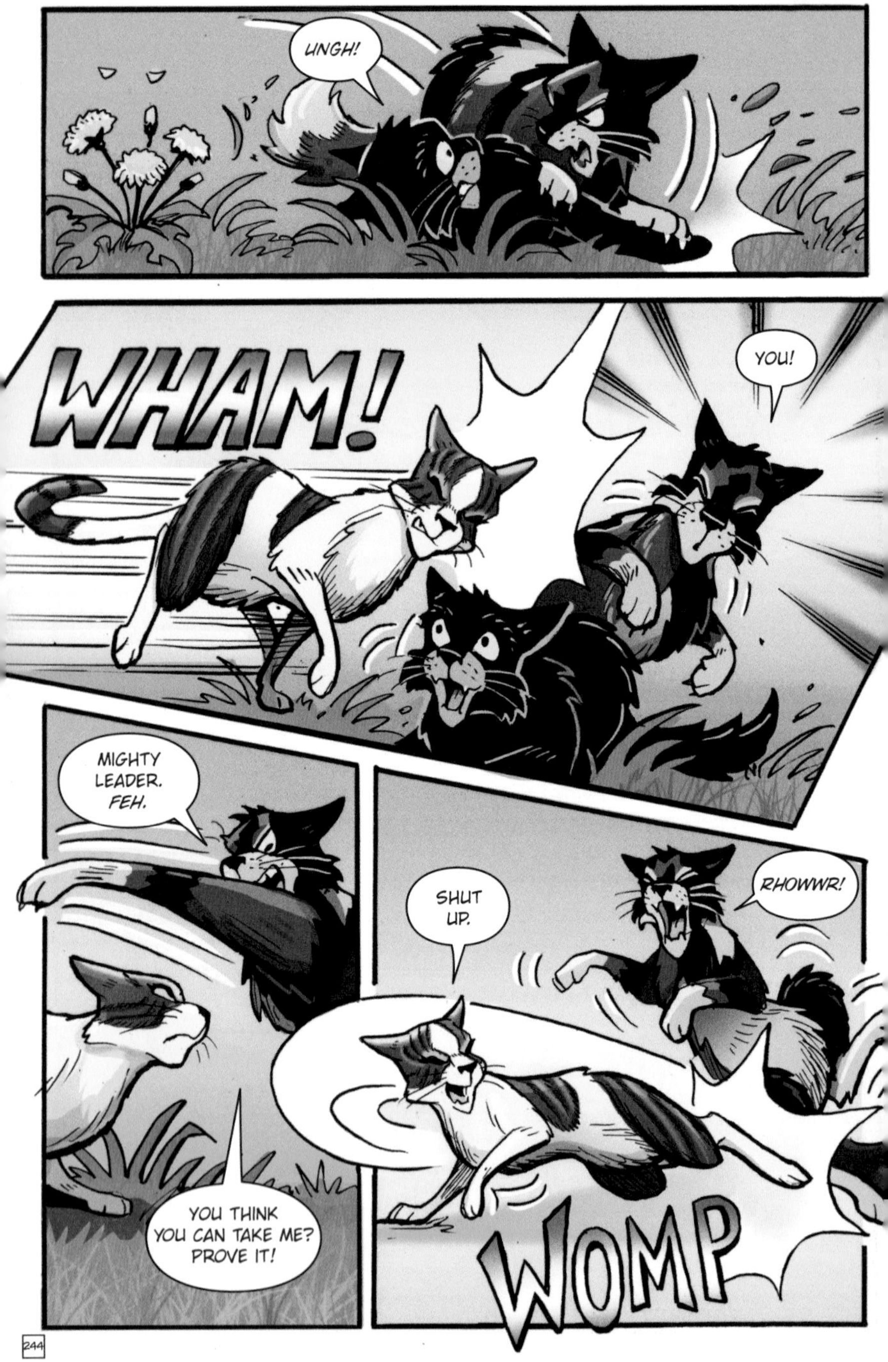
UNGH!
WHAM!
YOU!
MIGHTY LEADER. FEH.
YOU THINK YOU CAN TAKE ME? PROVE IT!
SHUT UP.
RHOWWR!
WOMP

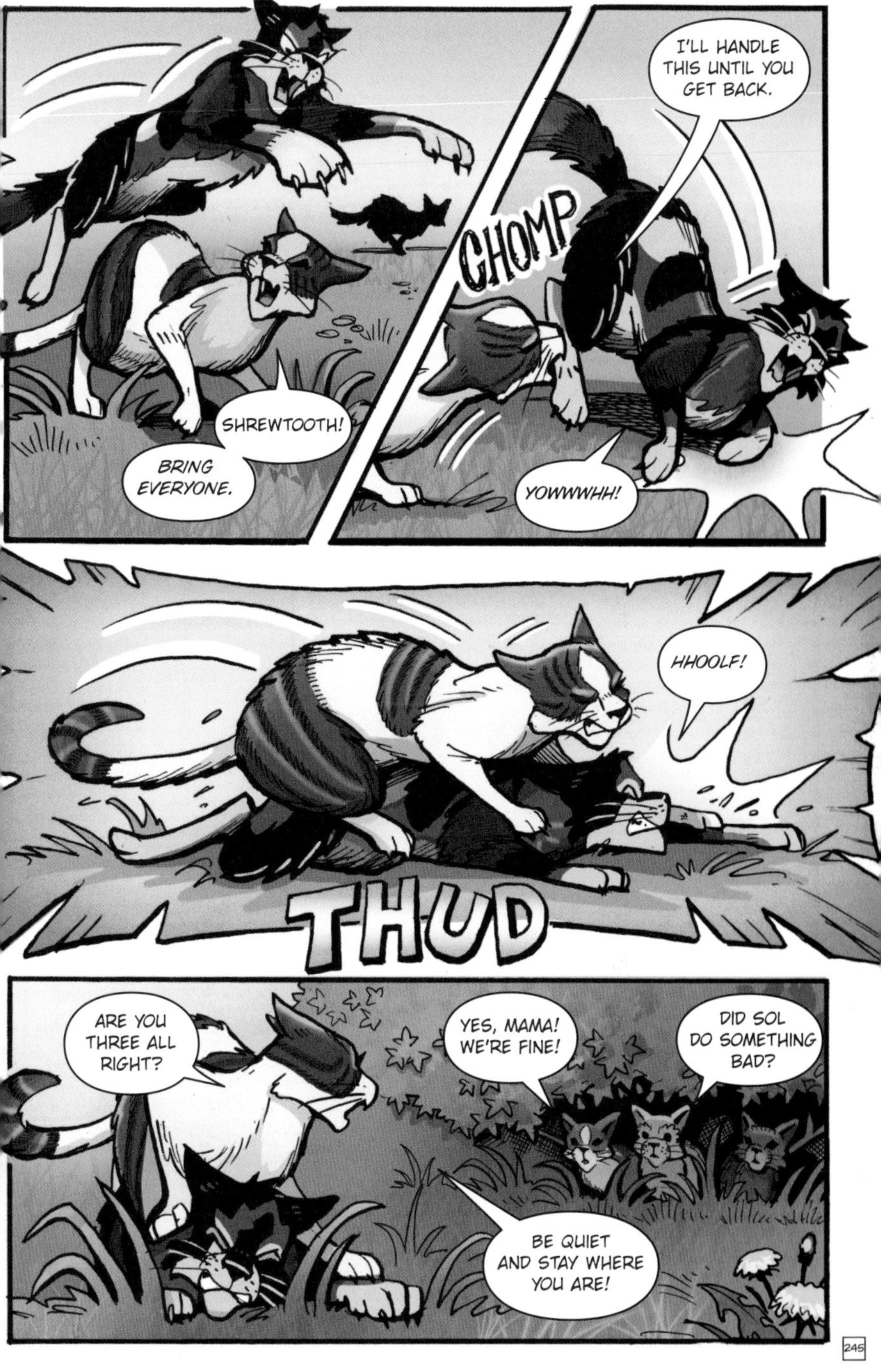
SHREWTOOTH!
BRING EVERYONE.
I'LL HANDLE THIS UNTIL YOU GET BACK.
CHOMP
YOWWWHH!
HHOOLF!
THUD
ARE YOU THREE ALL RIGHT?
YES, MAMA! WE'RE FINE!
DID SOL DO SOMETHING BAD?
BE QUIET AND STAY WHERE YOU ARE!

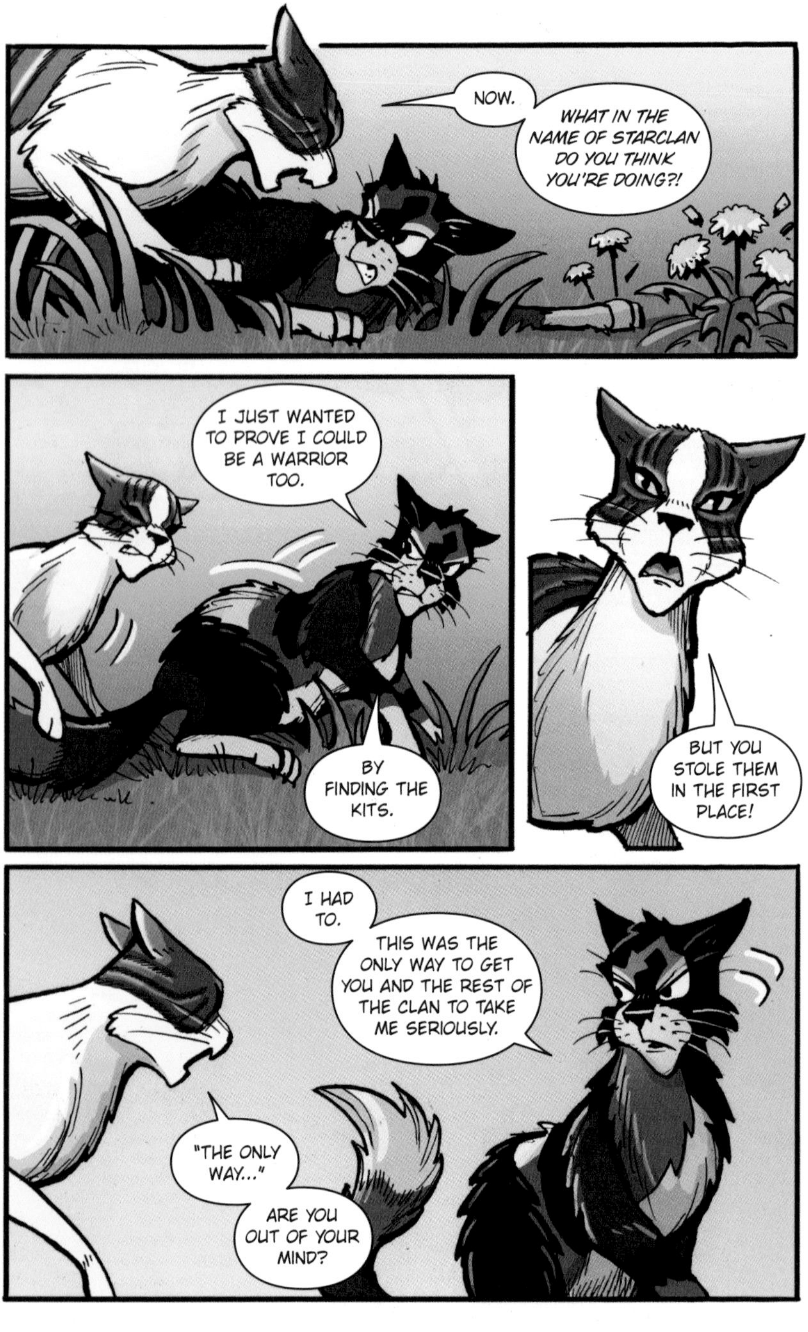
NOW.
WHAT IN THE NAME OF STARCLAN DO YOU THINK YOU'RE DOING?!
I JUST WANTED TO PROVE I COULD BE A WARRIOR TOO.
BY FINDING THE KITS.
BUT YOU STOLE THEM IN THE FIRST PLACE!
I HAD TO.
THIS WAS THE ONLY WAY TO GET YOU AND THE REST OF THE CLAN TO TAKE ME SERIOUSLY.
"THE ONLY WAY..."
ARE YOU OUT OF YOUR MIND?

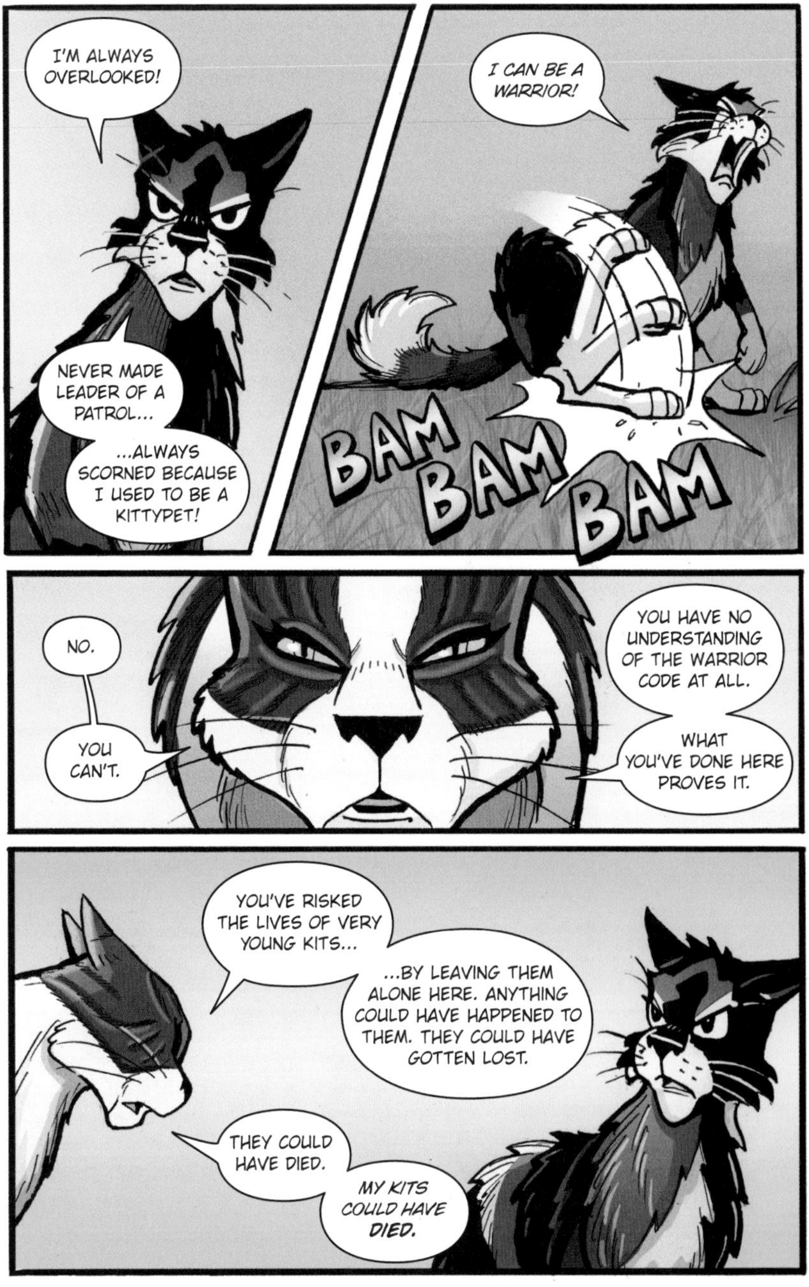
I'M ALWAYS OVERLOOKED!
NEVER MADE LEADER OF A PATROL...
...ALWAYS SCORNED BECAUSE I USED TO BE A KITTYPET!
I CAN BE A WARRIOR!
BAM BAM BAM
NO.
YOU CAN'T.
YOU HAVE NO UNDERSTANDING OF THE WARRIOR CODE AT ALL.
WHAT YOU'VE DONE HERE PROVES IT.
YOU'VE RISKED THE LIVES OF VERY YOUNG KITS...
...BY LEAVING THEM ALONE HERE. ANYTHING COULD HAVE HAPPENED TO THEM. THEY COULD HAVE GOTTEN LOST.
THEY COULD HAVE DIED.
MY KITS COULD HAVE DIED.

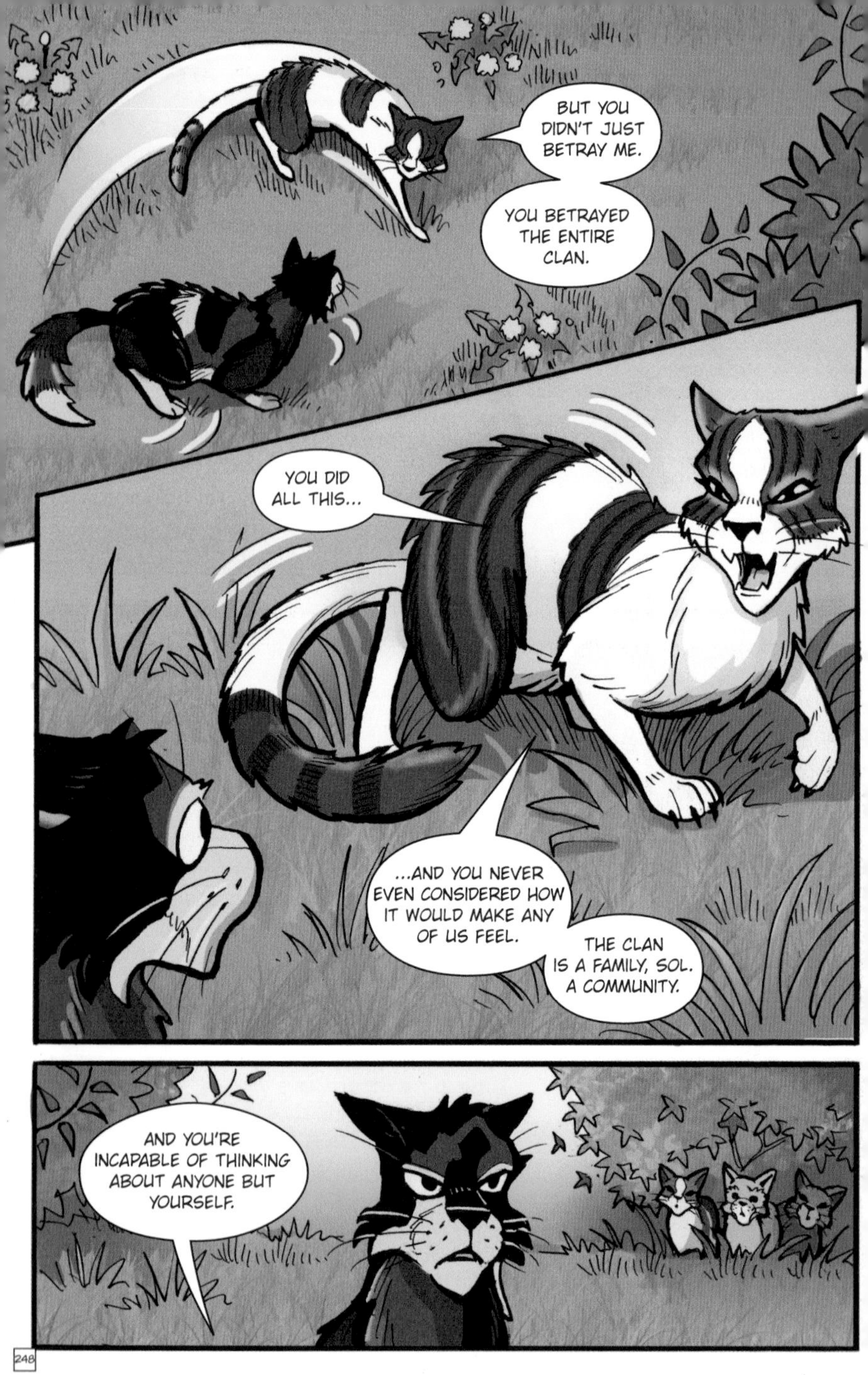
BUT YOU DIDN'T JUST BETRAY ME.
YOU BETRAYED THE ENTIRE CLAN.
YOU DID ALL THIS...
...AND YOU NEVER EVEN CONSIDERED HOW IT WOULD MAKE ANY OF US FEEL.
THE CLAN IS A FAMILY, SOL. A COMMUNITY.
AND YOU'RE INCAPABLE OF THINKING ABOUT ANYONE BUT YOURSELF.

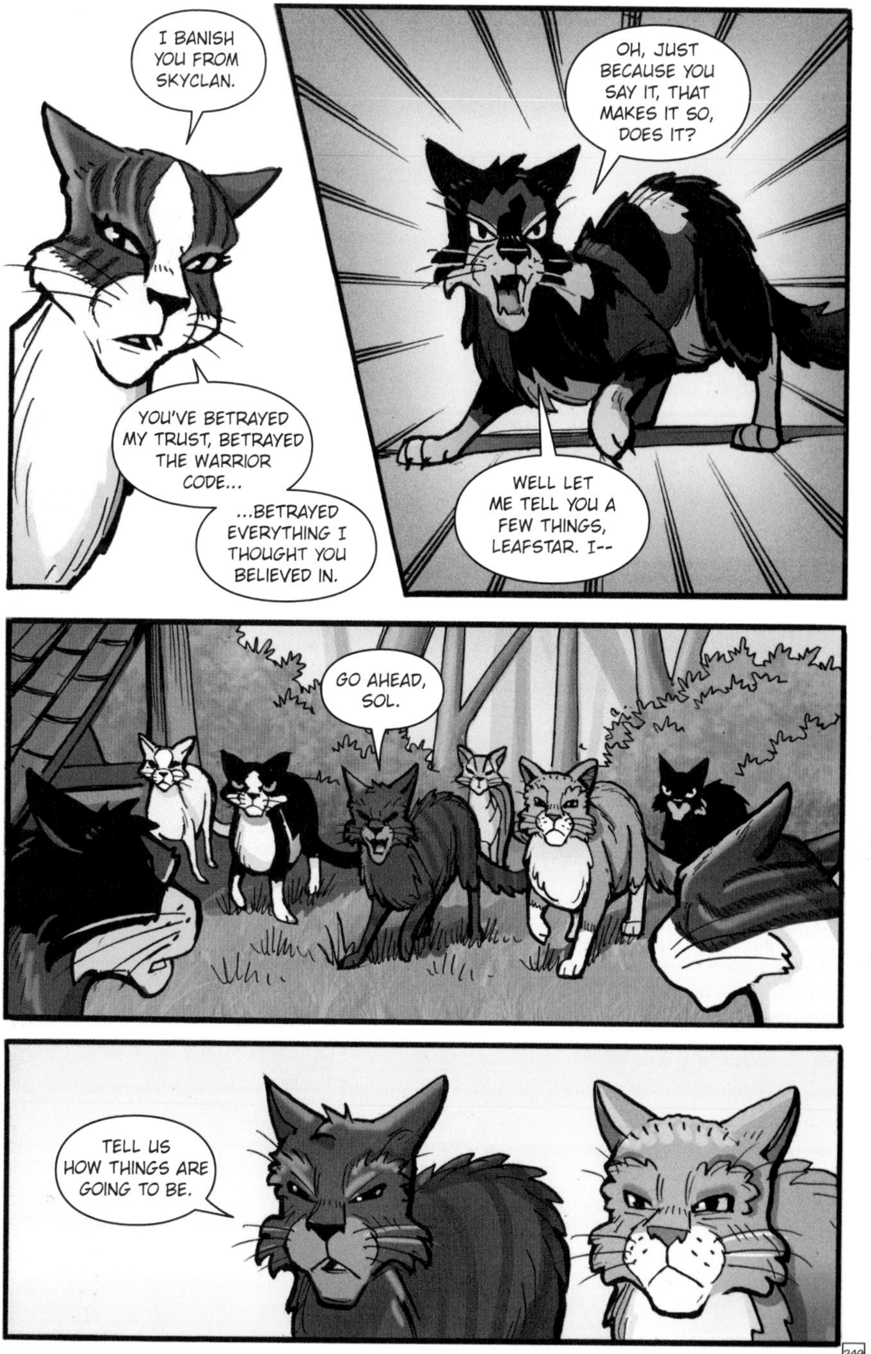
I BANISH YOU FROM SKYCLAN.
YOU'VE BETRAYED MY TRUST, BETRAYED THE WARRIOR CODE...
...BETRAYED EVERYTHING I THOUGHT YOU BELIEVED IN.
OH, JUST BECAUSE YOU SAY IT, THAT MAKES IT SO, DOES IT?
WELL LET ME TELL YOU A FEW THINGS, LEAFSTAR. I--
GO AHEAD, SOL.
TELL US HOW THINGS ARE GOING TO BE.

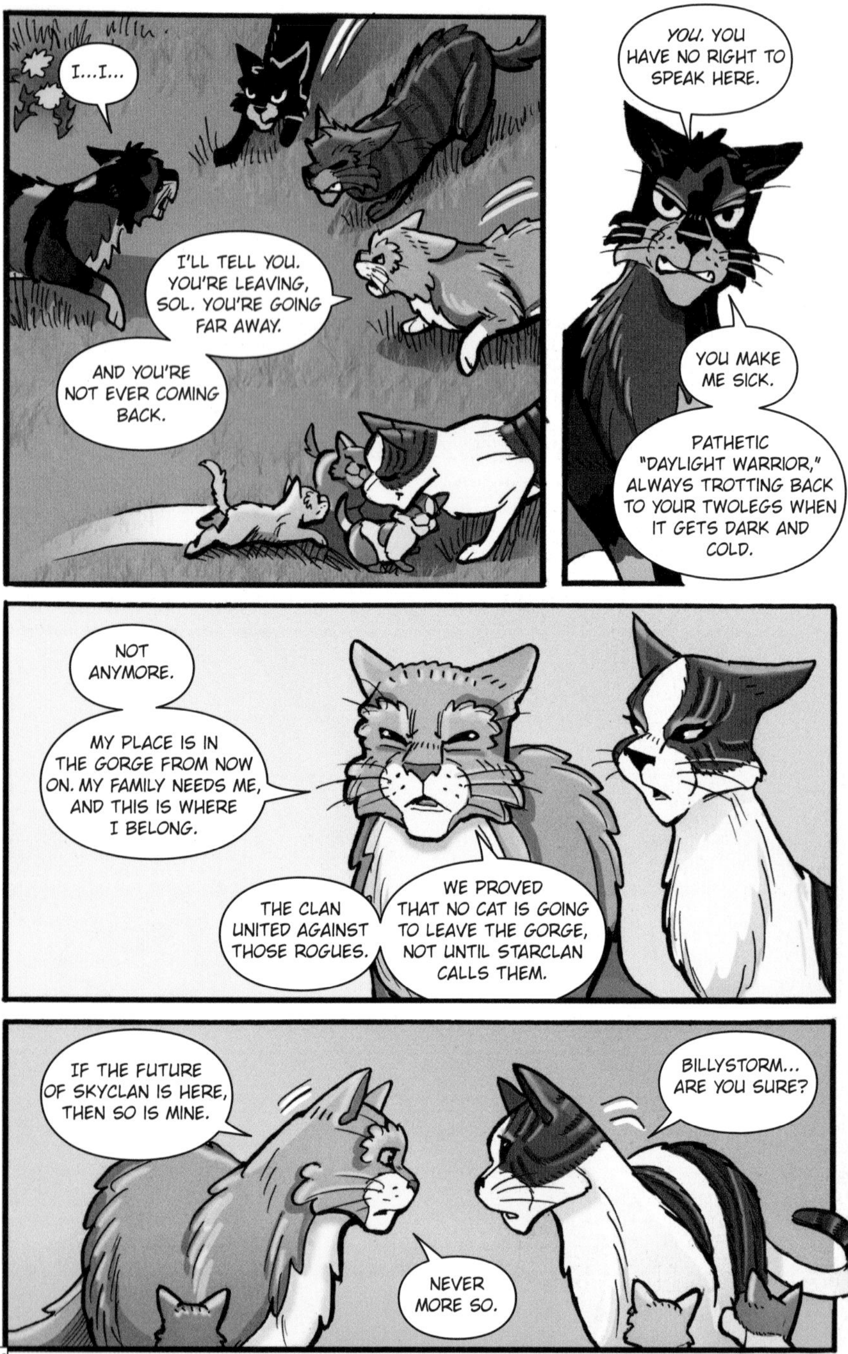
I...I...
I'LL TELL YOU. YOU'RE LEAVING, SOL. YOU'RE GOING FAR AWAY.
AND YOU'RE NOT EVER COMING BACK.
YOU. YOU HAVE NO RIGHT TO SPEAK HERE.
YOU MAKE ME SICK.
PATHETIC "DAYLIGHT WARRIOR," ALWAYS TROTTING BACK TO YOUR TWOLEGS WHEN IT GETS DARK AND COLD.
NOT ANYMORE.
MY PLACE IS IN THE GORGE FROM NOW ON. MY FAMILY NEEDS ME, AND THIS IS WHERE I BELONG.
THE CLAN UNITED AGAINST THOSE ROGUES.
WE PROVED THAT NO CAT IS GOING TO LEAVE THE GORGE, NOT UNTIL STARCLAN CALLS THEM.
IF THE FUTURE OF SKYCLAN IS HERE, THEN SO IS MINE.
BILLYSTORM... ARE YOU SURE?
NEVER MORE SO.

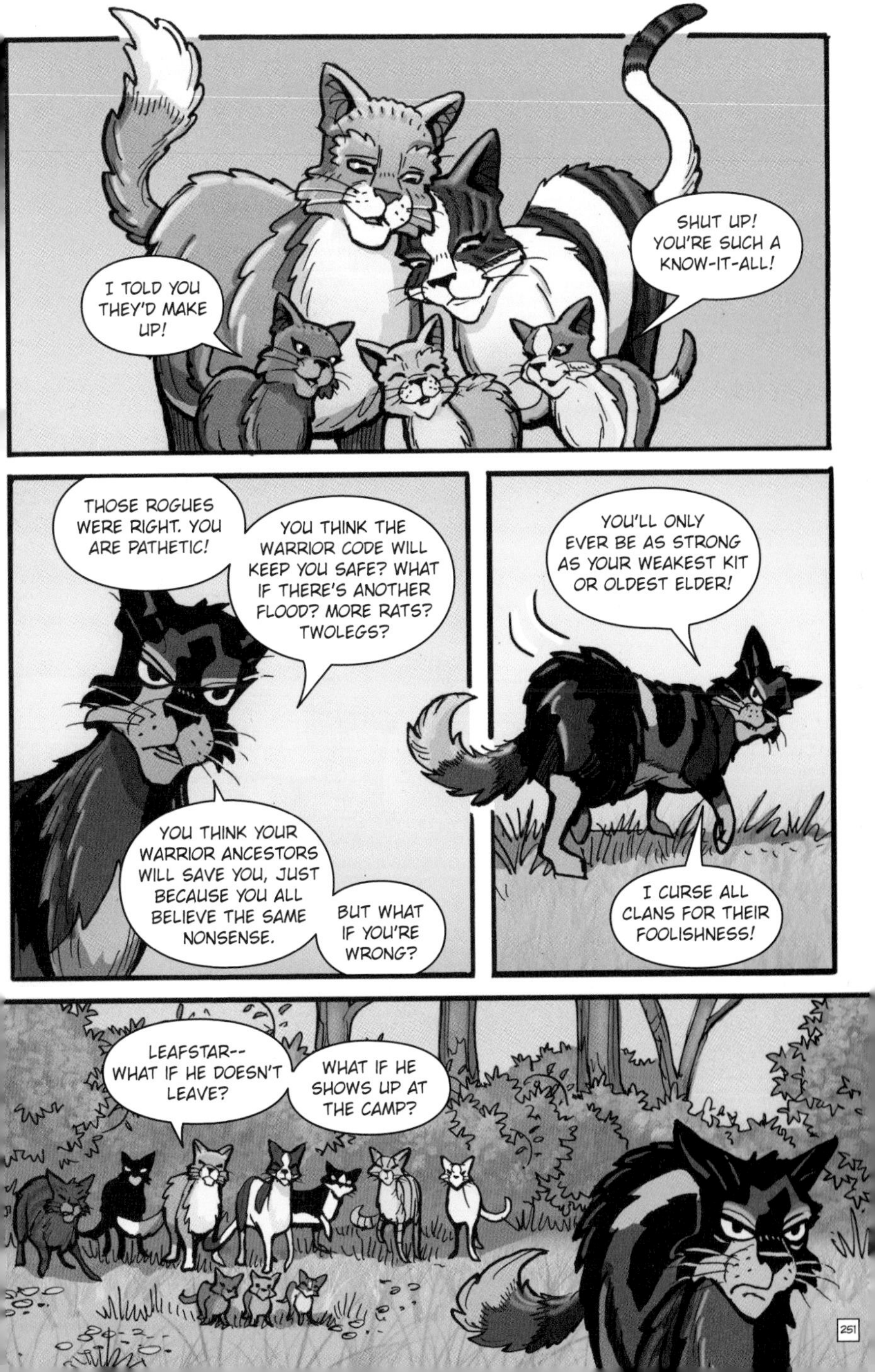
I TOLD YOU THEY'D MAKE UP!
SHUT UP! YOU'RE SUCH A KNOW-IT-ALL!
THOSE ROGUES WERE RIGHT. YOU ARE PATHETIC!
YOU THINK THE WARRIOR CODE WILL KEEP YOU SAFE? WHAT IF THERE'S ANOTHER FLOOD? MORE RATS? TWOLEGS?
YOU THINK YOUR WARRIOR ANCESTORS WILL SAVE YOU, JUST BECAUSE YOU ALL BELIEVE THE SAME NONSENSE.
BUT WHAT IF YOU'RE WRONG?
YOU'LL ONLY EVER BE AS STRONG AS YOUR WEAKEST KIT OR OLDEST ELDER!
I CURSE ALL CLANS FOR THEIR FOOLISHNESS!
LEAFSTAR-- WHAT IF HE DOESN'T LEAVE?
WHAT IF HE SHOWS UP AT THE CAMP?

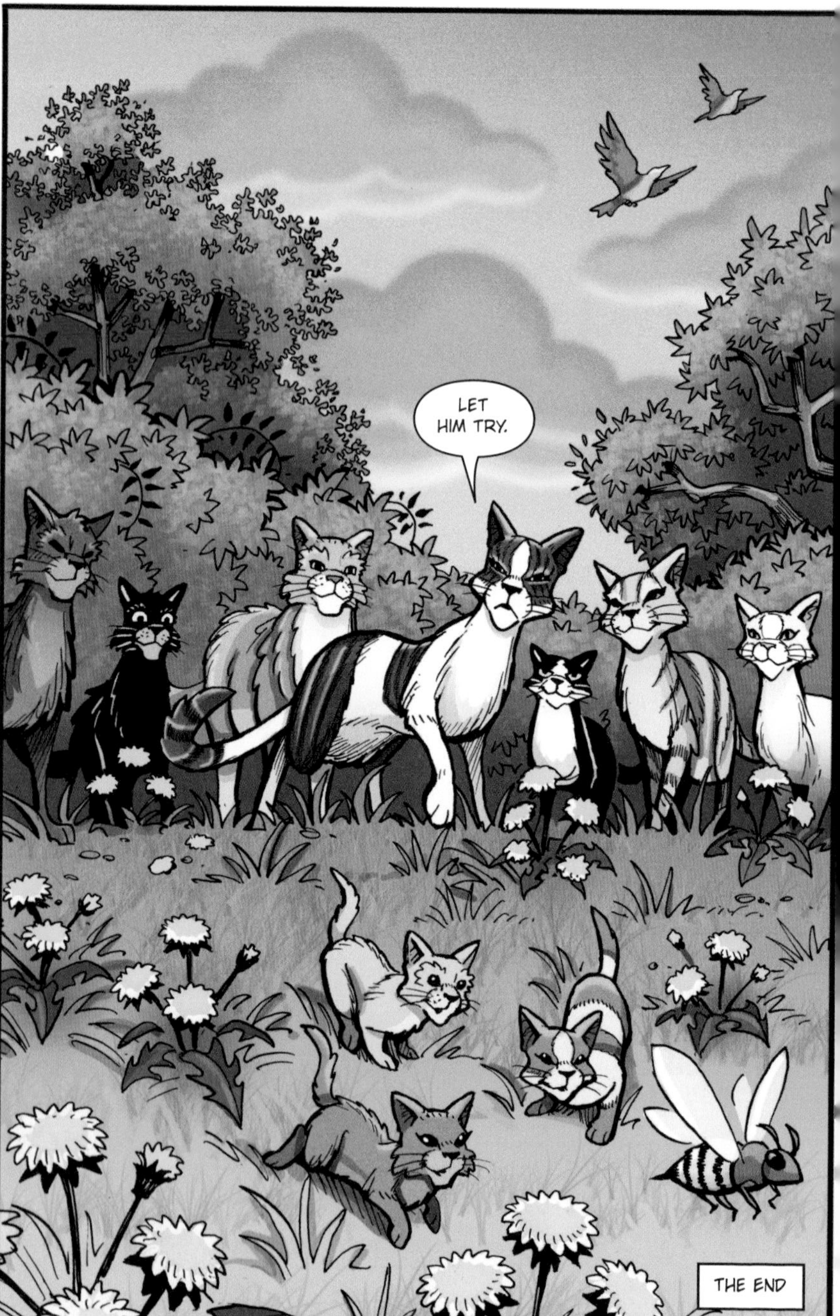
LET HIM TRY.
THE END

A NEW WARRIORS ADVENTURE BEGINS!

DON'T MISS

THE BROKEN CODE
WARRIORS
LOST STARS
BONUS! POSTER INSIDE
ERIN HUNTER
#1 NEW YORK TIMES BESTSELLING AUTHOR

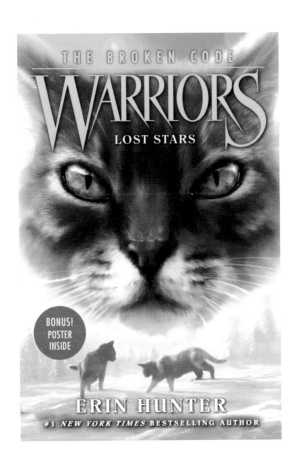

CHAPTER 1

❧

Shadowpaw craned his neck over his back, straining to groom the hard-to-reach spot at the base of his tail. He had just managed to give his fur a few vigorous licks when he heard paw steps approaching. He looked up to see his father, Tigerstar, and his mother, Dovewing, their pelts brushing as they gazed down at him with pride and joy shining in their eyes.

"What is it?" he asked, sitting up and giving his pelt a shake.

"We just came to see you off," Tigerstar responded, while Dovewing gave her son's ears a quick, affectionate lick.

Shadowpaw's fur prickled with embarrassment. *Like I haven't been to the Moonpool before,* he thought. *They're still treating me as if I'm a kit in the nursery!*

He was sure that his parents hadn't made such a fuss when his littermates, Pouncestep and Lightleap, had been warrior apprentices. *I guess it's because I'm going to be a medicine cat. . . .* Or maybe because of the seizures he'd had since he was a kit. He knew his parents still worried about him, even though it had been a while since his last upsetting vision. *They're probably hoping that with some training from the other medicine cats, I'll learn to control my visions once and for all . . . and I can be normal.*

Shadowpaw wanted that, too.

"The snow must be really deep up on the moors," Dovewing mewed. "Make sure you watch where you're putting your paws."

Shadowpaw wriggled his shoulders, praying that none of his Clanmates were listening. "I will," he promised, glancing toward the medicine cats' den in the hope of seeing his mentor, Puddleshine, emerge. But there was no sign of him yet.

To his relief, Tigerstar gave Dovewing a nudge and they both moved off toward the Clan leader's den. Shadowpaw rubbed one paw hastily across his face and bounded across the camp to see what was keeping Puddleshine.

Intent on finding his mentor, Shadowpaw barely noticed the patrol trekking toward the fresh-kill pile, prey dangling from their jaws. He skidded to a halt just in time to avoid colliding with Cloverfoot, the Clan deputy.

"Shadowpaw!" she exclaimed around the shrew she was carrying. "You nearly knocked me off my paws."

"Sorry, Cloverfoot," Shadowpaw meowed, dipping his head respectfully.

Cloverfoot let out a snort, half annoyed, half amused. "Apprentices!"

Shadowpaw tried to hide his irritation. He was an apprentice, yes, but an old one—medicine cat apprentices' training lasted longer than warriors'. His littermates were full warriors already. But he knew his parents would want him to respect the deputy.

Cloverfoot padded on, followed by Strikestone, Yarrowleaf, and Blazefire. Though they were all carrying prey, they had only one or two pieces each, and what little they had managed to catch was undersized and scrawny.

"I can't remember a leaf-bare as cold as this," Yarrowleaf complained as she dropped a blackbird on the fresh-kill pile.

Strikestone nodded, shivering as he fluffed out his brown tabby pelt. "No wonder there's no prey. They're all hiding down their holes, and I can't blame them."

As Shadowpaw moved on, out of earshot, he couldn't help noticing how pitifully small the fresh-kill pile was, and he tried to ignore his own growling belly. He could hardly remember his first leaf-bare, when he'd been a tiny kit, so he didn't know if the older cats were right and the weather was unusually cold.

I only know I don't like it, he grumbled to himself as he picked his way through the icy slush that covered the ground of the camp. *My paws are so cold I think they'll drop off. I can't wait for newleaf!*

Puddleshine ducked out of the entrance to the medicine

cats' den as Shadowpaw approached. "Good, you're ready," he meowed. "We'd better hurry, or we'll be late." As he led the way toward the camp entrance, he added, "I've been checking our herb stores, and they're getting dangerously low."

"We could search for more on the way back," Shadowpaw suggested, his medicine-cat duties driving out his thoughts of cold and hunger. He always enjoyed working with Puddleshine to find, sort, and store the herbs. Treating cats with herbs made him feel calm and in control . . . the opposite of how he felt during his seizures and upsetting visions.

"We can try," Puddleshine sighed. "But what isn't frostbitten will be covered with snow." He glanced over his shoulder at Shadowpaw as the two cats headed out into the forest. "This is turning out to be a really bad leaf-bare. And it isn't over yet, not by a long way."

Excitement tingled through Shadowpaw from ears to tail-tip as he scrambled up the rocky slope toward the line of bushes that surrounded the Moonpool hollow. His worries over his seizures and the bitter leaf-bare faded; every hair on his pelt was bristling with anticipation of his meeting with the other medicine cats, and most of all with StarClan.

He might not be a full medicine cat yet, and he might not be fully in control of his visions . . . but he would still get to meet with his warrior ancestors. And from the rest of the medicine cats he would find out what was going on in the other Clans.

Standing at the top of the slope, waiting for Puddle-shine to push his way through the bushes, Shadowpaw reflected on the last few moons. Things had been tense in ShadowClan as every cat settled into their new boundaries and grew used to sharing a border with SkyClan. Not long ago, SkyClan had lived separately from the other Clans, in a far-flung territory in a gorge. But StarClan had called SkyClan back to join the other Clans by the lake, because the Clans were stronger when all five were united. Still, SkyClan had needed its own territory, which had meant new borders for everyone, and it had taken time for the other Clans to accept them. Shadowpaw was relieved that things seemed more peaceful now; the brutally cold leaf-bare had given all the Clans more to worry about than quarreling with one another. They were even beginning to rely on one another, especially in sharing herbs when the cold weather had damaged so many of the plants they needed. Shadowpaw felt proud that they were all getting along, instead of battling one another for every piece of prey.

That wasn't a great start to Tigerstar's leadership. . . . I'm glad it's over now!

"Are you going to stand out there all night?"

At the sound of Puddleshine's voice from the other side of the bushes, Shadowpaw dived in among the branches, wincing as sharp twigs scraped along his pelt, and thrust himself out onto the ledge above the Moonpool. Opposite him, halfway up the rocky wall of the hollow, a trickle of water bubbled out from between two moss-covered boulders. The water fell down into the pool below, with a fitful glimmer as if the stars themselves were trapped inside it. The rippling surface of the pool shone silver with reflected moonlight.

Shadowpaw wanted to leap into the air with excitement at being back at the Moonpool, but he fought to hold on to some self-control, and padded down the spiral path to the water's edge with all the dignity expected of a medicine cat. Awe welled up inside him as he felt his paws slip into the hollows made by cats countless seasons before.

Who were they? Where did they go? he wondered.

The two ThunderClan medicine cats were already sitting beside the pool. Shadowpaw guessed it was too cold to wait outside for everyone to arrive, as the medicine cats usually did. Alderheart was thoughtfully grooming his chest fur, while Jayfeather's tail-tip twitched back and forth in irritation. He turned his blind blue gaze on Puddleshine and Shadowpaw as they reached the bottom of the hollow.

"You took your time," he snapped. "We're wasting moonlight."

Shadowpaw realized that Kestrelflight of WindClan and Mothwing and Willowshine, the two RiverClan medicine cats, were sitting just beyond the two from ThunderClan. The shadow of a rock had hidden them from him until now.

"Nice to see you, too, Jayfeather," Puddleshine responded mildly. "I'm sorry if we're late, but I don't see Frecklewish or Fidgetflake, either."

Jayfeather gave a disdainful sniff. "If they're not here soon, we'll start without them."

Would Jayfeather really do that? Shadowpaw was still staring at the ThunderClan medicine cat, wondering, when a rustling from the top of the slope put him on alert. Looking up, he saw Frecklewish pushing her way through the bushes, followed closely by Fidgetflake.

"At last!" Jayfeather hissed.

He's in a mood, Shadowpaw thought, then added to himself with a flicker of amusement, *Nothing new there, then.*

As the two SkyClan medicine cats padded down the slope, Shadowpaw noticed how thin and weary they both looked. For a heartbeat he wondered if there was anything wrong in SkyClan. Then he realized that he and the rest of the medicine cats looked just as skinny, just as worn out by the trials of leaf-bare.

Frecklewish dipped her head to her fellow medicine cats as she joined them beside the pool. "Greetings," she mewed, her fatigue clear in her voice. "How is the prey running in your Clans?"

For a moment no cat replied, and Shadowpaw could sense their uneasiness. *None of them wants to admit that their Clan is having problems.*

Shadowpaw was surprised when Puddleshine, who was

normally so pensive, was the first to speak up. Maybe the cold had banished his mentor's reserve and enabled him to be honest.

"The hunting is very poor in ShadowClan," he replied; Shadowpaw felt a twinge of alarm at how discouraged his mentor sounded. "If this freezing cold goes on much longer, I don't know what we'll do."

The remaining medicine cats exchanged glances of relief, as if they were glad to learn their Clan wasn't the only one suffering.

Willowshine nodded agreement. "Many RiverClan cats are getting sick because it's so cold."

"In ThunderClan too," Alderheart murmured.

"We're running out of herbs," Fidgetflake added with a twitch of his whiskers. "And the few we have left are shriveled and useless."

Frecklewish gave her Clanmate a sympathetic glance. "I've heard some of the younger warriors joking about running off to be kittypets," she meowed.

"No cat had better say that in my hearing." Jayfeather drew his lips back in the beginning of a snarl. "Or they'll wish they hadn't."

"Keep your fur on, Jayfeather," Frecklewish responded. "It was only a joke. All SkyClan cats are loyal to their Clan."

Jayfeather's only reply was an irritated flick of his ears.

"I don't suppose any of you have spare supplies of catmint?" Kestrelflight asked hesitantly. "The clumps that grow in WindClan are all blackened by frost. We won't have any more until newleaf."

Most of the cats shook their heads, except for Willowshine, who rested her tail encouragingly on Kestrelflight's shoulder. "RiverClan can help," she promised. "There's catmint growing in the Twoleg gardens near our border. It's more sheltered there."

"Thanks, Willowshine." Kestrelflight's voice was unsteady. "There's whitecough in the WindClan camp, and without catmint I'm terrified it will turn to greencough."

"Meet me by the border tomorrow at sunhigh," Willowshine mewed. "I'll show you where the catmint grows."

"This is all well and good," Jayfeather snorted, "every cat getting along, but let's not forget why we're here. I'm much more interested in what StarClan has to say. Shall we begin?" He paced to the edge of the Moonpool and stretched out one forepaw to touch the surface, only to draw his paw back with a gasp of surprise.

ERIN HUNTER

is inspired by a love of cats and a fascination with the ferocity of the natural world. As well as having great respect for nature in all its forms, Erin enjoys creating rich mythical explanations for animal behavior. She is also the author of the Seekers, Survivors, and Bravelands series.

Download the free Warriors app at www.warriorcats.com.